D0492681

CITY OF COVENTRY LIBRARIES

WITHDRAWN
FOR SALE

SOMETHING to LIVE FOR

Richard Roper was inspired by an article he read about the council workers who deal with situations when someone dies alone. Their days are spent sifting through the ephemera of those who've slipped through the cracks, searching for clues to a next of kin. Council workers are under no obligation to attend the funerals. Yet they do, sometimes dozens of them a year, just to make sure at least someone is there.

Richard Roper lives in London and loves listening to Ella Fitzgerald records on long train journeys. SOMETHING TO LIVE FOR is his first novel. It has sold in over twenty languages around the world and TV rights have been snapped up by Expectation Entertainment.

Connect with Richard @richardroper or visit his website www.richardroperauthor.com

SOMETHING
to LIVE FOR

Richard Roper

ORION

First published in Great Britain in 2019 by Orion Books,
an imprint of The Orion Publishing Group Ltd
Carmelite House, 50 Victoria Embankment,
London EC4Y 0DZ

An Hachette UK company

1 3 5 7 9 10 8 6 4 2

Copyright © Richard Roper 2019

The moral right of Richard Roper to be identified as
the author of this work has been asserted in accordance with
the Copyright, Designs and Patents Act of 1988.

'Blue Moon', Words by Lorenz Hart, Music by Richard Rodgers
© Copyright 1934 EMI Robbins Catalog Inc. EMI United Partnership Limited.
All Rights Reserved. International Copyright Secured. Used by permission of
Hal Leonard Europe Limited.

All rights reserved. No part of this publication may be
reproduced, stored in a retrieval system, or transmitted
in any form or by any means, electronic, mechanical,
photocopying, recording, or otherwise, without the
prior permission of both the copyright owner and the
above publisher of this book.

All the characters in this book are fictitious, and any resemblance to
actual persons, living or dead, is purely coincidental.

A CIP catalogue record for this book is
available from the British Library.

ISBN (Hardback) 978 1 4091 8559 8
ISBN (export trade paperback) 978 1 4091 8560 4

Typeset by Input Data Services Ltd, Somerset

Printed and bound in Great Britain by Clays Ltd, Elcograf S.p.A.

The Orion Publishing Group's policy is to use papers that are natural,
renewable and recyclable products and made from wood grown in sustainable forests.
The logging and manufacturing processes are expected to conform to the
environmental regulations of the country of origin.

www.orionbooks.co.uk

For Mum and Dad

Public Health (Control of Disease) Act 1984, section 46

(1) It shall be the duty of a local authority to cause to be buried or cremated the body of any person who has died or been found dead in their area, in any case where it appears to the authority that no suitable arrangements for the disposal of the body have been or are being made otherwise than by the authority.

Chapter One

Andrew looked at the coffin and tried to remember who was inside it. It was a man, he was sure of that. But, horrifyingly, the name escaped him. He thought he'd narrowed it down to either John or James, but Jake had just made a late bid for consideration. It was inevitable, he supposed, that this had happened. He'd been to so many of these funerals it was bound to at some point, but that didn't stop him feeling an angry stab of self-loathing.

If he could just remember the name before the vicar said it that would be something. There was no order of service, but maybe he could check his work phone. Would that be cheating? Probably. Besides, it would have been a tricky enough manoeuvre to get away with in a church full of mourners, but nearly impossible when the only other person there apart from him was the vicar. Ordinarily, the funeral director would have been there too, but he had called off sick.

Unnervingly, the vicar, who was only a few feet away from Andrew, had barely broken eye contact since he'd started the service. Andrew hadn't dealt with him before. He was boyish and spoke with a tremor that was amplified unforgivingly by the echoey church. Andrew couldn't tell if this was down to nerves. He tried a reassuring smile, but it didn't seem to help.

Would a thumbs up be inappropriate? He decided against it.

He looked over at the coffin again. Maybe he *was* a Jake, though the man had been seventy-eight when he died, and you didn't really get many septuagenarian Jakes. At least, not yet. It was going to be strange in fifty years' time when all the nursing homes would be full of Jakes and Waynes, Tinkerbells and Appletisers, with faded tribal tattoos that roughly translated as *'Roadworks for next fifty yards'* faded on their lower backs.

Jesus, concentrate, he admonished himself. The whole point of him being there was to bear respectful witness to the poor soul departing on their final journey, to provide some company in lieu of any family or friends. Dignity – that was his watchword.

Unfortunately, dignity was something that had been in short supply for John or James or Jake. According to the coroner's report, he had died on the toilet while reading a book about buzzards. To add insult to injury, Andrew later discovered first-hand that it wasn't even a very *good* book about buzzards. Admittedly, he was no expert, but he wasn't sure the author – who even from the few passages Andrew had read came across as remarkably grumpy – should have dedicated a whole page to bad-mouthing kestrels. The deceased had folded the corner of this particular page down as a crude place holder, so perhaps he'd been in agreement. As Andrew had peeled off his latex gloves he'd made a mental note to insult a kestrel – or indeed any member of the falcon family – the next time he saw one, as a tribute of sorts.

Other than a few more bird books, the house was devoid of anything that gave clues to the man's personality. There were no records or films to be found, nor pictures on the walls or photographs on the windowsills. The only idiosyncrasy was the bafflingly large number of Fruit 'n Fibre boxes in the kitchen cupboards. So, aside from being a keen ornithologist with a top-notch digestive system, it was impossible to guess what sort of person John or James or Jake had been.

Andrew had been as diligent as ever with the property inspection. He'd searched the house, a curious mock-Tudor bungalow that sat defiantly as an incongruous interlude in the terraced street, until he was sure he'd not missed something that suggested the man had any family he was still in touch with. He'd knocked on the neighbours' doors but they'd either been indifferent to, or unaware of, the man's existence, or the fact it was over.

The vicar segued unsurely into a bit of Jesus-y material, and Andrew knew from experience that the service was coming to a close. He *had* to remember this person's name, as a point of principle. He really tried his best, even when there was no one else there, to be a model mourner – to be as respectful as if there were hundreds of devastated family members in attendance. He'd even started removing his watch before entering the church because it felt like the deceased's final journey should be exempt from the indifference of a ticking second hand.

The vicar was definitely on the home straight now. Andrew was going to have to make a decision.

John, he decided. He was definitely John.

'And whilst we believe that John—'

Yes!

'—struggled to some extent in his final years, and sadly departed the world without family or friends by his side, we can take comfort that, with God waiting with open arms, full of love and kindness, this journey shall be the last he makes alone.'

Andrew tended not to stick around after the funerals. On the few occasions he had, he'd ended up having to make awkward conversation with funeral directors or last-minute rubber-neckers. It was remarkable how many of the latter you would get, hanging around outside, farting out inane platitudes. Andrew was well-practised at slipping away so as to avoid such encounters, but today he'd briefly been distracted by a sign on the church noticeboard advertising the troublingly jaunty 'Midsummer Madness Fete!' when he felt someone tapping him on the shoulder with the insistence of an impatient woodpecker. It was the vicar. He looked even younger close up, with his baby-blue eyes and blond curtains parted neatly in the middle, as if his mum might have done it for him.

'Hey, it's Andrew, isn't it? You're from the council, right?'

'That's right,' Andrew said.

'No luck finding any family, then?'

Andrew shook his head.

'Shame, that. Real shame.'

The vicar seemed agitated, as if he were holding on to a secret that he desperately wanted to impart.

'Can I ask you something?'

'Yes,' Andrew said, quickly deciding on an excuse for why he couldn't attend 'Midsummer Madness'.

'How did you find that?' the vicar said.

'Do you mean . . . the funeral?' Andrew said, pulling at a bit of loose thread on his coat.

'Yeah. Well, more specifically, my part in it all. Because, full

6

disclosure, it was my first. I was quite relieved to be starting with this one, to be honest, because there wasn't anybody here so it sort of felt like a bit of a practice run. Hopefully, now I'm fully prepared for when there's a proper one with a church full of friends and family, not just a guy from the council. No offence,' he added, putting a hand on Andrew's arm. Andrew did his best not to recoil. He hated it when people did that. He wished he had some sort of squid-like defence that meant he could shoot ink into their eyes.

'So yeah,' the vicar continued. 'How'd you think I did?'

What do you want me to say? Andrew thought. *Well, you didn't knock the coffin over or accidentally call the deceased Mr Hitler, so ten out of ten, I'd say.*

'You did very well,' he said.

'Ah, great, thanks mate,' the vicar said, looking at him with renewed intensity. 'I really appreciate that.'

He held out his hand. Andrew shook it and went to let go, but the vicar carried on, his grip unwavering.

'Anyway, I better be off,' Andrew said.

'Yes, yes of course,' said the vicar, finally letting go.

Andrew started off down the path, breathing a sigh of relief at escaping without further interrogation.

'See you soon, I hope,' the vicar called after him.

Chapter Two

The funerals had been given various prefixes over the years – 'Public Health', 'Contract', 'Welfare', 'Section 46' – but none of the attempted rebrands would ever replace the original. When Andrew had come across the expression 'Pauper's Funeral' he'd found it quite evocative; romantic, even, in a Dickensian sort of way. It made him think of someone a hundred and fifty years ago in a remote village – all mud and clucking chickens – succumbing to a spectacular case of syphilis, dying at the fine old age of twenty-seven and being bundled merrily into a pit to regenerate the land. In practice, what he experienced was depressingly clinical. The funerals were now a legal obligation for councils across the UK, designed for those who'd slipped through the cracks, their death perhaps only noticed because of the smell of their body decomposing, or an unpaid bill. On several occasions now, Andrew had found that the deceased had enough money in a bank account for direct debits to cover utility bills for months after their death, meaning the house was kept warm enough to speed up their body's decomposition. After the fifth harrowing instance of this, he'd considered mentioning it in the 'Any other comments' section on his annual job satisfaction survey. In the end he went with asking if they could have another kettle in the shared kitchen.

Another phrase he had become well acquainted with was 'The Nine O'clock Trot'. His boss, Cameron, had explained its origin to him while violently piercing the film on a micro-wavable biriyani. 'If you die alone' – stab, stab, stab – 'you're most likely buried alone too' – stab, stab, stab – 'so the church can get the funeral out the way at nine o'clock, safe in the knowledge that every train could be cancelled' – stab – 'every motorway gridlocked' – stab – 'and it wouldn't make a differ-ence.' A final stab. 'Because nobody's on their way.'

In the previous year Andrew had arranged twenty-five of these funerals (his highest annual total yet). He'd attended all of them, too, though he wasn't technically required to do so. It was, he told himself, a small but meaningful gesture for someone to be there who wasn't legally obligated. But in-creasingly he found himself watching the simple, unvarnished coffins being lowered into the ground in a specially designated unmarked plot, knowing they would be uncovered three or four more times as other coffins were fitted in like a macabre game of Tetris, and thinking that his presence counted for nothing.

As Andrew sat on the bus to the office, he inspected his tie and shoes, both of which had seen better days. There was a persistent stain on his tie, origin unknown, that wouldn't budge. His shoes were well-polished but starting to look worn. Too many nicks from churchyard gravel, too many times the leather had strained where he'd curled his toes at a vicar's verbal stumble. He really should replace both come payday.

Now that the funeral was over, he took a moment to

mentally file away John (surname Sturrock, he discovered, having turned on his phone). As ever, he tried to resist the temptation to obsess over how John had ended up in such a desperate position. Was there really no niece or godson he was on Christmas-card terms with? Or an old schoolfriend who called, even just on his birthday? But it was a slippery slope. He had to stay as objective as possible, for his own sake, if only to be mentally strong enough to deal with the next poor person who ended up like this. The bus stopped at a red light. By the time it went green Andrew had made himself say a final goodbye.

He arrived at the office and returned Cameron's enthusiastic wave with a more muted acknowledgement of his own. As he slumped into his well-weathered seat that had moulded itself to his form over the years, he let out a now sadly familiar grunt. He'd thought, having only just turned forty-two, that he'd have a few more years before he began accompanying minor physical tasks by making odd noises, but it seemed to be the universe's gentle way of telling him that he was now officially heading towards middle-age. He imagined that before too long he'd wake up and immediately begin his day bemoaning how easy school exams were these days and bulk buying cream chinos.

He waited for his computer to boot up and watched out of the corner of his eye as his colleague, Keith, demolished a hunk of chocolate cake and methodically sucked smears of icing from his stubby little fingers.

'Good one, was it?' Keith said, not taking his eyes off his screen, which Andrew knew was most likely showing a gallery of actresses who'd had the temerity to age, or something small and furry on a skateboard.

'It was OK,' Andrew said.

'Any rubberneckers?' came a voice from behind him.

Andrew flinched. He hadn't seen Meredith take her seat.

'No,' he said, not bothering to turn around. 'Just me and the vicar. It was his very first funeral, apparently.'

'Bloody hell, what a way to pop your cherry,' Meredith said.

'Better that than a room full of weepers, to be fair,' Keith said, with one final suck of his little finger. 'You'd be shitting piss, wouldn't you?'

The office phone rang and the three of them sat there not answering it. Andrew was about to bite but Keith's frustration got the better of him first.

'Hello, Death Administration. Yep. Sure. Yep. Right.'

Andrew reached for his earphones and pulled up his Ella Fitzgerald playlist. He had only very recently discovered Spotify, much to Keith's delight, who'd spent a month afterwards calling Andrew 'Grandad'. He felt like starting with a classic, something reassuring. He decided on 'Summertime'. But he was only three bars in before he looked up to see Keith standing in front of him, belly flab poking through a gap between shirt buttons.

'Helloooo. Anybody there?'

Andrew removed his earphones.

'That was the coroner. We've got a fresh one. Well, not a fresh body, obviously, they reckon he'd been dead a good few weeks. No obvious next of kin and the neighbours never spoke to him. Body's been moved so they want a property inspection A-SAP.'

'Right.'

Keith picked at a scab on his elbow. 'Tomorrow all right for you?'

Andrew checked his diary.

'I can do first thing.'

'Blimey, you're keen,' Keith said, waddling back to his desk. *And you're a slice of ham that's been left out in the sun*, Andrew thought. He went to put his earphones back in, but at that moment Cameron emerged from his office and clapped his hands together to get their attention.

'Team meeting, chaps,' he announced. 'And yes, yes, don't you worry – the current Mrs Cameron has provided cake, as per. Shall we hit the breakout space?'

The three of them responded with the enthusiasm a chicken might if it were asked to wear a prosciutto bikini and run into a fox's den. The 'breakout space' consisted of a knee-high table flanked by two sofas that smelt unaccountably of sulphur. Cameron had floated the idea of adding beanbags, but this had been ignored, as were his suggestions of desk-swap Tuesdays, a negativity jar – 'it's a swear jar but for negativity!' – and a team park run. 'I'm busy,' Keith had yawned.

'But I haven't told you which day it's on,' Cameron said, his smile faltering like a flame in a draught. Undeterred by their complete lack of enthusiasm, Cameron's most recent suggestion had been a suggestion box. This too, had been ignored.

They gathered on the sofas and Cameron doled out cake and tea and tried to engage them with some banal small talk. Keith and Meredith had wedged themselves into the smaller of the two sofas. Meredith was laughing at something Keith had just whispered to her. Just as parents are able to recognise variants in the cries of their newborns, so Andrew had begun to understand what Meredith's differing laughs denoted. In this particular instance, the high-pitched giggle indicated that someone was being cruelly mocked. Given that they kept very obviously sneaking glances in his direction, it seemed it was probably him.

'Rightio, lady and gents,' Cameron said. 'First things first: don't forget we've got a new starter tomorrow. Peggy Green. I know we've struggled since Dan and Bethany left, so it's super-cool to have a new pair of hands.'

'As long as she doesn't get "stressed" like Bethany,' Meredith said.

'Or turn out to be a knob like Dan,' Keith muttered.

'*Anyway*,' Cameron said, 'what I actually wanted to talk to you about today is my weekly . . . honk! honk!' – he honked an imaginary horn – '. . . fun idea! Remember, guys, this is something you can all get involved with. Doesn't matter how crazy your idea is. The only rule is that it has to be fun.'

Andrew shuddered.

'So,' Cameron continued, 'my fun idea this week is – drum roll please – that every month we have a get-together at one of our houses and we do dinner. A sort of *Come Dine With Me* vibe but without any judgment. We'll have a bit of food, I dare say a bit of vino, and it'll give us a chance to do some real bonding away from the office, get to know each other a bit better, meet the family and all that. I'm mega happy to kick things off. Whaddya say?'

Andrew hadn't heard anything past 'meet the family'.

'Is there not something else we can do?' he said, trying to keep his voice steady.

'Oh,' Cameron said, instantly deflated. 'I thought that was actually one of my better ideas.'

'No, no, it is!' Andrew said, overcompensating now. 'It's just . . . couldn't we just go to a restaurant instead?'

'Toooo expensive,' Keith said, spraying cake crumbs everywhere.

'Well, what about something else? I don't know – Laser Quest or something. Is that still a thing?'

'I'm vetoing Laser Quest on the grounds I'm not a twelve-year-old boy,' Meredith said. 'I like the dinner party idea. I'm actually a bit of a secret Nigella in the kitchen.' She turned to Keith. 'I bet you'd go crazy for my lamb shank.' Andrew felt bile stir in his stomach.

'Go on, Andrew,' Cameron said, confidence renewed by Meredith giving his idea her blessing. He attempted a matey arm punch that caused Andrew to spill tea down his leg. 'It'll be a laugh! There's no pressure to cook up anything fancy. And I'd love to meet Diane and the kids, of course. So, whaddya say? You up for this, buddy?'

Andrew's mind was racing. Surely there was something else he could suggest as an alternative? Life drawing. Badger baiting. *Anything*. The others were just looking at him now. He had to say something.

'Bloody hell, Andrew. You look like you've seen a ghost,' Meredith said. 'Your cooking can't be that bad. Besides, I'm sure Diane's a fabulous chef, amongst all her other talents, so she can help you out.'

'Mm-hmm,' Andrew murmured, tapping his fingertips together.

'She's a lawyer, right?' Keith said. Andrew nodded. Maybe there'd be some catastrophic world event in the next few days, a lovely old nuclear war to make them all forget about this stupid idea.

'You've got that beautiful old town house Dulwich-way, haven't you?' Meredith said, practically leering. 'A five-bed, isn't it?'

'Four,' Andrew said. He hated it when she and Keith got like this. A tag team of mockery.

'Still,' Meredith said, 'a lovely big four-bed, smart kids by all accounts, and Diane your talented, breadwinning wife. What a dark old horse you are.'

Later, as Andrew prepared to leave the office, having been too distracted to do any meaningful work, Cameron appeared by his desk and dropped down on to his haunches. It felt like the sort of move he'd been taught on a course.

'Listen,' he said quietly, 'I know you didn't seem to fancy the dinner party idea, but just say you'll have a think about it, OK, mate?'

Andrew needlessly shuffled some papers on his desk. 'Oh, I mean . . . I don't want to spoil things, it's just . . . OK, I'll think about it. But if we don't do that I'm sure we can think of another, you know, fun idea.'

'That's the spirit,' Cameron said, straightening up and addressing them all. 'That goes for all of us, I hope. Come on team — let's get our bond-on sooner rather than. Yeah?'

Andrew had recently splashed out on some noise-cancelling earphones for his commute, so while he could see the man sitting opposite's ugly sneeze and the toddler in the vestibule screaming at the utter injustice of being made to wear not one but two shoes, it simply appeared as a silent film incongruously soundtracked by Ella Fitzgerald's soothing voice. It wasn't long, however, before the conversation in the office started to repeat itself in his head, vying with Ella for his attention.

15

'Diane, your bread-winning wife . . . smart kids . . . Beautiful old town house.' Keith's smirk. Meredith's leer. The conversation dogged him all the way to the station and continued as he went to buy food for that night's dinner. That's when he found himself standing in the corner shop by multibags of novelty crisps named after celebrities and trying not to scream. After ten minutes of picking up and putting down the same four ready meals, feeling incapable of choosing one, he left empty-handed, walking out into the rain and heading home, his stomach rumbling.

He stood outside his front door, shivering. Eventually, when the cold became too much to bear, he brought out his keys. There was usually one day a week like this, when he'd pause outside, key in the lock, holding his breath.

Maybe this time.

Maybe this time it *would* be the lovely old town house behind that door: Diane starting to prepare dinner. The smell of garlic and red wine. The sound of Steph and David squabbling or asking questions about their homework, then the excitable cheers when he opened the door because Dad's home, Dad's home!

When he entered the hallway the smell of damp hit him even harder than usual. And there were the familiar scuff marks on the corridor walls and the intermittent, milky yellow of the faulty strip light. He trudged up the stairs, his wet shoes squeaking with each step, and slid the second key around on his keyring. He reached up to right the wonky number two on the door and went inside, met as he had been for the last twenty years, by nothing but silence.

Chapter Three

Five Years Previously

Andrew was late. This might not have been so much of a disaster if on the CV he'd submitted ahead of that morning's job interview he hadn't claimed to be 'extremely punctual'. Not just punctual: *extremely* punctual. Was that even a thing? *Were* there extremities of punctuality? How might one even go about measuring such a thing?

It was his own stupid fault, too. He'd been crossing the road when a strange honking noise distracted him and he looked up. A goose was arrowing overhead, its white underside lit up orange by the morning sun, its strange cries and erratic movement making it seem like a damaged fighter plane struggling back to base. It was just as the bird steadied itself and continued on its course that Andrew slipped on some ice. There was a brief moment where his arms windmilled and his feet gripped at nothing, like a cartoon character who's just run off a cliff, before he hit the ground with an ugly thud.

'You OK?'

Andrew wheezed wordlessly in reply at the woman who had just helped him to his feet. He felt like someone had just taken a sledgehammer to his lower back. But it wasn't this that stopped him finding the words to thank the woman. There was something about the way she was looking at him – a half-smile on her face, how she brushed her hair behind her ears – that was so startlingly familiar it left him breathless. The woman's eyes seemed to be searching his face, as if she too had been hit with an intense feeling of recognition and pain. It was only after she'd said 'Well, bye then' and walked off that Andrew realised she'd actually been waiting for him to thank her. He wondered if he should hurry after her to try and make amends. But just then a familiar tune began to play in his head. '*Blue moon, you saw me standing alone*'. It took all his concentration to shake it away, squeezing his eyes shut and massaging his temples. By the time he'd looked again the woman was gone.

He dusted himself down, suddenly aware that people had seen him fall and were enjoying their dose of *Schadenfreude*. He avoided eye contact and carried on, head down, hands thrust into his pockets. Gradually his embarrassment gave way to something else. It was in the aftermath of mishaps like this where he would feel it stir at his core and start to spread out, thick and cold, making it feel like he was walking through quicksand. There was nobody for him to share the story with. No one to help him laugh his way through it. Loneliness, however, was ever vigilant, always there to slow-clap his every stumble.

Though somewhat shaken after his slip, he was fine apart from a small graze on his hand. Now that he was nearing forty he was all too aware there was a small but visible spot on the horizon where such a standard slip would become 'having a little fall'. (He secretly welcomed the idea of a sympathetic stranger laying their coat over him as they waited for an ambulance, supporting his head and squeezing his hand.) While he hadn't suffered any damage to himself, unfortunately the same couldn't be said for his once-clean white shirt, which was now splattered with dirty brown water. He briefly considered trying to make something out of this and the graze on his hand to impress his interviewer. 'What, this? Oh, on my way here I was briefly diverted by diving in front of a bus/ bullet/tiger to save a toddler/puppy/dignitary. Anyway, did I mention I'm a self-starter and I work well on my own *and* as part of a team?' He decided on the more sensible option and dashed into the nearest Debenhams for a new shirt. The detour left him sweaty and out of breath, which was how he announced himself to the receptionist at the cathedral of concrete that was the council offices.

He took a seat as instructed and sucked in some deep, steadying breaths. He needed this job. Badly. He'd been working in various admin roles for the council of a nearby borough since his early twenties, finally finding a position that had stuck and which he had been in for eight years before unceremoniously being made redundant. Andrew's boss, Jill, a kind, rosy-cheeked Lancastrian with a 'hug first, ask questions later' approach to life, had felt so terrible at having to let him go that she'd apparently called every council office in London, asking about vacancies. The interview today was the only one that had come out of Jill's calls, and her email to him describing the job was frustratingly vague. From what Andrew could tell, it was similar to what he'd been doing before, largely admin, though it involved something to do with inspecting properties. More importantly, it paid exactly the same as his last job and he could start the following month. Ten years ago there was a chance he might have considered a fresh start. Travelling, maybe, or a bold new career move. But these days, just having to leave the house left him with an unspecific feeling of anxiety, so hiking to Machu Picchu or retraining as a lion tamer weren't exactly on the cards.

He tore at a loose flap of skin on his finger with his teeth, jiggling his knee, struggling to relax. When Cameron Yates finally appeared, Andrew felt certain he'd met him before. He was about to ask if that was actually the case – perhaps he'd be able to use it to curry favour – but then he realised that he only recognised Cameron because he was a dead ringer for a young Wallace from *Wallace and Gromit*. He had bulbous eyes that were too close together and large front teeth that jutted down unevenly like stalactites. The only real differences were his tufty black hair and Home Counties accent.

They exchanged some awkward small talk in the coffin-sized lift, and all the while Andrew couldn't tear his eyes away from the stalactites. *Stop looking at the fucking teeth*, he told himself, while staring directly at the fucking teeth.

They waited for someone to bring them two blue plastic thimbles of lukewarm water before finally the interview began in earnest. Cameron started by rattling through the job description, barely pausing for breath as he outlined how, if Andrew were to get the role, he'd be dealing with all deaths covered under the Public Health Act. 'So that's liaising with funeral directors to organise the services, writing death notices in the local paper, registering deaths, tracing family members, recovering funeral costs through the deceased's estates. There's an awful lot of the old paperwork malarkey, as you can imagine!'

Andrew made sure to nod along, trying to take it all in, inwardly cursing Jill for neglecting to mention the whole 'death' thing. Then, before he knew it, the spotlight was on him. Disconcertingly, Cameron seemed as nervous as he was, switching from simple, friendly questions to meandering, confusing ones, a harsher edge to his voice – as if he were playing good cop/bad cop by himself. When Andrew was afforded a second to respond to Cameron's nonsense, he found himself stumbling over his words. When he did manage to string a sentence together, his enthusiasm sounded like desperation, and his attempts at humour just seeming to confuse Cameron, who on more than one occasion looked past Andrew's shoulder, distracted by someone walking past in the corridor. Eventually it got to a point where Andrew felt so despondent he considered giving up on the spot and just walking out. In amongst his depression at how things were going he was still distracted by Cameron's teeth. For one thing, he'd started to question whether it was stalac*tites* or stalag*mites*. Wasn't there a thing about pulling down tights that helped you remember? It was at that moment that he realised Cameron had just asked him something – he had no idea what – and was now waiting for an answer. Panicked, he sat forward. 'Ermm,' he said, in a tone he hoped conveyed that he was appreciative of such a thoughtful question and thus needed to give it due consideration. But this was clearly a mistake, judging from Cameron's growing frown. Andrew realised the question must have been a simple one.

'Yes,' he blurted out, deciding to keep the answer short. Relief flooded him as Cameron's trampled Wallace smile reappeared.

'Wonderful. And how many?' he said.

This was trickier, though Andrew sensed a light-heartedness in Cameron's tone so this time plumped for a general, breezy response.

'Well, I suppose I sort of lose track sometimes,' he said,

trying a rueful smile. Cameron reacted with a false-sounding laugh, as though he couldn't quite tell if Andrew was joking. Andrew decided to fire back, hoping for more information.

'Do you mind me asking you the same question?' he said.

'Of course. I've just got the one myself,' Cameron said. He reached into his pocket and started rummaging. The thought briefly crossed Andrew's mind that the man interviewing him for a job was about to pull out a lone testicle, as if he asked this question of every man he met, hoping desperately for a fellow solo-ball owner. Instead, Cameron produced his wallet. It was only when he brought out a picture from within of a child trussed up in winter gear with skis on that Andrew understood what the question had been. He quickly replayed the conversation from Cameron's perspective.

'Do you have kids?'

'Ermm . . . Yes.'

'Wonderful, how many?'

'Well, I suppose I sort of lose track sometimes.'

Christ, had he just given the impression to a potential new boss that he was some sort of prolific Lothario who'd spent his life shagging around town and leaving a succession of women pregnant and homes broken?

He was still just looking at the photo of Cameron's child. *Say something!*

'Lovely,' he said. 'Lovely . . . boy.'

Oh good, now you sound like the childcatcher. That'll go down well. You start on Monday, Mr Paedophile!

He grasped his plastic water beaker, long since empty, and felt it crack in his hand. This was a fucking disaster. How could he have blown things already? He could tell from Cameron's expression that he was past the point of no return. Quite what he'd say if Andrew just admitted to accidentally lying about having children he wasn't sure, but it seemed unlikely that it would suddenly turn things around. He decided his best option now was just to get through the rest of the interview whilst saving as much face as possible – like continuing to do mirror, signal, manoeuvre on a driving test having just run over a lollipop lady.

As he let go of the plastic beaker he noticed the graze on his palm and thought about the women who'd helped him that morning. The wavy brown hair, that inscrutable smile. He could feel the blood starting to throb in his ears. What would it be like, to have a moment where he could just pretend? To play out a little fantasy all for himself. Where was the harm? Where, really, was the harm in spending the briefest moment imagining that everything had actually worked out fine?

He cleared his throat.

Was he going to do this?

'How old is he?' he asked, handing the photo back to Cameron.

'He's just turned seven,' Cameron said. 'And yours?'

Was he actually going to do this?

'Well . . . Steph's eight and David's six,' he said.

Apparently, he was.

'Ah, wonderful. It was when my boy Chris turned four that I really started to get the sense of what sort of person he was going to be,' Cameron said. 'Though Clara, my wife, always reckoned she could tell all that before he'd even left the womb.'

Andrew smiled. 'My wife Diane said exactly the same,' he said.

And, just like that, he had a family.

*

23

They talked about their wives and children for a while longer, but all too soon Cameron brought the interview back around to the job and Andrew felt the fantasy slipping away like water through his fingers. Before too long their time was up. Disconcertingly, instead of trucking out the usual line of whether Andrew had any questions for *him*, Cameron instead asked whether he had 'any last words', as if he were about to be taken away and hanged. He managed to dredge up some vague waffle about what an interesting role it seemed and how much he'd relish the chance to work in Cameron's dynamic-sounding team.

'We'll be in touch,' Cameron said, spoken with the sincerity of a politician pretending to like an indie band during a radio interview. Andrew forced a smile and remembered to make eye contact as he shook Cameron's hand, which was cold and wet, as if he'd been fondling a trout. 'Thanks for the opportunity,' Andrew said.

He found a café and used the free Wi-Fi to search for jobs, but he was too distracted to look properly. When he'd thanked Cameron 'for the opportunity' it had nothing to do with the job: it was because he'd been given the chance to indulge, however briefly, in the fantasy of having a family. How strangely thrilling and scary it had been to feel so normal. He tried to forget about it, forcing himself to concentrate. If he wasn't going to get another council job he'd need to expand his search, but it felt like an impossibly daunting task. There was nothing he could find that he seemed qualified for. Half the job descriptions themselves were baffling enough. He stared hopelessly at the large muffin he'd bought but not eaten, picking at it instead until it looked like a molehill.

Maybe he'd make other animal burrows out of food and enter the Turner Prize.

He sat in the café for the rest of the afternoon, watching important business people having their important business meetings and tourists thumbing excitedly through guidebooks. He stayed there long after all had left, pressing himself up against the radiator and trying to remain invisible to the young Italian waiter stacking chairs and sweeping up. Eventually the waiter asked Andrew if he wouldn't mind leaving, the apologetic smile leaving his face as he spotted the muffin molehill crumbs that had spilled on to the table.

Andrew's phone rang just as he stepped outside. An unknown number.

'Andrew?' the person on the end of the line said. 'Can you hear me?'

'Yes,' Andrew said, though he barely could with the combination of a blustery wind and an ambulance driving past, siren screaming.

'Andrew, it's Cameron Yates. I just wanted to give you a call to say that it was really good to meet you earlier today. You really seemed to get the can-do culture I'm trying to build here. So, to cut a long story short, I'm very pleased to say I'd love you to come on board.'

'I'm sorry?' Andrew said, jamming a finger in his free ear.

'We're offering you the job!' Cameron said. 'There'll be the usual formalities of course, but can't see any problems there, mate.'

Andrew stood there, buffeted by the wind.

'Andrew? Did you catch that?'

'Gosh. Yes, I did. Wow. That's great. I'm . . . I'm delighted.'

And he was. So delighted, in fact, that he beamed at the

waiter through the window. The waiter rewarded him with a slightly bemused smile.

'Andrew, listen, I'm just heading off to a seminar, so I'll ask someone to ping you an email with all the deets. I'm sure there'll be a few bits and pieces to chat through, but don't sweat any of that now. You get home and give Diane and the kids the good news.'

Chapter Four

It was hard for Andrew to believe that it was only five years since he'd stood in that windswept street, trying to take in what Cameron had just said. It felt like a lifetime ago.

He stirred listlessly at the baked beans currently spluttering in the travel saucepan on the hob, before depositing them on a crust of wholemeal he'd cut with his one still-sharp knife, its plastic handle warped and burnt. He looked intently at the square of cracked tiles behind the cooker, pretending it was a camera. 'So what I've done there is to combine the beans and the bread, and now I'll just add a blob of ketchup – I use Captain Tomato but any brand is fine – to make it a tasty trio. You can't freeze any of the leftovers, but luckily you'll have wolfed it all down in about nine seconds and you'll be too busy hating yourself to worry about that.'

He could hear his neighbour humming downstairs. She was relatively new, the previous tenants having moved out a few months ago. They'd been a young couple, early twenties, both startlingly attractive, all cheekbones and toned arms. The sort of aesthetically pleasing appearance that meant they'd never had to apologise for anything in their lives. Andrew would force himself to make eye contact with them and summon up a breezy greeting when they crossed paths in the hallway, but they never really bothered to reply. He was only aware that someone new had moved in when he heard the distinctive humming. He hadn't seen his new neighbour, but, oddly, he *had* smelled her. Or at least, he'd smelled her perfume, which was so strong that it lingered permanently in the hallway. He tried to picture her, but when he conjured the image of her face it was just a smooth, featureless oval.

Just then his phone lit up on the countertop. He saw his sister's name and his heart sank. He checked the date in the corner of his screen: 31 March. He should have known. He pictured Sally checking her calendar, seeing a red ring around the thirty-first and swearing under her breath, knowing it was time for their quarterly call.

He took a fortifying gulp of water and picked up.

'Hello,' he said.

'Hey,' Sally said.

A pause.

'Well. How are you, little bro?' Sally said. 'Everything cool?'

Christ, why did she have to speak as though they were teenagers?

'Oh, you know, the usual. You?'

'Can't complain, dude, I guess. Me and Carl are doing a yoga retreat this weekend, help him learn the teaching side of it and all that jazz.'

Carl. Sally's husband. Usually to be found guzzling protein shakes and voluntarily lifting heavy objects up and down.

'That sounds . . . nice,' Andrew said. Then, after the sort of short silence that clearly denotes it's time to move on to the most pressing matter: 'And how's it going with your tests and everything?'

Sally sighed.

'Had a bunch more last month. Results all came back

28

inconclusive, which means they still know sweet FA, basically. Still, I feel much better. And they think that it's probably not a heart thing, so I'm not likely to do a Dad and kick the bucket without warning. They just keep telling me the usual BS, you know how it is. Exercise more, drink less, blah blah blah.'

'Well, good that they're not unduly concerned,' Andrew said, thinking that if Sally shouldn't talk like a teenager he probably shouldn't talk like a repressed Oxford Don. He'd have thought that after all these years it wouldn't feel like they were strangers. It was still that simple checklist of topics: Work. Health. Family (well, Carl, the only person who came close to a shared family member). Except, this time, Sally decided to throw in a curveball.

'So, I was thinking . . . maybe we should meet up some time soon. It's been, like, five years now, after all.'

Seven, Andrew thought. And the last time was at Uncle Dave's funeral in a crematorium opposite a SnappySnaps in Banbury. And you were high. Then again, he conceded, he hadn't exactly been inundating Sally with invitations to meet up since.

'That . . . that would be good,' he said. 'As long as you can spare the time, of course. Maybe we could meet halfway or something.'

'Yeah, it's cool, bro. Though we've moved, remember? We're in Newquay, now – Carl's business, and everything? So halfway is somewhere else these days. But I'm going to be in London seeing a friend in May. We could hang then, maybe?'

'Yes. OK. Just let me know when you're coming up.'

Andrew scanned the room and chewed his lip. In the twenty years since he'd moved into the flat barely a thing had changed. Consequently, his living space was looking not so much tired as absolutely knackered. There was the dark stain where the wall met the ceiling in the area that masqueraded as a kitchen; then there was the battered grey sofa, the thread-bare carpet and the yellowy-brown wallpaper that was meant to suggest autumn but in fact suggested digestive biscuits. As the colour of the wallpaper had faded, so had the chances of Andrew actually doing anything about it. And his shame at the state of the place was only matched by the terror he felt at the thought of changing it or, worse, living anywhere else. There was at least one benefit to being on his own and never having anyone round – nobody could judge him for how he lived.

He decided to change the subject, recalling something Sally had told him the last time they'd spoken.

'How are things going with your . . . person?'

He heard a lighter sparking and then the faint sound of Sally exhaling smoke.

'My person?'

'The person you were going to see. To talk about things.'

'You mean my therapist?'

'Yes.'

'Ditched her when we moved. To be honest, dude, I was glad of the excuse. She kept trying to hypnotise me and it didn't work. I told her I was immune but she wouldn't listen. I've found someone new in Newquay. She's more of a spiritual healer, I guess? I bumped into her while she was putting up an advert next to Carl's yoga class one. What are the chances?'

Well . . . Andrew thought.

'So, listen man,' Sally said, 'there was something else I wanted to talk to you about.'

'Right,' Andrew said, instantly suspicious. First arranging to meet, now this. Oh God, what if she was going to try and make him spend time with Carl?

'So – and I normally wouldn't do this as I know that . . . well, it's not something we'd normally talk about. But, anyway, you know my old pal Sparky?'

'No.'

'You do, bud. He's the one with the bong shop in Brighton Lanes?'

Obviously.

'OK . . .'

'He's got this friend. Julia. She lives in London. Crystal Palace way, actually, so not too far from you. She's thirty-five. And about two years ago she went through a pretty shitty-sounding divorce.'

Andrew held the phone away from his ear. *If this is going where I think it's going . . .*

'But she's come out of the other side of it now, and from what Sparky tells me she's looking to, you know, get back in the saddle. So, I was just thinking, that, like, maybe you might—'

'No,' Andrew said. 'Absolutely not. Forget it.'

'But, Andrew, she's super-nice from what I can tell – pretty too, from the pics I've seen. I bet you'd like her.'

'That's irrelevant,' Andrew said. 'Because I don't want . . . that. It's not for me, now.'

'"*It's not for me*". Jesus, man, it's love we're talking about, here, not pineapple on pizzas. You can't just dismiss it.'

'Why not? Why can't I? It's not hurting anyone, is it, if I do? If anything, it's guaranteeing that nobody gets hurt.'

'But that's no way to live your life, dude. You're forty-two, still totally in your prime. You gotta think about putting your-self out there, otherwise you're, like, actively denying yourself potential happiness. I know it's hard, but you have to look to the future.'

Andrew could feel his heart start to beat that little bit faster. He had a horrible feeling that his sister was building up the courage to ask him about something they'd never ever discussed, not for want of trying on Sally's part. It was not so much the elephant in the room as the brontosaurus in the airing cupboard. He decided to nip things in the bud.

'I'm very grateful for your concern, but there's no need for it. Honestly. I'm fine as I am.'

'I get that, but, seriously, one day we're gonna have to talk about . . . you know . . . stuff.'

'No, we don't,' Andrew said, annoyed that his voice had come out as a whisper. Showing any sort of emotion was going to come across like an invitation to Sally to keep up this line of questioning, as if he secretly did want to talk about 'stuff' – which he definitely, absolutely, didn't.

'But, bro, we have to at some point, it's not healthy!'

'Yes, well neither is smoking weed your whole life, so I'm not sure you're in any position to judge, are you?'

Andrew winced. He heard Sally exhale smoke.

'I'm sorry. That wasn't called for.'

'All I'm saying,' Sally said, and there was a deliberateness to her tone now, 'is that I think it would be good for you to talk things through.'

'And all *I'm* saying,' Andrew said, 'is that I really don't feel like that's something I want to do. My love life, or lack there-of, isn't something I feel comfortable getting into. And when it comes to "stuff", there's really nothing to say.'

A pause.

'Well, OK, man. It's up to you, I guess. I mean, Carl keeps telling me to stop bothering you about it, but it's hard not to, you know? You're my brother, bro!'

Andrew felt a familiar pang of self-loathing. Not for the first time, his sister had reached out and he'd basically told her to take a running jump. He wanted to apologise properly, to tell her that of course it meant a lot to him that she cared, but the words stuck in his throat.

'Listen,' Sally said. 'I think we're nearly ready to sit down to eat. So, I guess . . . speak to you later?'

'Yeah,' Andrew said, screwing his eyes shut in frustration. 'Definitely. And thanks, you know, for the call and everything.'

'Sure. No problem, bro. Look after yourself.'

'Yes. I will. Absolutely. And you too.'

As Andrew made his way the short distance from the kitchenette to his computer he nearly walked straight into the *Flying Scotsman*, which chugged on unconcerned. Of all his locomotives, the *Scotsman* seemed to carry itself with the most cheerful insouciance (compared to the Railroad BR InterCity, for example, which always seemed petulant at being made to travel at all). It was also the very first engine, and the very first part of his model train collection as a whole, that he'd owned. He'd received it as a gift when he was a teenager, and he was instantly infatuated. Perhaps it was the unexpected source of the present rather than the thing itself, but over time he began to appreciate just how perfect it was. It took him years before he could afford to buy another engine. And then another. And then a fourth. And then track and sidings and platforms and buffers and signal boxes, until eventually all of the floorspace in his flat was taken up with a complicated system of interweaving tracks and various accompanying scenery: tunnels made to look as if they were cut into mountains, cows grazing by streams, entire wheat fields, allotments with rows of tiny cabbages being tended to by men wearing floppy hats. Before too long he had enough scenery to actively mirror the real seasons. It was always a thrill when he felt a change in the air. Once, during a funeral attended exclusively by the deceased's drinking pals, the vicar had made reference to the clocks going back as part of a clunky metaphor in his eulogy, and it was all Andrew could do not to punch the air with joy at the prospect of a whole weekend of replacing the currently verdant landscape with something more autumnal.

It was addictive, building these worlds. Expensive, too. Andrew's meagre savings had long since been spent on his collection and, other than rent, his pay packet now went almost exclusively on upgrading and maintenance. He no longer worried about all the hours, or sometimes whole days, he spent browsing the internet for ways to improve his set-up. He couldn't remember the point at which he'd discovered and then signed up to the *ModelTrainNuts* forum, but he'd been on it every day since. The majority of people who posted there made his interest seem positively amateurish, and Andrew thoroughly admired every single one of them. Anyone – anyone at all – who thought to log on to a message board at 2.38 a.m. and post the message: '*PLEASE HELP A NEWBIE: Stanier 2-6-4T Chassis CRACKED. HELP??*' was nearly as much of a hero to him as the other *thirty-three* people who replied within minutes offering tips, solutions and general words of encouragement. In truth, he understood about 10 per cent of all that was talked about in the more

34

technical conversations, but he always read them post by post, feeling genuine joy when queries, sometimes having lain dormant for months, were resolved. He would occasionally post on the main forum with general messages of goodwill, but the game changer was after he began regularly chatting to three other users and was invited – via private message no less! – to join an exclusive sub-forum. This little haven was run by BamBam67, one of the longest-serving members of the site, who had recently been granted moderator rights. The two others invited into the fold were TinkerAl, by all accounts a young and passionate enthusiast, and the more experienced BroadGaugeJim, who'd once posted a photo of an aqueduct he'd built over a running stream that was so beautiful Andrew had needed to have a lie down.

The sub-forum had been set up by BamBam67 to show off his new moderator privileges – and Bam *did* like to show off, often accompanying his posts with photos of his train set-up which seemed to be more about letting them see the size of his very beautiful home. They discovered early on that they all lived in London, except for BroadGauge, the enthusiastic, avuncular member of the group, who had been 'keeping it real in Leatherhead' for over thirty years, but the idea of them meeting up in real life had never been raised. This suited Andrew, who went by Tracker, just fine. Partly, because it meant there were times where he could modify his online persona to mask his real-life inadequacies – this, he had realised early on, was the entire point of the internet – but also because these were the only, and therefore best, friends he had, and to meet them in real life and find out they were arseholes would be a real shame.

There was a marked difference between what happened

on the main forum and the sub-forum. A delicate ecosystem existed in the former. Conversation had to be strictly on topic, and any user who flouted the rules was duly punished, sometimes severely. The most infamous example of this had been when TunnelBotherer6 had persistently posted about baseboards in a gears topic and had been branded a 'waste of space' by the moderator. Chillingly, TB6 never posted again. But in the sub-forum, away from prying main board moderator eyes, a slow shift occurred. Before long, it became a place where personal issues were discussed. It felt terrifying at first. It was like they were the Resistance, pouring over maps under a single lightbulb in a dusty cellar as enemy soldiers drank in the bar above. It had been BroadGaugeJim who'd been the first one to bring up an explicitly non-train issue.

'Listen chaps,' he'd written, *'I wouldn't normally want to bother you with something like this, but to be perfectly honest I'm not quite sure who else to ask. Basically, my daughter Emily got caught "cyberbullying" someone at school. Mean messages. Photoshopped pics. Nasty stuff, from what I've seen. She tells me she wasn't the ringleader, and feels really bad (and I believe her), but I still feel like I need to make sure she understands she can't be part of anything like that ever again, even if it means losing her mates. Just wondered if any of you might have any advice for a useless duffer like me!! No worries if not!!!!!'*

Andrew's scrambled eggs had gone cold as he waited to see what happened. It was TinkerAl who responded first, and the advice he gave was simple, sensible, yet obviously heartfelt. So much so that Andrew felt momentarily overwhelmed. He tried writing his own response, but he couldn't really think of anything better than what TinkerAl had said. Instead, he just backed up Tinker's suggestion with a couple of lines, and resolved, perhaps a little selfishly, to be the helpful one next time.

Andrew logged on, heard the reassuring sound of the *Scotsman* rushing past behind him, and waited in eager anticipation of the little breeze that followed in its wake. He adjusted his monitor. He'd bought the computer as a thirty-second birthday present for himself. At the time it had seemed like a sleek and powerful machine, but now, a decade later, it was impossibly bulky and slow compared to the latest models. Nevertheless, Andrew felt an affection for the clunky old beast that meant he'd cling on to it for as long as it still spluttered into life.

'*Hi all,*' he wrote. '*Anybody on for the night shift?*'

As he waited for the reply he knew would come within a maximum of ten minutes, he manoeuvred carefully across the rail tracks to his record player and thumbed through his LPs. He kept them in a wonky pile rather than in neat rows on a shelf – that diminished the fun of it. In this more ramshackle style of ordering he could still occasionally surprise himself. There were some other artists and albums in there – Miles Davis, Dave Brubeck, Dizzy Gillespie – but Ella vastly outnumbered all of them.

He slid *The Best Is Yet To Come* out of its sleeve but changed his mind and put it back. When he altered his railway landscapes that was because of the changing seasons, but there wasn't as straightforward a logic when choosing which of Ella's records to listen to. With her, it was just a case of what felt right in the moment. There was only one exception – her version of 'Blue Moon'. He hadn't been able to play that particular song for twenty years, though that didn't stop the tune filtering into his head on occasion. As soon as he recognised the first notes, pain would grow at his temples, his vision would fog, and then came the sound of piercing feedback and shouting, mixing with the music, and the uncanny sensation of hands gripping his shoulders. And then, just like that, it was gone, and he'd be looking at a confused cashier or realising he'd missed his bus stop. On one occasion a few years before, he'd walked into a record shop in Soho and realised that the song was playing on the shop's speakers. He'd left so hastily he'd ended up in a tense encounter with the shopkeeper and a passing off-duty police officer. More recently, he'd been channel-hopping and found himself watching a football match. Minutes later he was desperately searching for the remote to turn it off, because apparently 'Blue Moon' was what the Manchester City fans sang. To hear the actual song was bad enough, but fifty thousand people bellowing it out of sync was on another level. He tried to tell himself that it was simply one of those unusual afflictions people suffer and just have to tolerate, like being allergic to sunlight, or having night terrors, but the thought lingered that at some point, probably, he would have to talk to someone about it.

He ran his fingers down the uneven record pile. Tonight it was *Hello Love* that caught his eye. He carefully dropped the needle and went back to his computer. BamBam67 had been first to reply.

'Evening all. Night shift for me too. House to myself thankfully. Seen they're repeating that BBC thing from last year tonight? James May sitting in his shed rebuilding a Graham Farish 372-311 N Gauge steam loco. Apparently they did it all in one take. Anyway, don't bother with it. It's awful.'

Andrew smiled and refreshed. There was TinkerAl, right on cue:

'HAHA! Knew it wouldn't be your c.o.t.! I loved it, I'm afraid!'
Refresh. Here was BroadGaugeJim:

'Evening shift for me too, squires. I watched the May thing first-time round. Once he'd argued in favour of cork underlay over ballasted I'm afraid I couldn't really take the rest of it seriously.'

Andrew rolled his head around on his shoulders and sank down low in his chair. Now that the four of them had posted, now that Ella was crooning and a train was rattling around the room, defeating the silence, he could relax.

This was when everything came together.

This was everything.

Chapter Five

As Andrew's packed lunches went, this was another textbook effort, even if he said so himself. 'Ham *and* cheese,' he boasted to the camera. 'Blob of pickle goes central then we'll just spread it out to each corner. I like to imagine it's a traitor's body parts being sent to the four corners of England, but come up with whatever metaphor you want. Hang on, is this a bit of iceberg lettuce? You bet it is. So who's coming with? A packet of salt and vinegar from the multi-bag? Tick. And how about a satsuma from The Big Red Net? Ditto. Though do be careful to check it's not one of those sneaky ones that's pretending to be fine even though its bottom's gone mouldy. I always picture a vainglorious young soldier protesting he wants to go on patrol despite a shattered fibula, but again, do choose your own metaphor.'

He was about to launch into an explanation of his Tupperware system when he faltered, staring ahead as if the autocue had broken, the wholly unwelcome reminder of Keith and Meredith's tag-team interrogation coming into his mind.

Sitting on the train to work, wedged into the arm rest by a man whose legs were spread so far apart Andrew could only assume he was performing some sort of interpretive dance about what a *great guy* he was, he found himself thinking back to his very first day in the office. After his momentary excitement at getting the job, he'd spent the following days desperately panicking about how he was going to set things straight with Cameron about the small matter of his made-up family. He reasoned his best chance would be to get on with Cameron very, very quickly – to go against all instincts and actively befriend him. A few illicit chats in the corridor slagging other people off, a pint of lager after work on a Friday – that's what people did, wasn't it? – then he'd confess, say it had been a moment of madness between you and me, mate, and they'd chalk the whole thing up to one of those white lies everyone told in interviews.

Unfortunately, it wasn't to be. As is dictated by UK law, Andrew had said a brief hello to his new colleagues before immediately locking himself out of his emails and sitting in silence for an hour because he was too embarrassed to ask for help.

That's when he saw Cameron appear. This was Andrew's first big chance to get on friendly terms. He was just planning a witty opening gambit about his current admin crisis when Cameron, having interrupted to wish him a happy first day, went on to ask in a voice clearly loud enough that everyone else could hear, 'How's the family? Steph and David OK?'

So thrown was he that Cameron had blown the whole thing this early, he responded to the question of how his children were by saying, 'They seem fine, thanks.'

It would have been an appropriate response to an optician asking how his new lenses were, but not so much when referring to the wellbeing of his flesh and blood. Flustered, he gabbled on about them seeming to have lots of homework at the moment.

'Well,' Cameron said, when Andrew had finished rambling, 'Easter hols, soon. You and Diane off anywhere nice?'

'Um . . . France,' Andrew said.

'Oh, top banana,' Cameron said. 'Whereabouts?'

Andrew considered this.

'South,' he said. 'South France.'

And that was that.

In those early days, when conversation turned to family he was forced to think on his feet. He learned quickly that he could pretend to be distracted by something on his computer, or ask for a question to be repeated as if he hadn't quite caught it, to buy him time, but he knew he needed a more long-term strategy. In his second week there were a few days when nothing came up and he wondered if he might be out of the woods. Looking back, he'd been incredibly naive. This was *family*. This was what normal people talked about. The situation wasn't helped by the fact that Meredith seemed to exist on a diet of nosiness and gossip, constantly pressing Andrew for more specific information. A case in point had been when she, Keith, and a nervous graduate called Bethany were talking about weddings.

'Oh, it was so excruciating,' Meredith said, gloating about a friend's nuptials that weekend. 'They were standing there, up at the altar, and they just couldn't fit the ring on his big fat finger.'

'My dad thinks it's a bit namby-pamby for men to wear a wedding ring,' Bethany said, in her quivering voice that made her sound like she was perpetually being driven over a cattle grid.

'You seeeee?' Keith said, spreading his arms wide to make his point and revealing the sweat patches under his arms. 'That's what I've always said.'

'Oh, I don't know,' Meredith said. 'If my Graham didn't

wear one I know he'd have all sorts of slappers crawling all over him.'

She strained her neck to try and see over Andrew's screen.

'Do you wear one, Andrew?'

Stupidly, he actually checked his finger before saying no.

'Is that for any particular reason, or . . . ?'

Shit.

'No, no,' he said. 'I just . . . didn't think I'd like the feel of it.'

Nobody questioned this, but he could still feel his neck starting to burn with embarrassment. He realised then that it wasn't good enough just knowing the simple facts, having the general overview. He was going to have to accentuate the broad brushstrokes with finer ones. And so, later that evening, with Ella on in the background, he opened up a blank spreadsheet and began to fill in his family's story. He started by establishing as many 'factual' things as possible: middle names, ages, hair colours, heights. Then, over the following weeks, he began to add subtler details – remembering snippets of strangers' conversations from which he'd take some minor detail, or by asking himself how someone else's news might have been dealt with by his own family. Before too long you could have asked him almost anything and he'd have a response prepared. To look at the spreadsheet at random you might find that David enjoyed touch rugby but had recently sprained his ankle. He was shy and preferred playing on his own rather than with friends. He'd begged for months for a pair of trainers that had heels that lit up when you walked, until Andrew had finally relented.

Steph had terrible colic when she was a baby, but apart from the odd case of conjunctivitis now and then they rarely had to see a doctor with her these days. She asked scarily intelligent questions in public which often left them embarrassingly stumped. She had once played a shepherd at the nativity to mixed reviews from her co-stars, though of course they'd never been prouder.

It was the 'they' part – him and Diane – that he found more difficult. It had felt OK when he'd allowed himself to fantasise during the interview, but this was another level altogether. Nevertheless, the details were all there: Diane had recently been made partner in the law firm (her field was human rights), and though she worked long hours she'd now stopped checking the dreaded BlackBerry at weekends. Their wedding anniversary was 4 September, but they also had a mini-celebration on 15 November – the anniversary of their first kiss (standing outside in the snow after an impromptu party in a friend's halls of residence room). Their first proper date had been to see *Pulp Fiction* at the cinema. They went to her parents' for Christmas and tended to holiday in France in the summer and Center Parcs in the autumn half-term. They'd gone to Rome for their tenth wedding anniversary. When they could get a babysitter they'd go to the theatre, but nothing too avant-garde, because they'd decided their time and money was too precious to fritter away on something without at least one of the leads having been in a Sunday-night costume drama. Diane played tennis every Sunday morning with her friend Sue and was on the PTA at Steph's school. She used to wear bright orange-rimmed glasses before taking the plunge with laser surgery. She had a little scar above her eyebrow from where a boy at school called James Bond had thrown a crab apple at her.

All of this had been such a full-on job that Andrew had

barely found time to think about how his actual new role was going. He'd already been to two funerals and made difficult phone calls to several relatives. He'd even come along with Keith to his first property inspection and seen the room where a woman had taken her final breath. But all that felt like a walk in the park compared to keeping his deceit undiscovered. He was constantly on edge, waiting for the moment he got himself tangled up in knots or completely contradicted himself. But then a month passed, and another, and slowly he started to relax. All his hard work was paying off.

The moment that nearly changed everything came on a Friday lunchtime, Andrew having spent a fruitless morning searching for next-of-kin clues in a shoebox full of papers recovered from a property search. He was absentmindedly watching some shop-bought macaroni cheese rotate in the microwave and engaging in some idle chit-chat with Cameron, when the subject of allergies came up.

'That's the hard part,' Cameron was saying. 'You have to be totally prepared. It just means you're on edge rather a lot. Especially when it comes to nuts. With Chris, we just have to be extra vigilant, you know?'

'Mmm,' Andrew said, distractedly peeling back the plastic film and jabbing the pasta around with his fork. 'Steph's allergic to bee stings, so I know what you mean.'

It was only when he got back to his desk and was halfway through his lunch that he considered this little exchange. He hadn't needed to mentally refer to his spreadsheet or desperately improvise something; instead, he had quite calmly volunteered this information about Steph without even thinking about it, as if it had come from his subconscious. The fact that the detail had appeared so easily left him deeply unsettled. It may have helped his cause overall, another little piece of information to put meat on the bones, but it was the first time he'd really lost sight of why he was having to make things up in the first place. Allowing the fantasy to take over like that felt scary. So much so, in fact, that when he got home that evening, rather than updating his spreadsheet he spent the time looking for another job.

A week later, he had just come out of the church having attended the funeral of a seventy-five-year-old former driving instructor who'd drowned in the bath, when he turned on his phone to find a voicemail from an HR person asking him to interview for one of the jobs he'd applied for. Ordinarily this would have thrown him into a panic, but he always felt curiously numb after the funerals, so when he heard the message he felt calm enough to call back immediately to arrange the interview. This was his chance to escape and finally stop the lies.

Another week later and he was climbing the stairs at the council office and feeling horribly out of breath, trying to convince himself that this was because he was suffering from a disease – possibly fatal – and nothing to do with the fact he hadn't exercised for two decades, when his phone rang again. A few seconds later, he was wheezing that yes he'd be very happy to come in for a second interview. He spent the rest of the afternoon sitting at his desk and imagining how it would feel to tell Cameron he was handing in his notice already.

'You and the family up to anything nice this weekend, Andrew?' Bethany asked.

'Barbecue on Saturday if the weather's nice,' Andrew said. 'Steph's decided she's vegetarian, so not quite sure what's going to be on the menu for her.'

'Oh, I am too! It's fine – just do some halloumi cheese and some Linda McCartney sausages. She'll love it.'

They were still discussing weekend plans some minutes later when Andrew got an email from Adrian, the recruitment person who'd called him, asking him to confirm what dates he was free for the second interview. Andrew excused himself and went to find an empty toilet cubicle. He didn't want to admit to himself quite how warm and comforted he felt after little moments like this with Bethany and the others when discussing family stuff. The thought returned to him again: where was the harm in what he was doing? He wasn't upsetting anyone. People had *actual* families that they did *actual* diabolical things to, harming loved ones in all sorts of awful ways, and what he was doing wasn't comparable to that, was it?

By the time he'd got back to his desk he'd made up his mind. He had made peace with what he was doing. He wasn't going to turn back now.

'*Hi Adrian,*' he wrote, '*I'm really glad for the opportunity to have met with Jackie, but after a bit of soul-searching I've decided to keep on in my current role. Thank you for your time.*'

From then on, things started to get easier. He could happily join in with family chat feeling guilt-free, and, for the first time in a very long while, he felt happy more often than he felt lonely.

Chapter Six

Andrew emerged from the station and – soddiest of sod's laws – found himself walking just behind Cameron. He hung back and pretended to check his phone. To his surprise, he actually had a new text. To his disappointment, it was from Cameron. He read it and swore under his breath. He wanted to like Cameron, he really did, because he knew that his heart was in the right place. But it was hard to warm to a person who a) commuted on one of those mini-scooters which had suddenly been deemed acceptable for people above the age of five, and b) was unwittingly trying to ruin his life, having waited barely twelve hours before texting him to ask whether he'd had a chance to reconsider the dinner party plan.

The idea of losing his family didn't bear thinking about. Yes, there was still the occasional tricky moment in conversation that sent him briefly off balance, but it was worth it. Diane, Steph and David *were* his family now. They were his happiness and his strength and the thing that kept him going. Didn't that make them just as real as everyone else's family?

He made a cup of tea, hung his coat on its usual peg, and turned to see that there was a woman sitting in his seat.

He couldn't see her face because it was obscured behind his

computer, but he could see her legs, clad in dark green tights, under his desk. She was dangling one of her black pumps on her toes. Something about the way she was flicking it back and forth reminded Andrew of a cat toying with a mouse. He stood there, mug in hand, not quite knowing what to do. The woman was swivelling in his chair and tapping a pen – one of *his* pens – on her teeth.

'Hello,' he said, realising that even for him this was a record, to feel his cheeks reddening as the woman smiled and offered him a cheery hello in response.

'Sorry, but you're, um, sitting in . . . that's sort of technically my seat.'

'Oh God, I'm so sorry,' the woman said, jumping to her feet.

'It's OK,' Andrew said, adding, rather needlessly, another 'sorry' himself.

The woman had dark, rusty-red hair which was piled high on top of her head with what looked like a pencil poking through it, as if to pull it out would make her hair cascade down like some sort of *KerPlunk* Rapunzel. Andrew guessed she was a few years younger than him, late thirties perhaps.

'What a great first impression to make,' she said, getting to her feet. Then, seeing Andrew's confusion, 'I'm Peggy – it's my first day.'

Just then Cameron appeared and bounded over like a quiz-show presenter on a now-defunct digital channel.

'Excellent, excellent – you two've met!'

'And I've already stolen his chair,' Peggy said.

'Ha, *stolen his chair*,' Cameron said, laughing. 'So anyway. Pegs – do you mind if I call you Pegs?'

'Um . . . No?'

'Well, Pegs, Peggy – the Pegster! – You're going to be shadowing Andrew for a while just to get you up to speed. I'm afraid you're rather in at the deep end this morning as I believe Andrew has a property inspection. But, well, no time like the present to get stuck in, I suppose.'

He proffered a violent double thumbs up and Andrew watched Peggy recoil involuntarily, as if Cameron had just pulled out a knife. 'Righto,' Cameron said, oblivious to this, 'I shall leave you in Andrew's capable hands.'

Andrew had forgotten they'd got a new person starting, and he felt uneasy at the prospect of being shadowed. Entering a dead person's house was always strange and unsettling, and the last thing he wanted was someone else to worry about. He had his own methods, his own way of doing things. He didn't really want to have to keep stopping to explain everything along the way. At the start, Keith had been the one to show Andrew the ropes. He had seemed to take it relatively seriously at first, but before long he started to just sit in the corner and play games on his phone, pausing only to make crude jokes at the deceased's expense. Andrew might have welcomed a bit of gallows humour, though it wasn't really his style, but Keith didn't seem to possess a shred of empathy. Eventually, Andrew had approached him in the office kitchen and suggested he carry out inspections on his own. Keith had mumbled his agreement, barely seeming to notice what Andrew had said – though this may have been due in part to him struggling to extract his finger from the can of energy drink it was stuck in.

From then on, Keith stayed with Meredith in the office, registering deaths and arranging funerals. Andrew much preferred doing the inspections alone. The only problem with being unaccompanied was that news travelled fast when someone died. Suddenly a person who'd expired in complete solitude now had posthumous well-wishers and dear, *dear* friends who arrived during his inspections – caps in hand, beady eyes darting about the place – to pay their respects, and, just on the off chance, check if that watch the deceased had promised them in the event of their death, or fiver they owed them, happened to be on the premises. It was always the worst part, having to shoo these people away, the threat of violence hanging in the room long after they'd gone. So at least with the newbie alongside him he'd have a bit of backup, he conceded.

'I meant to say,' Peggy said. 'Before we left, Cameron cornered me and told me to try and persuade you that us all having "dinner party bonding sessions" together was a good idea. He said be subtle about it, but, well, that's not really my area of expertise . . .'

'Ah,' Andrew said. 'Well, thanks for letting me know. I think I'll just ignore that for now.' He hoped that was *that* nipped in the bud.

'Right you are,' Peggy said. 'Probably for the best as far as I'm concerned. Cooking isn't my bag, to be honest. I managed to get to the age of thirty-eight without realising I've been pronouncing bruschetta wrong all my life. Turns out it's not "brusheta", according to my neighbour. Then again, he does wear a pink jumper tied around his shoulders like he lives on a yacht, so I'm reluctant to take any of his advice.'

'Right,' Andrew said, slightly distracted, having realised they were running low on supplies ahead of the property inspection.

51

'I suppose it's a team building thing, is it?' Peggy said. 'To be fair, I'd prefer that than clay pigeon shooting or whatever it is these middle managers get up to.'

'Something like that,' Andrew said, pulling his rucksack around and searching it to see if he was missing anything.

'And so we're, um, actually going to see a house now where a bloke's just died?'

'Yes, that's right.' Shit, they *did* need supplies. They'd have to make a detour. He looked around in time to see Peggy puffing out her cheeks and then realised how unwelcoming he was being. He felt a familiar wave of self-loathing, but the words to rectify the situation wouldn't come, so they walked on in silence until they got to the supermarket.

'We just need to make a quick stop off here,' Andrew said.

'Mid-morning snack?' Peggy asked.

'Afraid not. Well, not for me. But feel free to get something for yourself. I mean, not that you need my permission. Obviously.'

'No, no, I'm fine. I'm actually on a diet anyway. It's the one where you eat an entire wheel of brie and then have a bit of a cry. You know the one?'

Andrew remembered to smile this time.

'I'll just be a minute,' he said, shuffling off. When he returned with everything he needed he found Peggy standing in an aisle by the books and DVDs.

'Just look at this lass,' she said, showing him a book whose cover showed a woman smiling to the camera, apparently halfway through preparing a salad. 'No one should look that delighted whilst holding an avocado.' She put the book back on the shelf and looked at the air freshener and aftershave in Andrew's basket.

'I've got a horrible feeling I don't know what I'm letting myself in for,' she said.

'I'll explain a bit more when we get there,' Andrew said. He made his way to the tills, watching Peggy as she strolled towards the exit. She had a curious way of walking, her arms flat against her sides but with her fists gently clenched and pointing out sideways, so that it looked like she had two treble clefs attached to her sides. As Andrew punched his pin into the card reader the tune of Ella and Louis Armstrong's version of 'Would You Like to Take a Walk?' drifted into his head.

They were standing at a crossroads, Andrew checking they were going the right way on his phone. Peggy filled the silence with a story about a particularly moving TV episode she'd watched the night before. 'Admittedly, I can't remember the name of the show, or the lead character, or when or where it's set – but if you can track it down it's brillo.' Satisfied they were going in the right direction, Andrew was about to lead the way when there was a sudden crash behind him. He span around to see where the noise had come from, and saw a builder leaning over some scaffolding, about to toss an armful of rubble down into a skip.

'Everything OK?' Peggy said. But Andrew was rooted to the spot, unable to take his eyes off the builder as he hurled another lot of bricks down with an even harsher clang. He began to clap dust off his hands, but saw Andrew looking at him and stopped.

'Problem, mate?' he said, leaning over the scaffolding. Andrew swallowed hard. He could feel pain beginning to grow at his temples, the sound of harsh feedback slowly filtering into his head. Underneath the static came the faint strains of 'Blue Moon'. With great effort, he managed to get his legs moving, and, to his relief, by the time he'd crossed the road and walked further on both the pain and noise had subsided. He looked around sheepishly for Peggy, wondering how he was going to explain his behaviour, but she was still standing by the skip, talking to the builder. From the expressions on their faces, it looked as if Peggy was patiently trying to teach an incredibly stupid dog how to do a trick. Abruptly, Peggy walked off.

'You all right?' she said when she'd caught up with him.

Andrew cleared his throat. 'Yes, fine,' he said. 'Thought I might have a migraine coming on, but thankfully not.' He nodded back at the builder. 'What were you talking to him about?'

'Oh,' Peggy said, still seeming distracted with concern for him, 'he made some unsolicited comments about my appearance so I took the time to explain that I sensed a deep, unquenchable sadness in his eyes. Are you sure you're OK, though?'

'Yes, fine,' Andrew said, realising too late that his arms were rigid at his sides, like a toy soldier.

They set off again, and even though he braced himself, the distant crash of rubble still made him jump.

The deceased's flat was part of the Acorn Gardens estate. The name was written in white on a green sign featuring the names of the various blocks on the estate: Huckleberry House, Lavender House, Rose Petal House. Underneath that someone had spray-painted: 'fuck cops' and underneath that a sketch of a cock and balls.

'Blimey,' Peggy said.

'It's OK. I've actually been here before. Nobody bothered me that time so I'm sure we'll be fine,' Andrew said, in part trying to reassure himself.

'Oh no, I'm sure it will be. I just meant that.' Peggy nodded at the sketch. 'Impressive detail.'

'Ah, right. Yes.'

As they walked through the estate Andrew noticed people closing their windows and parents calling their kids inside, as if it were a Western and he was an outlaw hell-bent on chaos. He just hoped his attempted friendly smile conveyed the fact it was a cagoule and some Febreze in his bag, rather than a shotgun.

The flat was on the first floor of Huckleberry House. Andrew paused at the bottom of the concrete steps and turned to face Peggy.

'How much detail has Cameron gone into with you about what happens at the property inspections?' he said.

'Not a huge amount,' Peggy said. 'It would be great if you could fill me in a bit more. Because I'll level with you, Andrew, I'm ever so slightly completely bloody terrified.' She laughed nervously. Andrew dropped his gaze. Part of him wanted to laugh along to reassure her, but at the same time he was aware that if there were any neighbours or friends of the deceased looking on it wouldn't look very professional. He squatted and reached into his bag.

'Here you go,' he said, handing Peggy a pair of surgical gloves and mask. 'So, the deceased's name is Eric White. He was sixty-two. The coroner referred the death to us because from what they can tell from the initial search by police there's no obvious sign of a next of kin. So we've got two goals today; firstly to piece together as much as we can about

Eric and find out if there really isn't a next of kin, and secondly try and work out if he's got enough money to pay for the funeral.'

'Wow, OK,' Peggy said. 'And what's the going rate for a funeral these days?'

'It depends,' Andrew said. 'Average cost is about four thousand pounds. But if the deceased hasn't got any sort of estate, and no relatives or anyone else willing to pay for it, then the council are legally obliged to bury them. Without frills – no headstone, flowers, private plot and whatever – that's about a grand.'

'Jeez,' Peggy said, snapping a glove on. 'Does that happen a lot?'

'Unfortunately,' Andrew said. 'In the last five years or so there's been about a 12 per cent increase in public health funerals. More and more people are passing away on their own, so we're always busy.'

Peggy shivered.

'Sorry, I know it's a bit bleak,' Andrew said.

'No, it's that expression – "pass away". I know it's meant to soften the blow, but it just seems so, I dunno, filmsy.'

'I agree, actually,' Andrew said. 'I don't usually say it myself. But sometimes people prefer it described that way.'

Peggy cracked her knuckles. 'Ah, you're all right, Andrew. I'm quite hard to shock. Ha – cut to me in five minutes' time legging it out of here.' From the couple of wafts Andrew had already smelled coming through the door, he wouldn't be at all surprised if that was what happened. What was the protocol then? Would he have to chase after her?

'So what else did the coroner have to say about this poor chap?' Peggy asked.

'Well, the neighbours realised they hadn't seen him for a while and called the police, who forced entry and found his body. He was in the living room and he'd been there for a while so was in a fairly bad state of decomposition.'

Peggy reached up and twiddled one of her earrings.

'Does that mean it might be a bit . . .' She tapped her nose.

'Afraid so,' Andrew said. 'It will have had time to air out a bit, but you can't . . . it's hard to explain, but . . . it's a very specific sort of smell.'

Peggy was starting to look a little pale.

'But that's where this comes in,' Andrew said quickly, holding up the aftershave, sounding unintentionally as if he was in an advert. He shook the bottle and sprayed it liberally inside his mask, then did the same for Peggy, who strapped her mask over her nose and mouth.

'I'm not entirely sure this is what Paco Rabanne had in mind,' came her muffled voice. This time Andrew smiled for real, and though Peggy's mouth was obscured he could tell from her eyes that she was smiling back.

'I've tried all sorts of different things over the years – but it's only ever the expensive stuff which seems to work.'

He took the keys from an envelope in his bag.

'I'll go and have a quick look first, if that's OK?'

'Be my guest,' Peggy said.

With the key in the lock, this was usually the point where Andrew took a moment to remind himself why he was there: that he was to treat the place with as much respect as possible, no matter how bad the conditions. He was by no means a spiritual person, but he tried to make sure he carried out his work as if the deceased were watching on. On this occasion, not wanting to make Peggy any more uncomfortable than she already was, he only went through this little ritual – putting his phone on silent, too – after he'd stepped inside and shut the door gently behind him.

When Peggy had asked him about the smell, he was glad he'd managed to censor himself. Truthfully, what she was about to experience would change her forever. Because, as Andrew had discovered, once you've smelled death it never leaves you. Once, not long after his first-ever house inspection, he'd been walking through an underpass and had caught the same smell of decomposition as he'd experienced at the house. Glancing to one side, he saw amongst the leaves and rubbish on the floor a small stretch of police tape. It still made him shudder whenever he thought about it, to feel so finely attuned to death.

It was hard to tell from the little hallway what condition the flat was going to be in. In Andrew's experience, the places fell into two categories: either they were immaculately clean – no dust, no cobwebs, not a thing out of place – or they were overpoweringly squalid. It was the former that Andrew found the most upsetting by far, because to him it never felt as simple as the deceased just being house-proud. Instead, it seemed more likely that they knew that when they died they were going to be found by a stranger and couldn't bear the thought of leaving a mess. It was like a more extreme version of people who spent the morning feverishly tidying in preparation for the cleaner. Of course there was a certain dignity to it, but it made Andrew's heart break to think that, for some people, the moments immediately following their death were more of a pressing concern than whatever time they had left to live. Chaos, on the other hand – clutter and filth and decay – never felt quite as upsetting. Maybe the deceased had just been unable to look after themselves properly in their last days, but Andrew liked to think that they were actually sticking two fingers up at convention. Nobody had bothered to hang around to look after them so why should they carry on giving a shit? You can't go gently into the good night when you're laughing uproariously imagining some mug from the council slipping on some shit on the bathroom floor.

The fact he was forced to shoulder open the door to the little living room suggested this was going to be the latter of the two scenarios and, sure enough, the smell hit him with an overwhelming intensity, greedily seeking out his nostrils. He usually refrained if possible from spraying air freshener, but to really be able to spend time there he would have to. He fired off a generous burst in each corner, picking his way through the mess, and reserved the most prolonged spray for the centre of the room. He would have opened the grimy window but the key was presumably lost somewhere in all the clutter. The floor was covered by an ocean of blue corner shop bags stuffed with empty crisp packets and cans of soft drinks. In one corner, a mound of clothes. In another, newspapers and post, mostly unopened. In the middle of the room there was a green camping chair, a can of cherry coke in each cupholder, opposite a television that was propped up on an uneven pile of telephone directories, so that it sloped to once side. Andrew wondered if Eric had suffered from a crick in his neck from having to angle his head at the listing screen. On the floor in front of the chair was an upturned microwave meal, yellow rice spilled all around it. That was probably where it happened. That chair. Andrew was about to make a start on the pile of post when he remembered Peggy.

'How is it?' she said when he stepped outside.

'It's pretty messy, and the smell isn't . . . ideal. You can always wait outside if you'd prefer.'

'No,' Peggy said, clenching and unclenching her hands at her side. 'If I don't do it first time then I never will.'

She followed him into the living room and, apart from the fact she was holding her mask to her face so firmly her knuckles were faintly white, she didn't seem too distressed. They surveyed the living room together.

'Wow,' Peggy eventually mumbled through her mask. 'There's something so . . . I dunno . . . *static* about all this. It's like the place died with him.'

Andrew had never really thought about it that way. But there *was* something eerily still about it all. They reflected in silence for a moment. If Andrew had known any profound quotes about death this would have been the perfect time for one. It was then that an ice-cream van went past outside, cheerily blasting out the *Match of the Day* theme.

Under Andrew's instruction, they began to sort through all the paper.

'So what am I actually looking for?' Peggy said.

'Photos, letters, Christmas or birthday cards – anything that might indicate a family member, their phone number, or a return address. Oh, and any bank statements so we can get a sense of his finances.'

'And a will, presumably?'

'Yes, that too. That usually depends on whether he's got a next of kin. The vast majority of people without one won't have a will.'

'Makes sense I guess. Here's hoping you had a bit of cash, Eric, old boy.'

They worked methodically, Peggy following Andrew's lead by clearing a space as best as possible on the floor and creating separate piles for documents depending on whether they contained any useful information or not. There were utility bills and a TV Licence reminder, along with a catalogue from the official Fulham Football Club shop, scores of takeaway menus, a warranty for a kettle and an appeal from Shelter.

'I think I've got something,' Peggy said, after twenty minutes of fruitless searching. It was a Christmas card, featuring some laughing monkeys in Christmas hats with the caption: 'Chimply Having A Wonderful Christmastime!' Inside, in handwriting so small it was as if the person were *trying* to remain anonymous, it read:

> *To Uncle Eric,*
> *Happy Christmas*
> *Love from Karen.*

'He's got a niece, then,' Peggy said.

'Looks like it. Any other cards there?'

Peggy dug about and did her best not to flinch when a horribly dozy fly was disturbed and flew past her face.

'Here's another one. A birthday card. Let's see now. Yep, it's from Karen again. Hang on, there's something else written here: "*If you ever want to give me a call, here's my new number.*"'

'There we go,' Andrew said. Ordinarily he would have called the number there and then, but he felt self-conscious with Peggy beside him so he decided to wait until they were back at the office.

'Is that it, then?' Peggy said, making subtle movements towards the door.

'We still need to see about his financial situation,' Andrew said. 'We know he had a small amount in a current account, but there might be something else here.'

'Cash?' Peggy said, looking around at all the mess.

'You'd be surprised,' Andrew said. 'The bedroom's usually a good place to start.'

Peggy watched from the doorway as Andrew headed for the single bed and dropped to his knees. The light coming from the window was catching the dust in the air. Every time he shifted on the floor another bloom of it billowed up, disturbing the rest. He tried not to grimace. This was the part that he found hardest, because it felt even more invasive to be poking around in someone's bedroom.

He made sure to tuck his sleeves into his protective gloves before reaching under the mattress at one end, slowly sweeping his hand along.

'Say he does have ten grand stashed away somewhere,' Peggy said, 'but he *hasn't* got a next of kin. Where would the money go?'

'Well,' Andrew said, readjusting his position, 'any cash or assets he has first of all go to paying for the funeral. What's left over is kept in the safe at the office. If nothing comes to light about someone who's clearly entitled to the money – extended family and so on – then it goes to The Crown Estate.'

'What, so old Betty Windsor gets her hands on it?' Peggy said.

'Um, sort of,' Andrew said, sneezing as some dust went up his nose. He found nothing on the first sweep, but after bracing himself and reaching in further he touched something soft and lumpy. It was a sock – Fulham FC branded – and inside was a bundle of notes, mostly twenties, held in place by an elastic band. For no discernible reason the elastic band had been almost entirely coloured in with blue Biro. Whether it denoted something vitally important, or was just an act of idle doodling, Andrew wasn't sure. It was this kind of detail that stayed with him long after the inspections: odd little elements of a forgotten life, the reasons for their existence unknowable, leaving him with a subtle feeling of unresolved tension, like seeing a question written down without a question mark.

From the amount of notes there he knew it was going to be enough for Eric to cover the cost of his funeral. It would be up to his niece how much she wanted to help out too.

'So, is that it?' Peggy said. Andrew could tell she was now really rather keen to be outside and breathe fresh air again. He remembered that feeling from his own first time – that first gulp of polluted London air was like being reborn.

'Yep, that's us done.'

He gave the place one final check in case they'd missed anything. They were just preparing to leave when they heard movement by the front door.

The man in the hallway clearly hadn't been expecting anyone to be there, judging from the surprise on his face and the fact he immediately took two steps back towards the door when he saw them. He was squat and noticeably perspiring – a bowling ball of a beer belly threatening to escape from under his polo-shirt. Andrew braced himself for confrontation. God how he despised encounters with these cynical, desperate opportunists.

'You police?' the man said, eyeing their protective gloves.

'No,' Andrew said, making himself look the man in the eye. 'We're from the council.'

The fact the man visibly relaxed at this point – even taking a step forward – was enough for Andrew to know why he was there.

'You knew the deceased?' he asked, trying to stand tall in the small hope the man might mistake him for a retired bare-knuckle boxer rather than someone who got vaguely out of breath watching Snooker.

'Yeah, that's right. Eric.'

A pause.

'Real shame about, you know, him passing on and that.'

'Are you a friend or relative?' Peggy said.

The man looked her up and down and scratched his chin, as if appraising a second-hand car.

'Friend. We were tight. Really tight. We went way back.'

As the man went to smooth what remained of his greasy hair against his head, Andrew noticed his trembling hand.

'How long we talking?' Peggy said.

Andrew was glad Peggy was taking the lead. The way she spoke, the steeliness of her voice, sounded much more authoritative.

'Oh, blimey, there's a question. A long old time,' the man said. 'You lose track of these things, don't you?'

Apparently confident that Peggy and Andrew weren't anything to worry about, he was now distracted by trying to look past them into the living room. He took another step forward.

'We were just about to lock up,' Andrew said, showing the key in his hand. The man eyed it with barely concealed magpie-like intent.

'Right, yeah,' the man said. 'I was just here to pay my respects and what have you. As I say we were good mates. I don't know if you found a will or anything . . .'

Here we go, Andrew thought.

'. . . but he'd actually said if he *were* to pass away, you know, suddenly and that, he'd want me to have a couple of his things.'

Andrew was about to explain, as calmly as he could, that anything that made up Eric's estate needed to remain untouched until everything was clarified, but Peggy got in ahead of him.

'What was it Mr Thompson was going to leave you?' she said.

The man shifted his feet and cleared his throat. 'Well, there was his telly, and truth be told he did owe me a little bit of cash too.' He flashed a yellow smile. 'To make up for all the drinks I'd bought him over the years, you know.'

'Funny that,' Peggy said. 'His name was Eric White. Not Eric Thompson.'

The man's smile vanished.

'What? Yeah, I know. White. What . . .' He looked at Andrew and spoke to him out of the side of his mouth, as if Peggy wouldn't be able to hear him. 'Why'd she do that, try and trick me, when a man's just died?'

'I think you probably know why,' Andrew said quietly.

The man was suddenly consumed by a hacking cough.

'Bollocks, you've no idea,' he spluttered. 'No idea,' he said again, yanking the front door open.

Andrew and Peggy waited a while before they went outside. The man had clumped down the steps and was now halfway across the estate, his hands in his jacket pockets. He turned briefly, back peddling as he looked back up and flicked a vee. Andrew took off his mask and gloves and Peggy did the same before wiping a sheen of sweat from her forehead.

'So what did you think of your first property inspection, then?' Andrew said, watching the man disappear around the corner with a final V-sign.

'I think,' Peggy said, 'that I need a stiff bloody drink.'

Chapter Seven

Andrew had assumed Peggy was joking even as she marched them into the first pub they came to around the corner from the estate. But then the next thing he knew she'd ordered a pint of Guinness and asked what he was having. He checked his watch. It had only just turned one o'clock.

'Oh, really? Well, I shouldn't . . . I'm not . . . um . . . OK, then. A lager, I suppose, please.'

'Pint?' the barman asked.

'A half,' Andrew said. He suddenly felt like a teenager again. He used to practically hide behind Sally as she'd confidently order them beers in their local. He'd had to hold the pint glass with both hands, like a toddler drinking milk from a bottle.

Peggy was drumming her fingers on the bar impatiently as the barman waited for her half-full Guinness to settle. She looked ready to jump over and drink straight from the tap.

Aside from a couple of regulars who looked so gnarled and settled in it was as if the structural integrity of the building depended on their presence, they were the only ones there. Andrew was still hanging his coat on the back of a chair when Peggy clinked her glass against his on the table, and drank three hearty gulps.

'Christ, that's better,' she said. 'Don't worry, I'm not an

alkie,' she added quickly. 'This is my first drink in about a month. That was just pretty intense for a first morning's work. Usually it's just seeing where the toilets are and forgetting the name of everyone you're introduced to. Still, better to properly go for it, I suppose. It's like getting into cold water, isn't it? And I've got enough holiday memories of slowly inching my way into the sea, like I could somehow trick my body into not realising what was happening, to know you've just got to get it over with.'

Andrew took a tentative sip of beer. He couldn't actually remember the last time he'd had an alcoholic drink, but he was fairly certain it hadn't been lunchtime on a Wednesday.

'How often do chancers like that guy turn up and try and scam money?' Peggy said.

'It's quite common,' Andrew said. 'The stories are usually very similar, though sometimes you get a person with something better prepared, more believable.'

Peggy wiped some foam off her lip.

'I'm not sure what's worse. Maybe the people who concoct a proper story are the real shits, not that dopey idiot back there.'

'I think you're right,' Andrew said. 'At least with Eric we've got what looks like a next of kin. That usually settles things – stops people chancing their arm when there's family on the scene.'

One of the locals at the bar began an impressively violent sneezing fit, entirely ignored by the others dotted around him. He eventually recovered enough to inspect whatever he'd hacked up into a handkerchief with a mixture of surprise and pride before ramming it back up his sleeve.

'Is it usually blokes who, you know, end up like this?' Peggy said, eyeing the sneezer as if he might be their next case.

'Nearly always, yes. I've only had one woman' – Andrew went red before he could stop himself – 'you know, a dead one.' *Oh God!* 'I mean . . .'

Peggy was trying very hard not to smile. 'It's OK, I know what you mean. You've only ever done one house inspection where the deceased was female,' she said, very deliberately.

'That's right,' Andrew said. 'It was my first inspection, actually.'

The pub door opened and an elderly couple came in, regulars too, it would seem, judging from the way the barman acknowledged them with a nod and began pouring a pint and a half of bitter without needing to be asked.

'What was that like, then, your first?' Peggy asked.

The memory of that day was still very clear in Andrew's mind. The woman's name was Grace, and she'd been ninety when she'd died. Her house had been so immaculate it was as if she might have expired as a result of a particularly vigorous clean. Andrew recalled the intense relief he'd felt when he and Keith had entered the house. Maybe it would always be like this: little old ladies who'd had a good innings and passed away in their sleep; savings in a Mrs Tiggywinkle money jar, *Brideshead Revisited* on VHS; a kindly next-door neighbour doing the weekly shop and replacing lightbulbs.

That was before he found the note under Grace's pillow.

'In the event of my death: make sure that evil bitch next door gets nothing. She'll be after my wedding ring – mark my words!'

He realised Peggy was looking at him expectantly.

'It was largely fine,' he said, deciding that dropping another grim tale into the mix might not be helpful.

They sipped their drinks and Andrew realised he should really ask Peggy some questions about herself. But his mind was blank. That was the problem when you spent your entire adult life treating small talk like it was Kryptonite. Luckily, Peggy had that rare quality of making a silence seem comfortable. After a while, she broke it. 'So is there nobody at the funerals if we've not found a next of kin?'

'Well,' Andrew said, 'and this isn't strictly part of the job, but if it doesn't look like anyone's going to turn up – no neighbours or ex-colleagues or anything – then I go myself.'

'That's very good of you. Going above and beyond, like that.'

'Oh no. Not really,' Andrew said quickly, squirming with embarrassment. 'It's quite common in this job, I think. I'm sure I'm not the only one.'

'Must be tough, though,' Peggy said. 'Are they usually OK – as much as they can be – the funerals? Nothing really distressing's happened?'

'Not so much distressing,' Andrew said. 'But there are unusual moments.'

'Like what?' Peggy said, leaning forward slightly.

Andrew immediately pictured the chair man.

'A man once turned up with a blue armchair,' he said. 'I'd not been able to find any friends or family, so I wasn't expecting anyone there. It turned out this man – Phillip – had been on holiday when his friend died. He was the one person who was allowed into the guy's house. The deceased was obsessed with this chair getting somehow damaged, though the colour had already begun to fade. Phillip wasn't sure why he was so attached to it, but he had a feeling his friend's late wife used to sit there. Phillip eventually persuaded the man to let him take it away and get the colour restored, but by the time he'd come to collect it from the repair place after his holiday, the man had died. Phillip saw the notice I'd put in the local paper that morning and headed straight to the funeral. He even brought the chair into the church so it was next to us during the service.'

'Wow,' Peggy said. 'That's heartbreaking.'

'It is, yes,' Andrew said. 'But . . .' He stopped abruptly, worrying that what he had been about to say was too weird.

'What?' Peggy said.

Andrew cleared his throat.

'Well, it actually made me determined to keep going to the funerals.'

'How come?'

'Oh, well, I'm not exactly sure,' Andrew said. 'It just felt like I sort of . . . had to.'

The truth of it – and he didn't think Peggy would necessarily benefit from him telling her this on day one of the job – was that it had made him see that everyone who died alone had their own version of that chair. Some drama or other, no matter how mundane the rest of their existence was. And the idea that they'd not have someone there to be with them at the end, to acknowledge that they'd been a person in the world who'd suffered and loved and all the rest of it – he just couldn't bear the thought of it.

Andrew realised he'd been spinning his glass on the table, not saying anything. He stopped and the liquid swirled for a moment before falling into a gentle rotation. When he looked up at Peggy, she seemed to be studying him, as if recalibrating something.

'Well, what a first morning on the job this has been,' she said.

Andrew took a big gulp of beer, enjoying the fact that

71

tipping liquid into his face meant the onus on him to talk briefly disappeared.

'Anyway,' Peggy said, seeming to sense Andrew's discomfort, 'we should talk about something more cheery. Like, who am I going to hate working with in the office?'

Andrew relaxed slightly. This felt like safer territory. He weighed the question up. If he was being professional about it he'd toe the party line and say that while of course it could be a challenging environment to work in, which meant there was the occasional personality clash, everyone always pulled together in the end. But then again he had just had half a pint of lager at 1 p.m. on a Wednesday, so sod it.

'Keith.'

'Keith?'

'Keith.'

'I think I remember him from my interview. He sat in with Cameron. He kept putting his finger in his ear and looking at what he pulled out.'

Andrew winced. 'Yeah, that's sort of the tip of the iceberg when it comes to his personal hygiene.'

Still feeling somewhat reckless, Andrew found himself divulging his theory that there was something going on between Keith and Meredith. Peggy winced.

'Sadly, Keith reminds me a bit of this boy I had a dalliance with in my teenage years. He smelled like unwashed PE kit and had long, greasy hair, but I was besotted. And I wish I could say that was because he was incredibly charming and kind, but he was a complete idiot. He *was*, however, the lead guitarist in a local band, a band I subsequently joined to play maracas in.' Andrew was instantly transported back to his teenage local and watching the first – and last – performance by Sally and then boyfriend Spike's band, Driftwood, where they nervously murdered Joni Mitchell covers in front of an audience of Andrew and twenty empty chairs. Sally had seemed unusually vulnerable that night, Andrew recalled, feeling a rush of affection for his sister.

'What was your band called?' he said to Peggy. She looked at him with an unmistakably mischievous glint in her eye. 'Get another round in and I'll tell you.'

It turns out that if you haven't had a drink for a long time, two halves of 4 per cent lager on an empty stomach will actually have quite a strong effect. Andrew didn't feel drunk as such, just fuzzy and warm and aware that he would happily punch a puffin if it meant he'd get some crisps.

As promised, Peggy revealed the name of the band she'd been in (Magic Merv's Death Banana), and they'd moved on to talking about their previous jobs. Peggy had also been axed from her position in a different part of the council and been shunted across. 'I was "business support officer" for the "Access, Inclusion and Participation Team",' she said, 'which was as fun as it sounds.'

Andrew had been trying to place her accent. He thought it was probably Geordie. Was it rude to ask that question? He rubbed at his eyes. God, this *was* a bit ridiculous. They should really have gone straight back to the office. Not that he had any desire at all to do so. But two beers, though. Two! At lunchtime! What was he going to do next – throw a television out of a window? Ride a motorbike into a swimming pool?

Just then the quiet was broken as a group of women bustled in, all talking loudly over each other. Their boisterousness was entirely at odds with the subdued atmosphere, but they didn't seem at all embarrassed, as Andrew would have been, to be causing any sort of disruption. He got the sense that this was a regular fixture, a midweek tradition, perhaps: the way they all headed for a particular table without deliberation. *Why is it that we find traditions comforting?* he thought, stifling a belch. He looked at Peggy and was suddenly struck by the promise of asking her this incredibly profound question. Inevitably, it didn't sound quite so clever when he said it out loud.

'Hmm,' Peggy said, not looking fazed, to Andrew's relief. 'I suppose it's probably just because it's a moment in time where you know exactly what's about to happen, so there are no nasty surprises waiting for you. I dunno, maybe that's a bit of a pessimistic way of looking at it.'

'No, I know what you mean,' Andrew said. He pictured Sally looking at the calendar, realising it was time for their quarterly call. Maybe there was some solace, some comfort, in the regularity of their interaction.

'I suppose it's about having a balance,' he said. 'You need to keep making new traditions, otherwise you start to resent the old ones.'

Peggy lifted her glass. 'I feel like I need to toast that. To new traditions.'

Andrew looked dumbly at her for a minute before quickly grabbing his glass and knocking it clumsily into hers with an ugly clink.

There was a collective cooing from the women in the corner. Peggy looked past Andrew's shoulder at them. After a moment she leaned forwards and looked at him conspiratorially. 'Be subtle,' she said, 'but don't you just love looking at everyone's reactions when someone's talking about getting engaged?'

Andrew swivelled around.

'Woah, woah, woah – I said subtle!'

'Sorry.'

This time, Andrew half turned in his chair and pretended to be inspecting a framed caricature of a drunken cricketer on the wall. He glanced as casually as possible at the group before turning back. 'Was there something specific I was supposed to notice?' he said.

'Look at their smiles. It's all in the eyes.'

Andrew was lost.

'Most of them are genuinely happy for her, but there are at least a couple of them who don't think this is a good idea,' Peggy said. She went to take a gulp of beer then decided what she had to say was more important. 'Me and my friend Agatha, right? For ages we had this game that whenever we found out someone we knew was getting married and we didn't really approve we'd guess what their first post-proposal argument would be about.'

'That's . . . that's a bit . . .'

'Mean? Awful? You betcha. I very much learned my lesson after I got engaged to my fella, Steve. When I saw Agatha I jokingly made her guess what our first fight had been. Unfortunately, it backfired in a pretty major way.'

'How so?'

'She guessed that it was because Steve had told me he was already having cold feet about the whole thing.'

'And what was it about really?'

'It was over a badly washed-up spatula.'

'Oh.'

'Yep. Turns out she'd never really approved of him at all. But we made up in the end, thankfully. All it took was five years of stubborn silence before bumping into each other, both hammered, in a kebab shop and putting the world to rights. She even bought me a spatula for mine and Steve's tenth wedding anniversary. Funnily enough, that was the first thing I reached for to chuck at his head the other night when he came back from a two-day bender having "just popped out for a quick drink". God, life's weird sometimes.' Peggy let out a hollow laugh and Andrew joined in, unsurely. Peggy took a long gulp of Guinness and landed her glass with a thud. 'I mean,' Peggy said, 'go out, get wasted, we've all been there, right?'

Thankfully, Andrew judged this to be rhetorical, and kept quiet.

'But just don't *lie* about it, you know?'

'Absolutely,' Andrew said. 'That's the last thing you should do.'

Peggy sighed.

'Sorry, this is stupidly unprofessional of me, banging on about my marital problems.'

'Not at all, it's fine,' Andrew said. He suddenly realised what he'd just opened the door to. He could sense the question coming a mile away.

'You married, yourself?'

'Mm-hmm.'

'So I can't now *not* ask you: what was your first post-proposal argument?'

Andrew thought for a moment. What would it have been? He had the feeling it should be something equally as trivial as Peggy's.

'Whose turn it was to put the bins out, I think,' he said.

'A classic. If only all the arguments were about domestic chores, eh? Anyway . . . just nipping to the loo.'

For one dreadful second Andrew nearly stood up, too, out of politeness. *Calm down, Mr Knightley*, he thought, watching Peggy disappear around a corner in search of the toilets. He looked around, accidentally catching the eye of a man sitting at the bar, who gave him the slightest of nods. *Here we are*, the look seemed to say, *on our own. As usual.* Well, not me this time, Andrew thought, feeling a prickle of defiance. When Peggy returned he looked at the man, feeling rather smug.

There was a shriek of laughter from the other table. However insincere her friends were being, the bride to be was very obviously glowing with happiness.

'Bloody hell,' Peggy said. 'Last time I smiled like that it was after I'd found a twenty-pound note in my dressing gown. I screamed so loud the dog farted.'

Andrew laughed. And perhaps it was just the beer on an empty stomach, or the fact he hadn't had to go straight back to the office to face another afternoon of Keith and the others, but he was feeling really rather happy and relaxed all of a sudden. He made a mental note to try and remember how it felt not to have his shoulders tensed so much that they were practically touching his ears.

'Sorry again for dragging you to the pub,' Peggy said.

'No, no it's fine. I'm actually having a good time,' Andrew said, wishing he hadn't sounded quite so surprised. If Peggy found this an odd thing to say, then thankfully her face didn't show it.

'By the way, how are you at pub quizzes?' she said, half distracted by a man on a mobility scooter edging his way through the door, shepherded by the barman.

'Pub quizzes? I'm . . . I don't really know,' Andrew said. 'Normal, I suppose?'

'A few of us get babysitters and do the one at the Rising Sun on the South Bank. We come last every time and Steve usually ends up getting into a fight with the quizmaster, but it's always a laugh. You should come.'

Before he could stop himself, Andrew said, 'I'd love to.'

'Champion,' Peggy yawned, rolling her head around her shoulders. 'And I hate to be the one to say this, but it's nearly two – I suppose we better get back?'

Andrew looked at his watch, hoping that there had been some sort of glitch in time so that they had another few hours. Sadly, it wasn't to be.

Even when they were approaching the office and climbing the rain-slick steps outside, which seemed especially keen to have him slip on them that afternoon, Andrew found he couldn't stop grinning. What an unexpectedly pleasant end to the morning that had been.

'Hang on a sec,' Peggy said as they came out of the lift. 'Remind me: Keith, Cameron . . . Melinda?'

'Meredith,' Andrew said. 'The one I've decided has a thing for Keith.'

'Oh yeah. How could I forget? A late summer wedding, maybe?'

'Hmm, spring, I think,' Andrew said, and in the moment it felt somehow perfectly natural for him to perform a semi-theatrical bow as he held the door, gesturing for Peggy to go through first.

Cameron, Keith and Meredith were sitting on one of the sofas in the breakout space and all got up straight away when Andrew and Peggy walked in. Cameron's face was ashen.

Oh shit, Andrew thought. *We've been rumbled. They know about the pub.* Maybe Peggy was just a stooge, hired as a one-off to investigate improper practices. The pub trip was all just a fucking ruse and it served him right for daring to hope to pretend he could be happy. But a quick glance at Peggy and he saw she was as nonplussed as he was.

'Andrew,' Cameron said, 'we've been trying to get in touch. Has someone managed to call you?'

Andrew pulled his phone out of his pocket. He'd forgotten to turn it off silent after leaving Eric White's flat.

'Is everything OK?' he said.

Keith and Meredith shared an uneasy glance.

'Someone called earlier, with some news,' Cameron said. 'Right?'

'It's about your sister.'

Chapter Eight

Andrew had been three and Sally eight when their father had died of a heart attack. Rather than this bringing the two siblings together, Andrew's early memories of his sister tended to feature her slamming doors in his face, screaming at him to leave her alone, and their occasionally vicious scraps when he was brave enough to stand up to her. He sometimes wondered how their relationship might have differed if their dad had been around. Would they have bonded more, or would their dad have had to be constantly intervening to stop them fighting, getting angry himself at their relentless squabbling, or perhaps using a gentler approach – telling them in a soft voice how they were upsetting Mum. For her part, their mother was never on hand to stop them fighting. 'She's taken to her bed', was the confusing expression Andrew had once overheard a neighbour say, unaware that he was lying in the border by the garden fence, recovering from Sally's latest pummelling. At the time he couldn't comprehend that his mum was crippled with grief. Nobody explained this to him. All he knew was that if she'd opened her bedroom blinds it was going to be a good day – and on good days he got sausage and mash for dinner. Occasionally, she'd let him climb into bed with her. She'd lie facing away from him, her knees pulled up to her chest. She would hum songs and Andrew would rest the tip of his nose on her back, feeling the vibration of her voice.

By the time Sally was thirteen she was already a good six inches taller than the biggest boy at school. Her shoulders grew broad, her legs meaty. There was a large part of her that seemed to embrace being different, stalking the corridors, actively looking for people to intimidate. Looking back, Andrew realised this was obviously a defence mechanism, a way for Sally to strike pre-emptively against any bullies, while also providing an outlet for her grief. He might have been more understanding if he hadn't been her punching bag of choice on quite so many occasions.

When some of the boys came back after summer holidays having had growth spurts, the bravest of them were confident enough to tease Sally, provoking her until she went for them, pursuing them across the playing fields, a manic glint in her eye, windmilling her arms at whoever she managed to corner.

One day, shortly after Andrew had turned eleven, he had waited until Sally had gone downstairs before creeping into her bedroom and just standing there, smelling his sister's smell, wanting desperately to perform some sort of spell that would change her and make her care about him. He had his eyes closed, tears pooling behind his eyelids, when he heard Sally hurrying up the stairs. Maybe the spell had worked; maybe Sally had felt the urgent call to find him and tell him everything was going to be fine. It only took Andrew a split second to realise that Sally's advance towards him was going to end with a punch in the gut, not an arm around the shoulder. He received a gruff apology later that day, though he couldn't be sure if it was guilt that made Sally do it, or a rare instance of their mother stepping in. In any case,

81

Andrew was only afforded a few days' respite before another scrap.

But then, out of nowhere, came along Sam 'Spike' Morris, and everything changed. Spike had only joined the school in sixth form, but he had a quiet confidence about him that meant he soon made friends. He was tall, with shoulder-length black hair and, much to the jealousy of his bumfluff-sporting male peers, possessed a full-on folk singer's beard. Almost immediately, the word went around that Spike had somehow incurred Sally's wrath, and that he was in for a windmilling if he crossed her again.

Andrew saw the telltale signs that a fight was happening somewhere as the other kids – as if by some innate instinct, like animals heading for higher ground before a tsunami – all began hurrying towards the terrapin huts. He got there in time to see Spike and his sister squaring up, circling each other warily. Spike, Andrew noticed, was wearing a badge with the peace symbol on it.

'Sally,' Spike said, in an unexpectedly soft voice, 'I don't know why you've got this beef with me, but I'm not going to fight you, yeah? Like I said, I'm a pacifist.' Sally had tackled him to the floor before the 'ist' was out of his mouth. It was at this point that Andrew got caught up in the melee of kids around him and was knocked to the floor, so for a few moments all he could hear was the approving roars as the fight continued out of sight. But then the roars suddenly gave way to jeers and wolf whistles. When Andrew finally managed to get to his feet to see what was happening, he was met by the sight of Sally and Spike locked in a passionate embrace, sharing an almost violent kiss. They broke apart briefly and Spike grinned. Sally returned the smile, then swiftly gave him a vicious knee to the balls. She marched away, hands raised in victory, but when she looked back at Spike writhing on the floor, Andrew was sure he saw concern tempering her triumph.

As it turned out, Sally clearly felt something deeper than just concern for Spike Morris's welfare and, against all odds, the two of them became an item. If Andrew was surprised at this, nothing could have prepared him for the effect it seemed to have on Sally. The change was instant. It was as if Spike had tinkered with a pressure valve somewhere and all her fury had been released. At school they were inseparable, loping around with hands clamped together, their long hair swaying softly in the breeze, handing out spliffs to the other kids they towered over, like benevolent giants who'd wandered down from the mountains. Sally's voice began to change, eventually morphing into a slow, monotonous drawl. At home, she started not only talking to Andrew, but inviting him to hang out with her and Spike in the evenings. She never acknowledged her previous reign of terror, but letting him spend time with them, watching films and listening to records, seemed to be her way of trying to make up for it.

At first, Andrew – like most of the other kids at school – thought this was some sort of psychotic, playing-the-long-game tactic; Sally was only sneaking him into pubs and inviting him to watch hammer horrors on ropey VHS to make the inevitable beatings afterwards unexpected and even more brutal. But no. Spike, it seemed, had softened her with love. That and the weed. There was the odd flash of anger, usually directed at their mother, whose torpor Sally took for laziness. But she would always apologise afterwards, and of her own volition.

Most surprisingly of all, shortly after Andrew turned thirteen, Sally went out of her way to source him a girlfriend. He'd been minding his own business, reading *Lord of the Rings* in his usual spot by the fight-zone terrapin hut, when Sally appeared at the other side of the playground along with two other girls Andrew had never seen before, one Sally's age, one closer to his. Sally strode over to him, leaving the other girls behind.

'Hey, Gandalf,' she said.

'Hello . . . Sally.'

'See that girl over there? Cathie Adams?'

Ah yes, he did recognise her now. She was in the year below.

'Yes.'

'She fancies you.'

'What?'

'As in, she wants to go out with you. Do you want to go out with her?'

'I don't really know. Maybe?'

Sally sighed. 'Of course you do. So now you need to go and talk to her sister, Mary. She wants to see if she approves. Don't worry, I'm doing the same with Cathie.' And with that she signalled to Mary with a thumbs up and pushed Andrew roughly in the back. He stumbled forwards, just as Mary shoved Cathie in his direction. They crossed in the middle of the playground and exchanged nervous smiles, like captured spies being exchanged across an exclusion zone.

Mary swiftly interrogated him, at one point leaning close and taking a tentative sniff. Seemingly satisfied, she turned him by his shoulders and shoved him back the way he'd come. A similar process had occurred with Sally and Cathie, it would seem, and the end result was that the next few weeks seemed exclusively to involve him holding Cathie's hand in mute acceptance as she paraded them around school at break times, her head held high in the face of jeers and sniggering. Andrew was beginning to wonder what the point of all this was when one evening, following a school play and two and a half bottles of Woodpecker cider, Cathie pinned him against a wall and kissed him, before he promptly vomited on the floor. It was the best evening of his entire life.

But such are the cruel twists of fate, only two days later Sally sat him down to deliver to him the terrible news, as passed on to her by Mary, that Cathie had decided to end things. Before Andrew had time to process this, Sally was hugging him ferociously, explaining that everything happened for a reason and that time was a great healer. Andrew had no idea how he felt about Cathie Adams's decision, but as he rested his head on Sally's shoulder, enjoying the pain that came from her fierce embrace, he thought whatever had happened was probably worth it.

The following Saturday, Andrew came back upstairs having been dispatched to make popcorn when he looked through a gap in the door and saw Sally and Spike kneeling, foreheads resting together, whispering softly. Sally opened her eyes and kissed Spike delicately on his forehead. Andrew had no idea his sister was capable of anything so tender. He could have kissed Spike Morris himself for performing this miracle. After everything, he'd finally got a big sister. Unbeknownst to him, that evening would be the last time he'd see her for years.

He had no idea how Sally and Spike had managed to sneak out of their separate homes and get to the airport, never mind how they'd afforded the flights to San Francisco, but it later transpired that when Spike turned eighteen he was entitled to a large sum of money that had been left to him by his grandparents. Andrew found a note in his sock drawer from Sally explaining that they'd 'gone to the States for a while. Don't want to cause drama, little bro,' she added, 'so please can you explain everything to dear old Mother, but not until tomorrow?'

Andrew did as he was told. His mum reacted to the news from her bed with a sort of affected panic, saying, 'Oh dear. Dearie, dearie me. Really, that's unbelievable. I can't believe it.'

There followed a surreal meeting with Spike's parents, who arrived outside the house in a VW Campervan and a haze of marijuana. Andrew's mum spent the morning fretting exclusively about which sort of biscuits she should put out and Andrew, terrified that she'd now gone entirely mad, scratched so hard at the spots on his cheeks that he bled.

He spied on the conversation by lying on the landing and peering down through the banister. Spike's father, Rick, and mother, Shona, were a jumble of long brown hair and pot bellies. Hippies, it turned out, didn't age well.

'The thing is, Cassandra,' Rick said, 'we kind of feel that as they're two consenting adults we can't stop them following their hearts. Besides, we went on our own trip at that age and it didn't do us any harm.'

The way Shona was clinging to Rick as if they were on a rollercoaster made Andrew ever so slightly doubt this statement. Rick was American, and the way he pronounced the word 'adults', with the emphasis on the second syllable, seemed so impossibly exotic to Andrew he wondered whether he might just up sticks and get on a plane across the pond, too. But then he remembered their mother. Sally might not have a conscience, apparently, but he still did.

At first, there was no word from Sally. But after a month a postcard arrived, post-marked New Orleans, with a picture of a jazz trombonist in smoky sepia.

'The Big Easy! Hope you're cool, dude.'

Andrew chucked it on his bedroom floor, furious. But the next day he couldn't resist the temptation to study it again, and then he found himself sticking it to the wall by his pillow. It would be joined later by Oklahoma City, Santa Fe, the Grand Canyon, Las Vegas and Hollywood. Andrew used up what little pocket money he had on a US map, tracking his sister's movements with a marker pen and trying to guess where she'd post from next.

By now his mother would oscillate wildly from angry rants about why Sally thought she could just go swanning off like that, and tearful laments about Andrew now being her only child – cupping his face in her hands and making him promise several times that he'd never leave her.

It was with grim irony, then, that five years later Andrew found himself sitting at what his mother now referred to, with no sense of how upsetting this was to him, as her deathbed. The cancer was aggressive and the doctor gave her weeks. Andrew was supposed to be going to university – Bristol Polytechnic – to read Philosophy that September, but he deferred to look after her. He hadn't told her he'd got a place at university. It was just easier this way. The problem was that he'd not been able to get in touch with Sally to tell her their mother was dying. The postcards had dried up, the last one coming the previous year from Toronto with the message, *'Hey, bud, freezin' here. Hugs from us both!'* But more recently there had been a phone call. Andrew had answered with a mouthful of fish fingers and nearly choked when the echoey sound of Sally's voice came through the receiver. The line was terrible and they barely managed a conversation, but Andrew did just catch Sally telling him she'd call again on 20 August when they'd be in New York.

When the day came he sat waiting by the phone, half willing the call to come, half hoping it never would. When it finally did he had to wait for it to ring several times before he could face picking up.

'Heyyyy, man! It's Sally. How's the line? Hear me OK?'

'Yeah. So listen, Mum's ill. As in, really ill.'

'What's that? Ill? Like, how bad?'

'As in not-getting-better ill. You need to get on a plane now or it might be too late. The doctors think it might be less than a month.'

'Holy shit. Are you serious?'

'Of course I'm serious. Please come home as soon as you can.'

'Jesus, bro. That's . . . that's nuts.'

Sally's return was as clandestine as her exit. Andrew was coming down for breakfast as usual when he heard the kitchen tap running. His mum hadn't been out of bed for weeks, let alone made it downstairs, and he felt a flash of hope: maybe the doctors had got it wrong. But it was Sally who was standing at the sink, a ponytail seemingly featuring all the colours of the rainbow stretching all the way down to her lower back. She was wearing what looked like a dressing gown.

'Brother, fuck!' she said, pulling Andrew into a bear hug. She smelt of something musty and floral. 'How the hell are you?'

'I'm OK,' Andrew said.

'Jesus, you've grown about twenty feet.'

'Yeah.'

'How's school?'

'Yeah, fine.'

'You do good in your exams?'

'Yeah.'

'What about girls? You got a new chick yet? Nah, too busy playing the field, I bet. Hey, you like my sweater? It's Baja. I could get you one if you want.'

No, what I want is for you to come and talk to our dying mother.

'Where's Spike?' Andrew asked.

'He's stayed out in the States. Gonna go back to him when it's all, you know . . . over.'

'Right,' Andrew said. So that answered that. 'Do you want to go up and see Mum?'

'Um, yep, OK. As long as she's up and everything. Don't wanna disturb her.'

'She doesn't really get up any more,' Andrew said, heading towards the stairs. He thought for a moment that Sally wasn't going to follow, but then he saw she was just kicking off her shoes.

'Force of habit,' she said, with a sheepish smile.

Andrew knocked on the door once, twice. Nothing. He and Sally looked at each other.

It was almost as if she'd planned to die before the three of them were together, just to make things extra painful.

'Classic Mum,' Sally said later in the pub, though she pronounced it 'Mom' and Andrew was very tempted to pour his pint over her head, suddenly no longer in awe of the accent.

Their mother's funeral was attended by two great-aunts

and a handful of reluctant ex-colleagues. It was impossible for Andrew to sleep that night. He was sitting on his bed, reading yet failing to follow Nietzsche on Suffering, when he was suddenly aware of the squawking starlings in the nest in the porch who'd mistaken the security light for dawn. He peered through his curtains and saw his sister, laden down with a backpack, walking away, and wondered if this time she was going for good.

As it turned out, it was only three weeks later – Andrew having spent the majority of that time lying on the sofa wrapped in the duvet from his mum's bed, watching daytime TV – when he came downstairs and found Sally once more standing by the sink. She'd come back for him. Finally, some-thing had got through that thick skull. When Sally turned around Andrew saw her eyes were puffy and red, and this time it was he who crossed the room and hugged her. Sally said something, but her voice was muffled against his shoulder.

'What's that?' Andrew said.

'He left me,' Sally said, sniffing violently.

'Who did?'

'Spike, of course! There was just a note in the apartment. He's gone off with some fucking girl, I know it. Everything's ruined.'

Andrew shook Sally off and took a step back.

'What?' Sally said, wiping her nose on her sleeve. Then a second time, louder, when Andrew said nothing. There it was again, that old anger flashing in her eyes. But this time Andrew wasn't afraid. He was too furious.

'What do you think?' he spat. And then Sally was advanc-ing on him and pushing him back against the fridge, an arm against his throat.

'What, are you fucking glad or something? Pleased that he's left me?'

'I couldn't care less about him,' Andrew gasped. 'What about Mum?' He struggled to pull Sally's arm away from his throat.

'What about her?' Sally said through gritted teeth. 'She's dead, isn't she? Dead as a doornail. How can you be that upset? That woman didn't have a maternal bone in her body. When Dad died it was all over for her. She just fell apart. Would she really have done that if we mattered to her?'

'She was ill! And given what a mess you are about getting dumped, I don't think you're one to judge about someone falling apart.'

Sally's face flashed with renewed anger, and she managed to free her arm to hit him. Andrew staggered backwards, his hands over his eye. He braced himself for another impact, but when it came it was Sally taking him gently in her arms, saying 'I'm sorry', over and over. Eventually they both slid down to the floor where they sat, not speaking, but calm. After a while Sally opened the freezer and passed Andrew some frozen peas, and the simplicity of the act, the kindness of it in spite of her being the reason for his pain, was enough to cause tears to leak from his uninjured eye.

The next few weeks followed the same pattern. Andrew would return from his job working in the chemist on the high street and cook pasta with tomato sauce, or sausage and mash, and Sally would get high and watch cartoons. As Andrew watched her suck up spaghetti strands, sauce dribbling off her chin, he wondered just what sort of an adult she would turn out to be. The fiery bully and the hippie were still living Jekyll and Hyde-like inside her. How long, too, before she left again? He didn't have long to wait, it turned out, but this time he caught her sneaking out.

'Please just tell me you're not going to try and find Spike?' he said, shivering in the doorway against the dawn chill. Sally smiled sadly and shook her head.

'Nah. My pal Beansie got me job. Or at least he thinks so. Up near Manchester.'

'Right.'

'I just need to get myself back on track. Time for me to grow up. I just can't do that here. It's too fucking grim. First Dad, now Mum. I was . . . I was going to come and see you. Say goodbye and everything. But I didn't want to wake you up.'

'Uh-uh,' Andrew said. He looked away, scratching at the back of his neck. When he looked back he saw that Sally had just done the same. A mirror image of awkwardness. This, at least, made them both smile. 'Well. Let me know where you end up,' Andrew said.

'Yeah,' Sally said. 'Deffo.' She went to close the door but stopped and turned. 'You know I'm really proud of you, man.'

It sounded like something Sally had rehearsed. Maybe she'd hoped to wake him after all. He couldn't work out how that made him feel.

'I'll call as soon as I get settled, I promise,' she said.

She didn't, of course. The call only came months later, by which time Andrew had got his place sorted at Bristol Poly, and already it felt like an unbridgeable gap had opened between them.

They did spend a Christmas together, though, where Andrew slept on the sofa in the little flat Sally shared with Beansie (real name Tristan), the three of them drinking

Beansie's home-brewed beer that was so strong that at one point Andrew was convinced, briefly, he'd gone blind. Sally was seeing someone called Carl, a lean, languid man who was obsessed with working out and the subsequent refuelling. Every time Andrew turned around he was eating something: a whole bag of bananas, or great slabs of chicken – sitting there in his workout clothes, licking grease from his fingers like an Adidas-clad Henry VIII before he'd let himself go. Eventually Sally moved in with Carl and that's when Andrew stopped seeing her altogether. The system of regular phone calls came into play – not through any spoken agreement, it was just how things began to work. Every three months, for the past twenty years. It was always Sally that called. Sometimes, back in the early days, they'd talk about their mother – enough time had passed for them to see some of her eccentricities through rose-tinted glasses. But as the years went by, their reminiscing became forced, a desperate attempt to keep alive a connection that seemed to diminish every time they spoke. These days, the conversations had become a real effort, and sometimes Andrew wondered why Sally still bothered to call him. But then there were moments – often in the silences, when there was only the sound of their breathing – when Andrew had still felt an undeniable bond.

Chapter Nine

Andrew left the office in a daze, shaking off offers from Cameron and Peggy to accompany him home. He needed fresh air, to be on his own. It took all his strength to pick up the phone and call Carl. But Sally's husband – Sally's widower – wasn't the one who answered. Instead, it was someone who introduced herself as 'Rachel, Carl's best friend' – a strange way for a grown adult to describe themselves, especially given the circumstances.

'It's Andrew. Sally's brother,' he said.

'Of course. Andrew. How *are* you?' And then before Andrew could actually answer: 'Carl says there's no room for you at the house, unfortunately. So you'll have to stay at the B & B down the road. It's very near the church . . . for the funeral and everything.'

'Oh. Right. Has that all been arranged already?' Andrew said.

There was a pause.

'You know our Carl. He's very organised. I'm sure he won't want to worry you with all of the little details.'

Later, as the Newquay-bound train pulled away from London and copses replaced concrete, it wasn't grief or even sadness that Andrew felt. It was guilt. Guilt that he hadn't cried yet. Guilt that he was dreading the funeral, that he'd actually considered the possibility of not going.

When the conductor appeared, Andrew couldn't find his ticket. When he finally found it in his inside jacket pocket he apologised so profusely for wasting the conductor's time that the man felt compelled to put his hand on Andrew's shoulder and tell him not to worry.

He spent a week in a damp B & B, listening to seagulls keening outside, fighting the urge to leave and get straight back on a train to London. When the morning of the funeral arrived, he ate a breakfast of stale cereal alone in the B & B 'restaurant', the proprietor watching on throughout, standing in the corner with his arms folded, like a death row prison guard observing him eating his final meal.

Walking into the crematorium, the coffin resting on his shoulder, he was aware that he had no idea who the other bearers, apart from Carl, were; it had seemed impolite to ask.

Carl – who had entered his fifties in disgustingly healthy and stylish fashion, all salt-and-pepper hair and wristwatch the value of a small market town – spent the service with his head raised stoically, tears spilling metronomically down his cheeks. Andrew stood awkwardly next to him, fists clenched at his side. At the moment the coffin went through the curtains, Carl let out a low, mournful howl, unburdened by the self-consciousness that consumed Andrew.

Afterwards, at the wake, surrounded by people he had never seen, let alone met, before, he felt more alone than he had in years. They were in Carl's house, in the room dedicated to his burgeoning yoga business, Cynergy. The room had been temporarily cleared of mats and exercise balls so there was space for trestle tables struggling to support the regulation wake spread. Andrew was reminded of a rare occasion he'd seen his mother laughing, having recalled the Victoria Wood line about a typical British reaction to the news that someone had died: 'Seventy-two baps, Connie. You slice, I'll spread,' she'd said in a perfect imitation, tweaking Andrew's ear and dispatching him to put the kettle on.

As he chewed on a damp sausage roll, he suddenly got the sense that he was being watched. Sure enough, Carl was looking at him from across the room. He had changed out of his suit into a loose white shirt and beige linen trousers, and was now barefoot. Andrew couldn't help but notice he'd kept his expensive watch on. Realising that Carl was about to make his way over, Andrew quickly put down his paper plate and was up the stairs as fast as he could and into the thankfully unoccupied bathroom. As he washed his hands his eye was drawn to a shaving brush on an ornate white dish on the window sill. He picked it up and ran his finger across the top of the bristles, specs of powder flicking off into the air. He brought it to his nose and smelt the familiar rich, creamy scent. This had belonged to his father. His mother had kept it in the bathroom. He couldn't remember talking to Sally about it. She must have formed an especially sentimental attachment to want to keep hold of it.

Just then someone tapped on the door and Andrew quickly slipped the brush into his trouser pocket.

'Just a minute,' he said. He paused and forced an apologetic smile on to his face. When he emerged, Carl was standing outside with his arms crossed, biceps straining against his shirt. Up close, Andrew could see that Carl's eyes were raw from crying. He caught the scent of Carl's aftershave. It was rich and overpowering.

'Sorry,' Andrew said.

'No problem,' Carl said, though he didn't move to let Andrew pass.

'I was thinking I might head off soon,' Andrew said. 'It's a long journey back,' he added, more defensively than he'd intended.

'Of course you were,' Carl said.

Andrew chose to ignore this comment. 'See you then,' he said instead, stepping around Carl and heading for the stairs.

'After all,' Carl said, 'this must be much easier for you now Sally's gone.'

Andrew stopped at the top of the stairs and turned. Carl was looking at him, unblinking.

'What?' Carl said. 'You don't agree? Come on, Andrew, it wasn't as if you were ever really there for her, no matter how much that obviously hurt her.'

That's not true, Andrew wanted to say. *She was the one who abandoned me.*

'Things were complicated.'

'Oh, I've heard all about it, believe me,' Carl said. 'In fact, there wasn't a week that went by when Sally didn't talk about it – going over it all again and again and again, trying to work out how to get through to you, how to make you care, or at least stop hating her.'

'Hating her? I didn't hate her – that's ridiculous.'

'Oh, is it?' Renewed anger flashed in Carl's eyes and he moved towards Andrew, who dropped down a couple of stairs. 'So you didn't hold such a grudge about her apparently "abandoning" you for America that you basically refused to ever see her again?'

'Well no, that's not—'

'And even when she spent weeks on end – months, actually – trying to reach out and help you sort your life out, you were so pathetically fucking stubborn that you wouldn't let her in, even though you knew how much it was hurting her.' Carl pressed his fist to his mouth and cleared his throat.

Oh God, please don't cry, Andrew thought.

'Carl, it . . . it was com—'

'Don't you *dare* fucking say it was complicated again,' Carl said. 'Because it's actually very simple. Sally was never really happy, Andrew. Not really. Because of you.'

Andrew dropped down another step and nearly stumbled. He swivelled and used the momentum to keep on going. He needed to be as far away as possible from this. *He's got no idea what he's talking about*, he thought as he slammed the front door behind him. But doubt had began to nag at him as he left, and it only intensified during the train journey home. Was there some truth to what Carl had said? Had Sally really been so cut up about their relationship that it had somehow contributed to her decline? It was a thought too painful to even consider.

With all the lights off, the brightness of the screen was harsh on Andrew's eyes. TinkerAl's forum avatar – a dancing, laughing tomato – usually a cheering sight, seemed malevolent tonight.

Andrew made himself look at the words he had typed and untyped so many times he'd lost count.

'I buried my sister today'

The cursor flashed back at him expectantly. He moved the

mouse until it was over the 'post' button, but took his hand away, reaching for his plastic tumbler of foamy beer instead. He'd been drinking in an attempt to recreate the comforting sense of warmth he'd felt in the pub with Peggy, before Cameron's awkwardly delivered bombshell, but it had just left him with a dull, repetitive throbbing behind his eyes. He sat up straight and felt the bristles of the shaving brush in his pocket poking into his leg. It was 3 a.m. Carl's words were swimming in his head, the confrontation still horribly vivid. What he'd give now for loved ones around him. Gentle words. Mugs of tea. A moment when a family was more than the sum of its parts.

He looked again at the screen. If he were to refresh, there would be tens, maybe hundreds of messages now shared between BamBam, TinkerAl and Jim. Something about spotting some limited edition rolling stock or a platform footbridge for sale. They were the closest he had to friends, but he couldn't bring himself to confide in them about this yet. It was just too hard.

He moved his finger to the delete key.

'I buried my sister today'

'I buried my'

'I buried'

'I'

Chapter Ten

Despite Cameron insisting he could take off as much time as he needed, Andrew went back to work two days after the funeral. He'd barely slept, but it had been bad enough spending one day sitting around with nothing to distract him – he'd much rather deal with dead people he'd never met. He braced himself for the onslaught of sympathy. The head tilting. The sad-eyed smiles. People not even being able to *imagine* how hard it was for him. He'd have to nod and say thanks and all the while he'd be hating them for saying such things and hating himself because he didn't deserve their sympathy. It was to his considerable confusion, then, that Peggy had spent the majority of the first hour that morning talking to him about moorhens.

'Very underrated birds, if you ask me. I saw a one-legged one once at Slimbridge Wetland Centre. It was in quite a small pond and it just seemed to be swimming in circles around the perimeter in a sort of sad victory lap. My daughter Maisie wanted me to rescue it so she could "invent it a new leg". Ambitious, eh?'

'Mmm,' Andrew said, batting a fly out of his face. Bearing in mind this was only Peggy's second property inspection, she seemed to have acclimatised remarkably well, especially given that Jim Mitchell's house was in an even worse state than Eric White's.

Jim had died in bed, on his own, at the age of sixty, having choked on his own vomit. The flat's kitchen, bedroom and living room were all in one, with a separate shower room covered in mildew, its floor boasting an impressive range of stains whose origins Andrew tried not to think about.

'This is the sort of room my estate agent would describe as a "compact, chic washroom",' Peggy said, sweeping a mouldy curtain aside. 'What the hell,' she yelped, stepping back.

Andrew rushed over. The whole bathroom window was covered in little red bugs, like blood spatter from a gunshot wound. It was only when one of them flapped its little wings that Andrew realised they were ladybirds. They were the most colourful thing in the entire flat. Andrew decided that they'd leave the window open in the hope it would encourage an exodus.

They were dressed in the full protective suits this time. Peggy had specifically requested this outside so that she could pretend to be a lab assistant in a James Bond film, having watched *You Only Live Twice* the previous evening. 'My Steve used to have a bit of Pierce Brosnan about him when we were first going out. That was before he discovered pork pies and procrastination.' She sized Andrew up. 'I reckon you might pass for – who's the baddy who was in *GoldenEye*?'

'Sean Bean?' Andrew said, moving over to the kitchenette.

'Yeah, that's the one. Reckon you've got a touch of the Sean about you.'

As Andrew caught sight of his reflection in the filthy oven door – the receding hairline, patchy stubble, bags under his eyes – he suspected that Sean Bean might be doing a lot of things at that moment in time, but he almost certainly wasn't scrambling around on the kitchen floor of a South London bedsit with a 'Mr Chicken!' takeaway menu stuck to his knee.

After twenty minutes of searching they went outside to take a breather. Andrew was so tired he felt almost weightless. A police helicopter went past overhead and they both craned their necks to watch it as it banked and flew back in the direction it had come from.

'Phew, they weren't after me, then,' Peggy said.

'Mmm,' Andrew murmured.

'You know, I've never had to talk to the police before. I feel like I'm missing out, somehow, you know? I just want to report a minor misdemeanour, or be called on to make a statement – that's the dream. Have you ever had to do anything like that?'

Andrew had zoned out.

'Sorry, what?'

'Ever had any encounters with the old bill. The rozzers. The . . . peelers? Is that one right?'

Andrew was transported back to the record shop in Soho. The sudden awareness that the song playing over the speakers was 'Blue Moon'. The blood draining from his face. Rushing to the exit and wrenching the door open. The strangled cry of the shop owner. 'Fuck! Stop him, he's nicked something!' Running straight into the man outside and bouncing off him on to the floor, lying winded. The man looming over him. 'I'm an off-duty police officer.' The furious face of the shop owner coming into view. Being hauled to his feet. Arms held. 'What have you taken?' The owner's breath smelling of nicotine gum.

'Nothing, *nothing*,' he'd said. 'Honestly, you can search me.'

'Why the hell'd you run then?'

What could he have said? That hearing that song crippled

him with pain? That even as he lay winded on the pavement its fading bars lodged in his head still made him want to curl into the foetal position?

'Bloody hell,' Peggy laughed, 'you look like you've seen a ghost!'

'Sorry,' Andrew said, but his voice cracked and only half the word came out.

'Don't tell me – you got done for pinching pick 'n' mix from Woolworths?'

Andrew's eyelid was twitching uncontrollably. He was desperately trying to stop the tune coming into his head.

'Or some naughty double yellow line action?'

Blue moon, you saw me standing alone.

'Oh, dear – it was littering, wasn't it?'

She nudged him on the arm and Andrew felt the voice coming up from somewhere deep inside him, sharp and unstoppable. 'Leave it, OK?' he snapped.

Peggy's face fell as she realised he wasn't joking.

Andrew felt a miserable wave of shame hit him. 'I'm sorry,' he said. 'I didn't mean to snap like that. It's just been a strange couple of weeks.'

They stood in silence for a long time, both of them clearly too embarrassed to speak first. Andrew could practically hear Peggy attempting to regroup, the cogs whirring as she decided to change the subject. This time he was going to be ready and attentive.

'My daughter's invented this game, right?'

'A game?'

'Yeah. And I'm not sure if I should be worried about her or not, but it's called the Apocalypse game.'

'Right,' Andrew said.

'So, the scenario is this: a massive bomb has gone off and everyone's been wiped off the face of the earth. It appears that you are the only person in the country to have survived. What do you do?'

'Not sure I understand,' Andrew said.

'Well, where do you go? What do you do? Do you find a car and go blasting up the M1 trying to look for people? Or do you just head straight to your local and drink the bar dry? How long before you try and make your way across the channel, or go to America, even? If nobody's there could you break into the White House?'

'And that's the game . . . ?' Andrew said.

'Pretty much,' Peggy said. Then, after a pause. 'I tell you what I'd do, right? I'd go to Silverstone and do a lap of the track in the Fiesta. Then, I'd either hit golf balls off the top of the Houses of Parliament or cook myself a fry-up in the Savoy. At some point I'd probably go across to Europe and see what's what – though I slightly worry I'd end up having to be part of some sort of resistance group, smuggling people across the border and that sort of thing. And I'm not sure I'm a good enough person to get involved in that if there's nobody left at home to see my Facebook post about it.'

'Understandable,' Andrew said. He was trying to think what he'd do, but his mind was blank. 'I'm afraid I can't really think of anything, myself,' he said. 'I'm sorry.'

'Ah well. It's not for everyone,' Peggy said. 'By the way, if you fancy heading off early I'm sure I can crack on by myself.'

'No, I'm all right,' Andrew said. 'Quicker with two of us anyway.'

'Right you are. Oh, I nearly forgot to say, I bought a flask of coffee today. Let me know if you want a mug. And I *attempted* flapjacks too.'

'I'm fine, thanks,' Andrew said.

'Well, let me know if you change your mind,' Peggy said, heading back into the house. Andrew followed her, a waft of fetid air hitting him before he'd even crossed the threshold. Luckily, before long, Peggy found something.

'It's one of those Christmas "round robin" things,' she said, her voice strained because of having to breathe through her mouth. She passed what she'd found to Andrew. The paper felt brittle, as if it had been screwed up and straightened out countless times. In amongst the pages detailing uneventful holidays and unremarkable school sports days, there was a photo of the family, their faces looking pixelated from where the paper had been scrunched up.

'I wonder how many times he nearly threw this out but couldn't quite bring himself to,' Peggy said. 'Hang on, look, there's a phone number there on the back.'

'Well spotted. Right, I'll give them a call,' Andrew said, reaching for his phone and turning it on.

'Are you sure you're all right to?' Peggy asked, her tone deliberately casual.

'I'm fine, but thank you,' he said. He dialled the number and waited for it to connect. 'I'm sorry again, about snapping,' he said.

'Don't be silly,' Peggy said. 'I'm just going to head outside for a second.'

'Sure,' Andrew said. 'See you in a minute.'

Someone picked up on the first ring.

'Sorry, Brian, lost you there,' the person on the line said. 'So like I said, this is just something we'll chalk up to experience.'

'Sorry,' Andrew said, 'this is actually—'

'No, no, Brian, time for apologies is over. Let's clean-slate this one, OK?'

'I'm not—'

'"I'm not", "I'm not" – Brian, you're better than this, yeah? I'm putting the phone down now. I'll see you in the office tomorrow. I don't want to hear any more about it, OK? Right, good. See you later.'

The line went dead. Andrew sighed. This was going to be a tricky one. He hit re-dial and walked over to the living-room window. At first he thought Peggy was doing some sort of exercise – she was squatting down and rocking on her heels slightly, as if she were about to bounce up into a star jump. But then he saw her face. She'd gone very pale. There were tears pooling in her eyes and she was taking in deep lungfuls of air. It was then that Andrew realised that of course she hadn't acclimatised at all to being inside a house that was in such a poor state. And then there was the coffee and the flapjacks and the games and the talking – all designed to cheer him up, without even a hint of patronising him or doing the sad head tilt. All that time she'd been feeling awful but pretending not to, and he hadn't even realised. Peggy's kindness, her selfless-ness, was so overwhelming that for a second Andrew thought he might cry.

The man who'd answered the phone was letting it ring out this time – presumably letting poor Brian stew in his own juice. Andrew watched Peggy stand up and take one final breath, before going towards the front door. He hung up the phone and cleared his throat, trying to get rid of the lump that had formed there.

'Not good?' Peggy said, eyeing the phone in his hand.

'He thought I was someone who he worked with calling him back and he wouldn't let me speak.'

'Oh.'

'And he used the term "clean slate" as a verb.'

'What a cock.'

'My thoughts exactly. I'll try him again later, I think.'

They stood still for a moment, looking around at the mess. Andrew scratched at the back of his head.

'I, um, just wanted to say thank you,' he said, 'for, being here and chatting and the flapjacks and everything. I really do appreciate it.'

Some colour returned to Peggy's cheeks, and she smiled.

'No bother, pal,' she said. 'So, back to the office?'

'You should go back,' Andrew said, not wanting Peggy to be there a second longer than she needed to. He pulled a roll of bin bags out of his rucksack.

'Is there not more to do, though?' Peggy said, looking at the bin bags.

'No, it's just . . . When it's as bad as this I like to clear up the worst of the rubbish. Just doesn't seem right to leave the place like this. Like I said, you can go back.'

Andrew wasn't quite sure what the look Peggy was giving him meant, but he felt as if he might have said something embarrassing.

'I think I'd rather stay,' Peggy said, arm outstretched. 'Chuck us a bag.'

As they cleared up, Andrew willed his imagination into action until, eventually, he had something.

'I'd go to Edinburgh, by the way,' he said.

'Edinburgh?' Peggy said, looking confused.

'During the apocalypse. I'd see if I could drive a train up

there, then try and break into the castle. Or climb Arthur's Seat.'

'Aha, not a bad shout at all,' Peggy said, tapping her chin contemplatively. 'I have to say, though, I still think I win with my Savoy fry-up or parliament golf plan. Just saying.'

'I didn't realise there was a winner,' Andrew said, folding up a pizza box which had chunks of greasy mozzarella stuck to it.

'I'm afraid there has to be. And given that I lose to my kids every single time, do you mind if I have this one? You know, to regain a bit of pride?'

'Fair enough,' Andrew said. 'I'd shake your hand to congratulate you, but there seems to be quite a lot of mouldy cheese on mine.'

There was a moment where Peggy looked at his hand in horror where Andrew thought he might have said something far too weird, but then Peggy let out a huge belly laugh and said, 'Jesus, what *is* this job?', and Andrew felt awake for the first time that day.

They'd worked their way through the majority of the rubbish when Peggy said, 'I wanted to say I'm sorry, you know, about your sister. I just didn't know when was the right time.'

'That's OK,' Andrew said. 'I'm . . . It's . . . I don't know, really . . .' He trailed off, caught halfway between saying how he felt and what he thought he was supposed to say.

'I lost my dad nine years ago,' Peggy said.

Andrew felt as if someone had stuck him on pause. 'I'm sorry,' he managed to say, after what felt like an age.

'Thanks, pet,' Peggy said. 'It's a while ago now, I know, but . . . I still remember afterwards, there were days – especially at work – where all I wanted was to hide away, but there were others when it was all I wanted to talk about. And that's when I noticed people avoiding me, deliberately not catching my eye. Of course, I realise now they were just embarrassed about not knowing what to say to me, but at the time it felt like I had something to be ashamed about, that I'd done something wrong and was inconveniencing everybody, somehow. What made it harder was that my feelings were all over the place.' Peggy gave Andrew a look as if wondering whether she should continue.

'How do you mean?' he said.

Peggy chewed her lip. 'Let's just say kindness wasn't exactly in my dad's DNA. The abiding memory of my childhood is sitting in the living room and holding my breath when I heard his footsteps on the drive. I could tell from how the sound varied what mood he was going to be in. He never hurt us, or anything, but he got in these moods where nothing me or my sister or my mam did was good enough, and he left us in no doubt as to exactly how we'd let him down. Then one day he just upped and left. Ran off with some lass from work, so my sister later found out. Mam never accepted that, though. That was the hardest part. She talked about him like he'd been God's gift, as if he were a war hero who'd drifted out to sea on a raft never to be heard of again, despite the fact he was shacked up with this woman four streets away.'

'That must have been hard,' Andrew said.

Peggy shrugged. 'It's complicated. I still loved him, even though I barely saw him after he left. People think loss is the same for everyone, but it's different in every case, you know?'

Andrew tied a bin bag closed. 'That's true,' he said. 'With my sister, I sort of . . . well, it's complicated, like you said about your dad. And the idea of people looking at me, all sympathetic . . .' He trailed off.

Peggy had joined him in picking up the remaining rubbish with a litter picker. 'Yep, I hear you,' she said. 'I mean, their hearts are in the right place, but if you've not been through it then it's impossible to understand. It's like we're in "the club" or something.'

'The club,' Andrew murmured. He felt a burst of adrenaline pass through him. It was the oddest feeling. Peggy looked at him and smiled. And Andrew, remembering his failed attempts at properly saying cheers in the pub, suddenly found himself raising his litter picker in the air, an empty packet of Hula Hoops in its pincers, and saying 'To the club!'. Peggy looked at him in surprise, and Andrew's hand wavered, but then she reached her own picker aloft. 'The club!' she said.

After a slightly awkward pause they lowered their pickers and carried on tidying.

'Now then, Andrew,' Peggy said after a while, 'back to more important matters.'

Andrew raised his eyebrows.

'Is this going to be about the apocalypse, by any chance?'

An hour later they were nearly done, Andrew having had a surprisingly enjoyable time clearing away rubbish and playing end-of-the-world-themed games, when Peggy said, 'If you want a slightly more structured mental test, it's that pub quiz I mentioned tonight if you fancy it.'

Maybe, actually, Andrew *did* fancy it. It would be something else to take his mind off things after all, and this way he could make it up to Peggy properly for snapping at her, if not with his ropey general knowledge then with pints of Guinness.

'Yes, why not,' he said, trying to sound like this was the sort of thing he was always doing.

'Top stuff,' Peggy said, and the smile she gave him was so warm and genuine that he actually had to look away. 'And bring Diane! I want to meet her.'

Oh yes. That.

Maybe Diane would magically appear in the bathroom mirror and find him a better shirt than this orange monstrosity. He'd panic-bought it after work on the way home, suddenly very aware that the last time he'd specifically bought clothes for a night out people were still worried about the Millennium Bug. He had no real idea what was fashionable, these days. Occasionally, he thought about replacing some of his particularly old stuff, but then he'd see someone young and apparently trendy wearing a shirt that looked exactly like one he'd hung on to since the early nineties, so what was the point?

He moved his face closer to the mirror. Maybe he should buy some cream or other to try and get rid of those dark circles under his eyes. But then again, he did feel an odd sort of attachment to them, perhaps because they were the closest thing to a distinguishing feature he had. Everything else about him was just so . . . normal. Part of him longed to have 'a thing' – like those men who decide to compensate for being five foot five by spending hours in the gym, ending up incredibly muscly yet still having to walk a bit faster than their friends to keep up. Or maybe he'd choose a dominating nose, or jutting-out ears – the sort of feature that, if possessed by a celebrity, would lead to them being described as 'unconventionally attractive' by the press. Ordinary-looking women were saddled with 'Plain Jane' but there didn't seem to be

111

an equivalent for men. Maybe, Andrew thought, he would take on that mantle. 'Standard Andrew'?' 'Standy Andy?' The benchmark for men with light-brown hair and unremarkably straight teeth. It would be one way to leave a legacy.

He stepped back and smoothed out a crease on his shirt-sleeve. 'You know what you look like? A Wotsit with a face drawn on it.' He puffed out his cheeks. What in God's name had he been thinking to agree to this? The Sentinel 4wDH was speeding around at a pleasing pace, hypnotic on the figure of eight track he'd set up. He'd deliberately chosen Ella's 'But Not For Me' – smooth and languid and beautiful – to try and calm him down, but it wasn't helping much. This was why he didn't socialise, because just the thought of it was making his stomach cramp up. The temptation to stay in and carry on his conversations on the forum was very much in danger of winning out. But in the end he forced himself to leave the house. Diane, he had decided, was having to pull a late one at work, but he'd managed to get a babysitter last minute.

He googled the pub before he left and was concerned that it might be dangerously close to 'cool', judging by the ominous photos of chalkboards by the door with their aggressive slogans promising – with 50 per cent accuracy – 'beer and good times', but when he got there he was relieved to see it looked fairly normal, from the outside at least. Nevertheless, he did three walk-bys, pretending to be on his phone so that if Peggy or her friends saw him from the inside he could pretend he'd just been finishing a call before he came in. The timing of his arrival was crucial. If he got there too early he'd be forced into making conversation. Too late, and he'd feel like an interloper. Ideally, he'd join them in time to say a quick hello *just* before the quiz began – then the focus would be on the questions and nobody would feel like they had to make an effort to include him in conversation.

The next time he passed by he glanced through the window and spotted a group of people in the far corner. It was them. Peggy was sitting next to a man in a leather jacket who had long brown hair and a goatee. Steve, presumably. He seemed to be in the middle of an anecdote, his gestures getting more expansive as he built to what was obviously the punchline. He banged the table as the others laughed. Andrew saw a few people standing at the bar looking round to see the reason for the noise. Peggy, he noticed, was only half joining in with the laughter.

He braced his hand against the door, but then he froze.

This wasn't him. This wasn't what he did. What if he literally didn't know one correct answer in this quiz, or was forced to take sides in a heated debate? What if they were on course to win and then he ruined it for everyone? And even then, it wasn't as if the quiz was continuous – there'd be gaps where people could question him about his life. He knew how to deal with people at work when it came to talking about his family. He could predict what things they'd ask him and knew when to duck out of conversations when he felt uncomfortable about where they were going. But this was unchartered territory, and he'd be trapped.

A car pulled up behind him and he heard someone get out and offer a familiar 'have a good night' – a farewell that could mean only one thing. He turned and saw the cab's yellow light, a welcoming beacon promising sanctuary. He rushed over and rattled off his address to the driver, yanking the door open and throwing himself inside. He sank down low into the seat, his heart racing as if he were in a getaway car leaving a bank robbery, and a quarter of an hour later he was outside his building, his evening over, twenty pounds down and he hadn't even bought a drink.

Inside the hallway there was an envelope on the mat. He picked it up, assuming it was just junk mail, but when he turned it over he saw his name and address were written in biro. He quickly stuffed the envelope into his pocket and hurried up the stairs. Inside his flat, his urgency to get music on and a train moving around the track felt even greater than usual.

He pushed the needle down roughly on the record player and turned the volume up, then knelt down and tugged at the rail track, pulling the middle of the eight apart and pushing it out to create one loop instead of two. He set the train running and sat in the newly created circle, his knees folded to his chest. Here, he was calm. Here, he was in control. Trumpets howled and cymbals crashed, and the train fizzed around the track, encircling him, guarding him, keeping him safe.

After a while he remembered the envelope in his pocket. He took it out and opened it, pulling out the message inside. As he did so he was hit by a waft of rich aftershave.

Your disappearing act meant you weren't around long enough to hear Sally's will being read this morning. You little bastard. Did you know? Because I certainly didn't. Twenty-five grand in her savings – you'd have thought she'd have mentioned that to me, wouldn't you? After all, we were trying to grow the business – that was the dream. So you can imagine it came as something of a shock to find out about it, and that she had decided to leave the money not to me, but to you.

Maybe now you'll begin to realise just how sick with guilt she was, all because you never forgave her, no matter how hard she tried to help you. You were like a brick tied around her ankles, weighing her down. Well, I hope you're happy now Andrew. It was all worth it, wasn't it?

Andrew read Carl's letter through several times, but it still didn't make sense. Surely, Sally giving him the money was some sort of administrative mistake? A wrong box ticked? Because the alternative explanation, that it was a last-gasp attempt to make things right, to rid herself of guilt that she had lived with and that he could, and should, have absolved her of, was too desperately sad for him to contemplate.

Chapter Eleven

For the next three months, each time Andrew returned home it was with trepidation at the prospect of another envelope addressed to him in Carl's spidery scrawl.

The letters arrived erratically. Some weeks there would be two or three – tear-stained and ink-blotted – then there would be four weeks without one at all. But Carl's anger never wavered as he continued to blame Andrew for conning Sally out of her money. '*You are pathetic and cowardly and worthless, and you don't deserve Sally's forgiveness*', was how he'd ended his latest note. Andrew wondered if Carl would be surprised to know that he was broadly in agreement with this assessment.

Each time he opened the door to find a letter he would trudge upstairs and sit on the side of his bed, turning the envelope around in his hands. He told himself to stop opening them, but he was trapped in an unforgiving cycle: the more he read, the guiltier he felt, and the guiltier he felt, the more he thought he deserved Carl's anger. This was especially true when Carl once more accused Andrew of contributing to Sally's ill-health by never reaching out to her, because the more he thought about it, the more he started to convince himself that this was true.

*

It was long enough now after Sally's death for some sense of normality to have returned in the way that people were treating him. Cameron had gone through a phase of putting a hand on his shoulder when he spoke to him, looking at him with his sad, bulbous eyes and knitted eyebrows and doing the head tilt, but thankfully that had now stopped. More of a relief still was the fact that Keith, who had briefly restrained himself, was now back to being a complete arsehole.

After several aborted attempts, he'd finally built up the courage to tell the sub-forum about Sally.

'Hi chaps. Sorry I've been a bit quiet of late. Had some sad news. I lost my sister. I'm still feeling a bit numb about it all, to be honest.' As soon as he'd hit 'post' he wondered if he'd done the wrong thing, but they'd all responded with sympathetic, well-judged messages and, in a move of touching solidarity, had changed their avatars from dancing tomatoes and cheerful fat controllers to match Andrew's plain, sky-blue square.

But while things were largely back to normal, there was something that had been brought sharply into focus, something that Andrew was finding hard to ignore. He had always justified continuing to lie about having a family on the grounds that it was harmless. But, subconsciously, the fact that Sally was still around (no matter how strained their relationship), meant that the fantasy he'd created just existed alongside his real life. But now, with her gone, he was feeling increasingly uncomfortable about Diane, Steph and David. As a result, when family came up in conversation with Cameron, Keith and Meredith, he no longer felt the little thrill he used to when inventing some mundane detail about how things were at school, or what his weekend plans were. But it was worse – much worse – when it came to Peggy. The day after he'd bailed on the pub quiz he'd been racked with guilt and apologised far more earnestly than was necessary, much to Peggy's amusement and confusion. After a few more weeks in her company Andrew realised she wasn't the sort of person to sweat the small stuff like that. She had continued to shadow him, so they had spent almost all their time at work together: attending more property inspections, as well as the office grind of registering deaths and compiling details of unclaimed estates to send on to the treasury.

And then there had been the funeral.

Andrew had mentioned in passing to Peggy that he was going to attend the service of Ian Bailey, having not been able to track down any friends or family. He wasn't expecting Peggy to ask if she could come.

'You don't have to,' he said. 'It's not compulsory – or technically part of the job, in fact.'

'I know, but I'd like to,' Peggy said. 'I'm just following your lead, really. If the point is to help see the person off with some company then me doubling the numbers is a good thing to do, right?'

Andrew had to concede that this was a good point.

'Not to sound patronising,' he said. 'But it's maybe worth taking a bit of time to prepare yourself for it. As I've said, they can be pretty bleak affairs.'

'Don't worry,' Peggy said. 'I was thinking I could do a bit of karaoke to cheer things along. "Africa" by Toto, something like that?'

Andrew looked at her blankly and saw her smile falter. God, why couldn't he just respond normally to things? He forced himself to try and rectify the situation.

'I'm not sure that'd be appropriate,' he said. Then, after a beat, 'I think "The Final Countdown" might be more fitting.'

Peggy chuckled while Andrew went back to his screen, torn between self-reproach at trivialising the funeral and relief and pride at managing to successfully devise and deliver a real-life joke to a real-life human being.

That Thursday they stood in church, waiting for Ian Bailey to arrive.

'It's nice – well, not *nice*, but, you know, a good thing, there being two of us today.' Andrew winced slightly at how clumsily this had come out.

'Three of us, actually,' Peggy said, pointing up at the rafters, as a sparrow flitted from one beam to another. They were quiet for a moment, watching the bird until it disappeared out of sight.

'Have you ever imagined your own funeral?' Peggy asked.

Andrew kept his eyes on the rafters. 'I can't say I have. You?'

Peggy nodded. 'Oh yeah. Loads. When I was about fourteen I got really obsessed and planned the whole thing, right down to the readings and the music. I seem to remember everyone was going to be dressed in white, so it was different from normal funerals, and Madonna was going to do 'Like A Prayer', a cappella. Is that weird? I mean, the planning of it, not the Madonna part – I *know* that's weird.'

Andrew watched the sparrow flit to another beam. 'I don't know,' he said. 'I suppose it makes sense. We're all going to have one, so why not think about how you want it to go?'

'Most people don't want to think about it, do they?' Peggy said. 'Understandably, I suppose. But then for some of us death is always at the back of our minds. I think that's the only real explanation why some people do such stupid, impulsive things.'

'Like what?' Andrew said, giving in to neck ache and lowering his head.

'Like people who embezzle money from their business even though they're *obviously* going to get found out. Or that woman who was on the news for getting caught pushing a cat into a wheelie bin. It's as if, in that moment, they're sticking two fingers up to death. *You're coming for me, I know you are – but watch this!* It's like a pure burst of living, isn't it?'

Andrew frowned. 'You're saying pushing a cat into a bin is a pure burst of living?'

Peggy had to cover her mouth to stop herself laughing, and for one dreadful moment Andrew thought they were both about to get the giggles, like naughty schoolchildren. Then a memory came to him, quite out of the blue, of him and Sally convulsing with laughter in a fish and chip shop as they exchanged fire with chips across the table, while their mother was distracted by a conversation with someone at the counter.

Try as he might, as the service proceeded he found it impossible not to think about Sally. Surely, there had been other moments like that? Had her leaving for America been such an all-consuming betrayal that it had biased his memory? After all, he thought, with a sudden pang of dread, there had been one particular memory that he'd spent the last twenty years trying to let go, where Sally had done her utmost to help him, and he hadn't let her. He pictured himself in his flat, routed to the spot, hearing the phone ringing on and on and on, unable to answer. When he'd finally picked up, he heard her voice, pleading with him to talk to her, to let her help. He'd let the phone slip from his hand. He told himself he'd answer the next day when she called, and then the day after that, and every day for the next month after, but he never did.

Andrew's mouth had gone horribly dry. He was only vaguely aware of the vicar's soft address. At Sally's funeral, he had been numb, miserably self-conscious next to Carl. But now, all he could think of was why he hadn't answered the phone.

His breathing had become shallow. The vicar had just finished delivering part of the service, and nodded to the back, whereupon an organ clunked into life. As the first chord filled the church, Peggy leaned over to Andrew. 'Are you OK?' she whispered.

'Yes, I'm fine,' he said. But as he stood there, his head bowed, listening to the music growing louder, the church floor swam in front of his eyes, and he had to grasp on to the pew in front with both hands to stop himself falling. His breaths were coming in shuddering bursts, and as the music echoed around the church, and he realised he was finally beginning to mourn his sister, he was vaguely aware of Peggy's hand gently rubbing his back.

By the time the service was over he had managed to compose himself. As he and Peggy walked out of the churchyard he felt it necessary to explain what had just happened.

'Back there,' he said, 'I was a bit . . . upset . . . because I was thinking about my sister. Not that I *wasn't* thinking about Ian Bailey, but . . .'

'It's OK, I get it,' Peggy said.

They walked on in silence for a while. Andrew began to feel the tightness leaving his throat, and the tension from his shoulders. He realised Peggy was waiting for him to be the one to speak first, but he couldn't think of anything to say. Instead, he found himself softly humming Ella's 'Something To Live For'. He'd been listening to it the previous evening – the version from *Ella At Duke's Place*. He'd always had an odd relationship with the song. He loved it for the most part, but there was a particular moment which for some reason seemed to leave him with a gnawing pain in his gut.

'There's a piece of music,' he said. 'It's one of my favourites. But there's this moment, right at the end, that's jarring, and loud, and sort of shocking, even though I'm expecting it. So when I'm listening to the song, as much as I'm enjoying it, it's always sort of spoilt by the fact I know this horrible ending is coming. But, there's nothing I can do about it, is there? So, in a way, it's like what you were saying earlier, about people who are comfortable with the fact that they're going to die: If I could just accept the ending's coming, then I could concentrate on enjoying the rest of the song so much more.'

Andrew glanced at Peggy, who seemed to be trying to suppress a smile.

'I cannot believe that you had that pearl of wisdom up your sleeve,' she said, 'when you let me wang on about someone pushing a cat into a bin.'

Peggy began to attend all the funerals with him from then on. Without really thinking about it, Andrew realised that he now felt relaxed around her, glad to have her company even. It was an odd sensation to feel so normal discussing everything from the meaning of life to whether the vicar was wearing a wig. He was even starting to hold his own when it came to playing along with the games she and her kids had invented. His proudest moment had been coming up with one of his own, devising a challenge where you had to argue in favour of arbitrary opponents: the colour red versus Tim Henman, for example. On occasion, at home in the evenings, he found his mind wandering, thinking about what Peggy might be up to at that moment.

Schedules permitting, they would have lunch in the pub every Friday where they would review the week, marking property inspections from 1–10 on the 'harrowing scale', reminding each other of the latest personal hygiene disaster from Keith or snarky comment from Meredith. It was as he was on the way to one of these lunches, enjoying the sun on his back after days of grey skies, when Andrew had a sudden realisation and stopped dead in the street, causing a man behind him to take evasive action. Could it really be true? He supposed it must be. No, there were no two ways about it: he was dangerously close to making a friend. The thought actually made him laugh out loud. How on earth had this happened? It was as if he'd managed to do it behind his own back. He carried on towards the pub with a new swagger, so much so that he overtook the man whose path he'd just accidentally blocked. As soon as he sat down, though, unable to stop grinning like an idiot, Peggy raised her eyebrows and jokingly speculated that he'd just popped over to Diane's office 'for a quickie or something'.

And therein lay the problem: the closer they got, the worse it was when he had to lie. It felt like a ticking time bomb – that it was only a matter of time before Peggy found out the truth and he'd lose the first friend he'd made in years. One way or another, he knew that something had to give. As it turned out, he didn't have to wait long.

The day had begun with a particularly gruelling house inspection, not helped by the fierce July heat. Terry Hill had slipped in the bath and lain there dead for seven months. Nobody had missed him. It was only when his overseas landlord finally stopped receiving rent that his body was found. The TV had still been on. A knife, fork, plate and water glass sat gathering dust on the kitchen table. Andrew had opened the microwave to find something festering inside and accidentally inhaled a great waft of rancid air, coughing and retching as he ran from the room. He was still feeling like he might be sick when Peggy, who valiantly dealt with the microwave horror while he recovered, turned to him and said, 'We've not talked about tonight, have we?'

'What's tonight?' Andrew said.

'So, the week you were off work, before the funeral, Cameron started on again about his stupid *Come Dine With Me* family dinner party thing. Every day it'd be an email or he'd mention it out of nowhere in a meeting.'

'Jesus,' Andrew said. 'Why is he so *obsessed* with this idea?'

'Well, I think there are probably two explanations.'

'Go on . . .'

'OK, one: it's something he's been taught to do on a course. It's a box-ticking exercise to show he's getting the team to bond, and he'll be flavour of the month with the bosses.'

'Hmm. And two?'

'He hasn't got any friends.'

'Oh,' Andrew said. The bluntness of it caught him off guard, but thinking about it, Cameron's general behaviour did seem to make more sense if that was the case.

'That would explain a lot,' he said.

'I know,' Peggy said. 'So anyway, he made us get a date in the diary – we delayed it as far down the line as possible, obviously. He didn't want to ask you about it when you were away, but I ended up saying I'd ask you, largely just to get him off my back for five minutes. I just haven't found the right moment to tell you. But as far as Cameron's concerned, you're coming.'

Andrew started to protest but Peggy interrupted. 'Look, look, I *know* it's a massive pain in the arse, but I for one cannot bear him going on and on about it all the time with his sad face all crumpled in disappointment when we put it off. He's going to host it tonight and the others and I are going. His missus will be there, but it's optional if we want to bring partners.'

Well that's one thing at least, Andrew thought.

'I think you should come,' Peggy said. 'It might be fine – OK, it'll definitely be awful, but . . . well, what I'm really saying is, *please* just come so we can get shitfaced together and ignore the others.' She put her hand on Andrew's arm, smiling hopefully.

Andrew could think of many things he'd rather be doing that evening – most of them involving his testicles, jam and some aggrieved hornets – but he suddenly felt a rather strong urge not to disappoint Peggy.

That evening he arrived at Cameron's carrying a bottle of off-licence Merlot and feeling firmly out of his comfort zone.

Who even likes dinner parties, anyway? he thought. Dutifully doling out compliments just because someone's managed to shovel some stuff into a pot and heated it to a point where it didn't kill anyone. And then there was all the competitive conversation about books and films: '*Oh you simply* must *see it. It's a Portuguese art-house epic about triplets who befriend a crow.*' What a lot of nonsense. (Andrew did take the occasional bit of enjoyment from hating things he'd never actually experienced.)

Keith and Meredith had been particularly abhorrent that afternoon, with Cameron in prime pillock mode. Quite why the man thought them all spending an increased amount of time together in an enclosed space was going to help, Andrew had no idea. It was like trying to force the negative ends of magnets together.

He was looking forward to spending time with Peggy, of course, although she'd seemed unusually subdued when she'd left the office, something that was possibly connected to the phone call he'd overheard her having on the back stairs, during which she had employed the word 'wazzock' several times. Delivered in her Geordie twang, it sounded like music to him.

He rang Cameron's doorbell and hoped to God that Peggy was already there. Ideally, they could just sit next to each other, ignoring the others and arguing whether Tiramisu was better than Michael Flatly, *Lord of the Dance*.

The door was answered by what appeared to be a very short Victorian dandy, wearing a velvet jacket complete with waistcoat and bow tie. It took Andrew a moment to register that this was, in fact, a child.

'Do come in. I'll take your coat?' the child said, holding Andrew's jacket between thumb and forefinger as if he'd been handed a sack of dog turds. Andrew followed him into the hall as Cameron appeared, aggressively brandishing nibbles at him. 'Andrew! You've met Chris, I see?'

'It's Christopher,' the boy said, turning from the coat hook, smiling frustratedly. Andrew had already got the impression that Christopher held his father to very high standards which Cameron rarely met.

'Clara?' Cameron called.

'What now?' someone hissed back.

'Darling, our first guest's arriiiiived!'

'Oh, just a second!' This voice bore almost no resemblance to the first. Clara appeared in an apron, smiling to reveal several thousand pristine white teeth. She had closely cropped auburn hair and was so pretty that Andrew felt flustered even before they exchanged an awkward handshake, which became a hug and then a kiss on each cheek, a three-for-the-price-of-one greeting, Clara pulling him towards her as if leading him in a ballroom dance. Cameron handed Andrew a bowl of cashew nuts and asked Clara how the starters were coming along. 'Well,' she said, through ever so slightly gritted teeth, 'if someone hadn't turned the hob all the way off we would have been bang on time.'

'Oh dear – guilty!' Cameron said, clapping his hand to the top of his head and gurning. Andrew looked at Christopher and the boy rolled his eyes as if to say 'tip of the iceberg'.

Meredith and Keith arrived together – not by coincidence, Andrew guessed, his suspicions confirmed by the fact that they were both clearly quite tipsy. Keith ruffled Christopher's neatly parted hair and the boy left the room with a murderous look in his eyes, returning – to Andrew's disappointment – brandishing a comb and not a revolver.

By the time Peggy pitched up they had already sat down for the starters. 'Sorry I'm late,' she said, hurling her coat on to an empty chair. 'Got stuck on a bus. The traffic was an utter bastard.' She glanced at Christopher. 'Oh, sorry, is that a child? Didn't mean to swear.'

Cameron laughed uncertainly. 'I'm sure you've heard worse from us, haven't you Chriss-o?' Christopher muttered something darkly into his soup.

Conversation was stop-start, in the way that magnifies every slurp of food and clink of cutlery. They all agreed that the soup was delicious, although Meredith did add a caveat that it was a 'bold choice' to have added quite so much cumin. Keith smirked at this, apparently enjoying the backhanded compliment, and Andrew was suddenly horribly aware that there was some knee-touching going on under the table. He wanted to bring this to Peggy's attention, if only to share the burden of horror, but she seemed distracted, pushing soup slowly around her bowl like a disillusioned painter mixing colours in their palette. Andrew felt a strong urge to get her away from the others and ask if she was OK, but it was hard when you had Cameron to contend with. He had clearly anticipated lulls in conversation, and was beginning to bring up a flurry of topics that were as disparate as they were fruitless, the latest being their taste in music.

'Peggy? What tickles your fancy in that regard?' he asked. Peggy yawned. 'Oh, you know, acid house, dubstep, Namibian harpsichord stuff. All the classics.' Meredith hiccuped and dropped her spoon on the floor, disappearing to retrieve it and nearly sliding off her chair in the process. Andrew raised his eyebrows at Peggy. He had never really understood the point in getting hammered at social events like this. Surely you were just more likely to say something stupid and then spend the rest of the evening regretting it? Then you'd need another drink just to get over that.

'That,' Peggy would later say to him, 'is drinking in a nutshell.'

Once they'd finished the main course, Clara asked with exaggerated winsomeness if Cameron could give her a hand in the kitchen.

'You're sure I won't just be in the way?' Cameron asked with a little chuckle.

'No, no. Just don't go near the hob,' Clara said.

Cameron headed after her with a 'you got me there!' gesture. A symphony of slammed cupboard doors occurred shortly afterwards.

'There may be trouble ahead,' Peggy sang quietly.

It was then that Meredith and Keith decided that they needed the toilet at exactly the same time. Andrew and Peggy listened to the sounds of excited footsteps on the stairs.

'Those two are definitely shagging, then,' Peggy said. 'Sorry for swearing again, Christopher,' she added. Andrew had entirely forgotten the boy was still there.

'Not at all,' Christopher said. 'I better go and see what's happening in the kitchen.'

Peggy waited till the door was closed, then leaned over to Andrew.

'At least the poor sod's got his mother's looks. Anyway, bollocks to this, I'm off.'

'Oh, are you? Don't you think you should just . . . wait?'

'Absolutely not,' Peggy said, swinging her coat on and making for the door. 'I've had a rubbish enough day as it is without having to endure another second of this. You coming or what?'

Andrew hesitated, but Peggy wasn't going to hang around for an answer. He swore under his breath and dashed to the kitchen, opening the door to find Clara in full flow.

'You *know* Wednesday is book club night, yet as usual you didn't give any bloody consideration to what I might— Andrew! Is everything OK?'

Cameron spun around.

'Andrew! Andy-boy. What's up?'

'Peggy's not feeling too clever so I thought I better make sure she gets home OK.'

'Oh, are you sure? There's ice cream!' Cameron said, eyes wide in desperation. Luckily, Clara stepped in and, with a bit too much intensity for Andrew's liking said, 'There'll always be ice cream, Cameron. It's chivalry that's in short supply.'

'Look, I better go . . .' Andrew said, hearing the argument renewed in earnest as soon as he'd closed the front door.

He had to jog to catch Peggy up. When he arrived at her side he was too out of breath to say anything, and Peggy only offered a quick 'all right?' before falling quiet. They walked on without speaking, Andrew's breathing finally levelling out, until gradually their steps were in sync. It was a comfortable silence, but it felt charged in a way that Andrew couldn't put his finger on. As they waited to cross the road at some traffic lights, Peggy pointed out a pool of dried blood on the pavement.

'I've walked past a patch like that on my road every day this week and it's barely faded,' she said. 'Why is it that blood takes ages to wash away?'

'I think it's because it carries all the proteins and iron and everything,' Andrew said. 'And it's so thick because it coagulates. Hard to get rid of, blood.'

Peggy snorted. '"Hard to get rid of, blood." Now that's the most serial killer-y thing I've heard in a while.'

'Ah. God, I hadn't . . . I just meant that—'

Peggy laughed and nudged him with her elbow. 'I'm only messing.' She puffed out her cheeks. 'God, I shouldn't have come out tonight. I really wasn't in the mood for it. Think anyone noticed?'

'I'm sure they didn't,' Andrew said, trying not to picture Cameron's forlorn face. 'Is everything all right?'

'Oh, I'm fine, really. I'm just having a bit of a hard time of it. With Steve, actually.'

Andrew wasn't quite sure how to respond, but Peggy didn't need a prompt.

'You remember I told you about my friend Agatha, the one who clearly didn't approve of him?'

Andrew nodded. 'The spatula. The one that you, well . . .'

'Chucked at his head? Yes, well. That's not the only thing I've felt like throwing at him recently. It's just so bloody hard, sometimes. When Agatha told me her doubts about him when he first proposed, I just couldn't even consider what she was saying. I was so fiercely proud of what I had, I thought she was just jealous. Sure, we used to row now and then, but then we'd always make up. Better that than those couples who never raise their voices but keep each other awake at night grinding their teeth.'

'And what seems to be the problem?' Andrew asked, wincing at how he'd managed to somehow sound like a 1950s doctor talking disapprovingly to his patient about their libido.

'So there's the drinking,' Peggy replied. 'I know things are on the verge of going tits up when he starts singing, and last night it was "Yes Sir I Can Boogie". Next thing he's getting all boisterous and asking complete strangers to dance, buying shots for everyone in the pub. Then he finally has too much and starts getting confrontational with people for no reason. But it's the *lying* about the drinking that I really can't stand. It's just relentless. Last night I went home before him as he was having 'one for the road'. He gets back steaming at 2 a.m. Usually I can handle him by giving him a quick bollock-wallop, but last night he was determined to go and say goodnight to the girls, but it was so late it was practically morning, and I didn't want him to go and wake them up, so then it became "oh, you're not letting me see my own kids". He ended up sleeping on the landing under a *Finding Nemo* duvet in some sort of protest. I left him there snoring. This morning my youngest, Suze, came out and saw him lying there. She looked at me, shook her head and said, "Pathetic." *Pathetic!* I didn't know whether to laugh or cry.'

An ambulance flashed past, lights on but no siren, ghosting through a gap in the traffic.

'You got an apology this morning, presumably?' Andrew said, not entirely sure why he'd decided to play devil's advocate.

'Not exactly. I tried to talk to him, but he gets this scrunched up face when he's hungover and it's hard to take him seriously. Honestly, it goes all mad and blotchy. Like he's a clumsy bee-keeper. We'd have had it out this evening if I hadn't had this nonsense to go to. The only reason I stayed as long as I did was because you were there. I mean, that lot are just the absolute worst, aren't they?'

'They really are,' Andrew said, wondering whether Peggy had seen just how wide he'd smiled about him apparently being the only reason she'd stayed.

'I wonder if Meredith and Keith are still up in that bath-room,' Peggy said with a shudder. 'Oof, it really doesn't bear thinking about.'

'It really, really doesn't,' Andrew said.

'And yet now I can't stop picturing them sweating away.'

'Oh God, *sweating*?'

Peggy sniggered and linked her arm into his.

'Sorry, there was no need for that, was there?'

'There absolutely wasn't, no,' Andrew said. He cleared his throat. 'I have to say, it's felt like a lifetime, having to deal with those idiots by myself, so it's nice . . . it's been really good to have, you know, a friend, to share the burden with.'

'Even when I make you think of them *at it*?' Peggy said.

'OK, maybe not then.' Andrew wasn't exactly sure why his heart was beating almost uncomfortably hard. Or, for that matter, why he'd allowed them to walk past at least three stops from where he could have caught a bus home.

Peggy groaned. 'I've just realised Steve's going to have written me an apology song on his stupid guitar. I actually can't stand the thought of it.'

'Hmm, well, we can always head back to Cameron's for pudding?' Andrew said. Peggy elbowed him again.

They were both quiet for a moment, lost in their own thoughts. A siren sounded in the distance. Perhaps it was the same ambulance that had gone past with just its lights on, Andrew thought. Had the paramedics been on the radio, waiting to hear if they were needed after all?

'Are your lot still going to be up when you get in?' Peggy said.

Andrew winced. *Not this. Not now.*

'Diane, maybe,' he said. 'The kids should be asleep by now.'

They were approaching the station Andrew guessed Peggy was getting her train from.

'Is it bad,' he said, fighting the voice in his head warning him that this wasn't a good idea, 'that sometimes I just sort of wish I could escape from it all?'

'From what?' Peggy said.

'You know, the family . . . and everything.'

Peggy laughed and Andrew immediately backtracked. 'God, sorry, that's ridiculous, I didn't mean to—'

'No, are you *kidding*?' Peggy said. 'I dream of that on a regular basis. The bliss of it all. The time you could actually spend doing things you wanted to do. I think you'd be mad *not* to fantasise about that. I spend half my life daydreaming about what I'd be doing with myself if I wasn't stuck where I was . . . and then that's usually when one of the kids ruins it by drawing something beautiful for me or being inquisitive or loyal or kind, and I feel like my heart's going to explode with how much I love them, and then it's all over. Nightmare, eh?'

'Nightmare,' Andrew said.

They hugged goodbye outside the station. Andrew stayed for a while after Peggy had gone, watching people coming through the ticket barriers, blank face after blank face. He thought of the property inspection that morning and Terry Hill with his knife, fork, plate and glass. And that's when the thought hit him so hard it practically winded him: living this lie would be the death of him.

He thought about how he'd felt in the brief moment Peggy had hugged him. This wasn't physical contact through the formality of an introductory handshake. Nor was it the un-avoidable touch of the barber or dentist, or a stranger on a packed train. It had been a genuine gesture of warmth, and for that second and a half he was reminded about how it felt to let someone in. He had resigned himself to the fate of Terry Hill and all those others. But maybe, just maybe, there was another way.

Chapter Twelve

When it came to model trains, one of the most satisfyingly simple things Andrew had learned was that the more you ran a locomotive, the better it performed. With repeated use, an engine starts to glide around the track, seeming to grow in efficiency with every circuit. When it came to making connections with people, however, he was less of a smoothly running locomotive and more a rusty rail-replacement bus.

After he'd left Peggy at the station he'd practically floated home, suddenly buoyed by possibility. He'd half considered turning on his heels and running after her to improvise some sort of grand gesture – perhaps spelling out 'I am terrified of dying alone and I think it's probably weird when adults make friends this late in life but shall we do it anyway?' in discarded Ribena boxes at the side of the tracks. In the end, he managed to contain himself and jogged halfway home, buying four cans of Polish lager from the corner shop, drinking them in quick succession and waking up hungover and afraid. He forced himself out of bed and fried some bacon while listening to 'The Nearness of You' – Ella and Louis Armstrong from 1956 – five times in a row. Each time the vocals kicked in he could feel the sensation of Peggy's arm interlinked with his again. If he closed his eyes tightly enough he could see the smile she'd given him as they parted from their hug. He looked at his watch and decided he'd got just enough time for one more spin of the record, but as he went to move the needle back, the miserable sound of 'Blue Moon' suddenly came into his head, as clear as if it was coming through the record player. *No, no, no! Not now. Stay in the moment for once.* He scrabbled to put 'The Nearness of You' on again and bent down by the speaker, his ear so close that it hurt, his eyes screwed shut. After a moment there was a piercing shriek and he opened his eyes to see the room was hazy with smoke, the alarm triggered by the now-cremated bacon.

It was still too early to go to work, so he sat at his computer with two cups of tea in an attempt to alleviate his hangover – taking sips from alternate mugs – and pondered on how he might go about cementing a proper friendship with Peggy, something that elevated things above just spending time together at work. Even the idea of suggesting they go for coffee, or to the cinema or whatever, left him firmly out of his comfort zone, and *God* how he loved that zone. It was a world where Pickled Onion Monster Munch were seen as the height of culinary experimentation, where ice-breaker games were punishable by death.

He thought about what he and Peggy had bonded over so far. Well, there were the chats about the meaning of life and loss, and the idea of 'the club'. But it wasn't as if he could go steaming in there and suggest they got matching litter-picker tattoos via a quick trip to Alton Towers, was it? At the heart of that conversation, though, had been the fact that Peggy had been trying to comfort him. She'd used the apocalypse game as a fun distraction – that had been a gesture of real kindness. And now it was Peggy who was clearly in a bad way because of Steve. If he was able to comfort her as she had him, then that would surely be the basis of a real connection. So what could he do to try and cheer *her* up?

What he really needed was advice, and there was only one place he could go to for that. A few clicks of the mouse and he was on the forum. The only issue was that he felt too embarrassed to just come straight out with it and ask for help. He'd have to improvise, see where that got him first. '*Morning, chaps,*' he wrote. '*I'm after some advice. I happened to meet someone recently who's having a bad time with a seller. They'd been promised a China Clay 5 Plank Wagon Triple Pack but the seller lied and ended up going with another bidder at the last minute. They're very upset, so any help on how to cheer them up would be greatly appreciated!*'

TinkerAl replied within seconds: '*Hmm. Well, it's the Beckenham & West Wickham Vintage Toy Train show next weekend. Could take them to that?*'

BamBam67: '*Why would they possibly have wanted a China Clay 5 Plank Wagon Triple Pack when for the same money they could probably have got a Dapol B304 Westminster?*'

Hmm. Andrew drummed his fingers on his knees. If he was actually going to get any useful advice he'd have to take the plunge properly. He wrote and rewrote a message several times, eventually hitting post.

'*OK, truth be told, the person I was talking about **is** having a bad time of it at the moment, but she's not actually into trains (for her sins!). I'm just a bit rusty when it comes to this sort of thing. Any advice on fun activities and the like would be really helpful.*'

BroadGaugeJim: '*Aha! She's not, isn't she? I'd been curious about whether there was a Mrs Tracker on the scene!*'

Tracker: '*No, no, it's nothing like that.*'

TinkerAl: '*Ah. Sounds like Tracker isn't that keen to expand on the specifics, Bam. But we're here for you, mate, if you do want to!*'

Andrew felt a pang of something between embarrassment and affection.

'*Thanks, TA. In all honesty, part of my being so rubbish at all this, hence why I'm asking for advice, is because I'm not exactly a people person. But it just feels a bit different with her. In a good way. It's been a very long time since I had someone in my life like this, and it's been really nice. But there's still a nagging doubt that I should just leave things as they are.*'

BamBam67: '*I can understand that.*'

TinkerAl: '*Yeah, me too.*'

BroadGaugeJim: '*Ditto. I'm not the biggest people person myself. Sometimes it's just easier to go it alone in life. No dramas that way.*'

Andrew went to the kitchen and put the kettle on (just a single tea, this time), thinking about what BroadGauge had said. He knew that he was comforted by how much control he had with this simple little life of his. It was consistent and unspectacular and he had absolutely no desire to jeopardise that. But there were moments – when he saw groups of friends sitting in neat, symmetrical rows on pub benches, or couples holding hands in the street, where he felt a wave of embarrassment that he, a forty-two-year-old man, hadn't exchanged so much as a cup of tea with an acquaintance or a flirtatious smile with someone on a train in years – that he scared himself with how intense the feeling of longing was. Because maybe, actually, he did want to find people to be close to, to make friends and perhaps even find someone to spend the rest of his life with. He'd got adept at sweeping that feeling away as quickly as he could, telling himself that it would only lead to unhappiness. But what if he let it grow – nourished it, in fact? Maybe that was the only way forward. The past was the past and maybe this time, once and for all, he could stop it dictating his life.

He sipped his tea and replied to BroadGauge.

'I don't know, BG, I thought maybe I was too stuck in my ways, but maybe not! Anyway, perhaps we should get back to train chat, eh? I appreciate the help, though. Opening up like this isn't really my forte. Feels a bit unnatural, like going for a poo with your coat on.' He decided, on balance, to delete this last line before posting.

TinkerAl: *'Well, let us know how you get on mate!'*

BroadGaugeJim: *'Absolutely!'*

BamBam67: *'Indeed!'*

Despite his newfound determination to get out of his comfort zone, to be part of Peggy's world and vice versa, Andrew was all too aware that honesty was something of a given when it came to friendship, and as far as Peggy knew he was a happily married father of two, living in relative luxury. He briefly considered the idea of Diane running away to Australia with a surfing instructor, taking the kids with her. But even then, say he managed to convince Peggy it was all just too painful ever to talk about, ten years down the line he still wouldn't be able to show her a picture of the kids, let alone explain why he hadn't been out to visit them. His only option was to hope they could get to a point where he could tell her the truth and pray that, somehow, against all odds, she'd accept it.

But his attempts to try and properly cement their friendship got off to a tricky start. Andrew had spent a frustrating

Tuesday afternoon working his way through the contacts on an old Nokia phone he'd recovered from a property search. Nobody he'd called had answered yet. As he plucked up the courage to call a contact saved as 'Big Bazza', he decided to craft what he hoped was a funny email to Peggy. He crowbarred in some in-jokes and generally tried to come across as charming and irreverent, signing off by suggesting they should run away to the pub 'right bloody now!!'.

Andrew had never before experienced regret quite as potent as he did immediately after hitting send. He was wondering whether he had time to locate a hammer and smash up the building's power supply, or his own face, when Peggy's response arrived.

'Ha, yeah.'

Oh.

A second message appeared. Here it was – the moment where she saw quite how brilliant and hilarious he was.

'By the way, I finally tracked down the will executor of that bloke who died on Fenham Street. Do you think "I want nothing to do with that bastard" counts as a "formal revocation of duty"?'

This was going to be harder than he thought. He knew he was being impatient, but what if Peggy decided she'd suddenly had enough for some reason and quit the job and moved away? What made things worse was that as each day passed he was increasingly aware of how much she was starting to mean to him, and the more he realised this the more ridiculous his behaviour became. How the hell was he supposed to seem like someone Peggy wanted to spend time with when he was sitting there worrying himself into a state of panic that he was looking at her left eye more than her right and, for reasons that were hopelessly unclear, talking to her for a very long time about artichokes.

What he really should just do was casually enquire if Peggy wanted to meet outside of work. If she didn't want to, then that was fine. He'd get the message that it was just a work friendship situation and that would be that. So the only thing for it was to be very calm and confident and ask her, very directly, if, perhaps, and fine if not, of course, she wanted to do something one evening, or at the weekend. On balance, he realised the Beckenham & West Wickham Vintage Toy Train Show was probably an ambitious opening gambit, but a drink, say, or dinner, that was what he should go for. And, just so there could be no backing out, he decided to set himself a deadline – Thursday that week seemed as good as any – where he had to ask her by the time they left work. He just hoped she could deal with him being weird until he'd worked up the courage.

There was, he admitted, a very, *very* slight chance that he was overthinking things.

Inevitably, by the time Thursday afternoon arrived he still hadn't asked her. In retrospect he might have decided that delaying things by a day or so was preferable to making his move as they sorted through rubbish in a dead man's home, but at the time it really felt like it was now or never.

Derek Albrighton had lived to the age of eighty-four before his heart stopped beating. His flat was right on the borough's boundary edge – one street across and he would've been dealt with by another team. The coroner had sounded unusually grumpy when she'd called Andrew and asked him to investigate.

'No obvious next of kin. Neighbours called the police after they'd not seen him for a couple of days. The attending officers were about as useful as a mudguard on a tortoise, as per. Would be great to get this one sorted as soon as poss, Andrew. I'm on holiday soon and I've got paperwork up to my ears.'

Derek's flat was one of those places you felt could never get warm, no matter how much you heated it. It was tidy, on the whole, apart from the dull white powder that was spread out on the kitchen lino, with footprints in it, as if it were a pavement covered in a thin layer of snow.

'It's flour,' Peggy said. 'Either that or rat poison. Did I mention I'm a crap cook? Ah, but what have we here?' She reached for a large biscuit tin that was sitting on top of the microwave. She cooed as she removed the lid, beckoning Andrew over to show him the still pristine Victoria sponge that was inside.

'Shame he didn't get to eat it after all the effort he clearly went to,' Andrew said.

'A tragedy,' Peggy said, reverently replacing the lid, as if it were a time capsule they were about to bury. Andrew decided to try out a lean against the kitchen counter, one leg crossed behind the other, an eyebrow raised in what he hoped suggested an irreverent take on early-years Roger-Moore Bond.

'So, you a big fan of . . . cake, then?' he said. Unfortunately, or, perhaps not, Peggy was busying herself with some paperwork she'd found and was only half paying attention.

'Yeah, course, who isn't?' she said. 'I wouldn't trust anyone who says they aren't a fan of cake, to be honest. It's like those people who say they don't like Christmas. Get over yourself, of course you do. What else don't you like? Wine and sex and bloody . . . tenpin bowling?'

Andrew winced. This wasn't going well. For one thing, he *hated* tenpin bowling.

'Nothing here, no phone book or anything either,' Peggy said, shuffling the bits of paper newsreader-style. 'Bedroom?'

'Bedroom. Sure thing . . . *you*,' Andrew said. He tapped out a little rhythm on the counter top to show how devil-may-care he was – how music ran through his soul – pausing only very briefly to deal with the massive coughing fit he was suffering as a result of his jaunty drumming disturbing yet more flour. Peggy was looking at him with a mixture of suspicion and confusion, like a cat that's seen itself in the mirror.

The bedroom was dominated by a surprisingly plush double bed, with purple satin sheets and brass headboard – incongruous next to the tattered blinds, worn carpet and cheap chest of drawers at the foot of the bed, on top of which sat an ancient-looking TV and VHS player. Andrew and Peggy knelt at either side of the bed and began checking under the mattress.

'I was thinking,' Andrew said, emboldened slightly by the fact Peggy couldn't see him, 'you know that pub we went to after your first property inspection?'

'Uhuh,' Peggy said.

'That was nice, wasn't it?'

'Not sure I'd say nice, but there was beer there and that always feels like a plus in a pub.'

'Ha . . . yeahhh.'

Not there then.

'I didn't see what the food was like,' he said. 'Do you have a favourite sort of cuisine for, you know, when you're out?'

Cuisine?

'Hang on,' Peggy said. 'I've got something.'

143

Andrew edged around to the foot of the bed.

'Oh,' Peggy said. 'It's just a receipt. For some socks.'

Andrew was starting to feel desperate. He was really going to have to say something now before he bottled it. 'So I was just, you know, wonderingifyoufanciedgoingfordinneror-somethingafterworksometimesoon,' he gabbled. As he went for another casual lean his elbow pushed a button on the television, which began to turn itself on with a series of clunks and whines, sounds that seemed to entirely encapsulate the 1980s. Moments later, the room was filled with the unmistakable sounds of sex. Andrew span around to see a middle-aged woman on the screen in nothing but a pair of high heels being taken from behind by a man who was naked apart from a white baseball cap.

'Oh my God,' Peggy said.

'Oh my God,' the man in the baseball cap answered.

'You like that, don't ya, ya dirty sod,' the woman grunted, rhetorically, it would seem. As Andrew backed away to fully take in the horror, he trod on something. It was a video case – the cover of which featured a shot of the couple on screen in mid flow. Block red capitals announced the film's title: *IT'S QUIM UP NORTH!*

Andrew slowly rotated the case so that Peggy could see. She had already been crying silently with laughter, but this, apparently, was the final straw, and she let out a loud, gleeful cackle. After a moment Andrew began edging towards the TV as if he were going back to a lit firework, weight on his back foot, one hand covering his face, jabbing randomly at the buttons until he hit pause and a grotesque tableau shuddered on the screen.

In the end, they managed to compose themselves enough

to finish the rest of their search with the requisite solemnity. It was Andrew who found a tattered document folder in a drawer that had a phone number for a 'Cousin Jean' written on the flap.

'Well, I for one am not calling Cousin Jean,' Peggy said.

'It does seem a bit strange after . . . that,' Andrew said.

Peggy shook her head, bewildered. 'I was going to suggest we should get a coin and toss for it, but that seems a horribly inappropriate thing to say now.'

Andrew snorted. 'I can't quite work out what to think about Derek Albrighton.'

'Well it's clear to me that the bloke had life absolutely figured out,' Peggy said.

Andrew raised his eyebrows.

'Oh, come on,' Peggy said. 'If I get to eighty-four and my day consists of baking a cake and celebrating that achievement with a wank then I'll be pretty bloody happy.'

'You two look pleased with yourselves,' Keith said, when they arrived back at the office.

'Thick as thieves,' Meredith said, clacking a biro between her teeth.

'Bit like you two at Cameron's the other night,' Peggy said calmly, which shut them up. She hung her coat on the back of her chair and winked at Andrew. He grinned back, goofily. Peggy might not have had time to answer his question about dinner – randy Derek Albrighton had put paid to that – but it had been such a fun walk back to the office that he couldn't feel too despondent. Cameron chose that moment to amble out of his office and, in an uncharacteristically solemn voice, asked them to join him in the breakout area. Ever since the disastrous dinner party he'd carried himself with the air of a well-meaning schoolteacher who'd let his students bring in a game on the last day of term only for them to spray silly string all over the place and write rude words on their desks. The five of them sat in a semi-circle and Cameron steepled his fingers against his chin.

'I've been mulling over whether to actually say anything, guys, but I've decided I'd like to talk to you all about what happened last week at my house. Before I speak, would any of you like to say anything?' The water cooler hummed. A strip light overheard flickered. Outside, a vehicle announced that it was reversing.

'OK,' Cameron said. 'Well, what I wanted to say to you was that – and, believe me, I hate to say this – I was really rather disappointed' – his voice cracked, and he had to stop and gather himself – '*disappointed* with you all. What with two of you running off early and two of you disappearing upstairs. What should have been a nice evening for all of us to bond ended up having the opposite outcome. I mean, talk about low-hanging fruit, guys.' He waited for this to sink in. Andrew hadn't realised he'd taken it this badly. 'However,' Cameron continued. 'I very much believe in second chances, so let's give this another go and see how we get on, OK, team? Meredith has kindly volunteered to host the next evening. Andrew, you can do it after that.'

Andrew instantly pictured the stain on his kitchen wall, the battered old sofa and the distinct lack of a family there, and bit down hard on his cheeks.

Cameron kept them for further blather about budgets and targets, then decided to regale them with a spectacularly dull anecdote about he and Clara losing each other in the supermarket, before finally they were all allowed to go back to their desks. Not long after, Peggy sent Andrew an email. *'I don't know about you, but all I was thinking about during that was whether they ever made* It's Quim Up North 2.'

'*Would you need to have seen the first one to understand the sequel?*' Andrew replied.

A minute later he received two messages at once. The first was from Peggy: *'Ha! Quite possibly. Oh, and, I forgot to say: Yes to dinner. Where are we going?'*

The second was a text from an unknown number: *'How many letters am I going to have to send you before you grow some balls and reply? Or are you too busy thinking about what you'll spend Sally's money on?'*

Chapter Thirteen

It took Andrew six attempts to dial Carl's number without hanging up before it connected. He hadn't thought about what he was going to say. He knew he just had to stop this.

'Hello, Cynergy?' A hollow sense of friendliness in the voice.

'It's Andrew.'

A pause.

'Oh. You finally decided to call, then.'

'These letters. Please – please just stop sending them,' Andrew said.

'Why should I?' Carl said.

'Because . . .'

'The truth hurts, doesn't it.' A statement, not a question.

'What do you want me to say?' Andrew said.

'How about an apology? It was *you* that made her ill. You did this.' Carl's voice was shaking already. 'Can't you see that? She spent her *whole* life trying to make things right, and you never let her. You were too stubborn to forgive her and her heart was a fucking wreck because of you.'

'That's not true,' Andrew said, unsure of the words even as he said them.

'You're pathetic, you know that? God, I just keep imagining

what Sally would be thinking now – how much she'd regret what she'd done. I bet she'd—'

'OK, OK – Jesus Christ, you can have the money. I never asked for it in the first place. As soon as I get it I'll transfer it over, but you have to promise to just . . . leave me alone.'

He heard Carl sniff and clear his throat. 'I'm glad you've come to your senses. I will "leave you alone", as you put it. But I'll be in touch again when I know you've got the money, you can be sure of that.'

Then the line went dead.

Andrew made some beans on toast and logged on to the sub-forum, eager to forget about his conversation with Carl.

I'm after a bit of restaurant advice, chaps,' he wrote. '*Some-where nice but not too expensive. Think LNER 0-6-0T "585" J50 Class rather than LNER 0-6-0 "5444" J15.*' Within minutes the sub-forum had come up trumps with several suggestions. Eventually, he settled on an Italian restaurant that was trendy enough not to put pound signs on the menu but not so fancy that the meals were described in a Tuscan mountain dialect.

The next morning they were at a property inspection and Andrew reminded Peggy of the plan. 'There's no rush, obvi-ously, but just – whenever you've got a mo – maybe ping me over some dates for when you're free for our dinner thing,' he said, as casually as possible, even throwing in a yawn for good measure. Peggy looked up from the Viennetta box containing the last will and testament of Charles Edwards, which she'd just discovered under the kitchen sink.

'Oh aye, will do. Next couple of weeks, I reckon. I'll check my diary back at the ranch.'

'Cool. Sure . . . like I said, no rush,' Andrew said, knowing that he would spend the rest of the day refreshing his inbox until he was on the verge of a repetitive strain injury.

When the day of their dinner arrived the following week, Andrew found himself immediately anxious from the moment he got up. By the time he was at the office he'd managed to work himself up so much that at one point Meredith sneezed and he spontaneously apologised. He tried to tell himself to calm down, that it was ridiculous to be so anxious. *It's just dinner, for God's sake!* But it was no good. Peggy had spent the morning in an adjacent room that held the office safe, storing away the unclaimed items of value from a recent property visit in preparation for their sale, and had been on a training course away from the office in the afternoon. This, he decided, was probably why he felt so tense. Not being able to see her to exchange a friendly word or two with all day meant it was hard not to think she'd rather be doing anything else than spending her evening with him.

As if to confirm his gloom, he knew the restaurant was a poor choice by the look the waiter gave him on arrival, as if he were a stray dog who'd wandered in looking for a place to die.

'Your . . . friend is on their way, sir?' the waiter asked after he'd been sitting there for less than five minutes.

'Yes,' Andrew said. 'I hope – I'm sure – she'll be here soon.'

The waiter gave him a seen-it-all-before smirk and poured two inches of water into his glass. Twenty minutes went by, during which Andrew refused and then reluctantly accepted some incredibly hard bread.

'Are you sure you don't want to order something now for when your friend arrives?' the waiter said.

'No,' Andrew said, annoyed at the waiter and annoyed at

himself for having the temerity to get out of the little box he lived in.

Then, with the muscles in his toes tensed as he prepared to rise and make as dignified an exit as possible, he saw a flash of colour at the door and there was Peggy in a bright-red coat, hair sopping wet from rain. She plonked herself down in the chair opposite with a half-mumbled greeting and thrust a crust of bread into her mouth.

'Christ,' she said. 'What's this I'm eating – a hubcap?'

'I think it's focaccia.'

Peggy grunted and, with some difficulty, swallowed.

'You know when you married Diane?' she said, ripping a bit of bread in two.

Andrew's heart sank. Not this. Not this already.

'Mm-hmm,' he said.

'Did you ever think that there'd be a point where you'd be staring at her as she sat on the living room floor with a beer can balanced on her belly like a drunk, horizontal Christ the Redeemer and think to yourself: how the hell have we ended up here?'

Andrew shifted awkwardly in his seat.

'Not word for word, no,' he said.

Peggy shook her head slowly, gazing into middle distance. There was a lock of rain-damp hair hanging down at the side of her face. Andrew felt a strange urge to reach over and tuck it behind her ear. Was that something he'd seen in a film? The waiter appeared at the table, his smirk replaced by a slightly disappointed, almost apologetic smile now that Peggy had shown up.

'Would you like to look at the wine list, sir?'

'Yes please,' Andrew said.

'Don't bother about asking me, mate,' Peggy muttered.

'I apologise, madam,' the waiter said, bowing theatrically before sauntering off.

'Annoys me, that,' Peggy said. 'For all he knows I'm an off-duty sommelier. The wazzock.'

On the one hand Andrew was enamoured by Peggy's righteous ire. On the other, he feared the chances of piss in their linguine had just been significantly increased.

After a glass of wine and the arrival of the starters, Peggy seemed to relax a little, but there was still an undercurrent of frustration and, as a result, conversation was hard-going. Andrew began to panic in the increasingly long stretches where they weren't talking. Being silent during meals was for married couples on holiday in brightly lit tavernas with only their mutual resentment of each other left in common. This wasn't going to plan at all. What he really needed was something to snap them out of it. His wish was granted, but perhaps not quite in the way he would have wanted, when a man in a yellow coat, stretched tightly over his enormous form, barged into the restaurant. His sleeves were pulled over his hands and he had his hood drawn tight over his head, the effect of which made it look like an incredibly large child was barrelling towards them. As he stomped closer he yanked his hood away from his face, showering some nearby diners with raindrops. Heads were turning. The look on each face conveyed that very particular fear when someone is behaving outside the normal boundaries in a public space, namely: *what is about to happen and am I going to be able to trample my way out first if it all kicks off?*

'I could be wrong,' Andrew said, trying to sound calm, 'but I think your husband's just walked in.'

Peggy turned around and immediately got to her feet. Andrew folded his hands in his lap and stared at them, feeling pathetically scared in the face of the inevitable confrontation.

'So you're following me now?' Peggy said, hands on hips. 'How long have you been standing out there? And where are the girls?'

'With Emily from next door,' Steve said in a voice so low it sounded like he was in slow motion.

'OK, and just to check, that isn't just another lie?'

'Course not,' Steve growled. 'And who the fuck's this little shite?'

Andrew somewhat optimistically hoped it wasn't him Steve was referring to.

'Never mind who he is,' Peggy said. 'What the hell are you doing here?'

'I'm just nipping to the loo,' Andrew said with a manic brightness, as if this would make him impervious to being punched. The waiter stood aside to let him past, the smirk returned to his face.

When Andrew plucked up the courage to return to the table, Peggy and Steve were nowhere to be seen, and Peggy's coat was gone. Some of the other diners were risking covert looks up at him as he took his seat. Others were looking out of the window, where Andrew could now see Peggy and Steve. They were standing in the street outside, hoods up, both gesticulating furiously.

Andrew hovered by the table. He should go out there. He should at least *pretend* to himself, if not the rest of the restaurant, and the snarky fucking waiter, that he was going to go out there. As he drummed his fingers on the back of his chair, still deciding what he was going to do, the yellow blob was suddenly gone, as if carried off down river by a strong current, and Peggy was heading back inside. She looked as if she'd been crying – it was hard to tell because of the rain – and mascara had snaked down her cheeks in two thin lines.

'Are you O—'

'I'm really sorry, but please can we just eat?' Peggy interrupted, her voice hoarse.

'Of course,' Andrew said, shoving some more shrapnel bread into his mouth and consoling himself with the fact he hadn't been punched in the face by a giant Geordie.

Peggy went to eat the last mouthful on her plate, changed her mind, and set her knife and fork down together with a clang.

'I'm sorry you got called a shite back then,' she said.

'No need to apologise,' Andrew said, thinking that it should really be him apologising for being such a coward. 'I'm guessing we'll skip the puddings, then?' he said.

The hint of a smile returned to Peggy's face. 'You're joking, I hope. If there was ever a time for emergency sticky toffee then it's now.'

The waiter came over and cleared their plates.

'I don't suppose sticky toffee pudding's on the menu?' Andrew said, with his best stab at a winning smile.

'As it happens, sir, it is,' the waiter said, seeming disappointed at this.

'Oh, champion,' Peggy said, offering the waiter a thumbs up.

They both finished their puddings at the same time, returning their spoons to the bowl with simultaneous clinks.

'Snap,' Peggy said. 'How much food have I got on my face, by the way?'

'None,' Andrew said. 'How about me?'

'No more than usual.'

'Glad to hear it. Actually, you have got a little bit of . . .'

'What?'

'Mascara, I think.'

Peggy snatched up her spoon and looked at her reflection. 'Ah, Jesus, I look like a panda – you should have said something.'

'Sorry.'

She dabbed at her cheeks with her napkin.

'Do you mind me asking if everything's OK?' Andrew said.

Peggy continued to dab. 'I don't,' she said. 'But there's not much to say, so . . .' She smoothed her napkin flat on the table. 'This might be a bit weird, but can I ask you to do something?'

'Of course,' Andrew said.

'OK, so close your eyes.'

'Um, sure,' Andrew said, thinking this was the sort of thing Sally used to make him do that would invariably end up with him in pain.

'Can you picture a moment, right now, where you and Diane were at your happiest,' Peggy said.

Andrew felt the heat rising on his cheeks.

'Have you got something?'

After a moment, he nodded.

'Describe it to me.'

'How . . . how do you mean?'

'Well, when is it? Where are you? What can you see and feel?'

'Oh, OK.'

Andrew took a deep breath. The answer came to him not from something written on a spreadsheet, but from somewhere deep inside.

'We're just out of university, starting our lives together in London. We're in Brockwell Park. It's the hottest day of the summer. The grass is completely dry, practically charred.'

'Go on . . .'

'We're sitting back-to-back. We realise we need a bottle opener for our beers. And Diane pushes her back against me to try and get to her feet. And she nearly falls, and we're just giggling, and giddy in the heat. She walks up to these strangers – a couple – to borrow their lighter. She knows this trick where you can use one to open a bottle. She cracks the tops off with a flourish and hands the lighter back. She's walking back to me, and I can see her but I can still see the couple, too. They're both looking at her. It's like she's left an impression on them in that moment that means they'll be thinking about her for the rest of the day. And I realise how lucky I am, and how I never want this day to end.'

Andrew was startled. Both at the clarity of what he'd just pictured, and by the tears pooling fast under his eyelids. When he finally opened his eyes, Peggy was looking away. After a moment, he said, 'Why did you want to know that?'

Peggy smiled sadly.

'Because when I try and do the same thing, I can't seem to see anything. It's that more than anything that's making me think I can't see a happy ending. The truth is, I've given Steve an ultimatum: to clean up his act or that's it. Trouble being, I don't really know which way I want things to go. Ah well, I'm sure whatever happens will be for the best.'

Andrew was feeling a peculiar mixture of emotions. Anger,

at the big flapping daffodil, and pain at the sight of Peggy, her posture slumped slightly, her defiance undermined by her watering eyes. But there was something else there, too. It struck him that, up until now, he'd been too eager to find an excuse to get close to Peggy, that this had been far too much about him, and the fear of where his life was heading. Part of him had *wanted* a reason to be able to step in and be there for her, which meant that perhaps part of him hadn't cared if she was upset. Well, if he was going to be that cynical and selfish, then he didn't deserve a friend. And now, as he desperately searched for something to say to Peggy, he realised the pain he was feeling concealed a different truth. In that moment, he didn't care about himself. All he wanted to do was make Peggy happy. The pain was there because he didn't know how.

Chapter Fourteen

The following fortnight was dominated by death. The coroner seemed to be on the phone practically every hour, struggling to remember which cases she'd discussed with them ('We talked about Terrence Decker, right? Newbury Road? Choked on a marshmallow? Oh, no, wait, that was someone else. Or possibly a dream I had.')

Such was the glut of property inspections they were having to do, at times Andrew and Peggy regretfully sacrificed respectfulness for pragmatism, sorting through the chaos and the mess or the soulless, empty rooms as quickly as possible. The houses varied from a cramped maisonette, complete with a dead rat sporting a grotesque grin on its face, to a seven-bedroom house backing on to a park, its interior overwhelmed with cobwebs, every room feeling pregnant with secrets.

Peggy had been struggling even before the frequency of the inspections increased. Whether Steve had messed up again and she'd been forced to act on her ultimatum, Andrew wasn't sure. The first time he'd seen her returning from the loos in the office with puffy red eyes he'd started to ask her if she was all right, but she very calmly interrupted and asked him a question about an upcoming job. From then on, every time he saw her looking upset or happened to hear her on the stairwell having an angry phone call, he made sure to make her a cup of tea, or email something silly and distracting about Keith's latest hygiene horror. He even attempted to bake some biscuits, but the end results had resembled something a child might use for a snowman's eyes, so he had abandoned them in favour of shop-bought. Somehow, it just didn't seem enough.

During a brief respite in the breakout area one afternoon, eating what Peggy referred to as 'alternative bananas' – a Twix and a KitKat Chunky respectively – Andrew happened to mention Ella Fitzgerald.

'She that jazz one?' Peggy said through a mouthful of nougat.

'"*That jazz one*"?' Andrew said. He was about to admonish Peggy for her description, but then an idea struck him. People still liked getting mixtapes, didn't they? And what could be better than Ella to cheer someone up? If she could have the same effect on Peggy as she'd had on him over the years, it could even be a revelation, a cornerstone of comfort like it had been for him since he'd first listened to her all those years ago. And so began a series of agonising evenings spent trying to choose songs that perfectly encapsulated Ella's essence. He wanted to capture the whole spectrum – upbeat and downbeat numbers, polished and loose – but also just how joyously, infectiously funny she could be on her live albums. The outtakes and the between-song badinage meant as much to him as the most soaring melody.

After evening five, he began to wonder if it was actually an impossible task. There was never going to be *the* perfect tape. He'd just have to hope what he'd chosen would have the right sort of alchemy to make it a source of comfort to Peggy whenever she needed it. He decided to give himself one more night to finish it, eventually collapsing into bed way past midnight, his stomach rumbling angrily, at which point he realised he'd been so engrossed he'd forgotten to have any dinner.

When he presented the end result to Peggy on the stairs outside the office, he affected an air of nonchalance to try and hide the nagging voice telling him this might have been a weird thing for him to have done. 'By the way, I knocked up an Ella Fitzgerald mixtape for you. Just chose a few songs I thought you would like. No pressure, of course, to listen to it straight away, or even over the next few days, or weeks, or whatever.'

'Ah, thanks, pet,' Peggy said. 'I solemnly swear to listen to it within the next few days, or weeks, or whatever.' She turned the CD over and read the back. It had taken seven attempts for Andrew to write the tracks out in acceptably neat handwriting. He realised Peggy was looking at him with a twinkle in her eyes. 'How long did it take for you to "knock this up" out of interest?' she said.

Andrew blew a dismissive and unintentionally wet raspberry. 'Couple of hours I suppose.'

Peggy opened her bag and dropped the CD inside.

'I've no doubt you're an excellent mixtape maker, Andrew Smith. But you're a terrible liar.' And with that she walked calmly into the office. Andrew stood there for a moment, grinning, albeit slightly confused as to why it felt like Peggy had taken his stomach, heart, and several other vital organs with her as she'd left.

There's nothing like a PowerPoint presentation to stamp out green shoots of happiness, especially one involving sound and visual effects. Cameron was particularly pleased at getting letters to spiral on to the screen soundtracked by typewriter clacks, jauntily revealing that there had been an increase of 28 per cent of elderly people describing themselves as feeling lonely and/or isolated. His *pièce de résistance* was an embedded YouTube clip of a mid 90s sketch-show skit which bore no relevance to the presentation but was just, he explained, 'a bit of fun'. They sat there in rigid silence, apart from Cameron, who chuckled away with increasing desperation. Just as it seemed the damn thing was finally about to end, an email notification appeared in the bottom right-hand corner of the screen:

MARK FELLOWES
Re: potential cutbacks

Cameron immediately scrabbled to close the window. But it was too late. The rest of the sketch played on, the studio audience's laughter horribly at odds with the new atmosphere. Andrew couldn't work out if anyone was going to say something. Clearly also anticipating this, Cameron shut down his laptop and made a swift exit, like someone who's just given a short statement outside court escaping the paparazzi, ignoring Meredith, who'd started to ask him the obvious question of what the email had been about.

'Shit the bed,' Keith said.

Later that morning, Peggy and Andrew arrived for a property inspection at 122 Unsworth Road feeling shell-shocked.

'I really can't lose this job,' Peggy said.

Andrew decided to try and stay calm rather than add fuel to the fire.

'I'm sure it'll be fine,' he said.

'And you're basing that on . . . ?'

'Um . . .' The calm quickly deserted him. 'Blind optimism?' He laughed nervously.

'I'm glad you're not a doctor giving life-expectancy odds to a patient,' Peggy said.

They got into their protective gear, and Andrew looked at the frosted glass window of number 122 and really rather wished he and Peggy were anywhere else but here.

'Nothing like sorting through a dead bloke's stuff as a cheery distraction, eh?' Peggy said, putting the key in the lock. 'Ready?'

She shunted the door open and gasped. Andrew braced himself for what lay beyond her. He must have carried out over a hundred property inspections in his time, and all these homes, no matter what their condition, left an impression on him, some little detail standing out: a gaudy ornament, a troubling stain, a heartbreaking note. Smells, too, stayed with him. And not just the horrendous ones. There had been lavender and engine oil and pine needles too. As time passed he stopped being able to match the memory to the person or the house. But once Peggy stood to one side and he saw past her, he knew for sure that he would always remember Alan Carter and 122 Unsworth Road.

At first, it wasn't clear what exactly he was looking at. The floors, radiators, tables, shelves – every available surface – were covered with little wooden objects. Andrew dropped down to the floor and picked one up.

'It's a duck,' he said, suddenly feeling a bit stupid for saying that out loud.

'I think they all are,' Peggy said, crouching down next to

him. If this was a dream, Andrew wasn't quite sure what his subconscious was going for.

'Are they little toys – was he a collector or something?' he said.

'I don't . . . Blimey, you know what, I reckon he's carved all of these himself. There's got to be thousands of them.'

There was a path through the middle of the carvings, presumably made by those first on the scene.

'Remind me who this guy is?' Peggy said.

Andrew found the document in his bag.

'Alan Carter. No obvious next of kin, according to the coroner. God, I know it's been busy but you'd have thought she'd have mentioned this.'

Peggy picked up one of the ducks from a dressing table and ran a finger across the top of its head, then down the curve of its neck.

'So the question currently running through my mind, other than "what the fuck?", of course, is . . . why ducks?'

'Maybe he just loved . . . ducks,' Andrew said.

Peggy laughed. '*I* love ducks. My daughter Suze actually painted me a mallard for a Mother's Day present a few years ago. But I'm not so much of a fan that I'd want to go and whittle a million of them.'

Before Andrew had a chance to speculate further there was a knock at the door. He went to answer it, briefly imagining a human-sized duck on the other side, there to offer its condolences in a series of solemn quacks. Instead, it was a man with beady blue eyes and Friar Tuck hair.

'Knock knock,' the man said. 'You from the council? They said you'd be around today. I'm Martin, from next door? It was me who called the police about Alan, the poor chap. I thought I might . . .' He trailed off as he saw the carvings.

'Didn't you know?' Peggy said. The man shook his head, looking bewildered.

'No. I mean, the thing is, I'd knock on Alan's door every now and then, say hello, but that was it. Come to think of it, he never opened the door more than to show his face. He kept himself to himself, as the saying goes.' He gestured to the carvings. 'Is it OK if I have a closer look?'

'By all means,' Andrew said. He exchanged a look with Peggy. He wondered if she'd been starting to think the same as him, that despite all the intricacy and craftsmanship, at some point they would likely have to work out if the ducks had any discernible value that could be used to cover Alan Carter's funeral.

When Martin the neighbour left, Andrew and Peggy reluctantly got on with the job they were there to do. An hour later they were packing up and getting ready to leave, a thorough search of the place for documents revealing only a folder with neatly filed utility bills, a *Radio Times* which looked as if it had been rolled up for the purposes of killing flies – but nothing that gave any clues to a next of kin.

Peggy stopped by the front door so suddenly that Andrew nearly walked straight into her, just about managing to keep his balance, like a javelin thrower post-throw.

'What is it?' he said.

'I just don't want to leave this one without trying absolutely everything to find out if he's got family, you know?'

Andrew checked the time. 'I suppose one more sweep couldn't hurt.'

Peggy beamed, as if Andrew was sanctioning one more go

on a bouncy castle rather than an additional search through a dead man's belongings.

'Take a room each?' he said.

Peggy saluted. 'Sir, yes sir!'

Andrew thought he might have something when he found a piece of paper that had fallen behind the drawers in a cupboard, but it was just an old shopping list, yellowed with age. It looked like they were all out of options, but then Peggy had a breakthrough. Andrew found her kneeling on the floor, reaching around the side of the fridge.

'I can see a bit of paper or something trapped there,' she said.

'Hang on,' Andrew said. He took hold of the fridge and rocked it back and forth in little jerks to move it to one side.

Whatever it was, it was covered in a thin layer of grime.

'It's a photo,' Peggy said, wiping it clean with her sleeve to reveal two people looking back at them. They wore slightly sheepish smiles, as if they'd been waiting a long time to be exposed by someone clearing the dirt away. The man was dressed in a wax jacket with a flat cap tucked under his arm. His silver hair was fighting a losing battle against the wind to stay in place. There were pronounced crow's feet around his eyes and wavy wrinkles on his forehead like ridges on a sand dune. The woman had frizzy brown hair tinged with grey. She was wearing a mauve cardigan and matching hooped earrings, an element of fortune teller about her. She looked to be in her fifties, the man perhaps in his sixties. The photographer had cut them off at the waist, making enough space for a sign above their heads which read: 'And a few lilies blow.' There were more signs behind that, but the writing was out of focus.

'Is that Alan, do we think?' Andrew said.

'I guess so,' Peggy said. 'What about the woman?'

'They're obviously together in the photograph. His wife? Or ex-wife? Hang on, is that a name badge on her cardigan?'

'It just says "staff", I think,' Peggy said. She pointed to the sign. '"And a few lilies blow." I feel like I should know that.'

Andrew decided that this was enough of a reason to break his usual rule and use his phone.

'It's from a poem,' he said, scrolling down the screen. 'Gerald Manley Hopkins:

> *I have desired to go*
>   *Where springs not fail,*
> *To fields where flies no sharp and sided hail*
>   *And a few lilies blow.'*

Peggy ran her fingertips slowly over the photo, as if hoping to glean information simply by touch.

'Oh my God,' she said suddenly. 'I think I know where this is. There's this big second-hand bookshop near where my sister lives – oh, what the hell's it called?' She flicked the photo back and forth impatiently as she tried to remember, and that's when they both caught a glimpse of something written on the back, in slanting blue pen:

B's birthday, April 4, 1992. We met after lunch at Barter Books and strolled down to the river. Then we had sandwiches on our favourite bench and fed the ducks.

Chapter Fifteen

Andrew watched the funeral director lay the simple wreath at the unmarked grave and wondered how long it would be before it wilted away to nothing. The council usually paid for the wreaths, but recently when he'd asked for funds to do so it had led to increasingly tedious and depressing exchanges of emails which got him nowhere. At least he was still able to pay for obituaries in the local paper, as long as the wording was kept to a minimum. In this particular case he'd only been able to achieve an acceptable length by omitting the deceased's middle name, the sparsity of the notice barely leaving room for sentiment: 'Derek Albrighton, died peacefully on 14 July, aged eighty-four'. He supposed one small advantage of the restricted word limit was that he couldn't act on the temptation to add, 'post-cake, mid-wank'.

He met Peggy in a café that overlooked some railway tracks.

'You know cranes, right?' she said, looking out of the window as Andrew sat down.

'The construction machine or the long-necked bird?' Andrew said.

'The former, obviously.'

'Obviously.'

'When you see one of those massive ones by a skyscraper,

do you ever wonder if they had to use another crane to build *that* crane. Or did it just get up there by itself? I suppose it's all a metaphor for how the universe was created. Or something.'

A commuter train rattled past.

'I'm glad I'm sitting down,' Andrew said. 'That's quite a lot to take in.'

Peggy stuck her tongue out at him. 'So how was it today – did anybody show up at the church?' she asked.

'Sadly not.'

'You see, this is what I'm worried about,' Peggy said, taking a swig of ginger beer.

'What do you mean?' Andrew said, wondering if maybe *he* should start drinking ginger beer.

Peggy looked sheepish and reached into her bag, bringing out the photo of Alan Carter and 'B'.

'I just can't stop thinking about this,' she said.

It had been a week since they'd visited Alan's house and Andrew had tried to convince Peggy that they'd done all they could, that she'd go mad if she kept thinking about it, but she clearly hadn't let it go. Reluctantly, he took the photo from her. 'And you're sure it's . . . where was it again?'

'Barter Books. It's a second-hand bookshop in Northumberland. I googled it just to make sure, and it's definitely the right place. My sister moved to a village nearby a few years ago and we usually pop in on the way to visiting her.'

Andrew studied the now familiar sight of Alan and his grinning companion.

'I just can't bear the thought of him being buried alone if there's someone out there who loved him and should be there – or at least be given the opportunity to be there.'

'But that's the point, isn't it?' Andrew said. 'Unfortunately, the cold truth of it is that when we get in touch with these people there's usually a reason they're not in contact with the person who's died.'

'Yeah, but that's not always the case, is it?' Peggy said, her eyes wide, imploring Andrew to understand. 'It's hardly ever because there's been some great dramatic falling out. At worst it's a stupid argument over money, and more often than not it's just out of laziness that they've fallen out of touch.'

Andrew went to speak but Peggy jumped in again.

'What about that woman you called last week – the one whose brother died. She didn't have a bad word to say about him – she was just embarrassed, more than anything, because she'd stopped bothering to call or visit him.'

Andrew immediately thought of Sally and felt his neck starting to prickle.

'I mean, what a sorry state of affairs society's in,' Peggy continued, 'and so utterly *British*, to be that stubborn and proud. I mean . . .' She stopped, seemingly aware from Andrew's body language that he was uncomfortable with where this was going. She quickly changed the subject and offered to buy him an 'overpriced, possibly stale' cookie.

'I couldn't possibly ask you to do that,' Andrew said, putting his hands up in mock earnestness.

'Oh, but I insist,' Peggy said. As she went up to the counter, Andrew looked at the photograph again. Perhaps he shouldn't have been so dismissive. Maybe there was a way of pursuing this without getting too deeply invested. He looked over at Peggy, who was taking the cookie-selection process very seriously despite the obvious impatience of the waitress. As usual, Andrew had made his textbook packed lunch that morning, but he'd pretended he hadn't when Peggy suggested they go out to eat. He looked again at the photo. Maybe there wasn't too much harm in hearing Peggy out.

'So, what do you want to do?' he said when she returned, proffering cookies.

'I want to go there,' she said, tapping the photo. 'To Barter Books. And find this woman – find "B".'

'Isn't that a bit . . . I mean, isn't it incredibly unlikely that she's still working there?'

Peggy scratched at an imaginary stain on the tablecloth. Andrew narrowed his eyes. 'Have you already contacted them?'

'Maybe,' Peggy said, her mouth twitching as she tried to hide a burgeoning smile.

'And?' Andrew said, and Peggy leaned forward and began to speak with a rapidity unusual even for her: 'I phoned a lass there and spoke to her about it and I explained about the photo and what I did for a living and that I was a regular visitor and I asked whether there was anyone working there who's name began with B who had brown and grey frizzy hair that might now actually be a bit more grey than brown and if they used to know someone called Alan.'

She paused for breath.

'Right. And?' Andrew said.

'*And*, well, she said she couldn't give out specific details about staff members, but there were some people who'd been working there for a good long while and I was very welcome to pop in the next time I was up visiting my sister.' Peggy opened her arms wide as if to say *see*.

'So you're saying you want to go to this bookshop on the off-chance that the person in the photograph with Alan is still working there?' Andrew said.

170

Peggy nodded emphatically, as if there had been a language barrier and she had finally broken through to him.

'OK,' Andrew said, 'to play devil's advocate—'

'Oh, you bloody love playing bloody devil's bloody advocate,' Peggy said, flicking a crumb in his direction.

'Say it *is* her, the woman in the photo, what will you say?' Andrew flicked the crumb back to signify the ball was in her court again.

Peggy thought for a moment. 'I think I'll just have to do that on the day. Busk it in the moment.'

Andrew went to speak but Peggy jumped in first. 'Oh, come on, where's the harm?' she said, reaching over and taking his hand, which was halfway to delivering a cookie to his face. 'Look, I've got it all worked out, right. I hadn't even thought about a holiday this summer, but God knows I need one – the kids, too, and,' she released Andrew's hand and a bit of cookie fell on to the table, 'Steve's been staying at a friend's, recently . . . Anyway, my plan is to go up and see my sister the week after next and drop in on Barter Books while I'm there.'

Andrew tilted his head from side to side, weighing this up. 'OK, well in fairness, if you're going up to see your sister, it's not quite as . . . mad.'

Peggy put the photo back in her bag.

'I'd invite you to come up too, but I assume you'll be busy with the family.'

'Ermm, well . . .' Andrew floundered, trying to think on his feet. It had seemed like a genuine invitation from Peggy, not simply out of politeness. 'I'll have to check,' he said, 'but, actually, Diane was planning to take the kids down to visit her mum that week. In Eastbourne.'

'And you're not going too?' Peggy said.

'No, probably not,' Andrew said, willing his brain into gear. 'I, um, don't really get on with Diane's parents. Bit of a long story.'

'Oh?' Peggy said. She wasn't going to let him finish there, clearly, but this wasn't something that had ever made it to Andrew's master spreadsheet.

'It's a bit complicated, but basically her mum never approved of us getting together in the first place, because I was always seen as a bit unsuitable. So we've never really been able to see eye to eye and it just causes tension whenever we meet.'

Peggy went to say something, then stopped.

'What?' Andrew said, a little too defensively, panicking that she wasn't convinced by this story.

'Oh, nothing. It's just. I can't imagine you being deemed unsuitable,' she said. 'You're far too . . . nice . . . and . . . you know . . .'

Andrew really *didn't* know. He took advantage of Peggy being flustered for once and thought about what he should do. The simplest option would be just to stay at home and avoid further questions about his family life. But there was just something about the idea of getting to spend a whole week with Peggy – on what felt like an adventure, too – that was too exciting and scary a prospect *not* to miss. If this wasn't going out of his comfort zone, then what was? He had to go for it.

'Anyway,' he said, as casually as possible, 'I'll have a think about Northumberland. There's a good chance I can come and it, er, wouldn't be weird or anything, for me to do that, would it?'

He hadn't quite thought this last bit through, and it came out halfway between a normal question and a rhetorical one.

Peggy seemed like she might be about to answer but luckily someone on a neighbouring table knocked an entire pot of tea on to the floor, whereupon five members of staff appeared from nowhere and cleared up the mess with the efficiency of Formula One mechanics in the pit lane, and the moment passed. Peggy seemed to use the distraction to do some weighing up of her own. 'If you were free then you should definitely come,' she said, once the pit lane crew had done their clean-up. Andrew recognised that tone. It was the way someone spoke when they were trying to convince themselves as much as the person they were talking to that what they were suggesting was a good idea.

They left the café and walked most of the way back to the office without speaking. Andrew glanced at Peggy, saw her furrowed brow, and knew that like him she was replaying the conversation from the café over in her mind. They crossed at some lights and stepped around either side of a woman with a pram. When they came back together their arms bumped and they both apologised at the same time, then laughed at their politeness, the tension of the silence broken. Peggy raised an eyebrow at him. It seemed like such a daring gesture, to Andrew. As if she was on the verge of acknowledging what they were both thinking about the trip, that it was much more important to both of them than they were letting on. Furthermore, Andrew had the sudden realisation that it was, in fact, one of the most spectacularly perfect eyebrows he'd ever seen, and that his heart was starting to beat uncomfortably fast.

'So what's Barter Books like, then?' he said, trying to restore normality to the conversation.

'Oh, it's amazing,' Peggy said. She was attempting to put her coat on but was having a hard time finding one of the armholes. 'It's a huge old place, rows and rows of books, comfy sofas dotted around.'

'Sounds lovely,' Andrew said. For some reason, putting one foot in front of the other had become an impossible task. Was this really how he walked? It seemed so unnatural.

'It really is,' Peggy said, finally getting her arm through the coat sleeve. 'It used to be a station and they've kept the waiting room and turned it into a café. The best part is there's a model train that runs all the way round the shop above the bookshelves.'

Andrew stopped dead in his tracks before hurrying to catch Peggy up.

'Say that again?'

Chapter Sixteen

To Andrew's dismay, the trip was nearly scuppered before they'd even booked train tickets.

Cameron, for reasons which were unclear, had taken to getting people's attention by whistling at them. At first it had been a sharp, enthusiastic toot. But recently, in parallel with his mood, the whistle had become a low, melancholy sound, like a farmer instructing his sheepdog on its last outing before it was to be put down.

It was by this method that Andrew was beckoned into Cameron's office. There were folders and documents all over the place, and he had to gather a bunch of them up and move them off a chair so he had somewhere to sit. Distressingly, Andrew realised the office had started to resemble a room he might usually find himself searching through with surgical gloves and a litter picker.

'Rightio then, Drew,' Cameron said. 'This holiday you've booked. In future please check with the others in the team about timings because Peggy's away at the same time and that's just not ideal. Please just be a bit more nimble about things, OK? It's so easy to cascade this sort of thing.'

'Ah right, yes,' Andrew said. He and Peggy hadn't deliberately concealed the fact they were going away together, but he couldn't help but enjoy how illicit that seemed to make it. He realised that Cameron was looking at him expectantly.

'I'll check next time,' he said quickly.

'Good. Thanks,' Cameron said.

Andrew hoped that was going to be the end of it, but the next day he was at his desk when he heard raised voices coming from Cameron's office. 'It's just absolutely outrageous,' Meredith was saying, with typical understatement. 'I'm sorry, literally the last thing I like doing is complaining, but you can't just turn around to me and say I can't take holiday when I want to, that's against my rights. I don't see why Andrew and Peggy can just swan off at the same time and I can't. It's ludicrous. It's completely unfair.'

Cameron followed her out, ringing his hands with an alarmingly tight-looking grip.

'As I have told you, Meredith,' he said, his voice ominously quiet, 'you *can* take a holiday. I have just asked you to *not* to go away the one week Peggy and Andrew are.'

'Well, how was I supposed to know when they were away? I'm not Mystic Meg, am I?'

'You're supposed to plan in advance and look at the log,' Cameron said.

'What?'

'*The log! The fucking log!*'

Cameron covered his mouth with his hands, seemingly more shocked than anyone about his outburst. It was at that point that Keith wandered into the office, humming something a semitone out and brandishing a heart attack in a bap. He looked at them in turn and took a massive bite, ketchup dripping on to his chin.

'What have I missed?' he said.

Andrew got to his feet. He had to act quickly so the trip wasn't endangered. 'Look, I think what Cameron was trying to say, Meredith, is that we just need to make sure this log . . . thing . . . is filled out from now on. It's a bit of miscommunication, that's all. I'm sure he didn't mean to shout. Right, Cameron?'

Cameron looked at Andrew as if only just realising he was there. 'Yes,' he said. 'Yes, that's right. Tough week. Clara and I . . . Not that I want to get into all that business but . . . I'm sorry.'

Andrew decided to ignore the Clara comment and quickly moved to settle things. 'I'm happy to take on some of your workload this week to make up for it, Meredith.'

Peggy was looking at him slightly curiously, perhaps as equally surprised as he was at him taking charge like this. It felt sort of liberating – for a moment he had a taste of what it would be like to send cold food back in a restaurant, or ask people to move down on the tube.

'Well,' Meredith said, 'it doesn't make up for not being able to go away. I was planning on going on a yoga retreat, so that will need rescheduling. Not ideal, as you can imagine. But yes, I am hugely snowed under as it happens. So thanks, I suppose.'

'Yoga, eh?' Peggy said, licking the lid of a yoghurt she'd produced seemingly out of nowhere. 'Downward dogs and all that bollocks?'

Andrew widened his eyes at her.

'I mean, good for the old joints and that, I'll bet,' she said.

'And flexibility,' Meredith said, glancing at Keith, who smirked and took another huge bite of bap.

'I know what,' Cameron said suddenly, with a startling

return to his usual bright self. 'How about I go out and buy us a cake?'

'A . . . cake?' Andrew said.

'Yes, Andrew. A cake. A big lovely cake. Right now. That's what you hardworking lot need.' And before anyone could say anything else Cameron walked out, not even stopping to pick up his coat despite the torrential rain.

Keith sucked his fingers clean.

'Fifty quid says he's in the papers tomorrow morning.'

Peggy rolled her eyes. 'Don't say things like that,' she said.

'I *do* beg your pardon,' Keith said, in his best attempt at a snooty voice. Meredith giggled. 'Besides,' Keith went on, 'if he's out the way maybe we keep our jobs.'

Nobody, it seemed, had a response to this. There was just the sound of Keith giving his fingers one final clean.

Come on, come on, come on.

Andrew was pacing back and forth – as much as you *can* pace back and forth in a train vestibule. The train was scheduled to leave King's Cross at 9.04, and he and Peggy had arranged to meet on the concourse at 8.30. In retrospect, alarm bells should have rung when she'd said '8.30 – or thereabouts.'

He'd messaged her three times so far that morning:

Just on the concourse. Let me know when you get here.' – sent at 8.20.

'It's platform 11. Meet you there?' – sent at 8.50.

'Are you near . . . ?' – sent at 8.58.

He couldn't write what he really wanted to, namely: *Where in God's name are you??* but he hoped the ellipsis would get the general gist across.

He planted his foot so that it was halfway out of the train

door, ready to defy every fibre of his being and jam it open. He could just get off, of course, although they *had* bought specific tickets for this time that *were* non-refundable – not that he cared about that sort of thing, *obviously*. He swore under his breath and dashed over to the luggage racks to retrieve his bag. Ideally, he would have been travelling with an elegant little suitcase, the sort of thing you saw BBC4 travel-documentary makers in white linen suits wheeling through Florence. But what he actually had was a great, cumbersome, bright purple backpack that at one time in his life he'd used to carry every single possession he had to his name.

While he hadn't upgraded his bag, or bought a linen suit for that matter, he had spent far too much money on an extensive clothes overhaul: four new pairs of trousers, six new shirts, some leather brogues and, most daringly, a charcoal grey blazer. On top of this he'd also had his quarterly haircut, choosing a more upmarket place than usual, and bought a bottle of the stinging lemon aftershave the barber had splashed unbidden on his cheeks, which made him smell a bit like a sophisticated dessert. At the time, looking at himself in the barber's mirror, in his new garb and new haircut, he was pleasantly surprised at his reflection. Would it be too much of a stretch to think he looked handsome? Perhaps even – dare he say it – Sean Bean-esque? He had been secretly quite excited to see what Peggy might make of his new look, but by the time he got to the station the unfamiliarity of it all was actually making him feel even more self-conscious than usual. It was as if everyone in the station was judging him. *Well, well, well,* the man in Upper Crust seemed to be thinking, eyeing his jacket scornfully, *a bold fashion choice for a middle-aged man who still clearly uses a combined shower gel and shampoo.*

Andrew felt something itching at his hip, and realised to his embarrassment that he'd left a label on his shirt. He twisted the material round and began pulling and yanking at the label, until eventually it snapped off. He shoved it into his pocket and looked at his watch.

Come on, come on, come on.

There were two minutes before the train was scheduled to depart. Resignedly, he swung his rucksack on to his back, nearly falling over in the process. He took one final look down the platform. And there, miraculously, flanked by her two girls, waving tickets at the guard and hurrying through the barriers, was Peggy. The three of them were laughing, urging each other on. Peggy too wore a ludicrously bulky rucksack, loosely secured, which was wobbling violently from side to side as she ran. Her eyes scanned down the carriages until she saw him. 'There's Andrew,' he heard her say. 'Come on you two slowcoaches – run to Andrew!'

They were only feet away from Andrew now and suddenly he was overcome with a desperate desire to stop and bottle the moment. To see Peggy rushing towards him like that, for him to be needed, to be an active participant in someone else's life, to think that maybe he was more than just a lump of carbon being slowly ushered towards an unvarnished coffin; the feeling was one of pure, almost painful happiness, like a desperate embrace squeezing air from his lungs, and it was then that the realisation hit him: he might not know what the future held – pain and loneliness and fear might still yet grind him into dust – but simply feeling the possibility that things could change for him was a start, like feeling the first hint of warmth from kindling rubbed together, the first wisp of smoke.

Chapter Seventeen

Andrew jammed the doors open, incurring both the anger of the guard on the platform and the unbridled tutting of passengers in the vestibule. Peggy frantically ushered the kids on to the train before jumping on herself, and Andrew released the doors.

'Well, that's probably the most rebellious thing I've ever done,' he said. 'I imagine this is the same feeling you get after a skydive.'

'What a hell raiser you are,' Peggy said, struggling to catch her breath. When she looked at him she seemed to do a double take. 'Wow, you look . . .'

'What?' Andrew said, running a hand through his hair self-consciously.

'Nothing, just . . .' Peggy picked a stray bit of cotton from his blazer. 'Different, that's all.'

They held eye contact for a moment. Then the train began to pull away.

'We should find our seats,' Peggy said.

'Yep. Good plan,' Andrew said, and then, suddenly feeling rather devil-may-care: 'Lead on Mac . . . lovely . . . duff.'

To Andrew's great relief, Peggy had turned to her daughters, who were waiting patiently behind her, and hadn't seemed to have heard this. He decided to leave devil-may-careness for another day. Perhaps when he was dead.

'Kids, say hello to Andrew,' Peggy said.

Andrew had felt apprehensive about meeting Peggy's girls, and had turned to the sub-forum for advice, waiting for a spirited but good-natured debate about the best way to replace valve gear pins from driving wheels to finish before bringing the conversation around to his nerves at meeting Peggy's children.

'*This might sound rather odd,*' BamBam wrote, '*but the best advice I can give is **not** to talk to them like they're children. None of that patronising, slow-talking nonsense. They'll spot such bullsh*t a mile off. Just ask lots of questions and essentially treat them like you would an adult.*'

So, with a general air of suspicion and mistrust, Andrew thought. Though he replied: '*Thanks, mate!*' and worried for two hours about the implications of him now being the sort of person who used the word 'mate'.

As it turned out, Peggy's eldest, Maisie, happily ignored them all for the duration of the journey – only lifting her head away from the book she was reading to ask where they were, or what a particular word meant. Her younger sister, Suze, on the other hand, conversed entirely through the medium of 'would you rather' scenarios, which made things infinitely easier than Andrew was expecting. She had a twinkle in her eye that made it seem as though she was constantly on the cusp of laughing, so Andrew was finding it hard to treat the questions with the gravitas they clearly warranted.

'Would you rather be a horse that can time travel or a talking turd?' was the latest conundrum.

'Would it be OK for me to ask follow-up questions?'

Andrew asked. 'That's what Peggy – your mum, I mean – and I normally do.'

Suze yawned as she deliberated. 'Yeahhh, OK,' she said, apparently satisfied that this was above board.

'OK,' Andrew said, suddenly aware that both Peggy and Suze were looking at him intently, and trying not to feel embarrassed. 'Can the horse speak?'

'No,' Suze said, 'it's a horse.'

'That is true,' Andrew conceded. 'But the *turd* can talk, though.'

'So?'

Andrew didn't really have a response to that.

'The problem you've got here,' Peggy said, 'is that you're trying to apply logic to the question. Logic is not your friend, here.'

Suze nodded sagely. Next to her, Maisie closed her eyes and took a deep breath, frustrated at the constant distractions. Andrew made sure to lower his voice.

'OK, I'm going to go with the horse.'

'Obviously,' Suze said, apparently baffled as to why it had taken Andrew so long to get there. She tore open a bag of lemon sherbets and, after briefly contemplating, offered the bag to Andrew.

As the train snaked into Newcastle, the Tyne Bridge sparkling in the sun, Peggy took out the photograph of Alan and 'B'.

'What do you reckon, kiddos. Think we're gonna find this lass?'

Maisie and Suze shrugged in unison.

'That seems about right,' Andrew said.

'Oi,' Peggy said, kicking him gently in the shin, 'whose side are you on?'

*

Peggy's sister, Imogen was, by her own admission, 'a cuddler', and Andrew had no option but to submit to her bosomy bear hug. She drove them to her house in a car with an alarming amount of gaffer tape holding it together, with Andrew sitting in the back next to the girls, feeling a bit like an awkward older brother.

Imogen had obviously been busy that morning as the kitchen was teeming with cakes, biscuits and puddings, many of which Andrew lacked the critical vocabulary to describe.

'I see you're catering for village fetes now,' Peggy said.

'Oh, give over, you all need fattening up,' Imogen said. Andrew was glad that while cuddles were compulsory, pokes to the belly were apparently restricted to family.

Later that evening, with the kids in bed, Imogen, Peggy and Andrew settled down in the living room and half-watched a romcom, Imogen thankfully interrupting a dire scene involving bodily fluids to ask about Alan and the ducks.

'You've never seen anything like it, honest to God,' Peggy said.

'Well, it's very sweet what you're doing,' Imogen said, stifling a yawn. 'I mean, you're both mental, obviously . . .'

Peggy started to make their case again. She was sitting with her legs tucked back to one side, her jumper slipped off her shoulder. Andrew felt an ache somewhere in the region of his stomach. It was then he glanced over and saw that Imogen was watching him. More specifically, she was watching *him* watching Peggy. He looked away and focused on the TV, glad the room was dim enough to hide his reddening cheeks. He got the impression that Imogen wasn't someone easily fooled, and just as he'd had that thought she cut across Peggy's questioning of the protagonist's Irish accent.

'So, what does your wife make of your chances of finding this person, Andrew?' she said.

Well, what *would* she make of them?

'She hasn't said much about it, truth be told,' he said.

'Interesting,' Imogen said.

Andrew hoped that was the end of it, but then Imogen spoke up again.

'Surely she must have been curious, though?'

'*Imogen* . . .' Peggy said.

'What?' Imogen said.

'I don't tend to talk too much about my work at home, to be honest,' Andrew said, which *was* technically true, he supposed.

'How long have you been with her?' Imogen said.

Andrew kept his eyes on the screen.

'Oh, a long old time,' he said.

'And how did you two get together?'

Andrew scratched at the back of his head. He really wasn't in the mood for this.

'We met at university,' he said, as casually as possible. 'We were friends for a while – mainly bonding over our shared hatred of all the idiots on our course, or the ones who'd taken to wearing berets, at least.' He took a sip of wine. He wasn't sure why, but he felt compelled to keep going. 'She had this way of looking at me over the top of her glasses. Used to make me feel a bit faint. And I'd never met anyone I found it so easy to talk to. Anyway, we were at this party and she took me by the hand and led me away from all the noise and people and, well, that was that.' Andrew looked at his hand. It was the strangest thing. He could practically feel the sensation of that firm grip, confidently pulling him out of the room.

'Ah, sweet,' Imogen said. 'And she wasn't particularly intrigued about you coming all this way . . . with Peggy,' she added pointedly.

'Imogen!' Peggy snapped. 'Don't be so bloody rude. You've just met the man.'

'No, no, it's fine,' Andrew said, keen that this didn't end up in an argument. Thankfully, a neat solution presented itself.

'In actual fact, I'd better give Diane a ring now, if you'll excuse me.' His left leg had gone numb from his sitting position, so he had to limp away to the guest bedroom as fast as he could, like an injured soldier retreating from no man's land. The room was freezing, the window having been left open on the latch. He wondered if he should actually fake the phone call in case anyone could hear him. He could just come out with some generic stuff about how the journey had been, what he'd had for dinner – the sort of thing he imagined most people would say in real life.

In real life. He was going to get fucking sectioned for this. He slumped on to the bed. Out of nowhere, the tune came into his head – *Blue moon, you saw me standing alone* – and then came the feedback and static, like a wave smashing against rock. He tried to shake it away, getting so desperate for it to end he found himself face down on the bed, pounding the duvet with his fists, shouting into the pillow.

Eventually, the chaos subsided. He lay still in the resulting silence, fists clenched, short of breath, praying that his shouts hadn't travelled. He looked at his reflection, pale and tired, in the dressing-table mirror, and suddenly he felt desperate to be back in the front room with a glass of wine in his hand and the rubbish telly on in the background and – even if half of it was suspicious about him – the company.

He wasn't sure what made him do it, but he found himself pausing outside the living-room door, which was open just wide enough for him to hear Imogen and Peggy speaking in hushed tones.

'You really think his missus is fine with this?'

'Why wouldn't she be? She's away herself, remember. With her parents. They don't get on with Andrew, apparently.'

'That's not what I meant, and you know it.'

'What, then?' Peggy hissed.

'Come off it, you really think he isn't interested in you?'

'I'm not answering that.'

'OK, well, are you interested in *him* then?'

A pause.

'I'm not answering that either.'

'I don't think you have to.'

'Please can we just change the—'

'I know things are shite with Steve, but this isn't the answer.'

'You've no idea what things are like with Steve.'

'Of course I do, I'm your sister. He's obviously up to his old tricks again. And the sooner you get out of that the better. It's just like Dad – constantly begging for forgiveness and saying it won't happen again. I can't believe you're being so naive.'

'Don't. Just don't, OK?'

There was a pause, then Peggy spoke again.

'Look. It's so lovely being here. You know how much the girls adore you, how . . .' her voice broke ever so slightly 'how I do, too. I just want to relax for a few days, get myself together again. If things go the way I think they are – with Steve, with work – I need to be in a good frame of mind to deal with it all.'

Another pause.

'Ah pet, I'm sorry,' Imogen said. 'I just worry about you.'

'I know, I know,' Peggy said, her voice muffled by what Andrew guessed was another bear hug from Imogen.

'Peg?'

'Yeah?'

'Pass us the biccies.'

'*You* pass *us* the biccies, they're equidistant.'

'Are they bollocks,' Imogen said, and Peggy let out a slightly tearful giggle.

Andrew retreated a few steps, both in an attempt to calm his thumping heart and to make his entrance seem more genuine.

'Hello, hello,' he said. Peggy was sitting on the sofa where he had been before so she could look at her phone, which was charging nearby, meaning he had to choose whether to sit next to her or Imogen. Peggy smiled at him as he hovered, the light from the TV showing the dampness in her eyes.

'Everything . . . OK?' he said.

'Oh, aye,' Imogen said, patting the space next to her. 'Sit yer arse down here.'

Andrew was glad to have his mind made up for him, even if it meant a missed opportunity to be closer to Peggy.

'Let's finish these buggers off then,' Imogen said, divvying up the remaining Hobnobs.

'You get through OK?' Peggy said.

'Huh? Oh, yes. Thanks.'

'Good-o,' Imogen said. 'The signal can be pretty patchy that side of the house.'

'My luck must have been in,' Andrew said.

It was then that his phone – which had been on the mantel-piece where he'd put it when he'd first arrived that afternoon – began to ring.

Chapter Eighteen

'So, yeah, I've got two phones. One's a work one that I got ages ago. I'm not sure if Cameron even knows about it so, you know, best keep shtum!'

Andrew kept replaying his garbled explanation over and over in his mind. Neither Peggy nor Imogen seemed to know what he was blathering on about, which just meant he carried on and on, digging an increasingly large hole. Thankfully, they'd continued to just look at him blankly, like two bored customs officials ignoring a foreign traveller's desperate attempts to explain their plight, and the climax of the romcom provided enough of a distraction for conversation to move on.

Andrew had assumed that they would be going to Barter Books the next morning, but Peggy and Imogen had other plans. What followed over the next couple of days were boat trips to the Farne Islands where Andrew was unceremoniously shat on by a puffin (much to Suze's delight), blustery coastal walks punctuated by tea and cake pit stops (much to Imogen's delight), followed by delicious dinners back at Imogen's and two occasions where Peggy fell asleep on Andrew's shoulder (much to Andrew's delight).

Alone in the guest room, he thought of the conversation he'd eavesdropped on.

'*OK, well, are you interested in* him *then?*'

'*. . . I'm not answering that.*'

'Interested in him'. Could that have meant anything other than romantic interest? Maybe it was from a purely anthropological point of view – that Peggy was planning to make scientific field notes: *A squat specimen, frequently observed making a twat of himself.* Either way, Peggy had refused to answer the question, and Andrew had watched enough episodes of *Newsnight* to know this meant she was avoiding telling the truth. He only wished Imogen had gone full-Paxman on her.

Finally, the following morning they headed to Barter Books. Andrew got the sense that Peggy had been delaying the visit, not because she'd somehow lost interest, but because she was scared that it was going to end in failure.

The kids had stayed behind with Imogen, who had promised to make them a cake so chocolatey it would send Bruce Bogtrotter into a diabetic coma. Peggy had taken Imogen's Astra, Imogen explaining all the car's various problems and how to cope with them, many of which involved punching things and swearing.

'Bastard,' Peggy grumbled, yanking the gearstick violently back and forth and making a joke about her first boyfriend's eyes watering that caused Andrew to wind down the window for a moment.

They passed a sign saying they were fifteen miles from Alnwick.

'I'm feeling a bit nervous,' Andrew said. 'How about you?'

'Dunno. Yeah. Sort of,' Peggy said, but her attention was on the rear-view mirror as they merged on to a dual carriageway.

The more miles they chewed up, the more fraught Andrew

felt, because the closer they got to the bookshop the closer they were to their adventure ending. Most likely they'd just be returning home, deflated with defeat, and Alan would be buried with just them and a disinterested vicar for company. Then it would be back to the daily grind.

They passed another sign for Alnwick. Five miles, now. Someone had somewhat unimaginatively graffitied the word 'shit' on to the sign in angry red. Andrew was reminded of something he'd seen coming back from a rare school trip to the Ashmolean Museum in Oxford. He remembered the evening sky being scorched pink, his eyes following the telegraph wires silhouetted against it like a blank musical score, when he noticed the letters painted white and bold on a fence in the distance: 'Why Do I Do This Every Day?' The memory had stayed with him despite him not understanding its commuter-baiting message at the time. It was as if his subconscious was saying: *this won't mean much to you at the moment because you're too young and your major concern is whether Justin Stanmore is going to Chinese Burn you again, but just give it thirty years or so and its significance will really hit home.*

He sat forward.

Maybe he'd just tell Peggy everything. Now. Here. In an overheating Vauxhall Astra on a dual carriageway.

He shifted in his seat, half exhilarated, half terrified at the possibility. Everything could be out in the open. Not just about his growing feelings for her, but about the big lie, too. Peggy would hate him, maybe never even talk to him again, but it would end just . . . *this.* This relentless misery – of still clinging on to something that barely provided him solace any more. The realisation came to him like a radio signal finding its way through static: a lie can only exist in opposition to the truth, and the truth was the only thing that could free him of his pain.

'Why are you wriggling around so much?' Peggy said. 'You're like my old dog dragging its arse along the floor.'

'Sorry,' Andrew said. 'It's just . . .'

'What?'

'. . . Nothing.'

Andrew lost Peggy almost as soon as they walked into the bookshop, his focus drawn immediately to what was happening five feet above his head. A beautiful, dark green engine – an Accucraft Victorian NA Class, if he wasn't very much mistaken – was sliding effortlessly around the tracks positioned above the bookstacks. The aisles beyond were bridged by signs bearing lines of poetry. The nearest read:

> *Yon rising Moon that looks for us again—*
> *How oft hereafter will she wax and wane*

The train flashed past again, a soft breeze rippling in its wake.

'I'm in heaven,' Andrew whispered to himself. If anything was going to slow his pulse back to normal after what had nearly just happened in the car, it was this. He was aware of someone standing next to him. Glancing to his side, he saw a tall man in a grey cardigan, his hands held behind his back, looking up at the train. He and Andrew exchanged nods.

'Like what you see?' the man asked. Andrew had only ever heard this phrase used by bolshy brothel madams in period dramas, but despite it seeming so out of context, at the same time he really *did* like what he was seeing.

'It's mesmerising,' he said. The man nodded, eyes briefly closing, as if to say: 'Welcome home, old friend'.

Andrew took a deep breath, feeling properly calmed now, and turned slowly on the spot so he could take in the rest of the place. He certainly wasn't the sort of person who would use the word 'vibe', but if he *were*, Barter Books' vibe was one he was very much 'down with', to borrow one of Sally's old phrases. It was so serene, so quiet. People were browsing the shelves with a sense of reverence, their voices lowered. When someone took a book off a shelf they did so with the delicacy of an archaeologist bringing ancient pottery out of the soil. Andrew had read that the shop's claim to fame was that it was where the original 'Keep Calm And Carry On' poster had been unearthed. And whilst it had spawned thousands of annoying variations – Meredith had a mug in the office with the slogan 'Keep Calm And Do Yoga' written on it, possibly the most prosaic sentence ever committed to ceramic – here it felt like the perfect emblem.

But they weren't here for the atmosphere. Andrew found Peggy sitting low in a chair that looked almost obscenely comfy, her hands linked behind her head, a contented smile on her face.

'Argh,' she moaned, as Andrew approached, 'I suppose we better get on with this, then?'

'I think we better had,' Andrew said.

Peggy looked at him determinedly and held out her hands. At first Andrew stared at them uncomprehendingly, then snapped into action and pulled Peggy to her feet. They stood side by side, shoulders touching, facing the polite queue by the tills.

'Right,' Andrew said, rubbing his hands together to suggest

industry. 'So are we just going to go up there and ask them whether a "B" works here?'

'Unless you've got a better idea?' Peggy said.

Andrew shook his head. 'Do you want to do the talking?'

'Nope,' Peggy said. 'You?'

'Not particularly, if I'm honest with you.'

Peggy pursed her lips. 'Rock Paper Scissors?'

Andrew turned so he was facing her. 'Why not?'

'One, two, three.'

Paper. Paper.

'One, two, three.'

Rock. Rock.

They went again. Andrew thought about going scissors, but at the last minute he changed it to rock. This time, Peggy went paper. She closed her hand over his.

'Paper covers rock,' she said quietly.

They were standing close, now, hands still touching. It felt for a second as if the hubbub had died away, that all eyes were on them, that even the books on the shelves were holding their breath. Then Peggy suddenly dropped her hand. 'Oh my God,' she whispered. 'Look.'

Andrew forced himself to turn around so that they were side by side once more. And there at the tills, cup of tea in hand, glasses around her neck on a chain, was a woman with green eyes and frizzy grey hair. Peggy dragged Andrew by the arm over to the waiting-room café.

'That's definitely her, right?' she said.

Andrew shrugged, not wanting to get Peggy's hopes up. 'It could be,' he said.

Peggy manhandled him once more, this time out of the way of an elderly couple who were slowly carrying trays laden with scones and mugs of tea over to a table. Once settled, the man set about spreading cream on to his scone with a trembling hand. His wife looked at him askance.

'What?' the man said.

'Cream before jam? Ya daft apeth.'

'That's the way it's supposed to be.'

'Is it heck. We have this argument every time. It's the other way round.'

'Nonsense.'

'It isn't nonsense!'

'It bloody is.'

Peggy rolled her eyes and gently prodded Andrew forwards. 'Come on,' she said. 'We've buggered about far too much already.'

As they made their way towards the counter, Andrew felt his heart starting to thump faster and faster. It was only when they reached the woman and she looked up from her cross-word that Andrew realised Peggy had taken his hand. The woman put down her pen and asked in the soft yet slightly raspy voice of a smoker how she could help.

'This is going to sound like a slightly strange question,' Peggy said.

'Don't worry, love. I've been asked some very strange questions in here, believe me. Belgian chap a few months ago asked me whether we sold books about bestiality. So fire away.'

Peggy and Andrew laughed slightly robotically.

'So,' Peggy said. 'We just wanted to ask, well, whether your name begins with "B".'

The woman smiled quizzically.

'Is that a trick question?' she said.

Andrew felt Peggy tighten her grip on his hand.

'No,' she said.

'In that case, yes it does,' the woman said. 'I'm Beryl. Have I sold someone a dodgy book or something?'

'No, nothing like that,' Peggy said, glancing at Andrew.

This was his cue to take the photograph from his pocket and hand it over. The woman took it from him and there was a flash of recognition in her eyes.

'Blimey,' she said, looking at them in turn, 'I think this calls for another cup of tea.'

Chapter Nineteen

Beryl responded to the news of Alan's death with a short, sad exhalation, like a week-old birthday balloon finally admitting defeat.

Andrew had only ever given news to relatives on the phone, never face-to-face. Seeing Beryl's reaction in person was a very uncomfortable experience. She asked him the questions he'd been expecting – how had Alan died, who had found him, where and when was the funeral going to be – but he got the sense she was holding back about something. And then of course, there was the other thing . . .

'Ducks?'

'Thousands of them,' Andrew said, pouring tea into their cups. He'd very nearly said 'I'll be mother', but managed to stop himself just in time.

Peggy showed Beryl Alan's note about feeding the ducks on the back of the photograph. 'We assumed it was something to do with this.'

Beryl smiled, but her eyes started to water too, and she reached into her sleeve and retrieved a hanky to dab them dry.

'I remember that day. It was miserable weather. As we were walking to our usual bench we saw an ice-cream van parked on the side of the road. The bloke inside looked so depressed we went and bought a 99 each just to cheer the poor bugger up. We ate it before we'd had our sandwiches – it felt so decadent!'

She lifted her mug to her lips with both hands and her glasses momentarily steamed up.

'Do you remember having the picture taken?' Peggy asked.

'Oh yes,' Beryl said, wiping her glasses with her hanky. 'We wanted a snap of us in the shop because that's where we first met. It took Alan about ten visits to pluck up the courage to talk to me, you know. I've never seen someone spending so long pretending to look at books on Yorkshire farm machinery of the eighteenth century. At first I thought he might just really love farming, or Yorkshire – or both – but then I realised he was only standing there because it was the best way to keep sneaking glances at me. Once I saw him holding a book about seed drills upside down. That was the day he finally came over and said hello.'

'And you became an item straight away?' Peggy said.

'Oh no, not for a long time,' Beryl said. 'The timing was rubbish. I'd just divorced my husband and it hadn't been the easiest of rides. Looking back now I don't know why I made such a fuss about waiting. It just seemed like I should pause for the dust to settle a bit. Alan said he understood that I needed time, but that didn't stop him coming in and pretending to still care about bloody farming for the next six weeks, sneaking over to say hello whenever there was a gap between customers.'

'Six weeks?' Peggy said.

'Every day,' Beryl said. 'Even when I had five days off for tonsillitis he still came in, despite my boss telling him I was going to be off for the rest of the week. Eventually, we had our first date. Tea and iced buns in this very café.'

They were interrupted by one of the staff who was noisily clearing away crockery from the adjacent table. She and Beryl exchanged slightly frosty smiles. 'She's the worst, that one,' Beryl said, when the woman was out of earshot, without providing further explanation.

'But you and Alan were together properly after that?' Peggy probed.

'Yes, we were inseparable actually,' Beryl said. 'Alan is – oh, I suppose I should say *was* – a carpenter. His workshop was in his house just down the road, near the little cemetery. I moved in just after Christmas. I was fifty-two. He was sixty but you'd never have known it. He could have passed for a much younger man. He had these great big strong legs like tree trunks.'

Andrew and Peggy looked at each other. In the end, Beryl realised what the unspoken question was.

'I suppose you're wondering why we weren't still together.'

'Please don't feel obliged to tell us,' Andrew said.

'No, no – it's fine.'

Beryl composed herself, polishing her glasses again.

'It was all down to my relationship with my ex-husband. We'd got married when we were twenty-one. Kids, still, really. And I think we both knew as soon as we came home on our wedding night and gave each other a chaste little peck on the cheek that we didn't properly love each other. We stuck it out for years but eventually I couldn't stand it any more and I decided to end it. And I made a decision then and there' – she rapped her knuckles on the table for emphasis – 'that if I were to ever find someone else to share my life with it would have to be for love and nothing else. I wasn't going to settle for the sake of it being the done thing, or just for companionship. And at the first sign of feeling like we were going through the motions, that we'd fallen out of love, that would be it. Bish, bash, bosh. I'd be out.'

'And that's what happened with Alan?' Peggy said.

Beryl took another sip of tea and replaced the mug carefully on its saucer.

'We were very much in love to start,' she said. She eyed Andrew mischievously. 'You might want to cover your ears for this part, but we practically spent the first few years in bed. That's the thing with someone who works with their hands. Very skilled, you see? Anyway, aside from *that* side of things, for a long time we were very happy. Even though his family had buggered off a long time before, and mine had never approved of the divorce, it didn't matter. It just felt like me and him against the world, you know? But then, after a while, Alan started to change. It was subtle at first. He'd say he was too tired to work, or he'd go for days at a time without shaving or getting out of his pyjamas. Occasionally I'd find him—' She broke off and cleared her throat.

Peggy leaned across the table and put her hand on Beryl's. 'It's OK,' she said, 'You don't have to . . .' But Beryl shook her head and patted Peggy's hand to show she was OK to continue.

'Occasionally, I'd find him sitting cross-legged on the living-room floor, back against the sofa, just looking out into the garden through the French windows. Not reading. Not listening to the radio. Just sitting there.'

Andrew thought of his mother in the dark of her bedroom. Inert. Hidden away. Unable to face the world.

'He was a proud old sod,' Beryl said. 'Never would have admitted to me that he was struggling with whatever it was. And I could never find the right words, or the right moment, to ask him about it all. Then his back went. Whether it was psychosomatic or what I don't know, but he had to sleep in another room because otherwise he'd disturb me by getting up – or so he said. Then one evening we were having tea, watching some rubbish on the telly, and out of nowhere he turned to me and said: "You remember what you told me right after we met, about what you'd do if you stopped loving the person you were with?"

'"Yes," I said.

'"Do you still believe that?" he said.

'"Yes, I do," I said. And I *did*. I should have said something reassuring of course, but I just assumed he knew I still loved him as much as I always had. I asked him whether he was OK but he just kissed me on the top of my head and went off to do the washing-up. I was worried, but I thought he was just having one of his difficult days. The next morning I went off to work as usual, but when I got home he wasn't there. And there was a note. I can still remember holding that piece of paper, my hands shaking like mad. He'd written that he knew I didn't love him any more. That he didn't want to put me through any pain. He'd just gone. Never left an address, never left a phone number. Nothing. I tried to find him, of course. But as you know there were no relatives to get in touch with, and he didn't have any friends I knew of. I did actually look into getting a whatchamacallit, a private investigator, but the thought always dogged me that maybe he'd just lied, that he'd run off with some other lass. Looking at this though' – she picked up the photograph – 'and hearing about this duck business . . . Well, you tell me.' At this, a sob escaped her, and she clasped both hands to her chest. 'Maybe I should have tried harder after all.'

After they'd made sure Beryl was OK, with promises to be in touch soon, Andrew and Peggy emerged from the shop like two people leaving a cinema: blinking into the sunlight, thoughts consumed by the story they'd just been told.

They stood in the car park and checked their phones. Andrew was really just scrolling up and down his short list of existing texts – offers from pizza companies he'd never ordered from, PPI scams, work nonsense. He couldn't shake the desperate sadness of Beryl's story.

Peggy was gazing into middle distance. An eyelash had fallen to her cheek. It looked like the smallest of fractures on a piece of porcelain. Somewhere nearby, a car horn sounded with one sharp blast and Andrew reached out and took Peggy's hand. She looked at him with surprise.

'Let's go for a walk,' Andrew said.

They left the car park and made their way towards the town centre, hand in hand. Andrew hadn't planned to go this way, but it just felt right, as if they were being drawn along by an invisible force. They walked along the high street, weaving past parents with pushchairs and a group of tourists who'd slowed to a stop in the street as if their batteries had run down, then on further to Alnwick Castle, with its red and yellow Northumberland flags strained taut by the breeze. Without exchanging a word they made their way around the castle, to the surrounding field, newly cut grass collecting on their shoes. Down, further, past kids throwing a dog-eared tennis ball around and pensioners resting on picnic tables watching the moody clouds closing in on the sun. Down, further still, along a path carved out by footfall, until finally they reached the river and found a solitary bench half covered in moss at the water's edge. They sat and listened to the gurgling water and watched the reeds struggling to stay upright against its flow. Peggy was sitting upright, her hands in her lap, one leg crossed over the other. They were both very still, at odds with the rushing river, like the model figures Andrew arranged on his living room floor. But even in that stillness, there was movement. Peggy's foot was stirring almost imperceptibly every second or so, like a metronome. It was, Andrew realised, not because of tension or nervousness, but purely because of the pulse of her heart. And suddenly he was gripped by possibility once again: that as long as there was that movement in someone then there was the capacity to love. And now his heart was beating faster and faster, as if the power of the river was pushing blood through his veins, urging him to act. He felt Peggy stir.

'So,' she said, the faintest of tremors in her voice. 'Quick question. With scones, do you go with jam or cream first?'

Andrew considered the question.

'I'm not sure it really matters,' he said. 'Not in the grand scheme of things.' Then he leaned across, took Peggy's face in his hands, and kissed her.

Somewhere, he could have sworn he heard a duck quack.

Chapter Twenty

It was fair to say, if you were to really drill down and examine the data, and then draw conclusions *from* said data, that Andrew was, to a certain extent, drunk. He was dancing around Imogen's living room, with a giddy and giggling Suze, singing along raucously to Ella's 'Happy Talk'. They were, by now, the firmest of friends.

Andrew still couldn't quite believe what had happened earlier that day. The moment he'd taken Peggy's hand and set off without knowing where he was going, it had felt like an out-of-body experience. The memory was somehow sharp and blurry all at once. They'd sat for a long time on the bench, their foreheads touching gently, their eyes closed, until Peggy broke the silence. 'Well now. I'm not entirely sure I saw this coming.'

As they made their way back to the car Andrew felt as though he'd been drugged. He spent the entire journey home trying to stop grinning. He watched the fields flash by, getting the occasional glimpse of the sea, sunlight shimmering on its surface. A sunny August day in England. Perfection.

'That was an eventful day, then,' Peggy said when they were back at Imogen's, as if they'd just been for a ramble and come across an unusual bird's nest on the ground.

'Oh, I dunno. Pretty run-of-the-mill stuff for me, all told,' Andrew said. He leaned across to kiss her but she laughed and gently nudged him away. 'Give over! What if someone sees? And before you say anything, earlier it would just've been a pensioner on a bench, not . . .' *Imogen or the kids*, was the unspoken thought. The spell might not have been completely broken, but it was certainly damaged. Andrew was about to get out of the car but Peggy made an exaggerated show of looking around before leaning over and giving him a peck on the cheek, then quickly fixed her make-up in the mirror. It was all Andrew could do not to skip up the drive, Morecambe and Wise-style.

Dancing around the living room to Ella would have to do instead. Maisie, who up until now had been summarily ignoring them in favour of her novel, waited until the song was over before asking who the singer was. Andrew put his hands together as if in solemn prayer. 'That, my friend, was Ella Fitzgerald. The greatest singer there's ever been.'

Maisie gave the subtlest nod of approval. 'I like her,' she said, with the tone of someone weighing in calmly to settle a fierce debate, before going back to her book.

Andrew was about to find a new tune – he was in the mood for 'Too Darn Hot', next – and, more importantly, get another lager from Imogen's booze fridge in the garage, when Peggy appeared at the living-room door and asked the girls to come and help her lay the table.

Andrew retrieved a fresh beer and flopped down on to the sofa, allowing himself a moment to take everything in. He let the music wash over him, listened to the animated voices coming down the hallway, and breathed in the delicious cooking smells drifting from the kitchen. All of it was intoxicating.

He decided this should be part of some government scheme: that everyone should be legally entitled to have at least one evening a year where they could sink down into soft cushions, their stomachs rumbling in anticipation of ravioli and red wine, listening to chatter from another room, and feel, for the briefest flicker of time, that they mattered to someone. It was only now he could truly see how deluded he'd been to think the fantasy he'd created could be anything more than the weakest facsimile of the real thing.

After he'd listened to 'Too Darn Hot', he headed to the kitchen and asked whether there was anything he could do.

'You could give the girls a hand,' Peggy said.

Andrew saluted, but Peggy had turned away and missed it. She and Imogen were having to chop, peel and stir in close proximity, but, as if carefully choreographed, they managed to avoid getting in each other's way. Andrew, on the other hand, now fully buzzed by the beer, quickly became an increasingly frustrating presence as he tried to help. There was something about being in another person's kitchen which meant everything he was looking for seemed to be in a totally illogical place. When he confidently opened the cutlery drawer all that was inside was a warranty for a sandwich toaster, and the cupboard that should have housed glasses contained just a novelty egg cup in the shape of a hollow-backed pig, and some birthday cake candles.

'Andrew, Andrew,' Imogen said, attempting to keep the frustration out of her voice as he tried to pull open a false drawer next to her, 'glasses top left, knives and forks here, water jug over there, salt and pepper here.' She pointed out each item like a football manager on the touchline indicating who the defenders should be marking, and Andrew called her 'Gaffer', a word which he didn't even know was in his vocabulary and which caused Imogen to briefly pause zesting.

Table now laid, Andrew sat down at it with a fresh beer and some Pringles Suze had brought him (two in her own mouth poking out to make it look like she had a duck's beak) and drank in the atmosphere. The kitchen, like the rest of the house, was well-kept but with lots of character – a bunch of flowers in a quirky vase on the windowsill, a print on the wall with a picture of a woman cooking and sipping from a glass with the caption '*I love cooking with wine – sometimes I even put it in the food*'. The windows had steamed up to reveal handprints and a wonkily drawn heart.

'I never know whether you're supposed to eat the top bits of peppers,' Peggy said to no one in particular. 'Don't want to make people ill, but don't want to be wasteful either. I end up walking to the bin, nibbling on it till I get there, then chucking what's left away.'

Jesus Christ, Andrew thought, unable to stifle a hiccup, *I think I'm in love.*

As the old drinking adage goes: beer before wine, then you'll be fine; *six* beers before *half a bottle* of wine then you'll be dizzy and believe the story you want to tell to be much more important than anyone else's.

'Yeah, so, yeah,' Andrew slurred. '. . . yeah.'

'You were in the kitchen?' Imogen prompted.

'Yes, Imogen, we were! But then we thought we'd check the bedroom because that's where they usually leave their money if they have any – cash, you know, rolled up in socks or in a Tesco's bag shoved under the mattress. So anyway, anyway, we went in there – didn't we Peggy?'

'Mm-hmm.'

'And the impression we'd had up till then was that the man had been fairly quiet, fairly normal . . .'

'Andrew, I'm not sure this is OK . . . the kids . . . ?'

'Ohhh it'll be fine!'

Peggy took his hand under the table and squeezed it firmly. It would only be much later that he'd realise this wasn't an affectionate gesture but an attempt to get him to stop talking.

'So, the bedroom's bare apart from a telly, and I accidentally turn it on and lo and behold—'

'Andrew let's talk about something else, eh?'

'—he'd been watching a dirty film called *Quim Up North*!'

Peggy had spoken over him, so the impact of the punchline was deadened.

'Come on, girls, shall we play cards or something?' Imogen said. 'Maisie, you can help teach Suze.'

While Maisie went to get the cards, Andrew – as is the preserve of the drunken – suddenly decided it was imperative he be as helpful as possible while doing so ostentatiously enough to be praised for it.

'I'll do the washing-up,' he announced determinedly, as if volunteering to go back into a burning building to rescue some children. After a while Peggy came up to him at the sink as he struggled to pull on washing-up gloves.

'Oi, you, you lightweight,' she said in a low voice. She was smiling, but there was a firmness to her voice which went some way to sobering Andrew up.

'Sorry,' he said. 'Got a bit carried away. It's just . . . you know. I'm feeling quite . . . happy.'

Peggy went to say something but stopped herself. She squeezed his shoulder instead. 'Why don't you go and relax in the living room for a bit? You're the guest, you shouldn't be doing the washing-up.'

Andrew would have protested, but Peggy was standing closer to him now, her hand on his arm with her thumb gently caressing it, and he very much wanted to do exactly as she asked.

The girls and Imogen had briefly abandoned cards to see how fast they could play pat-a-cake, pat-a-cake, baker's man, their hands a blur, collapsing into giggles as they finally lost co-ordination. Andrew heard the tail end of their conversation as he left.

'That pasta we just ate now,' Maisie said.

'Yes, pet,' Imogen said.

'Was it al dente?'

'I think it was Jamie Oliver, love,' Imogen said, cackling at her own joke. *At least I'm not the only one who's pissed, then*, Andrew thought. He slumped on to the sofa, feeling exhausted suddenly. All of this euphoria was very tiring, but it didn't stop him wanting the day to go on forever. He just needed to rest his eyes for a minute.

In the dream, he was in an unfamiliar house, dressed for a property search in his regular protective suit, except it was beginning to feel suffocatingly tight against his body. He couldn't remember what he was supposed to be searching for; he had a feeling it was to do with some documents. 'Peggy, what are we looking for again?' he shouted. But her reply was muffled, and though he looked in every room he couldn't seem to find her. And then he was lost – and more and more rooms kept appearing, so that every time he crossed a threshold he was in a space he didn't recognise, and he was calling Peggy's name and asking for help and his protective suit was starting to constrict him to the point where he thought he might pass out. And there was music – jarringly out of tune, so deep it was vibrating through his body. The song was Ella's, but her voice sounded like it was playing at half speed. *Bluuuue moooooon, you saw me standing aloooonnnne.* Andrew tried to shout for someone to turn it off, to play anything – anything – but that, but no sound came out of his mouth. And then suddenly he was in his own flat and Peggy was in the corner, her back to him, but as he approached and screamed her name, the music getting louder all the time, he saw it wasn't Peggy at all, but someone with brown, wavy hair, a pair of orange-rimmed glasses in her hand at her side, and then the glasses had slipped through her fingers and were falling in slow motion towards the floor—

'Andrew, are you OK?'

Andrew opened his eyes. He was on the sofa and Peggy was leaning over him, her hand cupping one side of his face.

Was this real?

'Sorry – I didn't know whether to wake you, but you looked like you were having a nightmare,' Peggy said.

Andrew's eyelids flickered and closed.

'You don't have to say sorry,' he mumbled. '. . . never . . . ever have to say sorry. You're the one who's saved me.'

Chapter Twenty-One

'Trust me, it'll help.'

Andrew took the can of Irn-Bru from Peggy with a trembling hand and took a tentative sip.

'Thanks,' he croaked.

'Nothing like a four-and-a-half-hour trip on a train that smells of piss to cure a hangover,' Peggy said.

Suze nudged Maisie and gestured for her to take her earphones out. 'Mum said "piss",' she said. Maisie rolled her eyes and went back to her book.

Andrew was never drinking again, that much he knew. His head was throbbing, and every time the train took a bend he felt a horrible pang of nausea. But far worse were the incomplete flashbacks from the previous night. What had he said? What had he done? He remembered Peggy and Imogen looking annoyed. Was that at the point when he'd started a sentence three times with increasing volume and urgency ('I was . . . So, anyway, I was . . . *I WAS*') because people didn't seem to be concentrating? He'd at least managed to get to bed rather than sleeping on the sofa, but – *shit* – he remembered now that Peggy had practically had to drag him there. Luckily, she hadn't lingered long enough for him to embarrass himself further. Ideally, now, they'd be recreating the spirit of excitement and adventure of the journey up there, but Andrew was having to focus all his attention on not puking himself entirely inside out. To make matters worse, there was a small child sitting directly behind him kicking his seat while asking his father a series of increasingly complex questions:

'Dad, Dad?'

'Yes?'

'Why is the sky blue?'

'Well . . . it's because of the atmosphere.'

'What's a atmosphere?'

'It's the bit of air and gas that sort of stops us getting burned by the sun.'

'So what's the sun made of?'

'I . . . Um . . . why don't we find you your bear, Charlie? Where's Billy the Bear gone, eh?'

I hope Billy the Bear is a nickname for a strong sedative, Andrew thought. He tried to will himself into unconsciousness, but it was useless. He noticed Peggy was looking at him, arms folded, her expression unreadable. He scrunched his eyes shut, falling into a horribly uncomfortable pattern of falling asleep but almost immediately jolting awake. Eventually he managed to doze, but when he woke, expecting to be south of Birmingham at least, it turned out they were stationary having broken down before they'd even got to York.

'We apologise for the delay,' the driver said. 'We appear to be experiencing some sort of technical delay.' Apparently unaware that he hadn't turned off the Tannoy, the driver then treated them all to a peek behind the magician's curtain: 'John? Yeah, we're fucked. Have to chuck everyone off at York if we can even get a shunt there.'

After said shunt finally materialised, Andrew and Peggy

hauled their bags off the train along with a few hundred other passengers whose phasers were all set to 'grumble', only to be elevated to 'strongly-worded letter' when they were told it would be forty minutes before a replacement train could get there.

The brief sleep had revived Andrew enough that he could now, with horrible clarity, consciously consider how much he'd ruined things. He was just deciding how to carefully broach the possibility that maybe he and Peggy could possibly *have a little chat, about, you know, everything,* when Peggy returned from the café with crisps and apples for the girls and coffees for her and Andrew and said, 'Right, we need to have a word.'

She bent down and kissed the top of Suze's head.

'Won't be a minute, pet. We're just going to stretch our legs, but we'll not go far.'

She and Andrew walked a little way along the platform.

'So,' Peggy said.

'Look,' Andrew said quickly, cursing himself for butting in but desperate to get his apology in as soon as he could. 'I'm so sorry about last night – as you said, I'm clearly a lightweight. And I know, especially, that to do that when that's what Steve's been doing is so stupid of me, and I just promise to you now – on my life – that it won't happen again.'

Peggy swapped her coffee from one hand to the other.

'Firstly,' she said, 'getting tipsy on a few beers and being a bit of a tit doesn't make you Steve. It makes you a bit of a tit. Steve's got an actual problem.' She blew on her coffee. 'I haven't told you this, but it turns out he's been sacked for drinking at work. He had a bottle of vodka in a drawer, the moron.'

'Jesus, that's awful,' Andrew said.

'He's getting help, so he claims.'

Andrew chewed his lip. 'Do you believe him?'

'I don't really know. In fact, to be truthful, the only thing I can be sure about right now is that everything's a huge mess and there's no way someone's not going to get hurt.' The jaunty musical jingle that precedes an announcement sounded and everyone on the platform pricked up their ears, but it was just warning them of an approaching train that was not stopping there.

'I know that things are complicated,' Andrew said, because that seemed like something people said in these sorts of conversations.

'They are,' Peggy said. 'And you can see that maybe my head's been a bit all over the place recently. That maybe I haven't been thinking straight, and that I've been a bit, well . . . reckless.'

Andrew swallowed, hard.

'You mean with you and me?'

Peggy scrunched her hair tight at the back of her head, then let it go.

'Listen, I'm not saying I regret what happened yesterday, not for one second, and I honestly mean that.'

There was a 'but' coming. Andrew could sense it hurtling towards him quicker than the onrushing train.

'But, the thing is . . .' As Peggy grasped for what to say next there came the familiar two-tone blast from the train, warning people to stand back. 'I just think,' Peggy said, stepping closer to Andrew, her mouth close to his ear to make herself heard over the noise of the train that was now tearing towards them, 'that I don't want you to get carried away, and that this should just be something lovely that happened. A one off. Because meeting you and becoming friends has been such a wonderful, unexpected thing . . . but friends is all we can be.'

The train thundered past and disappeared into the tunnel. Andrew wished, very much, that he was on it.

'Does that make sense?' Peggy said, taking a step back.

'Yeah, sure,' Andrew said, waving his hand in what he hoped was a casually dismissive way. Peggy took him by the hand.

'Andrew, please don't be upset.'

'I'm not upset. Honestly. Not in the slightest.'

He could tell from the way Peggy was looking at him that this pretence was pointless. His shoulders slumped.

'It's just . . . I really feel like we've got something, here. Can't we at least give it a chance?'

'But it's not as easy as that, is it?' Peggy said. Andrew had never felt so pathetically desperate. But he had to keep going, had to keep trying.

'No, you're right. But it's not impossible. We could get divorced, couldn't we? That's an option. It'll be hard – obviously – with the kids and everything, but we'd work it out. Find a way to be a family.'

Peggy put a hand up to her mouth, fingers splayed across her lips. 'How can you be so naive?' she said. 'In what universe does that happen so smoothly, so quickly, with all the logistics sorted and none of the fucking pain of it all? We're not teenagers, Andrew. There are consequences.'

'I'm getting ahead of myself, I know. But yesterday has to count for something, right?'

'Of course it does, but . . .' Peggy bit her lip and took a moment to compose herself. 'I have to think of the girls, and that means making sure I'm in the best possible state of mind so that I'm there for them whatever.'

Andrew went to speak but Peggy cut across him.

'*And*, at the moment, given what I've been going through with Steve, what I really need – even if this is hard to hear – is an understanding friend with a good heart, who's there to support me. Someone honest, that I can trust.'

They had been promised a replacement train, but in reality this just meant they were forced to cram on to the next service, which was already full. It was an every-man-for-themselves affair, but Andrew managed to get into position by a door to let Peggy and the girls on to the train first, before some opportunists snuck on before he could. In the end, with no hope of reaching the others, he was forced to perch uncomfortably on his stupid purple rucksack in the vestibule. The toilet door opposite was malfunctioning, perpetually sliding open and shut and letting out a cocktail of piss and chemical smells. Next to him, two teenagers with an iPad were watching a film where old ladies played by grotesquely made-up men farted and fell into cakes, all of which the teenagers observed without a flicker of emotion.

When they finally reached King's Cross and traipsed off the train, Andrew realised he'd lost his ticket. He didn't even bother to fight his case, shelling out more money instead so they'd let him through. At the other side of the barrier, Suze wore the telltale creased face of a grumpy child after a long journey. But, to Andrew's surprise, when she saw him she ran over and reached her arms up to hug him goodbye. Maisie opted for a rather formal if still affectionate handshake. As the girls bickered about who deserved the remaining strawberry bonbon, Peggy approached Andrew warily, as if he might try to carry on their earlier conversation. Sensing this, Andrew managed a reassuring smile and Peggy relaxed and leaned in to hug him. Andrew went to let go but Peggy took him by the hands. 'We shouldn't forget, in all of this, that we actually found Beryl!' she said. 'That was the reason for the trip, after all.'

'Absolutely,' Andrew said. It was too painful, this intimacy. He decided to pretend his phone was vibrating, apologising and backing away with one finger pressed to his free ear as if to block out the noise of the station. He made for a pillar, still holding the phone up to his ear and mouthing silently to nobody, as he watched Peggy and the girls walk away until they were lost in the crowd.

Later, he stood outside his shabby building, which had seemingly aged ten years in the last week, and considered finding a café or somewhere else where he could sit and pretend for another few hours at least that he wasn't home again. He thought back to how uncharacteristically rushed he'd been when he'd left the house, feeling jarred by the change in routine but dizzy with excitement at spending so much time with Peggy. He'd barely had time to turn off his PC before – weighed down by his backpack – he'd hurled himself down the stairs and out of the building.

Eventually he resigned himself to going indoors, into the shared hallway with its familiar scent of his neighbour's perfume, the scuff marks on the wall, and the flickering light.

He was about to unlock his front door when he became aware of a noise apparently coming from the other side. God, surely it wasn't a burglar? Gritting his teeth, he swung his bag up in front of him to make an improvised shield, unlocked the door, and threw it open.

Standing there in the semi-darkness, his heart pounding, he realised that the sound was coming from the record player in the far corner. In his haste to leave he must not have turned it off properly, so the needle was skipping, and the same note was stuttering away on a loop, over and over and over again.

Chapter Twenty-Two

His name was Warren, he was fifty-seven years old, and it had taken eleven months and twenty-three days for anyone to realise he was dead. The last record of him being alive was when he'd been to the bank to pay in a cheque, whereafter he'd returned home, died, and rotted away apologetically on a sofa under a throw patterned with hummingbirds.

The only other flat in the building was unoccupied, which explained the fact that the smell, which was currently causing Andrew to gag even before he'd set foot in the flat itself, hadn't been the thing to alert someone to Warren's death. In fact, the only reason it hadn't been longer before his body had been discovered was that direct debits for his rent and energy bills had bounced back at the same time. An unfortunate debt collector – who'd apparently been scrambled to the property with the urgency of a counter terrorist operative – had peered through the building's letterbox only to be met by a volley of flies.

Peggy had messaged him on Sunday evening, the day after they'd returned from Northumberland, to say she'd developed 'a stinking cold' and wouldn't be coming into work the next day. In truth, Andrew was quite relieved she wasn't with him. He wasn't sure how he'd be able to act normally around her after all that happened. And so it was that he found himself at his first solo property inspection in months, a heavily aftershave-soaked mask pressed to his face, bracing himself to enter. Though he'd tried to prepare himself as best he could, he was still unable to stop himself dry-heaving. He dropped his bag to the floor and batted away the flies excited from the disturbance. He worked as quickly as he could, separating bin bags of indiscriminate rotting food and soiled clothes as he looked for any sign of a next of kin. He searched for nearly two hours without finding anything. With all the usual places covered, he even forced himself to look inside the oven, which was caked in congealed fat, and the fridge, which was empty save for a single Petits Filous yoghurt. When he finally left, not having found a single trace of evidence that Warren had family, or any concealed cash, he headed to his flat rather than the office. As soon as he was inside he tore off his clothes and showered, turning the water as hot as he could bear and scrubbing feverishly at his skin, using a whole bottle of shower gel. All the while he struggled to think of anything other than Warren. What must his last few weeks before he'd died been like, living in all that filth? He'd always thought he preferred the chaos to the sterile, but on a purely sensory level it was hard to reconcile how someone could have lived like that. Surely he must have been of unsound mind not to know how bad it was. It made Andrew think of the frog boiling to death, unaware that the water's getting hotter.

Later, he headed back to the office smelling like the Body Shop had vomited on him, and arrived to find Cameron sitting on Meredith's yoga ball, his eyes closed in contemplation, a mug of what looked like swamp water steaming away next to him.

'Hello, Cameron,' Andrew said.

Cameron kept his eyes closed and showed Andrew the flat of his hand, like a sleepwalking traffic cop halting imaginary cars. There wasn't enough space for Andrew to squeeze around the exercise ball to his desk, so he had to wait while Cameron finished whatever the hell it was he was doing. Eventually, Cameron let out such a long, powerful breath that Andrew thought at first the ball had developed a puncture.

'Good afternoon, Andrew,' Cameron said, rising with as much dignity as is possible when clambering off an oversized plastic testicle. 'And how was the property inspection?'

'Truthfully, it was probably the worst one I've ever had to do,' Andrew said.

'I see. And how does that make you feel?'

Andrew wondered if this was a trick question.

'Well . . . bad.'

'I *am* sorry to hear that,' Cameron said, rolling his shirt-sleeves up to the elbow before changing his mind and rolling them back down again. 'No Peggy today, then, poor thing.'

'No,' Andrew said, slumping down into his chair.

'Meredith and Keith have taken a couple of days off,' Cameron said, running his finger along the top of Andrew's screen.

'Uh-huh.'

'So that means it's just us two here . . . holding the old fort.'

'Yep,' Andrew said, unsure where this was going, wondering if he should suggest that Cameron's next move towards enlightenment should be an enforced period of silence. It was horribly clear, though, that Cameron had some sort of an agenda. Andrew watched him go to walk away before making a big show of changing his mind, snapping his fingers as he turned back.

'Actually, do you mind if we had a quick chat? I can make you some herbal tea if you want?'

Andrew didn't know what was worse, the prospect of having a chat of *any* length with this silly prat, or the fact he'd just pronounced the word 'erbal'.

The breakout area had evolved since Andrew had been away. There were blue and purple throws over the sofas and a coffee table book about transcendental meditation artfully placed on a beanbag where the coffee table used to be. Andrew was just glad that there weren't any obvious hooks to hang wind-chimes from.

'Are you looking forward to Thursday night?' Cameron asked.

Andrew looked blankly back at him.

'It's Meredith's turn to host us for dinner,' Cameron said, clearly disappointed that Andrew had forgotten.

'Oh, yes, of course. Should be . . . . fun.'

'You think? Look, I know it was a bit of a funny old evening when Clara and I hosted . . .'

Andrew wasn't sure whether he was supposed to agree with this or not so kept his mouth shut. 'But I'm sure it'll be a more chilled out evening this time around,' Cameron said.

They sipped their tea and Andrew chanced a look at his watch.

'I'm glad it's just us two, actually,' Cameroon said. 'It gives me a chance to touch base with you about something.'

'Right,' Andrew said, resisting the temptation to scream, 'If you mean "talk" just say "talk, you maddening little bastard!"'

'You'll remember my presentation a little while back, where a certain notification appeared on the screen.'

Cutbacks. With all that had been going on, Andrew had barely had time to think about that.

'The truth is,' Cameron continued, 'I just don't know yet whether it's going to be *us* that'll need to have fewer people wearing more hats, or another department.'

Andrew fidgeted in his seat. 'Why are you telling me this, Cameron?'

Cameron flashed him a particularly desperate grin, his teeth on full display.

'Because, Andrew, it's been playing on my mind to the point of distraction, and I just felt I had to say something to someone here and because . . . we're mates, right?'

'Sure,' Andrew said, guiltily avoiding Cameron's eye. If Cameron was telling him this, did it mean he would be safe? His optimism quickly vanished when he realised that meant that Peggy could be the one to go.

'Thanks, mate,' Cameron said. 'Feels loads better getting that off my chest.'

'Good-good,' Andrew said, wondering if perhaps he should try and make the case for Peggy now.

'So how's the old fam-fam, then?' Cameron said.

The question caught Andrew off guard. Troublingly, it took a moment for him to realise Cameron meant Diane and the children. He made to reply but his mind was blank, no false anecdotes or news coming to mind as usual. *Come on, think! Just make something up like you normally do.*

'Um . . .' he said, then, panicking that Cameron would take his hesitation to mean something might be wrong, quickly followed up with, 'They're fine. Just all good, really. Listen . . .' He got to his feet. '. . . I've really got loads to do, so I better get back to it. I'm sorry.'

'Oh well if you're—'

'Sorry,' Andrew said again, nearly tripping over an errant throw on the floor as he hurried away, feeling suddenly short of breath, just making it to the toilets in time to cough up bile into the sink.

That evening, he chatted with BamBam, TinkerAl, and BroadGaugeJim, and tried not to think about what had happened with Cameron. It had been terrifying to go blank like that. Maybe he was just rustier than usual because his focus had been on Peggy. The closer he'd got to her, the more distant Diane had become. He'd neglected his 'family', the people he relied on for support, and the guilt he felt was deep and real. The strength of the feeling was horribly troubling. *This. Isn't. Normal*, he told himself, digging his fingernails into his thigh.

He felt bad for interrupting the current sub-forum conversation – '*Which type of rubberised horsehair is best for creating bush scenery?*' – but there was nowhere else for him to turn.

'*Chaps, not to bring the mood down, but remember when I told you about that person who I was starting to get along with really well? It turns out there was something more than just friendship there, but now I've blown it.*'

BroadGaugeJim: '*Sorry to hear that, T. What happened?*'

Tracker: '*It's a bit complicated. There's someone else in her life. But that's not even the main problem. Basically, I've been holding something back from her, and I know that if I come clean she'll probably never talk to me again.*'

BamBam67: '*Yikes, that does sound rather serious.*'

TinkerAl: '*Tricky one, mate. What I would say is maybe you should just be honest with her? Maybe you're right – she might never talk to you again, but if there's even the smallest chance she'll*' *be OK with it, then isn't that worth fighting for? This time in a week you could be together! Bit of a cliché I know, but isn't it better to have loved and lost, and all that???'*

The discordant 'Blue Moon' arrived in an instant, and the screeching feedback and stabbing at Andrew's temples was so severe that he had to slide to the floor and clap his hands to his head, drawing his knees up to his chest, waiting for the pain to subside.

He slept fitfully that night. He'd developed earache and a raw, scratchy throat, and his body was starting to ache all over. As he lay awake in the early morning, listening to the rain hammering at the window, he thought of Peggy, and wondered whether he'd caught this cold off her, or just a stranger.

Chapter Twenty-Three

Peggy was still off sick the following day. Andrew had texted her asking if she was feeling better, but there was no reply.

The cold he'd caught had evolved into something that sapped him of energy but left him too uncomfortable to sleep. Instead, he sat shivering or sweating under a duvet watching mindless action films, the moral of each story appearing to be if you drive a car fast enough a lady will take her top off.

He was halfway to work the following morning, feeling as if he was trudging through thick mud, when he suddenly remembered it was the day of Alan Carter's funeral. He forced himself to turn back and flag down a taxi.

The vicar – a squat man with piggy eyes – greeted him at the church's entrance.

'Relative?'

'No, council,' Andrew said, glad that he *wasn't* a relative given the brusqueness of how the vicar had spoken to him.

'Ah yes, of course,' the vicar said. 'Well, there's one lady inside. But it doesn't look like anyone else is coming so we better crack on.' He raised a fist to his mouth to cover a burp, his cheeks bulging like a frog's neck.

Beryl was sitting on the front row of the empty church. Andrew tucked his shirt in and flattened his hair down as he walked up the aisle. 'Hello, dear,' Beryl said when he arrived at her side. 'Gosh, are you OK? You look ever so peaky.' She put the back of her hand to his forehead.

'I'm fine,' Andrew said. 'A bit tired, that's all. How are you?'

'Not so bad, pet,' Beryl said. 'Have to say, it's been a long time since I've been in a church.' She lowered her voice to a whisper. 'I'm not exactly a believer in the beardy bloke upstairs. Neither was Alan, truth be told. I'm sure he'd have found all this palaver funny, really. Is Peggy coming, do you know?'

'I don't think so, I'm afraid,' Andrew said, looking back towards the door just in case. 'She's really poorly, unfortunately. But she sends her love.'

'Oh well, not to worry,' Beryl said. 'More for the rest of us.'

Andrew couldn't think what Beryl meant until he looked down to see she was holding an open Tupperware box full of fairy cakes. After a moment's hesitation, he took one.

The vicar appeared and stifled another belch, and Andrew feared the worst about the sermon, but thankfully the vicar's delivery was heartfelt enough. The only blip in the service came when a man wearing a baseball cap and waterproof trousers – a gardener, Andrew presumed – shunted the church door open and whispered 'oh bollocks' just loudly enough for them to hear before slipping back out.

Even with this interruption, Beryl remained composed throughout. Perhaps because Andrew had more of a personal investment than usual, he listened intently to the vicar's words and, to his intense embarrassment, found himself on the verge of tears. He felt a wave of shame hit him – he hadn't ever met this man; it wasn't his place to cry. And yet that guilt only made things worse and eventually he was unable to stop a single tear spilling down on to each of his cheeks. Luckily, he managed to wipe them away before Beryl saw. He'd have to blame his cold if she said anything about his puffy eyes.

As the vicar asked them to join him in reciting the Lord's Prayer, the realisation suddenly came to Andrew that he hadn't been crying for Alan, or even for Beryl, but for the future version of himself, his death unmourned at a service in a draughty church with only the walls to receive the vicar's perfunctory words.

They said polite if stiff goodbyes to the vicar – 'I don't trust men with handshakes that firm, you have to think they're over-compensating for something,' Beryl said – and were walking arm in arm along the churchyard path when Andrew asked Beryl whether she needed accompanying back to the station. 'Don't worry, love. I'm actually visiting a couple of old friends. Old being the operative word: I think they've got about seven teeth between them, these days, Sheila and Georgie.'

They'd reached the end of the path. The wind was rushing through the branches of the imposing yew tree that stood just inside the churchyard walls. They were only just into September, but the sublime August day in Northumberland seemed a long time ago.

'You got time for a cuppa before I go?' Beryl said.

Andrew scratched at the back of his head. 'Sadly not.'

'Time waits for no man, eh? Hang on, though.' Beryl scrabbled in her handbag and found a pen and paper. 'I'm around for another few days. Give me your number. I've got my special old-lady mobile phone the size of a brick with me, so maybe we could meet up later in the week or something.'

'That would be lovely,' Andrew said.

Another gust of wind came, stronger this time. Beryl readjusted her hat and took Andrew by the hand.

'You're a good man, Andrew, coming here today. I know my Alan would've appreciated that. You take care now.'

She walked away, looking brittle against the wind, but after a few steps she stopped and came back.

'Here,' she said, digging the box of cakes out of her bag. 'Share these with Peggy, won't you?'

Chapter Twenty-Four

Andrew stooped to double-check, but there were no two ways about it: he was looking at a dead mouse.

He'd been searching for a bucket because water was leaking from an unidentifiable hole in the ceiling above the back stairs. Cameron had called the maintenance team but they'd fobbed him off. His response had been to repeat some sort of mantra over and over under his breath, his eyes tightly shut.

'Back in a sec,' Andrew had said, backing slowly away.

As he opened the cupboard underneath the kitchen sink he was hit by the familiar stench of death and, sure enough, lying there on its back among bleach bottles and a hi-vis jacket, was a mouse. This wasn't exactly under Andrew's remit, but he couldn't just leave it there, so he put on a single washing-up glove and picked it up by its tail. He caught his distorted reflection in the shiny side of the coffee machine and saw the mouse swinging back and forth, as if he were performing some sort of macabre hypnotism. Not wanting to disturb whatever mindfulness ritual Cameron was going through, his only option was to go back through the office and out of the front entrance to find somewhere to dispose of the corpse. So it was with a horrible inevitability that he had managed to get all the way to the main doors without passing a soul only to be met by Peggy coming the other way. She was distracted by collapsing her umbrella and, making a split-second judgement, Andrew opened his coat pocket and stuffed the mouse inside it. Her umbrella now folded away, Peggy clocked Andrew and made her way over.

'Hello,' she said, 'how's tricks?'

Aside from the dead mouse in my pocket?

'Yes, OK. Nothing new, really. You're feeling better, then?'

He had meant it as a genuine question but in his flustered state it came out almost sarcastically. Thankfully, Peggy didn't seem to take it that way.

'Yep, much better,' she said. 'What's the craic today then?'

'Oh, just the usual.'

Mouse in my pocket, mouse in my pocket, mouse in my pocket.

'Keith and Meredith?'

'Not in yet.'

'Thank God for small mercies. And we've not been fired, yet?'

'Not that I know of.'

'Well that's something.'

For the first time since Andrew had known Peggy, there was an awkward pause.

'Well, I better crack on,' Peggy said. 'Coming?'

'Sure,' Andrew said. 'I've just got to . . . I'll see you in there.'

He disposed of the mouse in some weeds in a corner of the car park. He had only just got back inside when he looked out of the window to see Keith arriving on his scooter next to the burial ground. Such was his size relative to the machine it reminded Andrew of a clown on one of those ankle-height tricycles. Barely half a minute later Meredith parked up in her custard-yellow hatchback, and Andrew watched her and Keith take a sly look around before locking lips, Keith wrapping his arms around Meredith as the kiss became more passionate, so it looked as if she'd fallen into quicksand.

Andrew was trying to write an obituary for Warren but kept distracting himself by stealing glances at Peggy, who despite her earlier assurances that she was feeling better still looked pale and worn out. Though that might have been something to do with having to listen to Meredith banging on about some sort of 'mini-retreat' she'd just been on. He was considering going over to rescue Peggy, but things felt so different now. He couldn't bear the idea of her smiling warily as he approached, worried that he might try and bring up what had happened in Northumberland. Instead, he trudged to the kitchen and went to make tea. Someone had finished the milk and put the empty carton back in the fridge. Andrew sincerely hoped that whoever it was – and let's face it, it was Keith – would tread on an upturned plug in bare feet some time soon. From the kitchen doorway he could see into Cameron's office. Cameron was sitting at his computer, arms aloft, viciously squeezing stress balls in each hand. He saw Andrew and his grimace turned into a slightly pained smile, the same expression a baby pulls in the process of filling its nappy. At least today can't get any worse, Andrew thought, and as if Cameron had read his mind he chose that moment to wheel himself over on his chair.

'Remember, guys, it's Dinner Party Mark Two tonight.'

Chapter Twenty-Five

Andrew peered out from behind a tree across the street from Meredith's house, picking at the price label on the cheapest bottle of wine he'd been able to find in the corner shop. He was no expert, but he was pretty sure that Latvia wasn't famed for its rosé.

He braced himself to enter the fray. Cameron had been suspiciously quiet since the cutbacks conversation, and even though they were supposedly 'mates', Andrew wasn't going to assume for a minute that he was safe. He would have to be on his best behaviour tonight. Cameron was continuing to give a disproportionately large shit about these stupid dinner parties, so if pretending to be the sort of person who enjoyed talking about school catchment areas over an under-baked flan stood him in good stead, then so be it.

He was about to cross the road when a car pulled up outside and he shrank back as he saw Peggy climb out of the passenger side, waving goodbye to Maisie and Suze in the back seats. The window lowered and Andrew heard Steve's gruff voice. Peggy turned and leaned in through the window to retrieve the handbag Steve was proffering, and there was just enough light in the car for Andrew to see them kiss. He waited after Peggy had gone inside and watched as Steve cracked his knuckles before taking what was unmistakably a hip flask from the glove compartment and taking a deep swig before driving off, tyres shuddering against the tarmac.

Meredith opened the door and bestowed a kiss on each of Andrew's cheeks, a greeting he received while motionless, as if he were a statue she was kissing for luck. The music that was playing from concealed speakers throughout the house was, Meredith cheerfully informed him, by someone called Michael Bublé.

'It's jazz!' she added, taking the wine from him.

'Is it?' Andrew said, looking around for something hard and pointy to bash his face into.

The house looked as if it had been decorated by someone who might name their horse after a Nazi sympathiser. The others were all there. Keith, to Andrew's surprise, was dressed in a grey suit with a purple tie, the knot of which was largely obscured by the folds of his neck. He looked troublingly happy. Cameron – who was already sitting at the dining-room table with a large glass of red wine – was wearing a white shirt with three buttons undone, greying chest hair poking through, and had a bracelet of wooden beads around his wrist.

Andrew bumped into Peggy who was coming back from the loo and they performed an interminably awkward shuffle as each tried to let the other past.

'You know what, I'm just going to stand still and close my eyes until you've found a way past,' Peggy said.

'Good plan,' Andrew said, with a forced laugh. As he passed her he caught what smelled like a new scent – something subtle and fresh. For some reason this floored him even more than seeing the kiss. He felt his stomach plunge.

'I thought we'd start with a bit of a game, just to loosen us up,' Meredith said, once they were all assembled in the dining room.

Oh joy, Andrew thought.

'Let's go around the group, saying a word each, until we've improvised a story. It can be about anything. First person to go blank or crack up loses. Andrew, why don't you start.'

Oh God.

Andrew: 'Okay, um: We'

Peggy: 'all'

Cameron: 'went'

Meredith: 'to'

Keith: 'Meredith's'

Andrew: 'house'

Peggy: 'and'

Cameron: 'we'

Meredith: 'all'

Keith: 'really'

Andrew: 'hated'

Andrew looked over to Peggy. Why was she staring at him like that? Did that mean she'd lost? And then he realised what he'd said.

Thankfully, Peggy came to his rescue, laughing robotically so that the game ended. The dinner itself passed uneventfully. Meredith delivered several courses, all of them seemingly varieties on the theme of hedge cuttings, which left Andrew starving. He'd worked his way through most of his bottle of Latvian wine, which was surprisingly nice – so he was a racist as well as cheap – drumming his fingers on the table as he listened to the others talking about a Scandinavian crime boxset he'd yet to watch. Meredith prefaced her thoughts by saying 'this isn't a spoiler', before revealing the death of a lead character, two plot twists, and the dialogue from the final scene of the show in its entirety. He'd cross that one off his list, then.

Cameron had been his usual animated self, edging towards the giddy end of the spectrum. Andrew hadn't thought his behaviour particularly unusual, but when Cameron stood up to go to the loo he wobbled on his feet, grabbing on to a cabinet for support, before weaving unsteadily out of the room.

'He got here an hour early,' Meredith whispered gleefully. 'Got stuck into the Malbec like you wouldn't believe. I think there's trouble in paradise with Clara.'

'And where's your feller tonight?' Peggy asked, just as Keith went to brush a crumb from Meredith's sleeve. He withdrew his hand sharply but Meredith grabbed it, like a lion being fed a hunk of meat in a zoo, and slapped it down on the table, locking her fingers with his.

'Well, in fact,' she said, 'I was – *we* were – going to wait until after the home-made profiteroles, but we've actually got something to tell you.'

'You're shagging?' Peggy said, stifling a yawn.

'Well, there's no need to be so crude about it,' Meredith said, a fixed smile on her face. 'But, yes, Keith and I are officially partners. As in lovers,' she added, in case anyone thought they were about to float a company on the stock market.

The dining room door swung open and banged against the wall as Cameron staggered over to his chair. 'What have I missed, then?' he said.

'Them two are "lovers", apparently,' Peggy said. Andrew

went to top up her glass but she put her hand over it and shook her head.

'Well, that's . . . I mean, good . . . Good for you,' Cameron said. 'Now that's what I call team bonding!' He laughed raucously at his own joke.

'Keith, would you mind helping me in the kitchen for a moment?' Meredith said.

'Yeah, sure,' Keith said, the familiar leer back on his face.

'I'm just going to get some air,' Peggy said. She looked at Andrew and raised her eyebrows.

'I think I will, too,' Andrew said.

'There's a surprise,' Keith said quietly.

'What's that?' Peggy said.

'Nothing, nothing,' Keith said, hands raised defensively.

The four of them stood and Cameron looked up at them, confused, like a little boy lost in a crowd.

Outside, Peggy produced a cigarette and offered one to Andrew, who accepted, despite having no intention of smoking it. He lowered his arm, letting the cigarette burn, and watched Peggy inhale deeply.

'Cheek of that knobber, Keith,' Peggy said, tilting her head up as she exhaled smoke. Andrew again caught a hint of her new perfume and felt like he might overbalance. He wasn't sure why it was affecting him like this. He hummed tunelessly, the silence too much to bear.

'What?' Peggy said, seemingly taking this to mean he wasn't in agreement with her about Keith.

'Nothing,' Andrew said. 'He's a knobber, like you said.'

Peggy exhaled again. 'You haven't . . . said anything to him, have you?'

'No, of course not,' Andrew said, cringing.

238

'OK. Good.'

This was miserable. To hear the concern in Peggy's voice at the thought of their secret coming out, knowing that her primary concern was jeopardising her reconciliation with Steve, was torture. Should he tell her he'd seen Steve drinking as he'd driven off? Regardless of what had happened between them, surely she had a right to know if Steve was lying to her, especially if he was endangering the girls. Peggy was eyeing him suspiciously.

'Just so we're clear, you're not going to do anything silly are you? No mad gestures inspired by those two idiots in there? Because believe me, that won't work.'

This time, it was anger Andrew felt. He hadn't asked to come and stand in the cold and be humiliated like this.

'Oh, don't worry,' he said, 'I wouldn't dream of ruining things for you.'

Peggy took a final drag on her cigarette and threw it to the ground, crushing it with her boot heel, fixing Andrew with a steely expression.

'Just so you know,' she said, her tone so harsh it made Andrew take a step back, 'this hasn't been an easy week for me. It's been pretty gruelling, in fact, largely because I've spent the entire time doing what that moron Cameron would no doubt describe as a root-and-branch review of my marriage. But thankfully, for all the pain involved, it's resulted in Steve cleaning himself up and deciding to be a husband and a father again. And that's how things have to be for me. There's no other option. It's not my place to say, but if you're not happy with Diane then maybe you need to have an honest conversation with her, too.'

Andrew was going to let her walk back inside, but these last words had stung him too much and he couldn't stop himself.

'I saw Steve drop you off earlier,' he blurted out. 'With the girls in the car.'

'And?' Peggy said, her hand on the door handle.

'When you'd gone inside he took out a hip flask.'

Peggy bowed her head.

'I'm sorry,' Andrew said. 'I just thought you should know.'

'Oh, Andrew,' Peggy said. 'Did all that stuff we talked about before – about being friends, about being there for each other . . . did it not mean anything to you?'

'What? Of course it did.'

Peggy shook her head sadly.

'Yet you're fine with lying to me?'

'No, I—'

But Peggy didn't stay to hear him out, closing the door firmly behind her.

Andrew stood listening to the faint strains of music and voices coming from inside. He looked at Peggy's cigarette smouldering on the floor and realised he was still holding his own. He took aim and dropped his on to hers, then mashed them together with his heel.

For the rest of the evening he retreated into himself, picturing his Ella records and all the model train components he owned neatly laid out on the floor, debating what he could live with selling should he be the one to get sacked. There was *Souvenir Album*, maybe. It was probably the record he listened to the least. The DB Schenker Class 67 had seen better days, he supposed. It looked magnificent still, but barely made it around the track without slowing to a stop at least a couple of times, no matter how much he serviced it.

Peggy sat glumly while Cameron, Keith and Meredith entered the stage of drunkenness where one-upmanship masquerades as badinage. There were boasts of drinking sessions, crowbarred anecdotes about meeting celebrities and, most alienating of all, talk of sexual exploits.

'Come on then, come on then,' Keith said, raising his voice above the others. He had seemed unusually awkward earlier, before Meredith had made their affair public, but now he was relaxing into his old self, shirt untucked, tie loosened, like Mr Toad on dress-down Friday. 'Who here's done it in public?'

So far, Andrew had got away with staying quiet and eating his food, occasionally smiling or nodding to give the impression he was engaged with the conversation. But now their plates were cleared and he had nowhere to hide. Keith caught his eye and Andrew knew instantly that he wasn't going to miss the opportunity to embarrass him.

'Come on, Andy Pandy. You and your missus have been together how long?'

Andrew took a sip of water. 'A long time.'

'So come on, have you . . . ?'

'Have we what?'

'Got down and dirty somewhere public!'

'Ah. Um. No. Not to my knowledge.'

Meredith sniggered into her wine glass. Cameron laughed too, but his glassy eyes suggested he was too drunk to understand what was going on.

'Not to your knowledge?' Keith said. 'You do know how sex works, Andrew? It's not like you can do it behind your own back.'

'Well . . . depends how flexible you are,' Meredith said, with a horrible cackle. Andrew excused himself to go to the toilet. 'Don't think we've forgotten about you,' Keith called after him.

Andrew was in no hurry to return to the dining room-turned-school playground, but there was something disconcerting about Meredith's bathroom – namely the picture of her and, presumably, her now former partner. It was a professional shot – all fluffy white shagpile and unnatural body language. Andrew looked at the man smiling gamely at the camera and wondered where he was at that moment. Maybe he was out drowning his sorrows with friends, that same fixed smile on his face, telling everyone that no, seriously, honestly, this is the best thing that's ever happened to me.

Back in the dining room, there was no sign of things having calmed down, although Cameron did appear to have passed out. Keith was standing next to him holding a marker pen, apparently preparing to draw something on his face. Meredith was at his side, bouncing on her feet and wheeling her arms excitedly like a toddler who's just learned to stand unaided. Just as Andrew approached the table, he saw Peggy clearly lose patience and stomp over to Keith, making to whip the pen out of his hand.

'Oi!' Keith said, ripping his hand away. 'Come on, it's just a bit of fun.'

'Could you be any more immature?' Peggy said. She went to make another grab for the pen but this time Meredith stepped in front of her, eyes fiery with defending Keith. 'I don't know what your problem is, Mrs Uptight,' she hissed.

'Oh, I don't know,' Peggy said. 'How about the fact he's clearly in a bad way about his wife, as you so kindly brought up earlier? Just because you two are apparently so happy doesn't mean you get to humiliate him.'

Meredith tilted her head to one side and stuck her bottom lip out. 'Oh hun, you sound ever so stressed. You know what you need? A good yoga sesh. I know this great place – Synergy – where I was last week? Get all that frustration out of you, yeah?'

Synergy? Why does that sound familiar? Andrew thought, edging around the table to stand next to Peggy. He'd planned to try and calm things down, but Peggy had other ideas.

'You know what?' she said. 'Every time I've had to be in the same room as you these last few months, the only thing that's given me any sort of pleasure is trying to work out what exactly it is you both look like.'

'Peggy—' Andrew said, but she raised a hand. A hand that wasn't to be trifled with. 'And, I'm very pleased to say, I've finally reached my conclusion, because it's now very clear to me that you, Keith, look like a health warning on a pack of cigarettes.'

Meredith made a strange gurgling sound.

'And as for you, *hun*, you look like the result of a dog being asked to draw a horse.'

As much as Andrew was enjoying the looks on Keith and Meredith's faces he knew this silence was his last chance to stop things getting out of hand.

'*Look,*' he said, startling himself with how loudly he'd spoken, 'remember the cutbacks thing we saw in Cameron's presentation? You really think this sort of behaviour is going to go down well if he's got to make that decision? I know he can be an idiot, but he's still the most important person in this room.'

It was at that moment that Cameron began to snore.

'Ha, yeah, he looks really important right now,' Keith

said. 'You're just scared, as fucking usual. I, for one, am sick of trying to pretend he's anything other than a streak of chamomile-tea piss. Let him fire me, see if I fucking care.'

He took the lid off the pen with his teeth and spat it on to the floor, doubling down on his bravado. For the first time, Meredith looked uneasy, Andrew's words about the cutbacks clearly getting through to her at least. Andrew and Peggy exchanged a look. He wanted to tell her that they should just get out of there, let these two idiots seal their own fate. But before he could say anything Peggy darted towards Keith and grabbed the pen.

'You bitch!' Keith snarled, grasping at thin air as Peggy dodged him.

'Oi!' Andrew yelled, rushing over, banging his hip on the table in the process. Peggy feinted one way then doubled back and climbed up on to a chair where she held the pen aloft, Keith and Meredith straining to reach it. If a stranger had walked into the room they might have been under the impression that they'd just chanced upon a strangely angry morris dance. Just as Andrew reached the melee, Peggy pushed Keith away with her foot so that he stumbled backwards. Andrew could see the fury in Keith's eyes, and as he lurched back towards Peggy, Andrew instinctively reached out and pushed him in the side as hard as he could. Unbalanced, Keith stumbled away and slammed backwards into the wall with a horrible double thwack of back followed by head against the doorframe.

At that moment, several things happened at once.

Cameron woke with a start.

Keith reached for the back of his head, looked at the blood

on his fingertips, and promptly collapsed to the ground with a thud. Meredith shrieked.

And then, as Andrew's brain finally clicked – *Cynergy*, not Synergy – he felt his phone vibrating and pulled it out of his pocket. It was Carl.

Chapter Twenty-Six

Andrew wasn't sure how long he'd been in the bath (or why he'd decided to run one in the first place), but it had been scaldingly hot when he'd lowered himself gingerly in, and now it was barely lukewarm. He'd put Ella on in the living room, but the bathroom door had swung shut so he could only just hear the music. He'd considered getting out and opening the door, but there was something different about experiencing the music like this, where he had to train his ears so intently that he heard every key change, every subtle shift in vocal inflection, as if for the first time. He felt overwhelmed at Ella's capacity to surprise and thrill him after all this time, but now the record had come to an end and every time he shifted position he felt the coldness of the water seeping into his flesh.

He couldn't really remember leaving Meredith's earlier that evening. He'd stumbled out, his phone still ringing, vaguely aware that Meredith was screaming 'He's killed him! He's killed him!' as Peggy tried to calmly explain the situation on the phone to the emergency services. The next thing he could recall was the scuff marks and the strip light and his neighbour's perfume. Maybe he was in shock.

He finally worked up the courage to get out of the bath and

sat shivering on his bed with a towel wrapped around him, looking at his phone on the floor in the corner where he'd dropped it. He'd turned it off after the third time Carl called, but he knew he couldn't ignore him for much longer. Carl and Meredith. Meredith and Carl. There was no way Carl calling him now was just a coincidence. And then there was Keith. Maybe he should call Peggy first, see what had happened. He couldn't have hurt him that badly, surely?

He went to the living room and sat with his phone, switching between the two numbers, unable to make a decision. Eventually, he pressed call. Digging his fingernails into his arm, he waited for Carl to answer, the silence horribly absolute. He was suddenly desperate to puncture the stillness, and he rushed over to his record player and clumsily dropped the needle, Ella's voice filling the room. It was the closest to backup he was ever going to get. He walked around the train tracks in a figure of eight, the phone still ringing out.

'Hello, Andrew.'

'Hello.'

There was a pause.

'Well?' Andrew said.

'Well what?'

'I'm returning your call, Carl. What do you want?'

Andrew heard Carl swallow. A disgusting protein-shake no doubt.

'I met one of your colleagues last week,' Carl said. 'Meredith.'

Andrew's head swam violently and he crumpled slowly to his knees.

'She came to a yoga class of mine. Business has been slow, so it was only her and a few others. We've not been able to afford proper advertising, of course.'

'Right,' Andrew said, clinging on to the slimmest hope that Carl wasn't going where he thought he was with this.

'We got to chatting after the class,' Carl said. 'It was a bit awkward, really. She suddenly started going on about some miserable affair she's having. I don't know why she thought I'd be interested. I was desperate to get rid of her and then suddenly, out of the blue, she mentioned where she worked. And, lo and behold, it was with you. Small world, isn't it?'

Andrew considered hanging up. He could take the SIM from his phone and flush it away and never have to speak to Carl again.

'Andrew, are you still there?'

'Yes,' Andrew said, through gritted teeth.

'Good,' Carl said. 'I thought someone might be distracting you. Diane, perhaps. Or maybe the kids.'

Andrew balled his free hand into a fist and bit down on it hard until he could taste blood.

'It's funny how our memories distort,' Carl said. 'Because I could have sworn that you lived on your own in a bedsit just off the Old Kent Road, that you hadn't been in a relationship since . . . well . . . But according to this Meredith person you're a happily married father of two living in a fancy town house.' Carl's voice was vibrating with repressed anger. 'And there are only two explanations there. Either Meredith has got things spectacularly wrong, or it means you've been lying to her and God knows who else about having a wife and children – and Christ, I hope it's the first one, because if it's the second then I think that might be the most pathetic, awful thing I've ever heard. And I can only imagine what your boss would think of that, were he to find out. You're working with vulnerable people a lot of the time, and for the council too. I can't imagine such a revelation would go down particularly well, do you?'

Andrew brought his hand away from his mouth and saw the cartoonish bite mark on his skin. A memory came into his head of Sally throwing a half-finished apple over a hedge and protesting to their mother when she told her off.

'What do you want?' he said quietly. At first there was no reply. Just the sound of their breathing. Then Carl spoke.

'You ruined *everything*. Sally could have got better, I know she could, if only you'd made things right. But now she's gone. And guess what? I spoke to her lawyer today, and she tells me that the money – Sally's life savings, just to remind you, Andrew – will be paid to you any day now. Christ, if only she'd known the sort of person you really are. Do you honestly think she'd have done the same thing?'

'I don't . . . That's not . . .'

'Shut up and listen,' Carl said. 'Given the fact I now know just how much of a liar you are, let me make it very clear what's going to happen if you decide to go back on your promise to give me what's mine. I'm going to text you my bank details, right now. And if you don't transfer the money to me *the moment* you get it, then all it takes is one phone call to Meredith, and everything's over for you. Everything. Got that? Good.'

With that, he hung up.

Andrew took the phone away from his ear and gradually his brain tuned back in to Ella's voice: *It wouldn't be make-believe, if you believed in me*. He immediately logged into his online banking on his phone. When the screen showed his account, it took him a moment to realise what he was looking at: the money was already there. His phone vibrated – Carl's bank details. Andrew started a new transfer, entering Carl's account number, his heart racing. One more click, and the money would be gone, and this would be over. But, despite every instinct, something stopped him. For all of Carl's words about what Sally would make of his lies, would she really take a better view of what Carl was doing right now? This money was the last thing that connected him and Sally. It had been his sister's last gift to him. The last emblem of their bond.

Before he could stop himself, he'd hit cancel, dropping the phone on to the carpet and putting his head in his hands, taking long, calming breaths.

He'd been sitting on the floor, thoughts flitting between weary defeat and desperate panic, when his phone rang again. He was half expecting it to be Carl – that somehow he'd worked out Andrew had the money already – but it was Peggy.

'Hello?' he said. The background noise was chaotic, people shouting over each other, clamouring to have their voice heard.

'Hello?' he said again.

'Is that Andrew?'

'Yes, who's this?'

'It's Maisie. Hang on. Mum? MUM? I've got him.'

Andrew heard a collective 'Woah!' and the sound of blaring horns, then everything went muffled with the sound of fingers scrabbling at the phone.

'Andrew?'

'Peggy? Are you OK? Did Keith—'

'You were right about Steve. Got back and he was shouting at the girls, drunk out of his skull and on God knows what else. I can't do it any more, I just can't. Grabbed as much stuff as I could and shoved the girls into the car. Steve was too busy smashing the place up to stop me leaving but he jumped on his motorbike and came after me.'

'Shit, are you all right?'

Another horn blared.

'Yes, well no, not really. I'm so sorry, Andrew, I should have believed you earlier.'

'It doesn't matter, I don't care – I just want to know you're safe.'

'Yeah, we are. I think I've lost him. But the thing is, look, I know it's late and everything but I've tried everyone else and . . . I wouldn't normally ask but . . . could we come to yours, just for an hour or something, till I figure out what to do?'

'Yes, of course,' Andrew said.

'You're a lifesaver. We won't be a hassle, I promise. OK, what's your address? Maisie, grab that pen, darling, I need you to write Andrew's address down for me.'

Andrew felt his stomach somersault as he realised what he'd just agreed to.

'Andrew?'

'Yes, I'm here, I'm here.'

'Thank God. What's your address?'

What could he do? He had no choice but to tell her. And almost as soon as the words were out of his mouth the line went dead.

'It's fine,' he said out loud, the words swallowed by the yawning indifference of his flat, the four walls that comprised living room, kitchen and bedroom seeming to have encroached.

OK, let's look at this logically, he thought, trying to quell the rising panic inside him. Maybe this could be a second house? A little place he had all to himself for a bit of . . . what was that dreadful phrase Meredith had said the other day? 'Me Time', that was it. He turned slowly on the spot and took the place in, trying to imagine it was the first time he'd seen it. It was no good. It felt too lived in to be anywhere other than his home.

I'm going to tell her everything.

The thought caught him off guard. Moments later came the sound of a car pulling up outside. He looked around. Maybe he should try and clear up – though there was hardly any mess. As usual, there was one plate, one knife and fork, one glass, and a single saucepan on the draining board. Nothing else was out of place. God, what was the use?

He took one last look around then grabbed his keys and headed for the door. Down the stairs. Past the scuff marks. Through the faint cloud of perfume. The lower he got the colder the air became, and he felt his confidence starting to drain with it.

No, you've got to do it, he urged himself. *Do it. Don't turn back now.*

He was in the corridor, just one set of doors separating him from Peggy and the girls, their shapes blurred through the frosted glass.

Do it. No going back.

His hand was on the door handle. His legs were shaking so much he thought they might give way. *Things just have to get worse before they can get better. Do it, you fucking coward – do it.*

Peggy threw her arms around him and he felt her tears on his cheeks. He hugged her back so tightly he could feel her loosen her own grip in surprise.

'Hey now, hey,' she whispered, and the softness of it brought tears swimming into his own eyes. He could see Suze trying to carry three different bags out of the car at once, struggling to keep her balance. Maisie was at her side, her face pale, her arms folded tightly around herself. Peggy put her hands on Andrew's chest. 'Shall we go inside?' she said. Andrew watched her eyes searching his, concern now dawning.

'Andrew . . . ?'

Chapter Twenty-Seven

Andrew was sitting on a dead man's bed, wondering if he had a broken foot. It had ballooned up grotesquely since last night, fluid expanding underneath spongey flesh, and it was now throbbing and hot, as if infection was setting in. He hadn't been able to fit a shoe on it that morning – the best he could do was a knackered old flip-flop he'd found at the bottom of a cupboard. The pain was excruciating, but nowhere near as bad as what he felt when he closed his eyes and pictured again the disappointment dawning on Peggy's face.

It had all happened in such a blur – his garbled apology to her and the girls (no, sorry, they couldn't come in, he was so, so sorry, he'd explain when he could, it just wasn't possible tonight after all) – then the confusion on Peggy's face, and the hurt, and finally the disappointment. He'd fled inside, unable to watch Peggy shepherding her confused daughters back into the car, jamming his fingers in his ears so he couldn't hear them questioning why they were leaving already. He was back in the corridor, past the scuff marks and through the cloud of perfume, and up the stairs, and inside, and then he was listening helplessly as the car drove off, and when he could no longer hear its engine he looked down and saw the train set laid out with all its precision and care and expense and then he was kicking and stamping at it, bits of track and scenery slamming against the walls, until all that was left was carnage blanketed by silence. He hadn't felt a thing at first, but then the adrenaline wore off and the pain hit him in a dull, sickening wave. He crawled to the kitchen and found some frozen peas, then searched the cupboard next to him, optimistically hoping to find a first aid kit. Instead, there were two bottles of cooking wine covered in a thick film of dust. He drank half a bottle in one go, until his throat stung and the wine spilled over his mouth and down his neck. He shifted so he was sitting against the fridge, and that's where he eventually fell into a fitful sleep, waking just after three and crawling to his bed. He lay there, tears leaking down his cheeks, and thought of Peggy driving through the night, her face intermittently illuminated by street lights, pale and afraid.

He'd turned off his phone and thrown it in a drawer in the kitchen. He couldn't bear to hear from anyone about anything. He still had no idea what had happened to Keith. Maybe he'd already been fired for hurting him like that.

When the morning came, he couldn't think what to do other than carrying out the property inspection he'd been scheduled to do. He sat on the tube amongst the rush hour commuters, the pain in his foot now so severe it strangely emboldened him to stare at everyone in turn, feeling miserable at just how much he wanted someone to ask if he was OK.

The address for the property inspection had rung a bell, but it was only when he'd limped on to the estate that he recognised it as the place he and Peggy had come on her first day. (Eric, was that the man's name?) As he prepared himself to enter the property of the late Trevor Anderson, he looked across the rain-slick concrete slabs, a hopscotch still faintly visible, and saw a man carrying two off-licence bags' worth of shopping struggling to open the door to the flat where Eric had lived. Andrew wondered if the man knew about what had happened there. How many thousands of other people, in fact, might at that very moment be about to open the door to a house where the last occupant had died and rotted without anybody noticing.

According to the coroner, Trevor Anderson had died having slipped and banged his head on the bathroom floor, adding that conditions in the house were 'pretty poor' in the bored tone of someone reviewing a disappointing quiche from a gastropub. Andrew put on his protective clothes, forcing himself to ignore a fresh wave of pain in his foot, and observed his usual ritual of reminding himself why he was there and how he should behave, before going inside.

It was clear Trevor had found it hard to cope in his last days. Rubbish was piled up in the corner of the living room – the collection of stains on one particular spot of the wall suggesting various things had been thrown at it before sliding down to join the pile. There was a fiercely strong smell of urine because of the bottles and cans of all sizes filled to the brim, which were spread out in a halo around a small wooden stool just feet from a television on the floor. The only other things that could count as possessions were a pile of clothes, and a bicycle wheel resting up against a beige radiator shot with scorch marks. Andrew searched through the rubbish but knew in his heart of hearts that he'd find nothing. He got to his feet and peeled off his gloves. In the side of the room that functioned as the kitchen, the oven door hung open in a silent scream. The freezer buzzed for a moment, then clicked off again.

He hobbled into the bedroom, once separated from the living room by a door, but now just by a thin sheet secured by parcel tape. Both the duvet cover and pillowcases were Aston Villa-branded. Next to the bed was a mirror, flecked with shaving foam, leaning up against the wall along with a bedside table improvised from four shoeboxes.

The pain was suddenly too much and Andrew was forced to hop over and sit on the bed. There was a book on top of the shoeboxes, an autobiography of a golfer he'd never heard of, the cheesy smile and baggy suit placing it firmly in the 1980s. He opened the book at random and read a paragraph about a particularly arduous bunker experience at the Phoenix Open. A few pages on, a light-hearted anecdote about a charity match and too much free cava. As he flicked forward again, something came loose and fell into his lap. It was a train ticket, twelve years old: a return from Euston to Tamworth. On the back there was an advert for the Samaritans: 'We don't just hear you, we listen'. Below, in a small patch of white space, something had been drawn in green biro.

Andrew spent a long time studying Trevor's drawing. He knew it was Trevor's, because it consisted of three simple oblongs, each with a name and dates inside them:

Willy Humphrey Anderson: 1938–1980
Portia Maria Anderson: 1936–1989
Trevor Humphrey Anderson: 1964–????

The only other words: *Glascote Cemetery – Tamworth.*

Andrew had so many questions. Had the drawing been intended for someone specific to see, or purely for the first person who found it? How many years after this man had drawn where he wanted to be buried had he sat waiting for death?

257

Andrew wanted to think that Trevor Anderson had lived a life of glorious hedonism. That this little piece of admin was a rare moment of practical planning in amongst the carefree fun. Looking around at the grimy flat, Andrew realised this was a desperately optimistic thought. The reality would be that in the last few years Trevor would have opened his eyes each morning, checked for sure that he wasn't dead, and got up. Until one day he didn't.

It was the waiting, that was the worst part – when the days were exclusively about eating enough food and drinking enough water to keep yourself alive. Maintenance. That was all it was. Andrew suddenly thought of Keith's dull eyes the moment before he crashed to the ground. Christ, what had he *done*? At some point he'd have to face the consequences. And then there was Carl. How was he going to deal with that? He could simply fold and transfer the money. But would that really be the end of it? Carl seemed so angry and bitter. What was to stop him flipping at any moment and picking up the phone to Meredith? The waiting would be torture. He could never truly think about being happy with that hanging over him. What about Peggy? He thought of that afternoon in Northumberland. At the time he'd felt so full of possibility, convinced that everything was going to change. How wrong he had been. There was no way he could expect Peggy to understand his lies, not after he'd refused to help her when she'd needed him most.

There was, of course, one very simple way to fix everything. It was a thought that had occurred to him a long time ago, now. Not in some moment of crisis, but simply registering itself as a possibility, as he went about his business. He had been waiting in line somewhere. A supermarket checkout perhaps, or maybe the bank. As soon as he'd acknowledged the thought, it was with him permanently. It had been like a stone hitting a windscreen, leaving a tiny crack in the glass. A permanent reminder that, at any time, the whole sheet of glass could smash. And now, he realised, it made complete and utter sense. Not only did he have a way out, but, for once in his life, he would be in complete and total control.

He looked at himself in the mirror, his face partially obscured by a streak of dirt. He set the ticket down carefully on top of the book and got slowly to his feet, standing still for a moment, listening to the gentle hum of the estate – canned laughter from a television next door, gospel music coming from the flat below. He could feel his shoulders slacken. Decades of tension were beginning to lift. Everything was going to be fine. The opening bars of Ella's 'Isn't This A Lovely Day?' came into his head. There was a renewed flash of pain in his foot. But this time he barely registered it. It didn't really matter. Not now. Nothing did.

In the kitchen, the freezer buzzed into life for a few moments, shuddered, then clicked off.

He made one final pass of Trevor's flat and emailed a report to the office. Hopefully he'd given enough information for someone to make the funeral arrangements.

He took the bus home, standing with one leg raised like a flamingo, feeling liberated at how little of a shit he gave about the way people were looking at him. As soon as he was home he went straight to the bathroom and ran a bath. As he waited for it to fill he limped to the kitchen and, almost as if trying to hoodwink himself, reached into a drawer without looking until his hand touched what he was after. He ran his fingers against the scarred plastic handle of the knife, feeling oddly comforted by its familiarity. He ran it under the tap, supposing it should be clean, though it didn't really matter. He started towards the kitchen, but stopped and turned back. This wasn't going to change anything, he told himself, but it felt like he should check, just in case. He opened the drawer and pulled out his phone. It seemed to take an age to turn on. When it vibrated, Andrew nearly dropped it in surprise. But then he saw that the message was from Carl. '*Is the money with you yet? You better not be having second thoughts.*' He shook his head, slowly. Of course Peggy hadn't messaged him. He was already dead to her. He threw his phone on to the countertop.

He flicked through his Ella records and decided what he was going to play. Normally, it would be on instinct. But for this, he felt the need to find the album that encapsulated everything he loved about her. In the end he decided on *Ella in Berlin – The reissued import version*. He lowered the needle and listened to the volume fade up on the crowd, their excited applause sounding like rain on a windowpane. He undressed where he stood, half-heartedly folding his clothes and leaving them on the arm of a chair. He thought perhaps he should write a note, but only because that's what people did. What was the point if you didn't have anyone to say anything to? It would just be another piece of paper waiting for the litter picker's pincers.

By the time he'd lowered himself into the bath, gasping with pain as the hot water stung his foot, applause was ringing out again at the end of 'That Old Black Magic', and the gentle double bass and piano of 'Our Love Is Here To Stay' filled the air.

He'd intended to drink the rest of the wine, but had forgotten to bring the bottle from the kitchen. It was better this way, he decided. To be completely lucid. In control.

The rumbling thud of the bass drum and the rushed coda from the piano signalled the end of the song, and Ella thanked the crowd. Andrew always thought she sounded so genuine when she did that; it was never forced, never false.

He was beginning to feel woozy. He hadn't eaten for hours and steam was fogging the room and his senses. He tapped his fingers on his thighs under the water and felt the ripples go back and forth. He closed his eyes and imagined he was floating down a languid river somewhere on the other side of the world.

More applause, and now they were on to 'Mack The Knife'. This was where Ella forgot the words. *Maybe this time it would be different*, Andrew thought, feeling along the side of the bath until he found the plastic handle, gripping it tightly. But no, there was the hesitation, then the breathless, audacious reference to wrecking her own song, and now the cheeky im-provisation where she morphed into Louis Armstrong's rasp, the roar of the crowd. They were with her, cheering her on.

He lowered his hand into the water. Tightened his grip. There was barely time to pause for breath before the urgent drums of 'How High The Moon' and Ella launching into her scat-singing. The music chased after her words, but she was always too quick, always too quick. He twisted his arm and clenched his fist. He felt the sharpness of the metal, his skin straining against it, about to give way. But then there was another noise, cutting through the music, vying for his attention. It was his phone ringing, he realised, opening his eyes, his fingers unclenching from around the knife's handle.

Chapter Twenty-Eight

It was Peggy.

'You're in the shit for not being here. Cameron's properly fuming, and he's taking it out on the rest of us. Where the hell are you?'

She sounded angry. Glad, perhaps, to have an excuse to call and vent at him without explicitly mentioning the other night.

He'd managed to crawl to the bedroom where he was now sitting on the floor, naked, exhausted. It felt like he'd just woken from an incredibly intense dream. He had a sudden vision of blooms of scarlet muddying the clear bathwater and had to grip his knees to stop the sensation that he was falling. Was he still here? Was this still real?

'I'm at home,' he said, his voice thick and unfamiliar.

'You've thrown a sickie?'

'No,' he said. 'It's not that.'

'Right. Well, what's going on then?'

'Um, well, I think I sort of nearly tried to kill myself.'

There was a pause.

'Say that again?'

They met at the pub, once Andrew had refused Peggy's several demands to take him to hospital. The post-work, Friday evening drinkers would be descending soon, but for now the place was empty, save for a man sitting at the bar making conversation with the polite yet clearly bored barmaid.

Andrew found a table and slowly lowered himself on to a chair, folding his arms around his chest. He felt incredibly fragile all of a sudden, like his bones were made of rotten wood. A few moments later Peggy shoulder-barged the door open, hurrying over to him and smothering him with a hug that he accepted but couldn't reciprocate because he'd begun to shiver uncontrollably.

'Wait here, I know what'll sort you out,' Peggy said.

She returned from the bar with what looked like a glass of milk. 'They didn't have honey, so this'll have to do. Not a proper hot toddy, but ah well. My mam used to give them to me and Imogen when we had colds. At the time I thought it was a proper cure, but looking back she clearly just wanted to knock us out so she could get some peace.'

'Thank you,' Andrew said, taking a warming sip and feeling the not-unpleasant sting of the whisky. Peggy watched him drink. She looked anxious, fidgeting with her hands, twiddling her earrings – delicate blue studs that looked like teardrops. Andrew sat inert, opposite her. He felt so detached.

'So,' Peggy said. 'You, um, said on the phone about the whole, you know . . .'

'Killing myself?' Andrew said.

'That. Yes. Are you – I mean it's a stupid question I suppose but – are you OK?'

Andrew thought about it. 'Yes,' he said. 'Well, I suppose I feel a bit sort of . . . like I might *actually* be dead.'

Peggy looked down at Andrew's drink. 'OK, I really do

think we need to get you to hospital,' she said, reaching over and taking his hand.

'No,' he said firmly, Peggy's touch bringing him out of his daze. 'There's really no need. I didn't hurt myself and I'm feeling better now. This is helping.' He took a sip of whisky and coughed, clasping his hands together until his knuckles were white in an attempt to stop them trembling.

'OK,' Peggy said, looking sceptical. 'Well, let's see how you feel after this.'

Just then the door of the pub opened and four extremely loud sets of suits and ties containing men came in and arranged themselves at the bar. The old regular finished his pint, tucked his newspaper under his arm, and left.

Peggy waited until Andrew had finished his whisky, before seeming to remember she had a beer to drink, taking two large gulps. She sat forward and spoke softly. 'What happened?'

Andrew shivered in response and Peggy reached over and cupped her hands around his. 'It's OK, you don't have to tell me details, I'm just trying to understand why you'd . . . want to do something like that. Where were Diane and the kids in all of this?'

Andrew's synapses instantly fired as he searched for an explanation. But nothing came to him. Not this time. He smiled sadly, as the realisation hit him. This time, *this time*, he was going to tell the truth. He took a deep breath, trying to settle himself, to stamp down on the part of him desperately trying to stop him going through with this.

'What? What's happened?' Peggy said, looking even more worried. 'Are they OK?'

Andrew started to speak, hesitantly, having to pause every few seconds: 'Have . . . have you ever told a lie so big that you felt there was no way out of it . . . that you . . . that you had to just carry on pretending?'

Peggy looked at him evenly. 'I once told my mother-in-law that I'd criss-crossed the bottoms of sprouts when I hadn't. That made for a tense Christmas Day . . . but that's not quite what you mean, is it?'

Andrew shook his head slowly, and this time the words came out before he could stop them.

'Diane, Steph and David don't exist,' he said. 'It came from a misunderstanding, but then I kept the lie going, and the longer I did, the harder it was to tell the truth.'

Peggy looked as though she was thinking and feeling a hundred different things at once.

'I don't think I really understand,' she said.

Andrew chewed his lip. He had the strangest sensation that he was about to start laughing.

'I just wanted to feel normal,' he said. 'It started off so small but then' – he let out a strangely high-pitched bark of a laugh – 'it sort of got a bit out of hand.'

Peggy looked startled. She'd fiddled with one of her earrings so much that it came free in her hand and bounced on to the table like a little blue tear that had frozen as it fell.

Andrew stared at it, and then the tune came into his head. This time, though, he willed it on. *Blue moon, you saw me standing alone.* He started to hum the tune out loud. He could sense that Peggy was beginning to panic. *Ask me. Please*, he begged silently.

'So, just so I'm clear,' Peggy said. 'Diane just . . . doesn't exist? You invented her.'

Andrew grasped his glass and tipped the remaining liquid into his mouth.

'Well, not entirely,' he said.

Peggy rubbed her eyes with her palms, then reached into her bag for her phone.

'What are you – who are you calling?' Andrew said, starting to get to his feet, yelping at the pain, having forgotten about his bruised foot.

Peggy waved her hand at him, getting him to sit back down.

'Hi, Lucy,' she said into her phone. 'I'm just calling to check you're all right to look after the girls for another couple of hours. Thanks, pet.'

Andrew readied himself to speak but Peggy held up a hand. 'I'm going to need an oil change before we go any further,' she said, downing the rest of her drink, snatching their empty glasses and marching to the bar. Andrew clasped his hands together tightly. They were still so cold he could barely feel them. When Peggy returned with their drinks she had a new resolve about her, a steely look in her eyes that said she was prepared to hear the worst and not appear shocked by it. It was, he realised, exactly the sort of look Diane used to give him.

Chapter Twenty-Nine

Andrew had gone to Bristol Polytechnic the summer after his mother's death. With Sally in Manchester with her new boyfriend, it had been less about a yearning for higher education and more about finding some people to talk to. Without any real research he settled on some digs in a part of the city called Easton. The house was just off a stretch of grass with the optimistically bucolic name of Fox Park, which in reality was a tiny patch of green separating the residential street from the M32. As Andrew arrived outside the house, hauling his possessions in a bulky purple rucksack, he saw a man in the park, dressed entirely in bin liners, kicking a pigeon. A woman appeared from a bush and dragged the man away from the bird, but to Andrew's horror this was only so she could continue the assault herself. He was still recovering from having witnessed this harrowing tag-team display as he was ushered into his lodgings by the landlady. Mrs Briggs had a fierce blue rinse and a cough like distant thunder, and Andrew quickly realised she had a good heart underneath her stern exterior. She seemed to be constantly cooking, often by candlelight whenever the electricity meter ran out, which it regularly did. She also had an unnerving habit of slipping in criticism halfway through an unrelated sentence: 'Don't worry about that feller and the pigeon, my love, he's bit of a funny one that lad – gosh, you need a haircut, m'duck – I think he's one sandwich short of a picnic, truth be told.' It was the conversational equivalent of burying bad news.

Andrew soon grew fond of Mrs Briggs, which was just as well, because he hated everybody on his course. He was savvy enough to work out that Philosophy was going to attract a certain type, but it was as if they'd all been grown in a lab somewhere, purely to annoy him. The boys all had wispy beards, smoked shitty little roll-ups, and spent most of their time trying to impress girls by quoting the most obscure passages they knew from Descartes and Kierkegaard. The girls were denim-clad and seemed to spend all the lectures stoney-faced, anger boiling away underneath the surface. Andrew only worked out later that this was largely due to the male tutors, who engaged in lively debate with the boys but spoke to the girls the way you might to a rather intelligent pony.

After a few weeks he made a couple of friends, a pudding-faced, largely benign Welshman called Gavin, who drank neat gin and claimed to have once seen a flying saucer going over Llandovery rugby ground, and Gavin's girlfriend, Diane, a third-year who wore bright orange-rimmed glasses and didn't suffer fools gladly. Andrew quickly realised that Gavin was obviously the biggest fool of all, constantly testing Diane's patience in increasingly creative ways. They had been together since before uni – 'Childhood sweethearts, you see,' Gavin told him for the seventh time one evening, after his sixth gin – and Gavin had followed her to Bristol to do the same course. Later, Diane would confide that this had been less Gavin not bearing for them to be apart and more that the simplest of tasks were too hard for him. 'I came home once to find him trying to cook chicken nuggets in the toaster.'

For reasons that were unclear to Andrew, Diane was the only person he'd ever met in his brief adult life who he found completely unproblematic to talk to. He didn't stutter or stumble over his words when he was with her, and they shared a very specific sense of humour – dark, but never cruel. On the few instances they were alone – waiting for Gavin to meet them at the pub, or in snatched moments when he was in the toilet or at the bar – Andrew began to open up to her about his mum and Sally. Diane had a natural gift for helping him to find the positives in what he was going through without trivialising anything, so when he spoke about his mum, he found himself recalling the rare occasions when she'd seemed unburdened and happy, which usually occurred when she was gardening in the sunshine with Ella Fitzgerald playing in the background. When he spoke of Sally, he remembered a phase around the time they were watching Hammer horrors with Spike when she started to come back from the pub with presents she'd 'acquired', clearly from a dodgy regular who'd got them off the back of a lorry, including a Subbuteo set, a little wooden instrument apparently known as a Jew's Harp, and, most magnificently of all, an R.176 *Flying Scotsman* with apple-green engine and teak carriage. He loved that engine, but it was Diane who made him realise that it was more than just an appreciation of the thing itself – that it was also em-blematic of that brief period of time when Sally had been at her most affectionate.

Occasionally, through a haze of smoke in a rowdy pub, he would catch Diane looking at him. Unembarrassed at being caught in the act, she would hold his gaze for a second before rejoining conversation. He lived for those moments, to the point that they became the only thing keeping him going. He was failing in his coursework so badly that he'd completely stopped bothering with it. He was resigned to dropping out at Christmas. He'd get a job somewhere and save some money. He told himself he'd go travelling, but in truth he'd found it hard enough moving to Bristol.

One night, he, Diane and Gavin were invited to an impromptu party in a fellow philosophy student's halls of residence room, on the condition that they bring a crate of beer each. A large gang of them crammed into a bedroom, and cracked open cans. Nobody wanted to talk about uni work, but Gavin found a copy of *On Liberty* and began drunkenly reading out passages as everyone tried to ignore him. As Gavin searched for a new book – perhaps Voltaire was what this party needed! – Andrew reached for what he was 50 per cent sure was *his* Holsten Pils, but someone took his free hand from behind and pulled him outside. It was Diane. She led him through the corridor, down the three flights of stairs and out into the street, where snow was falling in thick clumps.

'Hello,' she said, putting her arms around his neck and kissing him before he could reply. By the time he opened his eyes again there was a carpet of snow.

'You know I'm going back to London later this week?' he said.

Diane raised her eyebrows.

'No! I didn't mean that . . . I just . . . I just thought I should tell you.'

Diane politely advised him to shut up and kissed him again.

They snuck back to Mrs Briggs's that night. Andrew woke the next morning and thought Diane had left without saying goodbye, but her glasses were still on the bedside table, pointing towards the bed as if watching him. He heard the toilet flushing and then the sounds of two different sets of footsteps meeting on the landing. A short stand-off. Awkward introductions. Diane climbed back into bed and punished Andrew for not coming to her rescue by clamping her ice-cold feet to his legs.

'Don't you ever warm up?' he said.

'Maybe,' she whispered, pulling the duvet over their heads. 'You'll just have to help me, won't you?'

Afterwards, they lay on their sides with their legs still entwined. Andrew traced his finger on the little white scar above Diane's eyebrow.

'How did you get this?' he asked.

'A boy called James Bond threw a crab apple at me,' she said.

Five days later, they stood on the train platform as the sun warmed them through a gap in the fence. They'd been on their first official date the previous night, to see *Pulp Fiction* at the cinema, though neither of them were able to remember a great deal about the plot.

'I wish I'd worked harder,' Andrew said. 'I can't believe I've messed this up so badly.'

Diane took his face in her hands. 'Listen, you're still grieving for goodness' sake. The very fact you managed to get out of the house is something you should be proud of.'

They stood huddled together until the train came. Andrew bombarded Diane with questions. He wanted to know everything about her, to have as much as possible to cling on to after he'd gone.

'I promise to come and visit you whenever I can afford the ticket, OK?' Andrew said. 'And I'll call. And write.'

'What about a carrier pigeon?'

'Oi!'

'Sorry, it's just you *are* talking a little bit like you're being shipped off to a war somewhere, not Tooting.'

'And remind me again why I can't just stay here?'

Diane sighed. 'Because a) I think you should spend some time with your sister, especially at Christmas, and b) because I think you need to move home for a bit and decide what you want to do next, independently of me. I have to concentrate on my degree, for one thing, and when that's finished I'll probably end up moving to London anyway.'

Andrew pulled a face.

'*Probably.*'

After a moment of silence he realised how unattractive his sulking was, but as Diane hugged him goodbye she gripped him so fiercely that he felt the warmth of her all the way back to London.

He moved into the spare room of a house currently occupied by two Dubliners who'd just discovered speed, and who he managed to largely avoid apart from when they'd summon him to help settle entirely incomprehensible debates, where he tended to side with the one who looked most likely to set fire to something if he wasn't declared the winner. He survived entirely on Rice Krispies and the thought of the next time he'd get to speak to Diane. They had an arranged time every week when he'd go down to the payphone at the end of the road and call her, Diane demanding they start every conversation with him telling her about the newest 'busty' or 'exotic' woman being advertised in the phone box. He kept an empty Nescafé jar on his bedroom windowsill where he saved up money for train fares to Bristol, having found work behind the till in a video rental store exclusively patronised by shifty-eyed drunk men buying porn, something he'd only told Diane after much carousing in the pub.

By this point he'd all but given up on the idea of going back to try and finish his degree. Summer was creeping towards them and it made him anxious just thinking about the idea of being back in classes again.

'So you're just going to sit about in London working in a porno shop?' Diane asked him. 'What happened to you making decisions, or is this really the height of your ambition? You need to find out what you want to do for yourself. If you're not going to finish your degree you need to work out how you're going to have a career.'

'But—'

She waved away his protests. 'I'm serious. I won't hear another word about it.' She put her hands on the side of his face and squeezed his mouth into a comedy fish. 'You need to believe in yourself a bit more and just bloody get out there. What's your dream job, your dream career?'

She released the fish and waited for him to answer.

What *was* his dream job? More importantly, what could he say that she wouldn't laugh at?

'Working in the community somehow, or something, I suppose.'

Diane narrowed her eyes, searching his face for signs of facetiousness.

'Well then, good,' she said. 'So that's the first positive step. You know the area you want to work. You just need some experience. That means an office job, first up. So as soon as you're back in London you're going to find one. Agreed?'

'Yeah,' Andrew mumbled.

'Don't sulk!' Diane said, and when he didn't respond she moved down the bed and blew a fierce raspberry on his belly.

'What about you, then?' Andrew said, laughing, pulling her up so that she was lying on top of him. 'What's *your* dream job?'

Diane rested her head on his chest. 'Well, as much as I spent my entire adolescence saying I'd do the complete opposite of my parents, hence the Philosophy degree, blah blah blah, I'm thinking about a law conversion.'

'Oh yeah? Brokering deals for drug-dealing informants, that sort of thing?'

'The fact that's your first thought makes me think you've been watching lots of terrible straight-to-video films from your shop.'

'It was either that or the porn.'

'And you've not watched any of that.'

'Absolutely not.'

'So if you want to have some "alone time" you just picture . . .'

'You. Exclusively you. Wearing nothing but a smock made out of pages from Virginia Woolf novels.'

'I thought as much.'

She rolled off him so they were lying side by side.

'So, you're going to be a lawyer, then,' Andrew said.

'Either that or an astronaut,' she said with a yawn.

Andrew laughed. 'You can't have a Welsh astronaut. That's ridiculous!'

'Um, why not?' Diane asked.

Andrew prepared his best Valleys' accent. 'Well, there now, rrrright. That's a small step for man, that is, and a great big giant one for mankind, see.'

Diane huffed and went to climb out of bed, but Andrew dived and grabbed her arm that she'd left deliberately dangling there. He loved it when she did that. Teasing him. Knowing that she would only get as far as a step away before he pulled her back towards him.

Back in London, he spent his time behind the video shop counter circling jobs in the paper. He'd just sold an horrific-looking video to a gaunt-faced man who explained that 'wanking helps me with the comedowns', when the phone rang. Five minutes later he replaced the receiver and considered the possibility that the woman who'd just asked him to come in for an interview might have been hired by Gavin as some sort of cruel act of revenge.

'Firstly, you're insane,' Diane said, when he spoke to her from the phone box later that evening (Bella, gorgeous busty blonde). 'Secondly, I'm pretty sure I'm entitled to say I told you so. So we can do that now or wait till after you've actually got the job. It's up to you . . .'

The interview was for an admin assistant at the local council. He borrowed one of the Irish boys' suits, which had once belonged to his father. Checking his pockets as he sat in the waiting room, he found a ticket stub from a 1964 production of a play called *Philadelphia, Here I Come!* which had been performed at the Gaiety Theatre, Dublin. Had Sally gone to Philadelphia when she was in the States? He couldn't remember, and he'd long since thrown away the postcards. He decided that the optimism of the title was a good omen.

The following morning, Diane's opening line as she picked up the phone to him was, 'I told you so.'

Andrew laughed. 'What would you have done if you'd said that and I hadn't got it?'

'Um, pretended it was one of my other boyfriends?'

'Hey!'

A pause.

'Wait, you are joking, right?'

A sigh.

'Yes, Andrew, I'm joking. Hamish Brown accidentally touched my boob whilst trying to fix an overhead projector last week, that's about as close as I've come to cheating on you . . .'

Despite himself, Andrew spent possibly 70 per cent (OK, 80, 90, tops) of the time worrying about Diane being enticed away by someone. He always pictured a floppy-haired rower called Rufus, for some reason. All broad shoulders and old money.

'Luckily for you, fictional Rufus is no match for a real-life skinny Philosophy drop-out who works in a porno shop and lives with two speed-freaks.'

Andrew was so nervous on his first morning at the council that he was forced to make a decision on whether it was less strange to spend the entire time on the toilet or to be sitting at his desk wincing with stomach cramps every five seconds. Thankfully, he managed to get through the day, and then a week, and then a month, without shitting himself or accidentally setting anything on fire. 'We really need to work on your benchmarks,' Diane told him.

Then the most glorious of days arrived: 11 June 1995. Diane's course was over and she was coming to London. Andrew said goodbye to the Irish boys, who seemed surprisingly emotional (though that could have been because they'd been up for three days straight), and piled all his stuff into the taxi waiting to take him to the flat he'd found for him and Diane, who'd managed to get everything into a couple of suitcases and taken the train from Bristol.

'Mum wanted to drive me,' she said, 'but I was a bit worried you might've rented us a crack den or something and I didn't want her having a panic attack.'

'Ah. Hmm. Funny you should say that . . .'

'Oh God . . .'

Andrew couldn't be sure the tiny flat he'd found off the Old Kent Road *hadn't* ever been used as a crack den – it was a rough-and-ready sort of building with scuff marks on the corridor walls and a dewy smell about the place – but as he lay in bed that night, Diane sleeping next to him, her knees curled up to her chest, he couldn't stop smiling. This already felt like home.

Their moving coincided with a summer that brought with it a fiercely cloying heat. July was particularly punishing. Andrew bought a fan and he and Diane sat in their underwear in the front room when it got too hot. They both became mildly obsessed with Wimbledon that month, Steffi Graf being a particular hero to Diane.

'This is just too bloody hot, isn't it?' Diane yawned, lying down on her front as Graf signed autographs before leaving Centre court.

'Might this help?' Andrew said, before fishing two ice cubes out of his glass and carefully dropping them on to Diane's back, innocently apologising as she half-shrieked, half-laughed.

The heat was unrelenting into August. People eyed each

other nervously on the Tube, looking out for potential faint-ers. Roads cracked and split. Hosepipe bans were out in force. On the hottest day of the year, Andrew met Diane after work and they sprawled on the parched grass in Brockwell Park as all around them people kicked off shoes and rolled up sleeves. They'd brought bottles of lager but had forgotten to bring an opener. 'Not to worry,' Diane said, confidently approaching a couple who were smoking and borrowing their lighter to somehow crack open the beers.

'Where did you learn that trick, then?' Andrew asked as they resettled themselves on the grass.

'My grandad. He could use his teeth, too, in an emergency.'

'He sounds . . . fun.'

'Good old Grandad David. He used to say to me' – she affected a deep, booming voice – '"if there's one lesson I've learned, Di, it's never go cheap on your booze. Life's too short." My granny would just roll her eyes. God, I loved him, he was such a hero. You know what, if I ever have a son I really want to call him David.'

'Oh yeah?' Andrew said. 'What about if you have a girl?'

'Hmmm.' Diane inspected her elbow, creased with a criss-cross patch from the grass. 'Oh, I know: Stephanie.'

'Another relative?'

'No! Steffi Graf, obviously.'

'Obviously.'

Diane blew the froth from her beer at him.

Later, at home, she straddled him on the sofa as lightning seared the sky.

The rain came while the city slept, a deluge of greasy water pounding the streets. Andrew stood by the window as dawn broke, sipping a cup of coffee. He couldn't tell if he was still a bit drunk, or whether there was a hangover lying in wait. One of those nasty ones that creeps up on you, the sort where you're eating bacon while its en route to the plate from the frying pan. He heard Diane stir. She sat up in bed and let her hair fall over her face.

Andrew laughed and went back to looking out of the window. 'Have you got a hurty head?' he asked.

'I've got a hurty everything,' Diane croaked. He heard her shuffle over and felt her arms go around his waist, her cheek resting at the top of his back. 'Shall we have a fry-up?' she said.

'Sure,' Andrew said. 'We'll just have to grab a few things from the shop.'

'Whadoweneed?' Diane said with a yawn that Andrew felt resonate through him.

'Oh, just bacon. And eggs. And sausages. And bread. Beans, possibly. Milk, definitely, if you want tea.'

He felt her grip slacken slightly and she groaned in defeat.

'Whose turn is it to *do a thing*?' he asked, innocently.

She buried her face into his back. 'You're only saying that because you know it's mine.'

'What? Never!' Andrew said. 'I mean, thinking back: I changed the channel, you put the kettle on, I put the bins out, you bought the paper, I did the washing-up . . . Oh, you're quite right, it *is* your turn to do a thing.'

She poked her nose into his back several times.

'Gerrof,' he said, eventually giving in and turning to take her in his arms.

'Do you promise everything will be better after bacon and beans?' she said.

'I do. I absolutely do.'

'And you love me?'

'Even more than bacon and beans.'

He felt her slide her hand into his boxers and squeeze him.

'Good,' she said, kissing him on the lips with an exaggerated 'mwah' and abruptly walking off to slip on some flip-flops and throw a jumper over her pyjamas.

'Well, that's not fair,' Andrew said.

'Hey, it's my turn to do a thing, I'm just going by the rules . . .' Diane said with a shrug, trying to keep a straight face. She reached for her glasses, grabbed her purse and left, humming a tune. It took Andrew a second to realise it was Ella's 'Blue Moon'. *Finally*, he thought, *she's a convert*. He stood there, grinning stupidly, feeling so hopelessly in love it was like he was a punch-drunk boxer desperately trying to stay upright.

He allowed himself two listens of 'Blue Moon' before heading to have a shower – guiltily hoping that by the time he came out he'd be able to smell bacon sizzling. But there was no sign of Diane when he emerged. And there still wasn't ten minutes later. Perhaps she'd bumped into a friend – a fellow Bristol Poly alumnus; small world and all that. But something about this just didn't feel right. He quickly dressed and left the house.

He could see the gathering of people from the other end of the street where the shop was. 'That's the thing,' he overheard someone in the gaggle muttering just as he reached them. 'All that hot weather and then suddenly a big old storm . . . bound to cause damage.'

There were police officers standing in a semi-circle, blocking anyone from going further. One of their radios crackled into life, a confusion of feedback and static that made an officer on one end of the ring wince and hold his radio out at arm's length. Then a voice cut through the interference: '. . . confirm it's one deceased. Falling masonry. No one's been able to ascertain who owns the building, over.'

Andrew felt the dread seeping into him as he moved through the last line of the crowd and towards the edge of the police ring. He was trembling as he walked, as if an electric current were flowing through him. Ahead, he could see some blue plastic sheets on the ground, rippling in the breeze, a pile of smashed slate to one side. And there, next to it, perfectly intact, looking just the same as on the bedside table in Mrs Briggs's house, was a pair of orange-framed glasses.

A policeman had his hands on his chest, telling him to get back. His breath smelled of coffee and there was a birthmark on his cheek. He was angry, but then he suddenly stopped shouting. He knew. He understood. He tried to ask Andrew questions but Andrew had crumpled to his knees, unable to support himself. There were hands on his shoulders. Concerned voices. Radio static. Then someone was trying to pull him to his feet.

The noise of the pub flitted back in and the policeman's hands became Peggy's, and it was as if he was coming up from under water, breaking the surface, and Peggy was telling him it was OK, squeezing him tightly, muffling his sobs. And even though he couldn't stop crying – it felt like maybe he'd never actually stop – he slowly became aware of a tingling in his fingers, warmth finally returning.

Chapter Thirty

He barely had the energy to get back to his flat. Peggy walked him there, half supporting his weight, and insisted that she come in with him. He protested half-heartedly, but now Peggy knew the truth there wasn't much point.

'It's either that or the hospital,' Peggy said, which settled the matter.

The model train set still lay wrecked, untouched since he'd smashed it up. 'Hence the limp,' he mumbled.

He lay down on the sofa and Peggy covered him in a blanket and then her coat. She made him tea and sat cross-legged on the floor, occasionally squeezing his hand, calming him down each time he jolted into consciousness.

When he woke, she was sitting in an armchair reading the *Ella Loves Cole* sleeve notes and drinking coffee from a mug he'd not used in a decade. There was a crick in his neck – he must have slept in a funny position – and his foot was still throbbing, but he felt more like himself. He had dreamt about Meredith's dinner party, and a question suddenly struck him.

'What happened to Keith?' he asked.

Peggy looked up at him. 'Morning to you too,' she said. 'Keith, you'll be glad to hear, is fine.'

'But I heard you calling an ambulance,' Andrew said.

'Aye. By the time it had arrived he was awake and trying to persuade the paramedics not to take him. To be honest, they seemed more worried about Cameron – silly sod sat there passed out with pen all over his face. I think they thought we'd kidnapped him into a mad cult, or something.'

'Is Keith back at work?'

'Yep.'

'Is he, you know, angry at me?'

'Well, he's not exactly delighted. But Meredith is treating him like a war hero, constantly fussing over him, so I think he's secretly quite enjoying it. She's the one you want to . . .' Peggy stopped herself.

'What?' Andrew said.

'She kept talking about getting Keith to press charges.'

'Oh God,' Andrew groaned.

'Don't worry, it's fine,' Peggy said. 'There is a chance I may have had a little word with her about it, and that she's not mentioned it since.'

Andrew couldn't be sure, but it seemed like Peggy was trying to suppress a smile.

'You sound like a Mafia boss,' he said. 'But I'm very grateful, whatever you said.' He looked across at the oven clock and scrabbled to sit upright.

'Jesus,' he said. 'Have I really been asleep for twelve hours? What are you still doing here? You should be at home.'

'It's all right,' Peggy said. 'I've Facetimed the girls. They're staying in Croydon with one of Imogen's friends. They got to stay up and watch something horrifically inappropriate on the telly last night, so they couldn't care less that I'm not there.'

She turned the record over. 'I've got a confession to make. I haven't listened to the mixtape you made me.'

'I'll let you off,' Andrew said. 'Like I said, it barely took any time to put together.'

Peggy placed the record carefully back on top of the pile.

'Your mam was a big fan, you said?'

'I don't really know. I've just got really vivid memories of her putting these records on and singing along as she did stuff in the kitchen, or playing them out of the window as she gardened. She always seemed, I don't know, like a completely different person when she let herself go like that.'

Peggy drew her knees up to her chest. 'I'd like to say I have similar memories of my mam when I was younger, but if she was dancing around the kitchen it was usually because she was trying to wallop one of us, or there was something on fire. Or both. Right, you look like you need some toast.'

'It's fine, I'll do it,' Andrew said, starting to get to his feet, but Peggy told him to sit still. Andrew just hoped to God she didn't judge him too much on the three cans of baked beans and possibly stale loaf of bread that made up the contents of his kitchen cupboards. Before he could make pre-emptive apologies his phone vibrated. He read the message and felt faint again. He waited until Peggy brought over a plate of generously buttered toast and a mug of tea.

'There's something else I need to tell you,' he said.

Peggy took a big bite of toast. 'OK,' she said. 'But I'll be honest with you, Andrew, after last night I'm not sure there's much you can say that'll shock me. But go for it.'

By the time he'd finished telling her about Carl and the blackmail, Peggy had lost interest in her toast, which she'd thrown on to her plate in disgust. She was pacing back and forth, hands on hips.

'He can't do that to you. There was a reason Sally gave you that money, and the fact he's threatening you is outrageous. You're going to call him right now and tell him to get fucked.'

'No,' Andrew said, 'I can't.'

'Why the hell not?'

'Because . . .'

'What?'

'It's not that easy. I can't . . . I just can't.'

'But it's just an empty threat, now, because it's not as if . . .' Peggy stopped pacing and looked at him. 'Because you *are* going to tell the others at work the truth about everything, right?'

Andrew didn't say anything.

'Well,' Peggy said, matter-of-factly, 'you're going to have to. In two weeks' time you're supposed to be hosting the next dinner party, so you haven't really got a choice.'

'What?' Andrew said. 'But what about what happened at Meredith's – that was a disaster. Surely Cameron doesn't want that happening again.'

'Oh, on the contrary, he's got it in his head that it's the perfect way for you and Keith to make up. He was so hammered that night he didn't really understand what had happened, other than that you and Keith had "fallen out". I managed to wipe his face clean and pour him into a taxi. He kept mumbling something to me about "redundancies", but God knows what's happening there.'

Andrew folded his arms.

'I'm not telling them,' he said, in a voice barely louder than a whisper. 'I can't.'

'Why not?'

'What do you mean, why not? Because I'll get fired! I can't afford for that to happen, Peggy. I've got no transferable skills, for one thing.'

They were silent for a moment. Andrew really wished there was music playing. Peggy moved over to the window and stood with her back to him.

'I actually think you do have transferable skills,' she said, 'that you could do something else. And I think you know that too.'

'What's that supposed to mean?' Andrew said.

Peggy turned around and went to speak, but then stopped, seemingly changing her mind.

'Can I ask you something?' she said, eventually.

Andrew nodded.

'How much has this place changed since you moved in?'

'How do you mean?'

Peggy looked around. 'When did you last buy new things? Have you, in fact, changed anything since the day Diane . . .'

Andrew suddenly felt horribly self-conscious.

'I don't know,' he said. 'Not a lot. A bit, though. The computer's new.'

'Right. And how long have you been doing your current job?'

'What is this, an interview?' Andrew said. 'Do you want another cup of tea, by the way?'

Peggy came to sit next to him and took his hand in hers. 'Andrew,' she said softly. 'I'm not even going to pretend to know how much shit you've had to go through, but I do know from experience what it's like to live in denial, to not confront things. Look at me and Steve. I knew in my heart of hearts that he wasn't going to change but it took me sinking to absolute rock bottom to do something about it. Didn't you have that same realisation last night? Don't you feel now that it's time to try and move on?'

Andrew felt a tightness in his throat. His eyes began to sting. Part of him wanted Peggy to keep on at him like this, part of him just wanted to be alone.

'People won't be as kind as you,' he said, quietly. 'And you couldn't exactly blame them. I just need more time – to think about how I'm going to do it, you know?'

Peggy lifted Andrew's hand and used hers to press it against his chest. He could feel his heart pounding against his ribcage.

'You've got to make a choice,' Peggy said. 'Either you can try and keep up with the whole pretence – pay that money to Carl, even though it's yours, keep on lying to everyone – or you can tell the truth and start accepting the consequences. I know it's hard, I really do, but . . . OK, that day in Northumberland. When we had our "moment", shall we say.'

Andrew really, *really* wished he didn't blush so easily.

'Yeah,' he mumbled, rubbing his eyes.

'Look at me. Please.'

'I can't.'

'OK, then just close your eyes. Think back and picture that moment. You don't have to tell me, but just think about how that made you feel. How lovely and *different* and . . . intense it was. I don't know. I'm only going on how it felt for me.'

Andrew opened his eyes.

'Later,' Peggy said, 'when you were falling asleep on the sofa. You kept saying "you've saved me". You thought I was your way out of all this. But – and you've got to trust me on this – only you can change things. It *has* to come from you.'

Andrew's eye was drawn to the railway debris. It was as if the crash had just happened.

Peggy looked at her watch. 'Look, I should probably think about going now. I need to make sure the girls have been given something else to eat other than Curly Wurlys.' She stood up – letting Andrew's hand go – and retrieved her coat and bag. 'Just think about what I've said, OK? And if you start feeling . . . you know . . . then call me straight away. Promise?'

Andrew nodded. He really didn't want her to leave. He wasn't going to be able to do this without her, whatever she might think. 'I'm going to do it,' he blurted out. 'I'll tell the truth, to everyone – but it just *can't* be now, when Cameron's talking redundancies. I just need to find a way of getting through the stupid bloody dinner party with my reputation intact, and then, when things have settled down, I'll fix everything, I promise. So all I'm asking is for a bit of help, short term, for how I'm going to . . .' His words petered out as he saw the disappointment in Peggy's eyes. She moved towards the door and he limped after her.

'What are you . . . please don't—'

'I've said my piece, Andrew. I'm not going to change my mind. Besides, I've got my own mess I need to sort out.'

Andrew just managed to stop himself begging her to stay.

'Sure,' he said. 'Of course. I understand. And sorry, I didn't mean to drag you away. And I'm sorry for lying to you. I wanted to tell you the truth, I really did.'

'I believe you,' Peggy said, giving him a peck on the cheek.

Andrew stood there for a long time after Peggy had gone. He looked down at the wine stain on the carpet. It was in the same spot where he'd stood the day after Diane's death, rigid in his own despair, the phone ringing and ringing as Sally tried to get him to speak to her. He felt impossibly guilty for how he'd behaved then – how cowardly and weak he'd been to hide himself away, too broken to face the funeral, refusing to let Sally comfort him. It was even worse now, thinking about how he'd indulged in the fantasy of how his life might have gone if Diane had never walked out of the house that morning. He couldn't believe how kind and understanding Peggy had been after she'd learned the truth. He'd expected her to run a mile. Unless of course she was just lulling him into a false sense of security before she dashed to the nearest mental hospital to report him as a deluded, dangerous fantasist . . . Surely, *surely*, nobody else would be as understanding as her, if he were to simply come out and tell them. He pictured Cameron's beady eyes widening, Keith and Meredith turning from stunned to scathing in the blink of an eye.

He heard his mobile vibrate again. Another message from Carl, no doubt. The autopilot in him wanted to put on some Ella, but he stopped by the record player, his hand above the needle. Without music or the gentle whooshing of a train he was more aware of what he could hear. He opened the window. Sparrows were singing. A bumblebee ambled towards him, then veered away.

Despite the fact he was feeling jittery from caffeine, he made himself another cup of tea, enjoying the comforting warmth of it as he drank, his thoughts percolating. He understood why Peggy was frustrated that he wasn't simply going to come clean with everyone now that he'd revealed the truth to her, but what she perhaps hadn't fully grasped was how potent the fantasy was, how tied to it he felt. It wasn't something he could just walk away from.

He stood and surveyed the train wreck. It was hard to tell

what damage was repairable and what was ruined for good. The locomotive he'd had set up at the time – an O4 Robinson class – was probably a write-off, as were the carriages. Thank Christ it hadn't been any of his really prized locomotives. Most of the scenery – the lighter stuff – was definitely irreparable. Trees and animals were flattened and bent. Figures lay prone on the ground. All of them, he realised, except three farm-hands who were still upright in what used to be an orchard, a look of defiance about them.

Peggy had told him he alone had to choose what to do, and maybe she was right. But what if that meant he chose only to tell people the truth when he actually felt ready? That was still him taking control, wasn't it? He ignored the dissenting voice at the back of his head by focusing on what he told himself was the more immediate concern: namely, the approaching dinner party. It was absolutely vital that he kept Cameron happy. What he really needed was some help. Peggy was out of the question. So that left . . . well, 'Nobody,' he said out loud. But as he looked again at the stoic farmhands, he remembered that, actually, that wasn't strictly true.

Chapter Thirty-One

Saturday afternoons weren't the busiest times on the sub-forum, but Andrew could still picture BamBam67, TinkerAl and BroadGaugeJim checking in before the evening was out – a quick glance as they waited for dinner to cook, just in case someone had posted to confirm that the new Wainwright H Class 0-4-4T really *did* justify the insane hype.

It worked in his favour that recent events had meant his activity on the forum had been limited in the previous week, as the last two messages mentioning him, from TinkerAl and BroadGaugeJim, were written with genuine concern:

'Tracker, you've gone a bit quiet. All good?'

'Was just thinking that! Don't say old T-bone's gone cold turkey??'

The fact that they were obviously concerned for his welfare made him feel a little more comfortable about asking for help like this. He composed a message in a blank document, tweaking and rewording from start to finish several times.

He was still finding it hard to get completely warm, so he'd rooted around in a cupboard and found some blankets which he'd washed and tumble-dried before wrapping them around his shoulders, so that it looked like his head was poking out through the top of a wigwam.

He copied and pasted his message into a new post on the

forum, gave it one final check, and then, before he could back out, he hit send.

Andrew took a sip of lager and made a note to remind himself that his instincts – much like burgers bought from lay-by vans and people who started sentences with 'I'll be honest with you' – were not to be trusted. He'd chosen the pub near King's Cross because it was called The Railway Tavern, and that felt like a good omen. He had visions of Barter Books – the same ambience, but substituting thick pints of bitter and interesting crisps for tea, scones and books. Instead, the pub felt like the sort of place you only ever heard mentioned in the same breath as phrases like 'fled the scene' and 'unprovoked attack'. Andrew had long since lost track of which clubs were battling it out at the top of Division One, or whatever it was called now, but the twenty or so other men in the pub were, to put it mildly, invested. Insults were levelled at the screen with furious relish. More confusingly, a man with ginger sideburns kept clapping whenever a decision went his team's way or there was a substitution, as if his applause could actually travel through the screen and reach the player coming on. Another man, in a leather jacket worn over his team's colours, periodically threw his arms up in the air and turned to try and make conversation with a group of fans who steadfastly ignored him. A young woman was standing further along the bar, pulling nervously at her purple hair, which looked like it had the consistency of candyfloss. Never had Andrew seen so many people in the same place, supporting the same team, wearing the same shirt, looking so alone.

Under other circumstances, he would have left and found somewhere else, but that wasn't an option. He'd concluded his message on the forum by naming the pub and the time. For all he knew, there might've been three instant replies, apologetic or otherwise, rejecting the plan, but he hadn't been able to face looking to see if anyone had responded. The closest he'd got was scrolling down with one hand over his face, peeping through a gap between his fingers, as if he were looking at an eclipse.

He fiddled nervously with a beermat, eventually giving in to the urge to tear it into strips, leaving a pile of cardboard on the table like a hamster's nest. He was suddenly very aware of how desperate he felt. He cringed at his cheery sign-off on the forum – *'Besides, it would be fun for us to actually meet up in person, no??'* – which now seemed glaringly ripe for dismissal and ridicule. It went against pretty much everything they stood for. The forum was a place where you could pretend to be someone else and, more importantly, do so naked while eating cheese if you wanted. How was real life supposed to compete with that?

He took a careful look around, remembering how Peggy had admonished him for his obviousness in the pub on her first day, hoping to see someone he thought might be one of the forum lot. He was doing his best not to make eye contact with the man in the leather jacket, who, when Andrew was ordering a pint from the grizzled barman, had turned to him showing his bloodshot eyes and grunted, 'All right?'. Andrew had pretended not to hear before scuttling away, also pretending not to hear the man muttering 'wanker' after him.

He straightened his coat lapel so that the little model train badge he'd affixed to it was visible. He'd hoped it was a subtle touch that would make him recognisable to the others without drawing undue attention. So it was all he could do not to burst out laughing when he looked up to see the man who'd just entered the pub was wearing a T-shirt bearing the slogan: 'Model Trains Are The Answer. WHO CARES WHAT THE QUESTION IS?'

Andrew half stood, half waved to the man, who – to his overwhelming relief – grinned back at him.

'Tracker?'

'Yes! My name's Andrew, you know, in real life.'

'Nice to meet you, Andrew. I'm BroadGauge – Jim.'

'Great!'

Andrew reached out and shook Jim's hand, possibly a bit too enthusiastically judging by Jim's expression, but Andrew felt too excited to be embarrassed. Somebody had come!

'Cracking badge, by the way,' Jim said.

'Thanks,' Andrew said. He was going to return the compliment about Jim's T-shirt when evidently a goal was scored and the pub erupted into howls of disapproval. Jim briefly appraised the commotion then turned back, his eyebrows raised.

'Sorry, it's a rubbish choice of venue,' Andrew said, quickly. Jim shrugged. 'Nah, it's fine. What are you drinking, then?'

'Oh, lager please,' Andrew said, waiting till Jim was heading to the bar before necking the last third of his pint.

As Jim returned with their drinks he was followed over by the young woman with purple hair, who'd just come out of the ladies. Before either Jim or Andrew could say anything she'd sat down at the table and offered them a tentative hello.

'Um, sorry,' Jim said, 'but we're actually waiting for someone.' Andrew gave the woman an apologetic smile.

'Yeah, that'd be me,' the woman said.

Andrew and Jim looked at each other.

'Hang on,' Andrew said, 'you're . . .'

'TinkerAl,' the woman said.

'But . . . but you're a woman!' Jim said.

'Well spotted,' the woman said. Then, when neither Andrew or Jim could work out how to respond, she rolled her eyes and said, 'The "Al" part comes from Alexandra. But people call me Alex.'

'Well,' Jim said, 'that's, you know . . . good for you!'

'Thanks,' Alex said, smothering a smile before launching into a passionate monologue about her latest acquisition. 'I honestly reckon it outclasses the Caerphilly Castle 4-6-0,' she said.

'No way!' Jim gasped, eyes nearly popping out of his head.

The three of them continued to talk trains, occasionally having to raise their voices over the men shouting at some perceived injustice on the big screen. Despite the occasional angry glare from leather jacket man, Andrew was beginning to relax. Though if BamBam wasn't going to turn up, that posed a big problem. He needed him the most.

It was during a melee of celebrations as the home team pinched an equaliser that a man sauntered through the door and pulled up a chair at their table. He was wearing a dark-blue denim shirt tucked into some beige slacks and smelled of expensive aftershave. He introduced himself as BamBam, then Rupert – which the others tried and failed not to seem surprised by. Jim watched Rupert shake Alex's hand and couldn't help himself. 'She's a woman!' he said.

'It's true,' Alex said. 'I've got a certificate and everything. Right, who wants crisps?'

The four of them drank and ate from bags of smoky bacon that were democratically opened out on the table. As they talked about new purchases and various upcoming conventions

– already promising to meet up at an exhibition at Alexandra Palace – Andrew was starting to wish he didn't have to upset the balance by bringing his plan into the mix. But after he returned from the toilet, the others clearly using the opportunity to discuss his message, Jim cleared his throat and said, 'So, Andrew, you, um, invited us here for a . . . thing?'

Andrew had carefully rehearsed what he was going to say, but he could still feel the blood thumping in his ears. He'd decided to get everything out as quickly as possible, revealing only as much as he had to. He spoke without pausing to draw breath, so much so that he was actually light-headed by the time he'd finished.

'That's it,' he concluded, taking a big gulp of beer.

There was a horribly long pause. Andrew grabbed another beer mat and started to tear and twist it.

Then Rupert spoke.

'Just to be clear,' he said, 'you need my house to host a dinner party in?'

'And for all of us to help you cook for said dinner party?' Alex said.

'And just generally be on hand to help out . . . and stuff,' Jim added.

'Because,' Alex said, 'redundancies are on the cards and you need to keep your boss on side.'

Andrew realised how mad it all sounded, laid bare like that. 'I honestly can't explain to you how insane my boss is,' he said. 'I thought he was just making us do these dinner parties because he wanted us all to be friends, but it seems like it's more to do with him trying to decide who he likes the most and who he can bring himself to let go. And I . . . well, I really can't afford to be that person.'

The others exchanged glances, and Andrew sensed they might want to confer.

'I'll get a round in,' he said. Despite worrying about what Jim, Rupert and Alex were deciding to do, he couldn't help but grin to himself as he made his way to the bar. *I'll get a round in* – so casual! As if it were the most natural thing in the world!

'I need to change the barrel for the pale ale,' the barman said.

'That's fine, take your time,' Andrew said, realising too late that this might have sounded sarcastic. The barman stared at him for a moment before heading to the cellar.

'You wanna be careful,' Leather Jacket man said. 'I've seen him kick seven shades out of a bloke for less. He's fine one minute, mental the next.'

But Andrew wasn't listening. There was a mirror just above the row of spirits, and in the reflection he could see the others deliberating at the table. He was suddenly very aware of the ebb and flow of noise from the fans around him, as if the groans and expletives and shouts of encouragement were the soundtrack to the conversation he was watching.

'Why you ignoring me, mate?' Leather Jacket man piped up.

Andrew acted oblivious and counted out his money for the round.

'Helllooooooo,' the man said, reaching over and waving a hand in front of Andrew's face.

Andrew pretended to be surprised. 'Sorry, I'm not really with it today,' he said, wishing he didn't sound quite so much like a flustered supply teacher.

'No excuse to totally ignore me like that,' the man said,

poking him in the shoulder. 'Basic fucking human politeness, that.'

Now Andrew was desperate for the barman to return. He looked at the mirror. The others still seemed to be in deep discussion.

'So what you reckon?' the man said, indicating the screen.

'Oh, I don't really know,' Andrew said.

'Have a guess, mate. Bit of fun.' The man poked him in the shoulder again, harder this time.

Andrew backed away as subtly as he could. 'A draw?' he said.

'Pah. Bollocks. You West Ham in disguise? Oi, everyone, this one's West Ham!'

'I'm not, I'm nobody,' Andrew said, his voice going falsetto. Luckily, no one paid them any attention, and to Andrew's relief the barman finally reappeared and finished pouring the drinks.

When he arrived back at the table it was to what felt like an awkward silence, and he realised he'd forgotten one vital point. 'I forgot to say, I'm not asking you to do this for free. We can work out, you know, a payment, whether that's cash or you taking your pick of my kit. I managed to damage my O4 Robinson recently, but there are my other locomotives, and scenery, so just let me kn—'

'Don't be silly,' Alex interrupted. 'Of course you don't need to pay us. We're just trying to work out logistics.'

'Oh. Good,' Andrew said. 'I mean, great, that you're on board and everything.'

'Yep, definitely,' Alex said. 'We're friends, after all,' she added, in a voice that made it sound like she was settling the issue. She widened her eyes at Rupert.

'Oh, yes, indeed,' he said, 'and you're welcome to have your soirée at mine. My partner's actually away with work next week, so the timing's decent. Though I'm a lousy cook, I'm afraid.'

Jim linked his fingers together and extended his arms, cracking his knuckles. 'You can leave the cooking to Jimbo,' he said.

'So. There we go. Sorted,' Alex said.

They talked a little more about the whens and wheres, but after a while conversation turned back to trains. For the second time that afternoon, Andrew had to concentrate on hiding the goofy grin that kept trying to wriggle on to his mouth.

The football was finished – it *was* a draw in the end – and most of the fans had already filed out, shaking their heads and grumbling. Leather Jacket man had other ideas, however, and Andrew groaned inwardly as he watched him meander over and pull up a chair at the table next to them.

'Model trains, eh,' he said, eyeing Jim's shirt before resting his feet on the back of Andrew's chair. 'Fuck me, do people still actually do that crap?'

Alex raised her eyebrows at Andrew. 'Do you know him?' she mouthed. Andrew shook his head.

'Sorry, mate,' Alex said, 'we're a bit busy. Mind giving us some space?'

The man made a big show of looking Alex up and down. 'Well, well, well, if I was ten years younger . . .'

'I'd still have utterly ignored you,' Alex said. 'Now go away, there's a good boy.' The man's leer turned into a scowl. He kicked the back of Andrew's chair. 'You wanna tell that bitch to shut her mouth.'

'All right that's enough,' Andrew said, getting to his feet. 'I'd like you to leave us alone now.' His voice was shaking.

'Yeah, and what happens if I don't?' the man said, standing and drawing himself up to his full height. This was the cue for Rupert, Jim and Alex to stand up, too.

'Jesus, look at you lot,' the man said. 'A wimpy prick, a slag, Fred Dibnah, and a shit Sherlock Holmes.'

'Well, that's not very nice now is it?' Rupert said, sounding remarkably calm. Andrew would have questioned whether such a sarcastic tone was the right approach, but then he noticed what Rupert already had. Namely, that unbeknownst to Leather Jacket man, the barman was walking towards him, rolling his head around his shoulders as if he were about to run the 100 metres. He waited for the man to take one more step towards Andrew before he advanced swiftly, grabbed him by his collar, hauled him towards the exit and shoved him through the door, aiming a kick at his backside for good measure. As he made his way back to the bar he even rubbed imaginary dirt off his hands, something Andrew had only ever seen in cartoons.

Andrew, Jim, Alex and Rupert all just stood there for a moment, nobody seeming to know what to say. It was Jim who broke the silence. 'Is anyone else quite impressed he knew who Fred Dibnah was?'

Chapter Thirty-Two

Peggy was worried about Andrew coming straight back into work. *You should take some time off, get your head together,* she texted him. *Remember how grim this job can be. It's not like you're a singer or an ice-cream taster.* But Andrew was struggling with being at home. It was just him and his own thoughts, and he hated his own thoughts – they were largely bastards. Since Peggy had come to his flat, he was also beginning to realise quite how ridiculous the state of the place was. He spent the evening after the sub-forum meet-up cleaning everywhere until he was sweaty and exhausted.

As he left the building the following morning he caught a tantalising glimpse of perfume woman's door closing behind her. He was so surprised to actually see evidence that she existed that he very nearly called out.

The evening of the dinner party coincided with Andrew and Peggy's first property inspection for two weeks – Malcolm Fletcher, sixty-three, massive heart attack on a lumpy futon. For once it only took them a few minutes before they had a breakthrough.

'Got something,' Peggy called from the bedroom. Andrew found her sitting cross-legged on the floor of a

walk-in wardrobe, surrounded by pairs of pristinely polished shoes, nearly identical suit jackets hanging above her,
as if she was a child playing hide-and-seek. She proffered
Andrew a posh-looking address book. He flicked through
but there was nothing written on any of the pages from
A to Z.

'Last page,' Peggy said, reaching up for Andrew to pull her
to her feet. Andrew flicked to the 'notes' section at the back of
the address book.

'Ah,' he said. *Mum & Dad* and *Kitty* were written at the top
of the page in small, neat handwriting, with corresponding
phone numbers next to them. He took out his mobile and
called *Mum & Dad*, but it was a young-sounding woman who
answered who'd never heard of anyone called Malcolm and
had no record of the previous occupants. Andrew had more
luck with Kitty.

'Oh goodness, that's . . . he's my brother . . . poor Malcolm.
God. What a horrible shock. I'm afraid we'd rather fallen out
of touch.' Andrew mouthed along with the last six words for
Peggy's benefit.

'So how are things?' Andrew said, as they left the flat, deciding to keep the question vague enough that Peggy could
respond however she wanted.

'Well, Steve came to collect the last of his things yesterday,
which was a relief. He told me he hadn't had a drink in ten
days, although he did smell like a distillery, so unless he got
very unfortunate and someone spilt an awful lot of gin on him
on his way over, I think he was probably lying.'

'I'm sorry,' Andrew said.

'Don't be. I should have done this a long time ago.

Sometimes you just need that extra little push. A reason to help you make the decision.'

Andrew could sense Peggy had turned her head to look at him, but he couldn't quite bring himself to meet her eye. He knew what she was getting at – and he didn't want to concede that she was right.

Just then, he received a text from Jim with the menu for that evening; the food sounding reassuringly posh – what, indeed, was kohlrabi? – and asking him to pick up booze. He shook the doubts from his mind. He had to focus on everything going perfectly tonight, no matter what Peggy thought.

'I just need to make a quick detour,' he said, taking them into Sainsburys and heading for the alcohol aisle.

'That person you spoke to today – Kitty, was it?' Peggy said.

'Mm-hmm,' Andrew said, distracted by reading the label on a Pinot Noir.

'She must've been the hundredth person you've heard saying "we'd rather fallen out of touch", right?'

'Probably,' Andrew said, reaching for a bottle of champagne and passing it to Peggy. 'Is this classy?'

'Erm, nope, not really. How about this?' She handed him a bottle with some silver netting around the neck. 'What I mean is,' she said, 'it's all very well doing what we do, but it all feels a bit "after the fact", you know? I mean, wouldn't it be nice if everyone did more to at least give people the option of finding company, to be able to connect with someone in similar positions, rather than this sort of inevitable isolation?'

'Yeah, good plan, good plan,' Andrew said. *Nibbles. Did they need nibbles? Or were nibbles passé, these days?* He hadn't felt that anxious up until now, but he was really starting to feel the nerves bubbling.

'I was wondering,' Peggy persisted, 'if there was, like, a charity that did that, or – I know this sounds a bit mad – whether we could actually look at setting one up ourselves. Or if not that, then finding a way to make sure at least *someone* other than one of us lot turns up to the funerals when we can't find a next of kin.'

'Sounds great,' Andrew said. *Why did paprika have such a monopoly on spice-flavoured crisps, anyway? Fuck, what if someone was allergic to paprika, or any of the food Jim was cooking? OK, just calm down. Deep breaths. Deep. Fucking. Breaths.*

Peggy sighed. 'And I'd also like to ride an elephant into the sea, naked, while singing the words to "Bohemian Rhapsody".'

'Mm-hmm, good plan. Hang on, what?'

Peggy laughed. 'Never mind.' She took the bottle out of his hands and replaced it with another.

'So, tonight . . .' she said.

Andrew winked. 'Got that all figured out,' he said.

Peggy stopped dead, waited for him to turn around and face her.

'Andrew, did you just wink at me?'

As soon as he got back to the office from the supermarket, Andrew walked straight over to Keith's desk.

Keith was eating a doughnut and chortling at something on his screen. But when he saw Andrew he dropped the doughnut and scowled.

'Hello, Keith,' Andrew said. 'Listen, I just wanted to apologise for what happened the other week. Things got really out of hand, but I am so, so sorry for pushing you like that. I really didn't mean to hurt you. I hope you can forgive me.'

He handed over the champagne Peggy had picked out, and offered Keith a handshake. Initially, Keith seemed taken aback by this charm offensive, but it didn't take him long to regain his composure. 'Costcutter own brand, is it?' he said, ignoring Andrew's hand and turning the bottle over to read the label, as Meredith hurried over to stand protectively at his side.

'Well, this doesn't exactly make up for it,' Meredith said.

Andrew held his hands up. 'I know. I agree. It's just a little gesture. I really hope that we can all get together tonight at mine, have a lovely time, and put everything behind us. What do you think? Sound like a plan?'

OK, OK, keep a lid on it, don't sound so desperate.

'Well,' Keith said, clearing his throat, 'I suppose that I was maybe being a bit out of order myself. And, well, I guess you weren't trying to deliberately knock me out.'

'No,' Andrew said.

'Obviously, given another day I'd have probably sparked you out for hitting me, if you'd not got that lucky shot in.'

'Definitely,' Meredith said, looking at Keith admiringly.

'But, for the sake of, you know, moving on, I'm happy to say bygones be bygones, and all that shit.'

This time Keith shook Andrew's proffered hand.

Just then, Cameron walked past, doubling back to see what was happening. He had dark rings under his eyes and looked horribly gaunt.

'Everything OK, chaps?' he said, slightly warily.

'Yes, absolutely,' Andrew said. 'We were just saying how much we're looking forward to dinner tonight.' Cameron searched Andrew's face for signs of sarcasm. Apparently satisfied of its absence, he smiled, put his palms together and said,

'Namaste', before backing away into the corridor and heading to his office with a new spring in his step.

'What a weirdo,' Keith said.

Meredith, realising that Keith's label was poking out of his shirt collar, reached over and tucked it in. Keith, Andrew noticed, looked a little embarrassed at this.

'So, Andrew,' Meredith said, 'do we finally get to meet Diane tonight?'

'No, afraid not,' Andrew said. 'She and the kids have tickets for a show. Crossed wires on the dates.' Even though he'd rehearsed this line several times, it still took all his concentration to make the words sound genuine. As he sat down at his desk, a fresh pile of paperwork in his in tray, a new lot of death to be tackled, he couldn't help but picture Peggy's reproachful look as he begged her to help him. *Only you can change things . . . It* has *to come from you.*

Chapter Thirty-Three

Andrew walked out of the office, laden down with booze, looked both ways before he crossed the road, and promptly dropped the bag of wine on the pavement, where it landed with a crunch. 'Unlucky mate,' called a white-van man, inevitably driving past at that moment. Andrew gritted his teeth and made his way to another Sainsbury's. What was it about going into a supermarket already carrying a bag of shopping that made it feel like you were returning to the scene of a botched murder?

He just about remembered which bottles of wine he'd previously bought and added another for good luck. The woman behind the till – Glenda, according to her name badge – scanned the bottles through and hummed approvingly. 'Big night tonight, m'love?'

'Something like that,' Andrew said.

Innocent though they'd been, Glenda's words opened the floodgates to Andrew's nerves. He could feel his heart starting to race as he hurried along, sweat beginning to pool under his armpits. He felt as though everyone he passed was giving him a meaningful look, as if there was something at stake for them, too, and every half-overheard snippet of conversation seemed to be charged with meaning. His anxiety wasn't helped by the fact that Rupert's directions to his house seemed needlessly complicated. He'd told them all to ignore Google Maps – 'It thinks I live in a shop called Quirky's Fried Chicken. I've sent several emails' – and go by his own instructions. When Andrew did eventually find the place, sweat was pouring off him and he was out of breath. He jabbed at the doorbell and heard a slightly pathetic and oddly discordant response, as if it were on the verge of breaking.

The door was answered by a cloud of smoke, followed by Jim.

'Come in, come in,' Jim said, coughing.

'Is everything OK?' Andrew said.

'Yes, yes, just a minor accident involving some kitchen paper and a naked flame. I'm cracking on with the starters nicely, though.'

Andrew was just about to ask whether there was a smoke alarm in the kitchen when it went off and he stood helpless, weighed down with the shopping, as Jim frantically flapped a tea towel in the air.

'Stick the wine on the island for now,' Jim said, indicating the pristine granite worktop, complete with wine rack and artfully arranged Sunday supplements. 'I need to work out what I'm pairing with what.'

'It's not an island,' came Rupert's voice from the doorway. 'According to our estate agent, anyway. It being connected to the wall on one side, it's actually a peninsula.' Rupert was wearing similarly smart attire to when they'd met in the pub, but with the addition of a purple dressing grown tied loosely at the waist. He noticed Andrew looking at it.

'It gets quite cold in my office but I can't bring myself to turn the heating up. Don't worry, I'm just an IT Consultant, not Hugh Heffner or anything.'

Jim pulled some ingredients from a bag and, having lined them up on the counter, began to scrutinise each item closely, as if he were judging a village fete competition.

'All good?' Andrew said.

'Yes. Absolutely,' Jim said, tapping a finger against his chin, his eyes narrowed. 'Absolutely.'

Andrew looked at Rupert, who raised an eyebrow at him.

Andrew was about to ask Jim if he was sure he knew what he was doing when the doorbell rang, the sound even more weary and out of tune than when he'd rung it himself. Rupert put his hands in his dressing gown pockets.

'Well, it's your house tonight, you better answer it.'

As Andrew left the room he heard Jim asking if Rupert owned a cleaver and felt his heart rate increase another notch.

Andrew opened the door to find Alex. Her hair was dyed a shocking white-blonde, although it wasn't altogether rid of the purple, which was clinging on in the odd streak.

'So I've got loads of decorations and stuff,' she said, thrusting one of the two bags she was holding into Andrew's hands. 'Gonna really set the mood and make it all massively, extremely fun! Look – party poppers!'

She skipped past Andrew and down the corridor.

'Um, Alex, when you say "massively extremely fun" – obviously I want it to be *fun* but I don't want anything too extreme or . . . or massive.'

'Sure, gotcha, don't worry about it,' Alex said. Andrew followed her into the dining room in time to see her enthusiastically scattering glitter on to the dining table.

'Shit,' she said suddenly, slapping a hand to her forehead.

'What's wrong?' Andrew said.

'Just realised I've left a whole bag of stuff at the shop. I'll have to go back.' When she took her hand away there was glitter in her hair.

Back in the kitchen, Jim was indiscriminately hacking at a butternut squash with a cleaver as if he were hastily dismembering a corpse.

'Everything all right?' Andrew said, hovering nervously.

'Yes, all good,' Jim said. 'Ah, that's what I was going to say: Rupert, do you have anything that we could use as a trolley to transfer the food to the dining room on?'

'A trolley? Can't I just carry it?' Andrew said.

'Yes, but I thought it might look quite fancy if you were to prepare the last bits and pieces of the main next to the table, Gueridon-style, you see?'

'Gueirdon?' Rupert said. 'Didn't he play left-back for Leeds?'

The doorbell warbled again. Andrew wondered about what else in the way of party decorations Alex might have returned with, but when he opened the door it was, with horror, that he found Cameron standing on the step.

'Hellooo!' Cameron said, stretching the word out as if he were calling into a tunnel to hear the echo. The smile disappeared from his face. 'Oh, crumbs, I'm not mega-early, am I?'

Andrew just about managed to regain his composure. 'No, no, of course not, come in, come in.'

'Something smells good,' Cameron said after he'd stepped inside. 'What's a-cookin'?'

'It's a surprise,' Andrew said.

'How intriguing,' Cameron said with a knowing grin. 'I've brought some vino rouge, but I'll probably stick to the Adam's

Ale this evening after my – how shall I put it – overindulgence last time.'

'Right, sure,' Andrew said, taking the bottle and guiding Cameron into the dining room.

'Clara and I had sort of clear-the-air talks when I got home that night, truth be told – unpacked everything and really drilled down. It always helps to talk things through, doesn't it?'

'Absolutely,' Andrew said, realising with some concern that Cameron looked even paler than earlier.

'Well, I like the glitter,' Cameron said. 'Very jazzy.'

'Thanks,' Andrew said. 'Take a seat and I'll be back with your water in a sec. Don't move!' he added, making a gun with thumb and forefinger. Cameron raised his hands meekly in surrender.

Andrew sprinted into the kitchen and closed the door. 'OK, we have a very big fucking problem,' he said. 'One of the guests – my boss, in fact – has arrived and is just sitting there in the dining room. So you need to keep as quiet as possible – and don't let anybody through this door who's not me.'

Rupert was swivelling back and forth on a tall chair, looking completely unfazed. 'Can't we pretend to be staff or something?' he said.

'No,' Andrew said. 'Too weird. They'll ask too many questions. Right, what am I doing? Ah yes, water.'

Andrew turned to the cupboards, looking for a glass.

'Hmm, slight issue,' he heard Rupert say.

'What? And where do you keep your glasses?'

'Top-left cupboard. And the issue is there's a woman just outside, staring at us.'

Andrew nearly dropped the glass as he spun around to look

at the window. Thankfully, it was Peggy. And as she caught his eye and smiled, one eyebrow slightly arched in amusement, Andrew was overwhelmed by how happy and relieved he was to see her – that this was always how he felt whenever she came into the same room as him.

He walked over and slid the French windows open.

'Hello,' Peggy said.

'Hello.'

Peggy widened her eyes, slightly.

'Shall I come in?'

'Oh, right, yes,' Andrew said, quickly stepping aside. 'Everyone, this is Peggy.'

'Hello . . . everyone,' Peggy said. 'I think your doorbell's kaput.'

Andrew started to garble an explanation but Peggy put up her hand to stop him. 'It's fine, it's fine, you don't have to explain. I'll go through, shall I?'

'Good idea,' Andrew said. 'Cameron's already here, actually.'

'Spectacular news,' Peggy said. 'Down here, is it?'

'Yep. Second – no, third – door on your right.'

Andrew watched her leave, then turned back to the counter top, leaning on it for support and taking some steadying breaths.

'She seems nice,' Jim said.

'She is,' Andrew sighed. 'So nice, in fact, that I *think* there's actually a very good chance I'm in love with her. Anyway, how's the butternut whatever coming along?'

When Jim didn't answer, Andrew looked around to see that Peggy had reappeared without him realising it. There was a moment when nobody did anything. Then Peggy stepped forward and reached past Andrew, avoiding his eye. 'Glasses in here are they? Lovely. Just getting Cameron's water.'

She filled the glass from the tap and left, whistling softly.

'Oh great,' Andrew said. He was about to follow this up with some less family-friendly words when there was a knock at the front door.

'I'll get it,' Andrew said, heading off down the hall. He opened the door to find a panicked-looking Alex bookended by a confused-looking Meredith and Keith, who were clutching bottles of white wine.

'Just picked up those things you asked for,' Alex said, robotically.

'Ah. Right. Yes,' Andrew said. 'Thank you very much.'

'No problem . . . neighbour.'

Andrew took the bag and ushered Meredith and Keith into the hallway, gesturing to Alex that she should go around to the French windows.

'Good luck!' she mouthed, giving him a double thumbs up.

'Can I use the loo?' Meredith said.

'Yes, of course,' Andrew said.

'Where is it?'

'Um, good question!'

Meredith and Keith didn't join in with Andrew's forced laughter. 'It's just through there,' he said, pointing vaguely down the hallway then scratching at the back of his head. Meredith went through a door and Andrew breathed a sigh of relief when he heard the bathroom fan come on. He showed Keith into the dining room and asked him to take Alex's bag in with him.

'Should be some fun bits and pieces in there. Party stuff, you know?'

He patted Keith on the back, wondering when it was he'd

become a back-patter, and dashed back into the kitchen.

Jim had his hands over his face, muttering through his fingers.

'What's happened?' Andrew said.

Jim took his hands away. 'I'm so sorry, mate. I don't know what's happened, but I think, in technical cooking terms, I've bollocksed it.'

Andrew grabbed a spoon and took a tentative slurp.

'Well?' Jim asked.

It was hard to adequately explain what Andrew's taste buds had just experienced. There was too much information to process.

'Well, it certainly has a tang to it,' Andrew said, not wanting to hurt Jim's feelings. His tongue was probing at his back teeth seemingly of its own accord. *Wine*, he thought. That was the answer. If they were drunk enough they wouldn't care about the food.

He uncorked two bottles of Merlot and headed to the dining room. As he came round the corner he was just thinking how ominously quiet it was – that it was the sort of silence that hung in the air following an argument – when he was met by a series of loud bangs. Startled, he felt both bottles slip from his hands. There was a moment where they all looked at the red wine spilling out on to the light-blue carpet, and the falling streamers from the party poppers nestling in the resulting puddle, before everyone burst into life, offering different advice.

'Blot it, you need to blot it. Definitely blot it,' Peggy said.

'But only with up and down movements not side to side – that just makes it worse, I saw it on QVC,' Meredith said.

'Salt, isn't it?' Keith said. 'Or vinegar? White wine?'

'I think that's a myth,' Andrew said, just in time to see Cameron leap forward with half a bottle of white wine which he deposited on to the carpet.

'He's going to kill me,' Andrew breathed.

'Who is?' Meredith said.

'No one. Everyone, please just . . . wait here.' Andrew dashed back down the corridor and into the kitchen. He explained the situation to Rupert, who listened to his rambling, took him by the shoulders and said, 'Don't worry. We'll sort it later. You need to give those people some food. And I rather think I've found a solution.' He pointed to the counter where five frosted Tupperware boxes sat. They were all labelled 'Cannelloni'.

Andrew turned to Jim, about to apologise.

'It's fine, do it,' Jim said. 'They might've found my dish a bit on the . . . challenging side anyway.'

A period of relative serenity followed as they cooked the cannelloni in batches in the microwave and cleaned up the mess. Andrew even felt relaxed enough that when Rupert wryly observed the absurdity of what they were doing, and Alex joked that she couldn't believe Andrew had talked them into it, he nearly dissolved into hysterics, having to shush the others good-naturedly. He periodically returned to the dining room to hand out breadsticks and olives, while Alex took on the role of continuity adviser on a film set, making sure he carried an oven glove over his shoulder and wiping a damp cloth on his forehead to give the impression of him slaving away at a hot stove.

When the food was finally ready to dish up, Andrew felt the most composed he had that evening. The cannelloni wasn't exactly awe-inspiring, and neither was the conversation, but it really didn't matter. Civility was exactly what was needed, and thus far everyone was on the same page. Keith, who had been quieter than usual, and less inclined to sarcastic asides, related a story, falteringly, about a voicemail he'd received the previous week. A woman had seen in the local paper the story of a pauper's funeral and had only then realised it was her brother, who she'd not spoken to in years. 'She told me they'd fallen out because of a table. They thought it was an antique passed down through ten generations. They'd fought over it when their parents died and eventually she came out on top. It was only after she'd seen that he'd died that she decided to get the thing valued, and it turns out it was a fake. A cheap knock-off. Barely worth a fiver.' Keith suddenly seemed uncomfortable in the reflective silence. 'Anyway,' he said. 'Just makes you think, I suppose. About what's important.'

'Hear hear,' Cameron said. They were quiet after this in the inevitable awkwardness created after someone's said something profound, nobody wanting to be judged for bursting the bubble by following up with something trivial in comparison.

It was Peggy who broke first. 'What's for pudding, then, Andrew?'

'You'll have to wait and see,' Andrew said, hoping that the others weren't beginning to get annoyed with all this vagueness when it came to the food. Given that the mains hadn't exactly been Heston Blumenthal-esque, there was no reason for them to be hoping for shaved ball bearings on a bed of whispers for pudding.

He headed back to the kitchen and took in the scene from the doorway. Jim, Rupert and Alex were all huddled around the counter where they were carefully adding strawberries and crushed pine nuts to bowls of something that looked genuinely delicious. Andrew stayed still for a moment, not wanting to announce his presence just yet. The three of them were hushed in their concentration, all working as a team, and Andrew felt the faint soreness of tears beginning to form behind his eyes. How kind these people were. How lucky he was to have them on his side. He cleared his throat and the others looked back, concern on their faces, smiles appearing when they saw it was him.

'Ta-dah!' Alex whispered, making up for having to lower her voice with some extravagant jazz hands.

Andrew brought the plates in to the dining room and received some admiring oohs and aahs.

'Blimey, Andrew,' Cameron said through a mouthful of ice cream. 'I didn't realise you were such a whiz in the kitchen. This one of Diane's recipes?'

'Ha, no,' Andrew said. 'She's . . .' He searched for the words. Something light. Something funny. Something normal. As he racked his brain, the memory came to him, crisp and clear, of Diane taking his hand and leading him away from the party, down the stairs, out into the snowy night. He shivered involuntarily.

'She's not here,' he said, eventually. He looked at Peggy. She was digging around with her spoon in her bowl, despite the fact there was nothing left, her expression betraying nothing.

Cameron was drumming his fingers on the table. He seemed to be waiting for them all to hurry up and finish, and Andrew noticed him check his watch surreptitiously. Peggy finally stopped pretending to eat and Cameron got to his feet.

'I actually have a few words I need to say to you all,' he said, ignoring the others exchanging nervous looks. 'It's been a challenging few months. And I think that sometimes the personal has got in the way of the professional – to some extent at least – for all of us at one point or another. On my part, I apologise for anything that I've done that's not sat well with you. I know, for example, that these evenings haven't been to everyone's taste, but I hope you understand it was simply an attempt to help bring us all together. Because, as you may have gathered by now, it was my feeling that the top brass were much less likely to try and break up a strong, cohesive team in the event of cuts. That, I suspect, was naive on my part. And you'll have to forgive me for that, and for not being as honest with you as I should have been, but I was just trying to do what I thought was best. However, it turns out that the statistics – and it feels strange to say this, I promise you – are on our side. The number of public health funerals rose even more sharply this year than any of us were expecting. And I'm incredibly proud of how you have dealt with that as a team. In truth, to be completely blunt, I have no idea what's going to happen next. A decision has been delayed on whether cuts are needed until at least the end of the year. Here's hoping that isn't the case. All I can promise is that, if it comes down to it, I will fight your cause to the absolute best of my abilities.' He looked at them all in turn. 'Well, thank you. That's it.'

They sat in silence as they digested the news. Clearly, Andrew thought, things were still up in the air, but it seemed they'd been given a few months' respite at least. After a while the atmosphere returned to something approaching how it had been before, though they were understandably more subdued. Before too long it was time for everyone to leave. Andrew fetched their coats. *You're nearly there*, he told himself. As he watched the others readying to go, he was expecting to feel a great wave of relief at having survived the evening, especially now that it seemed his job was safe, at least in the short-term. But instead, with each goodbye he said he felt not relief, but fear, and it seemed to spread up through his body like he was edging slowly into freezing water. He pictured Carl composing his next message – demanding to know where his money was, or maybe telling Andrew that he was about to bring his world crashing down instead. And then there was Diane. Ever since he'd told Peggy everything, the memories that he'd repressed for so many years had been begging for attention, and tonight they were coming to him thick and fast. It was as if a trapdoor had opened above his head and Polaroids were cascading down on him: A lingering look across a smoky room. Kissing as the snow fell. The fierce hug on the platform, the embers of that embrace warming him until he was home. The parched grass of Brockwell Park. The paleness of Diane's skin illuminated by lightning. Orange frames next to cracked slate.

Peggy leaned in to hug him goodbye.

'Well done,' she whispered.

'Thank you,' he said back, automatically. As she let him go, it felt as if all the breath had been taken from him, leaving him light-headed. Before he knew what he was doing, he'd reached out and taken Peggy's hand. He was aware of the others looking at him, but in that moment he just didn't care. In that moment, he realised that all he wanted was for Peggy to know how wonderful he thought she was. And even though the thought of saying those words was terrifying, the very fact he was considering doing it had to mean something. It had to mean he was ready to let go.

That was when Cameron opened the front door and a rush of cold air came down the hallway, eagerly searching out warmth to attack.

'Wait!' Andrew said. 'Sorry, everyone, but would you mind just waiting for a minute?'

After a moment, the others filed reluctantly back into the dining room like schoolchildren who'd been kept back after class.

'Um, Andrew . . . ?' Peggy said.

'I'll be right back,' he said. He could feel his heart starting to thump again as he skittered into the kitchen. Jim, Alex and Rupert all looked at the door, frozen in fear that they'd been discovered. When Andrew asked them to follow him they exchanged confused looks, but Andrew forced a reassuring smile.

'It's fine,' he said. 'This won't take long.' He ushered them down the corridor and into the dining room where he introduced the two equally perplexed groups.

'What's going on Andrew?' Cameron asked, once they'd arranged themselves in a semi-circle.

'OK,' Andrew said, 'I've just got a few things I need to tell you all.'

Chapter Thirty-Four

Andrew listened to the phone ringing out and gulped down half a glass of tepid Pinot Grigio.

'Andrew, what a pleasant surprise.'

'Hello, Carl.'

'Funny you should call – I've just checked my bank account and I still don't seem to have my money.'

'It's only just come into my account,' Andrew said, trying to keep his voice even.

'Well,' Carl said, 'you've got my bank details, so as long as you transfer it straight away we won't have a problem.'

'The thing is, though,' Andrew said, 'I don't think I *am* going to transfer it.'

'What?' Carl snapped.

'I said, I don't think I am going to transfer it.'

'You are,' Carl said. 'You *absolutely* are, because remember what happens if you don't. All I need to do is pick up the phone and you're fucked.'

'This is what I mean,' Andrew said. 'I appreciate that I may not exactly deserve this money – that perhaps my behaviour did cause some of Sally's unhappiness, and maybe more than that. But the thing is, we still loved each other, and I know that what I've been lying about might've been hard for her to deal with, but I think it would have been easier for her to understand that than the fact you're blackmailing me.'

'Oh, *please*. You really don't get this, do you? I am *owed* that money. I wouldn't be having to blackmail you in the first place if you'd just done what was right. So you listen to me. It's very simple, OK? If that money isn't in my account within twenty-four hours, then your life as you know it is over.'

The line went dead.

Andrew let out a deep breath and felt his shoulders slacken. He leaned forward in his chair and looked at his phone, which was on the dining-room table. There were seven others placed in a circle around it, all of which showed that they were still recording. There was silence in the room. Andrew looked down, his cheeks burning. There was a flash of movement, and for a second Andrew thought someone was about to attack him. But then, a split-second before she threw her arms around him, he realised it was Peggy.

Chapter Thirty-Five

Andrew waited until the taxi had wound its way out of the cul-de-sac, stopping to let a fox diligently trot across a zebra crossing, before he spoke.

'Am I going to get fired, then, do you think?'

Peggy handed him the bottle of wine she'd smuggled into the taxi and he took a surreptitious sip. 'Honestly? I've no idea,' she said.

The work lot had left in another cab. Jim and Alex had decided to stay a little longer at Rupert's, not being able to resist the opportunity to see his attic and its dedicated Rocky Mountains-themed train set-up.

'I couldn't quite tell how everyone reacted at first, when I told them everything.'

Andrew had only given the short version of events to the others, and describing his deception that way made it sound all the more stark. He'd braced himself for scathing interruptions from Keith and Meredith, but neither of them said anything. Nobody did, in fact, until he got to the part about Carl, at which point Alex launched into a furious rant about how they weren't going to let him get away with it. She demanded that Andrew call Carl right there and then, explaining to him impatiently exactly how he'd need to play the conversation to get

Carl to reveal unambiguously what he was doing. She cajoled the others into giving her their phones, lining them up on the table and setting them to record. Afterwards, they listened back on each one and decided that Meredith's recording was the clearest.

'Great, so you just need to send that to Andrew, now,' Alex told her.

'Oh right, yes. How do I . . .?'

Alex rolled her eyes and took the phone out of Meredith's hand. 'Andrew, what's your number? Right, there. Done.'

Afterwards, Rupert had suggested bringing out some 'decent' brandy to toast the plan working so well, but the suggestion was met with only a half-hearted response. Cameron, in particular, seemed eager to leave.

'Well. That was obviously . . . what a funny old evening,' he said to Andrew. 'I'm away for a few days, did I mention that? Training courses and whatnot. But we should talk properly when I'm back. About all this.'

'That could just mean he wants to talk to you and make sure you're OK,' Peggy said, as the cabbie casually veered across two lanes of traffic without indicating.

A thousand thoughts were clamouring for attention in Andrew's mind, and he didn't even notice that Peggy had slid across the seats until he felt her head on his shoulder.

'How are you feeling?' she asked.

Andrew puffed out his cheeks.

'Like someone's just removed a splinter I've had in my foot for a hundred years.'

Peggy rearranged her head on his shoulder.

'Good.'

The cabbie's radio crackled into life – the control room telling him he could go home after this job.

'God, it's no good, I'm falling asleep,' Peggy said. 'Wake me up when we're at Croydon, eh?'

'I think you're the first person in history ever to have said that,' Andrew said. Peggy elbowed him half-heartedly.

'So, earlier, when you came into the kitchen,' Andrew said, feeling unusually uninhibited given all that had just gone on. 'I couldn't tell if you'd heard what I'd just said. About, well, me maybe being in love with you.'

For a moment he thought Peggy was choosing how to respond, but then he heard the soft sounds of her breathing. She was asleep. He rested his head gently against hers. It felt entirely natural, in a way that made his heart soar and ache at the same time.

He'd be lucky if he'd get a minute's sleep that night, his brain was so wired. He had already sent the recording to Carl, but there had been no response. He wondered if there ever would be.

He found himself thinking of Sally – of the moment where she'd handed him that beautiful green model train engine, winking at him and ruffling his hair. Maybe, if they had their time again, they'd have been able to fix things. But he shook the thought from his head. He was tired of fantasising. He'd done enough of that for one lifetime. He drank the last dregs from the wine and raised the bottle in a silent toast to his sister.

Chapter Thirty-Six

Two mornings later Andrew woke with a start. He'd been dreaming about what had happened at Rupert's house – and for a horrible few seconds he couldn't be quite sure what was real and what his subconscious had decided to twist. But when he checked his phone the message Carl had sent him the morning after the dinner party was still there: 'Fuck you, Andrew. Enjoy your guilt money.'

Andrew knew that at some point he'd have to think about that guilt, and how he was going to deal with it – and what he was actually going to do with the money – but for now he was just hopelessly glad that everything with Carl was over.

He went to put the kettle on, feeling the unusual sensation of stiffness in his legs. The previous evening he'd been for what he'd ambitiously billed as a 'run', which in actual fact had been closer to a 'stagger' around the block. It had been agony at the time, but there was a moment when he'd got back – post-shower, post a meal made with something green in it – where he felt a rush of endorphins (previously something he'd imagined were mythical, like unicorns or something) so strong that he finally understood why people put themselves through this. There was life in the old dog yet, it seemed.

He fried some bacon and looked directly into the tile-camera.

'So you may have noticed I have accidentally burnt this rasher, but given I'm about to put a Lake Windermere's-worth of brown sauce on it, it doesn't really matter.'

He stretched his arms up behind his head and yawned. The whole weekend lay in front of him and, unusually, he had plans that didn't involve Ella Fitzgerald and browsing the forum.

It was going to be a long journey, but he was well prepared. He had a book and his iPod and had dusted off his old camera so he could take some snaps if the mood took him. When it came to his packed lunch he had gone entirely rogue, making sandwiches with white bread and experimenting with new fillings, one of which, in a move so daring he was barely able to contain himself, was crisps.

To his dismay, he got on to his train at Paddington with time to spare, only to find his reservation meant he was slap bang in the middle of a stag do, already getting stuck into the beers. It was three hours to Swansea, and that allowed for a lot more drinking time. They had personalised T-shirts commemorating 'Damo's Stag', and already seemed quite tipsy. But, against all the odds, they actually turned out to be pleasant company, offering snacks to everyone else in the carriage, helping people put their suitcases on the overhead shelves with faux-competitiveness, before breaking out crosswords and quizzes to pass the time. Andrew found himself so caught up in the general air of bonhomie that he ended up scoffing his packed lunch before midday, like a naughty schoolboy on a trip. The onward journey from Swansea was a more sombre affair, although a lady with purple hair knitting a purple bobble hat offered him a purple boiled sweet from a tin, like something out of an advert from a bygone era.

*

The station was so small it barely had a platform – one of those stops where you practically walk straight out on to the street as soon as you alight. Checking the route on his phone, Andrew took a turning on to a narrow lane where the houses on opposite sides seemed to lean towards each other. For the first time he began to truly feel the nerves that had been bubbling away under the surface ever since he'd left London.

The church was unassuming, its spire small enough to be concealed from view by two modest yews. The place had a wildness about it – the gate at its entrance covered with moss, the grass in the graveyard overgrown – but the early autumn air felt still.

He'd prepared himself for a lengthy search, a process of elimination. He half remembered holding the phone to his ear and a voice telling him that this was where the funeral was to be held, then the confusion and hurt following his mute response. The only detail he could remember was that the church was near the rugby ground where Gavin had claimed to have seen the flying saucer.

In the end, he'd barely walked past half a dozen headstones when he saw the name he was looking for.

Diane Maude Bevan.

He thrust his hands into his pockets, rocking on the balls of his feet, building up the courage to approach. Eventually he did, slowly, as if moving to the edge of a cliff. He hadn't brought anything with him – flowers, or anything like that. That just didn't feel right, somehow. He was in touching distance now. He dropped down to his knees and gently ran his hand across Diane's name, tracing each letter's contour. 'Well,' he said. 'I'd forgotten how much you hated your middle name.

It took me a whole Sunday to get it out of you, remember?'

He took a deep breath, hearing the tremor as he let it out. He leaned forward until his forehead was resting gently against the headstone.

'I know this doesn't count for much, now, but I am so sorry for never coming to see you. And for being so scared. You probably worked this out much sooner than I did, but, you know, I was never really able to accept that you were gone. After Dad, and Mum . . . and then Sally leaving . . . I couldn't let you go, too. And then somehow I got the chance to build this place, this world, where you were still here, and I couldn't resist. It wasn't supposed to be for long, but it got out of control so quickly. Before I knew it I was even inventing the *arguments* we'd have. Sometimes it was just silly stuff – you despairing about me and my silly model trains, mostly – but other times it was more serious: disagreements about how we were bringing up the kids, worrying that we'd not lived our lives to the full and hadn't seen enough of the world. That's the tip of the iceberg, really; I thought about everything. Because it wasn't just one life with you I imagined, it was a million different ones, with every possible fork in the road. Of course, every now and then I'd feel you pulling away from me, and I knew that was your way of telling me to let go, but that just made me cling on more. And, the thing is, it was only after the game was finally up that I was actually able to pull my stupid, self-absorbed head out of my arse and think about what you would have actually said if you knew, for one single second, what I was doing. I'm just sorry I didn't think of that sooner. I just hope you can forgive me, even though I don't deserve it.'

Andrew was aware that someone else had appeared to tend

to a grave a few feet away. He lowered his voice to a whisper.

'I wrote you a letter, once, very soon after we got together, but I was too scared to give it to you because I thought you might run a mile. It started life as a poem, too, so you were really let off the hook. It was full of hopelessly romantic sentiment that you would have, quite rightly, laughed your head off at, but I think one bit remains true. I wrote that I knew the moment we first held each other that something in me had changed forever. Up to that point I'd never realised that life, just sometimes, can be wonderfully, beautifully simple. I only wish I'd remembered that after you'd gone.'

He had to stop to wipe his eyes with his coat sleeve, smoothing his hand along the stone again. He stayed there, quiet now, feeling a pure and strangely joyful pain wash over him, knowing that, as much as it hurt, it was something he had to accept, a winter before the spring, letting its ice freeze and fracture his heart before it could heal.

The next train to Swansea was pulling into the station as Andrew got there, but he felt reluctant to leave so soon. He decided to stop in a pub nearby instead. As he approached the door, old habits kicked in and he hesitated just outside. But he thought of Diane watching on, no doubt mouthing swear words in his direction, and he pressed on. And though the regulars looked at him somewhat curiously, and the barman poured him a pint and threw a packet of salt and vinegar on the bar without much enthusiasm, their reaction to him was benign rather than unwelcoming.

He sat in the corner with his beer and his book, and felt, for the first time in a very long while, content.

Chapter Thirty-Seven

Andrew turned the pair of tights inside out and shook out a bundle of notes on to the bed.

'Bingo,' Peggy said. 'Enough to cover the funeral, do you reckon?'

'Should be,' Andrew said, leafing through the money.

'Well, that's something. Poor old . . .'

'Josephine.'

'Josephine. God, I'm the worst. It's such a lovely name, too. Sounds like the sort of woman who'd always bring loads of food to a harvest festival.'

'Maybe she did. Did she talk about church in the diary?'

'Only when she was slagging off *Songs of Praise*.'

Josephine Murray had penned scores of diary entries, as she'd noted, 'in an old Smith's notebook, using a chopping board resting on my lap as a makeshift desk, much like I imagine Samuel Pepys did'.

The diary's subject matter was largely mundane – short, spiky critiques of television programmes or comments on the neighbours. Often, she combined the two: 'Watched a forty-five minute advert for Findus Crispy Pancakes interrupted sporadically by a documentary about aqueducts. Could barely hear it over the noise of Next-Door-Left rowing. I really wish they'd keep a lid on it.'

Occasionally though, she'd write something more reflective:

'Got in a bit of a tizz this evening. Put some food out for the birds and felt a bit dizzy. Thought about calling the quack but didn't want to bother anyone. Silly, I know, but I just feel so embarrassed about taking up someone's time when I know I'm probably fine. Next-Door-Right were out having a barbecue. Smelled delicious. Had the strongest urge – for the first time in goodness knows how long – to take a bottle of wine round there, something dry and crisp, and get a bit tiddly. Had a look in the fridge but there wasn't anything there. In the end I decided that dizziness and tiddliness wouldn't have been a good mix anyway. That wasn't the tizz, by the way, that came as I was trying to drop off to sleep when I suddenly remembered it was my birthday. And that's why I'm writing this now in the hope it helps me to remember next year, if I haven't kicked the bucket by then, of course.'

Peggy put the diary in her bag. 'I'll have a proper look through this back at the office.'

'Right you are,' Andrew said. He looked at his watch. 'Sandwich?'

'Sandwich,' Peggy confirmed.

They stopped off at a café near the office. 'How about here?' Andrew said. 'I must have walked past this place a thousand times and I've never been in.'

It was warm enough to sit outside. They munched their sandwiches as a group of schoolchildren in hi-vis bibs were led along by a young teacher. She was just about managing to keep track of them all, while taking the time to tell Daisy that Lucas might not appreciate being pinched like that.

'Give it ten years,' Peggy said. 'I'll bet Lucas will be dying to get pinched like that.'

'Was that your flirting technique back in the day?'

'Something like that. Bit of pinching, few vodka shots, can't go wrong.'

'Classic.'

A man marched by them in an electric blue suit, shouting incomprehensible business jargon down the phone, like a peacock who'd managed to learn English by reading Alan Sugar's autobiography. He strode out into the road, barely flinching as a bike courier flashed inches past and called him a knobhead.

Andrew felt something vibrating against his foot.

'I think your phone's ringing,' he said, passing Peggy's bag over to her.

She pulled out her phone, looked at the screen for a second, then dropped the phone back in the bag where it continued to vibrate.

'I'm going to guess that was Steve again,' Andrew said.

'Mm-hmm. At least he's down to two calls a day now. I'm hoping he'll get the message soon enough.'

'How are the girls doing with it all?'

'Oh, you know, about as well as you'd expect. We've got a long old road ahead of us. But it's still absolutely for the best. By the way, Suze asked about you the other day.'

'Really? What did she say?' Andrew said.

'She asked me whether we'd be seeing "that fun Andrew man" again.'

'Ah, I wonder which Andrew she was thinking of there, then?' Andrew said, mock-disappointed, but unable to entirely conceal how proud he really was, judging from the smile on Peggy's face.

Peggy reached into her bag again and brought out Josephine's diary, flicking through the pages.

'She seems like such a lively old lass, this one.'

'She does,' Andrew said. 'Any mention of a family?'

'Not that I can see. There's lots more about the neighbours, though never by name, so I'm not sure how friendly they all were. I suppose if one lot of them was always rowing then maybe she didn't feel like talking to them. The others, though, the barbecuing lot – I might go back later and have a chat with them if I can't find anything here. Part of me's just intrigued as to whether she *did* ever decide to go round there for a drink or anything.'

Andrew shielded his face from the sun so he could look Peggy in the eye.

'I know, I know,' she said, holding her hands up defensively. 'I'm not getting too invested, honestly. It's just . . . this is yet another person who spent their final days completely alone, right, despite the fact she was clearly a nice, normal person. And I bet if we do find a next of kin it'll be another classic case of "Oh, dear, that's a shame, we hadn't spoken in a while, we sort of lost contact blah blah blah". It just seems like such a scandal that this happens. I mean, are we all really content to say to these people "Sorry, tough luck, we aren't even going to bother trying to help you poor lonely bastards", without at least offering them the chance to have the odd chat and a cup of tea with someone, or something?'

Andrew thought about what he might have done if, somewhere down the line, someone had offered him companionship. All he could really picture, unhelpfully, was a Jehovah's Witness standing at his door. But that figured, because, truth be told, he'd have rejected help outright. He said as much to Peggy.

'But it doesn't have to be like that,' she said. 'I wanted to talk to you about this, actually. I mean, I haven't exactly got it all mapped out, but . . .'

She began to root around in her bag, producing empty water bottles, an old apple core, a half-empty bag of Percy Pigs and fistfuls of receipts. Andrew watched, mesmerised, as she swore and continued to pull things out like an angry magician. Eventually she found what she'd been looking for.

'So it's just a rough outline,' she said, smoothing out a piece of paper. 'Really rough, actually, but it's a summary of what a campaign to help people could look like. The gist of it is that people can apply to have the option of a phone call or a visit from volunteers. And the thing is, it doesn't matter if you're a little old lady or a thirty-something high-flyer. It just gives you the option of having someone you can connect with.'

Andrew studied the paper. He was aware that Peggy was watching him anxiously.

'What?' she said. 'Is it mental?'

'No. It absolutely isn't. I love it. I just wish you'd told me about it sooner.'

Peggy narrowed her eyes.

'What?' Andrew said.

'Oh, nothing,' Peggy said. 'I was just thinking about a moment in Sainsbury's about a week ago when I nearly punched you in your stupid face.'

'Right,' Andrew said, deciding not to probe that one any further.

'There's something else I want to show you, too,' Peggy said, reaching into her Tardis bag again and pulling out her phone. 'Obviously, it's a bit too late to help poor old Josephine find company, bless her, but what do you reckon about this?' She passed her phone over to Andrew who wiped his fingers on a paper napkin before he took it. It was a post Peggy had drafted in Facebook.

'You know what?' Andrew said, once he'd finished reading it.

'What?'

'You're actually brilliant.'

Andrew wouldn't have thought Peggy capable of blushing, but her cheeks were definitely tinged pink.

'So shall I post it?' she said.

'Abso-bloody-lutely,' Andrew said. He handed her phone back and watched her upload the post just as his own phone started to ring.

'Yes . . . no, I understand, thanks, but like I said, that's out of my price range, I'm afraid. OK, thank you, bye.'

'"Out of my price range I'm afraid"', Peggy said. 'Are you buying a yacht or something?'

'That's next on the list, obviously. For now, I'm trying to move house.'

'Wow. Really?'

'I think it's for the best. Time to move on.'

'So now you're experiencing the joy of speaking to all those lovely lettings agents.'

'Yep. I've never had so many people lie to me in such a short space of time.'

'You have much to learn, my friend.'

Andrew rubbed his eyes and yawned. 'All I want is to live

in a converted train station on top of a mountain with sea views and Wi-Fi and easy access to central London, is that so much to ask?'

'Have another Hobnob,' Peggy said, patting him on the top of his head.

They were nearly back at the office – despite coming close to taking an executive decision to dedicate the afternoon to Scrabble in the pub.

Andrew had been building up the courage, again, to ask whether Peggy had overheard him in Rupert's kitchen, and this felt like the most opportune moment he'd had in the last few days.

'So, the other night . . .'

But he didn't get a chance to finish, because Peggy suddenly grabbed his arm. 'Look,' she muttered.

Cameron had arrived at the office ahead of them and was skipping nimbly up the stairs. He stopped to search for his building pass, only finding it once Andrew and Peggy had caught up with him.

'Hi, Cameron,' Peggy said. 'We weren't expecting you back till next week.'

Cameron busied himself with his phone as he spoke.

'Had to come back early,' he said. 'Last day of the course got cancelled. Salmonella, it would seem. I'm the only one who managed to escape it.'

The three of them walked down the corridor in silence. When they got to their office, Cameron held the door open so Peggy could go through, then turned to Andrew and said, 'Could we have a quick word in my office when you have a moment?'

'Sure,' Andrew said. 'Can I ask wha—'

'See you in a minute, then,' Cameron said, walking away before Andrew could say anything else. He didn't know exactly what was coming, but he could make a reasonable guess that he wasn't going to be awarded a knighthood.

A few weeks ago he would have been panic-stricken. But not any more. He was ready for this. He dumped his stuff by his desk and made his way straight to Cameron's office.

'Andrew!' Peggy hissed from across the room, her eyes wide with concern.

He smiled at her.

'Don't worry,' he said. 'Everything's going to be fine.'

Chapter Thirty-Eight

Another day, another funeral.

Today was the day Josephine Murray said goodbye to the world, and Andrew was the only one returning her farewell. He shifted his position on the creaky pew and exchanged smiles with the vicar. When Andrew had greeted him earlier that morning it had taken him a moment to realise he was actually the floppy-haired youngster who he'd watched conduct his very first funeral service. Though that had only been earlier that year, he already looked to have aged considerably. It wasn't just that his hair was neater, in a more conservative side-parting, it was also in the way that he carried himself – it was more assured. Andrew felt oddly paternal, seeing how much he seemed to have matured. They had spoken briefly on the phone beforehand and Andrew, after discussing it with Peggy, had decided to relate parts of Josephine's diary so that the vicar was able to add a bit more colour to the service, and make it more personal.

Andrew swivelled to look to the back of the church. Where, then, was Peggy?

The vicar approached. 'I'll give it another minute or so, but then I'll really need to start, I'm afraid,' he said.

'Of course, I understand,' Andrew said.

'How many were you expecting?'

That was the problem. Andrew didn't have a clue. It all depended on how Peggy had got on.

'Don't worry too much,' he said. 'I don't want to cause a hold-up.'

But just then the church door swung open, and there was Peggy. She looked flustered at first, but then relief flooded her face when she saw that the service hadn't started yet. She held the door for someone behind her – there was at least one other person, then – and made her way up the aisle. Andrew watched as first one, then two, then three people came in after her. There was a short gap, and then, to Andrew's amazement, a steady stream of people filed in until he lost count at over thirty.

Peggy arrived next to him. 'So sorry we're late,' she whispered. 'We had a decent response on the Facebook page but then we managed to round up a few people from Bob's Café across the road last minute.' She nodded at a man wearing a blue-and-white checked apron. 'Including Bob!'

The vicar waited until everyone was seated before making his way to his lectern. After the initial formalities he decided – spontaneously, it looked to Andrew – to leave his lectern, and his notes with it, so that he could be nearer to the congregation.

'As it happens, I have a little something in common with Josephine,' he said. 'My grandmother was her namesake – she was always Granny Jo to me – and they both kept diaries. Now, my granny's, which we were only allowed to read once she'd passed away, was, of course, of great intrigue to us. It was only when we were finally able to read it that we realised she'd written most of the entries after a couple of strong gin

and tonics, and so they were quite hard to read in places.'
There was a warm ripple of laughter from the congregation
and Andrew felt Peggy take his hand.

'From what I gather from the good people who've looked
after Josephine's affairs, her own diary shows her to be witty,
bright and full of life. And whilst she was someone not shy of
a strong opinion, especially when it came to television sched-
ulers or weathermen, her warmth and strength of character
are what leap off the pages.'

Peggy squeezed Andrew's hand and he squeezed back.

'Josephine may not have had family or friends around her
when she died,' the vicar continued, 'and today might well
have felt like a lonely occasion. So what a wonderful thing it is
to look out over so many of you who have given up your time
to be here today. None of us can be sure at the start of our
lives just how they will end, or what our journey there will be
like, but if we were to know, for sure, that our final moments
would be in the company of good souls such as yourselves, we
would surely be comforted. So thank you. May I invite you
now to stand and join me in a moment of contemplation.'

The service over, the vicar waited by the church door and took
a moment to thank everyone individually for coming. Andrew
even overheard him telling Bob that of course he'd love to pop
over later 'for a cuppa', but saying he'd probably pass on the
muffins. 'But they're massive!' Bob remonstrated. 'You won't
get a bigger one for miles around, honestly.'

'I think he's made about twenty new customers today,'
Peggy said. 'Good on him, the cheeky bugger.'

They strolled towards a bench and Andrew brushed away
some fallen leaves so they could sit down.

'So, are you actually going to tell me how it went with Cameron?' Peggy said.

Andrew leaned back and looked up at the sky, watching a distant plane leaving the faintest of vapour trails. It felt good, stretching his neck like this. He should do it more.

'Andrew?'

What was there to say?

The conversation had been meandering and inconclusive. Cameron was at pains to say how much he was on Andrew's side, how if it was up to him he'd let the revelations from the dinner party go. But then he started to pepper what he was saying with phrases like 'duty bound' and 'following protocol'.

'You understand I have to say something?' he concluded. 'Because, whatever the reasons for doing what you . . . did, it's all still rather troubling.'

'I know,' Andrew said. 'Believe me.'

'I mean, bloody hell, Andrew, if you were in my position, what would you do?'

Andrew got to his feet. 'Cameron, listen, I think you should do what your instincts tell you, and if that means reporting me to someone up the chain, or if it gives you a neat solution to the cutbacks issue were it to come up again, then I understand. I won't hold it against you.'

'But—'

'Honestly. To have everything out in the open, to have been able to move on, that's more important to me than keeping this job. If it helps you out with a tricky decision then I'm genuinely fine with that.'

God, what a relief it was to be able to speak as freely as this. To open himself up to new possibilities. He thought of Peggy's campaign. The more they discussed it, the more energised he felt.

'Besides,' he said to Cameron, 'it's about time I finally figured out what I'm going to do with my life.'

Peggy brought him back to the present as she took his hand. 'It's OK, we don't have to talk about it now.'

Andrew shook his head. 'No, we can. So, it looks like I'm going to be let go.'

'Oh my God,' Peggy said, clapping her hands to her mouth, eyes wide.

'*But*,' Andrew said, 'Cameron has promised to try and find me a position in another department.'

'And you'll go for it, you think?'

'Yes,' Andrew said.

'Right, well that's . . . good,' Peggy said, a tinge of disappointment in her voice.

'Though only temporarily,' Andrew said.

'Really?' Peggy said quickly, eyes searching Andrew's. He nodded.

'I've been doing a bit of research. About charity funding. I have the money Sally left me and I've not had any better ideas about how to spend it, and I know she'd be really happy with me using it for something like this.'

Peggy was looking at him with such a strong mixture of confusion and excitement that Andrew had to stop himself from laughing.

'I'm talking about your campaign idea, just in case you weren't quite there yet,' he said. 'And I was thinking, maybe you could, you know, help me. See if we can make a proper go of it.'

'This is . . . Andrew, I don't quite . . .'

'I'm not saying it's definitely possible,' Andrew said. 'We might fall at the first hurdle. But we can give it our best shot.'

Peggy was nodding at him very firmly. 'We can, we absolutely can,' she said. 'Let's talk about it more over dinner tonight – if the offer's still on, that is?'

'It very much is,' Andrew said. He'd found a new flat that morning – a chance spot on one of the four bewildering Apps he'd downloaded – and even though it meant he'd have to move the following week he'd made the decision to do it on the spot. Part of him did feel a little sad about moving, but at least with Peggy coming round that evening he'd be able to see the old place off in style.

'Quick question,' he said. 'You do like beans on toast, right?'

'My favourite, obviously,' Peggy said, looking at him with slightly narrowed eyes, not sure if he was joking or not. 'Although right now, I don't know about you, but I could murder a massive muffin.'

'Why not?' Andrew said.

They held each other's gaze for a moment. He pictured her and the girls rushing down the platform towards him at King's Cross, and his heart flickered once more with a sense of possibility. He had given up on how he was going to broach the subject of whether Peggy *had* overheard him talking about his feelings for her in Rupert's kitchen. All that mattered was that she was there now, at his side, knowing everything there was to know about him. That, he realised, was more than enough.

Acknowledgements

To my wonderful agent Laura Williams. Words can't express how grateful I am for everything you've done for me.

To Clare Hey at Orion and Tara Singh Carlson at Putnam. I am so lucky to be working with two such brilliant editors and publishers. Thanks for everything.

Thank you to everyone at Orion, especially Harriet Bourton, Virginia Woolstencroft, Katie Moss, Oliva Barber, Katie Espiner, Sarah Benton, Jen Wilson, Lynsey Sutherland, Anna Bowen, Tom Noble, and Fran Pathak. And to all at Putnam, especially Helen Richard, Alexis Welby, and Sandra Chiu.

To the awesome Alexandra Cliff – I shall remember that phonecall for a very long time. Also, to the brilliant Marilia Savvides, Rebecca Wearmouth, Laura Otal, Jonathan Sissons and everyone else at PFD.

To Kate Rizzo and all at Greene & Heaton.

Special thanks to Ben Willis, for reading this at an early stage and giving me invaluable advice in a Camberwell Wetherspoons, and for being there for me from the beginning. The same goes for Holly Harris (official). Thank you for everything, especially stopping me from going insane in Wahaca when I found out I was getting published. I am very lucky to call you both my friends.

To Emily 'half pint' Griffin and Lucy Dauman. You're the absolute best.

Thank you to Sarah Emsley and Jonathan Taylor – I couldn't wish for two more kind, wise and good-natured people as mentors and friends.

To the rest of the gang at Headline for being wonderful to work with, and whose celebratory messages to me the moment the news came out gave me so much joy. Special thanks to Imogen Taylor, Sherise Hobbs, Auriol Bishop, and Frances Doyle.

To the following, for their encouragement, support, advice and friendship: Elizabeth Masters, Beau Merchant, Emily Kitchin, Sophie Wilson, Ella Bowman, Frankie Gray, Chrissy Heleine, Maddy Price, Richard Glynn, Charlotte Mendelson, Gill Hornby, Robert Harris.

To Katy and Libby – wonderful, supportive sisters. Love you guys. And you too, JJ Moore – top 'BiL'.

Finally, to my mum, Alison, and dad, Jeremy, to whom this book is dedicated – this is all down to you.

This book must be returned on or before the date last stamped below, unless it is previously recalled by the Library.

An overdue charge is applied on late return of books
(See Library Regulations)

D0492683

g/dtp/datelabelrs100

About Island Press

Island Press, a nonprofit organization, publishes, markets, and distributes the most advanced thinking on the conservation of our natural resources—books about soil, land, water, forests, wildlife, and hazardous and toxic wastes. These books are practical tools used by public officials, business and industry leaders, natural resource managers, and concerned citizens working to solve both local and global resource problems.

Founded in 1978, Island Press reorganized in 1984 to meet the increasing demand for substantive books on all resource-related issues. Island Press publishes and distributes under its own imprint and offers these services to other nonprofit organizations.

Support for Island Press is provided by the Geraldine R. Dodge Foundation, The Energy Foundation, The Charles Engelhard Foundation, The Ford Foundation, Glen Eagles Foundation, The George Gund Foundation, William and Flora Hewlett Foundation, The John D. and Catherine T. MacArthur Foundation, The Andrew W. Mellon Foundation, The Joyce Mertz-Gilmore Foundation, The New-Land Foundation, The J. N. Pew, Jr., Charitable Trust, Alida Rockefeller, The Rockefeller Brothers Fund, The Rockefeller Foundation, The Tides Foundation, and individual donors.

ENVIRONMENTAL STRATEGIES FOR INDUSTRY

UNIVERSITY LIBRARY
NEWCASTLE UPON TYNE

WITHDRAWN

ENVIRONMENTAL STRATEGIES FOR INDUSTRY

International Perspectives on Research Needs and Policy Implications

Edited by KURT FISCHER
and JOHAN SCHOT

The Greening of Industry Network

NEWCASTLE UNIVERSITY LIBRARY
----
214 06468 3

658·4083 ENV
LONG

ISLAND PRESS

Washington, D.C. ❑ Covelo, California

Copyright © 1993 Island Press

All rights reserved. No part of this book may be reproduced in any form or by any means without permission in writing from the publisher: Island Press, Suite 300, 1718 Connecticut Avenue, NW, Washington, D.C. 20009.

Library of Congress Cataloging-in-Publication Data

Environmental strategies for industry : international perspectives on research needs and policy implications / edited by Kurt Fischer and Johan Schot.
    p. cm.
   Includes bibliographical references and index.
   ISBN 1-55963-193-7. — ISBN 1-55963-194-5 (paper)
   1. Industry—Environmental aspects—Management. 2. Factory and trade waste—Management. I. Fischer, Kurt, 1942– .
II. Schot, Johan.
HD69.P6E595 1993
658.4'08—dc20   92-33544
                                       CIP

Printed on recycled, acid-free paper

Manufactured in the United States of America

10 9 8 7 6 5 4 3 2 1

Contents

Preface

This book is a product of the Greening of Industry program, a U.S.-European partnership dedicated to studying the behavior of industrial firms around environmental issues. The program has established an international network of researchers, policy makers, and business leaders who meet in regular conferences to discuss their studies and experiences, publish results, and set research and policy agendas. Led by two multidisciplinary research organizations, the Center for Environmental Management at Tufts University and the Centre for Studies of Science, Technology, and Society at the University of Twente, the program seeks to improve existing policies and to find and exploit new ways of changing firm behavior.

The connections between the Center for Environmental Management and the Netherlands began in 1986 during a Tufts University study, conducted for the U.S. Environmental Protection Agency, of government and industry waste reduction initiatives in six countries. That study included waste reduction practices in the Netherlands, and the contacts established then, with individuals such as Frank van den Akker and Sybren de Hoo, advisors to the current program, opened up regular communications between Tufts and several Dutch researchers. We began working together as this volume's coeditors in 1989. Both of us were studying industry responses to environmental concerns but had difficulty finding other researchers working in the same area. Many interesting research questions were simply not being asked. Most government policies were based on a kind of input-output model that focused on what kinds of policy instruments (input) were needed to force industry to reduce emissions and pollution (output). Little attention was given to the internal processes of industrial firms. To reach out to other researchers and stimulate research, we devised plans for an international network, conference series, and publications series under the name of the Greening of Industry. The goal of this program is the promotion of empirical research, based in theory, that opens the black box that surrounds and conceals the inner workings of the firm to understand its environmental behavior.

The first convening of the network took place in Noordwijk aan Zee, the Netherlands, on November 17–19, 1991, and this volume grew out of the presentations, discussions, and agendas developed there. The next Greening of Industry conference will take place in Boston in 1993. An international advisory board with European and U.S. branches steers the project, providing representation from a number of countries and from perspectives in business, government, academia, and the public interest.

We wish to express our thanks to the program advisors. In Europe, the advisory group consists of Frank van den Akker, William Cannell, Olav-Jan van Gerwen, Sybren de Hoo, and Ferd Schellerman; and in the United States, Matthew Arnold, Joan Bavaria, Patricia S. Dillon, Thomas N. Gladwin, Christopher McGill, Abby Pirnie, and Henry Schilling.

We also express our gratitude to the organizations in Europe and the United States that have provided financial support for this program, making the Greening of Industry network a reality and this book possible: Commission of the European Communities, Directorate-General for Science, Research and Development, Strategic Analysis in Science and Technology; Corporate Affiliates Program of the Center for Environmental Management at Tufts University; International Association of Clean Technologies; Management Institute for Environment and Business; Ministry of Economic Affairs of the Netherlands; Ministry of Housing, Physical Planning, and Environment of the Netherlands; Netherlands Advisory Council for Research on Nature and Environment; Netherlands Organization for Technology Assessment; and the U.S. Environmental Protection Agency, Office of Research and Development.

Although this book is a product of the Greening of Industry program, the editors and chapter authors are completely responsible for its content, and no official endorsement by the sponsoring organizations should be inferred. We wish to thank especially all of the chapter authors for their hard work, patience, and cooperation with our editing direction and all of the network members who participated in the first convening and contributed to development of the research and policy agendas.

We wish to give special thanks to the many people who worked with us to bring this book to completion: to our colleagues Yvonne Ploum, Anne Chabot, and Colleen Singer for network planning and management; to Jodi Sugerman for tracking the chapters and coordinating the efforts of the authors and editors; to Carol Rougvie for her tireless, unflagging editing in record time; to Karen McDonald and her staff for preparation of the manuscript; and to William Moomaw and Anthony Cortese for their support throughout the project.

Kurt Fischer
Johan Schot
July 1992

ENVIRONMENTAL
STRATEGIES
FOR INDUSTRY

Introduction

The Greening of the Industrial Firm

Johan Schot and Kurt Fischer

Industrial firms exist in a world of change. They are confronted with a lot of challenges: rapidly evolving new technologies, shorter life cycles, globalization, increasing competition, and the need to reduce pollution substantially, to name a few. These challenges have been present since the 1970s and since then the existing growth model has been in crisis. This growth model is characterized by a search for mass production and mass consumption combined with a throwaway pattern of goods consumption. Within this model, firms have been able to pollute without constraints.[1]

In this book we clarify how industrial firms have managed the pollution aspect of the growth crisis; how in the 1970s and the beginning of the 1980s firms reacted in an ad hoc fashion and fought the need for more fundamental changes; and how during the 1980s they moved toward a more substantial and creative response to the crisis of the growth model. We discuss to what extent firms now acknowledge environmental management and cleaner processes and products as prime shaping forces for a new, sustainable growth model. The relationship between changes in firm behavior and external pressures is complex and subtle. This book explains this relationship, showing how diverse forces such as increasing commercial pressures, loss of credibility, increasing stringent government regulation, and increasing awareness on the part of investors have shaped the change process and forced firms to consider the pollution aspects of their business.

GROWING PRESSURES

The environmental crisis became visible in the 1970s. An explosion of environmental awareness took place. Governments issued many new laws. In all Western countries new government agencies were installed. In 1972 the United Nations Conference on the Human Environment in Stockholm and the Club of Rome's report *Limits to Growth* served as official confirmation of the importance of the environment. During the 1970s and 1980s the recognition grew that the natural environment itself is in an alarming state. It became clear that the production of pollutants and the consumption of energy need to be reduced substantially, while the opposite is happening. Globally, pollution is increasing, and following Heaton et al. (1991, 5), three long-term trends in the growth of pollution can be discerned in the Western world:

- From modest to huge quantities of pollutants: for instance, sulfur oxides increased by about 446 percent and nitrogen oxides by about 900 percent between 1900 and 1980. Other problems have multiplied correspondingly.
- From gross insults to microtoxicity: many synthetic organic compounds and radioactive materials are highly toxic in minute quantities and highly persistent in biological systems or the atmosphere.
- From local to long-term global effects: new environmental problems, such as global warming, acid rain, and the depletion of stratospheric ozone, are being discovered.

As a result of staggering pollution levels and the diversity of environmental concerns, a wide range of pressures is coming to bear upon firms from many sides. First, there are regulatory pressures, as regulations are becoming more stringent and encompassing. Second, there is credibility pressure. Although companies have taken a wide range of actions to reduce pollution, these actions have not yielded sufficient results. Goals have not been met, and accidents are still occurring on a regular basis. At the same time, the public expects improvement in environmental performance. Third are market pressures. Markets are changing. Consumers are appreciating more and more environmentally sound products, and consequently these products have an increasing degree of competitive advantage in the marketplace. Moreover, industrial customers are placing all kinds of environmental requirements on their suppliers. These trends offer new opportunities for competition and for newcomers to enter the market.

Fourth are financial pressures. Investors and insurance companies are incorporating environmental issues into their policies. For different reasons, banking and insurance companies are starting to use detailed questionnaires followed by full environmental risk surveys to assess solvency or insurability of each client. Some investors are showing a tendency to invest in firms that have a good reputation in the environmental field.

The intensity of these pressures varies by country, industry, sector, and firm. It is clear, however, that firms need to respond in order to ensure further use of scarce resources, public and political legitimacy, profitability, and financial assurance.

THE REACTIONS OF FIRMS

The varied responses of firms to mounting pressures can be categorized in two phases: 1970 to 1985 and 1985 to 1992.[2] The year 1985 is an arbitrary point of division. Nevertheless, somewhere in the mid-1980s firms changed from fighting or resistantly adapting to external pressures to embracing them and incorporating environmental considerations into their policies in a more rigorous way. (When we use the word *firm*, we refer to large companies of more than 5000 employees and multinational corporations. Little information on small and medium-size firms is available.) During both phases firms took a wide range of actions that included articulating more firmly their environmental policy statements, creating environmental staff functions, initiating to some extent performance measurement, and developing new technologies and new codes of conduct. These actions were part of a more fundamental pattern of dealing with environmental issues that could be labeled as environmental strategy. Quinn (1988, 3) defined a firm's environmental strategy as follows:

> The pattern or plan that integrates an organization's major goals, policies, and action sequences into a cohesive whole. A well-formulated strategy helps to marshal and allocate an organization's resources into a unique and viable posture based on its relative internal competencies and shortcomings, anticipated changes in the environment, and contingent moves by intelligent opponents.

Strategy not only is connected with goals, measures, plans, and actions, but also is a metaphor that guides the actions of the organization's members at different levels. Strategy implies the purposive force of mobilizing often imprecise and unarticulated visions and expectations to challenge dominating beliefs about the identity of the firm (Pettigrew 1987; Berg and Meima 1991).[3]

RESISTANT ADAPTATION, 1970 TO 1985

The overall picture in the period from 1970 to 1985 is one of firms resisting adaptation to growing regulatory and public pressures.[4] In the 1970s the majority of multinational corporations formulated written statements of corporate environmental objectives and policies. These policy statements most often contain a phrase such as "We will comply with all governmental laws and regulations." Only a few proclaimed the objective of going beyond regulation and taking leadership in environmental protection. In this period, environmental protection was seen as an operating constraint that needed to be taken care of because of outside pressures. Some policies were set for the entire corporation, but the implementation of these policies was weak and determined mainly by the local situation. Environmental protection was foremost a local task of facilities, not a corporate task of headquarters.

In the 1970s, most multinational corporations started to build small staff functions on local levels. These staffs served coordination, advisory, and external relations functions. In addition to staff units, in the early 1970s many multinational corporations installed corporate-level top management committees concerned with environmental problems. These committees served as a forum to discuss policy making. Their importance declined, however, at the end of the 1970s. Because of lack of corporate interest and the emphasis on compliance, most firms did not create an environmental performance measurement system. Emissions were seldom measured, nor was the environmental performance of managers and employees assessed. On the technological side, most firms created environmental specialist functions within their R&D departments. The research efforts were primarily of an applied rather than a fundamental character. The specialists helped facilities in meeting regulatory obligations, mainly through installing pollution control devices. In addition, some checks were created on R&D efforts and the products coming out of those efforts. For example, firms began to screen products for their toxicity. However, most firms did not fully integrate environmental issues into their business strategies and behavior. Environmental issues were not perceived as opportunities to gain competitive advantage (Steger 1988).

This profile is indicative of large company and multinational corporation behavior. In the period from 1970 to 1985, most small and medium-size firms probably did not formulate environmental policies at all, but instead dealt with environmental issues in an ad hoc way. This lack of policies is reflected in a 1974 survey that found that less than 40 percent of 516 responding companies, including small- and medium-size companies, had a formal statement of environmental policy (Gladwin and Welles 1976).

Following Petulla (1987), the picture of hesitantly adapting firms can be further described by dividing the reaction pattern into three categories. Each category can be seen as representing an overall pattern (strategy) that integrates goals, actions, and policies of firms. These patterns can be described as follows:[5]

- Crisis-oriented environmental management. This form of management still followed the earlier practice. There was no environmental policy strategy for compliance with laws and regulations. No separate environmental unit was established. Environmental conflicts with regulatory agencies or the community were managed on a crisis basis. Petulla found that the majority of the firms in his sample that fell into this category (29 percent in 1982) were small, with 50 to 1000 employees.
- Cost-oriented environmental management. According to Petulla, the major difference between the firms in this category and those in the previous one is that environmental regulations were officially accepted as a cost of doing business, and efforts were made to comply with them as efficiently as possible (if not enthusiastically). The firms that were in this category (58 percent in 1982) stayed at least in nominal compliance with environmental regulations, but delayed implementation as long as they could. These firms tended to be in the 5000-employee range, though at least one-quarter had fewer than 1000 employees.
- Enlightened environmental management. Firms in this category (9 percent in 1982) established strong corporate support that went beyond regulatory compliance. Good environmental practices had the complete support of top management, and these firms tended to have good relations with agency officials and community groups. Moreover, these firms tended to incorporate environmental goals into long-range environmental management.

In summary, the dominant pattern of the period from 1970 to 1985 was a lack of willingness to internalize environmental issues.[6] These issues were to some extent accepted as problems that should be managed, but only in reaction to outside pressures, notably regulation and public pressure. On the average, firms did not develop their own policies. As one manager put it in the Petulla research (1987, 171), "Just because we are keeping regulations, it doesn't mean that we agree with or like it." This statement expresses the kind of thinking that dominated this period. The nature of the reaction was highly fragmented and decentralized. No strong corporate policies were in place. On the technological side, most firms relied on pollution control, which implies that no changes occurred in basic process technology and products.

Embracing Environmental Issues Without Innovating, 1985 to 1992

Sometime during the mid-1980s, many firms realized that the existing approach would no longer satisfy government regulators and the public. Major accidents, such as the leak of methyl isocyanide at a Union Carbide plant in Bhopal, India, in 1984 and a chemical spill into the Rhine River following a fire at a Sandoz plant in 1986, acted as catalysts for intensified public hostility and distrust and inspired new regulations and new business action. Firms started defining environmental problems as their own responsibilities, as issues they could not ignore because they would threaten their very existence in the long run. As Loudon (1987), president of AKZO, put it, "History shows us that no industry has survived a permanent conflict with society. Dialogue, adjustment, and cooperation are therefore not a luxury but a necessity." Moreover, the first signals of coming pressures from consumers, industrial customers, and investors became visible.

In 1988 Arthur D. Little reviewed the policy statements of more than seventy-five firms in a variety of industries. These results, along with smaller surveys and in-depth case studies (Schot et al. 1991; Dillon and Fischer 1992), provide the following picture of changes:

- Almost all firms had a formal written policy statement by the end of the 1980s (Flaherty and Rappaport 1991, 10).[7]
- The policy statement was more demanding. In the Arthur D. Little survey (1988), 60 percent of the companies stated that they intended to go beyond compliance by committing both to compliance and to adoption of more stringent requirements where laws and regulations did not exist or were deemed inadequate.
- The policy statement was more specific and included: (1) statements of specific internal implementing requirements, such as "establish environmental, health, and safety programs, minimize emissions, ef-

fluents, and wastes, monitor environmental, health, and safety impacts" (Dillon and Fischer 1992), and (2) descriptions of responsibilities of corporate staff and facility managers, such as "conduct audits, provide staff support to operations, affiliates, and noncompany facilities."
- The policy statement contained issue-specific policies—for example, for groundwater protection, waste, water quality, and air quality. These issue-specific policies were often accompanied by reduction goals for longer time periods, such as "50 percent reduction of all waste in the coming five years."

Although policy statements address implementation issues, it can still be the case that a policy may not be implemented in reality or that policies may be fully implemented without mentioning it in the policy statement itself.[8] The marked change in the content and specificity of the policy statements revealed, however, at least a change in tone. Firms acknowledged their own responsibility for environmental problems. Moreover, the policy statements provided internal and external leverage. Internally, they were used to put environmental issues higher on the manager's and employees' priority list (Schot et al. 1991). Policy statements conveyed a simple statement of the direction in which the firm wanted to go. They provided a vision or metaphor for the firm and thus embodied a spiritual element that could mobilize internal forces (Tapon and Leighton 1991, 11). Externally, the firms could be examined on their performance by the public and by advocacy groups. A report by Friends of the Earth entitled *Hold the Applause! A Case Study of Corporate Environmentalism* (Doyle 1991) is an excellent example, showing that there are many gaps between DuPont's promises and its performance. It became clear during this period that the credibility and image of a firm would be negatively influenced if it could not meet its own standards (see Chapters 7 and 8).

In the 1970s large firms already had created dedicated environmental staff functions, mostly as part of an environment, health, and safety department. During the 1980s this trend continued. A clear expansion of staffing occurred. Multinational corporations created a whole infrastructure of units at different levels—corporate, division, and facility—as well as coordinating functions. In addition, many of them created positions of vice-presidents for environmental affairs. Smaller firms clarified responsibilities by making environmental management a part-time job of one of the company leaders. Environmental managers from different companies began to meet each other on a regular basis to exchange information and formulate policies at a branch level.

Tasks of environmental departments can be grouped into three categories (Ullman 1982):

- Monitoring: checking whether internal and external rules are observed, providing instruction, training, and advice to production management, and measuring and recording waste and emission flows.
- External contacts: maintaining contact with government agencies, the community, advocacy groups, and the general public.
- Innovation and strategic business policy development: influencing the company's strategic policy, for example, in the construction of new factories or in determining research and development strategies.

In this period, environmental departments spent most of their time, up to 80 to 90 percent, on the primary monitoring task and on related contacts with agencies and the public. The third, more strategic, task was a minor part of their activities (Rappaport et al. 1991; ECOTEC 1990; Kasperson et al. 1988). This reflects two things. First is the importance of enforcement and compliance on the company agenda. In this period, firms tended to plan consistently and rigorously for compliance and even future regulatory obligations. Second, firms had not yet integrated environmental issues into their strategic business goals and their policies.

To ensure compliance, firms rely on several controls. Most facilities gather information and report exceptions, such as noncompliance, spills, or accidents. Some facilities gather information on compliance and the progress of waste minimization efforts. To assess performance, an increasing number of firms are using several types of environmental audits. Most often they review the firm's compliance with government regulations and internal procedures. Other audits are done to assess new investments to ensure that real estate is free of contamination and that technology complies with regulation (Arthur D. Little 1984). In addition, companies have started to incorporate environmental criteria into the evaluation of line managers (ECOTEC 1990; Dillon and Fischer 1992).

Firms have embraced environmental management as vital for relationships with their external contacts (suppliers, clients, government, the public, and so forth) and for long-term survival. This is reflected in the fact that firms have constructed checks that integrate environmental impact assessments into decision-making procedures. Environmental considerations are most often taken into account in the capital investment decision-making process (Dillon and Fischer 1992). Firms evaluate the environmental performance of potential partners (Flaherty and Rappaport 1991, 9). In the chemical industry, new products are reviewed in a formal way. These review processes were set up in the 1970s but expanded during the 1980s to incorporate more aspects and to occur earlier in the design phase. Through these review processes the development of a certain product can be blocked (Groenewegen and Vergragt 1991; Schot 1992). Furthermore, planning documents from different functions and facilities are sometimes reviewed for environmental risks. This can be done on a formal and an informal basis. Firms have also discovered the economics of more rigorous policies to prevent waste and emissions. Under the influence of the "pollution prevention pays" movement, they have taken initiatives to prevent pollution by designing processes in which harmful emissions do not occur. When new plants are constructed, environmental considerations tend to be an integral part of the design process.

Thus, firms are optimizing their production processes to reduce pollution and are reviewing all kinds of decisions, including those for the development of new products, for negative environmental impacts. However, environmental considerations are seldom a factor in determining whether a product is made or which product is made. No routine attention is given to environmental aspects when R&D objectives are discussed. If R&D objectives aimed at solving environmental problems are formulated, this is done in reaction to a specific problem raised by regulatory or public pressures (Groenewegen and Vergragt 1991, 49; Schot 1992). A study of eight multinational chemical corporations found that when firms develop an environmentally sound product as a result of external pressure, they try to create two markets: a cheap mass market for the existing polluting products and a new upgraded market for the new environmentally sound product. Moreover, there is a strong tendency in industry to give preference to reuse and recycling of products rather than to the development of new alternative products (Schot et al. 1991).[9] Other indicators that companies are not integrating environmental considerations into their strategic policies are the following: (1) In a German survey of 197 companies it was found that firms did not conduct environmentally oriented strength-and-weakness analyses of their own products and competitive position, or those of their competitors (Kirchgeorg 1991). (2) Firms did not make use of environmentally oriented planning techniques, such as technology assessment and environmental impact assessment, or other strategic planning techniques, such as scenario analysis for identifying future risk and market opportunities, to pick up so-called weak signals in both respects (see Chapter 5). Further, environmental considerations were not addressed in decisions to acquire new businesses (Flaherty and Rappaport 1991).

FUTURE TRENDS

The overall pattern of change in the 1985–1992 period can be summarized in three trends, which will continue and deepen in the coming decade.

1. There is a clear institutionalization of environmental concern within firms. This is an expansion of a trend started in the 1970–1985 period. The localized and fragmented approach of that period has been replaced by a more rigorous and consistent corporate policy with strong top management support and enforcement.

2. Most firms perceive environmental problems as their own problems to solve. It is now part of their identity and goal setting to be environmentally friendly. Consequently, environmental issues are becoming part of business operations on all levels and in all functions. This implies that many firms have moved toward enlightened environmental management, as designated by Petulla. This is a shift from a defensive approach toward a more offensive or proactive approach (Steger 1988; Kirchgeorg 1991; Schot 1992). On the average, this may not be true for small and medium-size firms (see Chapter 4). In terms of Petulla's categories, these firms have moved from a crisis-oriented (passive, dependent) approach toward a cost-oriented (defensive) approach. Even enlightened environmental management, however, implies a preoccupation with regulation. A firm's commitment to going beyond regulation typically means anticipating regulation. On the average, firms do not develop their own policies but react to outside regulatory, public, and, to an increasing extent, market pressures.

3. A minority of firms are moving beyond a compliance-oriented approach. They are developing what could be called an environmentally innovative strategy. Such a strategy is based on the expectation that excelling in protecting the environment is necessary, creates new opportunities, and eventually could lead to competitive advantages. This strategy does not start in a single demonstration to produce a specific environmentally friendly product because of public or regulatory pressure. On the contrary, it aims first of all at increasing the firm's *capability* to develop environmentally sound product/market combinations. Second, firms employing an innovative strategy tend to be heavily engaged in waste and emission reduction at the source as a practice of continuous improvement, with a final goal of zero emission. A third characteristic of firms that follow an innovative strategy is transparency. To develop long-lasting and good relations with the public, consumers, and regulators, these firms tend to monitor emissions and waste streams and disclose information. In addi-

tion, they will allow external auditors to assess performance and publish results. At this point few companies have embraced all three features of an environmentally innovative strategy. However, the research of Kirchgeorg (1991, 144) (see Chapter 5 as well) showed that as many as 22.9 percent of the 197 firms in his sample are following what he called an environmentally oriented innovative strategy, defined as a rigorous internal environmental policy in combination with market-oriented environmental policy.

It is our expectation that in the coming decade more firms will shift from a compliance-oriented environmental management approach toward an innovative approach. At this time it is still profitable and viable to follow a compliance-oriented approach. However, the risks of this approach will become higher in the future. Regulatory and public pressures will become stronger and more powerful. More important, environmental considerations will enter the marketplace more forcefully. New markets will become more articulated and visible, which will create the danger that existing competitors or new firms will innovate and gain a competitive advantage (Steger 1988). To reduce financial risk and exploit new opportunities, investors will start looking more rigorously at the environmental practices of firms. In the same vein, Porter (1991, 96) claims that "the conflict between environmental protection and economic competitiveness is a false dichotomy. It stems from a narrow view of the sources of prosperity and a static view of competition. Strict environmental regulations do not inevitably hinder competitive advantage against foreign rivals; they often enhance it."

A shift to an innovative strategy will not come about easily. It is not a simple process. Taking an innovative stance means adding complexity, and firms already live in a world of increasing uncertainty and complexity. One significant obstacle is that some of the existing technological trends, such as shorter product life cycles, are at odds with environmental goals, such as extending product life cycles (see Chapter 13). But there are many more obstacles as well (see Chapter 9). Because of these problems, it is tempting to rely on a compliance-driven approach. Becoming green not only implies going beyond regulation, but also going beyond state-of-the-art behavior. Borrowing the phrasing of Kleiner (1991, 47), firms have to be better than the rest of industry and even better than the desires of their consumers. Is this too much to expect? No. If it were, no firm would ever innovate.

CONTENT OF THE BOOK

The five parts of this book explore in depth this account of recent patterns and trends in firm behavior. The chapters in Part I explore possible theoretical perspectives to study and explain how companies are dealing with the environmental challenge. Part II contains three chapters that are based on large surveys and case studies and that provide rich data on changing company behavior and the driving forces behind these changes. Parts III, IV, and V analyze in more detail three important driving forces—the public, government, and the industrial market—and subsequent changes of firm behavior. The Conclusion draws implications for policy making and identifies some key research needs for the future.

PART I: THEORETICAL PERSPECTIVES

As Gladwin indicates in his chapter, the collective track record of scholarship on the greening of industry so far has not been very impressive. A great deal of what is known is based on anecdotes published in business journals and on questionnaire research. This kind of research is generally long on description, short on analysis, and lacking theory. Available theoretical perspectives from strategic management, organizational studies, innovation studies, and psychology are not often used. The chapters in Part I explore three possible theoretical perspectives to explain the environmental behavior of firms. Thomas Gladwin discusses a broad array of organizational theories. Melissa Everett, John E. Mack, and Robert Oresick use the psychoanalytic psychology of the self to analyze the different personality structures of individuals who took unusual initiative in the interest of environmental responsibility, and those who did not. René Kemp develops an evolutionary, or neo-Schumpeterian, perspective to explain why companies develop new or adopt cleaner technologies.

We used the term *greening* in the title of this introduction, and it is used in some section heads and by some chapter authors as well because of its mobilizing power. It is a strong metaphor, conveying the vision that this book will discuss ways in which firms have reduced pollution and made their products environmentally friendly. In his chapter, "The Meaning of Greening: A Plea for Organizational Theory," Gladwin shows the ambiguity and complexity of the concept. It involves, for example, cognitions (thinking greenly), emotions (feeling greenly), and behaviors (behaving greenly). How these three components interact is, however, not clear and, as Gladwin contends, elusive. What is needed is greater theory development and application in empirical research. In this regard, Gladwin's chapter shows there is much to gain from the broad array of organizational theories that are already well developed or rapidly advancing. This argument is easily supported by the empirical material presented in this book.

Gladwin discusses the potential of six branches of theory. The first is greening as institutionalization. In this view, greening is foremost a result of firms seeking normative conformity and external legitimation. To this end, they will put pressure on each other to prevent "cowboy" behavior. The applicability of this theory is confirmed by other chapters in the book that show very clearly that image is an important driving force for firms to make changes. A second theory is greening as organizational learning. Organizations learn through a process of information acquisition, distribution, and storage. As Peter B. Cebon demonstrates in his chapter, this process is complicated and worthy of study because it clarifies how these learning processes can be optimized in their own local context. Third is greening as natural selection. This perspective makes clear that greening may be adaptive in the long run, but difficult and disruptive in the short run. The strength of inertial forces impedes adaptation. The chapters by Kemp, Ashford, and Dieleman and de Hoo discuss these impeding forces. Chapters by Steger; Williams, Medhurst, and Drew; and Cramer and Schot make clear, however, that the balance between impeding and stimulating forces is changing. Some external forces, such as markets and investors, are now pressing for change. In addition, too much emphasis on inertial forces obscures the fact that a small group of far-sighted companies has shown environmental leadership. This brings us to the fourth branch of theory, greening as strategic choice. In this perspective, greening is an outcome of purposeful action. Firms can choose to follow a specific strategy for different reasons. Gladwin discusses, among others, the following options: cost leadership through the pursuit of environmental efficiency, differentiation by developing environmentally friendly products for specific markets, and generic substitution of greener processes and products. (In his chapter, Steger elaborates on three additional options: defensive, offensive, and innovative strategies.) A fifth theory discussed by Gladwin is greening as transformational leadership. If one accepts a role for strategic choice, then it is appropriate to investigate leadership. Everett, Mack, and Oresick provide such investigation in their chapter. Sixth is the theory of greening as organizational evolution. In this perspective, structural forces and leadership are brought together. The question is asked: Under what conditions is leadership possible? This question suggests that deeper greening, involving deep-seated changes in core values and product and market strategies, depends on the experience of severe environmental shocks and crises that can threaten organizational survival. The history of greening is full of examples of such experience, as is shown in the chapter by Baram and Dillon.

Gladwin's chapter ends with a caveat, arguing that the greening of industry should not be equated with sustainable development. The latter concept entails broader, global issues related to sustaining the planet as a whole.

The shift to greening involves leadership and the reevaluation of existing beliefs—for example, from one in which environmental concerns and profitability are seen as at odds to one in which they are seen as mutually supportive. In their chapter, "Toward Greening in the Executive Suite," Everett, Mack, and Oresick address this issue. They compare two groups of corporate leaders: those who, in their own eyes, had taken some unusual risk or initiative in the interest of social or environmental responsibility, and those who had not. On the basis of in-depth interviews with twenty-four senior executives in publicly held corporations, the authors noted three significant differences between the two groups. These differences have to do with fundamental personality structure and what might be termed ways of viewing the world.

First, the two groups differed in their conscious norms of behavior. Harmony between personal values and business behavior, a form of what is known as self-consistency, was a matter of conscious concern for the unconventional risk takers. Second, the two groups varied in their personal efficacy—their appreciation of their personal power to affect matters or, in clinical language, their "agency." Agency refers to an inner source of authority for tough decisions and an ability to withstand institutional pressure. The third difference between the two groups of executives was the scope of their everyday awareness. While people are aware that they are part of a family, office, company, community, nation, species, and planet, their identification and empathy are most powerfully triggered at particular levels, depending on their subjective definition of the world they inhabit.

Everett, Mack, and Oresick conclude on the basis of their psychological portrait that a leader's capacity to focus attention on a major change of course, such as an environmental management initiative, may depend on deep personality structure. In each theme cluster in their model—self-consistency, agency, and scope of awareness—one response was associated with the capacity for greening of leadership more than the other. According to the authors, many factors unfortunately make corporations the breeding grounds for individuals who have highly developed institutional identities coupled with an underdeveloped core self, whose sense of personal agency is limited, and whose scope of awareness is constricted by the boundaries of daily functioning.

In his chapter, "An Economic Analysis of Cleaner Technology: Theory and Evidence," Kemp analyzes the process of innovation and diffusion of cleaner technologies. He views this process as endogenous, dependent on the environmental policy and the capabilities and incentives of firms to develop and supply cleaner technologies and on the goals and characteristics of potential users. He argues that the "greening of technology" process will necessarily be rather slow, despite the strong public call for it, due to the dominance of prevailing technological trajectories. These technologies are favored by the existing selection environment (for example, processes and actors influencing technological development) and benefit from dynamic scale and learning effects. New, cleaner technologies sometimes fail in the marketplace unless these barriers have been removed. Compared with other innovations, cleaner technologies depend much more on government regulation and subsidies and seem to be more riskier and less profitable, according to Kemp. As a consequence, market demand induced by government regulation is a crucial factor for the successful exploitation of technological opportunities. This conclusion is backed by case studies of three cleaner technologies: CFC substitutes, low-solvent paints and coatings, and membrane technology in the metal-plating industry.

PART II: THE ENVIRONMENTAL CHALLENGE: DYNAMICS OF FIRM BEHAVIOR

In their chapter, "Corporate Strategies for a Sustainable Future," Hugh E. Williams, James Medhurst, and Kirstine Drew identify a number of distinct, although partly overlapping, environmental pressures that are responsible for raising environmental awareness in industry and for stimulating industry responses. These include:

- Increasingly stringent environmental legislation and enforcement.
- Increasing costs associated with pollution control, waste disposal, and effluent disposal.
- Increasing commercial pressure from the supply, consumption, and disposal of both intermediate and final products.
- Increasing awareness on the part of investors of companies' environmental performance in view of the cost implications associated with liability and the "polluter-pays" principle.
- Increasing training and personnel requirements, together with additional information requirements.
- Increasing expectations on the part of the local community and the work force of the environmental performance of firms and their impact on the environment.

On the basis of a survey of 117 firms and detailed discussions with a selected sample of twenty-five firms in the United Kingdom, Williams,

Medhurst, and Drew have assessed the firms' responses to both current and future environmental pressures. Their analysis highlights the following conclusions:

- Firms do not have dramatically high net costs of pollution control when these costs are expressed as a percentage of turnover. Costs alone do not lead to major changes.
- The two main driving forces have been fear of developing a bad image and government regulation. The level of response is broadly related to the extent of the impact of environmental pressures. Firms exposed to more extensive environmental pressures have responded more than firms with less exposure to them.
- Related to the previous finding, the specific environmental problems that have been dealt with are those covered by the media and government regulation. These problems are mainly related to production processes and not so much to input (for example, raw materials) or to output (products).
- There is a recognition that, while pressures on production processes from the public and government regulation will increase in the future, there will be a much wider range of pressures from many more sources, including the market and investors.
- The current and future responses of firms do not match very closely the expected wider pressures. Almost none of the firms studied, except some larger multinational firms, have a full corporate-management response that includes comprehensive and continuous monitoring procedures for waste and emissions, emphasis on prevention instead of end-of-pipe technologies, and systematic auditing practices for their own company and suppliers.
- The level of impact and response seems to be determined by the size of the firm. Small firms are, with a few exceptions, relatively unaffected by environmental pressures and, given the relatively low level of importance attached to the issues, have not considered or prepared any real responses.

Companies have traditionally considered external regulatory and other pressures a nuisance. Ulrich Steger argues in his chapter, "The Greening of the Board Room: How German Companies Are Dealing with Environmental Issues," that companies should recognize the growing possibilities to use environmental issues as market and innovation potentials. New, clean technologies avoid pollution and costs, and consumers and user firms increasingly reward more environmentally sound products. Steger discusses to what extent corporations respond to this new approach. Do they shift from their traditional approach of just complying with the law toward an environmentally oriented approach in which environmental issues are integrated in their overall strategy? As a stepping-stone, Steger distinguishes three generic strategies that could be implemented in industry.

- The defensive strategy implies that in the given business there is no relevant market opportunity for the corporation. It is therefore rational just to comply with environmental legislation, mainly through the adoption of end-of-pipe technologies.
- The offensive strategy requires, above all, the development of environmentally sound products that provide an additional benefit for the consumer and therefore a competitive advantage for the corporation.
- The innovative strategy is, like any technology management, the most challenging, because the market potential can be achieved only by a major change in the production process or a complete new design of the products.

Steger concludes that only a minority of corporations are really implementing an offensive or innovative strategy and, thus, an all-inclusive environmentally oriented strategy. This conclusion is based on a comprehensive empirical study conducted by a research group on behalf of the Federal Environmental Protection Ministry in Germany. From 592 interviews with top managers across the different branches of German industry, it was determined that a majority perceive environmental protection as the task of top management. Environmental objectives are no longer perceived as conflicting with other important corporate market and profit objectives. However, only a small minority of top managers had motivated this change by recognizing the need to grasp new market opportunities. The majority were still driven by risk avoidance and compliance with the law. Steger ends his chapter optimistically by stating that although current practice is far from the attainable goal, firms are moving in the desired direction. Moving toward an environmentally oriented strategy calls for learning, and this requires, above all, time.

Peter B. Cebon's analysis opens the black box enclosing the internal workings of one particular company. In his chapter, "The Myth of Best Practices: The Context Dependence of Two High-performing Waste Reduction Programs," Cebon examines the constraints on FLECSOCO, a chemical manufacturer, in achieving waste reduction objectives, and the strategies the firm developed for overcoming these constraints. In exploring how two of FLECSOCO's divisions deal with these problems, he shows that the two divisions have quite different waste reduction programs, and even though they are both very good by industry standards, one is more effective than the other.

Cebon argues that managers have surprisingly little choice in the program designs they can select to achieve waste reduction objectives. A large number of political and structural obstacles, varying through time and across space, severely limit their options for program design. Yet, despite these apparently limited choices, the structures of the two FLECSOCO programs differ enormously, and this appears to be due primarily to the local context and the historical period in which the programs were developed.

Because successful programs appear to be constrained by context, no specific set of "best practices" for waste reduction management can be prescribed for industry in general or even for plants within a single firm or across corporations. Cebon's data suggest that the key to success appears to be an organizational capacity to allow sufficient flexibility in program design so that programs can be historically and locally sensitive and still be effective. Effectiveness is more likely if corporations can loosen the constraints on program design and if designers can be sensitive to constraints. In addition, Cebon's analysis suggests that participants in a waste reduction program need something to motivate them and that programs should not violate the territory of those people who supervise the participants.

PART III: TRUST AND CREDIBILITY

Industry has found that its environmental performance is under increasing public scrutiny. Caught in a tide of rising expectations, industry is experiencing something of a crisis of credibility and faces considerable public mistrust. Drawing on current research, Peter Simmons and Brian Wynne, in their chapter, "Responsible Care: Trust, Credibility, and Environmental Management," examine the response of the United Kingdom's Chemical Industries Association (CIA) to these pressures and its attempt to regain public trust by establishing environmental performance standards for the chemical industry through its Responsible Care program.

The CIA launched its Responsible Care program in March 1989. Based on a set of six guiding principles, it is an umbrella program with two avowed aims: improving the industry's performance in the areas of environment, health, safety, product safety, distribution, and relations with the public; and enabling companies to demonstrate that such improvements are taking place. The program has sought to influence the behavior and performance of member companies in the pursuit of greater public credibility. Most activities carried out by the association within the framework of the program have aimed to increase the commitment of individual member companies—for instance, by making compliance with its codes and guidance obligatory.

The CIA has not, however, imposed any sanctions. Encouragement is preferred to punishment. The CIA emphasizes peer pressure as the mechanism for ensuring the success of the program. Another recent development has been the introduction of performance indicators, in terms of percentage reductions of toxic emissions, transport incidents, complaints, and so forth, against a baseline score for year one. The association intends to release the figures after three or four years of results have been recorded. Raw data will not be published, and the results will be presented in aggregate form. The industry is afraid that otherwise the public will not understand the progress made. Thus, the essence of communication is education and not accountability. This is highlighted by the fact that the CIA resists the independent scrutiny of its members' environmental performance.

Although the Responsible Care program has stimulated improved industry performance through an extension of the network of mutual regulation, according to Simmons and Wynne, it has not addressed the underlying issues raised by the crisis of credibility, such as the grounded mistrust of the institutional system of organization and control within which the industry's operations are embedded and the culturally embedded basis of public mistrust. They conclude that simply telling people about improving environmental management will not be sufficient. As long as the industry remains convinced of the certainty of its knowledge and expertise and the irrelevance of that of outsiders, it will fail to overcome the mistrust of its various publics. According to the authors, steps are needed to increase public involvement and accountability. The public should not be regarded as a homogeneous entity. It consists of several constituencies: the regulatory community, neighbors, trade unions, the environmental movement, investors, and insurers. Appropriate mediating mechanisms must be created to connect developments internal to the industry to public experience. Open dialogue and active cooperation are required among industry, environmentalists, trade unions, and citizen groups, as well as government, to explore possible institutional mechanisms around which trust may be rebuilt. In building this trust in both directions, the greatest obstacle will be the mutual mistrust with which the industry and some of its publics view one another. Simmons and Wynne conclude, therefore, that the challenge for industry now is to exploit the opportunities for involving citizens in the policy process and improving the capacity for social learning.

Michael S. Baram and Patricia S. Dillon, in their chapter, "Corporate Management of Chemical Accident Risks," show how U.S. chemical companies have responded to the rising public concern about facility safety. Numerous accidents have occurred at industrial facilities during the past decade. Many of these accidents released hazardous chemicals, with tragic consequences for workers, community residents, and the environment. The Bhopal accident in 1984 prompted the U.S. Congress to enact the Emergency Planning and Community Right to Know Act (EPCRA) in 1986, requiring facilities to disclose chemical information to local officials and authorizing public access to the information. Before EPCRA, Bhopal had already motivated many large chemical manufacturers to take new voluntary actions to improve facility safety and strengthen emergency response. The enactment of EPCRA provided a further impetus for these corporate voluntary initiatives. On the basis of eight detailed case studies, the authors found that these initiatives fall into the following categories:

- Special evaluations of facility operations and the initiation of more stringent, periodic assessments of plant activities.
- Improvements in inventory management, including storage volume reductions and technical improvements to storage facilities.
- Changes in process technology, including hazardous material substitutions and technical improvements.
- Enhancement of monitoring systems to detect accidental releases.
- Establishment of accident reporting and internal accident evaluation procedures.
- Increased emphasis on securing information and technical assistance from chemical suppliers, advising and consulting customers, and oversight of suppliers' and contractors' activities that affect facility safety.

However, many firms subject to EPCRA have failed to comply with the reporting requirements, and many of those that have complied have not taken steps to reduce accident risks. Smaller firms in particular have high rates of noncompliance and provide little evidence of accident risk reduction. Given these mixed results, Congress took further steps in its enactment of the federal Clean Air Act Amendments (CAAA) in 1990. The deepest reforms are expected to come from the CAAA requirement that each facility develop a risk management plan for review by the U.S. Environmental Protection Agency.

The Bhopal incident and subsequent government regulation have stimulated not only private firms' activities but new efforts from major trade associations as well. The U.S. Chemical Manufacturers Association (CMA) has enacted Codes of Management Practice as part of its Responsible Care program. All CMA members have pledged to follow the ten guiding principles contained in these codes as a condition for retaining their CMA membership. Although, as in the United Kingdom's Responsible Care program, the CMA will not enforce compliance, private codes do form an important impetus for change. Private codes are public commitments, and chemical firms in particular realize that their performance must live up to their promises if they are to gain public trust and the confidence of their workers, customers, investors, and insurers. Furthermore, although not legally enforceable by regulatory agencies, such codes are legally relevant and indirectly enforceable. For example, regulators may compare a company's performance against its code to gauge the adequacy of corporate efforts to reduce risk and determine whether to carry out regulatory enforcement. Codes could be adopted as legal requirements, thereby making them directly enforceable by regulators. A code can also be introduced as evidence in lawsuits against a company as a means of measuring company performance and determining if performance failed to meet the promised standard of care or industry state of the art. Thus, private codes make companies more vulnerable in several ways, and this serves as an incentive for company performance that is consistent with its code. Baram and Dillon argue, however, that other forces are at work now as well. Firms are transforming the discussed fear factors (fear of regulation and negative image) into business opportunities for gaining economic and legal advantage. Environmental protection is seen as a basis to compete for market share, investor interest, and public trust.

PART IV: EFFECTIVE GOVERNMENT ACTION

How effective government action can be is shown by Hans Dieleman and Sybren de Hoo in the chapter entitled "Toward a Tailor-made Process of Pollution Prevention and Cleaner Production: Results and Implications of the PRISMA Project." The aims of the Dutch PRISMA project were primarily to show that the prevention of waste and emissions is possible in the short term and offers benefits both to companies and to the environment, and to formulate recommendations for an effective governmental prevention policy. Within the framework of PRISMA, ten experiments with prevention were carried out in various Dutch industrial companies, while in addition, studies were conducted to formulate recommendations for an effective prevention policy.

Significant results were achieved within the framework of PRISMA. In a number of companies the introduction of preventive techniques led to reductions in waste and emissions of 30 to 80 percent in two years. Occasionally it was possible to eliminate a noxious waste flow completely. The cost-benefit analysis of the prevention options carried out yields a varying picture with a few extremely favorable peaks. In general, the great majority of prevention options put into practice in the PRISMA companies were realized without financial problems.

On the basis of the PRISMA experiences, Dieleman and de Hoo conclude that prevention of waste and emissions is feasible and beneficial. Despite these results, most companies are still reluctant to develop prevention activities themselves. The authors identified obstacles to the development of prevention activities in firms and grouped them under five headings:

- Conceptual obstacles, such as the widespread viewpoint that preventing waste is costly business (PRISMA, however, has shown that this is not always the case).
- Organizational obstacles in the form of rigid structures within a company and between companies.
- Lack of information on prevention technologies.
- Technical obstacles, occurring when no alternatives are available.
- Economic obstacles, such as low charges for the disposal of waste streams, lack of funding opportunities, and incomplete calculation and allocation of environmental costs.

An essential ingredient for a policy aiming to overcome these obstacles is a system of knowledge transfer. Many such systems exist already; however, they do not stimulate pollution prevention because intensive interaction between companies and outside consultants is missing. This is shown in the PRISMA project and is also backed by innovation theories discussed by Dieleman and de Hoo. Governments should therefore give priority to stimulating such intensive interaction—for example, through the appointment of prevention teams that will stimulate, supervise, and advise companies. In addition, the authors contend that it is necessary to complement this interactive and voluntary approach by mandating industry to formulate and implement pollution prevention plans as part of the permit procedure.

In the chapter by Nicholas A. Ashford, "Understanding Technological Responses of Industrial Firms to Environmental Problems: Implications for Government Policy," similar issues are addressed in relation to regulation and innovation. On the basis of an historical review of U.S. experiences with regulation and its effects on innovation, Ashford demonstrates that standard setting can be used to encourage all the varieties of technological innovation as well as diffusion for both product and process change. U.S. experiences from 1970 to 1985 reveal significant innovation and essential compliance with very stringent regulation. Contrary to the widely held belief that too stringent a regulation inhibits innovation, Ashford argues that in some cases a standard that is not stringent enough may inhibit innovation.

The mid-1980s ushered in an antiregulatory federal government favoring the creation of economic incentives and voluntary action. Government regulations focused on information and reporting requirements and on negotiated rather than government-dictated rule making. It turned out that in the overwhelming majority of industrial firms, pollution control technology was in place, but the firms were not using the pollution prevention options open to them. According to Ashford, their first response was to undertake "housekeeping changes" and equipment modifications that could have been instituted much earlier. The firms also discovered that they could save money. Recycling increased and was financially attractive, partly because it was accompanied by material reclamation and partly because off-site waste treatment was becoming expensive. In other words, firms were so suboptimal in their industrial operations that almost anything they did yielded an improvement in the efficiency of pollution abatement.

What the record shows, however, according to Ashford, is that input substitution, process redesign, and product reformulation were rare events. They were rare events because environmental requirements were either not stringent enough on their face and/or there was inadequate enforcement to force technological change. From this analysis, Ashford derives that stringent and certain regulatory demands (such as emission, effluent, or exposure standards, or product bans and phase-outs) are necessary to effectuate pollution prevention. Voluntary action should be seen as a complement to, not a substitute for, regulatory requirements. To stimulate the development of cleaner technologies, strict standards are necessary with flexible provisions to allow and encourage innovative responses by industry. In addition, firms that are not in a position to innovate need governmental programs in technical assistance.

PART V: THE GREENING OF INTERFIRM RELATIONSHIPS

To realize product improvements, firms should no longer be concerned only with their own production process but also with other phases of the product life cycle. Since most firms are not involved in all phases of this cycle, cooperation between firms is necessary. This point is stressed in the chapter by Jacqueline Cramer and Johan Schot entitled "Environmental Comakership Among Firms as a Cornerstone in the Striving for Sustainable Development." The authors have coined the term *environmental comakership* to refer to the cooperation between firms on the environmental aspects of products. Current environmental comakership involves two developments. The first is exchange of information among firms about the environmental aspects of their (semifinished) products. A second, more committing development is for user firms to set demands on suppliers.

Is there already a visible tendency toward environmental comakership among firms, and what role can governments play in stimulating this process? These questions form the major issues dealt with in this chapter. On the basis of two empirical studies, Cramer and Schot conclude there is indeed a visible tendency toward environmental comakership. Although current information exchange about environmental aspects is still ad hoc and unstructured and is not yet common practice, there is a solid expectation that information exchange among firms will expand. In addition, companies have started to place requirements on one another. For example, the kind of stipulations chemical firms require their suppliers to meet are to supply the product without particular substances such as polyvinyl chloride, cadmium, and CFCs and to increase possibilities for reuse at the waste stage. These trends clearly link with another trend in industry in the field of quality control. Since the 1980s, many large user firms have decided, due to increasing international competition, to contract out more work to fewer firms. Strong relationships are built with a small number of suppliers. Part of this relationship is a substantial upgrading of quality standards and a growing interaction between user and supplier concerning the design of products. Environmental comakership could become part of this development and, as a consequence, gain more momentum.

According to Cramer and Schot, government could play a major stimulating role. First, it can develop data bases and methodologies to assess the environmental quality of products. Such initiatives are important to create a supply of information but will not suffice. Small and medium-size firms in particular do not easily make use of formal data bases set up by government. Firms rely on their own network of users and suppliers, which enables them to receive custom-made information. Thus, stimulating information exchange between companies could be a second important mechanism to create a supply of information. Government could stimulate the development of a more uniform system of data exchange, linking it to other systems, such as quality control. This supply-oriented policy should be complemented with a demand-side policy aimed at stimulating the use of information and articulation of demand for specific information. One way of doing this is to make manufacturers responsible for their own products through the entire life cycle. Another approach, the authors advocate, is the formulation of sustainability strategies. By a sustainability strategy they mean the conscious selection and putting into practice of a particular technological trajectory that, from the viewpoint of sustainability, should be given preference over other technological trajectories, and the implementation of which is considered feasible from a societal perspective.

Government's role is twofold. It should influence the process by setting the environmental objectives to be attained. It should keep watch over the particular industries, which all tend to defend their own survival, acting as an arbiter and distinguishing individual from collective interests. It should set the goals, while the industries should elaborate the best sustainability strategies for themselves considering the boundary conditions between individual and collective interests. Government can also provide structures that facilitate the establishment of networks between firms and user-producer relations in which environmental considerations have a place.

The chapter by Patricia S. Dillon and Michael S. Baram entitled "Forces Shaping the Development and Use of Product Stewardship in the Private Sector" discusses systematic company efforts to reduce risks throughout all or significant segments of a product life cycle—that is, from raw material acquisition through ultimate use and disposal. Product stewardship covers the initiatives of companies to redesign their products to make them safer or more environmentally acceptable and to transfer knowledge about the safe handling, use, and disposal of their products to downstream handlers and customers.

In this chapter, Dillon and Baram examine the forces promoting the development and use of product stewardship in the private sector, as well as current practices of U.S. corporations, with particular emphasis on technology transfer. The authors note that technology transfer has reached unprecedented levels in recent years, as suppliers voluntarily provide information and expertise on safe handling and use of their products to downstream customers and as customers demand more services and more environmentally acceptable products from suppliers. While some company efforts to address product risks are ad hoc (for example, in response to a specific incident or need), other initiatives by companies are part of a systematic effort to reduce the risks associated with their products.

Some companies, particularly in the chemical industry, have developed formal product stewardship programs that emphasize technology transfer. The pervasiveness of product stewardship efforts in the U.S. chemical industry has been advanced by the CMA's Responsible Care program and its members' commitment to counsel customers on the safe use, transportation, and disposal of chemical products. In addition to this general commitment, the CMA drafted Codes of Management Practice for product stewardship and product distribution that are an obligation of CMA membership.

Examples of the scope of the technology transfer initiatives are:

- Product warnings, labels, and other product information.
- Education and training programs set up by suppliers for their customers and other downstream users.
- Services provided by suppliers to promote the safe use, handling, and disposal of their products (for example, taking back used equipment from its customers for recycling).
- Access to company personnel and guidance documents.
- Purchasing contracts and product specifications.
- Notification, screening, and selection of suppliers, distributors, or customers.

According to Dillon and Baram, the increase in technology transfer can be attributed to a number of forces, such as the drive to reduce liability and regulatory costs, to improve competitive position, and to avoid negative publicity. The particular patterns of technology transfer and the type and quality of information vary depending on a number of factors related to the product, in particular the product's environmental risks and commercial characteristics. To encourage private sector initiatives, policy makers could identify obstacles to technology transfer and disseminate information on company initiatives for use by companies that want to develop new efforts or expand their voluntary efforts. In addition, Dillon and Baram suggest the development of an analytic tool, or matrix, for use by both policy makers and companies to assist in identifying product sectors or life cycle phases that could benefit from increased technology transfer activities.

A concrete example of cooperation between firms is presented in the chapter entitled "Solving the Automobile Shredder Waste Problem: Cooperation Among Firms in the Automotive Industry," by Frank den Hond and Peter Groenewegen. The authors describe the strategies adopted by several automobile manufacturers with regard to the management of shredder waste. In the past, automobile manufacturers have not shown any specific interest in the dismantling and shredder business. This has changed under pressure of government legislation that will make car manufacturers responsible for waste produced by old automobiles, as well as growing public concern and the expectation that future customers will regard recyclability as a selection criterion. To solve shredder waste problems, several automobile manufacturers, including Ford, Volkswagen, BMW, Mercedes-Benz, and Peugeot, have started pilot projects for automobile dismantling. In these projects they are learning how to disassemble automobiles, but at the same time they hope to convince governments that legislation is not necessary to solve the shredder waste problem.

Den Hond and Groenewegen classify strategies for vehicle disposal by individual automobile manufacturers according to whether they represent radical disposal innovations or reinforcement of current waste management practices. An innovation is considered radical when it deviates from current waste-handling technologies, which are characterized by disassembly of a certain number of parts for reuse and subsequent shredding and separation of metals. For example, Mercedes-Benz has developed a totally new melt-reactor. In current waste management practice, automobile production and vehicle disposal are activities in separate networks. The only linkage between production and disposal is via the retailing system. Automobile producers' strategies involve either linkages with existing waste management firms or development of their own in-house capability. From the authors' analysis, it is clear that individual automobile manufacturers have chosen diverse strategies. Although it is not clear to what extent new technologies and networks will evolve, the analysis shows that closing the loop involves not only environmental discussions, but also questions of innovation, and could result in structural changes in industry.

In the Conclusion the editors draw implications for policy development and identify future research needs. Most firms do not follow an innovative strategy despite the necessity of doing so to secure continuity and competitive advantage in most markets in the future. We define the government's central task as accelerating the process of change toward an innovative strategy. This task should be executed through the deepening and broadening of regulatory measures. "Deepening" implies that regulations need to be geared toward changing dynamics within firms. "Broadening" means expanding accountability and changing dynamics among firms as well as among firms and traditional stakeholders, such as investors, and emerging stakeholders, such as environmental groups. This movement toward the deepening and broadening of regulation requires a basic understanding of the dynamics of firm behavior, both within firms and among firms and stakeholders. Throughout the various chapters, research proposals and ideas are set forth for reaching this understanding. The editors conclude the book by highlighting the most prominent of these proposals.

ACKNOWLEDGMENTS

The authors acknowledge the helpful comments from Patricia S. Dillon, Peter Groenewegen, Tom Misa, and Yvonne Ploum on an earlier draft.

NOTES

1. Some authors label this growth model as Fordism (Van Tulder and June 1988; Green and Yoxen 1990). They contend that to solve the problems that have the last phase of expansion of Fordism, such as the increasing cost of labor and the increasing inflexibility of the production apparatus, a new set of basic technologies and accompanying management practices is necessary. On the technological side, microelectronics and biotechnology are widely discussed as the main candidates. They will form the core technologies of the factory, office, and farm of the future. On the management side, the need for decentralized management practices is emphasized. Unfortunately, in this discussion the pollution part of the crisis of Fordism is often neglected. New technologies and management cannot be viable unless they are sustainable.

2. The overall picture is different from industry to industry and from firm to firm. The research base is too small and too biased toward the chemical industry to provide a detailed account. Nevertheless, it is possible to make a global description of both phases.

3. Koolmann (1992) uses an analogue concept to describe technical change. In the German language this is termed *Leitbild*, meaning frame or vision.

4. The environmental behavior of firms during this period has not been extensively researched. The account in this chapter is mainly based on the seminal work of Gladwin and Welles (1976) (see also Gladwin [1977] and United Nations 1985, which is mainly based on the research by Gladwin). These authors examined in depth the adaptations of multinational corporations. They interviewed extensively North American and European executives of seventeen major petroleum, chemical, and metals multinational corporations.

5. Petulla's (1987) data base includes information on chemical, textile, petroleum, paper, and electroplating industries.

6. The picture is based primarily on larger companies and multinational corporations, but there are no reasons to assume that small and medium-size companies did not do better.

7. This is based on information from ninety-eight companies that responded between August and November 1990.

8. Dillon and Fischer (1992) contend that the comprehensive nature and level of detail of policy statements is a function of general organizational characteristics of the company, such as degree of centralization and company culture.

9. Some small firms are exceptions. They appear to be at the forefront of proactive responses to the new market opportunities. Remarkably, these small, proactive manufacturers of so-called green products do not seriously consider the impact of their production systems (Potter 1992).

REFERENCES

Arthur D. Little, Inc., Center for Environmental Assurance. 1988. *Environmental Health and Safety Policies: Current Practices and Future Trends*. Cambridge, Mass.: Arthur D. Little.

Arthur D. Little, Inc., Center for Environmental Assurance. 1984. *Current Practices in Environmental Auditing*. Report to the U.S. Environmental Protection Agency. Cambridge, Mass.: Arthur D. Little.

Arthur D. Little, Inc., Center for Environmental Assurance. 1981. *A Survey of Environmental Planning*. Cambridge, Mass.: Arthur D. Little.

Berg, Per Olof, and Meima, Ralph. 1991. "The Firm's Management of Its Ecological Role and Strategic Reconceptualization at PLM AB." Paper presented at the Strategic Management Society Annual Conference, Toronto, Canada, October 23.

Dillon, Patricia S., and Fischer, Kurt. 1992. *Environmental Management in Corporations: Methods and Motivations*. Medford, Mass.: Center for Environmental Management, Tufts University.

Doyle, Jack. 1991. *Hold the Applause! A Case Study of Corporate Environmentalism as Practiced at DuPont*. Washington, D.C.: Friends of the Earth.

ECOTEC. 1990. *The Impact of Environmental Management on Skills and Jobs*. Birmingham, England: ECOTEC.

Flaherty, Margaret, and Rappaport, Ann. 1991. *Multinational Corporations and the Environment: A Survey of Global Practices*. Medford, Mass.: Center for Environmental Management, Tufts University.

Gladwin, Thomas N. 1977. *Environment, Planning, and Multinational Corporations*. Greenwich, Conn.: JAI Press.

Gladwin, Thomas N., and Welles, John G. 1976. "Multinational Corporations and Environmental Protection: Patterns of Organizational Adaptation." *International Studies of Management and Organization* 9 (Spring/Summer): 160–84.

Green, Kenneth, and Yoxen, Edward. 1990. "The Greening of European Industry. What Role for Biotechnology?" *Futures*, June, 475–95.

Groenewegen, Peter, and Vergragt, Philip. 1991. "Environmental Issues as

Threats and Opportunities for Technological Innovation." *Technology Analysis and Strategic Management* 3(1): 43–55.

Heaton, George; Repetto, Robert; and Rodney, Sobin. 1991. *Transforming Technology: An Agenda for Environmentally Sustainable Growth in the 21st Century*. Washington, D.C.: World Resources Institute.

Kasperson, Roger E.; Kasperson, Jeanne X.; Hohenemser, Christopher; and Kates, Robert W. 1988. *Corporate Management of Health and Safety Hazards. A Comparison of Current Practice*. Boulder: Westview Press.

Kirchgeorg, Manfred. 1991. *Okologieorientiertes Unternehmensverhalten* (Environmentally oriented business behavior). Wiesbaden, Germany: Gabler.

Kleiner, Art. 1991. "What Does It Mean to Be Green?" *Harvard Business Review*, July/August, 38–47.

Koolmann, Steffen. 1992. *Leitbilder der Technikentwicklung: das Beispiel des Automobils* (Images of technological change: The case of the automobile). Frankfurt: Campus Verlag.

Loudon, A. A. 1987. "The Chemical Industry and the Environment." Paper presented at the European Conference on Industry and Environmental Management, Interlaken, Austria, October 12.

Pettigrew, Andrew M. 1987. "Context and Action in the Transformation of the Firm." *Journal of Management Studies* 24(6): 649–70.

Petulla, Joseph M. 1987. "Environmental Management in Industry." *Journal of Professional Issues in Engineering* 113(2): 167–83.

Porter, Michael E. 1991. "America's Green Strategy." *Scientific American*, April, 96.

Potter, Stephen. 1992. *The Design and Commercial Success of 'Green' Products in Small Firms*. Milton Keynes, Great Britain: Open University.

Quinn, J. B. 1988. "Strategies for Change." In *The Strategy Process: Concepts, Contexts, and Cases*, edited by J. B. Quinn, Henry Mintzberg, and R. M. James. Englewood Cliffs, N.J.: Prentice-Hall.

Rappaport, Ann; Taylor, Gary J.; Flaherty, Margaret; and Pomeroy, Geoffrey. 1991. *Global Corporate Environment, Health, and Safety Programs: Management Principles and Practices*. Medford, Mass.: Center for Environmental Management, Tufts University.

Schot, Johan. 1992. "Credibility and Markets as Greening Forces in the Chemical Industry." *Business Strategy and the Environment* 1(1): 35–44.

Schot, Johan; De Laat, Bas; Van der Meijden, Ronald; and Bosma, Harry. 1991. *Geven om de Omgeving. Milieugedrag van ondernemingen in de chemische industrie* (Caring for the environment. Environmental management in the chemical industry). The Hague: SDU.

Steger, Ulrich. 1988. *Umweltmanagement: Erfahrungen und Instrumente einer Umweltorientierten Unternehmensstrategie* (Environmental management: Experience and methods of environmentally oriented strategy). Wiesbaden, Germany: Gabler.

Tapon, Francis, and Leighton, Tony. 1991. *Green as Strategy: Lessons from the Chemical Industry*. Ecosource Discussion Paper No. 1991-17. Ecosource.

Tulder, Rob van, and June, Gerd. 1988. *European Multinationals in Core Technologies*. New York: John Wiley.

Ullman, Arieh A. 1982. *Industrie und Umweltschutz: Implementation von Umweltschutzgesetzen in Deutschen Unternehmen* (Industry and the environment: The implementation of environmental regulations in German enterprises). Frankfurt: Campus Verlag.

United Nations Centre on Transnational Corporations. 1985. *Environmental Aspects of the Activities of Transnational Corporations: A Survey*. New York: United Nations.

PART I

❦

Theoretical Perspectives

1

The Meaning of Greening:
A Plea for Organizational Theory

Thomas N. Gladwin

GREENING AND THE BLIND PROFESSORS

Building on the old Indian tale of the blind men and the elephant (Morgan 1986, 340), imagine a large university campus where a group of blind professors have assembled around a "thing" called greening and are trying to sense what it really is. The natural scientists, relying on their "supreme" laws, speak out first. The physicist, feeling matter and energy, proclaims that greening is obviously about minimizing entropy or disorder. The chemistry professor, sensing substances, retorts that it must involve reduced disruption of biogeochemical cycles that support life. The blind ecologist then pronounces that it must be about respect for ecosystem assimilative capacities, thresholds, and irreversibilities, by necessity halting the increased appropriation of annual photosynthetic product by humanity.

Farther down the academic pecking order, the softer social scientists then take the floor. The philosophy professor, perceiving values, suggests that this thing represents a shift from anthropocentric (human-centered) toward biocentric (ecosystem-centered) ethical systems, at the extreme even implying the abolishment of human privilege on the planet. The psychologist then posits that it must reside in human cognition about time and space, representing emergent biospheric consciousness. The wise old historian then reminds the audience that whatever it is, it represents perhaps the most significant change in human culture since the industrial revolution of the mid-eighteenth century.

Moving on, the political scientist speculates that this thing is about power, with Neo-Malthusians simply beginning to win out over Cornucopians in political arenas. The economist then efficiently argues that it is simply about internalizing environmental externalities. The sociologist stresses that it is really about changing social institutions and structures. The blind anthropologist then argues that it is cultural in nature, involving shifts in socially constructed systems of shared meaning about human-nature relationships. Looking very puzzled, a long-haired poetry professor breaks into the discussion, declaring that it is about language, offering a poem about it entitled "Nine REs": Reduce, Reuse, Return, Rethink, Repair, Replant, Recharge, Recirculate, Recycle. No one applauds.

Having waited patiently (probably while earning huge practice or consulting fees), the blind representatives of the professional schools finally chime in, with the medical professor stressing that the thing is basically about minimizing damage to human health and the lawyer claiming that it obviously boils down to normative conformity with governmental regulations. Finally, the business school professor says, "I think I've heard enough. This thing, at a minimum, is simply about harmonizing corporate environmental performance with stakeholder desires and expectations; but on second thought, it could also constitute a significant new source of competitive advantage, lower costs, expanded market share, and enhanced shareholder value; but on the other hand, of course, it all depends."

Now, throughout the academic convocation the thing has been standing still. Suddenly it begins to travel, moving into new areas in jolting fits and starts, fluctuating in size and intensity in seemingly random fashion, and changing its hue and form from seemingly familiar to unfamiliar. The thing's dynamism startles the gathered academics, complicating and casting doubts on their various interpretations of the phenomenon. With a passionate roar, the thing finally cries out, "Please help me: define me, describe me, theorize about me, study me, generalize about me, validate me, predict me, advise me!"

LESSONS OF THE PARABLE

What are the lessons of this intentionally exaggerated and maddening parable? Three central messages were intended: (1) greening, viewed as a process by which human activity is made compatible with biospheric capacity, is absolutely the most important phenomenon of our time, as human survival literally depends on it; (2) no matter what progress we make in the short term, the meaning of greening is bound to remain troublesomely ambiguous; and (3) the collective track record of academic scholarship on the greening of industry so far has not been very impressive. We are thus dealing with a great paradox here—with one of the most important processes or transformations of all time being woefully underdeveloped in terms of theory and underresearched from the standpoint of rigorous empirical testing. We share a common and vital mission of developing and validating models of how this thing called greening works.

IMPORTANCE OF GREENING

The Global Environment Program at New York University has recently analyzed the complete array of environmental and development challenges confronting humanity, including atmosphere, forests, biodiversity, water, land and agriculture, human health, human settlements, population growth, and mass poverty (Gladwin 1992a). Current data point to accelerated rates of soil erosion, stratospheric ozone depletion, urban congestion, acid deposition, wetlands destruction, coral reef damage, tropical rain forest depletion, groundwater overdrafting, desertification, and loss of plant and animal species. The data also confirm a steady deterioration in the quality of life for the world's majority, with the absolute number of people who are poor, illiterate, hungry, homeless, or without schooling, sanitation, and primary health care expanding every day (World Bank 1992). The problems are mutually reinforcing and deadly serious. Without significant changes over the next decade, including a substantial decoupling of the economy from adverse environmental impact, the probability is very high that our world could descend into a long decline as environmental, economic, and sociopolitical deterioration increasingly feed on one another to create an uncontrollable maelstrom (Brown, Flavin, and Postel 1991; Meadows, Meadows, and Randers 1992). Thus, the importance of greening as a big step (not the complete answer, as discussed at the end of this chapter) toward a sustainable world free of such devastation.

The critical importance of industrial greening, in particular, is highlighted by a consideration of the factors that contribute to large-scale environmental deterioration. As the World Resources Institute (Heaton, Repetto, and Sobin 1991; Smart 1992) has noted, the environmental burden on world ecosystems and natural resources can crudely be captured by the following equation:

$$\begin{array}{lcl} \text{Global} & & \text{(GNP} & \text{(Environmental} \\ \text{Environmental} = \text{(Population)} \times & \text{per} \times & \text{Impact} \\ \text{Burden} & & \text{Capita)} & \text{per unit} \\ & & & \text{of GNP)} \end{array}$$

In other words, environmental burden equals a product of population times affluence (traditionally defined) times (adverse) technology—that is, $E = P \times A \times T$ (Ehrlich and Ehrlich 1991). For purposes of analysis, P, A, and T can be set to 1 at the current time. The United Nations Population Fund (Lewis 1992) projects that world population will probably rise from 5.48 billion currently to 10 billion in 2050 before leveling off at 11.6 billion after 2100.

Ninety-seven percent of the population increase is projected to occur in developing countries, where population and poverty-induced environmental degradation is already rampant. Thus, the P variable will roughly jump from 1 to 2 by the middle of the next century. The A (affluence or resource consumption) term in the equation is also likely to increase substantially, given increased productivity, consumer aspirations, and the critical need for economic growth to reduce poverty and avoid sociopolitical instability in the developing world. By the year 2050, gross national product (GNP) per capita is projected to be two and a half times today's level (Smart 1992, 5). With the momentum of population and GNP per capita growth already in place, the forecast yields a projection of world economic activity five times the present level by 2050. Holding technology constant, the destructive burden of such growth on the Earth's ecosystems and services would also rise by a factor of five. (Note: Environmental degradation could also be exponentially higher if critical thresholds of ecosystem irreversibility are exceeded or if degradation rises in a nonlinear fashion with increased economic activity.) At a minimum, however, "it is obvious that to hold the global environmental burden constant or, better yet, to reduce it, will require a *dramatic reduction* in environmental impact per unit of GNP—a cut in excess of 80 percent, to less than 20 percent or less of today's level" (Smart 1992, 5). Given that the global environmental burden is currently mainly a product of the richest 20 percent of world population (which consumes roughly 80 percent of world resources and generates 75 percent of world pollution), it can be further argued that "Northern" lifestyles and technologies may need to become fully environmentally benign, or even net beneficial, to offset the increased global environmental burdens that "Southern" population expansion and rising resource consumption will produce.

AMBIGUITY OF GREENING

The second lesson of the parable can be summed up by abusing Elizabeth Barrett Browning's famous sonnet: "How do I green thee, let me count the ways." The motley collection of blind professors variously saw greening as involving entropy, biogeochemistry, ecosystem capacities, ethical values, human cognition, historical transformation, power shifting, externalities, social structures, cultural meanings, human health, normative conformity, corporate opportunity, and a poem with "Re" words. Dozens of other interpretations could be added. As an embryonic and "big idea of general usefulness" (Rodale 1987), greening is or involves all of these things, at one and the same time. It all depends on the angle taken and level of analysis chosen. But surely there must be limits. Greening can't be everything or else it is nothing.

To view greening merely in psychological terms reveals the many complexities involved in attempting to define the phenomenon. This author's crude content analysis of 250 newspaper and magazine articles with the term *greening* in their titles reveals that journalists collectively view it as a complex, dynamic system involving cognitions, emotions, and behaviors (Gladwin 1991). *Thinking greenly* is illustrated by frequent use of the term as a prefix ahead of awareness, attitudes, valuation, sensitivity, assessment, commitment, orientation, obligation, or conscience. *Feeling greenly* is indicated by connection of the phrase with positive emotions of admiration, respect, caring, closeness, hope, inspiration, compassion, and/or negative emotions such as guilt, shame, anger, fear, danger, sadness, and anxiety. *Behaving greenly*, which represents the main way authors tend to employ the phrase, entails association with acts of controlling, cleaning, preventing, protecting, conserving, preserving, reducing, remediating, and so forth.

As Sternberg (1987) has done for the concept of love, greening from a psychological perspective can be understood in terms of cognitive, affective, and behavioral components that together form the vertices of a triangle. Using this triangular conception of greening as the interaction of cognition, affect, and behavior stimulates a range of perspectives and analytical questions. For example:

- Amount of greening: the larger the triangle (i.e., the greater the amount of green thinking, feeling, and behavior of an organization), the greater the absolute amount of experienced greening.
- Time course of greening: different components of greening are likely to increase (and in some cases decline) at different rates over time—

that is, green behavior may rise or fall rapidly, whereas green affect will tend to grow slowly and steadily over a longer period of time.
- Geometry of greening: triangles of organizational greening may vary in both size and proportion, as the cognitive, affective, and behavioral components may vary in intensity at any given point in time (i.e., green thinking may lead or lag behind green behavior, etc.).
- Types of greening: nongreening (absence of green cognition, affect, or behavior), liking (only green affect), infatuated greening (only green behavior), empty greening (only cognition), romantic greening (mix of affect and behavior without cognitive commitment), fatuous greening (green cognition and behavior without congruent feeling), consummate greening (reinforcing green thought, feeling, and behavior), and so forth, are all suggested by Sternberg's analogous treatment of love (1987).

Conceptualizing greening as a mix of thought, affect, and behavior raises many questions about how the three components interact. Do organization members need to experience affective discomfort regarding adverse environmental impacts prior to changing their attitudes and cognitive processes? Or does green thought need to precede green feeling? Can green corporate action precede green thinking, with green-oriented goals, preferences, and rationality emerging from the action rather than guiding the action? Are green attitudes and behavior so loosely coupled that firms may profess green ideals they do not follow or utter green platitudes without examining their validity? Relationships between cognitions, emotions, and behavior are complex, elusive, and often very weak (see Fiske and Taylor 1984; Weick 1979; Zajonc 1980). James March provides a stern warning for those expecting rational choice models to explain organizational greening: "Choices are often made without respect to tastes. Human decision makers routinely ignore their own, fully conscious, preferences, in making decisions. They follow rules, traditions, hunches, and the advice or actions of others. Tastes change over time in such a way that predicting future tastes is often difficult. Tastes are inconsistent. Individuals and organizations are aware of the extent to which some of their preferences conflict with other of their preferences; yet they do nothing to resolve those inconsistencies . . . while tastes are used to choose among actions, it is also true that actions and experiences with their consequences affect tastes" (March 1978, 596).

INADEQUATE RESEARCH OF GREENING

A survey of recent reviews of the literature on the greening of industry (see Brewer 1992; Cairncross 1992; Dillon and Fischer 1992; Gladwin 1992a; Kiernan 1992; Kleiner 1991; Leighton 1992; Schmidheiny 1992; Smart 1992; Vandermere and Oliff 1991) yields ten rather critical general observations about the state of scholarship on the topic:

- Researchers have not offered precise definitions, often leading to confused and contradictory findings.
- Researchers have not produced, after two to three decades of attention, what anyone could rightfully consider as a great wealth of high-quality empirical findings.
- Researchers have not systematically built on one another's work—scholars of greening suffer from a "bias of the present," failing to cumulate research findings.
- Researchers have not been very enthusiastic about causal directionality—very little research has been conducted to determine the antecedents or consequences of greening in organizations.
- Researchers have not based much of their work on rigorous hypothesis-testing logic that rules out alternative explanations—empirically testable propositions are missing from the bulk of all greening research.
- Researchers have not conducted very much systematic comparison of their discoveries across industries, across firm size, and across societies.
- Researchers have not explicitly incorporated dynamics into their study designs, relying overwhelmingly instead on static, cross-sectional methodology—no programmatic, long-term, longitudinal research efforts on greening appear to exist.
- Researchers have not worked very hard at building and validating general models, instead being content to operate at the level of historical particulars.
- Researchers have not always distanced themselves from advocacy and ideology.
- Researchers have not attempted to place their work into broader streams of organizational research dealing variously with change, quality, ethics, globalization, leadership, transaction costs, and so forth.

If research on industrial greening is to be broadly utilizable, then three core criteria of the scientific method must be satisfied: (1) adequate description and classification; (2) generalizability of findings; and (3) predictability of conclusions. The review of existing work on industrial greening indicates that most of it is merely descriptive, boiling down to journalistic storytelling and case studies. Too little of it is driven by theory and rigorous methodology. As a consequence, greening is probably in an age of "superstition," which economist F. A. Hayek (1978, 31) defined as "a time when people imagine that they know more than they do."

How can we get from superstition to greater "truth" about how greening really works? Philosopher Blaise Pascal noted back in 1670 that "We know truth, not only by the reason, but by the heart" (Pascal 1950, 42). Most scholars of greening are probably sufficiently strong on heart, but could profit from a dose of enhanced reasoning. Thus, a plea for greater theory development and application in future research on greening. Many researchers have apparently assumed that greening is so embryonic, so different, so special, that work of a largely exploratory and pretheory nature is fully appropriate. But this misses a great opportunity, for as Kurt Lewin so memorably put it, "Nothing is so practical as a good theory" (Daft and Steers 1986, 23).

Without theory it is difficult to organize existing findings, to produce important generalizations accurately, to generate new ideas, to carefully shape and guide empirical inquiry, and to produce useful corporate and public policy interventions. If our work is to have greater impact, then it must become more theory-driven. We need more "truth" if we are to be influential in helping those who want to stimulate, enforce, or pursue greening. Better knowledge, in short, is needed for green action—that is, advising governmental bodies on appropriate political, regulatory, social, fiscal, monetary, and trade/investment policy transitions needed to push and pull organizations and individuals to green behavior; advising corporate leaders on how to overcome the resource, political, structural, and psychic blockages that impede greening of their organizations; advising community, labor, environmental, and social action groups on the best ways of influencing both governmental and corporate policies; and so forth.

The key to such action knowledge is knowing how greening really works: What is it? Why does it happen? Who does it happen to? When does it happen? Where does it happen? How does it happen? And what are the consequences of it happening? There is a critical need to begin the long journey toward creation of solid general explanatory theories about greening, along with maximal grounding of them in the empirical world. In this regard, scholars of greening have much to gain from linking with, and borrowing from, a broad array of organizational theories that are already well developed or rapidly advancing. Before reviewing the potential contributions of some of these theories, let us first highlight some key trends in the greening of business that await theoretical explanation and integration.

TRENDS IN THE GREENING OF BUSINESS

Trends in corporate environmentalism can be tracked by carefully monitoring journals (e.g., *Garbage, E Magazine, Tomorrow, The Economist*), annual environmental almanacs (e.g., produced by the World Resources Institute or by the editors of *Buzzworm*), business and environment sections of business newspapers (e.g., *Financial Times, Wall Street Journal*), and environmental newsletters (e.g., *Business and the Environment*). *Eco-Source*, based in Ontario, Canada, systematically and comprehensively collects environmental intelligence from dozens of major newspapers and environmental periodicals, cataloguing their findings in a computer data base. The ten most significant trends in the greening of business discerned from this data base as of 1992 (Leighton 1992), supplemented by corporate examples drawn from Gladwin (1992a), Cairncross (1992), and chapters in this volume were as follows:

1. Fundamental rethinking of traditional notions of disposability, risk, responsibility, and the right to pollute as indicated by pollution prevention and toxic reduction programs (e.g., 3M, Monsanto, Dow Chemical), total quality environmental management programs (e.g., members of the Global Environmental Management Initiative), large-scale conservation and demand-side management programs (e.g., Pacific Gas & Electric, Southern California Edison), design for disassembly efforts (e.g., BMW, Volkswagen, Mercedes), green lending guidelines (e.g., National Westminster Bank, BankAmerica, Royal Bank of Canada), debt-for-nature swaps (e.g., American Express, Bank of Tokyo, BankAmerica), industrial ecology experiments (e.g., industrial waste "food chain" involving Novo Nordisk, Kemira, Statoil, and the Asnaes power plant in Kalundborg, Denmark), and a variety of other innovative programs involving alternative agriculture, sustainable forestry, clean technology, and so forth.

2. The spread of holistic full cost and impact analysis involving increased environmental auditing, design for environment (e.g., AT&T), life cycle analysis (e.g., Procter & Gamble), cradle-to-grave product stewardship (e.g., Dow Chemical), total firm eco-audits (e.g., Esprit, Smith & Hawken, Patagonia, The Body Shop, Ben & Jerry's), and efforts toward national environmental accounting (e.g., Germany, Netherlands, Canada, Norway, Japan).

3. Greater environmental accountability being forced by accidents (e.g., Union Carbide—Bhopal, Exxon—Valdez, Sandoz—Rhine River), disclosure requirements (e.g., mandatory emissions reporting mandated by the U.S. Superfund Amendments and Reauthorization Act), community "not-in-my-backyard" pressures, and ethical/environmental screening by pension funds, mutual funds, religious investors, municipal and private portfolio managers, and credit-rating agencies.

4. Increased collaborative partnerships between corporations and environmental organizations (e.g., Fuji Photo Film and the Audubon Society, McDonald's and the Environmental Defense Fund, Merck and the National Institute of Biodiversity of Costa Rica, Safeway and Earth Island Institute, California and New England electric utilities and the Natural Resources Defense Council and Conservation Law Foundation).

5. Increased adoption and formalization of environmental policies, often catalyzed by industry associations (e.g., Responsible Care, International Chamber of Commerce, BAUM, Keidanren), extended internationally (e.g., Monsanto, Dow, ICI), focusing in a high-profile manner on waste reduction (e.g., Westinghouse, Chevron, 3M), and applied to suppliers (e.g., S.C. Johnson, Bell Canada, McDonald's).

6. Growing chief executive officer and board involvement in corporate environmental stewardship, with mindsets shifting from reactive to proactive, and focus shifting from operational to strategic (e.g., Edgar S. Woolard, chairman of DuPont; Alex Krauer, chairman of Ciba Geigy; Richard J. Mahoney, chairman and CEO of Monsanto; Denys Henderson, chairman of ICI; Helmut Sihler, president and CEO of Henkel; William D. Ruckelshaus, CEO of Browning Ferris Industries).

7. Growing pressure for environmental responsibility coming from company employees, labor unions, and prospective recruits (e.g., a McKinsey survey of 403 senior executives from around the world found that 68 percent of them agreed that "organizations with a poor environmental record will find it increasingly difficult to recruit and retain high-calibre staff" (McKinsey & Company 1991).

8. Increased external pressure for environmental performance via tightening of environmental regulations (e.g., European nations moving toward higher standards being set by Germany, Switzerland, and Denmark, or North American states following the leadership of California, Wisconsin, Minnesota, and Massachusetts) and strengthening of green consumerism assisted by product-labeling programs (e.g., Blue Angel, Ecomark, Environmental Choice, Green Cross, Green Seal).

9. Increased propensity of maverick companies deciding to turn envi-

ronmental improvement and resource efficiency to their competitive advantage, with "first movers" (Gladwin 1992a) appearing in appliances (e.g., Electrolux and AEG), automobiles (e.g., Honda and BMW), gasoline (ARCO and Shell), supermarkets (e.g., Tesco and Tengelmann), detergents (e.g., Ecover and Henkel), electricity (e.g., Pacific Gas & Electric and Southern California Edison).

10. Expansion of actual and potential legal liability for environmental damage caused by accidents (e.g., Exxon, Union Carbide), products (e.g., asbestos, pesticides), and past waste disposal practices (e.g., Allied Signal, Shell, General Electric), with criminal and civil damages for environmental harm skyrocketing and environmental liabilities beginning to pose significant credit risks.

APPLYING ORGANIZATIONAL THEORY TO GREENING

The formal analysis, diagnosis, organization, and extension of findings about greening such as those described above necessitates application of theory. While theories drawn from economics, political science, and other disciplines might be fruitful, this author's view is that sociological theory pertaining to organizations holds the greatest promise for improving our understanding of how greening works. (For surveys of organizational theory, see Daft 1992; Morgan 1989; Pfeffer 1982; Scott 1987; and journals such as *Administrative Science Quarterly, American Sociological Review, Organization Studies, Journal of Management Studies, Organization Science,* and *Annual Review of Sociology*.) Such theory focuses on basic characteristics of organizational participants, goals, social structure, technology, and external environment, at different levels of analysis (Scott 1987). It embodies multiple perspectives or frames of reference, viewing organizations variously as rational, natural, and open systems (Scott 1987), using a range of images or metaphors (e.g., organizations as machines, organisms, brains, cultures, political systems, psychic prisons, flux and transformation, and instruments of domination [Morgan 1986]).

GREENING AS INSTITUTIONALIZATION

The institutional approach to organizational analysis (see DiMaggio and Powell 1983; Meyer and Rowan 1977; Meyer and Scott 1983; Powell and DiMaggio 1992; Zucker 1987) suggests that changes in the features of organizations (such as greening) are often introduced to make organizations more aligned with the changing norms and expectations of the institutional environment. Isomorphism with public opinion, educational systems, laws, courts, professions, regulatory structures, awards, and certification and accreditation bodies confers a variety of survival advantages on organizations—for example, greater stability and predictability (DiMaggio 1988), enhanced legitimacy and status (Oliver 1990), greater ease of access to resources (Pfeffer and Salancik 1978), and greater invulnerability to questioning (Meyer and Scott 1983). Greening can thus be viewed as a process of normative conformity and/or external legitimation (see Chapters 7 and 8).

The institutionalist approach also argues (DiMaggio and Powell 1983) that firms within an "organizational field" come to resemble one another over time in their structures and practices. Competitive pressures serve to eliminate those firms that deviate from the norm, and a variety of institutional pressures encourage the remaining firms to imitate their more successful rivals to enhance their legitimacy. According to DiMaggio and Powell (1983), these include coercive pressures, such as laws that compel conformity; mimetic pressures, by which firms model themselves on others to reduce uncertainty; and normative pressures involving authorization or legitimation of organizational practices by superordinate collectivities (e.g., compliance with professional standards or guidelines). (See Chapters 7 and 8.)

Institutional theory may offer considerable guidance on the why, how, and when of greening. It may help, for example, to explain why firms establish green-related external institutional linkages, why they provide grants and donations to environmental causes (e.g., debt-for-nature swaps), why they create industry codes of conduct (e.g., International Chamber of Commerce, Keidanren, Responsible Care), why they create environmental associations (e.g., Global Environmental Management Initiative, Business Council for Sustainable Development), why they invest in public relations efforts to establish green identities (McDonald's, Mobil, Conoco), why they create cooperative efforts (e.g., Industry Cooperative for Ozone Layer Protection), why they go green at different rates and in different forms within different nations (i.e., structural isomorphism between structures of states and organizations operating under their jurisdiction [Carroll, Delacroix, and Goodstein 1990]), and why they green in waves via herd behaviors, contagion, and bandwagon effects (e.g., greenness rivalry among DuPont, Monsanto, and Dow in the U.S. chemical industry or between Southern California Edison and Pacific Gas & Electric in electric power in the state of California).

Greening as Organizational Learning

Theories of organizational learning focus on how past experience is mapped into actions appropriate to the novel present (Cohen and Sproull 1991). An organization learns "if, through its processing of information, the range of its potential behaviors is changed" (Huber 1991, 89). Four central constructs and processes are associated with organizational learning—knowledge acquisition, information distribution, information interpretation, and organizational memory—with more learning occurring when more of the organization's components obtain knowledge recognized as potentially useful, when more varied interpretations of it are developed, and when more organizational units develop uniform comprehensions of the various interpretations (Huber 1991, 90; Chapter 6 of this volume).

Viewing greening as learning holds great theoretical and empirical promise (see Levitt and March 1988 and Chapter 6 in this volume). How do organizations acquire green information or knowledge? How much of green learning is intentional versus unintentional or systematic versus unsystematic? Does greening involve organized experiments and/or arise from self-appraisal? How much of greening involves learning by doing, through trial and error? To what extent do firms learn vicariously, acquiring secondhand green experience from consultants, suppliers, joint venture partners, and competitors? How important is comparative environmental performance benchmarking? How influential are major accidents, such as the Union Carbide Bhopal explosion, as learning vehicles? How much and what types of environmental knowledge are transferred between corporations and environmental groups (e.g., National Wildlife Federation Corporate Conservation Council)? Do environment, health, and safety personnel serve effectively as learning agents via external scanning, focused searching, and performance monitoring? Through what means is green information distributed and communicated within organizations? Do some organizations learn about greening more quickly, reliably, and validly than others, and if so, does superior learning capacity yield competitive advantage?

Greening as Natural Selection

Natural selection, or population ecology, theory suggests that organizational survival is the result of external pressures that differentially select forms for retention in an organization's population (see Hannan and Freeman 1977, 1984, 1989). The focus is not on choices or problems of individual firms, but instead is concerned with the form and variety of entire populations of organizations over time. The theory downplays the consequences of managerial discretion or action and posits that organizational change is limited by strong inertial pressures. According to Haveman (1992), "The internal constraints are investment in plant, equipment, and specialized personnel; limits on the internal information received by decision makers; internal political constraints supportive of vested interests; and organizational history, which justifies past action and prevents consideration of alternative strategies. The external pressures for stability are legal and economic barriers to entry into new areas of activity; constraints on the external information gathered by decision makers; legitimacy considerations; and the problems of collective rationality and the general equilibrium."

The assumption of strong structural inertia implies that organizational change toward greening will tend to fall short of and/or lag behind external demands for greening. Greening may also render organizational performance less reliable or less efficient, thus hurting survival chances (Hannan and Freeman 1989). Organizational transformation toward greening (see Chapters 3, 9, and 10) may thus be adaptive in the long run, but difficult and disruptive in the short run. As such, greening may come about more because of selection and replacement (i.e., the creation and death of organizations and forms of organization) than because of organizational transformation. Adaptation, in other words, will largely be determined from without, with the external environment selecting green organizations and allowing only those firms with appropriate green variations to survive.

Ecological organization theory critically directs our attention to the strength of inertial forces impeding adaptation toward greening (see Chapters 3, 9, and 10). Does this explain why only a small group of far-sighted companies have apparently realized that environmental challenges represent vast new opportunities for strategic leadership and advantage, while "far too many corporations still don't care" about the environment, according to Stephan Schmidheiny, chairman of the Business Council for Sustainable Development (Sjoberg 1991)? The theory also calls attention to "speciation" events (Lumsden and Singh 1990)—that is, how do green firms originally get created and how do random green mutations in organizations occur? Why have environmentally progressive firms such as The Body Shop, Smith & Hawken, Patagonia, Ben & Jerry's, and Esprit been so successful? Are nuclear, coal, and oil firms being selected out of—and solar, wind, and biomass firms being selected into—the energy industry? Are stretch limousines, gas-powered motor vehicles, and supersonic jets being selected out of—and bicycles, electric cars, and mass transit being selected into—the transportation industry? Most important, is greening truly becoming a "selection criterion" by which organizations will either fail or survive and entirely new organizations will be created?

GREENING AS STRATEGIC CHOICE

Whereas natural selection reduces organizations and their leaders to inert observers of an uncontrollable "battle of the survival of the fittest," theories of strategic choice or behavior assume that managers do matter and that organizations purposively enact, define, and affect their domains (Hrebiniak and Joyce 1984; Hrebiniak and Joyce 1985; Hax and Majluf 1984; Lorange 1980; Miles and Snow 1978). Strategic action is viewed in this perspective as rational, deliberate, premeditated, and orderly, with firms pictured at the extreme "to be guided by a comprehensive and explicit strategy which is systematically planned and cooperatively executed" (Ansoff 1987, 505). General managers are seen to anticipate future threats and opportunities, engage in sound strategic analysis, set strategic objectives, and marshall, develop, and dynamically allocate resources to implement strategy (Aguilar 1992; Andrews 1980; Porter 1985, 1991; Wernerfelt 1984).

Greening, viewed as outcomes of rational strategic choice, may thus involve the search for different types of competitive advantage (Gladwin 1992a):

- Cost leadership through the pursuit of environmental efficiency throughout a company's value chain (e.g., 3M saving more than $537 million with its Pollution Prevention Pays program).
- Differentiation of products and services in environmentally oriented ways that command premium prices (e.g., AEG, Varta, Ecover, Henkel, Tesco, Tengelman, Audi, and other European firms gaining market share by targeting the green consumer).
- Leveraging core competencies associated with environmentally sound technologies that power individual business to adapt quickly to changing opportunities (e.g., Sanyo's patient strategy of developing and extending "soft" energy products such as rechargeable batteries and solar cells).
- Innovation and standard setting that sets the "rules of the game" (e.g., Arco announcing a new gasoline formula designed to sharply cut auto emissions).
- Generic substitution of greener processes, products, and services for

those that are more environmentally damaging (e.g., natural gas for coal or oil, compact fluorescent bulbs for incandescent bulbs, recycled products for virgin ones).

- Alliance creation that reduces the costs and risks of entering into new, environmentally beneficial businesses (e.g., General Motors, Ford, Chrysler, and the U.S. government teaming up to develop advanced battery technology for electric vehicles).

While some part of greening must surely arise from intentional strategic behavior, the processes of organizational choice are likely to be affected by considerable ambiguity, incrementalism, and bounded rationality (March and Simon 1958; Simon 1957). According to March (1981, 573), "Organizations do not always have a well-defined set of objectives; their preferences are frequently ambiguous, imprecise, inconsistent, unstable, and affected by their choices. As a result, problem solving and decision making assume some of the features of a garbage can process, learning becomes confounded by the ambiguity of experience, and actions become particularly sensitive to the participation and attention patterns of organizational actors." Streams of loosely coupled green problems, green solutions, green participants, and green choice opportunities therefore probably flow into organizations at different rates and become connected or decoupled according to temporal rather than causal logic (Cohen, March, and Olsen 1972). Greening may thus be a rather messy, disorderly, and fragmented process involving a "mix of rationality and foolishness" (March 1981). Green strategies probably "grow initially like weeds in a garden; they are not cultivated like tomatoes in a hothouse." They also are likely to "take root in all kinds of strange places, virtually wherever people have the capacity to learn and the resources to support that capacity" (Mintzberg and McHugh 1985, 194–96).

GREENING AS TRANSFORMATIONAL LEADERSHIP

If one accepts some role for strategic choice, then it is appropriate to inquire about the role that leaders play in the greening of industry (for a psychological view, see Chapter 2). Is rapid, proactive greening dependent on charismatic green leadership (Conger and Kanungo 1988), defined "as the force of personality that induces a high degree of loyalty, commitment, and devotion to the leader; identification of people with the leader and the leader's mission; adoption of the leader's values, goals and behavior; a sense of being inspired by the leader; a sense of self-esteem from relationships with the leader and the leader's mission; and a high degree of trust in the leader and the correctness of the leader's beliefs" (Daft 1992, 468)? Does such green charismatic leadership emerge most notably during corporate environmental crises, when leaders with the force of personality champion greening as the solution to the crisis?

To what extent does greening involve very extensive organizational change, innovation, and entrepreneurship—that is, "second-order change" (Levy and Merry 1986)? Deep versus shallow greening surely involves massive administrative change—fundamental transformations of mission, structure, and political, cultural, and technical systems (Tichy and Devanna 1986). As such, greening may necessitate "transformational leadership" whereby followers, especially top management teams (see Hambrick 1987), are motivated to "believe in the vision of corporate transformation, to recognize the need for revitalization, to sign on for the new vision, and to help institutionalize a new organizational process" (Daft 1992, 468), with leaders relying on charisma, inspiration, intellectual stimulation, and individual consideration (Bass 1985; Seltzer and Bass 1990).

A proactive corporate leadership agenda for achieving environmental sustainability includes: (1) inspiring a shared vision of the enterprise as environmentally sustainable; (2) creating an organizational culture that guides and supports sustainable corporate behavior; (3) encouraging quick organizational learning about the demands and opportunities that sustainable development presents; (4) empowering members of the organization to initiate, and take responsibility for, sustainable behavior; (5) developing the organizational expertise necessary for the company to perform sustainability; (6) persuading those who have a stake in the organization to support sustainable behavior; and (7) helping to transform public policies so that they reward sustainable development (see Gladwin 1992b).

The most important, and perhaps the most difficult, leadership task may be that of creating and maintaining green values within an organization. As Edgar H. Schein (1985, 317) noted, ". . . the unique and essential function of leadership is the manipulation of culture." Emergent values and ethics of the environmentally sustainable enterprise include stewardship, reverence, prevention, and humility in regard to ecology; frugality, permanence, simplicity, and sufficiency in regard to resources; fairness, compassion, appropriateness, and community in regard to society; and accountability, participation, proaction, and long-termism in regard to process (Gladwin 1992c). Substantial cultural leadership (Trice and Beyer

1991), symbolic management (Peters and Waterman 1982), and even evangelism (Weick 1979) will be needed to inculcate such green value systems within large organizations.

GREENING AS ORGANIZATIONAL EVOLUTION

Under what conditions is transformational leadership possible? A variety of organizational change theories are coming together to conceptualize change as a "punctuated equilibrium" (Gersick 1991; Tushman and Romanelli 1985). During periods of relative stability, change is incremental and convergent, by which organizational values, strategies, structures, power distributions, and control systems move into ever closer coalignment. Dramatic changes in technology (Tushman and Anderson 1986), regulatory shifts (Zucker 1987), radical disruptions in the socioeconomic environment (Tushman, Newman, and Romanelli 1986), and/or sustained performance declines are required to overcome the inertia of convergence. Only then can executive leadership initiate and implement discontinuous or "frame-breaking" change involving simultaneous and sharp shifts in strategy, power, structure, control, and so forth. "Reorientations" or "recreations" at these times demarcate and set the bearings for the next convergence period (Tushman, Newman, and Romanelli 1986).

This punctuated equilibrium model of organizational evolution suggests that only shallow corporate greening, managed by middle managers, is likely during convergence periods. Deeper greening, involving deep-seated changes in core values, product and market strategies, and resource allocation may thus depend on the experience of severe environmental shocks, jolts, and crises that threaten organizational survival (Starbuck, Greve, and Hedberg 1978). Frame-breaking upheavals resulting in deep greening may also necessitate fresh sets of senior executives brought in from outside the company who are unfettered by prior commitments to the status quo (Tushman, Newman, and Romanelli 1986). The relative paucity of fully green firms at the current time suggests that the period of revolutionary, quantum, disruptive, and metamorphic green reorientation has yet to arrive—the true "Eco-Industrial Revolution" (Kiernan 1992) thus lies ahead.

Rather than waiting to study revolutionary greening, scholars can today focus on incremental and partial green innovation by organizations. Such innovation represents "the development and implementation of new ideas by people who, over time, engage in transactions with others within an institutional order" (Van de Ven 1986). Abundant work exists on the motivations to innovate, the tasks of innovation, the stages of innovation, the role of champions of innovation, the barriers to innovation, the diffusion of innovation, and the risks/rewards of first-mover innovation. (For a survey, see Kanter 1990.) Much of this literature focuses specifically on technological innovation, so very relevant to greening of the transformation process of organizational inputs into outputs (Tushman and Nelson 1990). Such technological innovations often precede administrative innovation. Innovation, similar to strategic choice behavior, is increasingly viewed as a nonlinear, slightly chaotic, usually sloppy process (Kanter 1990, 278). Innovation theory allows us to hypothesize, however, that rates of green innovation are likely to be higher for organizations displaying higher complexity, stronger extra-organizational ties, more cosmopolitan orientations, greater boundary spanning, more intense communication integration, greater availability of resources, and more receptive social and legal environments (i.e., "fertile fields").

CONCLUSION

It should now be clear that a broad range of formal theory awaits application to the phenomenon of greening. Different organizational theories, of course, vary in their utility or soundness according to criteria of internal consistency, external consistency, scientific parsimony, generalizability, and verification (Kaplan 1964). The point, in any case, is that progress in the study of greening demands much greater application of the scientific method—that is: (1) observing real world facts; (2) formulating theoretical explanations using the inductive process; (3) generating predictions or hypotheses about the phenomena using the deductive process; and (4) verifying the predictions or hypotheses by returning to real world facts gathered through systematic, controlled observation (Stone 1978). Good theory and method will enable us to organize knowledge on greening into a pattern of relationships, will help us to summarize diverse findings about it, and will allow us to differentiate between important and trivial questions for future research (Hamner and Organ 1978). Regarding the future, it is important to keep the role of greening in proper perspective—thus, the caveat in the next section.

FINAL CAVEAT: GREENING VERSUS SUSTAINABILITY

Environmental management in rich nations (the focus of the vast majority of all research on industrial greening so far, including the work reported in this book), however vital, may not be enough to ensure an environmentally and socially secure world. Greening, in short, represents a necessary but not a sufficient condition for sustainable development (Brown, Flavin, and Postel 1991; Chiras 1992; Ehrlich and Ehrlich 1991; Gladwin 1992a; Gore 1992; Smith 1992).

Without substantial poverty alleviation and population stabilization on this planet, the future is likely to involve massive flows of ecological and economic refugees, major health crises, regional conflicts over resource use, mass famine and starvation, and even terrorist movements driven by grievances held by those perceiving gross inequity. There is no way in which the North can insulate itself from the adverse effects of a world majority experiencing widespread environmental destruction and sociopolitical disruption. No one can escape the effects of massive, mainly poverty-fed deforestation, species loss, dirty coal exploitation, or population displacement. In short, sustainability for the rich depends on sustainability for the poor, and vice versa. Unless we learn how to drastically shift economic opportunity, technology, capital, and primary socialservice provision toward the poor of this planet, then it is possible that greening in rich nations merely amounts to a rearranging of the deck chairs on a "Global Titanic."

REFERENCES

Aguilar, Francis J. 1992. *General Managers in Action*. New York: Oxford University Press.

Andrews, Kenneth R. 1980. *The Concept of Corporate Strategy*. Homewood, Ill.: Irwin.

Ansoff, H. Igor. 1987. "The Emerging Paradigm of Strategic Behavior." *Strategic Management Journal* 8: 501–16.

Bass, Bernard M. 1985. *Leadership and Performance Beyond Expectations*. New York: Free Press.

Brewer, Garry D. 1992. "Business and Environment: A Time for Creative and Constructive Co-existence." Paper prepared for William K. McInally Memorial Lecture, Ann Arbor, Michigan, March 31.

Brown, Lester R.; Flavin, Christopher; and Postel, Sandra. 1991. *Saving the Planet: How to Shape an Environmentally Sustainable Global Economy*. New York: W. W. Norton.

Cairncross, Frances. 1992. *Costing the Earth*. Boston: Harvard Business School Press.

Carroll, Glenn R.; Delacroix, Jacques; and Goodstein, Jerry. 1990. "The Political Environments of Organizations: An Ecological View." In *The Evolution and Adaptation of Organizations*, edited by Larry L. Cummings and Barry M. Staw, 67–100. Greenwich, Conn.: JAI Press.

Chiras, Daniel D. 1992. *Lessons from Nature: Learning to Live Sustainably on the Earth.* Washington, D.C.: Island Press.

Cohen, Michael D.; March, James G.; and Olsen, Johan P. 1972. "A Garbage Can Model of Organizational Choice." *Administrative Science Quarterly* 17: 1–25.

Cohen, Michael D., and Sproull, Lee S., eds. 1991. "Special Issue on Organizational Learning: Papers in Honor of (and by) James G. March." *Organization Science* 2: 1–145.

Conger, Jay A.; Kanungo, Rabindia N.; and Associates. 1988. *Charismatic Leadership: The Elusive Factor in Organizational Effectiveness.* San Francisco: Jossey-Bass.

Daft, Richard L. 1992. *Organization Theory and Design.* St. Paul: West Publishing.

Daft, Richard L., and Steers, Richard M. 1986. *Organizations: A Micro-Macro Approach.* Glenview, Ill.: Scott, Foresman.

Dillon, Patricia S., and Fischer, Kurt. 1991. *Environmental Management in Corporations: Methods and Motivations.* Medford, Mass.: Center for Environmental Management, Tufts University.

DiMaggio, Paul. 1988. "Interest and Agency in Institutional Theory." In *Institutional Patterns and Organizations: Culture and Environment*, edited by Lynne Zucker, 3–21. Cambridge, Mass.: Ballinger.

DiMaggio, Paul J., and Powell, Walter W. 1983. "The Iron Cage Revisited: Institutional Isomorphism and Collective Rationality in Organizational Fields." *American Sociological Review* 48: 147–60.

Ehrlich, Paul R., and Ehrlich, Anne H. 1991. *Healing the Planet: Strategies for Resolving the Environmental Crisis.* Reading, Mass.: Addison-Wesley.

Fiske, Susan T., and Taylor, Shelley E. 1984. *Social Cognition.* New York: Random House.

Gersick, Connie J. G. 1991. "Revolutionary Change Theories: A Multilevel Exploration of the Punctuated Equilibrium Paradigm." *Academy of Management Review* 16: 10–36.

Gladwin, Thomas N. 1992a. *Building the Sustainable Corporation: Creating Environmental Sustainability and Competitive Advantage.* Washington, D.C.: National Wildlife Federation.

Gladwin, Thomas N. 1992b. "Executive Summary of Building the Sustainable Corporation." Paper prepared for National Wildlife Federation Corporate Conservation Council Synergy '92 Conference, Laguna Niguel, California, January 16–17.

Gladwin, Thomas N. 1992c. "Toward Environmentally Sustainable Corporate Identity." Paper prepared for Business Briefing on the Earth Summit and Sustainable Development, New York, March 19.

Gladwin, Thomas N. 1991. "Green Cognition, Behavior and Emotion: A Content Analysis." Stern School of Business Working Paper. New York.

Gore, Al. 1992. *Earth in the Balance: Ecology and the Human Spirit.* Boston: Houghton Mifflin.

Hambrick, Donald C. 1987. "The Top Management Team: Key to Strategic Success." *California Management Review* 30: 1–20.

Hamner, W. Clay, and Organ, Dennis M. 1978. *Organizational Behavior: An Applied Psychological Approach.* Dallas: BPI.

Hannan, Michael T., and Freeman, John. 1989. *Organizational Ecology.* Cambridge, Mass.: Harvard University Press.

Hannan, Michael T., and Freeman, John. 1984. "Structural Inertia and Organizational Change." *American Sociological Review* 49: 149–64.

Hannan, Michael T., and Freeman, John. 1977. "The Population Ecology of Organizations." *American Journal of Sociology* 8: 929–64.

Haveman, Heather A. 1992. "Between a Rock and a Hard Place: Organizational Change and Performance under Conditions of Fundamental Environmental Transformation." *Administrative Science Quarterly* 37: 48–75.

Hax, Arnoldo C., and Majluf, Nicholas S. 1984. *Strategic Management: An Integrative Perspective.* Englewood Cliffs, N.J.: Prentice-Hall.

Hayek, F. A. 1978. *The Three Sources of Human Values: Hobhouse Lecture.* London: London School of Economics.

Heaton, George; Repetto, Robert; and Sobin, Rodney. 1991. *Transforming Technology: An Agenda for Environmentally Sustainable Growth in the 21st Century.* Washington, D.C.: World Resources Institute.

Hrebiniak, Lawrence G., and Joyce, William F. 1985. "Organizational Adaptation: Strategic Choice and Environmental Determinism." *Administrative Science Quarterly* 30: 336–49.

Hrebiniak, Lawrence G., and Joyce, William F. 1984. *Implementing Strategy.* New York: Macmillan.

Huber, George P. 1991. "Organizational Learning: The Contributing Processes and the Literatures." *Organization Science* 2: 88–109.

Kanter, Rosabeth Moss. 1990. "When a Thousand Flowers Bloom: Structural, Collective, and Social Conditions for Innovation in Organizations." In *The Evolution and Adaptation of Organizations,* edited by Larry L. Cummings and Barry M. Staw, 277–319. Greenwich, Conn.: JAI Press.

Kaplan, Abraham. 1964. *The Conduct of Inquiry.* San Francisco: Chandler.

Kiernan, Matthew J. 1992. "The Age of Eco-Strategy: Thoughts for the Earth Summit in Rio de Janeiro, June 1992." *International Executive* 34: 197–214.

Kleiner, Art. 1991. "What Does It Mean to Be Green?" *Harvard Business Review* 69: 38–47.

Leighton, Tony. 1992. "Putting It All Together: Ten Trends in Corporate Environmentalism." *Tomorrow* 2: 24–31.

Levitt, B., and March, J. G. 1988. "Organizational Learning." *Annual Review of Sociology* 14: 319–40.

Levy, Amir, and Merry, Urs. 1986. *Organizational Transformation.* New York: Praeger.

Lewis, Paul. 1992. "Food Production and the Birth Rate Are in a New Race." *New York Times,* May 10, 4E.

Lorange, Peter. 1980. *Corporate Planning*. Englewood Cliffs, N.J.: Prentice-Hall.

Lumsden, Charles J., and Singh, Jitendra V. 1990. "The Dynamics of Organizational Speciation." In *Organizational Evolution: New Directions*, edited by Jitendra V. Singh. Newbury Park, Calif.: SAGE.

March, James G. 1981. "Footnotes to Organizational Change." *Administrative Science Quarterly* 26: 563–77.

March, James G. 1978. "Bounded Rationality, Ambiguity, and the Engineering of Choice." *Bell Journal of Economics* 9: 587–608.

March, James G., and Simon, Herbert A. 1958. *Organizations*. New York: John Wiley.

McKinsey & Company. 1991. *The Corporate Response to the Environmental Challenge: Summary Report*. Amsterdam: McKinsey.

Meadows, Donella H.; Meadows, Denis; and Randers, Jorgen. 1992. *Beyond the Limits: Confronting Global Collapse: Envisioning a Sustainable Future*. Post Mills, Vt.: Chelsea Green.

Meyer, John W., and Rowan, Brian. 1977. "Institutional Organizations: Formal Structure As Myth and Ceremony." *American Journal of Sociology* 83: 340–63.

Meyer, John W., and Scott, W. Richard. 1983. *Organizational Environments: Ritual and Rationality*. Newbury Park, Calif.: SAGE.

Miles, Raymond E., and Snow, Charles C. 1978. *Organizational Strategy, Structure and Process*. New York: McGraw-Hill.

Mintzberg, Henry, and McHugh, Alexandra. 1985. "Strategy Formation in an Adhocracy." *Administrative Science Quarterly* 30: 160–97.

Morgan, Gareth. 1989. *Creative Organization Theory: A Resource*. Newbury Park, Calif.: SAGE.

Morgan, Gareth. 1986. *Images of Organization*. Newbury Park, Calif.: SAGE.

Oliver, Christine. 1990. "Determinants of Interorganizational Relationships: Integration and Future Directions." *Academy of Management Review* 15: 241–65.

Pascal, Blaise. 1950. *Thoughts*. Edited and translated by Henry F. Stewart. New York: Pantheon.

Peters, Thomas J., and Waterman, Robert H. Jr., 1982. *In Search of Excellence*. New York: Harper & Row.

Pfeffer, Jeffrey. 1982. *Organizations and Organization Theory*. Boston: Pitman.

Pfeffer, Jeffrey, and Salancik, Gerald R. 1978. *The External Control of Organizations: A Resource Dependence Perspective*. New York: Harper & Row.

Porter, Michael E. 1991. "Towards a Dynamic Theory of Strategy." *Strategic Management Journal* 12: 95–118.

Porter, Michael E. 1985. *Competitive Advantage: Creating and Sustaining Superior Performance*. New York: Free Press.

Powell, Walter W., and DiMaggio, Paul J., eds. 1992. *The New Institutionalism in Organizational Analysis*. Chicago: University of Chicago Press.

Rodale, Robert. 1987. "Big New Ideas: Where Are They Today?" *Bulletin of the Science and Technology Society* 7: 577–84.

Schein, Edgar H. 1985. *Organization Culture and Leadership*. San Francisco: Jossey-Bass.

Schmidheiny, Stephen, with the Business Council for Sustainable Development. 1992. *Changing Course: A Global Business Perspective on Development and the Environment*. Cambridge, Mass.: MIT Press.

Scott, W. Richard. 1987. *Organizations: Rational, Natural, and Open Systems*. Englewood Cliffs, N.J.: Prentice-Hall.

Seltzer, Joseph, and Bass, Bernard M. 1990. "Transformational Leadership: Beyond Initiation and Consideration." *Journal of Management* 16: 693–703.

Simon, Herbert A. 1957. *Models of Man*. New York: John Wiley.

Sjoberg, Claes. 1991. "Industrial Catalyst: Interview with Stephan Schmidheiny." *Tomorrow* 1: 34–40.

Smart, Bruce, ed. 1992. *Beyond Compliance: A New Industry View of the Environment*. Washington, D.C.: World Resources Institute.

Smith, Emily T. 1992. "Growth vs. Environment: The Push for Sustainable Development." *Business Week*. May 11, 66–75.

Starbuck, William G.; Greve, A.; and Hedberg, Bo L. T. 1978. "Responding to Crisis." *Journal of Business Administration* 9: 111–37.

Sternberg, Robert J. 1987. *The Triangle of Love*. New York: Basic Books.

Stone, Eugene F. 1978. *Research Methods in Organizational Behavior*. Glenview, Ill.: Scott, Foresman.

Tichy, Noel M., and Devanna, Mary Ann. 1986. *The Transformational Leader*. New York: John Wiley.

Trice, Harrison M., and Beyer, Janice M. 1991. "Cultural Leadership in Organizations." *Organization Science* 2: 149–69.

Tushman, Michael L., and Anderson, Philip. 1986. "Technological Discontinuities and Organizational Environments." *Administrative Science Quarterly* 31: 439–65.

Tushman, Michael L., and Nelson, Richard R., eds. 1990. "Special Issue: Technology, Organization and Innovation." *Administrative Science Quarterly* 35: entire issue.

Tushman, Michael L.; Newman, William H.; and Romanelli, Elaine. 1986. "Convergence and Upheaval. Managing the Unsteady Pace of Organizational Evolution." *California Management Review* 29: 29–44.

Tushman, Michael L., and Romanelli, Elaine. 1985. "Organizational Evolution: A Metamorphosis Model of Convergence and Reorientation." In *Research in Organizational Behavior,* edited by Larry L. Cummings and Barry M. Straw, 171–222. Greenwich, Conn.: JAI Press.

Vandermere, Sandra, and Oliff, Michael. 1991. "Corporate Challenges for an Age of Reconsumption." *Columbia Journal of World Business* 26: 6–25.

Van de Ven, Andy H. 1986. "Central Problems in the Management of Innovation." *Management Science* 32: 590–609.

Weick, Karl E. 1979. "Cognitive Processes in Organizations." In *Research in Organizational Behavior*, edited by Barry M. Staw, 41–74. Greenwich, Conn.: JAI Press.

Wernerfett, Birger. 1984. "A Resource-based View of the Firm." *Strategic Management Journal* 5: 171–80.

World Bank. 1992. *World Development Report 1992: Development and the Environment*. New York: Oxford University Press.

Zajonc, Robert B. 1980. "Feeling and Thinking: Preferences Need No Inferences." *American Psychologist* 35: 151–75.

Zucker, Lynne G. 1987. "Institutional Theories of Organizations." *Annual Review of Sociology* 13: 443–64.

2

Toward Greening in the Executive Suite

Melissa Everett, John E. Mack,
and Robert Oresick

It should not be a surprise that the term *greening* is difficult to define precisely. After all, it is a metaphor. As such, it encourages those of us who were trained in the sciences to think in new ways. This encouragement is essential, for the changes required in industry are not only in technologies, organizational structures, possible products, markets, and realistic definitions of development, although these are complex enough. What is truly required to bring about these changes is an overarching change in world view and sense of human possibility, a reordering of priorities, and a redefinition of accountability. Examples of the more far-reaching challenges to industrial structure and purpose include community right-to-know laws, dual bottom-line accounting, and the Valdez Principles (see Chapter 8).

As an organizing metaphor, greening suggests evolution rather than linear, inflexible change. It suggests adaptations that can support one another and, at each stage, open up unexpected possibilities for the next. Greening means investing the resources and encouraging the creativity needed to find solutions to long-standing problems. It means cultivating an atmosphere of accountability in which environmental considerations are seen as an integral part of designing a product or process, not as an afterthought.

The leadership challenge of greening is equally complex. A shift to sustainable industrial policies is likely to require significant personal adaptation on the part of those in charge, involving conscious and unconscious motivational factors. The good news is that such a greening in the board room could bring a highly desirable by-product: a healing of many of the ills and stresses that executives increasingly acknowledge in their professional and personal lives.

In facing environmental questions, the human beings who run corporations are just as complex, and at times contradictory, as any others. Two vignettes will set the stage for our discussion:

> . . . . Stanley Dudek, owner of a small coal company in St. Clairsville, Ohio, began reclaiming land he had strip mined so that it could be farmed again. Big operators, who were telling the public that it was physically and financially impossible to reclaim strip mined land, threatened Dudek and tried to shut him down. He kept right on, creating a model that convinced legislators to require reclamation from all mining companies.[1]

> . . . . When H. J. Heinz announced . . . that Star Kist tuna would be harvested in a way that protects dolphins, *CEO* magazine denounced chief executive Anthony J. F. O'Reilly for "capitulating" to "enviroterrorists." The Capitol Research Center in Washington publishes an annual volume of loyalists and traitors to the free-market cause, based on monies donated by the Forbes 250 companies. The 1990 volume, *The Suicidal Impulse*, criticized such firms as General Mills Corp., Aetna Life & Casualty, Inc., and DuPont Co. for giving to groups such as the Children's Defense Fund or the National Audubon Society. Bank of Boston was slammed for giving to the League of Women Voters Educational Fund, which the book says advocates school busing, quotas and "forced energy conservation."[2]

These are tough times for believers in completely rational decision making. The above cases suggest some of the psychosocial barriers to the adoption of clean technologies: group pressures and loyalties; the inertia of established patterns; and, at times, the simple inability of ordinary leaders to find the moral courage for this extraordinary era.

What psychological strengths distinguish those executives who find ways to incorporate necessary changes into their companies without jeopardizing what they have already created? What personal skills must be cultivated to help the upcoming generation of corporate leaders succeed in building healthy relationships among economy, environment, and society? To address those questions, we compared two groups of executives— those who, in their own eyes, had taken some unusual risk or initiative in the interest of social or environmental responsibility, and those who had not. It should be emphasized at the outset that this sample was not randomly selected; rather, the individuals studied were chosen on the basis of personal references as principled executives with a variety of social and environmental records who would be willing to speak with us candidly and confidentially. This was an exploratory study aimed at understanding, as wholistically as possible, how successful social and environmental innovators in business look at the world.

Psychology is not a unified, consistent discipline as is chemistry or engineering. It offers many alternative frames through which to look at the person, each bringing different qualities into focus and each supported by some empirical evidence. In that respect it is similar enough to management science that we expected quite interesting information to come from dialogues between psychologists and executives. Since we as psychologists have not run businesses ourselves, we know there are limits to our ability to understand the subjective experiences of corporate decision makers. We have done our best to serve as faithful translators. With expertise in humanistic clinical psychiatry and psychobiography, we did not approach this project as arbiters of what is or is not "normal," but to ask what is required of sane and productive people in the face of a monumental challenge.

The literature on executive psychology, extensive though it is, contains little of direct relevance to this question. But a number of qualitative studies provide useful, complementary findings on the personalities and styles of corporate decision makers. Michael Maccoby's classic, *The Gamesman*, describes a cluster of personality traits that stand out in executives who rise in corporations. Manfred Kets de Vries and Danny Miller's *Unstable at the Top* identifies five self-sabotaging management styles. Jeffrey Speller's *Executives in Crisis* reports on the stress symptoms and psychopathologies experienced, and often hidden, by senior executives. Ian Mitroff and Theirry Pauchant's *We're So Big and Powerful Nothing Bad Can Happen to Us* identifies many elements of managerial and decision-making style that are common in companies suffering from environmental and other crises. However, none of these studies looks directly at the qualities required to lead a turnaround in a corporation that is in trouble. Our research was conceived to be relevant to the environmental issue and to a range of other issues in which managers are called upon to adapt their policies and practices in response to new social imperatives.

Our approach is to consider the person, or the self, as a system encompassing behavior, thought, belief, emotion, memory, subconscious dynamics and images, relationships, and the deep structures of personality that govern the organization of all these elements. This places us in the tradition known as the psychoanalytic psychology of the self, framed by Harry Stack Sullivan, Heinz Kohut (1971, 1977), and others. This field of study has been revolutionized by the new theories on women's moral development of writers such as Jean Baker Miller (1991) and Carol

Gilligan (1982), who point out the essential role of "relational development" in shaping the moral reasoning of people of either gender.

Self, in its psychoanalytic usage, is both an intrapsychic and a social concept. On the one hand, it consists of those inner representations that together constitute the sense of "ourselves." On the other hand, self is social in that it comprises a system for connecting with others, who, through relationship, complete the sense of self. We also speak of a "core self," which, according to Daniel Stern (1985), begins to form in the three- to six-month period of life with the infant's sense of initiatory capability or agency. This core self becomes the subjective experience of identity, of personal continuity or consistency over time, more or less unassailable by life's stresses and vicissitudes.

We conducted in-depth interviews lasting from one to four hours with twenty-four senior executives in publicly held corporations. We focused on public corporations because their leaders are subject to the greatest constraints due to stockholder pressures and the threat of takeover—pressures that are often cited as barriers to more proactive environmental strategies. Our subjects included sixteen at the chief executive officer, chief operating officer, or board chair level; the rest were in top line and staff positions. They represented banking and finance, civilian and defense manufacturing, computers, chemicals, pharmaceuticals, engineering, architecture, entertainment, and communications.

Our interviews were confidential and generally were held in each executive's office. They were taped and transcribed. While our lines of questioning were flexible to ensure coverage of the major issues as defined by each subject, a cluster of core questions was asked in every interview. These were intentionally quite broad and included the following:

1. Please give a general history of your career path in terms of the values that have driven your choices and any major ethical turning points.
2. How would you summarize your working definition of your social and environmental responsibility as a business executive?
3. What dilemmas have you faced, in your corporate role, between your social or environmental responsibilities as you saw them and the practical constraints imposed by business concerns? How did you resolve each dilemma?

We grouped our subjects into two categories on the basis of their responses: those who had taken some personally significant risk or initiative in the name of social or environmental values (in their direct business decisions or job choices, rather than elsewhere in public life or in philanthropy), and those who had not. We dubbed the first group "principled risk takers" and the second "conventional decision makers." We emphasize that the two groups were each diverse and contained equally talented, dedicated, and principled executives.

The principled risk takers included executives who had taken unpopular positions on corporate policy in the name of social or environmental values; created job descriptions for themselves geared toward transforming their companies; changed their employers or career paths in the service of social or environmental values; discontinued products or refused contracts based on environmental criteria; and developed long-range, company-wide plans to shift to technologies they saw as cleaner.

ANALYTIC MODEL

The two groups differed significantly in three areas having to do with fundamental personality structures and what might be termed ways of viewing the world: self-consistency, personal efficacy, and scope of awareness. These differences were observed both in the whole sample and in a subsample of the sixteen highest-level executives.

SELF-CONSISTENCY

The groups differed in their conscious norms of behavior. Harmony between personal values and business behavior, a form of self-consistency, was a matter of conscious concern for the principled risk takers. It was seen as essential for coherent functioning. For the conventional decision makers, by contrast, the idea of different standards for business and private behavior was seen as obvious. Many commented, "Of course you use a different logic in making business decisions," and "I can't imagine it being hard to separate social values and business thinking."

One highly self-consistent executive is Mark, the CEO of a high-tech manufacturing company. As a vice-president, Mark took several initiatives to detach himself from projects involving technologies he saw as harmful and at times encouraged his superiors to keep the company as a whole out of those areas. He described himself as "a straight arrow" who found great satisfaction in a conservative lifestyle. One of his extracurricular activities was involvement, with his wife, in a group of couples interested in exploring the relationship between their values and their careers. He had also volunteered his time in several statewide environmental referenda. Speaking about his corporate choice, he said, "I had taken positions, spoken out on the issues. It seemed important to follow through in my own actions."

A similar sentiment was expressed by Norm, CEO of a large chemical company that had refused a lucrative government contract to manufacture an ingredient of binary nerve gas. In reaching his decision he had taken into account his employees' sentiments on the issue, his skepticism about the need for the product in national defense, and a corporate policy against selling weapons components to any government. At the same time, he feared adverse publicity and damaged government relations, which could have a significant effect on the company. Finally, he said, "You just have to be able to look at yourself in the mirror when you shave. If I had let that sale go through, I wouldn't have been able to."

The obverse of self-consistency is compartmentalization, the common capacity to think, feel, and act quite differently in different settings. Compartmentalization makes it possible to block from consciousness any concerns that are judged as irrelevant or that may be overwhelming in a given situation, even if they would trigger a passionate response in the same person in a different setting. In *Staying the Course: The Emotional and Social Lives of Men Who Do Well at Work*, Robert S. Weiss (1990, 58) described this as a mechanism for dealing with an endless stream of decisions: "Having chosen what seems the best of the available options, [successful men] compartmentalize any lingering uncertainty. They do not second-guess themselves; indeed, they do not permit themselves further attention to the problem."

Compartmentalization is illustrated by Ted, the CEO of a chemical engineering firm that had developed many lucrative environmental products and services. Initially he said he could not think of any dilemmas between his personal values and his corporate role. Later in the interview, however, in talking about the global nature of the company and his international travels, Ted volunteered this story: "You know the chemical plants in eastern Europe that are making the news, creating hell with all their environmental problems? We built a lot of them back in the early 1970s. *We told our clients at the time* that in the United States we would have had more stringent environmental controls. But they didn't want to pay for them. And we have always taken the position that *the customer is always right*."

Ted is torn between two concepts of "right"—what is required for human welfare and what appears to be required for business success. He can refer graphically to the deadly impact of the chemical plants and admit that he acted against his own best environmental judgment. But, at the same time, he is serious in the claim that the customer—no matter how ill-informed, short-sighted, or powerless—is, in a meaningful sense, right.

The dissonance between Ted's personal values and his business persona is so subtle that he does not seem to recognize the inconsistency. A more obvious, conscious form of compartmentalization is shown by Jim, a high-level officer in a bank that is heavily involved in financing nuclear power plants. Jim believes that the best way to manage stress and lead a well-rounded life is to preserve high barriers between private and business life. He does so by being a hard-driving executive by day and a community activist, serving on the boards of several nonprofit organizations, by night.

One of Jim's most compelling personal commitments is fund-raising for a hospice for children with cancer. Asked in the interview how he felt about the possible connection between the nuclear fuel cycle and the release of carcinogens, he jokingly rose from his chair and asked, "Are we done yet?" Then, to his great credit, he sat down and continued: "You know, the easy cop-out answer is that there isn't strict evidence that convinces you intellectually. I mean, I still think there is enough gray that it's hard to say what the cause and effect are. But it can't be good. Nuclear power. If we could do without it, it would be great. And this is a real cop-out, but I really feel I'm being sincere in answering it—hunger is hunger, and the person's dying because they don't have enough food. The disabled you can feel, touch. With nuclear power, it gets so esoteric to me. I don't know. I don't think I've paid enough attention to it . . . . Maybe it's almost denial."

Self-consistency does not mean a lack of complexity or even the absence of socially determined modes of operation. It does mean a relationship of mutual awareness, compatibility, communication, and even synergy among various social selves (Blasi and Oresick 1987).

A further distinction showed up between the principled risk takers and the conventional decision makers. The first group tended to justify their decisions by invoking universal values and supporting their arguments with imagery drawn from the world outside business. For example, they spoke of employees as an extended family. Said Norm, the CEO of the chemical company that had refused a lucrative contract to make a potentially dangerous product, "You get to thinking about your employees like your kids. Sometimes they need to be listened to, sometimes they need to be encouraged, and sometimes they need a good kick in the rear end."

The conventional decision makers, by contrast, used language and imagery that implicitly equated their personal well-being and range of options with the company's: "If I had accepted that contract, I—meaning the company—"; "As a senior attorney, we have to maintain 7000 jobs . . ."

Much more than the principled risk takers, the conventional decision makers tended to portray citizen advocates as adversaries and to see the prosperity of the private sector as a key to social welfare. Coupled with their tendency toward compartmentalization, this suggests a highly developed "corporate self" whose identification with the company's past and present may make change difficult. The principled risk takers, in contrast, may be more capable of independent judgment and less threatened by changing course because of a more autonomous sense of self apart from corporate life.

PERSONAL EFFICACY

Jim, the high-level bank officer, shows highly developed business and social selves with quite different value systems. He also shows a limited appreciation of his personal power to affect matters, or, in clinical language, agency. Agency is not just the ability to amass resources or give orders, but an underlying drive to act and an awareness of the impact of one's actions. One might think that, since they are trained as decision makers and leaders, all corporate executives would exhibit a high degree of agency. But in moral and creative terms, many of our subjects showed radical differences in this quality that had nothing to do with their actual economic or institutional clout. Although Jim has risen almost to the top in a major bank, he continues to feel he must prove himself and operates in the shadow of uncertainty, describing himself as "the classic C student who works hard."

Jim contrasts strongly with Harvey, an executive brought into a defense company to revitalize it and improve labor relations. In the process, he is initiating long-range planning efforts to diversify the company's products and make it less dependent on producing military technologies, in keeping with his personal concerns about weapons proliferation as well as his economic analysis. "I am not unusually bright or talented, but I am unusually confident," said Harvey. "Corporate America wants to make decisions, but it wants to make perfect ones. I am confident enough that I can make mistakes and bounce back. I knew I could bring some fresh air to the process."

Agency means an inner source of authority for tough decisions and a greater ability to withstand institutional pressure. Related to agency in many cases is a well-developed core sense of self independent of institutions (Deikman 1982). For some of our executives, that independent sense of self is rooted in a secure family life, an especially trusting friendship, or a commitment to community activities that have meaning. This well-developed core self was there from the start for some, and for others it was cultivated in psychotherapy, meditation, or walks in the woods. For still others, it involved a new level of identification that was not only separate from business life but broad enough to transcend it.

SCOPE OF AWARENESS

The third pattern of difference between our two groups of executives is the scope of their everyday awareness. This is not a value measure, not the same as depth or subtlety of understanding or degree of commitment. Although people rationally know that they are part of a family, office, company, community, nation, species, and planet, their identification and empathy are most powerfully triggered at particular levels, depending on their subjective definition of the world they inhabit.

Richard, once a rather typical executive in a big construction company, told of enormous changes in his life when he began seeing the planet as an integrated whole and consciously considered the meaning of his role as a global manager: "I was called to London to run a division which primarily did overseas work . . . everything from hotels in Jamaica to power stations in Saudi Arabia . . . . A friend in Australia gave me a book called *Limits to Growth*. I had never been involved in any sort of ecological thinking or concerns about the state of the planet. In those days, I traveled first class. I was on a jumbo jet traveling through from Sydney to London, and I went upstairs to the lounge on the jet and for twenty-four hours I just sort of toured the planet. It was a very powerful experience for me, because I realized that what I was doing, and what was the whole essence of my life—basically running building projects in the Third World using First World technology—might not be in the best interests of the planet." That realization led Richard to leave the company, spend several years in study and reflection, and finally help to create a new business using innovative technologies for solid waste management.

The concept of global consciousness is often invoked but rarely defined. As we use the term, it includes the ability to keep in mind large and complex systems; the capacity to assess impacts that are out of sight, based on indirect evidence; and the skill of systems thinking as it helps an individual to appreciate the ways in which, for example, a decision made in the United States can affect a particular expanse of forest in Brazil. Some wise voices have questioned the tendency to romanticize the global. As Wendell Berry (1990) wrote: "If you want to protect the environment, don't think globally. Think locally." We do not mean to suggest that the human mind is always able to register the global impact of human activity in its full scope and complexity. Not enough is known about the trade-offs between this broad awareness and focused, detailed knowledge of local concerns.

In most of our interview subjects, we saw difficult struggles between global and local focus, between general and particular concerns. A counterpoint to Richard is Pat, a senior attorney for a large manufacturing company that is known for both its enlightened attitudes toward employees and its pollution of local waterways. Pat felt most empowered not by grand visions but by tangible, local challenges. She chose to get involved as a community activist in housing and environmental issues, while for the most part declining to try to influence corporate policy on the same issues. She reflected, "Ours is hardly a community that is enlightened with respect to social services or the old affirmative action plan . . . but I can push for that. It's a very small speck, but we're going to make a dent in affordable housing. So global? Hardly. But I can feel and taste it, as opposed to, for example, engaging in a march."

There are many reasons why Richard was open to such a profound reassessment of the work that gave him livelihood and a sense of purpose, and why Mark and Harvey felt confident enough to try to change their companies' directions. Time did not permit a systematic gathering of information on these issues. But several of our interview subjects—those who saw themselves as having changed significantly with the development of their social and environmental concerns—volunteered detailed stories. In their accounts, several common themes recurred:

- Encounters with inspiring mentors and role models.
- Ongoing support, most commonly from a single close professional peer or a long-standing study/discussion group organized around a particular theme.
- Business loss or crisis forcing reevaluation.
- Illness or near-death experience.
- Spiritual awakening.

Because the interview subjects represented such wide variety in terms of life history, education, and generation, and because their companies covered such a wide range in industry, structure, culture, and financial health, the significance of these variations requires further exploration. To understand the potential of leaders for playing a constructive role, researchers and activists interested in greening must broaden their scope to include the less quantifiable but equally real realm of inner experience.

FROM DESCRIPTION TO PRESCRIPTION

The themes we have been discussing represent a cluster of significant personality traits, not a comprehensive model. They suggest that a leader's capacity to focus attention on a major change of course, such as an environmental management initiative, may depend on deep structures of personality as well as on the more commonly discussed factors, such as education and economics. Our examples illustrate the real struggles and trade-offs in the lives of corporate decision makers, especially those who have the mixed blessing of running global corporations. In each theme cluster in our model—self-consistency, personal efficacy, and scope of awareness—one response was associated with the capacity for greening of leadership more than the other. But it is easy to appreciate how either type of response could serve as an adaptation for the purpose of short-term self-preservation in a high-pressure corporate context. Understanding these perceived pressures and the likely adaptive responses of decision makers requires attention to the whole person and to the leadership context as it evolves.

Unfortunately, many factors render corporations breeding grounds for individuals who have highly developed institutional identities coupled with an underdeveloped core self, whose sense of personal efficacy is limited and whose scope of awareness is constricted by the boundaries of daily functioning. The frantic pace of many organizations—what management professor Peter Vaill calls "permanent white water"—leaves little time for self-reflection. And one of the strongest influences on a decision maker is the prevailing legal standard for fiduciary responsibility, by which an executive's decision not to pursue a legal profit opportunity, no matter how short-term, short-sighted, or harmful, can be cause for lawsuit or firing and can mark a company as a takeover target. In fact, Peter Drucker (1990, 231) argues that the pressure of takeover threats and the resultant crisis thinking "has become a dominant force—many would say *the* dominant force—in the behavior and actions of American management, and, almost certainly, a major factor in the erosion of American competitive and technological leadership." In this crisis climate, considerations of group loyalty and team playing take on emotional connotations of survival. The "corporate self" is reinforced, whether or not it makes decisions consistent with the whole person's highest values; whether or not it reflects a fully developed sense of personal power in keeping with the leadership challenge; and whether or not it is able to pay attention to the full impact of decisions made.

These factors compound the problem of executive stress, which is reaching critical levels. Yet those who suffer from it often respond with denial, seeing cracks in their public armor as weaknesses rather than as adaptive signs, according to Speller (1989). Conventional models of mental health have contributed to these unfortunate conceptions. For most of its history, mental health has been understood as adjustment to societal norms. Today, both supporters and critics of these norms must acknowledge that they are changing too fast and too radically to provide an anchor. For multinational and multicultural managers, this instability is especially acute. The nearly universal stress symptoms in Western cultures and the inadequacy of conventional clinical practice have for some years been forcing a reassessment of the field of psychology. The field that is emerging is less value neutral. Healthy functioning is seen as more than coping. It is seen as the full expression of human potential, including some commitment to the future of life on Earth.[3]

In this emerging view, much of the work of psychotherapists and other mental health professionals is to encourage fluidity among structures of the self, to bring more of the core identity into conscious awareness. A therapist does not ask, "How can you be a better soldier and adapt more fully to the expectations of others?" but "How can you bring *your* most basic values fully into your work, your relationships, and your life as an integrated whole?" The client is invited to view the available choices from a vantage point that is close to all the social selves but deeper than any. By this process, the issues are recontextualized in light of core values and needs. Agency is enhanced. Scope of awareness is shifted and expanded so that rigid institutional selves no longer dominate. One might begin a dialogue with the thought, "Risk losing my business? I'd die," and end in a very different position: "Risk losing my business? That would be hard. But I would get through it—and might even find something more exciting to do with the rest of my life."

The contribution of clinical perspectives to a discussion of corporate policy is in the light they shed on human beings' potential for change and the paths of individual adaptation that make coherent institutional change a possibility. Adults can become more aware of their fundamental personality structures. We all can choose to develop ourselves in ways that make changing our business practices easier. It is slow work, and demanding, calling forth human powers every bit as advanced as those required to run an organization. In fact, many of the skills that produce conventional business success can become powerful tools for personal development. Speller (1989) emphasizes that "Once executives break through denial, they move toward their goals for personal growth with the same dynamism they bring to conventional business challenges."

Leaders who want to integrate social and environmental vision with successful business practice will benefit from psychological literacy that will help them to:

- Understand that a split between private values and institutional decision making is not necessarily a long-term business advantage, and work to function as a whole person in the corporate setting.
- Appreciate the ways corporate identity may implicitly define "us" and "them" and shape the vantage points from which priorities are set— for example, in determining how much attention is paid to the environmental concerns of various constituencies.
- Recognize and resist the interpersonal pulls that can skew decision making.
- Cultivate a sense of agency and accountability that reflects the true significance of many of their business decisions.
- Consciously develop awareness of, and a sense of relationship with, all the constituencies their decisions affect, including the global community and future generations, and integrate that expanded understanding into viable business decisions.

Four recommendations for corporate adaptation emerge from our findings:

1. Curricula in environmental management and related areas of business ethics must address the whole person and not focus only on the array of technical choices. In many conventional curricula, the decision maker is intentionally portrayed as neutral and is rarely encouraged to consider his or her personal investments in a situation. But environmental decisions are not made only accordingly to theories of appropriate behavior. Just as important are the ego strength and moral courage to apply one's knowledge in real tests and the scope of awareness to recognize those tests when they arise. These can be cultivated only with time, care, and enough permission to counteract the pressures of convention. If theoretical understanding is divorced from personal growth, even the most carefully designed environmental management programs risk becoming training grounds for sophisticated rationalization rather than visionary leadership.

2. The cultures of corporations and business schools must be substantially reenvisioned to enable these lessons to take root. They must encourage the development of intrapersonal as well as interpersonal skills. This

means valuing and providing time for self-knowledge. It means honoring individual uniqueness in reality as well as in rhetoric. It means encouraging emotional as well as intellectual development, recognizing the role of emotion in decision making and particularly in changing course.

3. The swelling cadres of specialists—consultants, therapists, stress managers, even "executive coaches"—who help executives get through the day must be encouraged to take a fresh look at their services lest they find themselves serving as enablers for dysfunctional systems. They are in a position to teach powerful lessons that can assist decision makers in pulling themselves out of obsolete patterns and enhancing their creativity.

4. Finally, the laws and regulatory structures that govern business must be changed. The prevailing interpretation of fiduciary responsibility as maximizing profit within the letter of the law regardless of human and environmental impact must be reassessed. The perception of ceaseless and limitless stockholder pressure, whether or not this perception is accurate, keeps decision makers from looking too broadly outward, too deeply inward, or too far into the future. This is part of a broader reassessment, already under way in many corporations, of conventional thinking about the stakeholders who are entitled to a say in corporate decisions.

RECOMMENDATIONS FOR FURTHER RESEARCH

These interviews must be regarded as exploratory. They do show significant differences in personality and self-concept between the two groups we define as conventional decision makers and principled risk takers. These patterns of difference offer hope that the psychological dimension can complement other fields of research and contribute to more sophisticated strategies for cultivating environmentally responsible leadership.

Because our subjects represent such a wide range of personal and corporate variables such as age, education, and company size and financial health, we cannot draw conclusions about the relative importance of individual and institutional factors. What we can do is encourage larger-scale, more finely tuned psychosocial research in support of environmental management initiatives. To be useful, such research should simultaneously explore attitudes, beliefs, sources of information, emotional responses, and personality variables. It would include a search for connections between emerging styles of leadership and institutional factors such as type of industry, location, health of company, age of company, corporate culture, history of lawsuits, and history of takeover attempts. It would include systematic, detailed examination of the life histories of leaders who had experienced major changes in perspective leading to successful environmental initiatives.[4]

But there are intrinsic limits to the collection of facts divorced from a context. There is only an indirect connection between what people say they think and feel and how they will behave in a future situation. The most potent, psychologically sophisticated research in the service of environmental management is what we call "action research." For example, this includes examining actual corporate transformations in progress and working with the decision makers involved to test the emerging strategies for motivation and accountability. Two valuable approaches to this task would be: (1) reviewing existing environmental management case material from a psychological standpoint; and (2) bringing together corporate decision makers in a climate conducive to personal exploration and testing various educational methods for enhancing their commitment.

CONCLUSION

Environmental management has made its way onto the corporate agenda because serious concerns about public health have led to regulatory and consumer pressures and because corporate executives and their families are not immune to environmental dangers. Underlying every technological and economic decision is a cluster of questions about human relationships: Who is at risk? Who is responsible? What are the potential dangers? What standards of institutional responsibility and human justice apply in responding to them? These are highly charged questions of values, in some cases touching on the survival of individuals, communities, businesses, and ecosystems. Psychology permeates all these debates.

Individuals will always be shaped to some extent by the institutions in which they function. Making those influences conscious allows a decision maker the widest possible range of choices. By consciously directing the development of their own character strengths, as well as more conventional management skills, already talented executives can gain a crucial new set of survival skills for the future.

NOTES

1. *Giraffe Gazette* (Winter 1991), newsletter of the Giraffe Project, a nonprofit organization that rewards courage and service, located at 197 Second Street, Langley, Whidbey Island, WA 98260.
2. Jolie Solomon, "Taking a Stand," Boston *Globe*, July 21, 1991, 15.
3. For further discussion of this shift, see Philip Cushman, "Why the Self Is

Empty," *American Psychologist*, May 1990, 599–611; Sarah Conn, "Protest and Thrive: The Relationship Between Global Responsibility and Personal Empowerment," *New England Journal of Public Policy*, Spring/Summer 1990, 163–78.

4. For a rich discussion of priority-setting in social science research on the environment, see Paul C. Stern, Oran R. Young, and Daniel Druckman, eds., *Global Environmental Change: Understanding the Human Dimensions*. Committee on the Human Dimensions of Global Change, Commission on the Behavioral Sciences and Education, National Research Council. (Washington, D.C.: National Academy Press, 1992).

REFERENCES

Berry, Wendell. 1990. "Get Out of Your Car, Get Off Your Horse." *Harper's*, September.

Blasi, Augusto, and Oresick, Robert. 1987. "Self-consistency and the Development of the Self." In *The Book of the Self*, edited by Polly Yound-Eisendrath and James Hall, 69–87. New York: New York University Press.

Deikman, Arthur. 1982. *The Observing Self*. Boston: Beacon Press.

Drucker, Peter. 1990. *The Frontiers of Management*. New York: Harper & Row Perennial Management Series.

Gilligan, Carol. 1982. *In a Different Voice: Psychological Theory and Women's Development*. Cambridge, Mass.: Harvard University Press.

Kets de Vries, Manfred, and Miller, Danny. 1987. *Unstable at the Top: Inside the Troubled Organization*. New York: New American Library.

Kohut, Heinz. 1977. *The Restoration of the Self*. New York: International University Press.

Kohut, Heinz. 1971. *The Analysis of the Self*. New York: International University Press.

Maccoby, Michael. 1976. *The Gamesman: The New Corporate Leaders*. New York: Simon & Schuster.

Meadows, Donella; Meadows, Denis; and Randers, Jorgen. 1972. *Limits to Growth*. New York: Universe Books.

Miller, Jean Baker; Jordan, Judith; Kaplan, Alexandra; Stiver, Irene; and Surrey, Janet. 1991. *Women's Growth in Connection: Writings from the Stone Center*. Guilford Press.

Mitroff, Ian, and Pauchant, Theirry. 1991. *We're So Big and Powerful Nothing Bad Can Happen to Us: A Study of America's Crisis-prone Corporations*. New York: Birch Lane Press.

Speller, Jeffrey L. 1989. *Executives in Crisis*. San Francisco: Jossey-Bass.

Stern, Daniel N. 1985. *The Interpersonal World of the Infant*. New York: Basic Books.

Weiss, Robert S. 1990. *Staying the Course: The Emotional and Social Lives of Men Who Do Well at Work*. New York: Free Press.

3

An Economic Analysis of Cleaner Technology: Theory and Evidence

René Kemp

We live in a world that is more and more affected by technological change. In earlier times, pollution problems were viewed as undesirable but relatively unimportant side effects of industrialization and technology. The increase in the number and scope of pollution problems, due to the accumulation of "externalities" of growth, has put new demands on technology. Today there is a strong call for cleaner production and products to "engineer" our way out of the environmental crisis—representing a view of technological change as both the cause and cure of environmental problems.

This chapter explores the factors that promote and obstruct the development and use of cleaner technologies, defined as environmentally sound consumer products, low-emission processes, pollution control devices, recycling systems, or environmentally friendlier materials. In the first section of the chapter, a theory of environment-saving technological change is developed, building on the Neo-Schumpeterian theory of technological change. Within this Neo-Schumpeterian view, following the work of Nelson and Winter (1977, 1982), technological advance is seen as a complex, typically evolutionary process, endogenous to economic incentives, the pool of knowledge, and institutional structure. Furthermore, technological change is seen as the result of interactive heuristic search activities; it involves uncertainty and learning in a fundamental way and is characterized by certain paths or trajectories.

In this chapter it is assumed that technological change that preserves and protects the natural environment should also be viewed as an endogenous process, dependent on environmental policy, the capabilities and incentives of firms to develop cleaner technologies, and the goals and characteristics of potential users. It is argued that the process of "greening of technology" will necessarily be gradual and rather slow, despite the strong public call for it, due to the dominance of prevailing technological trajectories that have benefited from dynamic learning and scale effects and the adaptation of the selection environment.

In the second section, the unit of analysis is the firm. This section deals with the firm's decision to develop and to adopt cleaner technologies, given the general characteristics of technical change. The determinants of the firm's decision to supply a cleaner technology and the decision of the firm or the consumer to adopt a cleaner technology are identified and analyzed.

The third section contains findings from three case studies of cleaner technologies in the Netherlands and applies the theoretical framework in the analysis of the cases. The three technologies are: substitutes for chloro-fluorocarbons (CFCs), low-solvent paints and coatings, and membrane technology in the metal-plating industry.

In the fourth section, research needs related to cleaner technologies are discussed. One identified area of research is that of firms' strategies with respect to cleaner technologies, a topic that has not been discussed explicitly before. So far, a theory is lacking that enables researchers to understand strategic choices with respect to environmental issues. Possible elements of such a theory are identified, and the need for classification of firms with respect to the nature and source of environmentally friendly innovations is asserted.

The fifth section of the chapter presents some conclusions and policy implications.

AN ECONOMIC THEORY OF ENVIRONMENT-SAVING TECHNOLOGICAL CHANGE

The economic theory of environment-saving technological change developed here is based on the Neo-Schumpeterian, or evolutionary, theory of technological change. It is called an *economic* theory because, typically, economic assumptions are made about behavior; decisions about technologies are understood in terms of costs and benefits, and economic actors are assumed to pursue their own interests in a rational way. Although it may be labeled as an economic approach, it differs from the dominant neoclassical approach in economics by considering typical search heuristics of engineers, the systemic character of technology and economy, the importance of learning, and institutional factors.

In developing a theory, the concept of environment-saving technological change must first be defined. Unfortunately, in the Anglo-Saxon literature there is no generally accepted term that comprises all types of environment-saving technological change. Furthermore, the literature deals almost exclusively with one form: pollution control technology. With respect to this kind of technology, a distinction is often made between "end-of-pipe" (or "add-on") technology and "process-integrated" production changes (Hartje and Lurie 1984, 1985; OECD 1985). Other types of environment-saving technological change, such as input-saving technology, environmentally friendlier materials and substances, waste recycling technology, and cleaner consumer products, are also considered. The general term *cleaner technologies* is preferred and is defined as all techniques, processes, and products that avoid or diminish environmental damage and/or the usage of raw materials, natural resources, and energy.

With respect to these technologies, a distinction can be made between "clean" and "cleaning" technologies. Clean technology comprises input reduction or substitution, process-integrated changes that prevent pollution, recycling technology, and cleaner consumer products. Cleaning technology consists of end-of-pipe technology and other treatment, such as water treatment plants and waste facilities. Clean technology is preventive, whereas cleaning technology is curative. (See also Chapter 9.)

AN EVOLUTIONARY THEORY OF TECHNOLOGICAL CHANGE

Although technological change is widely recognized by economists as the engine of economic development, it has been at the periphery of economic analysis for a very long time. Except for the work of Joseph Schumpeter, who made innovation the cornerstone of his theory of economic development in capitalist societies, technological change remained to be treated in economic theory as an exogenous factor or as an unexplained residual, as in growth accounting studies. Only recently has this situation changed quite drastically. In a way, the work of Nelson and Winter (1977, 1982) was the starting point for a whole body of research into the economics of technological change.[1] In their seminal paper of 1977, they stressed that two important aspects of innovation should be incorporated in an economic theory of technological change: first, the involvement of uncertainty in research and development (R&D), and second, the institutional structure supporting the innovation. Their involvement in the study of technological change led them to develop an evolutionary theory of economic change as, in their view, a real alternative to neoclassical economics in terms of premises, scope, and method (Nelson and Winter 1982).

Within Nelson and Winter's evolutionary theory of economic and technological change, innovations are equivalent to biological variations or mutations, behavioral "routines" of organizations are equivalent to genes, and market selection (of firms, techniques, and products) is the economic equivalent of natural selection.[2] The focus on change and disequilibrium, uncertainty, and learning and adaptation processes, and the attention to the institutional structure are typical of the evolutionary, or Neo-Schumpeterian, view of technological change. This chapter builds on the concepts and findings of this literature in developing a theory of environment-saving technological change.

In this discussion it is assumed that environment-saving technological change should be viewed in a similar manner as normal technological change. Also, environment-saving technological change is an endogenous process, driven by economic demand and supply factors that are embedded in an environment of technical opportunities and socioinstitutional relations. Just like other innovations, cleaner technologies have to compete with existing production modes and products, either directly or indirectly. There is one important difference, however. Because the use, or abuse, of the environment is not sufficiently priced (for reasons not considered here), actors in the economic process do not receive appropriate signals from the market. Thus, environment-saving technological change depends to a large extent on government regulation, and its process differs from that of normal technological change in terms of both innovation and diffusion.

THE DIRECTION OF TECHNOLOGICAL CHANGE

Particularly in the last two decades, both the technical innovation process and the diffusion of technical innovations have been studied by many researchers in the field of economics of technical change, as well as those in related disciplines, such as the sociology and history of technological change. An important aim of such studies was to gain a better insight into the stimuli of innovation and innovation diffusion—to understand the "differential innovation puzzle," a term coined by Nelson and Winter (1977).

Many researchers have pointed to certain regularities in the process of technological change. Technological advance is considered to take place in certain directions and is not fine-tuned to changing demand and cost conditions (Nelson and Winter 1977, 56–57). Economists as well as sociologists and historians of technology have developed different concepts for this phenomenon that relate to technological opportunities, organizational capabilities, and typical search heuristics in the scientific and technical community. For example, Nelson and Winter (1977) describe common "natural trajectories," such as the exploitation of economies of scale, mechanization, and electrification, and other trajectories that are characteristic of a certain technique, in which case they speak of "technological regimes." Behind a technological regime or a natural trajectory is the sense of potential, of constraints, and of yet unexploited opportunities, which focuses the attention of engineers on certain directions in which progress is possible or worthwhile attempting (Nelson and Winter 1977, 57). Related to this idea are Rosenberg's concepts of "focusing devices" and "technological imperatives," such as bottlenecks in production, weaknesses of products, and clear objectives for improvement (Rosenberg 1976). Hughes, a historian of technology, speaks of "reverse salients" that develop as the technological systems expand. Reverse salients are components in the system that have fallen behind or are out of phase with others (Hughes 1989, 73).

The idea of focused search processes was further elaborated by Dosi, who made it the central concept in his analysis of technological change. Dosi speaks of "technological paradigms," which are analogous to Kuhn's concept of scientific paradigms. A technological paradigm, as used by Dosi, defines contextually the needs that are meant to be fulfilled, the scientific principles utilized for the search task, and the material technology to be used. A technological paradigm involves both an exemplar—an artifact that is to be developed and improved, such as a car, an integrated circuit, or a lathe, each with its particular technoeconomic characteristics—and a set of heuristics that provide directions for search and solutions—for instance, miniaturization of the integrated circuit. (See Dosi 1988a, 224–25; 1988b, 1127.) Examples of technological paradigms are the internal combustion engine, oil-based chemistry, and semiconductors. According to Dosi, the concept of technological paradigms explains why relatively ordered paths of technical change develop.[3] Such a path defined by a technological paradigm is called a "technological trajectory."

THE DOMINANCE OF TECHNOLOGICAL TRAJECTORIES

Although the concepts of technological paradigms and trajectories and related concepts are helpful in understanding the direction and pace of technical change, including environment-saving technological change, I believe they focus too much on the opportunities, constraints, and technical beliefs on the supply side and too little on economic supply and demand factors. In my view, the dominance of particular trajectories is to a large extent related to the adaptation of the selection environment and to the dynamic scale and learning effects that the older technologies have benefited from. The concepts of dynamic scale and learning effects and selection environment help explain why a large number of innovations fail in the marketplace; they explain the slow diffusion process in general and the dominance and stability of particular paradigms and trajectories. They also explain why the process of greening of technology will necessarily be slow, despite the strong public call for it.

Selection Environment

The term *selection environment*, stemming from evolutionary theory in biology, is borrowed from Nelson and Winter (1977, 1982) to explain how the relative use of technologies changes over time. The selection environment, as used here, involves the following elements: (1) the nature and size of the costs and benefits to potential adopters of a technology; (2) consumer and regulatory preferences and rules; (3) the transfer of information about successful innovations and the factors that facilitate or deter imitation; and (4) the systemic character of technology, economy, and social institutions. The influence exercised by the selection environment is not only *ex post*. The selection environment also generates feedback that strongly influences the R&D decisions of firms (Nelson and Winter 1982, 262).

The nature and the size of the costs and benefits of a product or process innovation to its adopters depend on the characteristics of potential users, the age and type of production techniques, the available skills and financial resources, and market conditions such as competition, product cycles, and prices of relevant inputs. Since industries and firms differ widely with respect to these characteristics, the selection environment is very heterogeneous.

The selection of technologies is also affected by changes in consumer preferences, such as fashion and lifestyles, or a higher preference for a cleaner environment, and by changes in government policy, especially regulation.

The mechanisms of information transfer and appropriability conditions surrounding a technological innovation also influence the selection of innovations. For any transaction to be completed, information transfer is necessary. This includes information about environmental problems, the availability of technologies, the characteristics of the product or process innovations, and its costs and benefits. Information transfer about an innovation may occur through several mechanisms, including direct contacts with suppliers, intermediary firms, journals, and recruitment of specialists. The appropriability conditions determine the extent to which an innovation can be secured against imitation. Examples of appropriability conditions are patents, secrecy, technical lead on competitors, learning curve effects, and the building up of a strong market position (Levin 1986). Imitation has a positive effect on the selection of an innovation; it increases the availability of certain technologies, stimulates competition between technologies, and reduces monopoly profits. Of course, imitation has a negative effect on the innovator's willingness to develop the innovation, as will be discussed later.

The fourth element in the selection environment is the systemic character of technology, economy, and social institutions. The selection environment can be thought of as a technoeconomic system or network of supplier-user linkages involving activities such as the production of materials, machinery, intermediate and final goods, and other activities, such as transport, marketing, finance, insurance, repair, and waste disposal. Within this network, economic activities are coordinated and have in the past been optimized.[4] A new technology, whether a new material, production technique, or product, must be integrated into this technoeconomic system and may require changes in several components of the system.

The concept of a selection environment helps explain why technological transitions will be necessarily slow and why certain trajectories will not be rapidly abandoned. New technologies must be embedded in a particular selection environment, which is adapted to older technologies. A new production technique, for instance, must be incorporated into the existing production processes of possible clients and must comply with diverse qualitative demands such as performance and user-friendliness. When a new technology is inadequate in certain technical respects or when the existing production routines of users have to be changed, the diffusion of the new technology will generally proceed slowly. New technologies sometimes also require different skills, education and training, and changes in regulatory legislation.

All this explains why manufacturers strive to develop so-called drop-in innovations that can be easily embedded in existing production processes and require few changes in the selection environment. For example, research efforts are directed toward the development of CFC substitutes for such uses as cooling in refrigerators, rather than toward the development of totally different production techniques and consumer products, such as a refrigerator with a totally different cooling system. Also, there is little incentive for firms to develop substitutes for their own products.

Dynamic Scale and Learning Effects

The success of a product or process innovation, however, does not depend only on the characteristics of the selection environment, but also on the characteristics of the innovation itself. These characteristics are not constant but evolve over time, due to dynamic scale and learning effects.

Prevailing technologies have, over time, benefited from these effects, which usually result in price reductions, evolutionary improvements (and sometimes also secondary innovations), and a better understanding of the process or product on the demand side. New technologies, as the outcome of R&D projects, must be embedded in a broad technical, economic, and social system and therefore confront all kinds of barriers, both internal and external to the firm.[5]

Learning is crucial in overcoming these barriers and includes learning about user needs, the manufacturing process, the new technology itself, and its effects on both costs and the organization of work for the user. These dynamic learning effects often lead to substantial manufacturing cost reductions and also to product improvements, including higher performance, wider applications, and increased reliability.[6]

Economies of scale (lower costs per unit of production related to higher production scales) may also lead to lower prices and stimulate the application of the technology. Economies of scale are particularly important in processing industries (such as the chemical industry and the food, beverage, and tobacco industries) and other industries involved in mass production.

It follows that new technologies—either new consumer products or new production methods—are in an unfavorable position, especially in the introduction phase. They are relatively expensive, not well known, and in some cases inadequately developed in terms of quality and user needs. They need to be improved with respect to both price and certain technical characteristics to be diffused more widely.[7] In addition, new technologies often require certain institutional changes because the skills of the work force, training, production routines, the organizational structure, and legislation are geared to the old technologies. New technologies may also confront social opposition from employees because of employment consequences and changes in tasks and rewards. All this explains why the diffusion of a new technique or method proceeds gradually or slowly and also explains the dominance of prevailing technological trajectories. The situation applies especially to radical innovations and new technological systems that entail vast possibilities for improvement and often require important changes in the selection environment, such as education, new supplier-user relationships, regulation, special government programs, and social acceptance.

The pace at which dynamic scale and learning effects take place is dependent on the diffusion process. The faster the diffusion, the faster firms can benefit from economies of scale and the faster learning effects take place. It is important for an innovation to reach the stage of market introduction; the experiences of customers are an essential source of information for improvements. Particularly, complaints and insurance claims from customers give important impetus to the further improvement of a product.

These concepts apply to all technologies, including cleaner technologies in the form of pollution control systems, recycling systems, and cleaner consumer products. However, the selection environment for cleaner technologies differs from that for normal technologies in a number of ways. First, the increasing environmental consciousness of consumers works in favor of cleaner production techniques and products. Second, environmental regulation and the anticipation of stricter environmental policies stimulate the innovation and diffusion of cleaner technologies.

On the other hand, other aspects of the selection environment and cleaner technologies work against the development and application of these innovations. First, the objective of cleaner production usually clashes with the dominant objective of making a profit. The public's demand for cleaner production does not translate into a strong demand for products that are more environmentally friendly, partly due to information gaps on the consumer side, partly because the environmental aspects are only one aspect of a product, and partly because of the "free-rider" behavior of individual consumers, who wait for other people to buy cleaner products and to change their behavior rather than doing so themselves. As a result, the willingness of firms to adopt more expensive pollution control technologies is rather low and depends strongly on government intervention. Second, in the introduction phase, cleaner technologies may have relatively higher prices and lower quality because of low-scale production and inferior materials (inferior from a non-ecological point of view). Third, information gaps are relatively large in the case of cleaner technologies. There are many environment-related aspects of processes and products that firms and consumers in particular have little knowledge of. Last but not least, environment-saving innovations may require wider institutional and organizational changes than other innovations. Not only do they depend on regulatory changes, but they sometimes require organizational changes, such as new departments and functions and different skills and training.[8] (In addition, cultural changes, such as feelings of responsibility for a cleaner environment and public health and well-being, may be important.)

Although the importance of factors in favor of cleaner technologies is growing, and numerous pollution control and recycling technologies and cleaner consumer products have been developed and introduced, in many cases these stimuli do not offset the negative stimuli. Consequently, the business of cleaner technologies is still rather uncertain and not very profitable.[9]

DETERMINANTS OF THE DECISION FOR CLEANER TECHNOLOGY

Several determinants are important in a firm's decision to *develop* cleaner technology; likewise, other important factors influence a firm's decision to *adopt* cleaner technology. Before these are discussed, however, a few distinctions that are common in the field of the economics of technical change need to be made. First, technical change consists of a number of phases. At the basis of technical change is technical and scientific research. This may result in a new finding or invention. The second phase of technical change is the development phase, in which "upscaling" of research takes place, from pilot configuration to pilot plant. This phase is relatively expensive compared to the first phase. Feasibility studies usually precede the third phase, which is market introduction. When the invention is available to the market, or when it is used by the innovating firm itself, we speak of it as an innovation. The final phase is diffusion, the process of adoption of the innovation over time. This discussion concentrates on the introduction, or innovation, phase and the diffusion phase.

Second, innovations can be divided into process and product innovations. A process innovation is a new or improved production technique— for example, a machine numerically controlled by a computer or a cleaning device. A product innovation is a new or improved consumer product.

Third, innovations can be subdivided into radical innovations (new techniques or products or important new applications) and incremental innovations (minor improvements to existing techniques and products). The following discussion focuses on the factors that influence the development and adoption of radical innovations rather than incremental innovations.

DEVELOPMENT OF CLEANER TECHNOLOGY

In the field of the economics of technical change, economists have fiercely debated whether innovations are determined by new knowledge and technological opportunities (the "technology push" or "supply push" view inspired by Schumpeter) or by economic stimuli, in particular, market demand (the "demand pull" or "market pull" view, with Schmookler (1966) as one of its important proponents). In the present discussion, this debate is less relevant; both factors are considered without elaboration of their relative importance.[10] Also relevant in the decision to develop an innovation in a market economy are the so-called appropriability conditions that determine the degree of protection against imitation and competition from other firms. As mentioned in the previous section, protection against imitation may take place in various ways, from legal protection in the form of patents to secrecy or a technical lead (Levin 1986). Following Dosi (1988a, 1988b) and Cramer and Schot (1990), this discussion distinguishes the three following factors as influential in the development of an innovation: (1) technological opportunities, (2) market demand, and (3) appropriability conditions.

Technological Opportunities
The technological opportunities to develop a particular technology for a certain environmental problem differ for each problem, industry, and firm. They are closely related to the existing pool of knowledge—that is, the whole of fundamental scientific knowledge and the knowledge that is embodied in machines, human beings, and organizations. Such knowledge is not immediately available or free of charge. Research effort and money are needed to draw on these technological opportunities, and there is always the risk that a project will fail, either technically or commercially.

The technological capabilities to develop an innovation also differ among various firms. These capabilities are related to the size and nature of the organization's knowledge base, which is shaped by its past activities. In actual practice, innovations are developed by certain firms, both within and outside the user sector. Process innovations are usually developed by special suppliers. Only the more knowledge-intensive sectors, such as the chemical and advanced electrotechnical industries, have the capabilities to develop cleaner production processes, either independently or with the help of special suppliers. Product innovations are usually developed by the manufacturers of the products.

Market Demand
The willingness to innovate depends on the expected market demand for an innovation. As a rule, the development of a new, cleaner technology for a firm's own use only is not profitable. The demand for cleaner production processes depends on the opportunities and willingness of

polluting companies to purchase cleaner techniques and to incorporate them in their production processes. The demand for cleaner production processes is realized mainly through environmental regulation, since cleaner production generally does not contribute to the sales of products but only increases costs.[11] The demand for cleaner consumer products occurs more easily through the market without government interference and is a stimulus for firms to develop these products.

Although environmental policy has become stricter, many firms that supply cleaner technologies face uncertain sales due to the unchallenging character of regulatory standards and uncertainty about environmental measures. On the other hand, it is clear that strongly emerging environmental awareness in general, increasing societal pressure, and anticipated stricter environmental policies enlarge the sales outlook for cleaner processes and products. In addition, firms that have developed cleaner processes can try to influence policy makers to prescribe their technologies to polluters or to tighten environmental regulation. Such behavior is referred to as "rent seeking" in the economic literature.

Appropriability Conditions

If a firm is to engage in R&D and develop an innovation, it must be able to appropriate the benefits from such an innovation. Imitations by competitors undermine this. The danger of imitation is generally high because the knowledge embodied in a new technology becomes available, at least in part, to others when the technology is introduced into the market. This knowledge usually can be reproduced or used by other firms at much lower development costs (Mansfield et al. 1981). Thus, the decision to develop an innovation depends on the appropriability conditions.

Levin (1986) distinguishes the following appropriability conditions: patents, as a means to protect from imitation and as a means to receive royalties; secrecy; the technical lead on competitors; learning curve effects; and the extent to which a strong market position can be built up through reputation or the establishment of distribution channels. Dosi (1988a) adds scale economies to these factors. Appropriability conditions differ according to the type of innovation. Research by Levin and others showed that technical lead and learning curve effects, along with additional marketing efforts, are the most important appropriability mechanisms for product innovations, whereas learning curve effects, secrecy, and technical lead on competitors are most important for process innovations (Levin 1986). Patents are additional appropriability conditions in most cases. They are important for some industries, such as the chemical and mechanical equipment industries, as well as for smaller companies.

To my knowledge, no specific research into the appropriability conditions of environment-saving innovations has been carried out. When the appropriability conditions for certain types of cleaner technologies are inadequate, this may be reason for government to lengthen patent life, to conduct or finance research itself, or to stimulate cooperation between companies.

ADOPTION OF CLEANER TECHNOLOGY

As mentioned earlier, market demand for cleaner technologies depends to a large extent on government regulation. However, several other factors also influence the decision to adopt cleaner technology. The following factors are distinguished in this discussion: (1) price and quality of the innovation, an important determinant of the costs and benefits of the innovation; (2) the transfer of knowledge and information that is required to realize a transaction; and (3) risk and uncertainty as to the economic consequences of the installation of a new technology.

Price and Quality

The price and quality (meaning the technical characteristics) of the innovation determine to a large extent its costs and benefits and, accordingly, its attractiveness for a potential user. These costs and benefits may involve different elements (e.g., the costs of purchasing the technology, implementation costs, financing costs, operating costs, and benefits such as improvement of the firm's public image and consumer satisfaction). The willingness to adopt cleaner techniques depends on the extent to which they increase costs and decrease profits. With respect to these costs and benefits, firms and consumers are considered separately.

For firms, the cost consequences of adopting cleaner technologies differ considerably. They depend not only on the purchase price of the technology but also on production quantities and the nature and age of the production process. Smaller firms often experience relatively high pollution control costs as a result of scale disadvantages. On the other hand, the environmental aspects of production and products play an increasingly important part in decision making. A bad environmental reputation may have a negative effect on the company's sales and may lead to personnel problems (such as motivation problems or difficulties in hiring people). However, such stimuli are still rather weak. (See Chapter 4.)

For consumers, the purchase of a cleaner product may also be hindered by price and quality characteristics. A hazardous product may be superior to its cleaner alternative in some respects. There is also opportunity for free-rider behavior by individual consumers, who may decide to rely on changes in the purchases and behavior of others, rather than making these changes themselves. On the other hand, consumer willingness to buy cleaner products is growing. It should also be noted that price and technical characteristics of the innovation are not constant but change over time as a result of dynamic scale and learning effects.

Transfer of Knowledge and Information

For the adoption of new technologies, transfers of knowledge and information are necessary. There are numerous problems relating to knowledge and information that hinder the adoption of cleaner technology. Knowledge about environmental effects and cleaner production methods has barely been organized in firms thus far. Apart from being unaware of the ecological damage resulting from their business activities, firms often do not know which cleaner technologies are available, or where to go for information about these technologies, or about the kinds of technical and financial support available. Small firms in particular face these problems. In addition, firms often require independent advice from external sources.

The transfer of knowledge and information may be accomplished in several ways through direct contacts with suppliers, demonstration projects, professional journals, informal contacts, data banks, congresses and trade fairs, or special intermediaries such as consulting firms. Many authors have pointed to the importance of knowledge transfer. Although I agree that more effective transfer of knowledge and information is important, I believe that the willingness of the demanders and suppliers—especially the demanders—of cleaner technologies to communicate with each other is far more important than the way in which knowledge transfer is organized.

Buyers of products also face problems relating to knowledge and information. Consumers have little knowledge of the environmental effects of their consumption and behavior. Furthermore, it is almost impossible for consumers to compare the environmental aspects of products, even if product information is given.

Risk and Uncertainty

Many firms do not adopt cleaner techniques because of their uncertainty and associated technical and economic risks. The adoption of a certain technique may require change in production routines and the organization of work (new functions, jobs, rewards, etc.) and may meet with both managerial and worker resistance. Moreover, personnel must gain knowledge of and experience with new machines. Process-integrated techniques that lead to radical changes in the production process particularly involve much risk and uncertainty (Hartje and Lurie 1984). Firms differ in their risk attitudes and in their perceptions of technical and economic risks.

THREE CASE STUDIES OF CLEANER TECHNOLOGIES

Little empirical research has been done concerning the factors affecting the development and adoption of cleaner technologies, particularly the effect of government regulation on the process of environment-saving technological change. In a 1990 research project of the Maastricht Economic Research Institute on Innovation and Technology (MERIT) and the Institute for Environmental Studies, the factors influencing the innovation and adoption of three kinds of cleaner technologies in the Netherlands were investigated. The technologies were CFC substitutes, low-solvent paints and coatings, and membrane technology in the metal-plating industry. Although the study took place in the Netherlands, the results are believed to apply to other Western countries as well. The research involved an extensive literature survey of the technologies as well as interviews with suppliers and potential adopters of the innovations.[12] Although this approach provided much qualitative information about the factors influencing the innovation and adoption of these technologies, it was not possible to assess the importance of the individual factors in a quantitative way. Despite this, the adopted research approach proved to be useful. Some conclusions and policy implications can be drawn from the case studies and these are discussed at the end of this chapter.

CFC SUBSTITUTES

CFCs have been employed in a broad range of products since their invention in the 1930s. Originally developed as coolants, they have also been used on a large scale as aerosol propellants, as foam blowers, sometimes as insulators, and as solvents in a range of cleaning applications in the metal and electrotechnical industries. Important properties of CFCs are their low toxicity and high level of stability (they are, for instance, nonflammable). However, their chemical stability eventually was found to be a crucial unfavorable property. CFCs reach the stratospheric ozone layer once they enter the atmosphere. There they destroy the ozone, which protects the Earth from ultraviolet rays. CFCs also contribute to the greenhouse effect. In the Montreal Protocol as amended in June 1990 in London, it was agreed that their production would be halted by the year 2000.

It is expected that about one-third of the current CFC market will disappear as a result of the transition to non-CFC technologies, such as the wider use of ammonia as a coolant or greater use of carbon dioxide instead of halons in fire extinguishers (UNEP 1989). For other CFC applications, a shift to "CFC-likes" will take place. These consist of hydrochlorofluorocarbons (HCFCs), so-called soft CFCs having a lower ozone-depletion potential, and hydroflourocarbons (HFCs), which do not contain chlorine or bromine and therefore do not affect the ozone layer. The use of CFC-likes is expected to replace about one-third of current CFC use. Another reduction of one-third will be achieved through a more careful use of CFC-likes, so that unnecessary losses of the compounds to the atmosphere are avoided.

Factors Influencing the Development of CFC Substitutes

Worldwide there are some twenty CFC manufacturers, six of which account for the bulk of CFC production. These are large chemical concerns, part of the "science-based" sector, which has ample technological opportunities to develop new substances and products. These companies have mainly focused their attention on the soft CFCs, continuing in the CFC trajectory so that they can benefit from the scale and learning effects achieved in that trajectory.

The possibilities for limiting HCFC emissions are in the hands of both the manufacturers and the users of HCFC-containing products. The prevention of unnecessary losses of HCFCs is a matter of good housekeeping combined with the use of relatively simple equipment, such as that used to recover CFCs from cast-off refrigerators. Alternative product design is another possibility. Alternatives to the CFC family may be developed by various firms, including those outside the chemical industry (e.g., the use of mineral or rock wool as an insulator instead of polyurethane foam and the replacement of propellant-driven aerosols by pump-driven aerosols).

Market demand for CFC substitutes is guaranteed by the future ban on CFCs. However, in the short term, market demand for these substitutes may be weak, especially for some applications. Except for aerosol propellants, autonomous market demand is not strong enough to establish a serious substitution of CFCs. In most applications, CFCs are "ideal" substances. Substitutes that perform as well as CFCs at a lower price are mostly flammable, toxic, and/or strongly reactive. Following is a brief exploration of the market demand for aerosols, refrigerators and cooling systems, foam, and cleansing and degreasing agents.

The buyers of aerosol products have played an important role in the transition toward CFC-free aerosols. Consumers identify CFC aerosols as products that are harmful to the ozone layer. They have come to be regarded as "contaminated" products. In response to this, large retailers decided to discontinue selling CFC aerosols. In this case, relatively cheap alternatives in the form of pump-driven aerosols were available.

Little initiative to replace CFCs is expected from the market for professional cooling systems. However, HCFC-22, a soft CFC, is increasingly used in larger equipment for technical and economic reasons. Consumer demand for environmentally friendly household refrigerators is a stimulus for manufacturers to take up the development of CFC-free products, but the cost of these refrigerators is still well above that of traditional ones.

Market demand for CFC substitutes in the foam industry, the biggest user of CFCs, depends strongly on government policy. In this sector, CFCs are used for the production of insulation material, which accounts for approximately two-thirds of total CFC use. Insulation of buildings and houses helps save energy and prevents pollution, so there may be a trade-off between different environmental goals. However, alternatives to foam are available; rock wool for insulation is an example. The demand for alternative insulation materials may be stimulated by government procurement and housing policies. Because soft foams are used in the furniture industry, for example—in mattresses and cushions—consumer demand may also exert an influence.

The demand for CFC substitutes as cleansing or degreasing agents is growing. Good and relatively cheap alternatives (such as water and soap) are available, and the demand for these may increase as knowledge of their cost advantages increases. The adoption of substitutes sometimes requires certain institutional changes, however. The use of CFC solvents to clean components of high-tech equipment is often prescribed by the customers. A well-known example is found in the specifications of defense ministries.

With respect to appropriability conditions, specific knowledge about CFC substitutes is concentrated in the larger CFC manufacturers. They have acquired a technical lead that obstructs market entry by other firms. In addition, the production of HCFCs calls for enormous investments, and economies of scale play an important role in the production of CFCs. Dynamic scale and learning effects are particularly important for CFC substitutes because of the more complex production processes. This also disadvantages potential newcomers to the CFC market. Patents are of minor importance as means to appropriate returns from R&D; the substances themselves cannot be patented, but sometimes the different components of the products can.

Factors Influencing the Adoption of CFC Substitutes

The price and quality of CFC substitutes do not so much influence the substitution of alternatives to CFCs, because substitution is inevitable. They do influence the direction toward which firms look for substitutes. Due to their complex production process, it is estimated that HCFCs will become two to five times as expensive as CFCs. The costs of a substitute technology are not, however, exclusively determined by the price of the substance, but also by the amount needed and the cost of the equipment in which it is used. In the market for coolants, the price/quality ratio is likely to favor HCFCs, whereas in the other areas of application, serious competitors will also be found outside the CFC trajectory.

For large users of CFCs, problems of knowledge and information about available alternatives are relatively few. These users are also involved in the CFC manufacturers' development and testing of CFC-replacing technology. Furthermore, in the Netherlands, sector-specific organizations play a significant part in the transfer of knowledge and information about alternative technologies through their involvement in the establishment of demonstration projects and so forth. Lack of information usually occurs in smaller firms. Consumers also have inadequate knowledge. The Dutch Ministry of the Environment has initiated an information and demonstration program aimed at reducing the use of CFC-113 as a solvent. Information transfer to consumers may be an efficient means to stimulate CFC substitution in other areas, based on the role of consumers with regard to aerosol products.

Although technical and economic uncertainty and risks are inherent in the shift to CFC substitutes in the various application areas, these are normal business risks that result from the shift to a new technology. Users tend to reduce the technical risk by making use of drop-ins—substitutes that can be used in existing installations with little adaptations—as much as possible. This is favorable for HCFCs. The economic risks for national industries that use CFCs are limited because all users, including those abroad, are faced with the need to switch to substitutes, so that competitive disadvantages in the international market will not occur.

Policy with Respect to CFCs

The dominant policy instrument relating to CFCs is direct regulation in its most extensive form: a future, general ban on their production and use.[13]

This ban can be considered a form of technology-forcing standard. It may be assumed that it will be a strong enough incentive for CFC-substitution innovations and their diffusion.

Economic instruments and information and communication have complementary roles. They can be used to accelerate and facilitate the transition to CFC substitutes. In the United States, for example, rights are allocated for CFC production and use. These rights are gradually reduced and are tradeable. The aim of fees for CFC use, which are also applied in the United States, is mainly to prevent windfall profits that may arise from the artificial scarcity of CFCs.

LOW-SOLVENT PAINTS AND COATINGS

In the 1950s, traditional linseed oil paints were replaced with paints based on synthetic binding agents. A basic component of most of these paints was organic solvents, usually present in percentages of 30 to 65 percent, but sometimes as high as 90 percent. It was not discovered until much later that the solvents, which are released during application, have negative effects on public health and the environment—for instance, through the formation of smog.

Low-solvent paints and coatings constitute a preventive environmental innovation. They are less damaging to health and the environment during application and production, as well as in the waste phase, although the prevention of damage during application is the most important aspect. There are various types of low-solvent paints: water-based (or waterborne) paints (5 to 10 percent solvents), "high solids" (20 to 30 percent solvents), powder coatings, and ultraviolet and electron-beam curing coatings. The first three types are appropriate for widespread application in both the architectural and industrial markets, although to different degrees.

Factors Influencing the Development of Low-solvent Paints and Coatings

Research into low-solvent paints and coatings started in the 1960s, particularly in the laboratories of the major paint manufacturers. Currently, practically all paint makers are developing water-based paints, for both the industrial and architectural markets. Small firms in the paint industry are strongly dependent on their raw materials suppliers (components of the large chemical concerns), which provide directive recipes for paints. The production of water-based paints is somewhat more complex than that of traditional paints. In some cases paint companies cooperate with one another or have research carried out by third parties. Large companies usually perform research in a more systematic manner by testing the paint on all kinds of materials and under all kinds of climatic influences. It can be concluded that vast technological opportunities for low-solvent paints are available to every firm in the paint industry. However, paint makers are sometimes criticized for conservatism and the undercapitalization of research efforts. Although many different formulations for new products are constantly being developed, only a small number reach the production stage.

The history of paints is strongly associated with changes in market demand. For example, the development of high-solvent paints was stimulated by the demand for paints with a shorter drying time than that of linseed oil paints. Demand by the automobile industry was an especially important influence in the development of these faster-drying paints. The demand for low-solvent paints has been mainly a derived one, dependent on government policy. Emission requirements in the 1960s and 1970s in the United States and West Germany (Rule '66 and TA-Luft, respectively) and legislation relating to working conditions in Scandinavian countries particularly increased the demand for low-solvent paints. Recently, the growing environmental awareness of consumers has stimulated the development of water-based paints and high solids for the architectural market. Industrial demand for low-solvent paints has been growing in the last few years, not so much because of the emission standards for organic solvents but for normal business reasons of lower labor costs and less material loss. In 1983 the market share for low-solvent paints for industrial application was 32 percent in the United States and 25 percent in Europe. In the Netherlands, the sales of powder coatings and water-borne paints for industrial application are currently increasing by 15 to 20 percent annually. The market share of low-solvent paints for other purposes (except wall painting) is much lower and increasing less rapidly.

The paint industry is unique with respect to appropriability conditions. Imitation of paint products is relatively simple. The composition of paints can be discovered quite easily by chemical analysis, although their production requires additional research work. Protection through patents is practically impossible, since paint preparation comes down to "mixing and stirring." To obtain a patent, new technical principles have to be developed. Suppliers of raw materials do patent new procedures more frequently than do paint manufacturers.

In the Netherlands, the most important protection of paint products lies in their distribution. The large paint manufacturers have their own distribution networks (service stations for professional users and paint shops for consumers), where customers can receive advice about the paint product to be used. Moreover, some paint manufacturers have "field workers" who visit their customers. Small firms especially rely upon such customer contacts. The situation in the Netherlands is quite different from that in Germany, where advice is much less important and paint is usually diffused via the wholesale trade.

The fact that paint companies sell their products through their own channels, however, is an obstacle rather than a stimulus to developing innovations. The innovating firm mainly reaches its own customers. Thus, a paint company's new products compete with its own existing products. This has a negative effect on the willingness of firms to perform R&D activities with respect to low-solvent paints.

Factors Influencing the Adoption of Low-solvent Paints and Coatings

Although the quality (in the sense of technical characteristics) of water-based paints differs considerably from that of high-solvent paints, water-based paints are generally market-ripe products. Yet, painters and private customers still have a strong preference for high-solvent paints. In addition to the familiarity of high-solvent paints and the claim (partially unfounded) that water-based paints require extra cleaning of old layers of paint, prejudices against the quality of water-based paints are a factor. In recent years the assortment of low-solvent paints has increased steadily. Today some high-gloss water-based paints are also available.

The price of water-based paints is about 10 percent higher than that of high-solvent paints. According to paint manufacturers, no major price decreases are expected as a result of economies of scale and learning effects. However, application and maintenance costs often favor low-solvent paints.

There is a serious lack of knowledge and information regarding the environmental damage caused by high-solvent paints and the availability of alternatives, as well as the quality and processing of low-solvent paints. These information gaps can pose problems for painters and private users in particular. Another obstacle results from past inflated claims concerning the merits of water-based paints. Such claims have led to disappointments in some cases.

Although there is some uncertainty about the quality of low-solvent paints (in terms of gloss, durability, etc.), and their use entails some risks for professional applicators (unsatisfactory results may lead to financial claims), the uncertainty and risks are relatively small, especially for nonindustrial users. For industrial use, it is often necessary to change production routines and the division of work, since the new paints and coatings require different machines and tools.

Policy with Respect to Low-solvent Paints and Coatings

Until recently most countries have only minimally pursued environmental policy regarding high-solvent paints. Policy has been directed toward emissions of organic solvents during production and application rather than toward products. At present, in the Netherlands, Germany, and Switzerland covenants are used to reduce the use of solvents in paints. These covenants are agreements between polluters and the government to reduce emissions and/or waste. Some countries (e.g., the Netherlands, Switzerland, and the United States) are considering the possibility of imposing fees on high-solvent paints. To my knowledge, product standards for solvents are not used or considered anywhere.

The effects of environmental policy on R&D activities to develop new and better low-solvent paints and coatings are relatively small. At present, low-solvent paints and coatings constitute a normal innovation, especially for the industrial market. Currently, there is less need for incentives to encourage innovations in the development of low-solvent paints than there is for incentives to promote the diffusion of the new products, particularly among professional painters and private consumers. A fee imposed on the use of solvents may contribute to the diffusion and further development of low-solvent alternatives, but such a fee will need to be considerable to be very effective. Information and communication are particularly important to increase acceptance of the new paint types and remove negative prejudices. Government procurement policies may also be helpful.

Membrane Technology in the Metal-Plating Industry

In the metal-plating industry, large amounts of heavy metals are released in wastewater. A policy adopted in the Netherlands in the 1970s was aimed at combating the discharge of these emissions into surface water. As a result, many firms in the metal-plating industry purchased an "ONO installation" (ONO in Dutch stands for detoxification, neutralization, dehydration), a technique whereby substances are extracted from industrial water. Although the resulting wastewater is cleaner, the technique produces chemical waste, which in turn must be taken care of. The ONO installation is a typical end-of-pipe solution that leads to a transfer of environmental problems.

In contrast, membrane technology can be considered a typical process-integrated technique. With this technology, metals can be removed from industrial water and reused. Thus far, the metal-plating industry has made little use of the various membrane techniques for the purification of industrial water.

Factors Influencing the Development of Membrane Technology for the Metal-plating Industry

Membrane separating or purification techniques were developed in the 1950s as a result of technological opportunities in the plastics-producing and -processing industry. On a world scale, the market for membranes is controlled by firms in the United States and Japan, where the governments put large amounts of money into research and development in this area in the 1960s. The research being carried out in the area of membrane technology is still not driven in any major way by potential market sales in the metal-plating industry, nor is such research specifically aimed at this industry.

For firms in the metal-plating industry, membrane technology is relevant to their process but not to their products. The application of membrane technology does not provide the firm with extra opportunities to increase sales by creating or conquering new markets.

It is to be expected that the demand for membrane technology in the metal-plating industry will increase, because the many end-of-pipe installations in this industry produce sludge containing heavy metals that has to be disposed of as chemical waste. The cost of treatment and disposal in the Netherlands will probably double or triple within the next few years.

The knowledge needed for the production of membranes and membrane installations is generally in the hands of their manufacturers. Protection of this knowledge is usually fixed in the form of patents, the most important appropriability condition in this industry. Application of membrane technologies in the metal-plating industry calls for tailor-made solutions, which constitutes a barrier to market entry. In this case, appropriability conditions are of little importance due to the small and difficult market for this technology.

Factors Influencing the Adoption of Membrane Technology in the Metal-plating Industry

The limited experience of metal-plating firms with membrane techniques is largely negative. There have been many technical problems with the installations, such as pollution of the membranes. In addition, follow-up attention from suppliers has often left much to be desired. Because of these negative experiences, membrane technology has a bad reputation in this industry. In general, the price of membrane equipment plays a lesser role. A well-functioning installation might lead to cost savings for some firms.

The potential for savings may rise substantially as the cost of transport and disposal of polluted sludge increases.

The knowledge potential users have about membrane technology is minimal and is limited to a number of bad experiences, which has a negative effect on demand. Furthermore, smaller firms especially lack the expertise to apply membrane technology. This is partly related to insufficient transfer of knowledge by the suppliers of membrane technology; these suppliers find the metal-plating industry a "difficult" and not very profitable market and direct their efforts preferably toward other markets.

Perceptions about the risks involved in the adoption of membrane technologies also obstruct their use in the metal-plating industry. Firms are afraid of breakdowns, which involve financial risks and time losses. Also, operation of the installations seems to absorb more time than indicated by the suppliers. Small firms, of which there are many in the metal-plating industry, particularly cannot afford the risk of spending much time on matters that do not directly benefit production.

Policy with Respect to Membrane Technology in the Metal-plating Industry

In the Netherlands a standards-based policy has been implemented with respect to heavy metals in the wastewater of the metal-plating industry. The standards were based on the "best-practicable-means" criterion. Since they pertain exclusively to emissions to water, the environmental problems have shifted and heavy metals are now released in the sludge. The fees imposed for discharge of heavy metals in wastewater have also contributed to this situation, as have investment subsidies, which have been used especially for end-of-pipe (ONO) installations. Because of the widespread use of ONO installations, the market for membrane technology is blocked for many years.

To make recycling of metals in the metal-plating process attractive, policy must focus on all the environmental effects of metal plating, which include pollution of the sludge with heavy metals. Because the metal-plating industry is heterogeneous, with widely varying production processes and, therefore, substantial differences in the costs of reducing heavy metals in emissions, economic instruments are preferred to direct regulation. For that matter, sharply rising costs for the disposal of chemical waste may have the same effect as a fee on the heavy metals in sludge. To prevent illegal dumping, a deposit premium for chemical waste may be considered.

Information and communication can be of great importance. Information should not only reinforce environmental awareness and convey knowledge of the various techniques for reducing heavy metal emissions, but also remove prejudices (whether unfounded or not) against process-integrated techniques such as membrane installations. Demonstration projects may make a significant contribution to this goal.

RESEARCH NEEDS

An earlier part of this chapter presented a theoretical framework for the analysis of environment-saving technological change. From the perspective of this framework, it is possible to discuss some research needs with respect to the greening of technology.

An obvious candidate for more research is, of course, the theoretical framework itself. Although this framework proved to be useful in the case studies, more empirical research is needed to assess its usefulness as a theory of environment-saving technological change. Dynamic scale and learning effects must be quantified in particular cases and their relevance to the diffusion process established. The usefulness of the concept of selection environment also needs to be investigated more thoroughly. Typical elements of the selection environment must be identified and their relevance assessed. As mentioned earlier, government policy constitutes an important, but not the only, stimulus in the selection environment. Its position and influence within the selection environment is still not well understood. Research in this area would involve assessment of not only the influence of particular regulation on firms' decisions, but also the influence of perceptions of and uncertainty about environmental policy. This might help policy makers design better policies to stimulate cleaner technology.

The relationship between market structure and innovation in and diffusion of cleaner technologies is another candidate for more research, as noted, for instance, by Nentjes and Wiersma (1988). The relationship between market structure and technological change has been studied quite extensively by economists (a survey can be found in Baldwin and Scott [1987]). In these analyses, the effects of such factors as firm size, market concentration, market organization (monopoly, oligopoly), and entry barriers on innovation and diffusion processes were investigated. Although these studies have led to solid conclusions with respect to the relationship between market structure and technological performance, and although structure and performance were found to influence each other, similar research with respect to innovation in and diffusion of cleaner technologies might contribute to our understanding of the process of the greening of industry. The incorporation of some factors in this chapter's theory of environment-saving technological change into these analyses, especially technological opportunities, mechanisms of learning, and appropriability conditions, might increase the usefulness of the research.

More research is also needed on corporate attitudes and organizational strategies with respect to environmental issues. In economic life, we can observe different technology strategies. With regard to innovations, Freeman (1982) identified six possible strategies: offensive, defensive, imitative, dependent, traditional, and opportunistic (or niche) strategies. The offensive strategy is designed to achieve technical and market leadership by putting the company ahead of competitors in the introduction of new products. Firms with such a strategy have strong R&D capabilities and special relationships with the science-technology system that transfers knowledge from universities to firms, and they are prepared to take a long-term view and high risks. Freeman refers to a defensive strategy when firms do not want to be the first innovator but are still quite innovative. Firms that adopt a defensive strategy do not want to incur the heavy risks of being the first to innovate and may imagine they can profit from the mistakes of the early innovators and their opening up of new markets. Firms that take an imitative strategy do not aspire to technical "leapfrogging" or keeping up with the game, whereas the firm with a dependent strategy does not attempt to initiate or even imitate technical changes in its product, except in response to specific requests from its customers or its parent companies. Freeman refers to a traditional strategy when firms do not change their products except for design reasons. Finally, an opportunistic, or niche, strategy exists when a firm identifies and exploits a new opportunity or market niche that does not require in-house R&D or complex design.

Although Freeman provides some explanation of these strategies, in terms of R&D capabilities and other capabilities such as production engineering, design, and marketing, and in terms of some appropriability conditions, he does not provide a systematic theory of innovation strategy. However, he points out several elements that should be incorporated into such a theory with respect to cleaner technologies. First is the fundamental uncertainty involved in innovation, because of which R&D behavior and innovation strategies cannot be understood in terms of given costs and benefits. The second element is differences in the capabilities of firms to develop an invention, produce it at sufficiently low cost, and market it successfully. The third element is differences in markets and corresponding stimuli such as prices, structure and size of demand, competition, market concentration, and entry barriers. Fourth is institutional factors such as the science-technology system, the education system, and appropriability conditions (patents).

The translation of general innovation strategies to strategies that pertain to environmental aspects has been attempted by Schot (1992), who uses a classification similar to that of Freeman. A theory of firms' strategies concerning environmental issues, however, is still lacking (although a start is made in Chapters 4 and 5 of this book). It should be noted that the identified strategies of firms with respect to environmental issues not only pertain to innovations in a firm's products (as in Freeman's analysis) but also relate to production and organizational factors (such as management styles and the introduction of environmental care systems). It will be interesting to compare firms' strategies with respect to environmental issues, which depend much more on government policy and pressures from local communities, with the innovation strategies discussed by Freeman. For example, a proactive strategy may be understood as an attempt to anticipate future regulation or as an attempt to prevent government regulation through self-regulation. A realistic theory of corporate strategy with respect to environmental issues must consider such firm-regulator relationships.

As explained earlier, these strategies also depend on the capabilities and strengths of individual firms (in terms of R&D, manufacturing, and marketing), the markets in which they operate, and other influence from the selection environment. To develop a theoretical framework, more empirical research is needed on the locus and motives of suppliers and adopters of cleaner technologies. Such research might result in a classification of industry sectors with respect to the nature and source of technical innovations, which may be a good basis for theoretical analyses. This type of research has been done by Pavitt (1984) for normal technical innovations. Comparative empirical studies might also be very useful. Studies of innovation and diffusion processes for cleaner technologies in different countries, incorporating different selection environments, may help researchers assess the particular influence of the different factors.

CONCLUSIONS AND POLICY IMPLICATIONS

This chapter has explored the factors that affect the decision to supply and adopt cleaner technologies, both theoretically and empirically. This final section attempts to derive some general conclusions about these factors and the way in which policy instruments can be used to stimulate the supply and demand of cleaner technologies.

In the three industries examined in the case studies, the technological opportunities and appropriability conditions do not appear to be distinct obstacles to the realization of cleaner innovations. One might conclude that this is hardly surprising, since if technological opportunities were absent and appropriability conditions insufficient, there would have been no new technologies to study in these industries. A more general conclusion, however, is that for almost all environmental problems, several technological opportunities for cleaner technologies are available and that firms in one way or another can protect an innovation against imitation for a sufficiently long period.

The multiple technological opportunities may confront policy makers with a dilemma. Since the success of a certain technology depends strongly on government policy, policy makers should be careful not to induce the selection of inappropriate technologies, and, as a result, lock in adherence to suboptimal technological trajectories. This point is less academic than it may seem. In the case of the metal-plating industry, the market for membrane technologies has been blocked for years because of the widespread adoption of end-of-pipe devices that resulted in the transfer of an environmental problem from one medium to another. In the case of CFC substitutes, policy makers face a similar dilemma: should HCFCs, which also affect the ozone layer but to a lesser extent, be allowed for a certain period, or should other solutions that currently are less suitable and more expensive be stimulated? The choice between technological solutions is very difficult, since a new technology's future costs and benefits (which depend on dynamic scale and learning effects) are unknown to both policy makers and suppliers of the technology. To address this policy dilemma, economic instruments may be preferred to direct regulation since they interfere less with the choice of technology. On the other hand, direct regulation may be better to induce a shift from a current nonsustainable technological trajectory, such as replacement of the internal combustion engine by a less polluting engine with a higher fuel efficiency. Direct regulation may be preferred in situations where the environmental risks are large and acute and when there is some consensus about the most viable technological solution, whereas economic instruments may be preferred when the transition costs involved are likely to be high and when there is much uncertainty about the best alternative technology or trajectory.

If the appropriability conditions are insufficient, policy makers can do little to improve them, except perhaps to subsidize certain R&D projects or stimulate cooperation between firms. As discussed, however, few technological opportunities are not exploited because of inadequate appropriability conditions, although they can be unfavorable, as in the case of low-solvent paints and coatings, and can, as a result, delay the development of new products.

Market demand seems to be the crucial factor for the successful exploitation of technological opportunities. As indicated, in the case of clean technologies, market demand depends strongly on government policy. Although there are other stimuli, such as pressure from local communities, the work force, investors, insurance companies, special environmental interest groups, and the larger public, these stimuli are still not very strong (see Chapter 4). The perspective of a certain policy can also provide an important stimulus. In the case studies, it was found that a clear policy objective for the interim period provided a strong push for the development of CFC substitutes and low-solvent paints and coatings.

The case studies also provided a lot of information about the factors that affect the adoption of cleaner technologies. We identified three factors that influence the adoption of a cleaner technology: the price and quality of the innovation, the transfer of knowledge and information about the environmental problem and the alternative technologies, and the degree of risk and uncertainty surrounding the adoption of the technology. In the case studies, these factors appear to be closely related. The risk and uncertainty regarding the adoption of the technology depend on the price and technical quality of the innovation and knowledge and information concerning adaptation problems. It is therefore essential to remove or reduce possible obstacles here, by addressing actual risks and lack of information and also by correcting distorted images or false information (see also Chapter 9 concerning conceptual barriers).

Even more important, it appears that the purchase price of a cleaner technology is often not the most important factor. A switch to another technology implies a simultaneous change in a number of financial and nonfinancial systems and measures of costs and benefits. As a result, the decision making surrounding a switch to a cleaner technology is often complex. However, this does not mean that price ratios will not play a crucial role at some point in the decision making.

With respect to the choice of policy instruments, this analysis suggests that no single instrument is optimal. Instead, the stimulation of cleaner technologies calls for a mixture of instruments, depending on the specific factors and circumstances. Suppliers and users of different cleaner technologies (environmentally friendly materials, pollution control and recycling technologies, and cleaner consumer products) function in strongly differing markets. The choice of policy instruments should be based on the different characteristics of those markets and the associated stimuli. In the case of heterogeneous users, effluent fees are generally preferred to standards. These fees are much more efficient than emission standards, giving equivalent environmental improvements at lower cost, and can be introduced more rapidly. The efficiency property makes effluent fees especially useful in stimulating input reductions and substitution and recycling of waste (in view of the many firms and industries involved). To stimulate pollution control and prevention technology, effluent fees and tradeable pollution permits are good alternatives to the emission standards that are used at present. Not only are they more efficient, but they also provide an incentive to reduce all emissions. Consequently, there is an incentive to develop and use more effective technologies, and the market for pollution control technologies may become less uncertain and more predictable.

Emission standards that are based on available, end-of-pipe technologies provide little incentive for the development of new, more effective technologies. To counteract this problem, technology-forcing standards and waivers for companies developing or adopting innovations can be considered. They may create a more certain and predictable market for new technologies. However, these instruments, particularly technology-forcing standards, are likely to lead to high costs for firms, unless the regulator is willing to soften and delay standards. However, this would have a negative effect on the willingness to develop innovations. Also, in the case of standards, the risk of being locked into a certain technology or trajectory, which may be suboptimal, is high.

Uncertainty about the demand for cleaner technologies, partly related to unpredictable government policy, may call for the use of R&D subsidies or loans. Subsidies for investments in cleaner technologies are less useful than loans. They clash with the polluter-pays principle and are expensive, and evaluation research in the Netherlands has proved them to be only minimally effective. There is also a risk that such subsidies can produce windfall gains for the firm receiving them. They should be used only when a switch to cleaner technology entails high costs and produces competitive disadvantages due to less strict regulation in other countries.

Communication instruments can be useful policy tools for addressing information problems related to products and processes. Environmental management systems (required in the Netherlands), demonstration projects, and information campaigns can be useful for ensuring that firms make full use of the possibilities available for emission reduction, as firms are often not familiar with available cost-reducing environmental measures. These profitable measures focus particularly on good housekeeping and waste prevention (Huisingh et al. 1986). (See also Chapter 9.) Information disclosure requirements, such as those in the United States that force firms to communicate information about the amount and type of emissions, can also be useful. Finally, instruments such as green labels and product information are believed to be not only useful but also necessary to stimulate the use of and demand for environmentally friendly products, considering the extensive lack of information about the environmental aspects of products.

It should be noted that the effects of these instruments depend not only on the instruments themselves, but equally on how they are implemented: their tightness, differentiation, time path, and flexibility.

Governments may promote ecological modernization of the economy not only through environmental policy, but also through policies pertaining to science and technology, educational programs, and the incorporation of environmental concerns in other policy areas, especially in the agricultural and transport industries. Public procurement could be used much more effectively for environmental purposes. Especially when an innovation is introduced to the market, before the technology has benefited to a great extent from dynamic scale and learning effects and the adaptation of the selection environment, a market niche may be created by a procurement policy that enables a cleaner technology to survive the tough market selection process for a certain period. This kind of policy may provide an important and decisive push for the further development and success of the technology.

Finally, this analysis suggests that in the short term, the transition to cleaner technologies can bring about high costs and serious adjustment problems for adopters. New and cleaner technologies will always be less suited for some adopters because of specific technical requirements or prohibitively high costs—for example, when existing production techniques in polluting firms have to be replaced early in their usable life. When technologies are improved in terms of price or technical characteristics, the overall costs of adopting the technologies may be much lower. Especially in the case of standards, the costs related to such a short-term transition can be high. This means that a combination of patience and persistence in environmental policy may be the optimal strategy.

NOTES

This chapter is based on a joint research project of the Maastricht Economic Research Institute on Innovation and Technology (MERIT) at the University of Limburg, Maastricht, the Netherlands, and the Institute for Environmental Studies (IVM) of the Free University in Amsterdam for the Ministries of Economic Affairs and the Environment in the Netherlands. The author thanks Sander Olsthoorn, Frans Oosterhuis, and Harmen Verbruggen for their work in the research project. Part of this chapter is a further development of an earlier paper, "Policy Instruments to Stimulate Cleaner Technology," prepared for the European

Association of Environmental and Resource Economists (EAERE) conference held on June 11–14, 1991, in Stockholm, Sweden.

1. For a survey of the literature on the economics of technological change, see Nelson (1981) and Dosi (1988b), and for a wide collection of new and important contributions see Dosi et al. (1988).

2. There is an important difference between biological and social evolution. In biological evolution, selection is deterministic, whereas in social evolution involving technological development, intentions and expectations are important, and actors make choices and anticipate the reactions of others (van den Belt and Rip 1989, 141).

3. A crucial implication of the general paradigmatic form of technological knowledge (and of the other concepts) is that innovative activities are strongly selective, finalized in quite precise directions, and cumulative in the acquisition of problem-solving capabilities (Dosi 1988b, 1128).

4. Four kinds of networks can be distinguished: (1) the firm as a network of activities (R&D, manufacturing, management, marketing); (2) the economy as a network of interacting suppliers and users, and involving a certain infrastructure; (3) the technological system (the whole of machines, techniques, components, technical standards); and (4) the socioinstitutional network (education and training, regulation, values, power balance, attitudes toward technology and change, etc.). It is within and through these networks that learning and adaptation take place. These dynamic learning effects are discussed later and elsewhere referred to as network externalities (Kemp and Soete 1992).

5. The notion of social and psychological barriers hindering the innovation process is a central element in Schumpeter's theory of innovation and economic development, in which he envisioned the character of the entrepreneur as a person of great will, energy, and vision (Schumpeter 1934, 73–94).

6. Three types of learning effects can be distinguished: (1) "learning by doing" in manufacturing as a result of optimization of the production process; (2) "learning by using" as a result of user information, as mentioned by Rosenberg (1982); and (3) "learning by interacting" as a result of contacts between supplier and contractor (Lundvall 1988). The two latter types of learning effects usually result in technical improvements, while the first results in lower prices.

7. The importance of improvements of an innovation in favor of a wide diffusion was noted by many historians of technical change, including Rosenberg (1976, 195), who writes: ". . . most inventions are relatively crude and inefficient at the date when they are first recognized as constituting a new innovation. They are, of necessity, badly adapted to many of the ultimate uses to which they will eventually be put; therefore, they may offer only very small advantages, or perhaps none at all, over previously existing techniques. Diffusion under these circumstances will necessarily be slow . . ." Rosenberg also points to the importance of complementary innovations (for example, in machine and tool development), infrastructure, and the availability of technical skills required.

8. The concept of selection environment also explains why, in the past especially, "end-of-pipe" technologies were applied in industry. These technologies could be easily added to the existing production modes at relatively low costs. Also, the typical "norm" policy of government, which was aimed at short-term successes and oriented to direct emissions into the air and water only (neglecting the waste problems related to end-of-pipe technologies), contributed to the dominance of end-of-pipe technologies over process-integrated solutions.

9. Research among suppliers of cleaner technologies in the Netherlands by IJlst et al. (1988) referred to the following factors as the most significant obstacles to offering cleaner techniques: unpredictable government policy (51 percent), profits (42 percent), and insecure market development (38 percent).

10. For a critical discussion of research that attempts to answer such questions, particularly the empirical research of the "demand pull" advocates, see Mowery and Rosenberg (1979).

11. Environment-saving technology does not always increase costs. The literature contains numerous examples of cleaner techniques that do lead to cost reductions (Huisingh et al. 1986). Profitable environment-saving techniques include, especially, recycling systems, energy conservation, and all kinds of improvements of existing processes relating to "good housekeeping." This has inspired governments to adopt "Pollution Prevention Pays" programs—for example, the PRISMA project in the Netherlands (see Chapter 9).

12. For references to the literature used in the case studies, the reader is referred to the original research report (Kemp et al. 1991), available only in Dutch.

13. "Use" is defined in the Montreal Protocol as production minus export plus import. Substances with a limited ability to affect the ozone layer (the so-called soft CFCs, or HCFCs) will be allowed until far into the next century according to the Montreal Protocol.

REFERENCES

Ashford, N. A.; Ayers, C.; and Stone, R. F. 1985. "Using Regulation to Change the Market for Innovation." *Harvard Environmental Law Review* 9: 419–66.

Baldwin, W. L., and Scott, J. T. 1987. *Market Structure and Technological Change.* Chur, Switzerland: Harwood Academic Publishers.

Belt, H. van den, and Rip, A. 1989. "The Nelson-Winter-Dosi Model and Synthetic Dye Chemistry." In *The Social Construction of Technological Systems: New Directions in the Sociology and History of Technology,* edited by W. E. Bijker, T. P. Hughes, and T. J. Pinch, 135–58. Cambridge, Mass.: MIT Press.

Cramer, J., and Schot, J. 1990. *Innovation and Diffusion of Environmental Technology: Opportunities for Research from a Technology-Dynamics Perspective.* RMNO Publication No. 44A. Rijswijk, Netherlands: Netherlands Advisory Council for Research on Nature and the Environment.

Dosi, G. 1988a. "The Nature of the Innovative Process." In *Technical Change and*

Economic Theory, edited by G. Dosi, C. Freeman, R. Nelson, G. Silverberg, and L. Soete, 221–38. London: Pinter Publishers.

Dosi, G. 1988b. "Sources, Procedures and Microeconomic Effects of Innovation." *Journal of Economic Literature* 26(3): 1120–71.

Dosi, G.; Freeman, C.; Nelson, R.; Silverberg, G.; and Soete, L., eds. 1988. *Technical Change and Economic Theory*. London: Pinter Publishers.

Freeman, C. 1982. *The Economics of Industrial Innovation*. London: Pinter Publishers.

Hartje, V. J., and Lurie, R. L. 1985. "Research and Development Incentives for Pollution Control Technologies." International Institute for Environment and Society (IIUG). Berlin: WZB.

Hartje, V. J., and Lurie, R. L. 1984. "Adopting Rules for Pollution Control Innovations: End-of-Pipe versus Integrated Process Technology." International Institute for Environment and Society (IIUG). Berlin: WZB.

Hughes, T. P. 1989. "The Evolution of Large Technological Systems." In *The Social Construction of Technological Systems: New Directions in the Sociology and History of Technology*, edited by W. E. Bijker, T. P. Hughes, and T. J. Pinch, 51–82. Cambridge, Mass.: MIT Press.

Huisingh, D.; Martin, L.; Hilger, H.; and Seldman, N. 1986. *Proven Profits from Pollution Prevention*. Washington, D.C.: Institute for Local Self-Reliance.

IJlst, P.; Stockman, C. T. M.; and Visser, E. T. 1988. *Informatieoverdracht en informatiebehoefte in de milieuproduktiesector in Nederland* (Information transfers and information needs in environmental industry in the Netherlands). Zoetermeer: EIM.

Kemp, R. P. M.; Olsthoorn, A. A.; Oosterhuis, F. H.; and Verbruggen, H. 1991. *Instrumenten voor de stimulering van milieutechnologie* (Policy instruments to stimulate cleaner technology). The Hague, Netherlands: EZ.

Kemp, R. P. M., and Soete, L. L. G. 1992. "The Greening of Technological Progress: An Evolutionary Perspective." MERIT Research Memorandum 91-011. *Futures* 24(5): 437–57.

Levin, R. C. 1986. "A New Look at the Patent System" *American Economic Review*, Papers and Proceedings, May, 199–202.

Lundvall, B. A. 1988. "Innovation as an Interactive Process: From User-Producer Interaction to the National System of Innovation." In *Technical Change and Economic Theory*, edited by G. Dosi, C. Freeman, R. Nelson, G. Silverberg, and L. Soete, 349–69. London: Pinter Publishers.

Mansfield, E.; Schwartz, M.; and Wagner, S. 1981. "Imitation Costs and Patents: An Empirical Study." *Economic Journal* 91: 907–18.

Mowery, D. C., and Rosenberg, N. 1979. "The Influence of Market Demand upon Innovation: A Critical Review of Some Recent Empirical Studies." *Research Policy* 8: 102–53.

Nelson, R. R. 1981. "Research on Productivity Growth and Productivity Differences: Dead Ends and New Departures." *Journal of Economic Literature* 19(3): 1029–64.

Nelson, R. R., and Winter, S. G. 1982. *An Evolutionary Theory of Economic Change*. Cambridge, Mass.: Harvard University Press, Belknap Press.

Nelson, R. R., and Winter, S. G. 1977. "In Search of Useful Theory of Innovation." *Research Policy* 6: 36–76.

Nentjes, A., and Wiersma, D. 1988. "Innovation and Pollution Control." *International Journal of Social Economics* 15: 51–71.

Organization for Economic Cooperation and Development. 1985. *Environmental Policy and Technical Change*. Paris: OECD.

Pavitt, K. 1984. "Sectoral Patterns of Technical Change: Towards a Taxonomy and a Theory." *Research Policy* 13: 343–73.

Rosenberg, N. 1982. *Inside the Black Box*. Cambridge: Cambridge University Press.

Rosenberg, N. 1976. *Perspectives on Technology*. Cambridge: Cambridge University Press.

Schmookler, J. 1966. *Invention and Economic Growth*. Cambridge, Mass.: MIT Press.

Schot, J. W. 1992. "Constructive Technology Assessment and Technology Dynamics: Opportunities for the Control of Technology—The Case of Clean Technologies." *Science, Technology and Human Values* 17(1): 36–57.

Schumpeter, J. A. 1934. *The Theory of Economic Development*. Cambridge, Mass.: Harvard University Press.

United Nations Environment Programme. 1989. *Technical Progress on Protecting the Ozone Layer*. Paris: United Nations Environment Programme.

Vollebergh, H., ed. 1989. *Milieu en innovatie* (Innovation and the environment). Groningen, Netherlands: Wolters-Noordhof.

PART II

❧

The Environmental Challenge: Dynamics of Firm Behavior

4

Corporate Strategies for a
Sustainable Future

Hugh E. Williams, James Medhurst, and Kirstine Drew

Environmental resources are fundamental to economic and social development. The reversal of environmental degradation and depletion of environmental resources is now recognized as being essential if growth in
economic activity is to be sustainable in the longer term. This principle has
received increasing recognition and acceptance by policy makers and the
wider community and represents a major break with the traditional view
that economic development could be based on the consumption of limitless environmental resources. Environmentally sustainable economic
growth is now widely accepted as being the goal for international, national, and regional economies, with the twin objectives of economic
development and improvements in environmental performance.

One of the major consumers of environmental resources and producers
of environmental damage and pollution is manufacturing industry, traditionally the bedrock of economic activity. Some business leaders now
widely acknowledge that environmental protection measures have become, and will continue to be, a growing influence on how companies
operate and, in some cases, on what they do. For some firms, environmental protection and green consumerism will provide new business opportunities; for many, adaptations will improve overall performance, bring
savings, and increase profitability. To others, however, meeting tougher
environmental standards will be costly and, in extreme circumstances, may
force closure. There is therefore a dynamic tension between maintaining

and increasing levels of economic activity and securing improvements in environmental performance.

In recognition that some companies will need assistance in developing responses to increasing environmental pressures, research into the character of environmental pressures and their potential impact on businesses is required. The authors have undertaken a number of studies (e.g., ECO-TEC 1991a, 1991b) to inform the development of policies that encourage companies to improve their environmental performance. The observations in this chapter draw heavily on this research.

The chapter first outlines the nature and range of environmental pressures on firms and, to provide some context for the empirical results, briefly indicates some aspects of the legislative context for firms in the United Kingdom. It then briefly describes the results of a study of the expenditures made by U.K. industry to respond to environmental standards. This provides one perspective on the driving forces—namely, costs—affecting company strategies. If firms are to make adequate responses to environmental pressures they must first have a full awareness of the issues. The chapter next describes the results of a detailed survey of firms in the West Midlands of the United Kingdom, considers the firms' awareness of environmental pressures and their responses, and draws some overall conclusions.

THE CHARACTER OF ENVIRONMENTAL PRESSURES ON FIRMS

A number of distinct, although interrelated, environmental pressures are responsible for raising environmental awareness in industry and for stimulating responses. These include:

- Increasingly stringent environmental legislation and enforcement.
- Increasing costs associated with pollution control, waste disposal, and effluent disposal.
- Increasing commercial pressure from the supply, consumption, and disposal of both final and intermediate products.
- Increasing awareness on the part of investors of companies' environmental performance in view of the cost implications associated with liability and the polluter-pays principle.
- Increasing training and personnel requirements, together with additional information requirements.
- Increasing expectations on the part of the local community and the

work force of the environmental performance of firms and their impact on the environment.

Each of these pressures is brought about by different actors, such as government agencies, consumers, and investors. The pressures each brings to bear are discussed below.

GOVERNMENT PRESSURE

It is not the purpose of this chapter to outline current and emerging legislation in the United Kingdom and the European Community (EC). It is necessary to note, however, that recent and upcoming European Community directives will result in much more stringent legislation requiring higher environmental standards to be achieved (e.g., in relation to effluents and atmospheric emissions). Moreover, this legislation is much more comprehensive and is likely to impact on a wider range of economic activities and industrial processes. This wider impact will also be brought about by encouraging other actors to press for improved environmental performance; for example, the eco-labeling proposal (see below) will allow consumers to exercise choice on the basis of environmental criteria.

The new legislation not only is aimed at preventing pollution by introducing higher standards, but also recognizes the vital importance of influencing the management behavior of industry and increasing the transparency of the firms' environmental management operations (e.g., the Environmental Audit Directive). The following are examples of the directives that are likely to cause these impacts:

1. A Hazardous Waste (Amendment) Directive has been proposed that will increase the number of waste streams defined as being hazardous.

2. The Draft Municipal Wastewater Directive primarily covers discharges from municipal wastewater treatment plants (vis-à-vis oxidizable organics, phosphorus, and nitrogen), but it also places similar biodegradable effluents from industry (e.g., food and drink) under the same controls.

3. The proposed Environmental Audit Directive, although likely to be voluntary at first, provides for rights of public access to the audited statement; as a consequence, companies could face increased exposure to financial risk. There will also be significant resource implications for industry in terms of the management time required to undertake the administrative procedures. If implemented as proposed, this directive will also have the effect of making companies take a much broader look at their environmental responsibilities.

4. A regulation was passed in March 1992 that provided for a community eco-labeling award scheme. Eco-labeling provides an official technical assessment of the life cycle of a particular product. The main aspects of the scheme embrace the concept of a "cradle-to-grave" approach whereby a product's environmental impact assessment takes account of extraction, manufacturing, packaging, and disposal. The scheme is voluntary, and the products included will be determined by the need for firms to promote eco-labeling as part of their marketing strategy and therefore will depend largely on consumer pressure in particular product markets.

To provide some context for the empirical results presented here, it is important to note that there have been two major pieces of legislation enacted recently in the United Kingdom—namely, the 1989 Water Act and the 1990 Environmental Protection Act.

There are three major implications of the 1989 Water Act. First, industry will be subject to more rigorous policing of discharge contents; second, industry will be subject to higher trade effluent and discharge charges; and third, industry will be subject to the possibility of the National Rivers Authority (NRA) imposing a cleanup program and associated costs where groundwater quality is threatened by leakage/seepage from a site.

The 1990 Environmental Protection Act introduces a system of integrated pollution control for major plants and more stringent control for all industry. Major plants are required to prevent prescribed substances from being released or, where this is not feasible, to use BATNEEC (Best Available Technology Not Entailing Excessive Cost) for pollution control on existing plants and best available technology for new investments. In addition, they must demonstrate proper management procedures and availability of adequately trained staff, provide for regular monitoring of the process, and maintain and make available records of emissions, effluents, and wastes.

Further, Part 2 of the act establishes a "Duty of Care" on waste producers and waste contractors. The main implication of this provision is that industry will have to increase its expenditure on waste management to ensure that its wastes are disposed of in a proper manner. Waste disposal costs will also increase significantly as waste operators implement higher standards.

While environmental legislation represents the main pressure, increasing costs associated with managing industrial emissions are also an important factor. In particular, the rapidly rising cost of waste disposal and of discharging liquid effluent to sewers or waterways is exerting severe financial pressure, thus providing a powerful incentive for industry to reduce both the volume and toxicity of its by-products. In addition, the cost implications of a major pollution incident (including remediation at the site, the effect on the company's image, potentially major fines, and lost production) provide a powerful incentive for firms to invest in measures that will reduce the probability or impact of such an incident.

Many companies will wish to manage environmental audits to assess their companies' performance and compliance with legislation and to provide the basis for future monitoring. This is likely to bring about significant investment and training requirements. Investment in pollution control is about not only short-term end-of-pipe solutions, but also the development of clean and cleaner technologies and plant management techniques that reduce waste and pollution discharges. This means the improvement of existing operations or the introduction of new plants and processes. Hence, programs of improved management or of process adaptation may need to be put in place to meet both environmental and financial criteria, and businesses will have to realign management practices to respond to environmental objectives in addition to other company objectives. All of this implies increased management as well as investment costs. Furthermore, the increased costs resulting from environmental regulation will affect companies not only directly, but also indirectly, as environmental costs feed through into the prices of raw materials, energy, water, and so forth.

CONSUMER AND SUPPLIER PRESSURE

Customer awareness of environmental issues represents a significant secondary pressure that has resulted in an increase in corporate awareness and the adoption of a range of responses by industry. Consumers are increasingly better informed and more aware of the environmental content and impact of consumer products and are thus demanding that industry improve the environmental performance of its products. This has resulted in material substitution and the development of "green" products—for example, detergents. Firms are also increasingly seeking to purchase intermediate products that will minimize their waste disposal, pollution control, and energy costs. In addition, suppliers are providing advisory services to their customers on the use of particular products and the development of alternative products in order to minimize their environmental impact. For example, certain chemical companies are helping their customers deal with the problems of disposing of used solvents by taking back solvents after use and assuming responsibility for their treatment and disposal.

INVESTOR PRESSURE

Investors are increasingly examining the environmental records of potential investments, and some are showing a tendency to invest in "greener" companies. This behavior is based on the expectation that these companies will benefit commercially from their green image and that there are efficiency gains associated with the adoption of cleaner technologies. However, also of concern are the cost implications of liability issues. Legislation introducing liability for environmental damage is not well developed in the United Kingdom. However, the experience of the U.S. Superfund, administered by the U.S. Environmental Protection Agency to fund the cost of cleaning up contaminated sites, has demonstrated that the costs associated with cleaning up contamination can be immense. Liability issues are likely to become increasingly prominent in the United Kingdom through measures such as the Duty of Care (breach of which will result in criminal liability) and the draft EC directive introducing civil liability for damage caused by waste. A more general liability directive for environmental damage is also possible. The 1989 Water Act introduced a provision whereby the NRA can clean up any site threatening groundwater quality and recover the costs it incurs in so doing. The ever-changing standards in environmental legislation introduce a new element of uncertainty into decision making with regard to the specification of new capital for plant and investment, thus increasing risk factors and costs.

COMMUNITY PRESSURE

Local communities represent a powerful pressure for improved environmental performance, particularly where firms are located in close proximity to residential areas. Where problems and nuisance associated with noise, vibration, and odor occur, local communities, both directly and indirectly through complaints to local environmental health departments, are capable of bringing considerable pressure to reduce environmental problems.

WORK FORCE PRESSURE

The interests and aspirations of the work force and of trade unions represent potential pressure where a strong interest in the environmental performance of a specific plant occurs.

A FRAMEWORK FOR CONSIDERING ENVIRONMENTAL PRESSURES ON FIRMS

The environmental pressures discussed above affect firms at all stages of activity, influencing the nature and cost of inputs, the required product specification, and sales service and responsibilities (see Figure 4.1). For example, introduction of a carbon tax may affect energy prices and will certainly increase transport costs. Water charges in the United Kingdom are also particularly affected by the need to pass on the costs of increased investment in protection of water resources. The nature of the product produced (and the materials or intermediate products used) also may be significantly affected by environmental pressures—for example, legislation and conventions banning the manufacture of CFCs, customer pressure regarding the use of tropical hardwoods for furniture, or the impact of green legislation and attitudes on the design of motor vehicles.

It has also been possible to identify a range of actors that influence, firm by firm, the way environmental pressures are articulated and managed. These actors, listed in Figure 4.1, act unilaterally and independently, but also under the influence of the other actors' interests and agendas. Thus, government pressures, particularly in the form of enforcement measures, influence the roles and impacts of other actors. For example, in the United States, the required improvement in the public reporting of firms' environ-

FIGURE 4.1.
ENVIRONMENTAL PRESSURES ON A FIRM

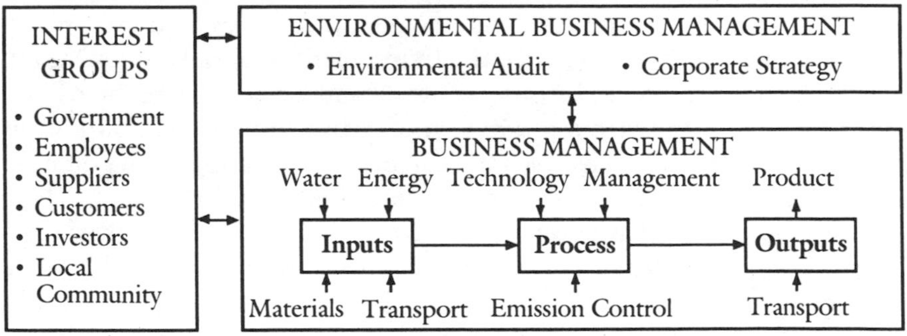

SOURCE: ECOTEC (1991b).

NOTES:
[1] Business Management: The conventional activity of business management.
[2] Interest Groups: Groups that mediate in the process of environmental management and influence the nature of pressures and the response.
[3] Environmental Business Management: The practice of managing a business with attention to the environmental sustainability of the activity and in response to environmental pressures.

mental performance improves the access of the community to information and, hence, its impact. Another example, in the United Kingdom, is the legal requirement to prepare registers of land ownership of land that is potentially contaminated. This could considerably affect asset values and, hence, the interest and impact of investors.

The box in Figure 4.1 labeled "Environmental Business Management" signifies the arrival of a new but necessarily integrated management responsibility to monitor and improve environmental performance, which reflects the pressures in force throughout a company's operation and as articulated by different actors. This new management responsibility is likely to be facilitated by the use of environmental auditing tools and to require the revision of corporate strategy.

Corporate responses have to deal with all of these pressures, which have both short- and long-term time frames. The chapter next examines the scale of the most obvious impact on industries in the United Kingdom—namely, the costs of pollution control. These costs are the most visible to a company and are frequently cited as reasons for not taking up the environmental challenge. Comparing pollution control costs with sales revenue places environmental pressures in the wider context of industry's activities as a whole and hence gives some perspective to these pressures.

INDUSTRY'S EXPENDITURE ON ENVIRONMENTAL PROTECTION

In 1988, ECOTEC undertook a detailed survey of the expenditures made by some 117 firms in the United Kingdom. Firms were asked to supply detailed information on the following components of expenditure: pollution control equipment (PCE), PCE installation, and PCE operation (including charges for emissions, effluents, and waste). These three components add up to what we have termed gross costs. In addition, firms were asked to consider possible financial benefits resulting from pollution control measures, due, for example, to improved plant efficiency. These benefits, where they have been quantified, are subtracted from gross costs to provide an estimate of net costs. All costs were annualized to give average annual figures.

The net costs are presented in Table 4.1. The first column reports the net costs per £1000 of sales revenue. The highest expenditure on pollution control for a given level of output is made by the chemical industry, while the lowest expenditure per £1000 of sales revenue is made by the engineering industry. These costs represent a first-order indication of the relative propensity of industrial activities to generate pollution. The high expendi-

TABLE 4.1
NET ANNUAL COSTS OF POLLUTION CONTROL IN
SELECTED INDUSTRIES, 1988

SELECTED INDUSTRY	NET COST (£ PER £1000 OF SALES REVENUE)	NET COST (PERCENTAGE OF SALES REVENUE)	NET COST
Fuel Processing	3.6	0.4	32.2
Metal Manufacture	11.8	1.2	267.3
Quarrying/Cement	5.5	0.6	8.8
Chemicals	13.7	1.4	379.3
Engineering	2.9	0.3	117.7
Food Processing	11.5	1.2	314.7
Paper and Pulp	8.8	0.9	190.2

SOURCE: ECOTEC (1989).

NOTES:

[1] All figures for 1988 are in 1986 prices. For equivalent sterling purchasing power in 1990 prices, multiply values by 1.24. From 1988 to 1992, real growth in expenditure can be expected.

[2] Industries listed in the table are still likely to be the most significant sectors in terms of environmental activity.

tures incurred in the chemical industry, for example, are due in part to the requirement to control very dangerous substances, especially in the organic pharmaceutical industry. By comparison, the engineering industry generates relatively smaller amounts of less harmful substances.

The second column expresses net costs as a percentage of sales revenue. It can be seen that there are significant variations between broad industry sectors. However, it is important to note that no sector has dramatically high net costs when expressed as a percentage of sales revenue.

The third column indicates the estimated net cost of pollution control in each of the selected industries. The highest level of expenditure is incurred by the chemical industry, as anticipated in the prior assumptions for the survey.

The net costs for selected industries, expressed as a percentage of company sales revenue, were also analyzed by size of company. This analysis should be treated with some caution given the limited number of respondents in certain firm size categories. The analysis, summarized in Table 4.2, indicates a broad direct relationship between firm size and the relative importance of pollution control expenditures. This relationship occurs in three of the five industries listed. However, in two industries the relation-

TABLE 4.2

NET ANNUAL COSTS OF POLLUTION CONTROL IN SELECTED
INDUSTRIES BY FIRM EMPLOYMENT SIZE

| | NET COSTS AS A PERCENTAGE OF TURNOVER | | | |
SELECTED INDUSTRY	Small (<100 Employees)	Medium (100–500 Employees)	Large (>500 Employees)	All Firms
Metal Manufacture	1.0 (5)	1.2 (13)	2.6 (2)	1.2 (20)
Quarrying/Cement	0.2 (3)	0.6 (3)	1.0 (2)	0.6 (8)
Chemicals	0.1 (17)	1.6 (26)	1.3 (11)	1.4 (54)
Food Processing	2.4 (5)	0.3 (2)	0.4 (6)	1.2 (13)
Paper and Pulp	0.1 (1)	0.7 (6)	1.7 (2)	0.9 (9)

SOURCE: ECOTEC (1989).

NOTES:
[1] Numbers in parentheses indicates number of respondents.
[2] Responses from the fuel-processing and engineering industries were insufficient to allow size analysis.
[3] See footnotes to Table 4.1.

ship does not occur. In the chemical industry, which had the largest number of respondents, there appears to be a size threshold above which pollution control expenditure becomes a much more significant item of expenditure—that is, when a firm employs more than 100 people. Moreover, a slight decrease in the relative importance of pollution control expenditure occurs for the largest firms. In the food-processing industry, the converse is the case. Small firms in this industry appear to have particularly high costs; for firms above a certain size (more than 100 employees), pollution control expenditure appears to be significantly lower.

The survey revealed two forces driving expenditure on pollution control: the "carrot" and the "stick." The carrot is improved market performance, which results from a "clean" image. A number of larger firms indicated that new corporate policies aimed at generating a better reputation for environmental responsibility were leading to new investment in pollution control. The sticks are stronger or more vigorous enforcement practices and the prospect of more stringent environmental policies. A number of firms were investing in pollution control to stay "ahead of the game." The carrot and stick phenomenon as an influence on pollution control expenditure is also related to company characteristics. The acceptance of greater environmental responsibility is also part of a wider recognition that the generation of wastes and pollutants indicates inefficient company practices. Investment in pollution control is therefore seen as an investment in a more efficient production process. On the other hand, companies that respond to the stick are those that perceive investment in pollution control as a cost burden to be minimized at all times.

To some degree, these aspects are reflected in the survey findings related to the financial benefits that firms attributed to pollution control expenditures. Financial benefits accrue mainly from the selling and recycling of waste products. For example, one major oil-refining company is able to halve the costs of crude oil inputs by replacing them with oil wastes from the refining process. These benefits are generally gained only by larger companies. With a few limited exceptions, no firms with sales revenue below £5 million attributed any financial benefits to pollution control. This reflects in part the greater awareness of larger firms concerning the benefits to be gained from well-planned and well-managed pollution control procedures and their need for efficient use of resources and reduction of waste to improve economic efficiency.

The estimated percentage of gross PCE costs that financial benefits represent, as shown in Table 4.3, varies from 14 percent in the quarrying/cement and paper and pulp industries to 3 percent in the metal-manufacturing industry. Across the industries included in this study, financial benefits account for some 7 percent of gross costs. To an extent, these benefits represent an understatement of the full level of financial benefits, since firms readily admit to being unable to quantify all the benefits they receive, or indeed admit to having not considered that benefits might actually occur. Variations between industries should therefore be inter-

TABLE 4.3

ANNUAL FINANCIAL BENEFITS ATTRIBUTED TO POLLUTION CONTROL IN SELECTED INDUSTRIES

SELECTED INDUSTRY	FINANCIAL BENEFIT (£ MILLION)	PERCENTAGE OF GROSS COST
Fuel Processing	1.3	4.0
Metal Manufacture	9.3	3.3
Quarrying/Cement	14.3	14.4
Chemicals	10.5	2.7
Engineering	8.4	6.7
Food Processing	31.2	9.9
Paper and Pulp	32.1	14.4

SOURCE: ECOTEC (1989).

NOTE: All figures are in 1986 prices.

preted carefully, since they reflect in part the ability of individual firms to quantify financial benefits.

The fact that pollution control costs as a percentage of sales revenue generally increase as firm size increases suggests, not surprisingly, that larger firms are more aware of the environmental pressures on them, even if only those pressures arising primarily from legislation and enforcement. One might also expect that the prospect of potential savings from better pollution control equipment or management practices might also influence firms' responses.

CORPORATE AWARENESS OF ENVIRONMENTAL PRESSURES

An earlier part of this chapter discussed the wide range of environmental pressures that bear upon firms and the different aspects of firm activity they can affect, from the purchase of inputs through process control and changes to the product itself. Such an analysis suggests that firms should be responding to environmental pressures as a part of overall strategic management, affecting decisions on product development, future process technology, and so forth, as well as current costs. ECOTEC therefore undertook a series of detailed discussions in 1991 with a selected sample of twenty-five firms in the subregion of the West Midlands of the United Kingdom. Table 4.4 shows the industry sectors, firm sizes, and number of firms surveyed.

A full corporate management response that examines not only the current position of the firm, but also possible future conditions, implies that the firm will have a view as to the nature of current environmental pressures and how these will change in the future. Thus, a series of scenarios of future developments were discussed with firms in the survey, both to check their awareness of potential future environmental pressures and as a basis for assessing their responses to both current and future pressures. The following discussion summarizes the views of the firms surveyed with regard to the impact of environmental pressures. The discussion is set out in terms of each of the key business management elements in Figure 4.1: inputs, processes, and outputs.

Impact of Environmental Pressures on Inputs

The impact of environmental pressures on a firm is partly influenced by the relative contribution to total production costs of the different inputs. On the basis of the interviews, it is evident that there is a variation in the

TABLE 4.4
A Profile of the Firms Interviewed

Industrial Activity	Firms Employing <100	Firms Employing 100–500	Firms Employing >500	Total Firms Surveyed	Total All Firms	Total Employment
Vehicle and engine manufacturing (3510)	0	0	3	3	31	15,000
Motor vehicle parts (3530)	2	3	0	5	48	5,100
Mechanical engineering (3289)	3	0	0	3	258	5,300
Engineers' small tools (3222)	2	1	0	3	177	3,600
Basic electrical equipment (3420)	1	2	0	3	16	4,300
Finished metal products (3169)	2	1	0	3	141	3,100
Aerospace equipment (3640)	0	0	2	2	16	4,800
Telecommunications equipment (3441)	1	0	1	2	9	6,800
Chemicals (25)	0	1	0	1	32	2,200
Total Firms Surveyed	11	8	6	25	—	
Total All Firms	673	41	14	—	728	
Total Employment	10,900	9,500	29,800			50,200

source: ECOTEC (1991b).

note: Numbers in parentheses represent headings of the Standard Industrial Classification.

character of production costs between small and large companies, as illustrated in Table 4.5. In large firms, raw materials and energy costs represent a higher percentage of production costs and labor costs a lower percentage, reflecting the greater capital intensity of production in larger firms.

Raw Materials

Raw materials costs generally account for the largest proportion of total production costs. The impact of environmental pressures on raw materials purchased by the firms interviewed stems principally from suppliers, particularly overseas suppliers. These suppliers, especially of metal products, are having to raise the price of raw materials in response to environmental pressures. Examples include overseas supplies of brass, metal, and aluminum and domestic supplies of steel products with a high selenium/cadmium content. Prices of these types of materials are increasing on the order of 10 to 12 percent per year, principally because of environmental pressures.

The impacts of price increases are increased costs and reduced profitability, because firms are severely curtailed in their ability to pass on price increases to their customers. Some companies said they would seek to source more widely to avoid incurring additional costs.

In a few firms, raw materials price increases have also led to some changes in production methods, particularly to minimize the amount of waste produced. For example, a tube-making operation altered its production process to minimize the amount of scrap steel produced.

Energy

Energy costs are a significant item in the production costs of most firms; they can account for up to 40 percent of production costs. Most of the

TABLE 4.5
A TYPICAL BREAKDOWN OF PRODUCTION COSTS

Cost Item	Small Firms	Large Firms
Raw Materials	50	60
Labor	40	25
Energy	5	10
Other (Including Water and Waste)	5	5
Total Costs	100	100

SOURCE: ECOTEC (1991b).

respondents think that energy prices will increase by some 5 percent in the near future, although some believe that price increases in the next five years could be substantially higher.

High energy users have considered the effects of higher energy costs, having undertaken energy audits. In particular they have investigated the opportunities for switching to more fuel-efficient sources, especially for space heating; plant layout is, however, a particular constraint in this regard. Energy efficiency measures are undertaken for commercial reasons and are not perceived to be a reaction to environmental pressures.

Labor

In the firms surveyed, the significance of environmental performance criteria in recruiting and retaining staff is not considered to be great. The recession has in many cases reduced the work force and increased the supply of skilled labor. In this context environmental criteria are less significant than pay and working conditions in attracting and retaining staff. However, a number of firms accept that in the future the perceptions held by potential recruits in relation to the firm's environmental performance could become a significant factor.

Raw Water

The firms surveyed generally did not consider increases in raw water charges to be a significant issue. Heavy users of water have already installed metering and are attempting to reduce consumption.

Conclusions

The main impacts of environmental pressures on inputs are increasing costs of energy and raw materials. Responses that minimize costs are being made, especially in relation to energy costs. Energy costs and increases are not perceived to be environmentally determined.

IMPACT OF ENVIRONMENTAL PRESSURES ON PROCESSES

The views held by firms clearly determine their judgment about the impact of environmental pressures, especially regulatory pressure. (There is a marked absence of information in most firms about the nature and volume of emissions, and therefore about the effect of environmental pressures on the industrial process.) These views are determined in part by the level and nature of the contacts firms had with regulatory agencies. This is an important point, since it illustrates the degree to which firms are still reacting to externally generated pressures rather than making environmental issues part of the internal management agenda. Responses specific to the key environmental media were found.

Water Pollution

Two separate pressures with regard to water pollution can be identified: higher wastewater charges for companies disposing of effluents to sewers/ water systems, and higher standards designed to reduce the concentration of pollutants in wastewater streams. The respondents recognized that current charges would increase; some firms believed that since charges in 1990 had risen 5 percent above inflation, even higher increases could be expected. Firms suggested that the effect of higher charges would not necessarily be significant and would be mitigated to some extent by their previous and current measures to reduce effluent volumes and concentrations.

Air Pollution

The respondents, particularly small firms, had an extremely limited appreciation of the current and future effects of air pollution control on their activities. Very few of the firms surveyed have undertaken any analysis of gaseous emission content, volume, or concentrations, and most, with the exception of the larger companies, are ignorant as to the nature and volume of their gaseous emissions. Judgments of the effects of higher air quality standards were therefore difficult for the firms to make.

A number of firms suggested that the effect of higher standards is directly related to the level of enforcement. Limited enforcement activity would allow firms to continue to operate at lower standards, knowingly or unknowingly. Respondents cited the difference between air pollution control and water pollution control, where greater contact with water pollution regulators has led to improved levels of pollution control.

Waste Management

All of the firms interviewed generate wastes, such as paint sludges, metal swarf, soluble cleaning oils, and so forth. In a limited number of cases, the wastes generated are hazardous. The majority of firms use specialist waste contractors to collect and dispose of their waste, but a small number of the larger firms have their own waste treatment and disposal operations.

The general lack of awareness in relation to gaseous emissions is matched by a similar lack of awareness of the provisions of the Environmental Protection Act in relation to waste management. Only the largest firms were aware of the Duty of Care provision, and a number of these firms had not thought through the possible implications of this provision, particularly in relation to liability and land contamination. The majority of companies surveyed are not aware of what happens to their waste after collection and do not consider that they have any responsibility for the waste once it is collected. Ensuring the use of licensed waste contractors is a responsibility recognized by most companies, but the survey identified only two companies that had carried out a thorough investigation of waste disposal operations.

In terms of waste disposal charges, companies expect a sharp increase in these costs. This view is based on the realization that landfill capacity is bound to decline and that incineration is more expensive, rather than on any understanding of Part 2 of the Environmental Protection Act. These higher charges are not generally considered to have a significant effect and have not, of themselves, led to revised waste management procedures.

Technology

The impact of environmental pressures on the technology, production, and pollution control methods of companies has been extensive; most of the companies surveyed have had to make investments and incur costs in response to environmental pressures. Significant expenditures have been made, for example, for noise and vibration reduction, with firms having to take action not only for health and safety reasons. In a few cases, the impacts have been so great as to put the commercial viability of the firm at risk, and these risks still persist.

In general, the respondents consider the impact of future environmental pressures on production and pollution control technologies to be uncertain. The most significant effect the firms identified is the likely requirement for the installation of pollution monitoring and sampling procedures, although firms are unclear as to the techniques and equipment that will be required. The uncertainty results from a lack of information in relation to new environmental standards and a lack of guidance as to the best technologies to use. Until these uncertainties are reduced, future environmental pressures are unlikely to lead to significant changes in production or pollution control technology in most firms.

Management

In firms that are responding widely to environmental issues, the amount of time allocated to environmental management tasks is generally perceived to have increased over the past two years by up to 30 percent in some of the larger firms. In the larger firms, and in highly polluting firms, there are examples of new positions being created specifically to carry out environmental responsibilities. Some companies have established environmental committees that meet at regular intervals. The effect of environmental pressures in quantitative terms ranges from approximately one-half to one person-year of additional management time.

The impact of environmental pressures on training is related to the type of company response to these pressures, particularly the technical response, as changes in process and equipment create a demand for training of both operators and managers. Also, some companies that are subject to severe environmental pressures, particularly in relation to compliance with legislation, believe that managers must be kept up-to-date on both legislation and new methods of pollution control and prevention. Some of the medium-size and larger companies surveyed suggested that training will become necessary if they are to implement monitoring and auditing procedures successfully in the future.

Conclusions

The main impacts of environmental pressures on technology in the firms surveyed are felt in relation to pollution control, especially effluent control and disposal. Firms had adopted an extensive range of technical responses to comply with environmental standards. In terms of management, firms are mainly reacting to the agenda set by government through legislation rather than promoting a positive environmental management response according to an internally generated agenda. Firms are slow even to perceive the development of policies by government.

IMPACT OF ENVIRONMENTAL PRESSURES ON OUTPUTS

Products

Most firms in the survey produce intermediate products and, consequently, do not consider their products subject to environmental pressures from customers or final consumers. Discussions with these firms do reveal, however, that certain pressures exist. Legislative pressures exist for environmental reasons, such as noise performance standards, and commercial pressures exist as customers require supplier firms to assist them in producing products that have fewer environmental effects resulting from use and disposal. This is particularly true of vehicle manufacturers. A response from the intermediate product manufacturers that is perhaps typical of these manufacturers in the United Kingdom is that they are very slow at innovation and regard their role as one of responding to customer company specifications.

Distribution

Distribution costs are generally insignificant as a proportion of operating costs, except where the company serves an export market, in which distribution costs can rise as high as 25 percent of total operating costs. The effect of higher fuel prices (reflecting environmental pressures) on distribution costs is likely to be mitigated by reviewing shipment loads. However, four companies suggested that a switch to rail is a possibility if fuel prices rise sufficiently.

Conclusions

Producers of intermediate products have focused little attention upon the potential impact of environmentally driven customer requirements. Large companies producing final products are much more aware of, and responsive to, green consumer pressures.

SOURCES OF ENVIRONMENTAL PRESSURE

Government

The survey respondents clearly perceive environmental legislation as the most powerful pressure. However, considering that firms are affected by legislation only to the extent to which it is enforced, some firms believe that this pressure may not be so great. In this situation some firms believe that commercial pressure, from both suppliers and customers, will become more significant.

The importance attached by different firms to legislation is also influenced by the extent to which they are exposed to environmental pressures in other countries. Firms operating in northern European countries and the United States are far more aware of the potential effect that the Environmental Protection Act and BATNEEC guidance could have on their U.K. operations than are firms that are essentially U.K.-based. This distinction is partly due to the size of the firm, since transnational firms are larger, but large, U.K.-based firms are also less well informed and less aware of the importance of environmental legislation than are firms with overseas ownership.

Local Communities

A small number of companies in the survey are currently severely affected by local community pressures to the extent that they have modified their processes and working operations and implemented pollution control activities. Some firms are still required to take corrective action that may threaten their viability. Others for whom the impact has not been so great expect that this type of pressure will heighten as public and community groups become more aware and better informed due to increased public access to information on firms' environmental performance, provided for in the Environmental Protection Act, and a general increase in concern for the environment.

Customers

Customers, as noted above, are not perceived to be a source of environmental pressure, although there is recognition that a number of existing and future pressures are driven by environmental improvement objectives. In particular, suppliers of motor vehicle components recognize that they will need to address the requirements of vehicle manufacturers as they respond to environmental pressures.

Suppliers

As discussed above, a perceived source of pressure is the suppliers of raw materials, particularly copper, aluminum, and steel, who pass on price increases to firms as a result of higher environmental costs. However, another significant issue that emerged in the survey was the environmental pressure arising from the use of particular material inputs in production processes that either have become subject to a ban or restriction (e.g., cadmium, CFCs, asbestos, and some solvents) or cause releases that are subject to increasingly stringent control (e.g., paints). The impact with regard to solvents and paints is likely to be very significant for companies in the survey, as these materials are heavily used in a wide range of processes (e.g., degreasing, painting and coating, shot blasting, and pickling) that are common to a number of the industry sectors surveyed.

Employees and Trade Unions

The work force and trade unions are not currently perceived by companies in the survey to be exerting pressure for improvements in environmental performance. This finding stems partly from the low presence of unions in the companies surveyed (particularly among the small companies) and partly from the fact that trade union activity on environmental issues has been fairly limited to date, with health and safety issues having the main impact on firms. The trade unions have been slow to address environmental issues due to a perceived conflict between their commitment to protecting jobs and the potential job losses associated with good environmental practice. However, there has recently been a shift in position in recognition of the link between good environmental practice and health and safety in the workplace, and due to concern for the living conditions of workers' families, who often live close to the workplace.

Investors

The firms surveyed do not currently believe that investors exert pressures for improved environmental performance. The majority of these firms have not considered the likelihood of such pressures emerging. However, a small number of the larger, well-informed companies are aware of the possible future implications and have begun to address the issue. In this context, it is worth noting that few of the firms in the survey recognize the potential liabilities associated with the possible contamination of their sites. The large majority of firms own their sites and have been established there for an average of thirty years, and, in some cases, for much longer periods. Thus, while pressure from investors is generally not recognized by firms, this does not imply that it does not exist.

Conclusions

Government legislation and enforcement remains the most tangible source of pressure on firms and the one that determines the character of company responses. Perceptions of the impact of other actors, and of the necessity of responding to these actors, are generally very limited.

CORPORATE RESPONSES TO ENVIRONMENTAL PRESSURES

The overall model in Figure 4.1 of how environmental pressures affect firms suggests that firms should be developing responses that integrate environmental considerations into all aspects of management for both current operations and future planning. However, as the above discussion shows, few firms recognize that the pressures are as wide-ranging as the model suggests. It is therefore not surprising that few of the firms interviewed had developed an environmental strategy or clear corporate environmental policies. The responses they have made are summarized below.

ENVIRONMENTAL AUDITS

The undertaking of an environmental audit—not just a compliance audit but one covering all business operations—is clearly a prerequisite for the preparation of environmental strategies. Some of the firms surveyed have conducted partial or complete environmental audits, most often energy audits as a basis for undertaking energy conservation measures. Even in the largest companies, comprehensive and continuous procedures for monitoring solid waste, effluents, and gaseous emissions are frequently absent, partly because of the high costs involved and partly because of uncertainty over the very recent developments in monitoring techniques and equipment. The general absence of monitoring is a particular feature in the response (or lack of response) by firms. However, despite the absence of a framework provided by an environmental audit, the majority of medium-size and larger firms have prepared some form of response to environmental pressures, particularly where technical solutions are required, in response to noise, effluent, fume, or odor problems.

Very few firms have considered undertaking environmental audits of their suppliers, and they seem to be skeptical of the idea. Exceptions include, for example, vehicle manufacturers, who propose to instigate environmental audits of their suppliers, albeit at a technical rather than a corporate level. A number of supplier firms are having to respond to the decision of British Aerospace, under the influence of the Minister of Defense, to audit their suppliers. This suggests that the customer–intermediate supplier chain will only work to transmit environmental pressures in certain circumstances.

TECHNICAL RESPONSES

The technical responses of the firms in the survey vary greatly. Firms at one extreme are investing heavily to remove or reduce environmental problems, while firms at the other extreme are undertaking only minimal responses. A number of larger firms have brought in new waste minimization and waste recycling operations associated with production processes. Examples include selling back solvents to suppliers, selling scrap metal, selling packaging for reuse, and reusing wastewater within the production process. A number of companies have invested heavily in R&D to remove pollution problems through the introduction of clean production techniques. A good example is the investment by a number of manufacturers in the vehicle industry in water-based paints and integrated pollution control as a means of mitigating emissions of volatile organic compounds.

Despite significant investment, substantial technical problems remain for many firms. Investment in noise reduction has typically occurred as a result of health and safety considerations and regulations. However, a number of firms believe that ensuring compliance with permitted noise levels requires further investment, which would cause substantial financial difficulties. Other difficult technical problems are related to treatment of effluents, particularly those contaminated with metal (copper and nickel), in the light of likely increases in standards.

The majority of firms are still largely dependent on end-of-pipe pollution control techniques. The range of potential technical responses is extensive, and the gradual introduction and assimilation of guidance in relation to BATNEEC will generate extensive investment in production and pollution control technologies. The detailed characteristics of this future investment are, however, unclear to many firms.

WASTE MANAGEMENT

The waste management practices of companies have not generally been subject to review or revision resulting from changes affecting the waste management industry. In the companies surveyed, awareness of these changes is very limited. Firms experiencing substantial increases in waste disposal charges and anticipating further increases have not changed their waste management practices and do not anticipate doing so. Some larger firms, while not fully conversant with Part 2 of the Environmental Protection Act, do recognize a need to review legal responsibilities in relation to waste management, but the majority do not. Some firms are undertaking waste audits with a view to clarifying their legal responsibilities and knowledge about the required levels of compliance.

PRODUCT REVIEW

The response to customer pressure is most developed in companies producing final consumer products; vehicle manufacturers are a good example. These large firms are responding to the need for more energy-efficient vehicles as the primary consideration, and weight reduction is their principal aim. The pressures associated with vehicle disposal are also being addressed with standardization and reduction in the number of vehicle parts. Some issues remain, however: new recycling procedures involving vehicle manufacturers in the collection, recycling, and scrapping of used vehicles are still to be developed.

The response of firms producing intermediate products is generally to accept that any market-driven environmental pressures will be articulated by their customers through changes in product specifications. Future responses are unlikely to develop very far from this position. The exceptions to this reactive approach occur in firms that produce intermediate products that are hazardous in use and disposal, such as chemicals. These firms have developed procedures and practices to advise and assist customers with the safe use and disposal of their products.

SECTOR AND SIZE OF FIRM

One major finding of the survey is that differences between companies in different industrial sectors in terms of both environmental impact and environmental response are not as significant as expected. A number of factors account for this. First, only two to five interviews were carried out in each sector, so that it was difficult to establish commonalities. Second, a number of environmentally significant processes—mainly, painting and coating, plating, degreasing, welding, and metal working—are common in many of the sectors studied. Hence, to a large extent, many of the companies interviewed are experiencing, or in the future will experience, similar problems. Third, many of the companies are simply not aware of the scale or nature of their environmental impacts and thus are unable to discuss the particular pollutants associated with their processes. Fourth, it is evident that size of the company and whether it operates independently or as part of a group are far more significant factors that tend to dominate the response.

Within this context it is possible to identify key findings pertaining to the different industry sectors.

Environmental pressures exerted through the supply of raw materials are most significant for companies working with metals—aluminum, steel, and brass.

Pressures related to emissions are most felt by companies operating coating and painting processes and degreasing and cleaning processes. These pressures affect component suppliers, vehicle manufacturers, small metal parts manufacturers, and printed circuit board manufacturers.

Pressures related to noise are evident throughout a number of industry sectors, primarily those involved with metal working, and particularly companies operating presses, working with metal on metal, and doing machine tooling. These include light engineering, heavy engineering, and vehicle manufacture.

Analysis of the responses to environmental pressures suggests a range of responses, governed by varying degrees of perception on the part of each firm as to the character and development of environmental pressures. The twenty-five firms surveyed have been mapped in Figure 4.2 according to the extent of the impact of environmental pressures and the degree of response, as judged by ECOTEC.

The assessment of the impact of environmental pressures takes into

FIGURE 4.2.

A SUMMARY OF THE IMPACT OF, AND RESPONSE TO, ENVIRONMENTAL PRESSURES BY FIRMS IN THE STUDY AREA

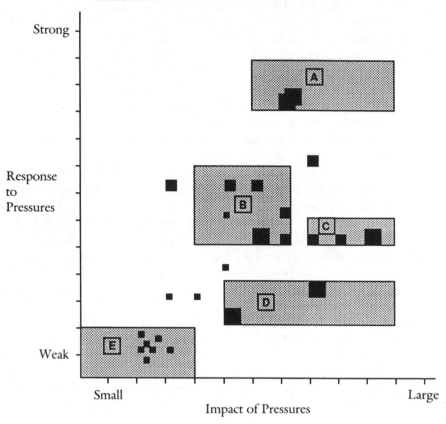

KEY

■ Small Firm (<100 employees)

■ Medium Firm (100–500 employees)

■ Large Firm (>500 employees)

SOURCE: ECOTEC (1991b).

account both current and future pressures; therefore, ECOTEC's judgment may differ from that of some of the firms, as they often have had only a very limited understanding of potential future pressures. In addition, ECOTEC's assessment of each firm's response takes into account the degree of success of the response in dealing with environmental pressure. Thus, a firm that has made an extensive investment in response to an environmental problem but has not succeeded in reducing the problem was judged to have weaker response than a firm that has taken relatively minor steps to address a particular problem but has succeeded in removing the problem.

The analysis highlights two important points. First, the level of response is broadly related to the extent of the impact of environmental pressures. Firms exposed to more extensive environmental pressures have responded more than firms with less exposure. Second, the extent of impact and level of response are determined by the size of the firm. Small firms (those employing less than 100 people) are, with a few exceptions, relatively unaffected by environmental pressures and, given the relatively low level of importance attached to the issues, have not considered or prepared any real responses.

The analysis also highlights particular groups of companies that experience similar impacts and have undertaken similar levels of response. Group A in Figure 4.2 comprises large, multinational, overseas-owned companies that are exposed to significant environmental pressures and have taken, and/or are planning to take, a broadly corporate response that goes beyond simply responding at a technical level to particular pollution control problems.

Group B comprises mostly medium-size companies that are not exposed to the highest impact of environmental pressures and have developed some mainly technical responses in response to particular problems. However, these firms are significantly less well advanced in their response and lack a coherent or strategic response to environmental pressures. Issues pertaining to waste management, liability, BATNEEC, and market pressures are largely unaddressed in these companies.

Group C comprises those firms that are most exposed to environmental pressures, ranging from noise and air pollution abatement to material-handling difficulties, and are under pressure from regulators and local communities. These firms typically have invested heavily in attempting to address technical problems but are still a long way from resolving their difficulties. They are currently the most commercially vulnerable firms as a consequence of environmental pressures.

Companies in Group D are under some environmental pressures, in some cases quite extensively so, without fully realizing that these pressures exist. As a consequence, their environmental management response is substantially limited. Although this situation is not an immediate problem in the firms interviewed, there are likely to be longer-term problems unless there are some changes in perception and response.

Companies in Group E are small firms that have a limited exposure to environmental pressures. As a consequence, responses are very limited. However, while issues relative to waste management and BATNEEC are less critical for these companies compared with larger firms, there remains a significant lack of awareness as to the nature of environmental pressures and suitable responses.

CONCLUSIONS

Figure 4.3 summarizes the general responses to environmental pressures by firms in the detailed survey. The first two columns of boxes express the areas of current and future environmental pressures on companies in the survey. These pressures are taken across the full range of issues presented in Figure 4.1. The final column shows the current and planned responses of firms. The following three general points may be made:

- Current pressures are seen to bear primarily on the production process itself and arise primarily from legislation and the local community.
- There is a recognition that, while pressures on production processes will increase in the future, there will be a much wider range of pressures on the company as a whole from many more sources.
- It is both interesting and significant that the current and planned responses of firms do not match very closely the expected wider range of pressures. Indeed, while many firms have started to respond to potential cost changes for energy and other inputs, technical responses to tighter process control legislation and to wider market/customer/investor considerations are lacking.

Like other surveys and much anecdotal evidence, this survey shows that it is the larger, multinational firms that are taking a more corporate and strategic view of environmental pressures. The cost data indicate that it is the larger firms that bear the highest costs of pollution control and that this might account for the high level of awareness and response to environmental pressures. However, it should be noted that a correlation exists between sectors dominated by large firms and sectors that are subject to a significant

FIGURE 4.3.
A SUMMARY OF THE GENERAL RESPONSES OF FIRMS TO ENVIRONMENTAL PRESSURES

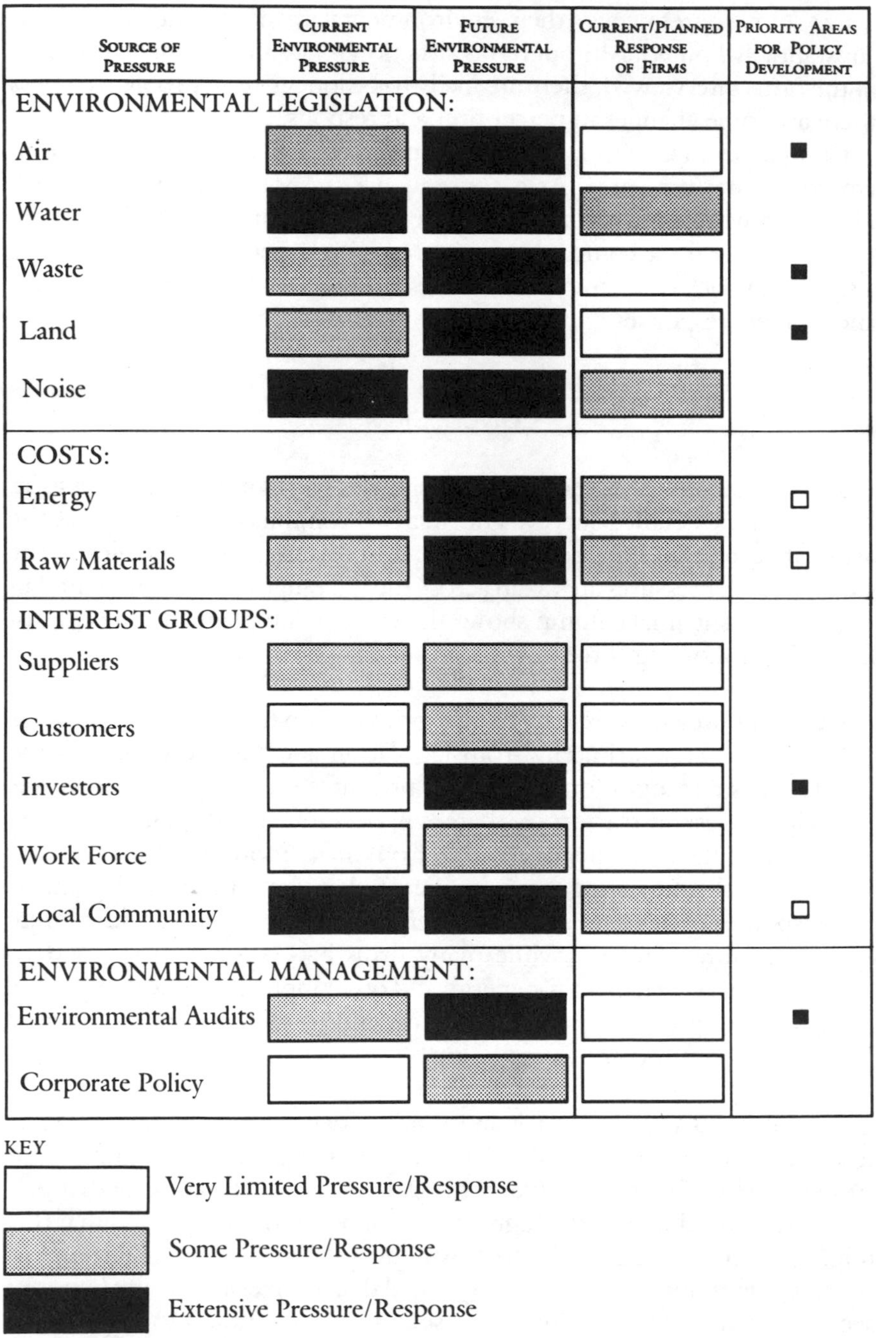

SOURCE OF PRESSURE	CURRENT ENVIRONMENTAL PRESSURE	FUTURE ENVIRONMENTAL PRESSURE	CURRENT/PLANNED RESPONSE OF FIRMS	PRIORITY AREAS FOR POLICY DEVELOPMENT
ENVIRONMENTAL LEGISLATION:				
Air	Some	Extensive	Very Limited	■
Water	Extensive	Extensive	Some	
Waste	Some	Extensive	Very Limited	■
Land	Some	Extensive	Very Limited	■
Noise	Extensive	Extensive	Some	
COSTS:				
Energy	Some	Extensive	Some	□
Raw Materials	Some	Extensive	Some	□
INTEREST GROUPS:				
Suppliers	Some	Some	Very Limited	
Customers	Very Limited	Some	Very Limited	
Investors	Very Limited	Extensive	Very Limited	■
Work Force	Very Limited	Some	Very Limited	
Local Community	Extensive	Extensive	Some	□
ENVIRONMENTAL MANAGEMENT:				
Environmental Audits	Some	Extensive	Very Limited	■
Corporate Policy	Very Limited	Some	Very Limited	

KEY

☐ Very Limited Pressure/Response

▨ Some Pressure/Response

■ Extensive Pressure/Response

SOURCE: ECOTEC (1991b).

degree of public and legislative pressure (e.g., chemicals, oil refining, vehicles). Indeed the cost data suggest that the costs of pollution control alone are unlikely to have brought about major changes in management approach; it may well have been wider issues of customer image and legislative control on products that influenced many large multinationals.

The same pressures are clearly not felt by smaller firms and particularly many producers of intermediate products. It is not clear that the producer-supplier chain is yet transmitting the signals very strongly, at least in the United Kingdom. However, if we are to move to an industrial structure that overall is more sustainable, it is clear that all firms must start to adopt the wider model of environmental awareness outlined in Figure 4.1 and an appropriate and equally wide corporate environmental management response. The introduction of eco-labeling or audit trails, which go beyond the firm to its suppliers and also consider the product, may be two ways to transmit signals more strongly through the economy as a whole. The other approaches would draw on many of the well-known strategies for helping smaller companies adopt new innovations (e.g., closer supplier-customer links and demonstration schemes).

There is much discussion as to how industry in general can be motivated to adopt more sustainable strategies. At one end of the scale is what might be called the "normative model," in which best-practice company management is carried out together with the articulation of the wider social responsibilities of companies. The International Chamber of Commerce's program "Business Charter for Sustainable Development" is an example. A second model is built around the notion of environmental standards and implemented through the market mechanism with the use of economic instruments such as effluent charges and taxes.

Some broad conclusions emerge regarding these two different models —the normative model and the market model—for encouraging industry to move toward more sustainable strategies. It is not surprising that the larger multinational companies are adopting the normative model, which is illustrated in Figure 4.1. This is partly because of their wider exposure to pressures (consumer, image, and enforcement pressures) and the sensitive or high-profile nature of some of their products (e.g., chemicals). It may well also reflect the corporate cultures of such firms, which are more likely to respond formally to social or community responsibility issues and to integrate total quality management—of which environmental control may be seen as a part.

Given the slow adoption of innovative management approaches by independent and small to medium-size firms in the United Kingdom, it also is not surprising that most of the companies surveyed do not follow the normative, best-practice management approach. The literature on both management innovation and barriers to diffusion gives clear, a priori indications that these results are to be expected.

The market approach also appears to lack influence on company behavior. There are at least three reasons for this. First, the easily observable direct costs of pollution control, such as charges for waste disposal and effluent treatment, are not large compared to other fixed costs and overheads and hence do not emerge strongly as costs for consideration. Second, these firms (particularly small and medium-size enterprises) clearly lack data on the environmental pressures and requirements affecting them and therefore have little idea of the current costs of meeting these requirements. Third, if the direct costs of current pollution control and waste disposal practices do not appear to be large, or firms are unaware of them, it is much more difficult to identify and quantify future costs or impacts that might be passed down the supply chain; hence, lack of information and possibly the low financial impact will inhibit the passing of signals through the market.

REFERENCES

ECOTEC. 1991a. *The Black Country Environmental Initiative*. Report prepared for the West Midlands Regional Office, Department of Environment, United Kingdom. Birmingham: ECOTEC.

ECOTEC. 1991b. *The Implications of Environmental Pressure for Industry*. Report prepared for Warwickshire County Council, Coventry City Council, and the BOC Foundation, United Kingdom. Birmingham: ECOTEC.

ECOTEC. 1989. *Industry Costs of Pollution Control*. Report prepared for the Department of Environment, United Kingdom. Birmingham: ECOTEC.

5

The Greening of the Board Room:
How German Companies Are Dealing
with Environmental Issues

Ulrich Steger

Environmental protection traditionally is regarded as a collective good: once it is produced, nobody can be excluded from its benefits. However, nobody is willing to pay for it (the free-rider problem), so the government must step in and set and enforce standards and regulations.

In an economic sense this means that environmental goods, which previously were unlimited and free, are now scarce and therefore have a price. Instead of setting a price or limiting the amount of environmental goods, the government normally prefers to protect the environment by setting emission or effluent standards for industry to limit the amount of pollutants discharged to air or water. These standards transfer into costs for control technology such as sewage treatment and scrubbers, the "price" of environmental protection. This price is different from plant to plant, and therefore such standards are economically not very efficient. This is the most important argument (aside from the bureaucratic red tape it creates) against this type of regulation.

With the regulatory approach, corporations are passive "victims" of political decisions, because they are unable to take a proactive stance. Corporations are still primarily oriented to this kind of environmental protection policy. It is rational for a company under these circumstances just to comply with the law and try to minimize the costs imposed by environmental regulation. Basically, regulatory standards are met by using end-of-pipe technologies, and often no other technical option is available in the required time schedule (Steger 1988; Antes 1991). However, this situation is changing, for three reasons.

First, end-of-pipe technology has altered the cost advantages of using standard technology, so that new, "integrated" technologies that avoid or prevent pollution in the production process are becoming profitable and leading to new considerations for innovative management (see Chapter 9). Second, companies that are paying the costs of end-of-pipe treatment are trying to substitute hazardous inputs to avoid pollution or other economic undesirables such as containers with residual toxic chemicals, which are regarded as hazardous waste. Thus, through these buying policies, suppliers are being forced into environmental protection (see Chapters 11 and 12). Third, and most important, consumer behavior is changing so that environmentally sound products increasingly have a competitive advantage in the market. As a recent survey indicates (Steger and Tiebler 1990), increasing environmental consciousness is becoming part of a change in values. More precisely, a reshuffling of priorities is occurring in the value systems of individuals through a continuous learning process that is taking place in all modern, industrialized, democratic countries. Thus, the change is not a short-term trend, but a more long-term one.

Environmental awareness influences consumer behavior at the point of sale through a complex "trickle-down" process: if the cognitive discord between a person's environmental conscience and actual behavior grows too large, at a certain point the gap is closed by a change in behavior. Factors that influence this process are mainly the knowledge of ecological interrelationships, the extent to which the individual is affected personally, the perception of personal responsibility (whether one can "make a difference"), the intention to change behavior, and readiness for change. Socio-demographic indicators of such changes in attitude are high income and high educational level (which are correlated with each other). Age and gender are no longer significant indicators.

The areas in which consumers exert this changing behavior are mainly those in which they feel personally affected; for example, environmentally hazardous products may be reevaluated if they are perceived as a direct personal risk. In this situation environmental protection is no longer a collective good, but an individual good, and therefore a relevant market demand factor.

Product areas in which that demand is developing (Steger and Tiebler 1990, 122) are nutrition, cleansing agents, cosmetics, and detergents, as well as furniture or other consumption goods, which bestow prestige because they enable individuals to show an environmentally oriented lifestyle. The list of products is rapidly increasing.

Experience shows, however, that environmental soundness—except in narrow market segments—is not a substitute for basic product performance and quality, but only an additional benefit.

This chapter focuses on an important question. In dealing with the development of a new environmental awareness, do corporations go beyond compliance with the law to tap market potential and opportunities for innovation with an environmentally oriented strategy?[1]

In basic terms, a company is environmentally oriented if it has integrated environmental issues into its overall strategy and has organized environmental protection in an appropriate way. This includes a systematic effort—beyond mere compliance with environmental protection laws—to identify environmentally sensitive market opportunities, develop and use clean technology and environmentally sound products, and search for the potential to reduce costs through environmental protection. Such an approach does not necessarily determine a particular option.

To meet this requirement, it is necessary to integrate environmental protection into the goal structure of the corporation. Using a differentiated set of goals, it is reasonable to assume that the most important objective (or "vision") of a company is survival—that is, strengthening its resources and capabilities to meet the requirements of changing business and gain a competitive edge (see Figure 5.1). At the next level are strategic goals (or "missions"), which include profit and market objectives as well as basic objectives. The latter are objectives that a corporation has to fulfill and to include in its missions to ensure long-term survival, such as vocational training, social benefits, and—a new factor—environmental protection.

Studies show that profit and market objectives are positively correlated with each other. The interesting question is how they relate to the basic objectives, especially environmental protection. Traditionally, it has been assumed that environmental protection is a conflicting goal, because it carries additional cost, which implies a decline in (at least international) competitiveness.

A variety of examples in companies, such as 3M in the United States, as well as new empirical studies (Steger 1990) indicate that this is not generally the case. The situation depends very much on the applied technology, the market conditions, the gains in efficiency, and the cost savings due to energy or water conservation and avoided waste disposal costs. It is therefore reasonable to assume that strategic planning can bring about an appropriate strategy that coordinates different goals or minimizes conflicts between goals.

Figure 5.1.
Goal Structure of a Corporation

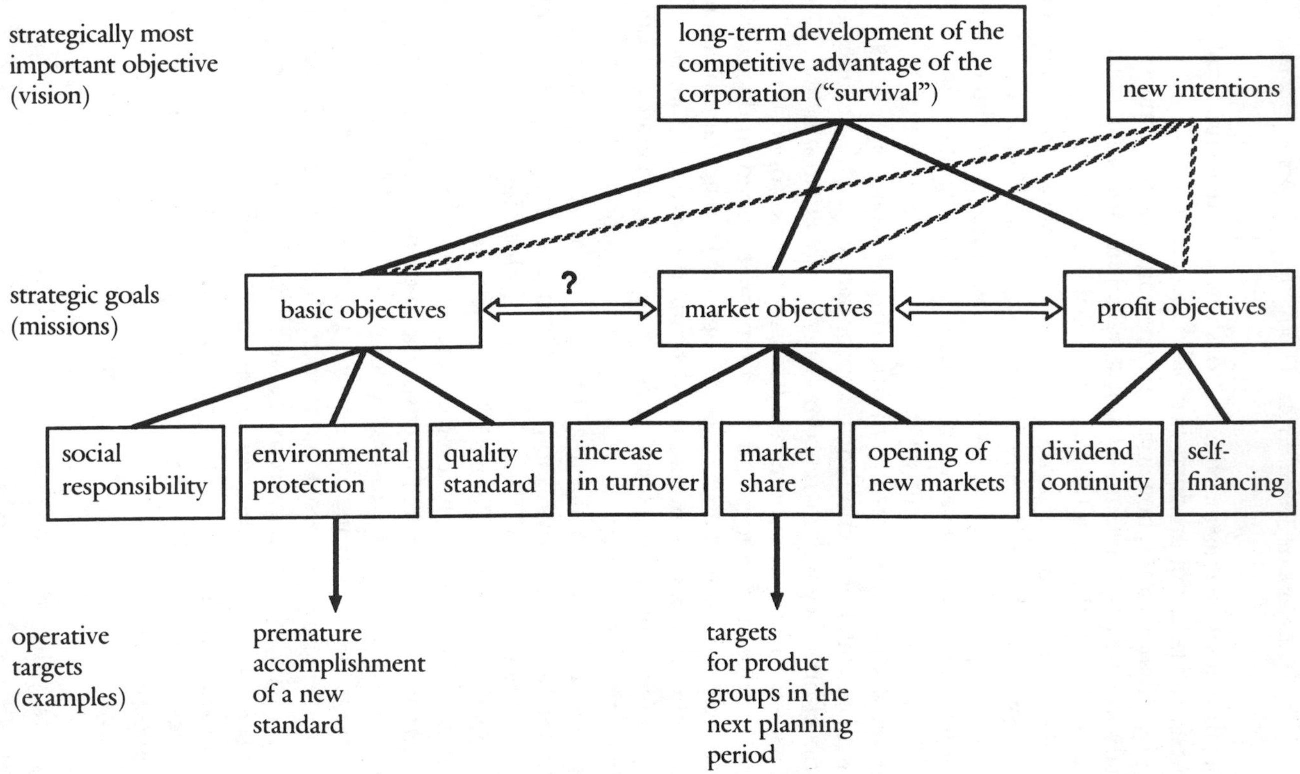

In Figure 5.2, four possible types of generic strategies—offensive, defensive, innovative, and indifferent—are shown. The type of strategy is determined according to two conditions: the company's potential for market opportunities resulting from an environmental protection stance, and the level of environmental risk inherent in the company's activities. The indifferent strategy is not discussed here because under the set of company conditions for this strategy (small potential for market opportunities and small environmental risk), environmental protection is of no strategic importance, although the company could institute some beneficial environmental practices such as purchasing recycled paper or investing in energy-saving measures.

A defensive strategy implies that, for the particular company, there is no relevant market opportunity in being environmentally oriented. It is therefore rational just to comply with environmental legislation. This situation is typical in the fossil fuel–based, electricity-generating industry. However, because of high environmental risks, such as air pollution, the company will be a primary target of environmental regulation. Furthermore, because of extensive fitting of its processes with end-of-pipe technologies, it may incur considerable increases in production costs, as external effects—in this case environmental costs—are internalized into the company's financial picture. This increases the incentives for buyers to switch to substitutes or for competitors to introduce new technologies (in the

FIGURE 5.2.
STRATEGIES BASED ON MARKET OPPORTUNITIES AND
ENVIRONMENTAL RISKS

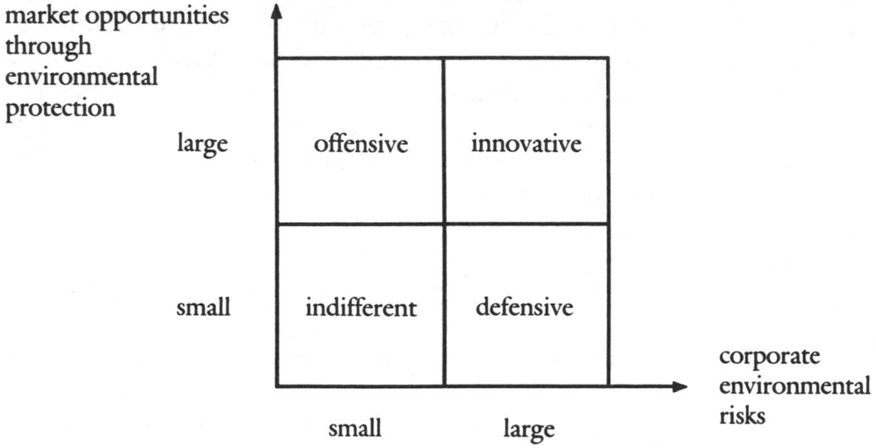

market opportunities through environmental protection

	small	large
large	offensive	innovative
small	indifferent	defensive

corporate environmental risks

case of power generation, for example, pressurized fluidized bed combustion). Only in highly stable markets in which technological improvements are marginal and price elasticity is low can this strategy therefore be regarded as sustainable.

An offensive strategy requires, above all, the development of environmentally sound products, or perhaps only product modifications, that provide an additional benefit to the consumer and therefore a competitive advantage for the corporation. A typical example is the food-processing industry. Critical factors are time (because competitors are in a similar situation, and a "me too" position is normally not as successful as a leadership position) and the ability to communicate the products' environmental advantages through marketing efforts. This requires not only the consumer's knowledge of the environmental improvement over former products, but also no relative discrimination of other products under the same brand (for example, the elimination or substitution of chemical preservatives must be possible over the complete range of products in certain types of food).

An innovative strategy—like any management innovation—is the most challenging because the market potential is tapped only by a major change in the production process or a complete new product design. Large segments of the chemical industry are subject to these conditions. For example, development of a completely degradable pesticide that leaves no residues in food would be a tremendous market opportunity. The positive market opportunities for an innovator are obvious and include profits of early learning experience, the freedom to set product standards, product differentiation, increased product appeal and image, and avoidance of future environmental regulation costs. The risks include high R&D costs, uncertainty of demand, information deficit on the part of customers, inability of new products to meet quality standards, and inability of old products to hold their competitive position due to further technological progress. All that is already known about balancing the risks and opportunities of innovation is applicable in this situation (see Chapter 3). An innovative strategy can therefore be justified only if there is potential for long-term success and a clear environmental advantage of the new product or process.

A SURVEY OF CORPORATE ENVIRONMENTAL STRATEGIES

The findings discussed here are based on the core of a survey, called the FUUF study (1991), of 592 German manufacturing and service companies. The survey had two primary aims: (1) to provide comprehensive assessment of pro-environmental corporate management in German industrial, service, and trading companies and financial services institutions, and (2) to identify market potentials that were equally pro-environmental and value-additive—that is, cost-cutting or revenue-increasing—and the prerequisites for their systematic implementation.

Surveys were carried out at 592 companies of all sizes in all branches of industry, including service companies, trading companies, and financial services institutions. The survey consisted of the following components:

- Direct questionnaire interviews of one-and-a-half to two hours' duration with members of the board—or the equivalent in the case of small or medium-size companies—of the 592 companies.
- Depending on applicability, independent completion of a total of nine division-specific questionnaires by division heads in the production, materials management, research and development, marketing, accounting, controlling, administration, personnel, and public relations divisions. For small and medium-size companies (fewer than 500 employees) the division-specific part of the survey was considerably reduced and consisted of selected questions from the nine divisional questionnaires.

The ten questionnaires together comprised 204 questions, some of which had subdivisions. The response rate for the divisional questionnaires ranged from 19.4 percent (production division) to 15.2 percent (administration division) of the total of 592 companies that responded to the main questionnaire.

Many of the survey questions were multiple-choice questions. The following limitations should be noted:

- There may have been a tendency toward socially desirable answers. Statements to the effect that environmental protection is undertaken by companies for reasons of "social responsibility," for example, must be viewed with a certain caution.
- Differing terminological interpretations between practitioners and academics may have resulted in distortions.
- The results are confined within a framework of prescribed questions and possible answers.

In general, it can be said that the assessments called for in the questions are subject to change, and therefore a time series survey would have been more enlightening than a one-time recording of the status quo.

In view of the scope of the FUUF study, results presented in this chapter are highly compressed. For the entire study, see FUUF (1991) and Antes, Steger, and Tiebler (1991). Of prime relevance here is the evaluation of the company management response (Antes, Steger, and Tiebler 1991), supplemented by selected results from the division-specific questionnaires.

COMPANY MANAGEMENT

1. Board members of corporate management assign environmental protection a high level of importance in their own companies. However, the motives for this are more strongly based on longer-term risk considerations—that is, safeguarding of corporate viability—and only secondarily on the exploitation of opportunities for cost reduction and/or revenue increase.

2. Of the conditions that are of importance for a successful pro-environmental company management, board members perceive external factors (market relations and market partners—suppliers, customers, and competitors) as being less favorable than internal ones. They view the current attitudes of consumers as the main factor inhibiting a wider variety of environmentally acceptable products. Nevertheless, 56.2 percent of the companies note a growing market segment of environmentally oriented consumers.

3. Environmental protection was only occasionally listed as an independent corporate objective. However, as is clear from the relationship between corporate and environmental objectives as viewed by the board members polled, this does not necessarily mean that environmental protection is subordinate to other objectives. The respondents emphasized that pro-environmental objectives are neutral or complementary to other important corporate objectives, rather than in competition with them. This applies above all to the most important corporate objective, according to 57.6 percent of the respondents—namely, the "safeguarding of corporate viability"; 59.9 percent view the relationship here as being a complementary one, 34.1 percent as a neutral one, and only 6.0 percent as a competing one. An opposing relationship is seen to a significant extent only with revenue objectives (33.1 percent) and liquidity objectives (32.2 percent). In contrast, the complementarity of environmental protection with "soft" factors, such as public image (86.8 percent), the acceptance of social responsibility (84.4 percent), or employee recruitment and motivation (72.4 percent) is outstanding. However, a realistic view must be taken of how much, or rather, how little, such soft factors actually count against "hard" sales and revenue objectives when it comes to a choice. It is

reasonable, however, to suppose that there have been considerable shifts in the perception of the complementary or conflicting nature of objectives since the 1970s, which undoubtedly has had a decisive effect on the approach of companies.

4. When more penetrating inquiries are made as to motives for the significance accorded to environmental protection, ecological and social responsibility are frequently quoted as the first reasons. It is very likely that social desirability of response is a major influence here. Table 5.1 gives a detailed breakdown of responses to this inquiry. It is conspicuous that value-adding potentials as yet hardly represent a motive for corporate environmental protection.

5. In respect to planning instruments, the main emphasis is clearly on traditional concepts (market analyses, strength/weakness analyses, competition analyses, and industry structure analyses). Newer planning instruments (diffusion curve concept, cross impact, and environmental scenario analyses), on the other hand, have a subordinate significance. About one-third of board members claim to already integrate environmental aspects into the above-mentioned traditional instruments, or to use ecology-related planning instruments (such as eco–balance sheets). Altogether, a growing receptivity to ecology-related planning can be expected in the future, with the inclusion of ecological measures in traditional instruments preferred (38.3 percent) to the introduction of specifically ecological planning instruments (25.5 percent).

6. The extent to which individual functions and divisions are affected by environmental considerations is assessed differently for different functions by board members. The divisions most affected ("very strongly"/ "strongly") are said to be those with a predominantly technical focus, such as production and, less so, research and development and materials management. Accordingly, environmental risks are countered in most cases with technical measures (77.5 percent); organizational and personnel-related measures are insignificant in comparison (14.5 and 8.0 percent, respectively).

A certain sensitization to the integrative or cross-sectional character of corporate environmental protection can be discerned insofar as one-half of the board members regard strategic planning as being very strongly/ strongly affected by considerations of environmental protection. On the whole, however, cross-sectional functions such as administration, personnel management, and controlling/accounting are viewed to a distinctly lesser degree as starting points for corporate environment policy than of the primary functions. It is interesting to note that, of the latter, marketing is regarded as being the least affected by environmental matters. With the

TABLE 5.1

MOTIVES FOR THE IMPORTANCE ASSIGNED TO ENVIRONMENTAL
PROTECTION IN COMPANIES

What reasons or motives are significant in your opinion for the importance attached to environmental protection in your company today?

REASON/MOTIVE*	FIRST	SECOND	THIRD	TOTAL**
Ecological/social responsibility	30.5% (172)	23.3% (100)	2.6% (25)	1./741
Legislation/government regulations	22.5% (127)	13.1% (56)	12.6% (25)	2./314
Safeguarding of corporate viability/risk aspects	12.1% (68)	8.9% (38)	11.1% (22)	3./302
Image/public relations	9.2% (52)	11.9% (51)	18.6% (37)	4./295
Employee protection	8.3% (47)	14.0% (60)	13.6% (27)	5./288
Market pressure/market potentials/sales possibilities	7.8% (44)	13.5% (58)	16.6% (33)	6./281
Protection of the environment quality of life	8.2% (46)	10.7% (46)	10.6% (21)	7./251
Value-adding potentials/ revenue	1.4% (8)	4.7% (20)	4.5% (9)	8./73
Total	100.0% (564)	100.0% (429)	100.0% (199)	
No details/not applicable	(28)	(163)	(393)	803

  * At evaluation the self-declared reasons and motives were collected into homogeneous groups.

** The total figure was ascertained by weighing the most important reason with three points, the second most important with two points, and the third most important with one point.

exception of accounting, the ranking shown in Figure 5.3 is confirmed to a remarkable degree by responses to the divisional questionnaires.

7. Defensive and remedial measures have predominated in corporate environmental protection. Divisional heads regarded environmental matters as highly integrated in the organizational process: by 91.5 percent in

FIGURE 5.3.

THE EXTENT TO WHICH CORPORATE FUNCTIONS ARE AFFECTED BY ENVIRONMENTAL CONSIDERATIONS (VERY STRONGLY/STRONGLY) AS PERCEIVED BY MEMBERS OF COMPANY MANAGEMENT

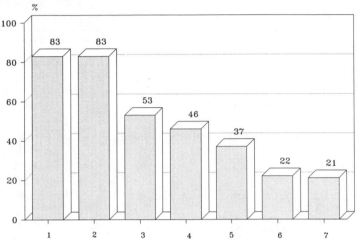

1: Own environmental consciousness
2: Fulfillment of government provisions
3: Image improvement
4: Reduction of liability risk

5: Sales-related considerations
6: Cost savings
7: Public pressure

the design of work and production processes, by 81.7 percent in plant and equipment design, and by 71.8 percent in job design. As descriptions of previous and current environmental measures, the statements "Environmental protection has up to now consisted of the fulfillment of statutory provisions" and "Environmental protection has up to now consisted of the elimination of existing environmental pollution" were chosen most often by corporate managers (57.4 percent and 60.6 percent, respectively). However, according to the information given by the respondents, these measures are likely to diminish in importance compared with more innovative and preventive measures. Thus, 61.5 percent expect the importance of avoidance of pollution to increase, whereas only 2.2 percent (13 of 592) expect it to diminish. There will also be a strong increase in the reduction of pollution, according to the responses, which are similar to those concerning avoidance (53.4 percent increasing significance and 3.9 percent decreasing significance). On the other hand, there is a clear discrepancy with regard to expectations about the importance of elimina-

TABLE 5.2
MOTIVES FOR ENVIRONMENTAL PROTECTION–ORIENTED MODIFICATIONS
TO THE ORGANIZATIONAL STRUCTURE (N = 90)

MOTIVE	PERCENTAGE OF THOSE INTERVIEWED*
Statutory obligations	43.3% (39)
Better efficiency of environment protection management	37.8% (34)
Exploitation of market opportunities	17.8% (16)
Better motivation and identification of employees	32.2% (29)
Better public image	34.4% (31)
Environmentally oriented change in individual divisional policies	27.8% (25)
Environmentally oriented change of business policies	7.8% (7)

* Multiple responses were possible.

tion. Only 31.1 percent assume that elimination of pollution will increase in importance, but as many as 19.8 percent think it will decrease in importance.

8. The motives are given in Table 5.2. Of outstanding importance is environmental legislation (statutory obligations) (43.3 percent). The exploitation of market opportunities is of relatively low significance. In general, environmental protection–oriented modifications to the organizational structure have until now been rather partial. Cross-divisional concepts are the exception.

9. It cannot be said of the majority of companies that their organizations are permeated with environmental orientation. As a rule, separate organizational units are concerned with environmental protection. The most widespread form of this is the legally required director of environmental protection (62.2 percent). Far less frequent are staff departments (34.4 percent), project teams (24.4 percent), and environmental committees (21.1 percent). The almost complete identification of corporate environmental protection with technical functions is confirmed by this survey.

Thus, environmental protection departments, or personnel entrusted with environmental tasks, are almost without exception found in the technical divisions.

INFORMATION

1. Currently, the most important environmental information sources, according to responses given by board members and heads of administration and controlling divisions, are the daily papers, specialist literature, and association publications. Official bulletins, weekly publications, seminars and congresses, and trade fairs and exhibitions rank much lower, and environmental protection data bases are practically insignificant. The most important internal information source is the director of environmental protection. Also of importance are the chambers of industry and commerce and, in some cases, external consultants.

2. Although only a minority of companies use ecologically modified or ecologically specific planning instruments, some two-thirds (64.7 percent) of the companies polled carry out risk analyses, by far the largest number of which (86.2 percent) relate to environmental protection. This result is consistent with the high degree of significance accorded to environmental protection for the safeguarding of corporate viability.

3. Calculations of costs and revenues related to environmental protection are done at only a minority of the companies polled. The information given by board members indicates that 36.0 percent of companies carry out such cost and revenue calculations. According to information from the accountant division, 37.5 percent of the divisions have the possibility of apportioning revenue lost or increased costs resulting from pro-environmental activity. The most frequent example of such apportionment occurs with remediation of environmental damage (25.5 percent). In fact, the more frequently remediation occurs, the more unequivocally environmental protection costs are identifiable as such. Specific apportioning of costs and revenues for environmental protection is most often possible for media-related protection technology (such as water protection and waste disposal technology) (30.5 percent) and to a far lesser extent for investment objects (18.6 percent), organizational units (16.8 percent), or product lines (10.2 percent). The statement by 64.7 percent of companies (383 of 592) that they have implemented revenue-increasing or cost-reducing environmental protection measures should therefore be viewed with some caution. Table 5.3a summarizes the companies' responses, and Table 5.3b lists specific measures that were mentioned.

TABLE 5.3A
COMPANY RESPONSES ON IMPLEMENTED OR
PLANNED REVENUE-INCREASING OR COST-REDUCING
ENVIRONMENTAL PROTECTION MEASURES

N = 592 RESPONDENTS	IMPLEMENTED	PLANNED
No information received on implemented or planned environmental protection measures.	11 (1.9%)	239 (40.3%)
NO Environmental protection measures are not implemented or planned.	198 (33.4%)	1 (0.2%)
YES Environmental protection measures are implemented or planned.	383 (64.7%)	352 (59.5%)
	100%	100%

PERSONNEL

1. The most important mechanism or conditions for promoting environmental awareness are thought to be ease of access to environmental information (59.5 percent) and use of the company's employee suggestions program (55.4 percent). Other mechanisms are the recognition of special service and ideas for environmental protection (29.1 percent), higher awards for environmental protection suggestions in the company's suggestions program (19.2 percent), systems of rewards for environmental protection ideas (16.9 percent), and incentive systems for the avoidance of environmentally harmful behavior (15.1 percent).

2. Just under one-half (46.9 percent) of the divisional managers polled claim to incorporate environmental aspects strongly or very strongly into company training programs. The technical bias of corporate environmental protection is also reflected in attitudes about further training. The main emphasis is quite clearly on production (77.5 percent), research and development (67.3 percent), and materials management (45.9 percent). Marketing (20.4 percent), strategic planning (19.4 percent), personnel (13.3 percent), administration (10.2 percent), controlling (4.1 percent), and accounting (2.0 percent) rank lower. Accordingly, the training courses offered are dominated by technical content. The only exception is content on environmental legislation, which is ranked second (28.4 percent). Training in substitution of alternatives to toxic materials is clearly in the lead at 36.3 percent. The minimization of energy consumption also has a

TABLE 5.3B

IMPLEMENTED AND PLANNED REVENUE-INCREASING OR COST-REDUCING
ENVIRONMENTAL PROTECTION MEASURES (IN DETAIL)

MEASURE	IMPLEMENTED	PLANNED
1. Savings (energy, water, raw materials, operating materials)	270 (45.6%)	150 (25.3%)
2. Substitution (materials, processes)	161 (27.2%)	157 (26.4%)
3. Emissions reductions (exhaust air, waste-water, solid waste, noise)	131 (22.1%)	156 (26.4%)
4. Recycling/reuse of raw materials	90 (15.2%)	72 (12.1%)
5. New markets (diversification)/new applications (market developments)	41 (6.9%)	47 (7.9%)
6. Improvements to working conditions (e.g., noise reduction, extractor systems, alleviation of work)	8 (1.4%)	19 (3.2%)
Total Responses (Multiple responses were possible)	701	601

particular significance. The ranking of training areas differs for personnel at the management level. The most frequently covered areas for this group are the development of environment-friendly processes and, again, environmental legislation.

MATERIALS MANAGEMENT

1. The heads of materials management divisions assessed the degree to which their own divisions are affected by environmental concerns even more highly than did corporate managers (74 percent compared with 63 percent). The reason becomes especially clear in reference to the goals and objectives of materials management divisions. Although environment-related goals are not at the top of the list, their significance approaches that of traditional materials management goals (e.g., material cost reductions, delivery, and capability). There is also a marked complementarity between traditional materials management goals and environmental protection goals, especially between those for material cost reduction and those for economical reuse of materials.

2. The essential motivational force for environmental protection measures in materials management comes from statutory provisions (83 percent of companies). Sales considerations (37 percent) and cost savings (22 percent), on the other hand, are gaining only slowly in significance (see Figure 5.3).

3. Among the four areas of materials management (purchasing, logistics, stores, and inventory control), pro-environmental measures have hitherto been concentrated in purchasing (which is also credited with having the greatest potential for innovation) and disposal logistics. The possibilities for environmental protection collaborations in the entire area of logistics are scarcely exploited. In general, this area of materials management is as yet accorded only a low significance in terms of implementing environmental protection to increase revenue or reduce costs.

PRODUCTION

1. Because it is the source of operating emissions, production encounters environmental protection issues and production managers feel a particular responsibility in this regard. This is evident in the setting of objectives for production divisions. Although, as a rule, environmental protection does not represent a production objective in itself, environmental aspects are among the highest objectives for production divisions.

2. Integrated environmental protection technologies have now achieved an extremely high level of acceptance. From a cost point of view, 88 percent of the production divisional managers polled see advantages in using integrated technologies, with energy and materials savings being the decisive factors. Among reasons for the use of add-on technologies, 54 percent of production divisional managers state that integrated technologies are not known. Skepticism as to the degree of technical maturity of these technologies plays only a subordinate role (28 percent). Cost-cutting effects of environmental protection measures can already be shown in numerous production sectors. In 65 percent of all production divisions polled, cost reductions have been achieved through modifications to manufacturing processes, production cost reductions in 49 percent, and energy and material cost reductions in about one-third of companies (36 percent and 33 percent, respectively).

RESEARCH AND DEVELOPMENT

1. In the survey of R&D divisional managers, the assessment of corporate management that company R&D is strongly affected by environmental matters is only partially supported. While, as a rule, environmental protec-

tion aspects are integrated into R&D philosophies and principles, environmental protection is seldom an expressed objective of the R&D division. Thus the development of more environmentally acceptable products, materials, and production or use plays only a subordinate role in the R&D group of objectives.

2. The departments and/or personnel responsible for environmental matters, such as the director of environmental protection, have only limited rights of intervention in corporate R&D. Only in exceptional cases are they seen to have a potential role in determination of involvement in R&D objectives. On the other hand, just under two-thirds of internal environmental protection departments have a consultant role. Even in the context of ideas generation in R&D, ideas stemming from environmental departments seldom are taken up.

3. In the evaluation of R&D projects, an expansion of traditional assessment methods (such as calculation processes) to include environmental aspects is regarded as inappropriate. Yet a fairly large number of companies apply specific environmentally related evaluation methods, such as technology effect analysis or environmental acceptability tests.

MARKETING

1. Generally speaking, while the marketing managers polled demonstrated knowledge of the relevance of environmental protection, they do not give it great consideration in practice. The social dimension of environmental protection is recognized, but only one-half (56.2 percent) of the companies also see in it a growing market segment. This makes clear, above all, the dominance of environmentally oriented public relations over other marketing instruments.

2. The somewhat low consideration given to environmental aspects may be, among other things, the result of the focus of market research. Sixty-four percent of the marketing divisions polled gather information on environmental protection, the main emphasis being on technological development and the activities of competitors. Analyses of consumers' environmental consciousness, altered requirements, and changes in purchasing behavior are given attention as yet by only one-fifth of the companies.

CONCLUSION

Environmental concerns are increasingly becoming a market issue. In the industrial and consumer markets, environmental requirements are being integrated into demand policies. In addition, the prevention or reduction of emissions and waste is often profitable from an economic point of view: it reduces costs. Consequently, there are increasing opportunities for corporations to use environmental concerns as market and innovation potentials. Environmental protection can no longer be seen as a mere cost burden. Measures directed toward compliance are still necessary but not sufficient by themselves. Because of new environmental market pressures and innovation potentials, firms can no longer justify reliance on a defensive strategy. A switch to an offensive or innovative strategy is timely and needed.

The basic finding of our empirical research is, however, that corporations do not fully realize this. Most corporations are not implementing an offensive or innovative strategy. A comprehensive, environmentally oriented approach is missing. This does not mean that these corporations have not undergone positive change. On the contrary, we found that most corporations no longer perceive environmental objectives as conflicting with other important corporate market and profit objectives. There are also indicators of change. A fairly large number of companies recognize a growing market segment for environmentally friendly products. Corporations are moving toward the implementation of more preventive measures. They are planning to incorporate ecological factors into their tradition planning instruments. Nevertheless, it is clear that motives for change are more strongly founded on avoiding risk than on grasping new market opportunities. Compliance is still a very important inducement for company behavior. Environmental issues are still connected mainly with production (process modifications) and technical issues. The influence of environmental issues on the full range of company activities is not taken into account—for example, R&D activities are seldom driven by environmental considerations. Marketing personnel neglect these considerations in their daily practice as well.

In conclusion, it can be stated that in current practice, corporations are still far from the attainable goal of a comprehensive environmental strategy. But simultaneously, it is clear that a majority of corporations are moving toward this goal. Even more so, a few of them are already experimenting with the implementation of such a comprehensive strategy. Thus, the process of learning has started and needs, above all, time.[2]

NOTES

A short version of this chapter was published in a special issue of *Business and Society Review* in 1990 and in a report of the Institut für Ökologie und Unternehmensführung in 1991.

1. Since the pioneering work of Strebel (1980), an increasing number of business administration scholars have studied this issue and its strategic dimension, and only the most important books are referenced here (Pfriem 1986; Kreikebaum 1990; Strebel 1980; Steger 1988, 1991; Kirchgeorg 1990). Other publications have focused on certain corporate functions (Stahlmann 1988; Brandt 1988; Raffée et al. 1988; Türck 1990) or served as lecture books (Schreiner 1988). A recent bibliography contained more than 800 publications on ecological marketing alone in five recent years (Antes and Tiebler 1990).

2. It should be noted that this conclusion is based on a survey of German companies. The companies must deal with tighter regulations than those in most other European countries and the United States.

REFERENCES

Antes, R. 1991. "Umweltorientierte Unternehmensführung im Handel" (Environmentally oriented corporate strategy in the business). In Umweltbundesamt (Hrsg.), Umweltorientierte Unternehmensführung: Möglichkeiten zur Kostensenkung und Erlössteigerung. Durchgeführt von: Forschungsgruppe Umweltorientierte Unternehmensführung. Berlin: Erich Schmidt Verlag.

Antes, R.; Steger, U.; and Tiebler, P. 1991. "Ergebnisse des Interviews mit Mitgliedern der Geschäftsleitung der Unternehmen zum Themenbereich 'Unternehmensführung' (Results of an interview with members of the administration from different firms on the theme of "corporate strategy). In Umweltbundesamt (Hrsg.), Umweltorientierte Unternehmensführung: Möglichkeiten zur Kostensenkung und Erlössteigerung. Durchgeführt von: Forschungsgruppe Umweltorientierte Unternehmensführung. Berlin: Erich Schmidt Verlag.

Antes, R., and Tiebler, P. 1990. "Bibliographie Öko-Marketing" (Bibliographie eco-marketing). Oestrich-Winkel: Arbeitsbericht Nr. 11 des Instituts für Ökologie und Unternehmensführung.

Brandt, A. 1988. *Öko-Marketing* (Eco-marketing). Frankfurt/New York: Campus-Verlag.

Collin, P. H., ed. 1988. *Dictionary of Ecology and the Environment.* Middlesex, Great Britain: IBD, Ltd., Publishing UK.

FUUF (Forschungsgruppe Umweltorientierte Unternehmensführung). 1991. "Modellversuch Umweltorientierte Unternehmenführung" (A model for environmentally oriented corporate strategy). In Umweltbundesamt (Hrsg.), Umweltorientierte Unternehmensführung: Möglichkeiten zur Kostensenkung und Erlössteigerung. Durchgeführt von: Forschungsgruppe Umweltorientierte Unternehmensführung. Berlin: Erich Schmidt Verlag.

Kirchgeorg, M. 1990. *Ökologieorientiertes Unternehmensverhalten* (The conduct of ecology-oriented firms). Wiesbaden, Germany: Gabler-Verlag.

Kreikebaum, H. 1990. *Integrierter Umweltschutz—Eine Herausforderung für das Innovationsmanagement* (Integrated environmental protection—A challenge for innovations management). Wiesbaden, Germany: Gabler-Verlag.

Pfriem, R. 1986. *Ökologische Unternehmenspolitik* (Ecological business policy). Frankfurt/New York: Campus-Verlag.

Raffée, H.; Förster, F.; and Krupp, W. 1988. *Marketing und Ökologieorientierung* (Marketing and ecology orientation). Mannheim: Institute for Marketing.

Schreiner, M. 1988. *Umweltmanagement in 22 Lektionen* (Environmental management in 22 lessons). Wiesbaden, Germany: Gabler-Verlag.

Stahlmann, V. 1988. *Umweltorientierte Materialwirtschaft—Das Optimierungskonzept für Ressourcen, Recycling, Rendite* (Environmentally oriented material Industry—The optimization concept for resources, recycling and gains). Wiesbaden, Germany: Gabler-Verlag.

Steger, U. 1991. "Auswertung des Investitionsprogramms zur Verminderung von Umweltbelastungen im Bereich des Immissionsschutzes bei Altanlagen" (The evaluation of the investment program to reduce the environmental pollution in the field of emissions protection). In Umweltbundesamt (Hrsg.), Umweltorientierte Unternehmensführung: Möglichkeiten zur Kostensenkung und Erlössteigerung. Durchgeführt von: Forschungsgruppe Umweltorientierte Unternehmensführung, Kapitel 4. Berlin: Erich Schmidt Verlag.

Steger, U. 1988. *Umweltmanagement—Erfahrungen und Instrumente einer umweltorientierten Unternehmensstrategie* (Environmental management—Experiences and instruments of an environmentally oriented business strategy). Wiesbaden, Germany: Gabler-Verlag.

Steger, U., and Tiebler, P. "Wahrnehmung des Umweltschutzes durch den Verbraucher" (The perception of nature-conservation by the consumer). Unpublished.

Strebel, H. 1980. *Umwelt und Betriebswirtschaft—Die natürliche Umwelt als Gegenstand der Unternehmenspolitik* (Environment and business administration—The natural environment as a topic for business policy). Berlin: Erich Schmidt Verlag.

Töpfer, K. 1987. "Risikoakzeptanz. Aufgabe der Politik oder der Wissenschaft?" (Risk acceptance. Task of policy or science?). In AGF-Mitteilungen, Sondernummer vom Dezember 1987.

Türck, R. 1990. *Eigenschaften, Erfassung und wettbewerbsstrategische Umsetzung ökologische Produkte* (Quality, registration and competition-strategical transformation of ecological products). Frankfurt/New York: Campus-Verlag.

6

The Myth of Best Practices:
The Context Dependence
of Two High-performing
Waste Reduction Programs

Peter B. Cebon

Consider three streams of pollution prevention literature. The first (e.g., Lovins and Lovins 1991) argues that there is so much "low-hanging fruit" out there (particularly in the form of wasted energy) that simply harvesting the fruit will enable us to resolve many of our policy problems. The second is exemplified by the story of an economist walking down the street with his daughter. When she suggests picking up a twenty-dollar bill lying on the sidewalk, he says not to bother: if it were real, someone would have picked it up already. That is, the hidden costs of achieving waste reduction and energy conservation must exceed the benefits, or the market would already have discovered them. Between these extremes is a group of authors (e.g., Hirschhorn and Oldenburg 1991; Royston 1979) who acknowledge that there are some managerial obstacles to pollution prevention, but who suggest that adhering to a number of simple principles and practices ("best practices") will enable those obstacles to be overcome with ease. For example, Michael Royston and Donald Huisingh suggested at the Greening of Industry Conference (November 17–19, 1991, in Noordwijk aan Zee, the Netherlands) that the key ingredients were top management commitment and problem solving on the shop floor. At other times we hear of the need for direct incentives and extensive data collection.

Hirschhorn and Oldenburg (1991) go well beyond a few simple prescriptions. In their sophisticated analysis of managerial strategies they argue that industrial waste reduction is a four-stage process and that each stage presents unique obstacles to performance that are often compounded with obstacles from prior stages. In the first stage, people should "exploit readily visible, easily implemented, low cost, and low risk opportunities" (p. 76). In the second stage, firms should aim to discover waste reduction opportunities that are not readily apparent. The third stage involves implementation of technology where there "is economic uncertainty because of substantial changes in technology and equipment" (p. 95). The final stage involves creation of dramatically new clean technologies. For each obstacle these authors describe a preferred managerial solution. Many of these preferred solutions correspond to the prescriptions of other authors.

This chapter compares two waste reduction programs in one company, the Florida and East Coast Synthetic Olefins Corporation (FLECSOCO) (a pseudonym), one of the twenty largest firms in the chemical industry. The company emits remarkably little waste, given its production volume. These low emissions levels result from the selection of relatively clean products, the construction of relatively clean plants, and the progressive improvement of existing processes to reduce waste emissions. The chapter compares programs in the third category, the progressive improvement of processes, at two plant sites, one located in Marbletown and the other in Schisttown. The success of these programs suggests that there is probably more fruit out there than even the optimists imagine and that it can be plucked cost-effectively. However, when the programs were examined closely, it was seen that many of the absolutist prescriptions and "best practices" that have been written about were violated. For example, at neither site did data collection drive problem solving. Instead, intensive data collection was reserved only for identified problems and solutions. Likewise, at neither site were direct financial incentives offered to participants. These were seen as liabilities for a program. Similarly, at both sites, all four of Hirschhorn and Oldenburg's temporal stages were pursued simultaneously, not serially. By the same token, at the site with a program that achieved superior waste reduction, problem solving was not pushed to the shop floor, while at the site with the less successful program it was.

It is not the intention here to develop an alternative set of best practices. Such an approach can work only if Hirschhorn and Oldenburg were correct when they asserted that the four stages represent a temporal ordering rather than different aspects of the task, if there were one best way of attacking each aspect, and if that best way were independent of the firm, the industry, and the location.

Instead, this chapter will show that the managers observed had to manage a tension between two competing demands. On the one hand, particular aspects of the waste reduction problem are best solved by particular individuals with particular skill sets and access to particular information sources. Housekeeping problems are best solved by the operators; process design changes by the production engineers assisted by operators; and research and development conundrums by specialists. Therefore, the first demand is to construct programs that use the groups most relevant to the specific problems at that site.

On the other hand, waste reduction managers rarely have free or guaranteed access to these target people. Most of the time they compete with a number of other functional managers who also have "top management commitment" (e.g., managers for safety, energy conservation, affirmative action, and training). Furthermore, the target people have very limited time, since most of it is devoted to producing chemicals. Therefore, the second demand is to design programs that make it possible to obtain the people and resources needed for effective waste reduction.

When waste reduction took precedence (e.g., for compliance problems), the first demand did also. That is, waste reduction managers could easily obtain the specific resources they needed. Most of the time, however, the second demand dominated. To get the resources they needed, the waste reduction managers had to do two things. First, they had to avoid conflicts with other actors' interests. Second, they had to offer more than waste reduction, or even waste reduction with a high return on investment. They made their programs more attractive to line management and participants by offering joint gains between their own objectives and those of other people on the site (see Bachararah and Lawler, 1990).[1] The political and structural obstacles that defined the constraints and created the possibilities for joint gains varied across time and between the sites. At Marbletown, the program designer, an energy conservation manager, could develop a program that targeted the most effective group on the site, the junior engineers. At the Schisttown program, this was not the case. Although the Schisttown program, which targeted the operators, was inferior in terms of its narrow waste reduction goals, this is not necessarily the case once benefits to other goals, accrued through joint gains, are considered.

THE TWO SITES

The Marbletown site, located in the southeastern United States, is the only plant site in FLECSOCO's Marble Division and one of the largest chemical facilities in the state. It comprises twenty-four processes producing mainly commodity chemicals, but also some specialty chemicals, a power supply, an incinerator, and a biological oxidation plant. It employs about 3200 people, including about 1000 maintenance contractors. It is nonunion and has been since opening in 1958. Within each process in the Marble Division, as in the Schist Division, there are three or four hierarchical levels of line engineers under one of the twenty superintendents. Each superintendent reports to one of four production managers, who, along with people such as the human resources manager, are known as major managers.[2] The major managers report to the facility general manager.

The Schisttown site, located in the western United States, is one of the company's three production facilities in the Schist Division and one of the largest chemical facilities in the state. It was purchased in 1938 and employs between 900 and 1200 production workers in thirteen plants under seven superintendents. It produces a mixture of commodity and specialty chemicals as well as power for the site. Most of the specialty chemicals are intermediaries for biocide production. Since the processes are on a smaller scale, production at the site is much more labor-intensive than at the Marbletown site. The union was decertified in 1971 after a prolonged campaign that began when neither of two competing unions could obtain a clear mandate from the employees. Unlike the Marbletown plant, the Schisttown plant has neither a hazardous waste incinerator for solid waste nor a biological oxidation facility for aqueous waste.

DATA COLLECTION

Most of the data were collected through interviews of fifty to ninety minutes' duration. Five interviews were longer, lasting two to three hours. Key interviewees were interviewed several times. Company employees were interviewed at corporate headquarters in September 1989 (eight interviews); at various plants, specifically Marbletown in May 1990 (eleven), Schisttown in June 1990 (sixteen), Hornfelstown, in the Hornfels Division, in October 1990 during a visit to discuss safety management (one); and at various seminars, conferences, and other opportunities (four). Four interviews were carried out by telephone, and many were also followed up by telephone.[3] The interviews at corporate headquarters included senior managers responsible for various aspects of health, safety, and environmental management as well as government and public affairs. In the plants, the principal interviewees were the program designers. However, other interviewees included design and production engineers, production managers, senior site management, and managers in a number of functional specialties such as research, technical services, and community relations. Key interviews and sections of interviews were transcribed. In addition, trade literature and company publications were reviewed and the records of an "ethical investment" firm were examined. Finally, the author discussed the work and exchanged literature with a journalist who writes about the company. An earlier draft of the manuscript was read by key people in the two divisions and corporate headquarters. This proved to be a valuable source of new data, insights, and clarification. Differences were discussed and changes were made at the discretion of the author.

Attempts to gather quantitative data to illustrate the argument were generally unsuccessful. While FLECSOCO keeps good emissions records, waste production records tend to be unsystematic—that is, they are good for the waste streams that are measured, but many streams are not. Data are stored in individual production units. Data on specific waste reduction projects are embedded in company-confidential data bases. Further, it is often very difficult to disaggregate the waste reduction portion of a project from the capital expansion part. Interestingly, even if personnel at the two sites had been prepared to provide the data they possessed, which they said would have required days of work, those data would not have been comparable. One site did not even bother to record one class of projects— very low cost initiatives—until 1990, they were considered relatively unimportant. The other site concentrated most of its ongoing programmatic waste reduction efforts in that area.

Because the two sites have such different technology, and because the Schisttown site has virtually no aqueous or solid waste treatment facilities (cf. Thompson 1967), it could not be shown empirically that waste reduction efforts at Schisttown are less effective than those at Marbletown. Therefore opinions were sought from three people with direct experience in environmental management at the two sites. All three said without hesitation that the Marbletown program is more effective. One, the youngest, believed that the difference was due to technology alone. The other two believed emphatically that the differences were managerial. On the basis of this, as well as the refrigeration system example presented later in the chapter and the fairly sketchy quantitative data that it was possible to gather (particularly on project size), it is the author's conclusion that the Marbletown site's program is more effective and that the differences are principally due to differences in program design.

A MAP OF THE CHAPTER

In the next section, the company's definition of waste reduction is bisected to correspond to two distinct sets of activities observed at each plant site. This yields four cases, two at each site, which are then described in detail. Two analytic sections follow. The first shows that an information-processing lens can explain why differences in program design lead to differences in performance. This leads to the first demand above, that the program design should engender the information flows that maximize performance. But why would managers choose designs that appear to be inferior? The second analysis argues for the second demand, political acceptability, and asks whether side benefits to other actors compensate for lower levels of performance when measured in terms of narrow corporate goals. The argument is bolstered with data from other programs in the Hornfels and Schist divisions.

TWO TYPES OF WASTE REDUCTION

Pollution management is generally divided into two categories: pollution control and pollution reduction. Pollution control refers to the treatment of a waste stream to curtail emissions to the environment. Pollution reduction involves the redesign or modification of processes or operations procedures so that less waste is produced in the first place. At FLEC-SOCO, all pollution-reducing technical changes are given one name: "waste reduction." However, it was observed that waste reduction projects fall into two distinct categories that have different objectives and therefore are assessed using different criteria. The author labeled one type "compliance-oriented waste reduction" and the other "savings-oriented waste reduction." For compliance-oriented waste reduction the project focus is on the amount of waste reduced. For a given waste reduction goal, people design systems as cost-effectively as possible. For savings-oriented waste reduction, the amount of waste reduced is generally subordinated as a goal to the rate of return on investment (ROI).[4] Although the Marble Division has accomplished most of its pollution reduction through savings-oriented waste reduction projects, the Schist Division has reduced most of its pollution through compliance-oriented waste reductions.

Compliance-oriented waste reduction projects are often initiated in response to either a regulation or a management policy decision to change the base assumptions for running the plant. These changes tend to alter dramatically the economics of disposal. For example, once Schist Division management decided to close the Schisttown site's surface impoundments, the cost avoided by eliminating the liquid waste stream of 64,000 tons per year was absolutely enormous. However, without that decision, the emissions reduction project would have seemed inordinately expensive. Therefore, it is rarely meaningful, except in a relative sense, to talk about ROI for compliance-oriented waste reduction projects.

COMPLIANCE-ORIENTED WASTE REDUCTION

Marbletown

Examples of compliance-oriented waste reduction projects at Marbletown include a recovery system that captures fugitive emissions from a hydrocarbon loading dock and returns them to the process; a special filter that captures fugitive emissions through vents in such a way that they can be trapped and released back into the process (instead of the whole filter being burned); improved procedures for purging vinyl chloride from vessels before maintenance or after leaks are discovered in loaded tank cars; and increased retention of polymers so the entrained monomer can be released to the air in a sealed storage area and returned to the process.

Compliance-oriented waste reduction projects are initiated by the plants themselves during normal operations, during biennial compliance reviews, or with plant expansions. The biennial compliance review is a formal meeting between the plant superintendent, his or her key staff, and key members of the environmental staff. At that meeting they review the plant's permits and discuss noncompliance events, permit exceedences, and recurring problems. If these are thought to be excessive, particular waste streams will be targeted and systems designed to deal with problems. Emissions are reduced during plant expansions for two reasons. First, and principally, capital expansions require repermitting of the plant. Because the region does not attain the national ambient air quality standard for volatile organic compounds, a new permit that allows the plant to increase its emissions would require the firm to find an offsetting reduction in another process on the site or buy a reduction from another plant in the region. Therefore, management refuses to submit applications that require emissions increases. Hence, the increased emissions from increased capacity must be compensated for through design changes elsewhere. Second, a capital expansion itself is a change moment in the plant's life. It opens up the whole technical system for negotiation much more than do routine operations. At that time, a lot of the barriers to change are not present; the plant will be down for a protracted period, people are thinking and talking about redesign, and a request for large capital, onto which an environmental request can easily be appended, is going to the board. The environmental staff like to help the process engineers, production engineers, and research engineers exploit that moment to ensure that emissions improvements are brought about.

Schisttown

Schisttown's compliance-oriented waste reduction efforts technically are extremely impressive. After a decision in 1984 to close the thirteen acres of surface evaporation ponds that had been used to receive the site's liquid waste, a team of 156 engineers and operators was put together. The team came up with twenty projects that reduced the quantity and toxicity of waste from the various streams and then cleaned up the waste sufficiently to feed back as an input to the facility's brine cells, where it could be made back into chlorine gas and sodium hydroxide (caustic soda). One stream, which had a high fluoride content, had to be sent off-site to a hazardous waste management facility to prevent poisoning the cell electrodes. In 1989, for an additional $1,300,000, that stream was virtually eliminated. Unfortunately, because the law changed shortly after the decision to close the ponds, the waste reduction process had to be accelerated. Because there wasn't time to work out how to remove impurities from the waste already stored in the evaporation ponds, the salt had to be encased in concrete, rather than processed through the brine cells. This left a "tomb" in the middle of the site.[5]

People at the site have also eliminated 63 percent of the waste sent off-site. One-half of this was the fluoride waste, and significant amounts were reduced with two other projects, one that eliminated white water from a synthetic rubber plant and one that eliminated waste from a research plant. It may well be that these should be classified as savings-oriented waste reduction rather than compliance-oriented waste reduction, but data are not available with which to make this determination. Chemical emissions that must be reported under Section 313 of SARA Title III (Emergency Planning and Community Right-to-Know Act) were reduced by 30 percent between 1987 and 1989.

SAVINGS-ORIENTED WASTE REDUCTION

Marbletown

The Marbletown savings-oriented waste reduction program is FLEC-SOCO's flagship initiative. It has been extremely successful and phenomenally profitable. FLECSOCO has had limited success transferring the program to other locations, however.

The program began in 1980 as an attempt to control energy costs. The division's long-term fuel gas supply contract had expired, so the long-run marginal cost of gas had risen significantly. Division management asked a senior engineer to investigate ways of reducing energy usage. The program he developed, a variation of a program developed in the company's Gneiss Division, was disarmingly simple: junior engineers were invited to submit designs for cost-effective energy conservation projects with a capital value of $10,000 to $200,000 to a competition committee comprising senior engineers, some superintendents, engineering managers, and a representative from the capital planning economic evaluation area. The projects had to offer an ROI exceeding 100 percent.[6] The submissions did not have to be formal, but they had to provide data and sketches that would substantiate the energy savings the engineers claimed. The competition committee reviewed the submissions, declared some of them "winners," and provided a ranked list of projects to division management. The review consisted of an oral presentation by the person submitting the project, a more detailed financial analysis, and a check of the engineering details to ensure that the works would operate as claimed. In return for their efforts, each of the submitters of winning projects received a plaque at an awards ceremony and the opportunity to oversee the detailed design and construction of the project. They did not (and still do not) receive any financial rewards.

The winning projects were placed into a pool with other projects submitted to the division for small capital allocations. Division management then allocated the capital money to the process areas and always included money for the winning projects. The money was then invested, at the discretion of the major manager overseeing the process, either in the projects or for some other need.

The success of the program has amazed everyone in the corporation, in terms of both its longevity and its effectiveness. Everyone thought the division would run out of energy conservation projects after the usual program life of two or three years. On the contrary, the plant engineers and operators have been able to come up with more and more projects each year. For the 1991 contest there were 144 entries, of which 128 were winners. Aspects of the history of the competition are highlighted in Table 6.1. Interviewees now believe that there are "almost an infinite number of projects out there."

The competition has changed a little since its inception. First, the hurdle ROI dropped to 30 percent with the price of energy.[7] Second, the categories of projects have increased to include all small-capital projects (i.e., up

TABLE 6.1

RESULTS OF THE MARBLETOWN COMPETITION[1]

TYPE OF PROJECT	1982	1983	1984	1985	1986	1987	1988	1989	1990	1991	1992
Non-WRFP projects above ROI cutoff[2]	27	32	38	59	60	90	71	42	78	73	74
WRFP projects above ROI cutoff							23	22	37	35	35
Cross-subsidized WRFP projects							1	3	16	18	19
Total projects	27	32	38	59	60	90	95	67	131	126	128
Investment ($MM)[3]	1.7	2.2	4.0	7.1	7.1	10.6	9.3	7.5	13.1	8.6	6.4
Annual Savings ($MM)[4]	3.0	7.6	8.3	10.2	8.3	11.5	18.0	37.0	17.6	27.6	20.3

SOURCE: Company materials.

NOTES:

[1] Table presents only those projects with a capital cost of less than $2 MM ($2,000,000). In addition, there were a few projects each year with a larger capital cost. Capital for these is allocated differently.

[2] Energy conservation, yield, maintainability, etc.

[3] Investment and savings are for projects with ROIs above the ROI cutoff.

[4] Total annual savings accruing from that year's projects.

to \$2,000,000 instead of \$200,000), large-capital projects (more than \$2,000,000), and expensed projects. Expensed projects and large-capital projects are not funded from the small-capital pool, however. Also, the \$10,000 minimum cost criterion was changed to a \$10,000 minimum savings criterion. Finally, the categories of projects have been increased to include yield improvements, maintenance cost reduction projects, waste reduction projects (in 1986), and a few small-capital expansions. Waste reduction projects have a different investment criterion, however. There is no formal ROI requirement. The criterion was changed in 1989 to state that the ROI for the group of projects from a given plant must exceed 100 percent.[8] This enabled the rate of waste reduction to be accelerated by packaging projects that save a lot of waste with projects that save a lot of money. Projects include such things as redesigned refrigeration systems, preheating fluids, reconfigured distillation columns, and removal of bottlenecks in processes.

Schisttown

More than fifty savings-oriented and compliance-oriented waste reduction projects were carried out at Schisttown between 1984 and 1989. However, it is often difficult to tell which projects fall into which category. Once constraints are imposed on emissions—in this case the decision to close the surface impoundments—the economics change enormously, so that virtually any project becomes attractive. In 1989 a total of thirteen projects in both the savings-oriented and compliance-oriented waste reduction categories were proposed at Schisttown. All of these involved investments of less than \$200,000. By comparison, in the same year, Marbletown implemented fifty-five savings-oriented waste reduction projects, many of which had a relatively high capital value. In addition, there were a large number of expensed projects at both sites.

The clearest way to differentiate the compliance-oriented from the savings-oriented waste reduction projects is in the process that those on the site claim to use to approach the problem. For compliance-oriented waste reductions, the approach is quite formulaic. Engineers develop a quantitative scheme for ranking the waste streams. For example, they might give volume a weight of five and toxicity a weight of seven. They collect data and rank the streams against the weights to determine which stream is most important. They then use a number of techniques to work out how to reduce the waste. For savings-oriented waste reduction, however, the approach is quite different. Instead of collecting data first and then working out how to act, the employees develop an idea for attacking the problem and then collect data to substantiate their approach. That is, while compliance-oriented waste reduction is essentially a deductive process, savings-oriented waste reduction is a much more creative and inductive process.

Two projects were clearly cost-effective waste reduction projects and involved significant engineering. The first involved the recycling of catalyst from a specialty chemical plant. The addition of new catalyst was causing a huge amount of tar to form. Hence, the more catalyst added, the more material had to be drained from the process to get rid of the tar. This created a vicious cycle. Over the prior three years, the company had carried out a series of research projects to determine whether or not recycling the catalyst would cause explosions or lead to the buildup of materials toxic to the process or the product. However, according to one interviewee, "there was no incentive for catalyst recycle until one day the source of disposal went away and we just had to sit there and eat it." Most of the waste had been sent to a local thermal oxidizer, and the excess was sent to either Marbletown or Hornfelstown for incineration. One day the thermal oxidizer went down and the plant was stuck with a "huge stream" of waste. The engineers decided to simply recycle it by running a pipe from the tail end of one process to the front of a prior one. It was a "no-cost no-brainer" that saved three dollars per pound of waste.[9] As a result, the disposal problem went from one of disposing of tar full of fresh catalyst to one of disposing of spent catalyst. This halved the waste volume. In a subsequent stage, production engineers hoped to reduce the waste by a further 80 percent by changing the process to reduce the amount of catalyst added.[10]

The second project illustrates one of the core differences between the Schist Division and the Marble Division. In 1985, as part of a plant modification, an engineer at Schisttown was asked to design a refrigeration system for a chemical stream. The engineer worked out that he could use a countercurrent heat exchanger to cool a hot effluent stream with an influent stream. This would be cheaper and more reliable than a chlorofluorocarbon-based system and would leak much less. However, the design was unusual and a bit complicated. Although the heat exchanger was installed eventually, the engineer had a lot of trouble justifying it to plant management. If this had occurred in Marbletown, it would have been installed readily; it would have been funded as part of the energy/waste competition.

Most of the other savings-oriented waste reduction at Schisttown occurs on a much smaller scale, through programs in the individual plants. The programs vary from plant to plant, and the two examined by the author, representing seven production facilities, are presumably the best. The programs are overseen by a committee comprising employees from the shop floor and an engineer. These committees attempt to solicit waste reduction ideas from others on the shop floor. It was observed that suggestions came principally from one of two sources.

One plant had a suggestion box. The plant superintendent brought the idea of using suggestion cards with him when he transferred from the Hornfels Division.[11] Suggestions were collected and acknowledged daily. In 1989, 165 were received. At its monthly meeting, the committee authorized funding for projects and awarded a small prize to the two best suggestions for the month. Not surprisingly, the scale of these projects is much smaller than those in the Marble Division. The ten biggest projects in 1989 yielded savings of $125,000.[12]

Implicit at this plant, and explicit at the second Schisttown plant examined, is the use of techniques of statistical quality control for the generation of savings-oriented waste reduction projects. At the second plant, savings-oriented waste reduction was integrated into operator training. In particular, in an attempt to push decision making down the organization under the rubric of continuous improvement, management had provided operators with training in a number of process management techniques. As part of that training, the operators were required to go back into the plants and apply the techniques to the management of a waste stream. This had led to a number of projects that reduced waste.

INFORMATION AS A KEY TO PROGRAM EFFECTIVENESS

Because waste reduction is a difficult information-processing problem, by analyzing the informational aspects of each of the four waste reduction programs one can understand differentials in program success. The core problem is that people can process only limited amounts of information (Simon 1976), and they must search for the information they need to make decisions (March and Simon 1958). Therefore, factors such as the context within which decision making occurs shape the availability of different types of information. This prejudices the information search and leads to local rationality that may be quite different from the global rationality expected (Cyert and March 1963).

In previous work, the author elaborated on these ideas for energy conservation decision making, a form of waste reduction, in universities (Cebon 1990, 1992). It was observed that three distinct classes of solution-specific information had to be brought together for a given solution to be adopted. The first class, technical information, generally defines the characteristics of the technology to be implemented and includes such things as its specification, performance, and price. This information generally comes from sources outside the organization. The second class, contextual information, describes the location in which the technology will be situated and hence the precise interfaces the technology must satisfy to fit into that location[13] (i.e., the requirements for the technical system, with all its idiosyncrasies, and likewise for the people directly affected).[14] This information is generally embedded in the workplace. The third class, connected information, deals with aspects of the technology and its implementation relevant to other functions. A particular technological change may affect worker safety, satisfaction, or skills, for example. This information comes from groups within the organization that are functionally or geographically removed from the site of the technology (Lawrence and Lorsch 1967). The author found that in the relatively mechanistic (Burns and Stalker 1961) universities he studied, changes in structure that increased access to one class of information generally reduced access to the others. Therefore, energy management decisions appeared highly structure-dependent, and solutions requiring high technical and contextual information were selected only in extraordinary circumstances, such as when the senior university administration was devoting a lot of attention to energy conservation.

If one considers three different types of waste reducing technological changes, different mixes of these types of information are seen. Housekeeping changes require very little technical information but lots of contextual information. As a general rule, the amount and complexity of the technical information required increases markedly as changes become more capital-intensive. The person or group identifying and appraising the problem needs a conceptual understanding of the relationships between larger and larger parts of the plant. For example, to eliminate waste oil that is dripping into a sump, the oil can be stopped at the source or intercepted before it enters the sump. To eliminate an entire refrigeration step, the whole production process must be understood, as well as a number of alternatives to refrigeration. Also, possible technical solutions and ideas may come from increasingly diverse parts of the environment. Ideas about valves can come from any chemical plant. Ideas about homeomorphic sets of steps may have to come from particular plants halfway around the world. Valves come from valve suppliers, but special equipment may need to be designed or purchased from obscure sources. For R&D projects, contextual information is probably of limited use once the problem has been defined. The requirements for connected information are probably independent of project type.

One can understand the differences in the effectiveness of the two savings-oriented waste reduction programs at the Marbletown and Schist-town sites by considering the differences in their location in the company's information-processing system. The Marbletown program involved engineers being assisted by operators, while the Schisttown program involved operators being assisted by engineers. When the engineers are the focus of the program, they will use both the contextual information that the operators give them and that which they gather themselves to enhance their understanding of the technical system as a whole. Given a much more abstract set of skills, an understanding of the larger spatial extent of the plant, and much better access to FLECSOCO's technical information-processing network, the engineers can solve problems better. For example, a number of engineers interviewed discussed the ease with which they could call or e-mail people they hardly knew halfway across the world to discuss particular technical issues (cf. Granovetter 1973).[15] Therefore, because the junior engineers have access to the right mix of information and because the projects are just the right size to excite them, a political climate that enables them to do the work and motivates them to want to do it will lead to the generation of many projects.

When the program involves operators being assisted by engineers, however, as at Schisttown, we can expect to find fewer large projects for two reasons. First, the operators have limited conceptual understanding of the process, a limited spatial domain in which they can act, and virtually no access to FLECSOCO's technical network. Very good contextual information without good technical information will result in housekeeping modifications. Although the engineers are supposed to help the operators with the savings-oriented waste reduction work, helping is very different from having the responsibility and incentive themselves. Second, the techniques used by the operators, such as statistical charting, assume that the basic technology is fixed, and they look for incremental improvements, particularly in operation, of the basic technology. As illustrated by the catalyst recycling and refrigeration projects described earlier, however, the big savings come through changes in core technology. Those changes will not flow from the techniques the operators are taught.

POWER AND JOINT GAINS AS KEYS TO PROGRAM ACCEPTABILITY AND SURVIVAL

The above analysis of the information structuring of the problem leaves two questions. A fairly simple analysis of the problem structure suggests that an approach to savings-oriented waste reduction that focuses on the junior engineers, as does the Marbletown program, will be much more successful. Since the Marbletown program had been in existence for six years before the Schisttown program was set up, why did the manager at Schisttown choose to focus on the operators? Second, why isn't the difference between the two savings-oriented waste reduction programs replicated in the case of compliance-oriented waste reduction?

These two questions can be answered by considering the politics of organizational decision making. Waste reduction decision making requires bringing together resources from throughout the organization and hence winning the support of the parties that control each resource. Two aspects of this are noteworthy. First, and most obviously, environmental managers tend to be much less powerful than production managers and need significant resources that are controlled by production management. The production manager must allow the production process to be changed. This may well be disruptive. In addition, because waste reduction solutions are highly contextual, the changes are best designed by the production employees themselves, though not necessarily by the operators, removing them from the production process. Simultaneously, managers from many other equally important, yet low-powered functional specialties—such as quality, safety, automation, and training—are vying for the same production resources.

Second, and more subtly, large organizations tend to have trouble allocating small amounts of capital efficiently (see Ross [1986], for example). Although some waste reduction investments are large, most tend to be small, so difficulties can be expected. Compounding this, many corporations try to ensure that capital is used efficiently by deliberately allocating applicants less capital than is requested. Waste reduction projects, being optional and proposed by low-powered environmental managers, are likely to be eliminated after such rationing.

OBSTACLE-FREE COMPLIANCE-ORIENTED WASTE REDUCTIONS

Early in the chapter it was argued that to survive, a program such as a waste reduction program must attract all parties whose participation is needed for success. Many of the power, informational, and ethical obstacles to compliance-oriented waste reduction are avoided by timing the projects with the company's capital cycle and giving them a compliance orientation. When demands press, managers have no trouble getting resources—people or money—so that pragmatic, rather than elegant, solutions are developed. Therefore, no context-driven differences appear.

The power obstacles revolve around securing resources from superintendents and the board. Superintendents can be won over, particularly in the allocation of design engineers' time, if there is any threat to regulatory approval of capital projects. "It really gets the skids moving," noted one interviewee. The board is generally supportive of these sorts of projects, despite their cost, once the need for compliance is established. Second, the "moment" created by either the capital project or the biennial compliance inspection frees up communications and information sharing. Finally, in the mid-1980s the Corporation's board created a special capital pool for environmental projects. This has almost certainly removed any stigma associated with doing capital projects for compliance. In fact, the stigma tends to be attached to not doing them soon enough to enable them to be done properly.

MANAGING SAVINGS-ORIENTED WASTE REDUCTION

When managers must compete with one another for access to people in the core of the organization, however, they are constrained to creating programs that do not conflict with other programs and that provide something extra—often joint gains—to the people in the core and, to a lesser extent, to other functional managers.

It is important to realize that the people managing waste reduction programs all have extensive experience as plant superintendents. Therefore, any discussion of power or interests does not imply the existence of conflict. The program designers are fully aware of the superintendents' incentive structure and the constraints under which they operate. They are fully capable of completely avoiding any sign of conflict arising from program design. One program manager said, ["The positions to organize programs like this are generally taken by people with lots of experience . . . . You need experience to know how to maneuver to get the right support at the right level to make these things work. You need to know who these people are and how to get them on your side."]*

Another noted: ["These programs tend to be run by very experienced people. You have to be very experienced. If the guy running the program is not experienced he is going to get wrapped up in doing stuff for its own sake. An experienced guy, however, will look at the resources he has available and how far to go in this to use about the right amount of resources . . . so as not to overemphasize your program vis-à-vis other areas."]

Later, the same interviewee added: ["The key is the leader of the pro-

---

* Quotes delineated with brackets ([ ]) are reconstructed from notes. They are not verbatim quotes.

gram. He has to understand what he is trying to do. If he doesn't understand that, he has no chance of succeeding. . . . The guy must design the program to match the situation he is working in and make it a successful thing."]

What might be conflicts in some organizations are simply seen as realistic constraints here.

CREATING SUCCESS AT MARBLETOWN THROUGH JOINT GAINS

Before one can see why the waste reduction manager at Schisttown would have been unlikely to succeed if he had tried to implement the Marbletown savings-oriented waste reduction program, it is necessary to understand why the Marbletown program works. It will be shown that the superintendents and engineers had strong incentives to support the initiation and continuation of the program, virtually irrespective of its energy and waste reduction performance. Furthermore, the program did not risk opposition from parties who could obstruct it—top management and other functional managers.

Initial Support from Plant Superintendents

In the early 1980s, the Marbletown plant superintendents were feeling two cost pressures. First, between 1981 and 1982 the company, having suffered badly in the market as a result of oil price shocks, decided to diversify into specialty chemicals. This meant limited capital funds for the commodity processes that predominate at the site. Second, because energy prices were high and commodity processes are energy-intensive, the inefficiency of some processes at Marbletown was a concern. An important way the superintendents of these processes could get money would be through the divisional small-capital funds, which are allocated to the site rather than the business. The best way they could compete for these funds was on the basis of ROI. Therefore, a group of superintendents were strong early supporters of the energy conservation project competition. They used the competition to fund projects that allowed them to do things they wanted to do, but incidentally gave them energy conservation gains. For example, one superintendent used the competition to increase the capacity of his process by 30 percent while justifying the projects on the basis of energy savings.[16] As additional benefits at his process, the competition projects improved operating efficiency at low capacity, made the process easier to run, and increased enormously the production range in which the plant was profitable. The company saw this when the market for the product picked up in the late 1980s.

In 1980, the company saw its chief resource for this type of problem solving as its junior engineers rather than its operators.[17] After a couple of years, the competition organizer realized that in addition to providing challenging and interesting work, the competition projects provided excellent training opportunities for the junior engineers. As the competition organizer stated, ["There's a lot of training involved in the projects. The engineers take a project to completion. They use decision-making tools. They learn the process of getting ideas, collecting data, evaluating projects, making presentations, doing detail design, and supervising construction."]

He went on to add: ["Get people making decisions early in their careers. The important thing is that decision making is not guessing. There is a technique. People need to get a feeling for the number of facts they need to gather before making a decision. . . . As you move on, the mistakes become more expensive."]

Over time, engineers found that by involving the operators they supervised in the process, they could generate more projects. Therefore, the competition also enhanced their management skills.

Support from Junior Engineers

While training may be a virtue, it doesn't explain why the junior engineers would participate in the competition enthusiastically. To understand this, the structure of FLECSOCO's internal labor market must be considered.

The plant superintendents have managed to enact a shared belief, which may or may not be true, that excellence in the energy/waste competition is vital for junior engineers wanting promotions. The argument is quite simple. First, the competition enables participating engineers to stand out from the other engineers and be seen by the superintendents of other processes. There is a public awards ceremony and winners get a paragraph in the division newsletter. Only one or two other activities in the division offer this sort of prominence. As one interviewee described it:

> And, what [the competition organizer] successfully did is he convinced plant superintendents and engineers that if you did not participate in that program; if you did not turn [in] a WRFP [Waste Reduction for Performance] or energy project, and if you were not at the big meeting every year to receive an award [when] all the major managers were sitting there and you got to walk up the aisle, and the general manager handed you your award and shook your hand; if you weren't one of those guys, you weren't going to get very far in FLECSOCO.

Second, if an engineer can do well in the competition, he or she has a set of skills that the company values. That engineer can work with data, work with and inspire the people he or she supervises, make decisions, write capital requests, oversee detail design, and supervise construction. Therefore, the claim has very high face validity to all involved. It is this high face validity that enables the shared enactment. Without it, the whole system fails.

Consider the counterexample of the safety and environment superintendent, one of the routes to a plant superintendent's job. This position was created to try and alleviate some of the pressure on the plant superintendents as they attempted to meet safety, environmental, quality, and productivity objectives simultaneously. It was also seen as a training exercise. The hope was that these people, when they became plant superintendents, would have a strong safety or environmental focus.[18] Each safety or environmental superintendent oversees four or five plants. One interviewee described what happened after the position was created: "We titled the job 'superintendent' to try to impress upon the people in the division that it was a serious job. We even came out with letters to say that we had put our best people in those jobs."

Unfortunately, the best people weren't put in the jobs. This interviewee continued:

> This meant that the superstars go straight to running the plant [as production supervisors]. This is an important point, because if we had successfully sold the job as being an intermediate step to plant superintendent, we would have had more of our superstars ask for the job. . . . [We couldn't sell this idea because] in FLECSOCO [we] will never promise a guy his next job. We could pick a safety superintendent, and we could insinuate that he will be the next plant superintendent, but we will never promise that. . . . And, unless it actually works out that way, the superstars perceive very quickly that it is all false.

Over time, the safety and environment superintendent's job has become more routinized, and so it has become less of a position for superstars. However, in its more routine form, it could still be seen as an important job for ascending junior professionals.[19]

Continued Support from Superintendents

Finally, one must ask why the plant superintendents continue to support the project competition. Three reasons seem apparent. First, while it is possible to fund any worthwhile project at FLECSOCO, that money is not necessarily easy to obtain. Superintendents always seem to have an incentive to get more money. Therefore, once the competition was in existence and using up 25 percent of the site's small capital, the superintendents had a big incentive to participate. Second, the superintendents are in "friendly" competition with one another. Their plants are constantly being compared to other plants on the site and to others making the same product.[20] Plants are evaluated regularly on the basis of a scorecard, a set of measures of plant performance. Since the initial placement of plants on various dimensions on the scorecard is a function of the basic technology, the relative rankings of the plants at a particular point in time are not terribly important. However, changes in those rankings over time are. Therefore, superintendents are constantly trying to improve the performance of their plants. Third, one area in which superintendents derive their status is in their ability to promote junior members of the company. If superintendents believe the project competition provides the route to success and want their engineers to be successful, they will support the competition.

AVOIDING CONFLICT WITH OTHER PROGRAMS AND INTERESTS

While the Marbletown program provides joint gains to superintendents, engineers, training personnel, and, from the point of view of energy conservation, waste reduction and maintenance personnel, it is important to realize that it also avoids a number of important conflicts.

Capital

The first conflict avoided is over capital. As noted earlier, the program is unusual in that the money is allocated after the projects are selected, rather than from within a fixed budget as might be expected. Asked why, the competition organizer responded, "The competition started in Gneiss [Division]. . . . [The program designer] made a mistake of trying to commit capital. It meant that every year he had to fight to get capital. Therefore, I avoided any control over capital. I didn't want to do it and I didn't want to compete with the major managers. I'd lose. . . . The managers are under a lot of pressure to fund the projects anyway."

Asked what that pressure was, the organizer explained that the competition process creates expectations from a large number of parties, particularly the engineers who have come up with the designs, to spend the money on the winning projects even though the superintendents don't have to. The problem with the Gneiss Division approach is that in a company where both the program managers and the division managers change jobs about every three years, it would not be long before either a program manager or a general manager would arrive who was not interested in either making a pitch for funds or providing them.

Time and Rewards for Engineers and Other Line Employees

For the same reason, no financial awards are given in the competition to the engineers who come up with the designs. As the organizer explained, "There are no financial rewards, since it competes with the line. A program cannot compete with the organization. That is, WRFP has no bureaucracy and no budget." Instead, the plant simply gives out a plaque that could be interpreted as a symbolic promise of financial rewards later on.

Another potential conflict might be that the competition takes up too much of engineers' time. An engineer who was interviewed explained that it didn't. He came up with projects by thinking about savings-oriented waste reduction and energy conservation opportunities as he walked around the plant. The competition took only a little time to keep notes, collect relevant data, and do brief write-ups of proposals.

Other Functional Groups

A further conflict might be that the group that is formally responsible for capital project appraisal would be offended that another group on the site had started to usurp its role. After all, the competition involves a committee formally evaluating engineers' proposals. Serendipitously, the program designer avoided this conflict by inviting a member of the capital planning/economic evaluation staff to join the competition committee. Initially, he felt he needed assistance with the economic evaluation aspects of the program. Subsequently, he realized that the program really "treads on their toes" significantly. However, since the capital planning people were brought in from the start, and learned more about technical evaluation—an area where they needed help—there were no problems.

A final conflict was pointed out in discussions of the program with the organizer of a similar energy conservation program at another site. He pointed out that programs like this could cause antagonism because they encouraged managers to underallocate their annual monies to some areas in the hope of picking up money for those areas through the competition. The Marbletown contest managed to avoid this conflict by opening itself up to a large number of functions (maintenance, savings-oriented waste reduction, yield improvements) in addition to energy conservation.

In summary then, the program organizer at Marbletown had a successful program because he managed to pitch it to the right people in the organization, the junior engineers. At the same time, he offered them and their supervisors reasons to support the program that were completely independent of their belief in energy conservation (and subsequently waste reduction). These included capital and engineer training for the superintendents and recognition for the engineers. Finally, by design and by accident, he managed to avoid conflicts with the superintendents and major managers, other functions, and the capital allocation staff.

Explaining Success at Schisttown

The beginning of the widespread use of quality circles in the United States in 1981 is a good marker for the start of concern about operator empowerment and skills. The Marbletown savings-oriented waste reduction program, which began in 1980, predated this.[21] By 1987, when the Schisttown program was created, the need for operator empowerment and skills development was well embedded in company ideology, and "continuous improvement" was seen as fundamental to corporate success.[22] Continuous improvement, which is part of total quality management, uses specific techniques to analyze problems. The Schisttown program was designed to provide continuous improvement training for operators.

A program designer explained that at most sites the rate of turnover of top site management is very high and that new initiatives are risky. Program designers are never sure how much effort programs are going to entail or how well they are going to work. Therefore, unless the program managers have sufficient power to have a program stand on its own, they have to piggyback it onto something else. That something should be relatively enduring in corporate strategy. This will enable them to sell it to the next general manager; it will give them support from other functional managers; it will be more attractive to superintendents; it will give them a reasonably good idea of how well it is going to work; and it is likely to stay institutionalized as long as the company is pursuing that particular strategy. This would explain why the program designer at Schisttown chose to align his program so closely with the continuous improvement effort.

Another interviewee picked up on the use of operators and hinted at another important advantage:

> I think it gives the operator a focus on really understanding cost-effective changes. And the other thing I believe is [that] when I talk to our employees, from the president to the newest hire . . . I really think our people really do have a significant environmental sensitivity, so if you can figure the right formula to capture that personal enthusiasm for the environment into job enrichment, and [identify] projects which will do something good for the environment as well as FLECSOCO, to which our employees are really dedicated, then I think you have a combination which is really win-win, in

that you have something our people can get excited about. As long as you do that cost-effectively with these high returns on investment, you hit a home run.

Attaching the program to the operators offered the company two other important advantages. FLECSOCO had to manage a major crisis in the mid-1980s when problems with one of the effluent streams at the Gneiss Division set off a public scare. This came on top of fifteen years of adversarial relations with the government and bad relationships with the public. A key part of the crisis was the realization that employee morale had dropped precipitously. In addition, the company reconceptualized its relationship with its institutional environment (cf. Bartunek 1984). It started to see the community, rather than the government, as the initial source of regulations.

The Schisttown site is in a part of the country with a very high environmental sensitivity. Thus, one advantage of using operators is that those who actively participate in environmental management are less likely to feel they are working for a polluting company and more likely to sell the company's environmental record in the local community. A second advantage is that this particular program design takes up very little of the organizer's time, as opposed to the Marbletown program, which requires that every project be examined before and audited after. At Schisttown, because of the region and because the company wanted to build an incinerator there, community relations are much more important than marginal waste improvements. It was more important that the waste reduction manager spend time educating the community on the enormous amount of waste the plant had already reduced (principally through the off-the-ponds project) than ensuring that future waste reduction projects are the best possible.

Note, however, that several important waste reduction projects did not come out of the operator-level program, but rather, came from the engineers. These include the refrigeration system project and the project to eliminate the fluoride waste stream.

Thus, at Schisttown, the program designer could not construct a program like the one at Marbletown without creating conflicts. Because the program was situated at a different time in a different place, he had to pitch it to the operators. Therefore, we see, once again, a program that offers joint gains for the participants and the superintendents that have nothing to do with waste reduction and the implementation of a design that avoids conflicts with the interests of others at the site.

A DIFFERENCE BETWEEN PROGRAM OUTCOMES: THE SCHISTTOWN REFRIGERATION SYSTEM

Given the above explanations, it is now clear why the Schisttown engineer had trouble funding the heat exchanger for the design of the refrigeration system. At Marbletown, the energy/waste competition projects are assessed on the basis of relative waste and energy merits independent of the concerns that dominate the plant superintendent's thinking, such as minimizing the amount of time taken in making decisions, focusing attention on decisions that affect the core operations of the plant, and emphasizing the dimensions on which he is evaluated. At Marbletown, the heat exchanger would almost certainly have been funded. At Schisttown, the project would come out of a superintendent's budget or capital submission directly. Superintendents within FLECSOCO are assessed on the basis of a scorecard with a number of unit ratios for operation of the plant (dollars per pound of product, accidents per hundred worker-years, energy per pound, and so forth). Until the recent ozone hole controversy, because refrigeration was not part of the core process of the plant, chlorofluorocarbon (CFC) usage was of no importance to plant management. Therefore, it wasn't measured and it wasn't on the scorecard. The particular refrigeration system to be designed would use a trivial amount of energy compared to the rest of the plant. Therefore, plant management would have been perfectly happy with a standard CFC-based refrigeration system. In other words, although the heat exchanger was better in terms of corporate profitability and waste reduction objectives, it didn't fit into the local definitions of either (Cyert and March 1963).

MORE DIFFERENCES: THE SCHISTTOWN AND HORNFELS COMPETITIONS

To round out the discussion, two other programs must be considered: one in the Schist Division and one in the company's Hornfels Division. The Hornfels program aimed at energy conservation and, like the Marbletown energy conservation competition, was modeled after the Gneiss Division program. The program at Schisttown was an attempt to implement the Marbletown competition, without the waste reduction component, as a part of Schisttown's continuous improvement effort. Although, on the surface, these two programs were virtually identical to the Marbletown program—both involved engineers submitting competitive designs for consideration by a committee—slight differences undermined support from key actors.

The Schisttown competition, which started in 1987, ran for two years. In both years projects totaling about $8 million were designated as winners, for an average ROI in excess of 100 percent. The organizing committee decided to scrap the program in the third year. The differences at Schisttown revolve around the way capital is allocated. Each division is given money to allocate as small capital for projects of less than $2 million. Two equity-based principles are commonly used to allocate capital to the individual plants: the replacement value of the capital and the amount allocated in the previous year. Plants might be allocated 4 percent of their replacement capital, for example. At the Marbletown, Gneiss, and Hornfels divisions, the energy/waste competition added a third principle. Instead of allocating all the small capital on equity-based criteria, a portion of it was put into the competition and therefore allocated on the basis of efficiency. At Schisttown, the program oversight committee couldn't persuade the general manager to do this. Instead, the general manager insisted that, irrespective of the competition outcomes, all the small capital would be allocated according to the equity-based criteria. In so doing, he immediately eliminated most of the incentive the superintendents might have had for participating in the competition. Instead of the engineers' submissions being seen as a source of extra capital, they were seen as a time sink. Once sufficient projects had been identified to use the annual budget wisely, there was no point in wasting time on fancy proposals. As the organizer explained, ["At the superintendent level, they didn't want to see guys writing these up and submitting them. They would rather see their guys working on the projects themselves."]

The Hornfels program started in 1983 and lasted about five years. It was scrapped in 1988 when the number and quality of projects submitted started to decline. In the third and fourth years there were about forty worthwhile projects; the fifth year yielded only thirty. While the organizer suggested in an interview that there was less energy conservation potential there, that appears implausible, as the Hornfels Division is several times the size of the Marble Division. It cannot be said that the program was a failure, given that the organizer may not have wanted the program to take off to the same extent as that at Marbletown. That is, it cannot be assumed a priori that the organizer was trying to create a successful program when it would have been easier to create a satisfactory one. But since the program died as soon as energy prices dropped, it can be said that it was not well institutionalized.

In the author's assessment, three aspects of the Hornfels program design prejudiced its success. First, as with the competition at Gneiss, funds were allocated before the winners were picked. As noted, the organizer at Marbletown saw this as a liability at Gneiss. Presumably, it was a liability at Hornfels also, and the program would have been much harder to fund once energy prices started to fall. Second, the Hornfels Division is huge—consisting of more than 150 plants—and there isn't the same dominance by commodity plants as in the Marble Division. For this reason the competition organizer had concentrated on the energy-intensive plants and had advised the specialty plants not to bother participating in the competition. The superintendent of one specialty plant, who was asked about engineers in that plant participating in a subsequent version of the competition set up for savings-oriented waste reduction, he said that this was discouraged because the big savings are in the commodity plants and so there is no point in competing with them.[23] Third, with such a huge site and such an enormous staff, it may be hard to create the perception that the program enhances a person's chances for promotion. That is, the facility is so large that everyone is anonymous and differences in technology that normally are compensated for rise up as obstacles. The shared belief is not enacted.

A corporate reader of a draft of this chapter suggested a fourth reason. Another difference between the Hornfels and Marbletown programs was that Hornfels accepted proposals for the competition four times yearly instead of once. In such a situation, the frequency of competition deadlines makes it relatively easy for people to indefinitely defer putting effort into writing submissions.[24]

CONCLUSION: BEST PRACTICES REVISITED

By examining two high-performing waste reduction programs in detail, it has been shown that by looking at particular aspects of the waste reduction problem, it is possible to identify key actors to solve the problem. The most efficient programs will engage those actors. However, before a program can be excellent, it has to survive. To do that, it must engage the target people, motivate them, and provide them with sufficient information and resources to do a good job. In addition, the program must have full and continuing support from the managers who supervise the participants. Programs that do not do so will not survive more than a couple of years and will be difficult to sustain in the meantime.

The data presented here suggest that there are a number of very important principles that managers must keep in mind when designing programs—principles in which, not surprisingly, the best practices of which one reads are subsumed. For example, participants need something to motivate them to participate. However, we cannot say, a priori, whether that should be a financial reward, a pat on the back, a veiled promise of promotion, an appeal to the health and welfare of the community, exhortations from top management, or an opportunity for a diversion from routine work. While we can expect some of these incentives to be more effective in general, which one is best in a particular instance depends on many things occurring in other functions and at other locations in the plant, elsewhere in the corporation, elsewhere in the industry and supplier networks, and within the local community.

Another important principle is that a program cannot violate the territory of the people who supervise the participants. Furthermore, a good program offers something that will make these people want to actively support it. It will also offer something to people from other functional groups. Finally, as far as possible, a good program will situate itself in the corporate information-processing system in a manner appropriate to the technical problem at hand. There may be a number of other key principles that were not demonstrated in this comparison of two cases.

ACKNOWLEDGMENTS

The author thanks the many people at FLECSOCO who generously gave of their time to participate in this study. Berit Aasen, John Ehrenfeld, Tad Homer-Dixon, Hans Klein, Jim Maxwell, Yiorgos Mylonadis, Michael Piore, Johan Schot, and participants in the MIT Organization Studies seminar provided valuable feedback. This research was supported in part by the MIT Hazardous Substances Management Program.

NOTES

1. In addition, they emphasized the importance of waste reduction and made it seem easier by arguing that corporate decision makers should employ the same processes for waste reduction that they do for safety.

2. The number of major managers at a site varies over time, depending on demand. As managers become more experienced, their responsibilities increase and so the number of managers needed declines.

3. Telephone interviewees were given an opportunity to review the interview notes, since the telephone interviews weren't taped, as the personal interviews were.

4. More formally, compliance-oriented waste reduction programs aim to maximize (pounds reduced) / (dollars invested). Savings-oriented waste reduction pro-

grams aim to maximize (dollars saved) / (dollars invested). For a given waste stream and a rational organization, these criteria are identical. A compliance-oriented waste reduction exercise should subsume all the savings-oriented waste reduction projects. However, we will see that the projects tended to be quite different.

5. People outside the division thought these projects were well engineered but that the division had acted too late. Because the division lacks a biological treatment facility or aqueous discharge permits, it was very vulnerable to a change in regulations. People in the organization had seen federal and state regulations coming, but the division did not act until the regulations were upon it. The author inferred from interviewees' comments that they felt this made the works more expensive and was part of the reason for having to encase the prior waste. This prediction is exactly opposite to the prediction that would follow from Jackall's (1988) argument at the "Alchemy" firm he studied. He would have expected management to wait until the last possible moment so they would not have to be held accountable for the expenditure.

6. Only operating (noncapital) savings were to be considered.

7. The original high ROI criterion was used because savings were in short-run energy acquisitions. The price of fuel was high in 1980, but there was no guarantee that it would stay high. As the price of fuel dropped, the hurdle ROI dropped to 30 percent. A project yielding 100 percent ROI in 1981 would have yielded about 30 percent ROI in 1988.

8. More specifically, the company has no formal requirement that a WRFP (Waste Reduction for Performance) project should have an ROI exceeding a particular value. However, competition organizers wanted to encourage personnel to ferret out both the very high return projects and those that reduced much waste but weren't very profitable. Therefore, they partitioned the projects into three categories—those with an ROI less than 30 percent, those with an ROI between 30 percent and 100 percent, and those with an ROI greater than 100 percent. The organizer added the criterion that the mean ROI for projects in the first and third categories must exceed 100 percent for a given plant.

9. Half the savings were in avoided disposal costs and the other half were in saved materials.

10. By developing techniques to keep up the activity of the catalyst, the engineers hoped to reduce the tar production.

11. It appears that parts of FLECSOCO have used a suggestion card system very similar to this one for many years. Such a system was used in the main research laboratory in the 1930s.

12. Expenditure figures were not available, but none of the projects appear to have required significant capital.

13. Contextual information differs from tacit information (that based in skill) in that contextual information can be communicated if the person wanting the information knows what question to ask.

14. One interpretation of the findings of a recent study on the impact of

maintenance contracting on safety in the chemical industry is that one of the reasons contractors have more accidents than permanent employees is that they are not sufficiently informed of the contextual idiosyncrasies of the processes on which they are working (Wells et al. 1991, 150).

15. A number of corporate artifacts show the company's emphasis on communication. The corridors in corporate headquarters are wide enough for people to walk eight abreast. This undoubtedly facilitates conversation. Similarly, when the company designed its new main research laboratory in the 1930s, the floor plan was organized to force everyone past everyone else's desk regularly. Finally, one of the plant sites was building a process similar to one located in Germany. The operators of the German facility participated actively at several stages in the design review for the new process.

16. All ROI calculations assumed that the superintendent was running the plant at the capacity demanded by the market at that time.

17. For a capital-intensive company, a key source of competitive advantage lies in its ability to design efficient processes and construct them quickly and well. Therefore, engineers who are good at design and construction are a vital resource.

18. It is the author's understanding that these positions have been very successful in terms of assuring safety and environmental performance. However, the point is that they have failed to achieve one of their goals: to provide environmental or safety sensitivity training for all upcoming managers. Notwithstanding, about 50 percent of plant superintendents have some sort of safety or environmental experience.

19. One can only speculate as to why it was easier to create the shared enactment in one case than the other. The author uses two plausible explanations. First, it is very easy to see if safety superintendents are being promoted, but it is much harder to work out whether competition winners are. Many more people win in the competition, and it is always assumed to be a relatively marginal thing. Second, there may be a professional/cultural reason. Knowing how to manage safety is something the company asserts is important, but knowing how to design, build, and manage things is something any junior engineer knows is important.

20. For example, FLECSOCO has seventeen plants globally making one common plastic.

21. The Marbletown site formed several quality circles in 1987. They have been successful and have endured.

22. The firm has pushed waste reduction to various extents since the 1960s.

23. This interviewee was selected by the safety staff as an excellent safety manager. It may well be that the managers at Marbletown who are overly concerned about safety also discourage their engineers from worrying about waste. The author did not investigate this, however, since Marbletown interviewees were selected by the environmental staff.

24. At both the Hornfels and Schisttown sites, the program organizer stayed in the division after the competition was terminated. Therefore, we can eliminate the

hypothesis that these programs died because the organizers weren't around long enough for the programs to be institutionalized.

REFERENCES

Bacharach, Samuel B. and Lawler, Edward J. 1980. *Power and Politics in Organizations: The Social Psychology of Conflict, Coalitions, and Bargaining*. San Francisco: Jossey Bass.

Bartunek, Jean M. 1984. "Changing Interpretive Schemes and Organizational Restructuring: The Example of a Religious Order." *Administrative Science Quarterly* 29(3): 355–72.

Burns, Tom, and Stalker, G. M. 1961. *The Management of Innovation*. London: Tavistock Publications.

Cebon, Peter B. 1992. "Twixt Cup and Lip: Organizational Behavior, Technical Prediction, and Conservation Practice." *Energy Policy* 20(9): 802–14.

Cebon, Peter B. 1990. "The Missing Link: Organizational Behavior as a Key Element in Energy/Environment Regulation and University Energy Management." Master's thesis, Department of Civil Engineering, Massachusetts Institute of Technology, Cambridge, Mass.

Cyert, Richard M., and March, James G. 1963. *A Behavioral Theory of the Firm*. Englewood Cliffs, N.J.: Prentice-Hall.

Granovetter, Mark S. 1973. "The Strength of Weak Ties." *American Journal of Sociology* 78(6): 1360–80.

Hirschhorn, Joel S., and Oldenburg, Kirsten U. 1991. *Prosperity Without Pollution: The Prevention Strategy for Industry and Consumers*. New York: Van Nostrand Reinhold.

Jackall, Robert. 1988. *Moral Mazes*. New York: Oxford University Press.

Lawrence, Paul R., and Lorsch, Jay W. 1967. *Organization and Environment: Managing Differentiation and Integration*. Boston: Graduate School of Business Administration, Harvard University.

Lovins, Amory, and Lovins, L. Hunter. 1991. "Least-Cost Climate Stabilization." *Annual Review of Energy* 16: 433–531.

March, James G., and Simon, Herbert A. 1958. *Organizations*. New York: John Wiley.

Ross, Marc. 1986. "Capital Budgeting Practices of Twelve Large Manufacturers." *Financial Management*, Winter, 15–22.

Royston, Michael G. 1979. *Pollution Prevention Pays*. New York: Pergamon.

Simon, Herbert A. 1976. *Administrative Behavior: A Study of the Decision-making Process in Administrative Organization*. New York: Free Press.

Thompson, James D. 1967. *Organizations in Action*. New York: McGraw-Hill.

Wells, John C.; Kochan, Thomas A.; and Smith, Michal. July 1991. "Managing Workplace Safety and Health: The Case of Contract Labor in the U.S. Petrochemical Industry." A Report to the Secretary of Labor for the Occupational Health and Safety Administration.

PART III

❧

Trust and Credibility

7

Responsible Care: Trust, Credibility, and Environmental Management

Peter Simmons and Brian Wynne

Public interest in environmental issues has increased sharply in the last twelve months and these concerns are being reflected by all the main political parties. The chemical industry has played a major part in improving the quality of life since its very beginnings. It has a good record of improving its environmental performance in recent years, but society rightly expects more rapid change—and we, in our industry, have to respond. The Chemical Industries Association launched its "Responsible Care" program in March; members' initial response has been encouraging and their enthusiastic support will do much to ensure the long term success of the program *and help regain society's trust*.[1]

In recent years the chemical industry has found its environmental performance under increasing public scrutiny and has been caught in a tide of rising expectations. It is experiencing a crisis of credibility and faces considerable public mistrust, which brings existing institutional arrangements into question and raises levels of uncertainty within the industry. Drawing on recent research in Britain, this chapter examines the response of the chemical industry to these pressures and its attempt to recuperate public trust by the promotion of environmental management standards and improved public communication through its Responsible Care program. After a brief sketch of the way in which the uncertainty of economic actions can be reduced through the formation of institutions and trust relations, the chapter describes the credibility problems faced by the chemical industry in Great Britain and how they led to the adoption of Responsible Care, and identifies some of the publics to whom the program is directed. The text then outlines the development of the program and explores some of the issues that have been raised, including its implications for commercial relations with other economic actors outside the industry. A theme of the analysis is the interplay between symbolic action initiated for credibility reasons and heightened regulatory pressures resulting from the altered identities, expectations, and relationships thereby engendered. The final section discusses a number of problems that must be addressed if the program's objective of reestablishing trust is to be achieved and if its potential contribution to improved social learning processes regarding environmental problems is to be realized.

UNCERTAINTY, INSTITUTIONS, AND TRUST

Broad cultural changes have led to a shift in social values concerning our relationship to the natural environment. Industrial activity has been identified as one of the major sources of environmental harm. Existing norms governing economic behavior are being brought into question. One result of this for industry has been a disruption of commonly shared expectations and an undermining of social trust. The consequent increase in levels of uncertainty for economic actors creates pressure for industry to respond to newly emerging expectations in order to recover its credibility with society and retain its license to operate.

The reduction or domestication of uncertainty is a central concern of all social actors, who function best when everyday life can be more or less predictable. Institutions—that is, any form of constraint that limits the choices of actors—reduce uncertainty by providing structure to everyday life by establishing the rules of the game (North 1990). One way in which institutions achieve this is by establishing diffuse relations of trust—that is, relations based on shared expectations about the social rules that govern a particular activity or situation (Holzner and Marx 1979). In other words, trust reduces the uncertainty faced by organizations by reducing the complexity of their environments (Luhmann 1979). However, trust has to be produced, and when institutions come into question, or are no longer accepted, uncertainty is increased. In personal relations and exchanges the production of trust can be based on personal characteristics, knowledge of past encounters, or other criteria, such as membership in the same family or community. In relations with institutional actors, such as firms, these means of producing trust do not hold. The problem then becomes one of developing institutional mechanisms for the production and maintenance of impersonal trust (Shapiro 1987). Zucker identified three types of mechanisms for producing trust in impersonal economic actors: (1) individual or firm-specific characteristics that signal a commitment to conform to societal and constitutive expectations; (2) regulations or formalized rules governing behavior; and (3) the use of third-party intermediaries, such as financial auditors, to provide a form of guarantee that an accepted set of rules is being followed (Zucker 1986).

The chemical industry's responses to the credibility pressures that it currently faces demonstrate a search for mechanisms that will rebuild social trust. The strategies that have been developed, either collectively or on the part of individual firms, display elements of all three types of trust-producing mechanisms. This chapter outlines some of these responses, focusing on the development of the British Responsible Care program, but first it places them in context by outlining the credibility problems that are faced by the industry.

CREDIBILITY PROBLEMS OF THE BRITISH CHEMICAL INDUSTRY

The Chemical Industries Association (CIA) represents the major part of the British chemical industry. It is estimated that its membership accounts for 90 percent of sales and 85 percent of employment in the sectors covered.[2] The CIA's view of its role is outlined in its 1978 activities report:

> In terms of an industry's survival and future prosperity the work of a trade association is closer to farming than it is to the hunting stage of Mankind's development. By this we mean that the operating environment of member companies is improved not so much by sudden dramatic actions on the part of the CIA as by the long term investment of effort and the painstaking cultivation of those various audiences, opinion formers and decision takers on whom we depend.[3]

The CIA engages in a range of activities on behalf of its members and considers itself to be one of the most effective British trade associations. According to a former president of the CIA, its activities fall into three broad categories: representational, aimed at achieving a better business, social, political, and operational environment for the manufacture and sale of chemicals; mutual help, whereby the CIA encourages and facilitates interfirm cooperation on problems of mutual concern; and direct provision of services to member companies.[4] There is particular emphasis within the chemical industry on the benefits of collective representation and public relations (PR) (Grant 1983, 63). In 1989, after financial write-offs and the payment of its operating expenses, which included its routine PR and press office activities, the association had a working budget of about £500,000, more than half of which was spent on PR programs and on running its Chemicals in the Community mobile exhibition.

In the past few years the task of communicating with the public has become more complex and demanding, and this is a matter of serious concern for the CIA. From the time of its formation in the mid-1960s, the CIA has commissioned regular opinion polls to monitor the public image of the industry. Since 1980 the polls have shown a consistent decline in the British public's evaluation of the industry (ENDS Report 1991). In the 1970s about half of the people polled expressed a favorable view of the industry. This had dropped to only 20 percent by 1990. Over the same period the proportion holding an unequivocally negative view of the industry grew from less than 10 percent to 33 percent. Only the nuclear industry elicits a stronger adverse reaction. This unfavorable view of the industry is associated in the surveys with a lack of public familiarity, the vast majority of respondents feeling that they know little or nothing about the chemical industry. Public concern centers in particular on pollution and the disposal of chemical wastes, although concerns about the safety of chemical plants and the storage and transportation of chemicals also figure to a significant extent.

PUBLICS AND PERCEPTIONS

In speaking of the public's perceptions and mistrust of the industry, it is important to recognize that the public does not constitute a homogeneous entity. It is fragmented into many different publics, reflecting the lack of a common consciousness or a common experience, so shared perception of effects is therefore limited. This sociocultural fragmentation supports the existence of multiple frames of reference and thereby militates against simple consensus (Holzner and Marx 1979). At the same time, these publics are "interdependent in multiple and complex ways—what one element does affects all elements, but many of the consequences are delayed and indirect" (Stone 1985). The chemical industry has a number of salient publics whose perceptions of its environmental effects impinge on one another and directly or indirectly affect its activities.

Given the CIA's aim of forestalling excessive government intervention in the industry's activities, one important public is the regulatory community. An association's internal effectiveness impinges on its external credibility with regulators (Kelley 1990). If the association's efforts to defend a degree of self-regulatory autonomy are to receive political credence, its policies for maintaining acceptable standards within the industry must be perceived to be effective. This view was expressed recently by John Cox, the CIA's director general, when he commented that an effective Responsible Care program might mean less regulation (ENDS Report 1991). However, despite the good standing that the CIA enjoys in government circles, policy makers in both Westminster and Brussels have shown themselves to be increasingly sensitive to public demands for increased regulation to mitigate the environmental impact of industrial activity. The credibility of the association's proposals with government regulatory bodies will be influenced, therefore, by its credibility with the wider public. Its aim of limiting state intervention to a level that is acceptable to the industry therefore depends on both demonstrating the effectiveness of its internal management of environmental risks and successfully rebuilding public trust.

The communities in the vicinity of chemical plants constitute another public that has been the focus of industry communication programs. Since the mid-1980s many British plants have run educational initiatives and open-door days aimed at local communities, in an attempt to increase public familiarity and cultivate a more favorable view of the industry. These initiatives have been encouraged by formal requirements under the 1982 European Seveso Directive to inform local communities about the hazards and emergency procedures for sites with major accident potential (Council Directive 1982). The industry's efforts also reflect a concern with the recruitment implications of a general climate of suspicion and mistrust.

However, even if the industry feels itself to have achieved some success, the underlying problem may go rather deeper. A lack of openly expressed disquiet does not necessarily confirm the existence of public trust. As Wynne argued elsewhere, when individuals or communities are faced with large corporations on whom their livelihoods may depend, differences in the power of the actors make it necessary for those who are socially dependent to rationalize their situation and act *as if* they trust a corporate actor when in fact they may feel an underlying and persistent ambivalence (that is not to say that acting *as if* trust existed only serves to rationalize behavior under conditions of dependency; it may also, as discussed later in the chapter, play a more positive role in the learning process) (Wynne 1987, 1990). Such ambivalence is rooted in a culturally embedded awareness of risk that has developed in contemporary industrial societies, the implications of which are discussed in the concluding section of this chapter.

There are also a number of other less proximate publics whose view of the industry can, either directly or indirectly, have a serious impact upon its operations. In terms of influencing wider social perceptions of the industry's activities, one of the most significant forces is the environmental movement. Environmental pressure groups have become adroit at using the media to draw attention to the industry's shortcomings. Despite claims from some quarters of the industry to a Pauline conversion and a professed commitment to environmental improvement, prominent groups such as Greenpeace and Friends of the Earth continue to keep up the pressure by subjecting public claims to critical scrutiny. The CIA has been understandably cautious about entering into formal relationships with its critics. Similarly, liaison initiatives with local communities have often been conducted with a sense of hostility toward outside interests such as national environmental groups and have attempted to exclude them. However, views within the industry show some signs of changing in this respect.

A final example of a public whose perceptions of the chemical industry's environmental problems can have serious consequences for its members is insurers. As a result of losses faced by the insurance industry in the United States throughout the 1980s, insurers have been increasingly reluctant to insure some classes of environmental risks, particularly gradual pollution. This has led to a virtual collapse of the market for gradual pollution coverage. Responding to what was fast becoming a critical situation, the CIA perceived a gulf of understanding between themselves and insurers, largely due to a perception on the part of insurers that equated greater technical complexity with greater danger and risk and that focused on consequences rather than probabilities. The CIA's efforts have been directed toward trying to modify this perception and to communicate the contrary view that greater technological sophistication is accompanied by more sophisticated risk management techniques (Posner 1989). Despite the CIA's efforts to provide evidence of the chemical industry's reliability, insurers' perceptions have been shaped by a number of financially painful experiences that tend to validate their underlying mistrust. The difficulty of invalidating mistrust is fundamental to understanding the vicious circle out of which the industry is attempting to break and is considered further in this chapter's concluding discussion.

The preceding sections have described some of the credibility pressures faced by the British chemical industry and have identified some of the publics whose perceptions of its environmental performance have implications for the industry's commercial operations. (Other stakeholder groups likely to become sources of significant pressure in the near future include employees and investors. Both show signs of a growing concern with the environmental performance of firms and are beginning to press for greater accountability in this respect.) With public confidence declining dramatically toward the end of the 1980s, a trend undoubtedly accelerated by growing public awareness of chemical-related environmental problems and the highly publicized incidents of Bhopal, Sandoz, and the *Karin B,* environmental performance has survived the impact of recession on the industry and is firmly established as a top priority. To meet the intertwined challenges of improving its performance and regaining public trust, the CIA has initiated an industry-wide program under the banner of Responsible Care. While it could be seen as simply another PR program, Responsible Care differs from simple image building in that it aims to transform not merely the image but also, in a significant sense, the identity of the industry.

THE CIA RESPONSIBLE CARE PROGRAM

The CIA launched Responsible Care in March 1989. Responsible Care takes its name from a program initiated by the Canadian Chemical Producers Association in 1985. It establishes an umbrella program with two avowed aims: improving the industry's performance in the areas of environment, health, safety, product safety, distribution, and relations with the public; and enabling companies to demonstrate that such improvements are taking place. Similar programs are now being established by other national industry associations and are being promoted by bodies such as Conseil Europeén des Fédérations de l'Industrie Chimique (CEFIC), the European chemical industry federation. Backed by many of the major multinational corporations, Responsible Care is becoming the flagship program of the international chemical industry in its efforts to redeem itself in the face of widespread criticism of its environmental record and deepening mistrust.[5]

The U.K. Responsible Care program, launched just a few months after the U.S. program, was the first of its kind in Europe. It had its beginnings in 1987, when the key debate concerning the industry centered on self-regulation. It is perhaps not surprising, in this context, that at the highly promoted press launch of a new set of CIA guidelines on waste management, the following question was raised: What does the CIA do to ensure that its members follow its guidance? The answer was, in effect, very little, beyond hoping that members would respond. In keeping with the less legalistic style of U.K. regulation generally, the CIA had a long tradition of producing "good practice" guidelines for its member companies but hitherto had not attempted to enforce compliance with its recommendations. However, the question of implementation touched at the heart of the industry's claims to be able to balance an acceptable regulatory framework with effective industry self-regulation and prompted the association to look at what might be done to ensure the effectiveness of its guidance.

A meeting held in February 1987 arrived at two conclusions: that there was a need for the association to be more than just a collection of members and that company self-regulation alone was not enough. These conclusions suggested two interrelated objectives: constructing a collective identity and moving beyond a compliance-oriented approach. As will be shown, these objectives underpin the CIA's subsequent development of Responsible Care. This view was endorsed by the CIA Council, and its Chemical Industry Safety, Health, and Environment Council (CISHEC) was asked to develop it further. As a result, a pilot study team was set up that, during the period from March 1987 to June 1988, drew up a set of guiding principles, developed and tested self-assessment questionnaires for completion by chief executive officers and site managers, and considered the options for monitoring progress. Initially, opinion was divided on whether or not the completed questionnaires should be returned to the CIA for monitoring. It was decided finally that the CIA should not be in the position of policing and judging members' performance, which was seen by many members as being out of keeping with the accepted role of the association. The entire CIA membership of about two hundred companies are now signatories to the program, and acceptance of its principles has become a condition of membership for companies joining the association.

The document that was signed affirms the commitment of CIA members to "managing their activities so that they present an acceptably high level of protection for the health and safety of employees, customers, the public and the environment," a commitment that is based on six guiding principles (see Figure 7.1).

SELF-REGULATION AND SOCIAL CONTROL

The acceptance of an obligation by member companies to conform to CIA guidelines implies a significant change in the relationship between the CIA and its members. However, even with industry members publicly committed to these principles and to working in accordance with the best practice guidelines produced by the CIA, there still remains the question of enforcement. That implies a sanctioning mechanism. Sanctions can take many forms, ranging from physical or economic coercion to attempts to persuade and give advice (Zald 1978).

FIGURE 7.1
GUIDING PRINCIPLES OF THE CIA'S RESPONSIBLE CARE PROGRAM

Members of the Chemical Industries Association are committed to managing their activities so that they present an acceptably high level of protection for the health and safety of employees, customers, the public and the environment.

The following Guiding Principles form the basis of this commitment:

- Companies should ensure that their health, safety, and environment policy reflects the commitment and is clearly seen to be an integral part of their overall business policy.
- Companies should ensure that management, employees at all levels and those in contractual relationships with the Company are aware of their commitment and are involved in the achievement of their policy objectives.
- All Company activities and operations must be conducted in accordance with relevent statuary obligations. In addition, Companies should operate according to the best practices of the industry and in accordance with Government and Association guidance.

In particular, Companies should:

- Assess the actual and potential impact of their activities and products on the health and safety of employees, customers, the public and environment.
- Where appropriate, work closely with public and statutory bodies in the development and implementation of measures designed to achieve an acceptably high level of health, safety and environmental protection.
- Make available to employees, customers, the public and statutory bodies, relevant information about activities that affect health, safety and the environment.

Members of the Association recognize that these Principles and activities should continue to be kept under regular review.

SOURCE: Chemical Industries Association.

Disciplinary or punitive sanctions would be one mechanism that might persuade a skeptical public that environmental performance is being taken seriously by the industry. Nevertheless, the use of such sanctions has been resisted by the CIA on the grounds that encouragement is preferable to punishment; they would also, of course, bring the CIA into a policing role that its members are not willing to accept. The CIA is able to exert some influence on the behavior of members, but its regulations do not have much bite when it comes to sanctioning noncompliance or poor performance. However, even the threat of expulsion, were it invoked, would carry little weight in an industry where association membership is voluntary and by no means universal. All of this undermines the likely effectiveness of the CIA's role as a mechanism for self-regulation. Certainly, if it were proposed as a substitute for other forms of surveillance and control, its effectiveness would be a major cause for concern. The main regulatory issue for the CIA, however, is not one of replacing state regulation with self-regulation, but rather of negotiating a balance between the two that satisfies both the normative requirements of regulators and the operational preferences of its members. In fact, research seems to indicate that "there are grounds for pessimism that the most compliance-conscious trade associations can ever deliver the self-regulation of which the most compliance-conscious individual companies are capable" (Braithwaite and Fisse 1987, 244).

This would seem to endorse the industry's decision not to construct a quasiregulatory role for the CIA. But if it is unlikely to be effective as a formal control agent, what of the informal control that it exercises?

The CIA emphasizes the use of peer pressure as the primary mechanism for ensuring the implementation of the program. Peer pressure has been effective in persuading less enthusiastic members to put their signatures to Responsible Care, although signatures and promises may be easier to secure than behavioral change. It is also being used, reportedly to some effect, to promote adoption of a similar program by related trade associations, but evidence of this remains to be seen. The problem with informal mechanisms of control is that, however well they may work, they are invisible to outsiders, and their lack of accountability does little to enhance trust in their effectiveness. If the process is to be more transparent, a first step is to elucidate the mechanisms by which peer pressure can operate.

Far from being the abstract constructions of economic models, markets are characterized by networks of social relations. These relations are embedded in social expectations and norms and in the ties between individuals (Granovetter 1985). This chapter has already illustrated some of the relations that exist with stakeholders outside the industry and the problem of matching expectations. Within the industry, too, there are networks of relations and normative expectations. For example, direct links exist at a senior level among company executives participating in national or regional CIA committees. Similarly, some environmental managers have links with their functional counterparts in other companies. However, these connections are far from being uniform throughout the industry and in some cases do not exist at all. The CIA itself constitutes a collective voice, enabling it to bring influence to bear on a nonconforming company on behalf of its peers. However, research on the prevention of corporate crime also casts doubt on the effectiveness of trade associations as agents of informal social control (Braithwaite and Fisse 1987).

Even though the CIA is unlikely to be effective as a primary agent of control, it has an important role to play in promoting the wider adoption of practices developed by the more environmentally conscious firms. This is where its capacity to exert its influence through informal networks and encourage institutional innovation is a major contribution. Any wider value that the CIA's initiative may have, then, beyond its immediate PR benefit to the industry, lies in the extent to which it enhances the responsiveness of its members to environmental concerns and contributes to restructuring the networks of commercial relations in ways that reinforce environmentally beneficial behaviors.

LEARNING NETWORKS AND SOCIAL CONTROL

Although the CIA has sought to promote a self-regulatory compliance consciousness within the industry, thus complementing state regulation, a major aim of Responsible Care is to go beyond that and encourage within the industry a culture that is responsive to public concerns about environment, safety, and health risks and motivates continuous improvement. The cultural change that this entails implies a continuous process of collective learning. Learning here does not refer to the simple acquisition of information, but rather to changing the theories in use and the organizational routines that guide a firm's behavior (Nelson and Winter 1982). To initiate and maintain such a process can be difficult within an individual firm. To attempt it across a whole industry requires not merely exhortation and encouragement but mechanisms to translate it into practice.

An important step in the evolution of the Responsible Care program has been the creation of a growing number of local experience exchange networks, or "cells," as the CIA calls them. These cells are made up of senior-level representatives from five or six member companies operating within about twenty miles of one another, who, together with a facilitator from the CIA, meet on a regular basis. Their main purpose is to provide a forum for sharing experience related to the implementation of Responsible Care, although they have been extended in a number of cases by inviting representatives of local governmental councils, customers, or other large nonchemical industry firms in the area to participate. By formalizing the boundary-spanning environmental activities of senior managers and collectivizing those activities in a problem-solving network, the Responsible Care cells establish an interorganizational structure that facilitates learning by both individual firms and the industry as a whole.[6]

Creating these small face-to-face groups also institutes a mechanism through which peer pressure may operate. All of the participants stand to gain, both as individual firms and as members of the industry, if the groups are successful; equally, nobody wants their reputation to suffer, even by association. By wedding self-interest to collective performance the groups establish a basis for mutual monitoring and control through peer pressure, which in turn may serve to motivate individual and collective search strategies as problems arise. Thus, they may perform a dual function, as learning mechanisms and mechanisms of social control, by facilitating processes of collective learning and of mutual regulation. However, the question of how effective peer pressure can be as a mechanism of social control in the face of incentives to act otherwise still remains.

DISCLOSURE OF INFORMATION

In a move to monitor the practical results of the program and to provide some solid evidence of improvement, the CIA has begun collecting from its members data designed to monitor progress in the management of environment, safety, and health risks. Based on a system developed by the French multinational Rhône Poulenc, each site records percentage changes in a number of indicators of performance, such as toxic emissions, transport incidents, complaints, and an environmental index, against a baseline score for year one. The CIA intends to release the figures once three or four years' results have been recorded. Raw data will not be published, and the results will be presented in aggregate form, combining the figures for individual sites to give an overall picture of the industry's progress in improving its performance. Part of the rationale behind this approach is the view that raw emissions data would be less comprehensible and open to misinterpretation by members of the lay public.

At a policy level, the performance indicators can be viewed as an exercise in symbolic politics, signaling the industry's willingness to meet demands for more information about the environmental impact of its activities. The CIA's attempt at increasing the availability of information to outside interests has, however, met with some skepticism. The environmental index that the CIA is including in its site performance indicators, representing emissions of unnamed pollutants that have been identified by site managers as being of particular concern for their site, has been criticized by Friends of the Earth as "inventing your own ruler." The credibility of this simplified and anonymous form of disclosure may be further undermined by the decision of a number of prominent CIA member companies, such as Imperial Chemical Industries (ICI) and BP Chemicals, to publish quantified emissions data of the type required in the United States under the provisions of the Emergency Planning and Right-to-Know Act, Title III of the Superfund Amendments and Reauthorization Act (SARA Title III).[7] At best, the CIA's performance index can be seen as a transitional step toward a much fuller form of disclosure that may well involve both the publication of raw data and the compilation of indices against which to monitor progress. Indeed, some within the industry accept the inevitability of the pressure for the publication of environmental data, particularly in light of moves by the Commission of the European Communities (CEC) to make the information held by regulatory bodies publicly available and to encourage companies, at the very least, to publish environmental statements in their annual reports.[8] Perhaps the real significance of the CIA initiative is as a small step in the cultural change to which the industry is submitting itself, a step toward accepting the right of the public to know about the unmarketed products of its operations.

The industry is very cautious about the types of data that it makes available, and it is clear from the discussions at the Responsible Care seminar in 1989 that some members wish to distinguish between those categories of information that should be made freely available and more sensitive information, such as that concerning air emissions, waste, "incidents," and "near misses," which they would prefer to keep in the private domain.[9] Behind this reticence to release the "wrong" sort of information lies the industry's view that the public simply does not understand it: ". . . Responsible Care is mainly about improved performance, but with the results of the recent MORI Poll showing that our public image is still deteriorating, we must obviously review how we can describe our improved performance *in a way that the public can understand.*"[10]

This view has strong parallels with that of the British scientific community, which, believing that it lacked popular support, perceived the problem as being a need for improved public understanding of science. Like the protagonists in the mainstream of the science debate, the CIA is viewing the problem as one of *misunderstanding* due to a lack of familiarity with the knowledge, methods, and processes on which its operations are based, when instead it may reflect a different *understanding*, and grounded mistrust, of the institutional system of organization and control within which the industry's operations are embedded.[11] This perception of the problem has its roots in the culture of the industry, which is discussed later in this chapter. What is at issue is not simply a matter of education, although that undoubtedly has a part to play, but one of accountability. Accountability is central to the whole problem of building trust in the industry.

A formal community awareness program, with much greater involvement of local interests, is the next priority for the Responsible Care task force. A community awareness program has been in existence in the U.S. chemical industry since 1985 and has now been integrated into the Chemical Manufacturers (CMA) Responsible Care program. This reflects the stimulus provided by the 1984 Bhopal disaster, the subsequent incident at Union Carbide's West Virginia plant, and the SARA Title III legislation passed as a consequence by the U.S. Congress in 1986.[12] In Great Britain, however, while there has been a community information requirement under regulations governing major hazardous sites, legislative requirements have been nowhere near as extensive, and a broadly based program of communication with local communities by the industry is a new development. Although the goal is to develop closer links with local groups, it remains to be seen, in light of observations already made, whether this will result in a monologue or a dialogue.

There are signs, however, that the CIA has recognized that improving environmental management within the industry and then simply telling people about it is not a sufficient foundation on which to rebuild public trust. Members of the association are discussing the role that might be played by an independent advisory panel. An advisory panel was set up by the CMA within the U.S. Responsible Care program. Part of its task is to monitor the questionnaires completed by members, an arrangement that has already been rejected by the CIA. On the other hand, some within the U.K. industry favor establishment of a panel, which would include environmentalists, to sensitize the industry to the perceptions and concerns of its publics and to involve outside interests in formulating acceptable responses. While this would represent quite a radical initiative for the CIA, a greater engagement with other interests at both the policy formation and implementation stages would be an important step in the development of Responsible Care, one that, as will be argued later, could be crucial to achieving its goal of recovering society's trust.

EVALUATING PERFORMANCE

A step that until now has not figured in the CIA's program is the independent scrutiny of environmental performance under Responsible Care.

With the exception of one or two individual firms, there has been general resistance to the idea of involving interests from outside the industry in evaluating its performance.[13] However, externally conducted and accredited evaluation is likely to carry more weight with the public than internally constructed and produced performance indicators.

The CIA is already committed to promoting the adoption of the quality assurance approach throughout the industry and, significantly, is now pursuing recognition of the Responsible Care program for certification under the ISO 9000/BS 5750 quality assurance standard. British Standards certification, because it is seen as both authoritative and independent, is likely to confer considerably more credibility on a company's environmental management system—rightly or wrongly—than endorsement by the industry's own association.

However, filtering Responsible Care through the philosophy of quality assurance itself raises a number of important issues. Foremost among these is that BS 5750 (as well as its new environmental counterpart, BS 7750) is a management *systems* standard. Its main focus is on the detailed specification of all stages of an operation and on establishing adequate documentary controls to ensure that procedures are carried out and standards are met. As such it can be a useful management tool, greatly increasing the capacity for monitoring and control, although detractors see it as a self-generating paper chase. In practice, BS 5750 is aimed at increasing organizational control to consistently meet a set of performance standards defined by management. It is, then, primarily about consistency rather than quality. The quality objectives that the system is intended to achieve, and therefore the criteria against which performance is to be evaluated, still need to be defined and will accordingly reflect the values, interests, and goals of those doing the defining. Thus, BS 5750 and the related environmental management systems standard, BS 7750, can confirm that a system is being adhered to, but in themselves they say nothing about the content of systems or about environmental performance. Nor do they address the differing definitions of quality and competing conceptions of value that are central to public debates about environmental standards. Bringing Responsible Care within the framing ideology of quality management may give the industry a reassuring sense of being in control, and British Standards certification may even function in some respects as a surrogate for direct monitoring and control. But it will not address the culturally embedded basis of public mistrust, rooted in a pervasive consciousness of risk that has become characteristic of contemporary industrial cultures.[14]

COMMERCIAL NETWORKS OF CONTROL

It has been shown how Responsible Care seeks to influence the behavior and performance of member companies in the pursuit of greater public credibility. The CIA also recognizes that the behavior of other firms with whom their members transact can impinge directly on public perceptions of their industry. The importance of these relationships is indicated by the Responsible Care principle that exhorts members to ensure that "those in contractual relationships with the Company are aware of [its] commitment *and are involved in the achievement of [its] policy objectives*" (emphasis added). One example of how this works in practice is the Responsible Care guidelines on the hiring of waste management contractors. These guidelines recommend that an examination of contractors prior to their selection should consider not only the technical adequacy of the facility but also a number of other specific points, including the reputation of the operating company, the competence of its employees and managers, its relationship with waste disposal and water authorities, its financial soundness, and whether it has insurance coverage.[15] Drawing on a CIA study of current auditing practices among member companies, guidelines have also been published on conducting safety audits of road haulage contractors and on the responsible use of landfill. Similar measures have already become standard practice in many firms, and in addition to statutory controls, their widespread diffusion creates a further pressure on contractors to maintain high standards of operation and management. Work is now in hand to produce a set of product stewardship guidelines that will incorporate the best practices being developed within the industry. (See Chapter 12 for a study of developments in product stewardship in the United States.)

These developments illustrate the move to institutionalize as standard industry practice risk management techniques that have been developed by individual companies to reduce interface risks. Thus the self-regulatory controls promoted by Responsible Care formalize informal practices of this kind, promote their diffusion and adoption, and thus extend the network of mutual regulation. As social expectations grow to demand ever higher standards of environmental performance, firms are only able to ensure that these expectations are met by increased levels of surveillance and control. In an important sense, this is a means of controlling uncertainty and its associated threats by reorganizing and extending the means of social control and mutual identity. These practices are being encouraged by the CIA not to add to the short-term profitability of the industry but as a longer-term investment in securing confidence and thereby reducing the uncertainties generated by antipathetic, unpredictable, and rapidly evolving public demands.

REGAINING SOCIETY'S TRUST

While it is too early to begin to assess the environmental benefits of Responsible Care in terms of improved industry performance, one can discern a number of issues that have implications for the underlying objective of regaining society's trust and therefore need to be addressed.

IDENTITY AND CULTURE

Perhaps the most immediate challenge, if the changes implemented by the CIA are to be more than merely symbolic gestures, is that of reconstructing the identity of the industry. This means not merely revamping its image to give it "green" credibility but transforming the industry's culture: changing how it sees itself, not just how others see it. The CIA's Responsible Care program has already taken some steps toward establishing the conditions for cultural change. First, there has been an important change in the structural relationship between the CIA and its members that recasts the role of the CIA by making compliance with its codes and guidance obligatory, although at present this still stops short of conceding disciplinary powers to the association. Second, enlisting the support of industry leaders and securing commitment from top executives in each company meet an important prerequisite for cultural change.[16] Finally, by constructing a collective identity under Responsible Care, the industry is also in a significant sense collectivizing its environmental responsibility, subsuming the efforts of its individual members, and creating a "community of fate" (Heimer 1985). Together with public statements of commitment and intent, this creates a powerful incentive for members to comply and for those companies that are making a considerable investment in their environmental performance to keep up the pressure on their peers to do likewise.

The CIA is attempting to engineer this change by embedding environmental concerns in every aspect of the industry's operations, from research and development to waste management. For example, the self-assessment questionnaires covering research and development and distribution, developed in addition to the original questionnaires for chief executive officers and site managers, are designed to provoke a more critical examination of the impact of a firm's activities and to instigate an iterative learning process. The total quality management philosophy of continual improvement that is being encouraged attempts to translate the results of this learning into new behavior patterns by scrutinizing all aspects of industry operations and by much more intensive and extensive monitoring of performance. However, these measures are directed at the surface culture of the industry; they do not question some of the underlying assumptions that characterize aspects of the industry's world view.

Fundamental to the identity of the chemicals sector is its sense of being a science-based industry. This is deeply ingrained in the industry's culture, and beliefs about the validity and authority of science frame its view of outside groups. These beliefs are reflected in the argument that has been made to legitimate the industry's claim to self-regulation—that its unmatched knowledge and expertise make the industry's own experts the people best suited to audit and regulate the environmental effects of its activities. The certainty of such knowledge has been brought into question by studies, such as those in the sociology of science, that highlight the uncertainties and indeterminacies of scientific and technical knowledge. Such studies also illustrate the relevance and validity of the local knowledge of those publics with whom the industry wishes to communicate.[17] As long as the industry remains convinced of the certainty of its knowledge and expertise and the inadequacy or irrelevance of those of outsiders, however, it will have difficulty overcoming both its own mistrust and that of its various publics.

Proof and Trust

Similarly, for all the improvements in standards of environmental management and in related learning processes that are being achieved, providing evidence in whatever quantity is unlikely to rebuild the trust that the industry seeks: "if evidence could solve the problem of trust, then trust would be no problem at all. . . . The point is that trust itself affects the evidence we are looking for. While it is never that difficult to find evidence of untrustworthy behavior, it is virtually impossible to prove its positive mirror image" (Gambetta 1988).

As Gambetta points out, this makes deep mistrust very difficult to invalidate through experience, either because it prevents people from engaging in appropriate forms of social experiment or because it results in behavior that reinforces the foundation of mistrust so that mistrust becomes self-fulfilling by generating a reality consistent with itself.[18]

As long as the Responsible Care program is founded on the premise that furnishing the public with evidence of its improvement will rebuild trust in the chemical industry, it is unlikely to achieve the recuperation of public confidence that the CIA is hoping for; societal expectations and demands will continue to outstrip the efforts of industry to anticipate and respond to them. Although it will result in continuing incremental improvements of one sort or another, Responsible Care, as presently conceived, does not address the underlying, and in a fundamental sense political, issues raised by the crisis of credibility with which the industry is faced.

CONCLUSION: PARTICIPATION AND SOCIAL LEARNING

This chapter has examined the evolution of the British chemical industry's Responsible Care program from 1987 to 1992. Responsible Care can be viewed as a form of symbolic action by the industry to address the declining confidence and disruption of trust that it faces in its relations with various publics and the crisis of legitimation to which this gives rise. The action taken entails various forms of institutional change. The discussion illustrated how the program, by encouraging the diffusion of new communication and control mechanisms, has simultaneously enhanced processes of industry learning and of mutual as well as self-regulation.

The institutional mechanisms being developed by the CIA to produce trust correspond broadly to those identified by Zucker (1986) and outlined earlier in the chapter: (1) firm-specific, and, in this case, industry-specific actions aimed at demonstrating the industry's commitment to conform to societal expectations; (2) regulatory mechanisms specifying operating standards and codes of practice, although their effectiveness is likely to be undermined by the lack of a clear sanctioning mechanism; and (3) the use of third-party intermediaries as a source of legitimation. This final mechanism has still to be developed, but a minimal version is likely to entail independent inspection and certification of members' Responsible Care programs to ISO 9000/BS 5750. Whether the CIA will go any further than this is not yet clear.

Perhaps the main conclusion suggested by the discussion so far is that the industry's attempt to bootstrap itself from its predicament is unlikely to achieve its long-term objective unless steps are taken to increase public involvement and accountability. Peer pressure may well be a positive mechanism for promoting responsiveness to environmental concerns within the industry, but seen from the outside, it is likely to confirm the opinion held by many that the scheme is simply another PR exercise. The different and often conflicting constructions of the problem with which the industry and its stakeholders are operating suggest that the challenge is not simply one of industry learning but of promoting a constructive form of social learning, one in which social understanding of the issues and the stakes is increased, rather than one in which learning is hampered by posturing and deception (Stone 1985).

It is important to clarify the use of the word *learning* as a metaphor for the process that is being advocated here. The rhetoric of organizational learning has been used in ways that lend themselves to a technocratic depoliticization of the process of change. In much of the literature on organizational learning, for example, political processes are frequently identified as obstacles to learning. What is being suggested here, however, is not a technocratic reduction but a fundamentally political conception of the learning process, one that captures many of the developments already described in relation to the development of Responsible Care: "Organizational learning is not a harmonious, conflict-free process of accommodation to environmental change. It is a political process involving the resolution of conflicts within organizations, the renegotiation and redesign of the partnerships with their environing networks of publics, and the redistribution of power" (Metcalfe 1981, 526).

To achieve this reconstitution in the face of the consistently turbulent nature of the organizational environment to which the chemical industry is attempting to adapt, appropriate mediating mechanisms are needed to connect developments internal to the industry with public experience. Such mechanisms would undoubtedly entail greater involvement of outside interests in the industry's policy-making process. This would require open dialogue and active cooperation among industry and environmentalists, employee and citizen groups, and government to explore possible institutional mechanisms around which trust might be rebuilt. What is needed is a forum that involves these different interests in addressing the industry's environmental problems and that creates the conditions for a more open dialogue, a forum in which the standing of interlocutors is equalized and the roles of "expert" and "public" are recast into a more collaborative process of participatory expertise (Fischer 1990). To create such an institution would require a considerable extension of the tentative *glasnost* with which the chemical industry is currently experimenting. At the present time this seems utopian, but there are signs of openings in this direction if the industry's nerve holds and the involvement of stakeholder groups is not limited to an exercise in legitimation.

One practical form that this development might take, following Metcalfe (1978, 51), is to bring the different interests together within a "network organization" that constitutes an interpersonal model of the larger network of pluralistic relations:

As microcosms of the larger scale political forces, network organizations provide a mechanism for exploring the interconnections among problems as perceived by different interests and a context for thinking through ways of arriving at mutually acceptable solutions. Network organizations facilitate the emergence of a shared frame of reference and the means of dealing with areas of conflict, but do not presuppose an identity of views or complete consensus.

Given that the objectives of the Responsible Care program embrace both industry-wide policy making and improved performance and communication at the level of the individual firm, two possible loci for the development of network organizations are suggested. At the national level, the advisory committee that is already envisaged could be constituted as a multilateral forum within which problem definition and policy formation could benefit from a direct engagement with alternative perspectives. Similarly, at the local level, the Responsible Care cell or, for larger firms, the site liaison committee, might provide the basis for a complementary forum that would foster simultaneously an improved learning capacity at the level of the individual organization, greater accountability to local publics, and a consequently enhanced legitimacy for the industry's activities.

The possibility that such an extension of Responsible Care might result in an effective relegitimation of the industry's activities does, however, raise one very considerable concern: if the program is successful in achieving its objective and reestablishes public trust, will it not remove what we have argued to be a significant pressure on firms to improve their performance?[19] This is a genuine dilemma and one that is impossible simply to dismiss given the virtual inevitability of unanticipated consequences arising from any intervention in a complex system of relations. There are, nevertheless, reasons for suggesting that an abatement in public pressure and a relaxation of effort by the industry would not ensue.

First, the point made earlier about public mistrust was that it was not simply mistrust of the industry but also of the institutions responsible for monitoring and regulating it. Any trust rebuilt on the basis of new institutional arrangements would only persist if those arrangements were themselves perceived to be effective and trustworthy. Any assumption that the public would readily concede trust to a legitimating façade seems unwarranted in light of some of the studies of public risk perception referred to earlier. The mechanisms would be reinforced by the wider public scrutiny made possible by an increasing availability of environmental data in many of the countries where Responsible Care programs are being instituted.

There is a need to acknowledge the danger of oppositional voices being silenced through accommodation, but, nonetheless, institutionalization fixes concerns in societal memory in a way that prevents them from being readily forgotten. If it is reinforced by pressures that do not allow selective amnesia, whatever the inclinations of the actors involved, the institutional dynamic that is set in motion can be maintained (Paehlke and Torgerson 1990, 299).

Second, far from encouraging recidivism, mechanisms of the kind proposed would help to ensure the long-term persistence of a culture of openness by institutionalizing new patterns of relations and communicative norms.[20] The problem is rather one of preventing the inflexibility and reduced learning capacity that can result from a rigid system of controls. Finally, then, the type of arrangements outlined here aims to stimulate not simply problem-solving but also problem-setting capacities, which are vital for adaptive flexibility, by facilitating the encounter of a plurality of perspectives.

These arguments do not eliminate concerns about the possibility of new institutional arrangements being open to manipulation, but they do offer reasons for believing that, rather than eliminating an important motivation for improved industry performance, they may constitute a means for ensuring a long-term proactive approach to environmental problems by the industry.

There is now a recognized need to enlist the cooperation of all sectors of society in addressing the complex problems posed by environmental change.[21] The greatest obstacle will be the mutual mistrust with which the chemical industry and some of its publics view one another—it has been observed that trust has to be built in both directions. Nevertheless, as Gambetta has suggested, even in the absence of "thick" trust, it may be rational to trust, to act *as if* one trusted. Unlike other commodities, trust can increase through use, and acting as if trust existed—that is, conceding trust—may actually generate the behavior that seems to be its precondition (Gambetta 1988).

To be sure, Responsible Care has been developed by the chemical industry as a strategy for reducing uncertainty in the face of unpredictable or destabilizing actions by other interests. The CIA is a strategic actor whose primary motivation is to protect and further the interests of its members. Nevertheless, as Rip reminds us, this inevitable strategizing can put into motion processes that create points of leverage and opportunities for change. To realize the opportunities created by these developments, however, the perspective within which they are framed needs to be broadened to embrace societal processes (Rip 1986). In the case of Responsible

Care, the effort to develop an institutional framework for the production of trust is pushing the chemical industry in the direction of greater responsiveness and social accountability in its management of environmental risks and in setting standards of performance. The industry has already demonstrated a capacity to experiment and innovate in its search for an effective response. With these industry-level developments set in the broader context of social and political processes, the challenge facing industry, policy makers, and researchers is to cooperate in exploring the opportunities that they engender for building institutions that increase participation in the policy-making process and improve the capacity for social learning.

ACKNOWLEDGMENTS

The research upon which this chapter is based was funded under the Countryside Change, Risk and Pollution program of the British Economic and Social Research Council, grant number W104251001. The authors would also like to acknowledge the helpful comments received from Kurt Fischer and Johan Schot and from Theo de Bruin on an earlier draft.

NOTES

1. Frank Whiteley, deputy chairman of ICI plc, Statement by the President, Chemical Industries Association, *Annual Report and Accounts 1989,* 5 (emphasis added).

2. On the associational structure of the British chemical industry and the CIA's role, see Grant (1983).

3. Quoted in Grant (1983, 21–22).

4. Robert Horton, managing director of British Petroleum, Statement by the President, Chemical Industries Association, *Annual Report and Accounts 1984,* 4.

5. For a review of developments around the world, see the special July 17, 1991, issue of *Chemical Week*, which is devoted to Responsible Care.

6. At the Greening of Industry Conference held in Noordwijk aan Zee, the Netherlands, November 17–19, 1991, Yiorgos Mylonadis presented a case study, "Environmental Concerns as a Source of Organizational Learning," that illustrates how environmental concerns can result in organizational learning.

7. Some skepticism was expressed during interviews by contacts in the industry about who benefited most from the disclosure requirements of SARA Title III. It was reported that the majority of requests for information had come not from community groups but from other, presumably competing, firms.

8. This proposal appears in the Fifth Action Program on the Environment (Commission of the European Communities 1992, 67).

9. Proceedings of the First Responsible Care Seminar, Chemical Industries Association, London, October 27, 1989.

10. R. J. Grainger, director, Product and Regulatory Affairs, CIA Responsible Care Seminar, London, June 20, 1990 (emphasis added).

11. This argument is developed in relation to the public understanding of science in Wynne (1992).

12. A study of corporate responses to SARA Title III can be found in Baram, Dillon, and Ruffle (1990).

13. For example, toxic waste incineration specialist Rechem International, now part of the Shanks and McEwan Group, responded to deepening public mistrust concerning its operations by appointing a former Friends of the Earth campaigner to its board of directors.

14. On this view of risk and culture, see Holzner and Marx (1979) and Beck (1992).

15. The imposition of a Duty of Care on waste producers under the Environmental Protection Act of 1990 and the attendant criminal sanctions have created a powerful incentive for increased monitoring of waste management contractors, particularly as the onus seems to be on the contracting parties to ensure compliance.

16. On the importance of leadership commitment in processes of organizational change, see Schein (1985). The enthusiasm of chief executive officers does not, of course, guarantee change. For this, the active involvement of the entire work force is needed, a point of which the CIA is well aware.

17. See, for example, Wynne (1989).

18. A similar point is made by Metcalfe (1978), whose description of how the resulting vicious circle can lead to a downward spiral of deepening mistrust captures precisely the situation in which the chemical industry finds itself.

19. The authors are grateful to Theo de Bruin for raising this question.

20. On the importance of institutionalization for cultural persistence, see Zucker (1977).

21. Shared responsibility is a central theme in the CEC's Fifth Action Program on the Environment, due to take effect in 1993, which calls for greater cooperation between industry and other interests (Commission of the European Communities 1992).

REFERENCES

Baram, Michael; Dillon, Patricia S; and Ruffle, Betsy. 1990. *Managing Chemical Risks: Corporate Responses to SARA Title III*. Medford, Mass.: Center for Environmental Management, Tufts University.

Beck, Ulrich. 1992. *The Risk Society: Towards a New Modernity*. London: Routledge. (Originally published as *Risikogesellschaft: Auf dem Weg in eine andere Moderne*. Frankfurt: Surkamp, 1986.)

Braithwaite, John, and Fisse, Brent. 1987. "Self-Regulation and the Control of

Corporate Crime." In *Private Policing*, edited by Clifford D. Shearing and Philip C. Stenning, 221–46. Beverly Hills: SAGE.

Commission of the European Communities (CEC). 1992. *Towards Sustainability. A European Community Program of Policy and Action in Relation to the Environment and Sustainable Development*. COM(92) 23 final, vol. II. Brussels: CEC.

Council Directive. 1982. "Council Directive of 24 June, 1982, on the Major Accident Hazards of Certain Industrial Activities." 82/501/EEC. *Official Journal of the European Communities*, L230, vol. 25, August 5, 1982.

ENDS Report. 1991. "A New Phase for Responsible Care." *ENDS Report*, no. 194, 16–18.

Fischer, Frank. 1990. *Technocracy and the Politics of Expertise*. Newbury Park: SAGE.

Gambetta, Diego. 1988. "Can We Trust Trust?" In *Trust: Making and Breaking Cooperative Relations*, edited by Diego Gambetta, 213–38. Oxford: Blackwell.

Granovetter, Mark. 1985. "Economic Action and Social Structure: The Problem of Embeddedness." *American Journal of Sociology* 91: 481–510.

Grant, Wyn. 1983. *The Organization of Business Interests in the U.K. Chemical Industry*. International Institute of Management/Labor Market Policy Discussion Paper (IIM/LMP) 83-3. Berlin: WZB.

Heimer, Carol. 1985. *Reactive Risk and Rational Action: Managing Moral Hazard in Insurance Contracts*. Berkeley: University of California Press.

Holzner, Burkart, and Marx, John H. 1979. *Knowledge Application: The Knowledge System in Society*. Boston: Allyn and Bacon.

Kelly, Patricia C. 1991. "Factors That Influence the Development of Trade Associations' Political Behaviours." In *Research in Corporate Social Performance and Policy*, edited by William C. Frederick and Lee E. Preston, 12: 93–142. Greenwich, Conn.: JAI Press.

Luhmann, Niklas. 1979. *Trust and Power*. New York: John Wiley.

Metcalfe, Les. 1981. "Designing Precarious Partnerships." In *Handbook of Organizational Design, Vol. 1: Adapting Organizations to Their Environment*, edited by Paul C. Nystrom and William H. Starbuck, 503–30. Oxford: Oxford University Press.

Metcalfe, Les. 1978. "Policy Making in Turbulent Environments." In *Interorganizational Policy Making: Limits to Coordination and Central Control*, edited by Kenneth Hanf and Fritz W. Scharpf, 37–55. Beverly Hills: SAGE.

Nelson, Richard R., and Winter, Sidney G. 1982. *An Evolutionary Theory of Economic Change*. Cambridge, Mass.: The Belknap Press of Harvard University Press.

North, Douglass C. 1990. *Institutions, Institutional Change and Economic Performance*. Cambridge: Cambridge University Press.

Paehlke, Robert, and Torgerson, Douglas. 1990. "Environmental Politics and the Administrative State." In *Managing Leviathan: Environmental Politics and the Administrative State*, edited by Robert Paehlke and Douglas Torgerson, 285–99. Ontario: Broadview Press.

Posner, Tamar. 1989. "Liability Insurance and the Chemical Industry." *Chemistry & Industry*, September 4, 560–62.

Rip, Arie. 1986. "Societal Processes of Technology Assessment." In *Impact Assessment Today*, edited by H. A. Becker and A. L. Porter, vol. 1, 415–33. Utrecht: Uitgeverij Jan van Arkel.

Schein, Edgar H. 1985. *Organizational Culture and Leadership*. San Francisco: Jossey-Bass.

Shapiro, Susan P. 1987. "The Social Control of Impersonal Trust." *American Journal of Sociology* 93: 623–58.

Stone, Clarence N. 1985. "Efficiency versus Social Learning: A Reconsideration of the Implementation Process." *Policy Studies Review* 4: 484–96.

Wynne, Brian. 1987. "Risk Perception, Decision Analysis and the Public Acceptance Problem." In *Risk Assessment and Hazardous Waste Management: Implementation and the Dialectics of Credibility*, edited by Brian Wynne. New York: Springer-Verlag.

Wynne, Brian. 1989. "Sheepfarming after Chernobyl. A Case Study in Communicating Scientific Information." *Environment* 31: 10–15, 33–39.

Wynne, Brian. 1990. "Major Hazard Communication: Defining the Challenge for Research and Practice." In *Communicating with the Public About Major Industrial Accident Hazards*, edited by H. B. F. Gow and H. J. Otway, 599–612. London: Elsevier.

Wynne, Brian. 1992. "Public Understanding of Science Research: New Horizons or Hall of Mirrors?" *Public Understanding of Science* 1: 37–43.

Zald, Mayer. 1978. "The Social Control of Industries." *Social Forces* 57: 79–102.

Zucker, Lynne G. 1986. "Production of Trust: Institutional Sources of Economic Structure, 1840–1920." *Research in Organizational Behavior* 8: 53–111.

Zucker, Lynne G. 1977. "The Role of Institutionalization in Cultural Persistence." *American Sociological Review* 42: 726–43.

8

Corporate Management of
Chemical Accident Risks

Michael S. Baram and Patricia S. Dillon

Chemical accidents at industrial facilities plague modern society despite the intensification of corporate safety efforts and government regulation following the 1984 Bhopal tragedy. These accidents, which range from minor spills to major explosions and releases of toxic chemicals, contaminate natural resources, disrupt communities, and frequently destroy the lives of workers and community residents. They also destroy corporate property and impair productivity.

Recent studies have sought to discern why chemical accidents occur and what further steps should be taken to reduce their incidence and magnitude and mitigate their consequences. These studies have found that traditional approaches to corporate safety, which focus on reducing human error and equipment failure, are insufficient because they do not address accident "preconditions," the deeper causes of chemical accidents that are imbedded in facility design, business decisions, and management systems.

Because of these findings and growing public concern, the 1990 Clean Air Act Amendments (CAAA) mandate that two federal agencies develop regulations that will require corporate management to carry out comprehensive safety audits for estimating accident hazards, risk management plans for delineating and performing corrective actions, and emergency plans for mitigating accident consequences. The law also requires that the agencies evaluate the corporate studies and plans, intervene when they are inadequate, and make the plans available to the public.

In addition, the federal government has launched a vigorous program for criminal prosecution of companies and their officials who violate federal laws. Fear of criminal prosecution and imprisonment has made top corporate officials and plant managers much more vigilant about compliance with federal laws.

These and other developments have prompted firms that make or use toxic chemicals, and their trade associations, to develop new private codes of conduct and voluntary standards. The codes are designed to structure corporate initiatives and promote the changes in organizational culture and behavior that are needed to assure continuing progress in accident prevention. To rectify weaknesses in earlier efforts at corporate self-regulation, the new codes also provide for self-evaluation and private enforcement.

This chapter discusses what has been learned about chemical accidents and examines the new approaches being taken in the United States by regulators, prosecutors, and companies to address deficiencies in safety management. Particular attention is given to new federal regulations that make corporate risk management more "transparent" and vulnerable to public pressure and to the new codes of conduct now being implemented.

CHEMICAL ACCIDENTS

The incidence of chemical accidents at industrial facilities in the United States is alarming. An Environmental Protection Agency (EPA) data base of "acute hazardous events" recorded 10,933 chemical accidents in the 1980s, based on an incomplete survey of media reports and other sources, and New York State has independently reported more than 2000 chemical accidents between 1983 and 1988. Thirty major accidents at petrochemical facilities in 1989 have been investigated by the Occupational Safety and Health Administration (OSHA), and reports by insurance companies further verify the high incidence of chemical accidents.[1]

Most accidents (36 percent) occurred at "primary production facilities" in the chemical and petroleum product sectors of American industry, according to the EPA's data base. Accidents also occurred at "secondary producer" facilities (13.9 percent), "end user" facilities (11.3 percent), and distributor facilities (7.4 percent). At these facilities, high-volume, industrial commodity chemicals were the class of chemicals most frequently released in accidents, with sulfuric acid, chlorine, anhydrous ammonia, and hydrochloric acid at the top of the list.[2]

Accidents include spills, vapor cloud releases, fires, and explosions. Although spills were most common (68.9 percent), vapor cloud releases most frequently caused evacuations (>75 percent) and deaths or injuries (>60 percent), and the smaller number of fires and explosions caused most deaths (85 percent) and injuries (35 percent). Under certain conditions, accidents have had catastrophic effects, as the international examples in Table 8.1 indicate.[3]

Accidental releases of toxic chemicals also cause chronic diseases and contamination of natural resources. There is no data base for such long-term effects, and one would be difficult to develop. However, studies of recent spills at a Basel, Switzerland, chemical plant and a Pennsylvania oil storage facility, and the 1976 release of a dioxin vapor cloud at a chemical plant in Seveso, Italy, clearly indicate that such releases contaminate rivers, drinking water, soil, livestock, and other property, and cause evacuations and hospitalizations.[4]

Extensive studies have been conducted to determine the causes of chemical accidents at industrial facilities, and various findings have been made by government agencies, company personnel, unions, and consultants.

TABLE 8.1
CATASTROPHIC INDUSTRIAL ACCIDENTS

ACCIDENT	EFFECTS
1947 ship explosion in Texas City Harbor	561 deaths, 3000 injuries, and destruction of one-third of city
1974 cyclohexane release in Flixborough, Great Britain	28 deaths, 89 injuries, and 2000 homes damaged
1975 propylene explosion in Beek, the Netherlands	14 deaths and 107 injuries
1984 gas pipeline explosion in Brazil	508 deaths and widespread destruction from fires
1984 liquid gas explosion in Mexico City, Mexico	550 deaths, 2000 injuries, and 350,000 homeless
1984 methyl isocyanate gas leak in Bhopal, India	2500 deaths and 200,000 injuries

For example, OSHA investigations of petrochemical facility accidents in 1989 found six major contributing factors: inadequate worker training, inadequate engineering controls, insufficient management supervision, improper tools and equipment, inadequate emergency response programs, and inadequate personal protective equipment. An insurance broker's study of 150 accidents in the "hydrocarbon-chemical industries" found that mechanical failure accounted for 41 percent of the accidents, operational error for 19 percent, process upset for 10 percent, natural hazard for 5 percent, and design error and sabotage for 4 percent each.[5]

But other experts have concluded that "business decisions" are a major causal factor of petrochemical accidents—for example, cost-cutting that seeks to "downsize" regular staff and increase company reliance on less costly contract workers, part-time workers who often lack the skills, training, and responsibility of regular employees. Regular employees cost more in terms of salaries, training, medical benefits, and pension programs and cannot be readily terminated during slack business periods. Management decisions to meet increased market demand by operating facilities at or beyond maximum capacity levels, and management inattention to safety hazards during plant start-up and shutdown, or allowing "on-line maintenance" to avoid process shutdown, are also implicated in the new studies.[6]

Recent evaluations have also gone beyond traditional findings that human error or equipment failure are the causes of accidents by pointing to other fundamental causes in many cases. These deeper causes are characterized as "accident preconditions" in that they establish a plant's ripeness for an accident. The preconditions include rigid plant design that does not sufficiently accommodate minor or foreseeable variations in employee behavior, and management overreliance on having employees follow safety rules without attentiveness to "precursors" that indicate accident potential, such as breakdowns in the water pressure needed to cool a process or to suppress a fire.[7]

The causes of chemical accidents fall into four broad categories: technical inadequacy, human error, business stressors, and management systems that fail to improve organizational behavior. Thus, corrective measures must be redirected to cognizant corporate officers and facility managers who have the authority and opportunity to prevent the causal conditions.

GOVERNMENT REGULATION

Companies that make, store, or use hazardous chemicals in the United States are subject to numerous regulations for preventing accidents and protecting workers, community residents, and the environment. Many of these regulations were enacted by state and local authorities in keeping with their traditional function of protecting the public from fires, accidents, and other threats to community safety. Today, state and local fire, safety, building code, land use, and public health officials have sufficient authority to identify and correct virtually all chemical accident risks. However, their performance varies from state to state and is generally considered inadequate for chemical process safety due to their lack of financial and technical resources, lack of expertise and information from industry, and lack of public interest or pressure until a major accident occurs.

The inadequacy of local controls and the shock of the Bhopal accident in 1984 prompted Congress to establish more effective regulatory programs at the local level and create new federal-level regulatory functions as well. In 1986, it enacted the Emergency Planning and Community Right to Know Act (EPCRA) to be administered by the EPA. EPCRA does not impose technical standards for equipment, facility design, processes, or safety, but requires firms that make, store, or use hazardous chemicals to report information on the chemicals to local emergency planning committees (LEPCs), for the purpose of having the LEPCs use the information provided by companies to develop various safety measures and emergency response plans that would be followed in the event of a facility accident. Virtually all the information provided by companies to LEPCs is publicly available on request, as are the response plans.[8]

This federal initiative, primarily directed at emergency response planning, has had mixed results. It has brought about greater awareness of facility accident risks by local officials and the development of emergency plans. However, performance varies over fifty states and more than 3000 LEPC jurisdictions. It has promoted greater community awareness of chemical accident risks and stimulated pressures on local officials and facility managers to improve safety. However, public awareness and action-forcing activities remain much lower than many had anticipated. It has forced company officials to compile data and reports and thereby stimulated greater management attention to chemical risks, particularly since the reports are publicly available and may stimulate public pressures. However, many firms have failed to comply with the report requirements, and of those that have complied, many have not taken steps to reduce accident risks. Smaller firms, in particular, have high rates of noncompliance and provide little evidence of accident risk reduction.[9]

Given these mixed results in LEPC and corporate performance, and the continuation of chemical accidents following the enactment of EPCRA, Congress took further steps in its enactment of the CAAA in 1990. The

CAAA contains an extensive agenda of measures for improving facility safety, to be administered by the EPA and OSHA, in addition to the continuation of EPCRA requirements.[10] This agenda is now being implemented with the development of new regulations by the EPA and OSHA, and assessment of its practical effects will not be possible for several years.

The CAAA agenda establishes that companies have the "general duty" of ensuring safe operations at facilities that make, store, or use hazardous chemicals and requires the EPA to designate the chemicals of concern and enforce this general duty. The ambiguity of the general duty requirement means that each company can be held accountable for *any* recognized risk factors at a specific facility by EPA and, in addition, must comply with technical standards applicable to its facilities. The EPA is authorized to enact technical regulations and guidances to prevent accidental releases into the ambient air, which will "cover the use, operation, repair, replacement and maintenance of equipment to monitor, detect, inspect and control releases." But the deepest reforms are expected to come from CAAA requirements that each facility conduct a comprehensive safety audit and "hazard assessment," develop a "risk management plan" (RMP) for review by the EPA, state and local agencies, and the public, and take necessary corrective measures under the RMP to improve facility safety and prevent accidental releases. Unless a firm follows this procedure to EPA satisfaction, the facility will not be permitted to operate.[11]

By requiring public access to corporate RMPs, Congress has made further use of the right-to-know approach to increase corporate transparency and public demands for safety far beyond EPCRA's accomplishments. EPCRA requires the disclosure of abstract information about chemical hazards and data on releases. But the CAAA now requires corporate disclosure of foreseeable risk scenarios and the measures needed to prevent them, and this RMP information is likely to have a greater effect on public perceptions of facility safety and corporate credibility.

The CAAA also retains and reinforces a parallel safety effort by OSHA. Since enactment of the Occupational Safety and Health Act in 1970,[12] OSHA has inspected facilities, enforced a general duty for companies to protect worker health and safety, and enacted and enforced numerous technical standards. In 1985, it promulgated a "worker right to know" standard to assure that workers are informed and educated about the hazardous chemicals to which they are exposed.[13] OSHA has intensified its process safety efforts in recent years because of major accidents at petrochemical facilities that have killed and injured numerous workers and has developed a "special emphasis" program for inspecting petrochemical plants. It also published a proposed "process safety" regulation with the intention to enact the final rule in late 1991.[14]

Congress, in enacting the CAAA in 1990, affirmed this OSHA initiative on process safety and mandated that the agency issue its process safety rule by November 15, 1991.[15] The rule will require employers to conduct "workplace hazard assessments" to identify conditions that have the potential to cause accidental releases at each facility subject to the rule and to thereafter develop and implement accident prevention plans. The plans are to involve operating procedures, employee training, emergency response measures, maintenance and inspection of equipment, investigation of accidents and "near misses," and other measures.[16]

Thus, EPA and OSHA regulatory responsibilities for preventing chemical accidents overlap considerably and will require close coordination. The agencies have therefore agreed to conduct joint inspections, data exchange, coordinated training, and enforcement. This new federal involvement in how industry manages safety is superimposed on an extensive array of state and local activities. Nevertheless, it is clear that industry remains ultimately responsible for identifying and correcting accident risk factors and for developing more vigilant management systems.

CORPORATE INITIATIVES

Accident prevention is a traditional corporate management function necessitated by concern for public safety, community relations, and the protection of valuable corporate facilities. For most firms, it has been viewed as a function to be carried out by the manager of each facility within the annual budget provided by corporate headquarters. But facility managers also have other concerns, such as improving productivity, reducing costs, and improving profitability, and they are often evaluated for their short-term performance on these matters (e.g., every six or twelve months). Obviously, the economic concerns can become dominant and suppress improvements in accident prevention that may be costly or impair productivity.

As facilities have become larger and more complex and make, store, or use a wide variety of chemicals, accident prevention has become a more demanding task requiring sophisticated management and the coordinated use of several types of expertise (e.g., design, engineering, health, and environmental specialists, and highly trained workers). This message was vividly brought to industry by the Bhopal tragedy in December 1984 and has been repeated in a series of major accidents at chemical and petroleum facilities in recent years.

Bhopal revived corporate concern about safety and stimulated many large chemical manufacturers, in particular, to take new voluntary actions immediately to improve facility safety and strengthen emergency response. Top corporate officials required facility managers to thoroughly assess accident hazards and propose corrective measures and related budgets. New teams were formed at such firms to carry out these tasks, develop management incentives and training programs, and facilitate financing. These voluntary activities were reinforced and expanded by the 1986 enactment of EPCRA, which required facilities to disclose chemical information to local officials and authorized public access to the information. The disclosures exposed chemical hazards to the public and local officials and increased the likelihood of controversies, thus providing further impetus for corporate voluntary initiatives.

A study by researchers at the Center for Environmental Management at Tufts University examined eight companies that make, process, or use hazardous chemicals to determine whether EPCRA was stimulating voluntary initiatives by these firms to reduce accidental and routine releases of the chemicals. The report, published in 1991, provides detailed case studies of each firm and the overall findings.[17]

The study found numerous interactions between "upstream" chemical producers and their "downstream" industrial customers (both secondary producers and end users) to foster improvements in managing chemical risks throughout the commercial life cycle of each chemical.

The study focused on firms making and using three industrial chemicals with different life cycle characteristics—chlorine as a bulk commodity chemical widely used in many sectors of industry and implicated in numerous accidents; vinyl chloride as a notorious toxic chemical often "captively" used within the chemical industry; and arsine as a highly hazardous gaseous form of arsenic used in small quantities in the high-tech semiconductor industry.

Among its conclusions, the study found that recent company initiatives to reduce the occurrence, magnitude, and impact on the community of an accidental release of chemicals fall into the following categories:

- Safety audits of facility operations and the initiation of more stringent, periodic assessments of plant activities.
- Improvements in chemical inventory management, including storage volume reductions and technical improvements to storage facilities.

- Changes in process technology, including hazardous material substitutions and technical improvements.
- Enhancement of monitoring systems to detect accidental releases.
- Establishment of accident reporting and internal accident evaluation procedures.
- Increased emphasis by chemical producers on providing risk information and technical assistance to downstream customers and advising and consulting on safety procedures for customers.

In addition to these private-sector initiatives, communities hosting company facilities were found to have mounted efforts to further protect their citizens by requiring additional information disclosures from the companies and were restricting company activities to designated areas and pressuring companies to improve chemical-handling practices.

The company initiatives were found to be diverse and shaped by corporate culture and resources as well as by the unique set of risk characteristics posed by the chemical and the facility—for example, toxicity, process, and potential release characteristics; worker exposure history; population density and community exposure potential; and community-company relationships. However, the larger firms had developed generic or corporate-wide policies for risk evaluation and safety improvement that were being applied at all their facilities. Enactment of the CAAA and forthcoming regulations by the EPA and OSHA, discussed earlier, reinforce these developments at the firms studied and will undoubtedly promote similar activities at other firms.

Bhopal and EPCRA have also stimulated collaborative efforts by major producers of chemical and petroleum products and by professional associations. Four months after Bhopal, the Center for Chemical Process Safety was formed by the American Institute of Chemical Engineers, with industrial support. It has since carried out technical studies and training programs for facility personnel, published guidances on process safety and hazard evaluation, and sought to transfer safety expertise to smaller companies.[18]

CODES OF CONDUCT

The most important private-sector activities thus far have been conducted by the major trade associations, the Chemical Manufacturers Association (CMA) and the American Petroleum Institute. The CMA has enacted a code of conduct for its 180 member firms entitled Responsible Care and consisting of ten "guiding principles." All CMA members have pledged to follow these principles as a condition for retaining their CMA membership. The principles emphasize company "outreach" (e.g., to "respond to community concerns"); to promptly report risk information to officials, employees, customers, and the public; and to counsel customers on the safe use of chemical products.[19]

The CMA is now preparing detailed guidances for member firms in the form of Codes of Management Practice and training programs and manuals for use by facility managers, marketing personnel, and other company officials. Two of the codes apply directly to accident prevention: Community Awareness and Emergency Response (CAER) and Process Safety. Each code also contains a self-evaluation form to be completed by each firm and submitted to the CMA for evaluation of progress. These are intended to measure company performance and provide the CMA with information to report to agencies and the public in order to convince the public of the seriousness of Responsible Care and CMA credibility as a self-regulator. According to the CMA, the codes are intended to "cause each company to stretch to continually improve performance."

The Community Awareness and Emergency Response code requires communication and dialogue between facility managers, employees, and community residents on chemical risk concerns, development and rehearsals of emergency response plans, and the sharing of information and experience. CMA training programs are now being conducted for facility managers, and member firms are revising their corporate policies to comply with this code.[20] The more extensive Process Safety code and supplemental manuals are "designed to prevent fires, explosions and accidental chemical releases."[21] Each member company is expected to follow detailed guidances on "management, technology, facilities and personnel" to improve process safety on a continuing basis.

Both codes are now being evaluated as potential models for adoption in other industrial sectors, and the National Association of Chemical Distributors, with several hundred firms as its members, has announced plans to promulgate a code consistent with the CMA's.[22] The American Petroleum Institute has also published a guidance for the management of process hazards. This private code for firms in the oil and gas industry sets forth a management system and technical standards for addressing eleven aspects of process safety, including hazards analysis, facility modifications, and employee training, for example. It is intended for application at member facilities where chlorine, ammonia, hydrogen sulfide, and hydrogen fluoride are used and where there is "potential to release 5 tons of gas or vapor in a period of a few minutes."[23]

The development of private codes for improving process safety by individual companies and trade associations is encouraging. Private codes are public commitments, and chemical and oil firms, in particular, realize that performance must live up to promise if they are to gain public trust and the confidence of their workers, customers, investors, and insurers. Although not enforceable by regulatory agencies, such private codes are legally relevant and "indirectly enforceable." For example, regulators may compare a company's performance against its code to gauge the adequacy of its efforts to reduce risk and determine whether to carry out regulatory enforcement (e.g., penalties or corrective orders) or criminal prosecution.[24] In many instances, Congress and government agencies have adopted private codes as legal requirements, thereby making such codes directly enforceable by regulators.[25] A code can also be introduced as evidence in personal injury lawsuits against a company as a means of measuring company performance and determining if performance failed to meet the promised standard of care or industry "state of the art."[26] Thus, private codes have legal implications that make companies more vulnerable to regulation, liability, and public attitudes, and this serves as an incentive for company performance that is consistent with its code.[27]

COMPANY ACCOUNTABILITY

Companies that make or use toxic chemicals are now subject to externally imposed regulatory requirements and self-imposed private codes and voluntary standards for preventing accidents. However, they still retain much discretion. For example, how much progress to make? At what pace? At what price? How safe is safe enough? What should be spent for a safety audit? When is more safety too costly in highly competitive markets? Will smaller firms muster the resources needed? Will entrenched cultures and bureaucracies in firms be capable of addressing and rectifying organizational and management systems that produce accidents?

How company officials will use their discretion in pursuing facility safety is the critical issue. From a traditional legal perspective, proper use of company discretion will be motivated by fear of vigorous regulatory enforcement and criminal prosecution by government agents and by fear of liability, transaction costs, and other losses arising from civil actions (e.g., tort litigation) brought by persons who have suffered injury as a result of a chemical accident. From a traditional business perspective, proper use of company discretion will be motivated by fear of negative public attitudes and negative insurer and investor responses to facility accidents. Thus, legal and business "fear factors" can be expected to promote company progress toward accident prevention, particularly at this time of extensive media coverage and public skepticism of company behavior.

But other forces are now at work on company discretion. Many larger firms have decided to compete for market share, investor interest, and public trust on the basis of their environmental reputations and track records, as well as price and productivity. Their managers are being given new goals, including accident prevention, and are being trained in how to achieve them. Lawyers are now counseling these firms on the legal advantages to be gained from disclosing and sharing risk information and vigilantly managing facility safety. Insurers are beginning to price coverage on the basis of the quality of management systems for process safety.

Thus, the legal and economic fear factors are being transformed into business opportunities for gaining competitive advantage over the long term, a healthier stimulus for the use of company discretion to prevent chemical accidents. Recognizing this, the EPA, OSHA, and similar agencies in the European Community are beginning to offer diverse inducements for corporate voluntary action on the discretionary aspects of facility safety.

We are witnessing a complex evolutionary process for addressing the significant problem of chemical accidents in industrial society. New regulatory strategies and private codes of conduct are creating higher standards of corporate responsibility. The hope is that performance will measure up to promise.

NOTES

1. See Industrial Economics Inc., *Acute Hazardous Events Data Base;* Attorney General, State of New York, *New York Under a Cloud: The Need to Prevent Toxic Chemical Accidents;* and OSHA, *The Phillips 66 Company Houston Chemical Complex Explosion and Fire* (discussing OSHA investigations and insurance association studies).

2. Industrial Economics Inc., *Acute Hazardous Events Data Base.*

3. Accident data taken from John Gray Institute, *Managing Workplace Safety and Health: The Case of Contract Labor in the U.S. Petrochemical Industry* and from Otway, "Risk Communication Policies in the European Community: Background, Status and Trends."

4. See discussion of Seveso in Otway, "Risk Communication Policies in the European Community."

5. See review of findings on causal factors in Baram et al. *Non-Regulatory Strategies for Preventing, Detecting, and Correcting Accidental Releases of Hazardous Air Pollutants.*

6. Ibid. See, for example, Visser, *Development of Safety Management in Shell Exploration and Production*, paper presented to Workshop on Control of Safety, Bad Homburg, Germany, May 1991; and OECD, *Prevention of Accidents Involving Hazardous Substances: The Role of the Human Factor in Plant Operations*.

7. Ibid. See also OSHA, *The Phillips 66 Company*.

8. EPCRA was created by Title III of the Superfund Amendments of 1986, 42 USC 11000. Sections 304, 311, 312, and 313 require reports of accidental releases, chemicals on site and their amounts and locations, and an inventory of all releases each year. The inventory, which includes routine releases and fugitive emissions as well as accidental releases, is provided to the EPA, which includes the data in its annual *Toxic Release Inventory* for public review.

9. See Baram, *Risk Communication as a Regulatory Alternative for Protecting Health, Safety and the Environment*.

10. Public Law 101-549, Title III, amending section 112 of the Clean Air Act of 1970. See Environmental Protection Agency, *Fact Sheet: Chemical Accident Prevention and Clean Air Act Amendments of 1990*.

11. Other provisions authorize the EPA to enforce and penalize and to seek court orders to prevent company activities that pose "imminent or substantial endangerment" to public health or the environment; and establish an independent federal board to investigate and report on accidental releases that lead to a fatality or substantial property damage.

12. 29 U.S.C. Sec. 651.

13. See discussion of this standard in Baram, *Risk Communication as a Regulatory Alternative*.

14. See discussion in OSHA, *The Phillips 66 Company*.

15. The rule was subsequently enacted in February 1992.

16. Public Law 101-549, Sec. 304.

17. Baram, Dillon, and Ruffle, *Managing Chemical Risks: Corporate Response to SARA Title III*. SARA Title III is an alternative designation for EPCRA.

18. See *Annual Reports* of the Center for Chemical Process Safety, New York, N.Y.

19. Chemical Manufacturers Association, *Responsible Care: Guiding Principles and Summary Description*. Also see discussion of Responsible Care in the United Kingdom in chapter 7 of this volume.

20. Chemical Manufacturers Association, *Community Awareness and Emergency Response: Code of Management Practices*.

21. Chemical Manufacturers Association, *Process Safety: Code of Management Practices*.

22. Personal communication from National Association of Chemical Distributors, October 8, 1991. The European counterpart of the CMA is the CEFIC, based in Brussels. The CEFIC is now in the process of adopting Responsible Care for its European member firms. *CEFIC News*, no. 2, 1991.

23. American Petroleum Institute, *Recommended Practice 750: Management of Process Hazards*.

24. U.S. Department of Justice, *Factor in Decisions on Criminal Prosecutions for Environmental Violations in the Context of Significant Voluntary Compliance or Disclosure Efforts by the Violator.*

25. See discussion of private codes in Baram, *Alternatives to Regulation.*

26. A current example is provided by litigation between *Gellman Scientific, Inc. v. Dow.*

27. See Jack Doyle, *Hold the Applause!*, a critical review of DuPont, alleging that its environmental performance sharply contrasts with its policies and public relations.

REFERENCES

American Petroleum Institute. 1990. *Recommended Practice 750: Management of Process Hazards.* Washington, D.C.: API.

Baram, M. 1990. *Risk Communication as a Regulatory Alternative for Protecting Health, Safety and the Environment.* Report to the Administrative Conference of the United States.

Baram, M.; Dillon, P.; and Ruffle, B. 1992. *Managing Chemical Risks: Corporate Response to SARA Title III.* Chelsea, Mich.: Lewis Publishers.

Baram, M., and McAllister, K. 1982. *Alternatives to Regulation: Managing Risks to Health, Safety, and the Environment.* Lexington, Mass.: Lexington Books.

Baram M., and Partan, D., eds. 1990. *Corporate Disclosure of Environmental Risks: U.S. and European Law,* Stoneham, Mass.: Butterworth Legal Publishers.

Baram, M.; Stricoff, S.; and Ragusa, M. October 1991. *Non-Regulatory Strategies for Preventing, Detecting, and Correcting Accidental Releases of Hazardous Air Pollutants.* Report to the U.S. Environmental Protection Agency. Cambridge, Mass.: Arthur D. Little, Inc.

CEFIC News, no. 2, 1991.

Center for Chemical Process Safety, 1982. *Annual Reports.* New York: Center for Chemical Process Safety.

Chemical Manufacturers Association. 1991. *Community Awareness and Emergency Response: Code of Management Practices.* Washington, D.C.: CMA.

Chemical Manufacturers Association. 1991. *Process Safety: Code of Management Practices.* Washington, D.C.: CMA.

Chemical Manufacturers Association. 1991. *Responsible Care: Guiding Principles and Summary Description.* Washington, D.C.: CMA.

Doyle, J. 1991. *Hold the Applause! A Case Study of Corporate Environmentalism.* Washington, D.C.: Friends of the Earth.

Environmental Protection Agency. December 1990. *Fact Sheet: Chemical Accident Prevention and Clean Air Act Amendments of 1990,* Washington: EPA.

Industrial Economics Inc. 1989. *Acute Hazardous Events Data Base.* Report to EPA. Cambridge, Mass.: Industrial Economics Inc.

John Gray Institute. 1991. *Managing Workplace Safety and Health: The Case of*

Contract Labor in the U.S. Petrochemical Industry. Report to OSHA. Washington, D.C.: John Gray Institute.

New York State Attorney General. 1989. *New York Under a Cloud: The Need to Prevent Toxic Chemical Accidents*. Albany, N.Y.: New York State Attorney General's Office.

Occupational Safety and Health Administration. 1990. *The Phillips 66 Company Houston Chemical Complex Explosion and Fire*. Report to the President. Washington, D.C.: OSHA.

Organization for Economic Cooperation and Development. April 1991. *Prevention of Accidents Involving Hazardous Substances: The Role of the Human Factor in Plant Operations*. Tokyo Workshop report. Paris: OECD.

U.S. Department of Justice. July 1, 1991. *Factors in Decisions on Criminal Prosecutions for Environmental Violations in the Context of Significant Voluntary Compliance or Disclosure Efforts by the Violator*. Washington, D.C.: Department of Justice.

Visser, J. May 1991. *Development of Safety Management in Shell Exploration and Production*. Paper presented to Workshop on Control of Safety. Bad Homburg, Germany.

PART IV

❦

Effective Government Action

9

Toward a Tailor-made Process of Pollution Prevention and Cleaner Production: Results and Implications of the PRISMA Project

Hans Dieleman and Sybren de Hoo

Sustainable development has become a policy objective in many countries throughout the world. The concept of sustainable development is based on a system view of the world, in which the globe is portrayed as one large ecosystem. Within this ecosystem, the effects of all activities act on each other, change the balance of the system, and alter the specific combination of relations, influences, and interactions among the diverse subsystems. The globe is always in a certain state of equilibrium, and human activities should be organized according to the specific demands of the ecosystem and that equilibrium. An interesting aspect of the report *Our Common Future*, by the World Commission on Environment and Development (the Brundtland Commission) (WCED 1987), is that it not only focuses on the biosphere as a separate system, but expands the view by incorporating technology and human organization in one unified system. Through better management and the use of cleaner technologies, it may therefore be possible to maintain a certain level of prosperity without endangering the biosphere and the condition of future generations.

In many countries, the Brundtland report evoked a debate over the need for new policy instruments and new approaches to pollution prevention and the introduction of cleaner production processes (van Weenen 1990). In the Netherlands, the Brundtland report, together with the report *Concerns for Tomorrow* (Federal Institute for Public Health and Environmental

245

Hygiene [RIVM 1988]), a research document revealing the poor state of the environment in the Netherlands, initiated a broad national awareness of the environmental crisis. *Concerns for Tomorrow* clearly stated that fundamental changes in production, consumption, and transportation were needed and that reductions of 70 to 90 percent in emissions and waste flows would be necessary. Moreover, the document questioned the potential of end-of-pipe technology in achieving these goals.

Consequently, the Dutch government, in its National Environmental Policy Plan, initiated many new approaches and policy directions. For business and industry, the new policy directions are diverse and include the development of "structural source-oriented measurements," focusing on the development of entire new production processes; the introduction of an "integral chain approach," focusing on the handling of substances within an entire production chain; the introduction of "environmental care systems," focusing on the integration of the environment into business management; several product-oriented policies and the introduction of a "volume-oriented policy track," focusing on the possibilities for phasing out the use of certain substances or products, or even the existence of specific economic sectors. For this reason, one might conclude that the Dutch National Environmental Policy Plan is one of the most comprehensive policy plans ever made and can be regarded as one of the most advanced, or maybe even *the* most advanced, policy plan worldwide.

This said, however, the many new policy approaches that have been introduced and that primarily aim for pollution prevention, cleaner production processes, and cleaner products, are mostly still in the research and development phase. Usually, the development and testing of new technologies is regarded as a step that should precede their introduction in industry. As a result, the potentials of pollution prevention and waste minimization can only be fully explored in the years to come, once technologies are developed, tested, and available. Thus, to many governments, the switch to cleaner technologies, cleaner products, and cleaner production processes is necessarily a long-term approach.

At the same time, many case studies of pollution prevention have shown that reduction of waste and emissions can be realized immediately through the application of existing technologies, management tools, and control mechanisms. Especially in the United States, the birthplace of the concept of pollution prevention, many case studies show surprising results, with companies realizing reductions in specific waste flows of up to 90 percent within a very short time frame and with substantial financial savings (Huisingh et al. 1986). These studies show that pollution prevention is enormously appealing because it combines quick results in waste reduction with financial savings for the companies involved. Moreover, it challenges governments and existing environmental regulations, since it clearly shows the many possibilities for waste reduction that have not been realized with traditional pollution control strategies.

Against this background, in 1988 the Netherlands Organization for Technology Assessment (NOTA), together with the Erasmus Centre for Environmental Studies (ESM) at Erasmus University of Rotterdam and the Interfaculty Department of Environmental Sciences (IVAM) at the University of Amsterdam, launched a large-scale investigation into the prevention of waste and emissions in Dutch industrial companies. This project was given the name PRISMA (Project Industrial Successes with Waste Prevention).[1] The main question posed by the project was: Is it possible to develop a pollution prevention methodology or approach that can be repeated at various locations in the Netherlands? The PRISMA project and its implications for effective government policies that stimulate the greening of industry are described in this chapter.

GOALS AND TERMINOLOGY

The many case studies of pollution prevention in industries outside the Netherlands show that prevention can be practiced with success in industry and is often an appropriate starting point for a company's environmental policy. By practicing pollution prevention companies are able to:

- Reduce potential environmental risks.
- Show concern for health in general and the health and safety of the company's employees in particular.
- Become actively involved in environmental protection.
- Save money by reducing the cost of treating and/or removing waste and emissions as well as raw material and overall operating costs.

To find out whether these results could also be attained in Dutch industry, the PRISMA project was designed with the following research objectives:

1. To show that in Dutch industry, too, the prevention of waste and emissions is possible in the short term and offers benefits both to companies and to the environment.
2. To test the usefulness and efficiency of a systematic approach in order

to discover and implement possibilities for pollution prevention in companies.

3. To assess obstacles to the introduction of pollution prevention in companies and formulate conditions under which prevention can actually be given shape.
4. To formulate recommendations for an effective pollution prevention policy.

Since the terms *pollution prevention, waste minimization, source reduction*, and the like are often used in a multiinterpretable way, the central concepts used throughout the PRISMA project were first defined for purposes of clarity throughout the project. This terminology has been documented in the *Handleiding voor Preventie van Afval en Emissies*, a modified version of the U.S. Environmental Protection Agency's (EPA) *Waste Minimization Opportunity Assessment Manual*.

In the project, *prevention of waste and emissions* is a term that covers only categories 1 and 2 of the hierarchy of five action points for controlling emissions to land, water, and the atmosphere (Figure 9.1).

The working definition of *waste and emissions* is as follows: all solid, liquid, and gaseous substances introduced into the atmosphere, water, and land.

Under the terms of PRISMA, the following definition of *prevention* was developed: "The prevention of waste and emissions means preventing or limiting the creation of waste and emissions by a reduction at source, by onsite reuse and/or a reduction of the total harmfulness to the environment."

This definition differs from the interpretation given to the concept of prevention by certain Dutch government bodies. According to the PRISMA definition, off-site reuse does not come under the heading of prevention. On the other hand, the concepts of waste and emissions are broadly defined; in the context of PRISMA, the focus is on the prevention of both solid and chemical waste, and emissions into water, soil, and air, representing a multimedia approach.

The techniques used to achieve pollution prevention are shown in Figure 9.2.

As part of PRISMA, various experiments concerning the prevention of waste and emissions were conducted in ten Dutch companies. Companies in the Rotterdam and Amsterdam regions whose management was prepared to invest time and energy in the prevention experiment were approached. The companies selected were from the following branches of industry: food products (three companies); electroplating (two com-

FIGURE 9.1
HIERARCHY OF ACTION POINTS FOR ENVIRONMENTAL POLICY

<table>
<tr><td>

P
R
E
V
E
N
T
I
O
N

</td><td>

1 **Reduction at source:** minimization of the amount and/or harmfulness of waste and emissions at source by:
—change of product,
—changing the process technology and the process itself, including change in input of raw materials/additives.

2 **Internal recycling:** the recycling of waste products and emissions whereby these are
—recycled as the raw material in either the same or a different production process,
—processed with the intention of recovering material, or
—used for a different useful application.

</td></tr>
</table>

Also of importance in terms of controlling waste and emissions are:

3 **External recycling:** the recycling of waste and emissions outside the company, or as a (secondary) raw material or for the purpose of material recovery or another useful application.

4 **Incineration/treatment:** destruction, neutralization, detoxination, and immobilization of waste and emissions to less hazardous substances.

5 **Storage/dumping:** the dumping of waste products on land, making use of storage facilities, limiting leakage and the control of emission to surrounding areas.

---

panies); metal working (two companies); public transportation (two companies); and chemicals (one company).

METHODOLOGY

The above-mentioned terminology is the result of the first phase of the project, in which the development of a methodology for the study and the organization of the work was carried out. This methodology was based on the U.S. EPA's publication *Waste Minimization Opportunity Assessment Manual*. The outcome was the publication of the *Handleiding voor Preventie*

FIGURE 9.2.
TECHNIQUES FOR THE PREVENTION OF WASTE AND EMISSIONS

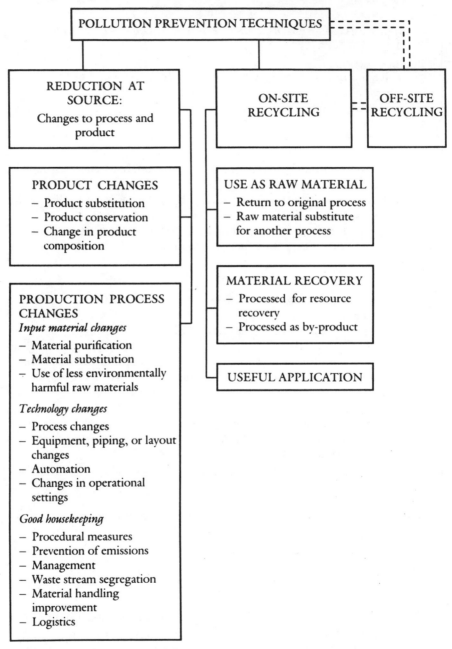

van Afval en Emissies in April 1990. The development and documentation of a methodology ensured that the work carried out in each of the companies would be more or less the same. The methodology was developed to be specific to the Dutch situation and was greatly improved upon throughout the course of the project. The major characteristics of the company approach are shown in Figure 9.3.

The PRISMA project manual offers a method of analyzing the flow of substances through and from a company and a procedure ("stages plan") for discovering and putting into practice possibilities for preventing waste and emissions on the basis of this analysis. The methods and procedure as described in the manual were tried out in ten companies and supervised by PRISMA researchers. Separate reports have been published on each of the companies.

The analysis of the flow of substances and the search for prevention options are embedded in the stages plan. The plan's four stages can be characterized as follows:

1. Planning and organization: the structure of the project, the motivation of those involved, the first inventory of bottlenecks and prevention possibilities, and the initial establishment of priorities.
2. Assessment: the analysis of substance flows and business activities, the appointment of teams to generate prevention options, and the first evaluation of the prevention possibilities that have been discovered.
3. Feasibility study: the technical and cost-effectiveness evaluation of the prevention options discovered.
4. Implementation: decision making concerning the necessary adaptations and investments, the application of preventive measures, the evaluation of results, and the establishment of a continuous prevention program.

In each of the ten companies this approach resulted in the establishment of a coherent package of prevention options. This result was achieved with a relatively limited input of time and effort on the part of managers, employees, and external researchers. The preliminary research required an average of ten person-days from the managers and employees, as well as approximately ten advisory days from the researchers. The assessment phase took twenty to sixty working days for the company, depending on the scale and complexity of the prevention options ascertained, and ten to fifteen advisory days for the researchers. The time needed for feasibility studies was more varied; particularly where large investments were involved, more time was needed.

FIGURE 9.3.
THE PRISMA COMPANY APPROACH. (FOR THE MOST PART, THIS IS COMPARABLE WITH U.S./EPA RECOMMENDATIONS.)

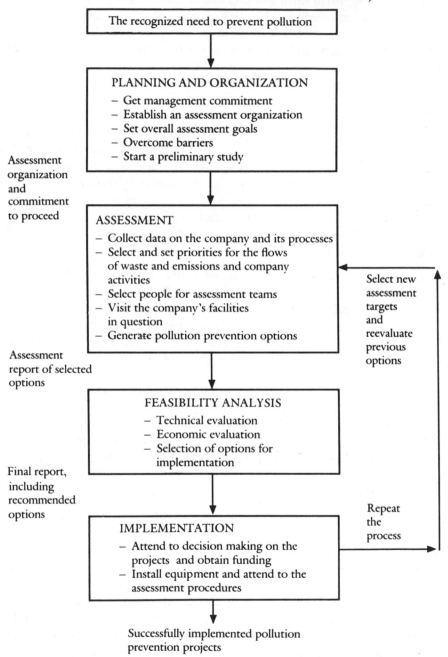

RESULTS

In each of the ten participating companies, the most potentially successful "areas of priority" activities that looked promising from the viewpoint of prevention were first selected. An area of priority might be a complete process, the use of certain raw and input materials, or a waste flow or emission. A total of thirty-five areas of priority were investigated in the ten companies. For each area a full analysis of the pollution load was conducted so that environmental effects in all "compartments" (water, soil, and air) were taken into account. Within the areas of priority a total of 164 "prevention options" (possibilities for preventing waste and emissions) were established. These included both minor changes in procedures and installations and drastic innovations in products or processes.

In 1991, at the end of the PRISMA project, the situation with regard to the 164 established options was as shown in Table 9.1.

In addition to the forty-five prevention options already implemented, another sixty-six options would, according to the researchers and company decision makers, be put into practice within eighteen months to three years following the conclusion of PRISMA. For ten of the options such extensive investments in equipment and research and development are needed that the implementation will take longer. For some other options it was not possible to ascertain the period within which they could be implemented. (See Table 9.2.)

Putting the prevention options into practice sometimes led to very substantial reductions in waste and emissions. Certain good-housekeeping measures effected 25 to 30 percent reductions in the use of chemicals. In a number of companies the introduction of technological changes achieved reductions in waste and emissions of 30 to 80 percent. Occasionally it was possible to eliminate a noxious waste flow completely. The use of alternative raw and input materials caused a 100 percent reduction in the emission of substances such as cyanide (in the zinc-plating process at electroplating companies) and solvents (for the degreasing of work items in garages and metal companies). (See Table 9.3.)

The cost-benefit analysis of those prevention options already executed yields a varying picture with a few extremely favorable peaks. With an investment of $1429, one company has saved approximately $137,143 per year. Another company has recouped an investment of nearly $457,143 within a year, saving altogether more than $500,000 per year.

Of the forty-five prevention options implemented, twenty have turned out to be cost-saving and nineteen cost-neutral. Thus, the great majority of

TABLE 9.1
OVERVIEW OF THE OPTIONS ACCORDING TO STAGE OF IMPLEMENTATION

COMPANIES	IMPLEMENTED	CONSIDERED FEASIBLE	FEASIBILITY STUDY STARTED	FEASIBILITY STUDY NOT YET STARTED	CONSIDERED UNFEASIBLE	TOTAL
B&S	6	4	0	0	8	18
Campina/Melkunie	8	2	0	2	2	14
Chromolux	4	3	1	4	9	21
DSM-resins	3	2	3	5	1	14
GVB	1	1	7	14	0	23
Heijchroom	4	1	6	1	0	12
Marvelo	6	0	4	4	0	14
Nestlé	4	3	1	2	2	12
RET	6	2	8	7	2	25
Stork	3	2	0	0	6	11
Total	45	20	30	39	30	164
Total		134				

TABLE 9.2
IMPLEMENTATION PERIOD OF THOSE OPTIONS CONSIDERED FEASIBLE

COMPANIES	<1.5 YEARS	1.5–3 YEARS	>3 YEARS	
B&S	6	4	0	
Campina/Melkunie	8	4	0	
Chromolux	4	6	2	
DSM-resins	3	7	2	
GVB	1	18	0	
Heijchroom	4	5	2	
Marvelo	6	7	0	
Nestlé	4	3	1	
RET	6	10	3	
Stork	3	2	0	
Total	45	66	10	Total = 121
Total		111		

these prevention options could be realized without financial problems. (See Table 9.4.)

It was found, moreover, that in many companies the preventive measures brought indirect benefits, such as an improvement in product quality. Many participating companies also appreciated the fact that thanks to PRISMA they are now more able to anticipate future changes in laws and regulations because they have a better view on their own production of waste and sources of waste flows. All ten companies have meanwhile completed plans for continuing the preventive activities. A few companies have already reserved financial resources for this purpose for the ensuing years.

These experiences show that preventive measures can yield significant results in both the short and the long term that will benefit the environment as well as the companies themselves. In more detail, the conclusions that can be drawn with respect to the first two of the project's four research objectives are as follows:

Conclusion 1: PRISMA has revealed that there are a multitude of possibilities for the prevention of waste and emissions in Dutch industry.

Conclusion 2: PRISMA has shown that many possibilities for preventing waste and emissions in companies can be realized within a period of one to three years.

Conclusion 3: In the ten PRISMA companies it has proved possible to reduce specific waste flows by 30 percent with a variety of prevention techniques. In special cases, reduction percentages of up to 80 percent

TABLE 9.3

SOME REDUCTION PERCENTAGES FOR CONSTITUENT FLOWS PER
PREVENTION TECHNIQUE

PREVENTION TECHNIQUE		%
Reductions from good housekeeping:		
B&S	extension of lubricating oil renewal period	30
Chromolux	chemicals recording	25
Heijchroom	good housekeeping vapor-degreasing installation	30
Marvelo	prevention management	5
Campina/Melkunie	optimizing the cleaning process	23
Campina/Melkunie	no rinsing between certain batches	2.5
Reductions from technological modifications:		
DSM-resins	replacement of sampling system	80
Marvelo	overhaul of coffee-packaging machine	33
RET	magnetic valve for motor oil	30
Reduction from change of input material:		
Chromolux	cyanide-free electroplating	100
Reduction percentage from a combination of measures:		
DSM-resins	different filter/good housekeeping synthetic resins	90

have been realized. Thus, in the areas of priority, results have been achieved that meet the requirements for sustainable development. Those involved in PRISMA believe that similar reductions are feasible in large sections of Dutch industry.

Conclusion 4: In many cases the implementation of preventive measures in companies presents no financial problems. Often measures can be taken without any effect on costs, while in certain cases considerable savings can be achieved.

Conclusion 5: With the use of the PRISMA manual and external supervision by PRISMA researchers, a coherent package of preventive measures could be established for each of the ten companies. Thus, the PRISMA approach is eminently useful and effective.

Conclusion 6: By following the PRISMA manual, an internal prevention survey can be carried out in a company with limited person-power (both internal and external). The PRISMA approach is therefore efficient.

TABLE 9.4
COST ASPECTS AND PAYBACK PERIODS PER MEASURE

COMPANY	UNKNOWN	COST-NEUTRAL	COST-SAVING PAYBACK PERIOD			COST-INCREASING	TOTAL
			<1 Year	<2 Years	<3 Years		
B&S	2	2	1	0	0	1	6
Campina/Melkunie	0	0	7	1	0	0	8
Chromolux	0	0	4	0	0	0	4
DSM-resins	0	0	2	0	1	0	3
GVB	0	1	0	0	0	0	1
Heijchroom	0	4	0	0	0	0	4
Marvelo	1	4	0	1	0	0	6
Nestlé	0	2	2	0	0	0	4
RET	0	3	0	0	1	2	6
Stork	0	3	0	0	0	0	3
Total	3	19	16	2	2	3	45

Conclusion 7: Three elements are lacking in the manual—namely, a feasibility study, an environmental hygiene evaluation, and a care system to safeguard environmental management in a company.

Conclusion 8: The procedure and methodology described in the manual, supported by external supervision, have proved satisfactory in practice. However, the procedure and methodology have to be adapted to the specific circumstances of each company in a creative and flexible manner.

OBSTACLES TO PREVENTION OF WASTE AND EMISSIONS

Within the framework of the PRISMA project, the specific obstacles that arise in companies when preventive measures are introduced have been studied at length to find ways of dealing with them. These obstacles can cause the introduction of preventive measures in companies to stagnate. It is therefore important to tackle them with a wide range of measures. Practical experience obtained through PRISMA suggests that intensive supervision by external consultants can remove a significant portion of the existing obstacles.

The main obstacles that must be overcome so that companies can develop activities for the prevention of waste and emissions are listed here. How these obstacles were tackled within the framework of PRISMA is also shown. Using the outcomes of the PRISMA project as a foundation, the text then describes the conditions under which a preventive approach can be based and subsequently developed.

The obstacles are grouped in five main categories: conceptual obstacles, organizational obstacles, obstacles related to the availability of knowledge, technical obstacles, and economic obstacles. This categorization is based on a study of the literature, the experiences of Dutch and other researchers engaged in pollution prevention studies, and the way in which prevention activities proceeded in the companies that participated in the PRISMA project.

CONCEPTUAL OBSTACLES

The view that "preventing waste is a costly business" is quite common in our society. Some people who believe this to be true consequently make no attempt to search for prevention options. Yet such a view is seldom, if ever, based on practical experience or experiments. This is a perfect example of a conceptual obstacle to the introduction of policy on the prevention of waste and emissions. Conceptual obstacles are often not recognized as such. Further study shows that various obstacles, even though formulated in economic or technical terms, are conceptual.

During the preparatory work for the PRISMA project a great deal of thought went into how conceptual obstacles could be overcome in the participating companies. The PRISMA team decided to place emphasis on conveying prevention concepts, opportunities for preventing waste and emissions, and the benefits that can be derived from their implementation. This approach was based on the view that concrete success stories from comparable companies could encourage the participants to adopt a proactive and prevention-oriented attitude. To ensure this transfer of information, workshops were organized for the participating companies and incorporated as part of the whole project. The researchers also hoped that intensive guidance of the companies throughout the duration of the project would help overcome any conceptual obstacles that might be present.

Conceptual obstacles can be grouped in five categories:

1. Underrating of the environment in company policy.
2. Narrow view of the relationship between company policy and the environment, resulting in confusion about the definition of prevention; the idea that prevention is possible only in the long term; the idea that protecting the environment is costly; and inadequate demand articulation.
3. Resistance to change.
4. Legally established standards as the only goal and guideline for environmental policy in companies.
5. The view that the production process is a "black box"—that is, that the inputs to the process can be altered in an attempt to control outputs without understanding the internal workings of the process.

Table 9.5 lists each type of obstacle along with the resulting problem and the solutions found.

ORGANIZATIONAL OBSTACLES

Obstacles can also exist within the organization of a company, in the way companies collaborate, and in the relations between companies and government. Bureaucratic and rigid structures make it difficult to introduce new ideas. Organizational obstacles can be grouped in three categories:

TABLE 9.5

OVERVIEW OF CONCEPTUAL OBSTACLES AND SOLUTIONS

OBSTACLE	PROBLEM	CONDITION OR SOLUTION
Underrating of environment in company policy	Too little willingness in company to make personnel and funds available for prevention activities	Present prevention of waste and emissions as a challenge for positive development of company
Narrow view of relationship between company policy and the environment, resulting in:		
a) Confusion as to the definition of prevention	a) Necessity for and benefits of preventing waste and emissions are not acknowledged	a) Clearly define prevention and disseminate prevention concepts
b) The idea that prevention is possible only in the long term	b) Preconceived idea that prevention of waste and emissions is only a thing of the future	b) Provide success stories of similar companies that prove the opposite
c) The idea that protecting the environment is costly	c) Preconceived idea that environmental measures are always costly	c) Provide success stories of similar companies that prove the opposite
d) Inadequate demand articulation	d) Inadequate explan-ation of factors that determine scope and composition of waste stream	d) Conduct material-oriented analysis of processes that leads to unambiguous definition of the problem; set up prevention strategy
Resistance to change	Prevention (like any other change) incites resistance	Make upgrading a challenge; involve entire company in prevention activities

Table 9.5 (*Continued*)

Obstacle	Problem	Condition or Solution
Legal standards as the only goal	Only those waste streams or emissions that exceed government standards are considered environmental problems	Have companies set their own priorities for internal environmental standards in company environmental policy; stimulate a proactive attitude
The view that the production process is a "black box"	Environmental policy takes shape only if preconditions are set with regard to production	Present production as most important link for preventing waste and emissions

1. Organization of the company.
2. Collaboration between companies (in the same vertical production column).
3. Organization of government environmental policy.

When the PRISMA project was launched, the researchers already had a picture of the organizational obstacles that could arise when introducing pollution prevention in companies. However, they were unable to change organizational structures to create favorable conditions for pollution prevention. All they could do was work with the companies to search for solutions that, given the existing organizational obstacles, would nevertheless achieve pollution prevention. Table 9.6 describes the organizational obstacles, the resulting problems, and the solutions found.

OBSTACLES RELATED TO THE AVAILABILITY OF KNOWLEDGE

The introduction of pollution prevention activities requires not only technical knowledge, but also knowledge of economics, social psychology, organizational sociology, and environmental protection. The knowledge required must be easily accessible to companies. The lack of pollution prevention knowledge and/or the lack of a sound infrastructure for the dissemination thereof can present obstacles. Of importance here is a solution-oriented multidisciplinary knowledge of the environment. Moreover, in contrast with technical knowledge—information about

TABLE 9.6
OVERVIEW OF ORGANIZATIONAL OBSTACLES AND SOLUTIONS

OBSTACLE	PROBLEM	CONDITION OR SOLUTION
Organization of company	Lack of clarity as to division and/or compartmentalization of environmental tasks and responsibilities; organization not geared to analysis of incoming and outgoing material streams	Embed pollution prevention within the organization so that environmental tasks and responsibilities can be created for projects that investigate opportunities for preventing waste and emissions in different company units
Collaboration between companies in same production column	a) Losing sight of prevention opportunities in other stages in production column, as prevention is limited to possibilities within company	a) Establish coordination between companies as to possibilities of avoiding environmental problems by bringing about changes in preproduction and postproduction lines
	b) (Presumed) demands by consumers and customers can be met only by existing technologies and processes	b) Promote consultation between manufacturers and consumers/users on product specifications; create room for prevention of waste and emissions
Organization of government environmental policy	Compartmentalized structure of environmental policy that inhibits integral analysis of production of waste and emissions and consumption of raw and input materials	Integrate environmental policy: coordinate formulation of short- and long-term environmental regulations (progressive standardization)

technological prevention options—such knowledge encompasses all the environmental compartments: air, water, and soil.

In the preparatory work for PRISMA, obstacles that arise from poor dissemination of knowledge were taken into account. To avoid such obstacles, the university research teams were required to make knowledge of pollution prevention technologies available to the participating companies. (See Table 9.7.)

TECHNICAL OBSTACLES

Technology is always involved in the prevention of waste and emissions. Prevention is achieved by making changes to installations, tools, input materials, processes, and production. Therefore, technical obstacles can arise when prevention activities are introduced, and they are encountered in all three stages of technological development—namely, development, demonstration, and dissemination. The actual boundaries between these stages are difficult to define with precision. In the preparatory work leading up to PRISMA, particular attention was paid to obstacles that emerge due to the poor dissemination of technology. (See Table 9.8.)

TABLE 9.7

OVERVIEW OF OBSTACLES RELATED TO THE AVAILABILITY OF KNOWLEDGE AND SOLUTIONS

OBSTACLE	PROBLEM	CONDITION OR SOLUTION
Development of knowledge	Knowledge required to generate and assess pollution prevention options is as yet underdeveloped	Widen prevention knowledge through further research
Dissemination of knowledge	Available knowledge on prevention of waste and emissions is segmented and difficult to access so that companies that could benefit from that knowledge are unable to do so	Optimize dissemination of prevention knowledge to companies by means of "prevention consultants" and data banks, for example

TABLE 9.8

OVERVIEW OF TECHNICAL OBSTACLES AND SOLUTIONS

OBSTACLE	PROBLEM	CONDITION OR SOLUTION
Development of technology	Very little technology developed from a waste and emissions prevention perspective	Initiate technology development by investigating factors that influence scale and composition of waste streams from production processes
Demonstration of technology	No overview of technological prevention options; many options also lack practical demonstration	Provide overviews and demonstrations of technological prevention options
Dissemination of technology	Information on technological prevention options is compartmentalized and difficult to access	Optimize dissemination of technological prevention options to companies using consultants, for example

ECONOMIC OBSTACLES

The prevention of waste and emissions is, among other things, achieved by improving the utilization of input materials. This is the basis for the hypothesis that prevention can be financially attractive ("pollution prevention pays"). In addition to a reduction in costs, prevention can also lead to an improvement in the quality of the product and result in more advanced innovations in processes and/or products. Prevention in companies can be restrained by financial obstacles, however, despite the potential cost savings. The PRISMA team identified four types of financial obstacles:

1. Vested interests.
2. Low charges for the disposal of waste streams.
3. In-company investment policy.
4. Incomplete calculation and allocation of environmental costs.

These financial obstacles are seen in the various stages of introducing the prevention of waste and emissions. Vested interests and incomplete calculation and allocation of environmental costs are significant obstacles to the initiation of a pollution prevention assessment in a business enterprise. They form a barrier to the search for prevention options within the company. Low costs for the disposal of waste streams and current in-company investment policies are significant obstacles that occur in the decision-making process about whether or not to execute proposed preventive measures. (See Table 9.9.)

CONDITIONS FOR PREVENTION OF WASTE AND EMISSIONS

In its own way, each of the various kinds of obstacles can delay or even block the prevention process. It is therefore essential to establish prevention policy as broadly as possible and tackle the whole spectrum of potential obstacles. The experiences from the PRISMA project show that intensive guidance and company-oriented consultancy can eliminate a substantial number of these obstacles. The instrument of well-equipped prevention teams, working in the background to assist the companies, is appropriate to overcome most of them.

There is a set sequence in which obstacles appear when waste and prevention is introduced in companies. The first obstacles faced by both companies and the government are conceptual ones. These become evident in various misunderstandings about the possibilities for preventing waste and emissions and the benefits that can be gained from their implementation. This means that when prevention is encouraged in companies, a great deal of attention must be devoted first to overcoming these conceptual obstacles.

Once conceptual barriers have been broken, companies are often next confronted with obstacles related to organization and/or knowledge in the search for prevention options. Later, in the actual implementation of preventive measures or prevention policy, obstacles of a financial or technical nature often emerge. Some of the obstacles encountered are present in the companies themselves. Others are presented by various societal actors or can be a part of the views and attitudes that exist in the whole of society. The conditions that must be created to overcome various kinds of obstacles are summarized as follows:

Conceptual: dissemination of prevention concepts in industrial circles and citizen and governmental organizations to promote awareness and acceptance of the benefits and possibilities of pollution prevention in general. This dissemination of information should be based on success stories in other companies working in the same field and should present prevention as a challenge for positive industrial development. Production

TABLE 9.9
OVERVIEW OF ECONOMIC OBSTACLES AND SOLUTIONS

OBSTACLE	PROBLEM	CONDITION OR SOLUTION
Vested interests	Various industries (e.g., waste processors and suppliers of end-of-pipe technology) benefit from present practices	Disseminate information about successful prevention projects in other companies to encourage viewing the source of waste streams as the main issue so that prevention emerges as the best solution
Low charges for the disposal of waste streams	Charges for removing waste and discharge or emission charges are too low to encourage companies to undertake prevention activities	Use financial measures to discourage waste of raw and input materials and generation of waste streams
In-company investment policy	Investments in preventive measures must be based on economic profitability	Stimulate investments in preventive measures above others (environmental investments); evaluate investments in preventive measures as production-linked investments
Incomplete calculation and allocation of environmental costs	Incomplete calculation of environmental pollution costs and failure to allocate costs to various company units, leading to underestimation of potential financial benefits from pollution prevention	Stimulate complete calculation and allocation of environmental costs via dissemination of information and development of appropriate tools

processes have a central role here as they are the basis for preventive measures. This information should serve to stimulate companies to adopt a proactive attitude toward the environment. It should encourage them to systematically assess and analyze all substances and materials entering and leaving the company.

Organizational: embedding of the prevention concept in the company organization through the delegation of tasks and responsibilities and the creation of latitude for scheduled prevention assessments in individual sections of the company; coordination between companies with a view to avoiding environmental problems in production activities by introducing changes in the preproduction and postproduction line; integration of environmental policy and time-related, more stringent standards.

Availability of knowledge: research to increase knowledge for generating and assessing prevention options; optimizing the dissemination of prevention knowledge (e.g., through consultants and data banks).

Technical: initiation of technological development for the prevention of waste and emissions; listing and demonstration of technological prevention options; optimizing the dissemination of technological prevention options to companies (e.g., through consultants).

Economic: financial discouragement of the spilling of raw materials and additives and the output of waste; consideration of prevention options as production-related investments and not additional (environmental) investments; dissemination of information to promote full calculation and allocation of environmental pollution costs.

TOWARD AN EFFECTIVE GOVERNMENT PREVENTION POLICY

The PRISMA project has shown that intensive interaction between companies and outside consultants, focusing on conceptual obstacles, knowledge transfer, and an analysis of production processes, can bring about the realization of pollution prevention in a relatively short period of time. The policy recommendations formulated at the end of the PRISMA project in 1991 are to a large extent based on this lesson. Consequently, improvement of knowledge transfer systems is the key policy recommendation. This section focuses on recommendations pertaining to the improvement of the knowledge transfer system. Other recommendations—such as the use of financial policy instruments, for example—are not discussed. (For a discussion of these policy instruments, see Dieleman et al. [1991].)

It is important to realize that many forms and systems of knowledge transfer already exist in Dutch society. They often do not result in changes in production processes, however, because of the fact that intensive interaction is missing. Knowledge transfer should take the form of technical assistance within a company, aimed at an interactive search process and based on an assessment of waste flows and prevention options. The use of prevention teams looks to be the most promising mechanism for achieving this kind of knowledge transfer. Therefore, the most important recommendation is as follows:

Recommendation I: The government should give clear priority to the appointment of prevention teams that will stimulate, supervise, and advise companies.

These prevention teams can function as a first line of assistance for industry. However, they must be supported with an infrastructure that can provide them with the necessary knowledge and legitimacy. Therefore, Recommendation I is backed up with related recommendations Ia to Ie:

Recommendation Ia: The government should be responsible for national coordination and for ensuring that the activities of the prevention teams are in line with one another.

Recommendation Ib: The government should determine the framework within which educational material on the prevention of waste and emissions is developed.

Recommendation Ic: The government should give greater priority to prevention-oriented demonstration projects in companies.

Recommendation Id: Better adjustment and coordination should be accomplished at a regional level between the various organizations currently involved in the transfer of knowledge. This will stimulate a well-planned, regional approach to prevention activities.

Recommendation Ie: The government should contribute to the establishment of an easily accessible data bank containing Dutch and international information on the prevention of waste and emissions.

Along with the establishment of prevention teams to stimulate industry, it is necessary to incorporate this communicative and interactive approach in the framework of government regulations, permits, and licenses. In that regard, Recommendation II has been formulated:

Recommendation II: There should be a direct link between government regulations and a prevention-oriented approach to waste and emissions. For this purpose, the formulation and implementation of company prevention plans should be compulsory conditions for the granting of a license.

This recommendation is also backed up with a number of related recommendations, which together provide for a compulsory prevention policy:

Recommendation IIa: An integrated environmental license should be introduced.

Recommendation IIb: To guarantee an effective enforcement policy, government policy should aim for a more intensive monitoring of prevention plans and of the progress made with the implementation programs.

Recommendation IIc: Focused training programs need to be developed for supervisory and enforcement bodies.

INNOVATION THEORY REVISITED

The diffusion and adoption of cleaner technology is a process that is difficult to get started. Several authors (Dieleman et al. 1991) discuss this and offer various reasons. Reference is made to various factors that form obstacles to the diffusion and adoption of cleaner technologies, especially in the literature on innovation theory; recommendations are also made for improving this situation. The obstacles described in this chapter are also mentioned in innovation theory, and attempts are made to come up with solutions for each.

On the basis of PRISMA experience, it is possible to interrelate the various obstacles and place them in sequence to obtain a better picture of their effects on the diffusion and adoption of cleaner technologies, as well as their effects on each other. The solutions put forward can thus be more easily interrelated.

Using the PRISMA experience, it is possible to attach elucidating, subtle distinctions to a number of the obstacles described in innovation theory.

PRIMARY CONDITIONS FOR THE DIFFUSION AND ADOPTION OF CLEANER TECHNOLOGY

A major problem in the diffusion of cleaner technology is that for a number of reasons companies react defensively to stimuli from their surroundings. In this context, various authors (Frank and Swarte 1986; Baas and Dieleman 1989; Cramer and Schot 1990) point out that the search process for cleaner technologies is often prompted by legal standards imposed by government within the scope of environmental policy. This generally leads to the application of cost-raising end-of-pipe technology. The emphasis on end-of-pipe technology mainly gives rise to the conceptual obstacles described earlier in the chapter.

When PRISMA started, a great deal of disbelief and skepticism had to be overcome. Nevertheless, the obstacles were overcome successfully. This can be explained by the procedure and methods used by the PRISMA researchers. The PRISMA approach turned out to be an essential link, both within and between the diffusion and adoption processes, and was apparently of great importance in attending to the following factors.

Diffusion as a Tailor-made Process

The application of technology is almost always specific to a certain location. Diffusion processes must therefore be tailored to the specific application. On the basis of research in three different countries, Allen et al. (1983) conclude that technology is seldom transferred through written information. Written information in the form of material such as brochures and folders is usually far too general. To truly have an effect, technology must be translated from the general to the location-specific. This implies interaction between the suppliers of technology and the potential users of that technology. The PRISMA project established this interaction by providing encouragement, supervision, and advice. The dissemination of knowledge for promoting the prevention of waste and emissions must be aimed at cultivating these processes of interaction.

Diffusion Through Interaction on the Basis of Equality

Attention also must be devoted to the actual nature of the interaction. One aspect that is quite often forgotten is that this interaction ought to take place between equal partners. At present, it occurs between suppliers who are expert in the area of environmental technology and companies that are inexpert in this area. Frank and Swarte (1986) point out that small and medium-size companies often have difficulty defining the exact problem that needs to be resolved. In such cases, the suppliers of environmental technology strongly dominate the interaction, and the selected solutions often are characterized by add-on technology. When companies adopt the PRISMA approach, a search process is launched to discover the origin of waste and emissions, and in this process the company and the providers of environmental technology face each other more as equals. At the start of the PRISMA project, most of the participating companies were, for example, incapable of identifying concrete areas requiring special attention for pollution prevention. Only after the preliminary research phase were they capable of asking pertinent questions. Mobilizing such interaction on the basis of equality also appeared to be an essential requirement for initiating an ongoing diffusion process within companies. Interaction around unilateral problems pointed out by the researchers alone would most probably have resulted in the termination of the process. One very important requirement for the successful diffusion of innovation is to encourage joint research into company-specific and process-related causes of waste and emissions.

Thus, interaction is an essential feature of a successful innovation diffusion process. Promoting innovation should be seen primarily as a social process that takes shape at the level of face-to-face relations. If this condition fails to be met, then it is most difficult to initiate the process of diffusion and adoption of cleaner technologies.

SECONDARY CONDITIONS FOR THE DIFFUSION AND ADOPTION OF CLEANER TECHNOLOGY

Based on the PRISMA experience, several other factors described in innovation theory should be considered as secondary conditions. These factors relate to the knowledge infrastructure and are important in ensuring the sound progress of the actual innovation process.

Availability and Accessibility of Information

Some of the problems with regard to the diffusion and adoption of cleaner technologies are to be found in the degree of availability and accessibility of information. The large volume of information, especially, is a problem here. Companies are often flooded with brochures, newspapers, and folders (Frank and Swarte 1986). The pertinent information is difficult to find (Moret, Ernst and Young 1990), and the outcome is that the available knowledge is insufficiently used. To solve this problem it has been proposed that information and documentation systems be improved and data banks established. However, Cramer and Schot (1989) state that the effectiveness of such systems is often extremely limited. They believe that knowledge systems have little effect since they are insufficiently consulted, especially by those in small and medium-size companies. Research supports this supposition. Yet this by no means implies that such knowledge systems are not useful if set up for the appropriate target group.

It is the authors' belief that two distinct phases in the diffusion trajectory are needed: (1) the dissemination of information to intermediary organizations, and (2) the dissemination of information to companies. Knowledge systems can be of great use, especially in the first phase. Intermediary organizations can have at their disposal the whole range of information available in the system and thus can offer each company selected information based on a joint analysis of the specific causes of waste and emissions in that company.

The importance of knowledge systems therefore should not be under-estimated. The dissemination of information available in these systems should, however, be tailored to the needs of the various participants in the diffusion process.

Availability of Cleaner Production Expertise in the Environmental Technology Sector

Cramer and Schot (1989) state that the main reason for the lack of diffusion of cleaner technology is that the suppliers of environmental technology have little knowledge about cleaner production processes. They have specialized completely in add-on technology, such as treatment plants, filters, and waste treatment technologies. The PRISMA project confirms this observation. It was difficult to get concrete prevention-oriented knowledge and technology from the existing environmental production sector. Yet the significance of this must not be overestimated. It is apparent that there is a reasonable amount of knowledge available within companies in this sector about alternative technologies and methods of production. Offering a method for determining the causes of the production of waste and emissions leads to a creative process within these companies in which a great deal of the available knowledge and experience can be used. However, the existing environmental production sector is not geared toward identifying areas requiring special attention for prevention of waste and emissions, but mainly toward putting forward concrete solutions for handling existing waste streams and emissions.

On this basis, it can be concluded that the main problem in companies offering environmental technology is not a lack of technological knowledge and skills. The problem is in the strategy they use, which consists of providing ad hoc solutions instead of stimulating the systematic search for process-related causes and thinking about solutions to those causes.

Prevention and the Technological Paradigm

Another factor referred to by Cramer and Schot (1989) is the fact that the suppliers of environmental technology are often "caught prisoner" in the end-of-pipe technology trajectory. The question these authors raise is whether the shift from end-of-pipe technology to cleaner technology in-volves a radical change of paradigm, or whether the prevention of waste and emissions is feasible within the existing technological paradigm.

The experiences gained from the PRISMA project show that a number of prevention options can very often be achieved within the existing technological paradigms and trajectories. To explore the potentials of these options, the most important change that must be made is related to the structure of knowledge transfer and information dissemination.

The PRISMA project has not yielded enough information, however, to indicate whether these relatively easy prevention options will stimulate a search for more substantial changes in production processes and lead to exploration of new technological paradigms and trajectories. It is the authors' impression that—especially by linking practical prevention assessments with research and development programs—in-company assessments can indeed lead to the assessment of the limits of existing technological paradigms and trajectories.

CONCLUSIONS

On the basis of the PRISMA project, it can be concluded that a substantial amount of pollution can be prevented in a short period of time, provided that the many obstacles to prevention are dealt with in appropriate ways. This chapter has presented a number of conditions for achieving the prevention of waste and emissions. These conditions are related to conceptual, organizational, knowledge-based, technical, and economic obstacles.

The authors' central policy recommendation is that a network of prevention teams be established by the government to assist industry in a search process for prevention options, based on a systematic assessment of waste flows and their sources. The *Handleiding voor Preventie van Afval en Emissies*, a modified version of the U.S. EPA's *Waste Minimization Opportunity Assessment Manual*, has proven to be an effective instrument for conducting such an assessment. The integration of prevention activities into compulsory prevention plans is also recommended.

In terms of innovation theory, the PRISMA experience has permitted review of the various conditions for the diffusion and adoption of cleaner technology that are found within innovation theory. The most important research finding is the distinction made between primary and secondary conditions for the diffusion and adoption of cleaner technology.

NOTE

1. Within the framework of PRISMA, experiments were carried out at ten companies; in addition, policy studies were conducted (by IVAM, ESM, and the Centre for Technology and Policy Studies [TNO]). As the principal, NOTA was in charge of management of the project. In addition, the Advisory Council

for Research on Nature and the Environment (RMNO) was actively involved in the implementation of PRISMA. The project has been partly financed by the Ministry of Economic Affairs (regional and industrial policy) and the Ministry for Housing, Regional Development and the Environment (Waste Management Group).

REFERENCES

Allen, T. J. et al. 1983. "Transferring Technology to the Small Manufacturing Firm: A Study of Technology Transfer in Three Countries." *Research Policy* 12: 199–211.

Baas, L. W., and Dieleman, J. P. C. 1989. "Kansen en Belemmeringen voor Afvalpreventie in het midden en Kleinbedrijf" (Opportunities and constraints for waste prevention in medium-size and small industries). In *Milieu en Innovatie* (Environment and innovation), edited by H. Vollebergh. Groningen, Netherlands: Wolters Noordhof.

Berkel, C. W. M. van. 1991. *The Prevention of Waste and Emissions at Heychroom.* PRISMA Company-Specific Final Report. The Hague: SDU.

Berkel, C. W. M. van. 1991. *The Prevention of Waste and Emissions at Marvelo.* PRISMA Company-Specific Final Report. The Hague: SDU.

Berkel, C. W. M. van. 1991. *The Prevention of Waste and Emissions at Nestlé Amsterdam.* PRISMA Company-Specific Final Report. The Hague: SDU.

Berkel, C. W. M. van. 1991. *The Prevention of Waste and Emissions at Stork Amsterdam.* PRISMA Company-Specific Final Report. The Hague: SDU.

Cramer, J., and Schot, J. 1989. *Problemen rond innovatie en diffusie van milieutechnologie: Een onderzoeks programmeringsstudie verricht vanuit een technologiedynamica perspectief* (Problems with innovation and diffusion of environmental technology: A research programming study conducted from a perspective of technology dynamics). RMNO publication series, no. 44. Rijswijk, Netherlands: RMNO.

Cramer, J. and Schot, J. 1990. "Stimulating Cleaner Technology Through Economic Instruments. Possibilities and Constraints." *Industry and Environment Review* 13: 46–53.

Crul, M. R. M. 1991. *The Prevention of Waste and Emissions at GVB (Rayon Noord).* PRISMA Company-Specific Final Report. The Hague: SDU.

Dieleman, J. P. L.; van Berkel, R.; Reijenga, F.; de Hoo, S.; Brezet, J.; Cramer, J.; and Schot, J. 1991. *To Choose for Prevention Is to Win; Towards a Preventative Environmental Policy for Government and Industry.* PREPARE experiences and manual. Euronviron, Green Umbrella, Eureka. The Hague: Ministry of Economic Affairs.

Frank, R., and Swarte, H. 1986. *Milieutechnologie, toepassing in kleine en middelgrote ondernemingen* (Environmental technology, application in small and medium-size industry). Erasmus Center for Environmental Studies, publication series, no. 1. Rotterdam: Erasmus University.

Hofman, H. D., and Dieleman, J. P. C. 1991. *The Prevention of Waste and Emissions at Campina/Melkunie Maasdam*. PRISMA Company-Specific Final Report. The Hague: SDU.

Hofman, H. D., and Dieleman, J. P. C. 1991. *The Prevention of Waste and Emissions at RET*. PRISMA Company-Specific Final Report. The Hague: SDU.

Hofman, H. D., and Koppert, P. C. 1991. *The Prevention of Waste and Emissions at B&S*. PRISMA Company-Specific Final Report. The Hague: SDU.

Hoo, S. de; Brezet, H.; Crul, M.; and Dieleman, H., eds. 1991. *Manual for the Prevention of Wastes and Emissions*. PREPARE experiences and manual. Euronviron, Green Umbrella, Eureka. The Hague: Ministry of Economic Affairs.

Huisingh, D.; Martin, L.; Hilger, H.; and Seldman, N. 1986. *Proven Profits from Pollution Prevention. Case Studies in Resource Conservation and Waste Reduction*. Washington, D.C.: Institute for Local Self-Reliance.

Koppert, P. C., and Dieleman, J. P. C. 1991. *The Prevention of Waste and Emissions at DSM-Resins Hoek van Holland*. PRISMA Company-Specific Final Report. The Hague: SDU.

Koppert, P. C., and Hofman, H. D. *The Prevention of Waste and Emissions at Chromolux*. PRISMA Company-Specific Final Report. The Hague: SDU.

Moret, Ernst and Young. 1990. *Milieu en onderneming, wanneer slaat de balans door? Enquete-rapport*. (Environment and business, when is the balance breaking through?). Utrecht: Moret.

RIVM (Federal Institute for Public Health and Environmental Hygiene). 1988. *Nationale milieuverkenningen, Zorgen voor Morgen* (Concerns for tomorrow). Tjeenk Willink, Alphen a/d Rijn.

Rosenberg, N. 1982. *Inside the Black Box: Technology and Economics*. Cambridge: Cambridge University Press.

Schot, J. 1991. *Maatschappelijke sturing van technische ontwikkeling. Constructive technology assessment als hedendaagse ludisme* (Societal control of technology. Constructive technology assessment as a Renaissance of Luddism). WMW publication series, no. 9. Enschede, Netherlands: Twente University.

VROM (Ministry of Housing, Physical Planning, and Environment). 1989. *To Choose or to Lose*. National Environmental Plan. The Hague: SDU.

Weenen, J. C. van. 1990. "Waste Prevention, Theory and Practice." Thesis research, Delft University, Castricum, Netherlands.

World Commission on Environment and Development. 1987. *Our Common Future*. New York: Oxford University Press.

10

Understanding Technological Responses
of Industrial Firms to Environmental Problems:
Implications for Government Policy

Nicholas A. Ashford

TECHNOLOGICAL CHANGE AND POLLUTION PREVENTION

Technological change is now generally regarded as essential in achieving the next major advances in pollution reduction. The necessary technological changes must include: (1) the substitution of materials used as inputs, (2) process redesign, and (3) final product reformulation. Initiatives for focusing on technological change must address multimedia pollution and reflect fundamental shifts in the design of products and processes. Distinguished from end-of-pipe pollution control, those new initiatives are known as *pollution prevention, source reduction, toxics use reduction,* or *clean technology* (OECD 1987). The practices of in-process recycling and equipment modification are sometimes also included in the approach. The term *waste reduction* is also used, but it appears to be less precise and may not include air or water emissions. Pollution prevention has also been discussed as a preferred way for achieving sustainable development, giving rise to the term sustainable technology (Heaton et al. 1991).

This chapter argues that the key to success in pollution prevention is to influence managerial knowledge of and managerial attitudes toward both technological change and environmental concerns. Encouraging technological changes for production purposes (i.e., main business innovation) and for environmental compliance purposes must be seen as interrelated, rather than separable, activities that must be fully integrated (Ashford, Heaton, and Priest 1979; Kurz 1987; Rip and van den Belt 1988; Schot 1992). To bring about this integration, management must be committed to expanding the "problem space" of the engineer/scientist/technologist to include environmental and safety concerns so that those concerns are reflected in both design and operational criteria of a firm's technology. This may require a fundamental cultural shift in the firm. A related cultural shift in the regulatory agencies that influence how firms respond to environmental demands is also essential.

The above discussion addresses managerial factors that influence technological change. The technology of the firm, however, also influences managerial style and may limit the kind and extent of technological changes that are likely or possible. Thus, the design of governmental (or corporate) policies for encouraging a fundamental shift in the technologies of production must rest on an appreciation of the different kinds of technological change, as well as the dynamics of achieving those changes under a regulatory stimulus.

TECHNOLOGICAL CHANGE DEFINED

Technological change can involve both technological innovation and diffusion. *Technological innovation* is both a significant determinant of economic growth and important for reducing health, safety, and environmental hazards.[1] It may be major, involving radical shifts in technology, or incremental, involving adaptation of prior technologies. Technological innovation is fundamentally different from *diffusion*, which is the widespread adoption of technology already developed. The term *technology transfer* is somewhat imprecise, sometimes referring to the diffusion of technology from government to industry, or from one industry to another. If that transfer involves significant modifications of the originating technology, the transfer can be said to result in incremental or minor innovation. Finally, the term *technology forcing* is used to describe regulation and is similarly imprecise, usually meaning forcing industry to innovate, but sometimes meaning forcing industry to adopt technology already developed and used elsewhere.

THE DYNAMICS OF REGULATION-INDUCED TECHNOLOGICAL CHANGE

Several commentators and researchers have investigated the effects of regulation on technological change.[2] On the basis of this work and experience gained from the history of industrial responses to regulation during the past twenty years, it will later be argued that it is now possible to fashion regulatory strategies for eliciting the best possible technological response to achieve specific health, safety, or environmental goals. Underlying a regulatory strategy aimed at stimulating technological change and achieving a significant level of pollution prevention is a rejection of the premise that regulation must achieve a *balance* or compromise between environmental integrity and industrial growth, or between job safety and competition in world markets.[3] Rather, such a strategy builds on the thesis that health, safety, and environmental goals can be *co-optimized* with economic growth through technological innovation (Ashford, Ayers, and Stone 1985).[4] Although a new technology may be a more costly method of attaining current environmental standards, it may achieve stricter standards at less cost than adaptation of existing technology. Figure 10.1 illustrates the difference.

Suppose it is determined (by either market demand or regulatory fiat) that a reduction in health risk from point A in Figure 10.1 to the risk represented by the longer dotted line is desirable. Use of the most efficient existing technological capabilities would impose a cost represented by point B.[5] However, if it were possible to stimulate technological innovation, a new technology "supply curve" would arise, allowing the same degree of health risk reduction at a lower cost represented by point C. Alternatively, a greater degree of health protection could be afforded if expenditures equal to costs represented by point B were applied instead to new technological solutions represented by point D. Note that co-optimization resulting in "having your cake and eating it too" can occur because a new *dynamic* efficiency is achieved.[6] Because end-of-pipe approaches have been used for a long time and improvements in pollution control have probably reached a plateau, it is argued that the new technology curve or frontier will be occupied predominantly by pollution prevention technologies—that is, new products, inputs, or production processes. The use of initiatives to bring firms into environmental compliance using new technologies is termed *innovation-driven pollution prevention*.

A MODEL OF THE EFFECTS OF REGULATION ON TECHNOLOGICAL CHANGE

Prior work has developed models for explaining the effects of regulation on technological change in the chemical, pharmaceutical, and automobile industries.[7] Figure 10.2 presents a modified model, structured to assist in

FIGURE 10.1.
AN INNOVATIVE RESPONSE TO REGULATION

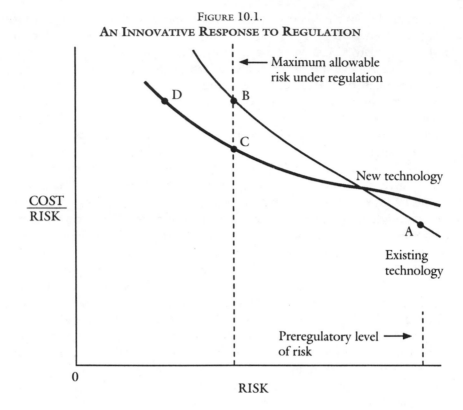

designing regulations and strategies for encouraging pollution prevention, rather than simply to trace the effects of regulation on innovation.

THE REGULATORY STIMULUS

Environmental, health, and safety regulations affecting the chemical-using or chemical-producing industry include controls on air quality, water quality, solid and hazardous waste, pesticides, food additives, pharmaceuticals, toxic substances, workplace health and safety, and consumer product safety.[8] These regulations control different aspects of development or production, change over time, and are "technology forcing" to different degrees.[9] Thus, designers of regulations should consider that the effects on technological innovation will differ among regulations that: (a) require demonstration of product safety prior to marketing (pesticides, food additives, pharmaceuticals, and, in some cases, new chemicals)[10]; (b)

FIGURE 10.2.

A MODEL FOR REGULATION-INDUCED TECHNOLOGICAL CHANGE

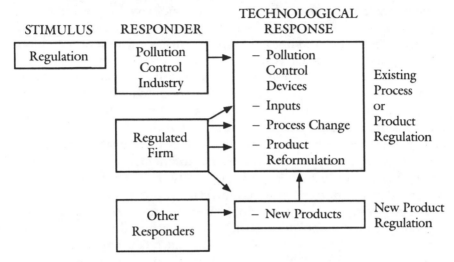

require demonstration of the efficacy of products prior to marketing (pharmaceuticals)[11]; (c) require proof of safety or the control of product use after marketing (existing chemicals under the Toxic Substances Control Act, worker protection, and consumer products)[12]; (d) control production technology to reduce risks to workplace health and safety[13]; and (e) control emissions, effluents, or wastes (air, water, and hazardous waste regulation).[14]

Furthermore, the internal structure of regulations may alter the general climate for innovation. Elements of that structure include: (a) the form of the regulation (product versus process regulation); (b) the mode (performance versus specification standards); (c) the time for compliance; (d) the uncertainty; (e) the stringency of the requirements; and (f) the existence of other economic incentives that complement the regulatory signal.

The distinction between regulation of products and regulation of processes suggests yet a further division.[15] New products differ from existing products, and production process components differ from unwanted by-products or pollutants.[16] Regulations relying on detailed specification standards or on "best available technology" may discourage innovation while prompting rapid diffusion of state-of-the-art technology. Similarly, although a phased-in compliance schedule may prompt only incremental improvements in technology, it allows a timely industry response.

An industry's perception of the need to alter its technological course often precedes promulgation of a regulation. Most environmental regulations arise only after extended scrutiny of a potential problem by government, citizens, workers, and industry. Prior scrutiny, according to a study done by the Massachusetts Institute of Technology,[17] often has greater effects on industry than formal rule making, because anticipation of regulation stimulates innovation. For example, formal regulation of polychlorinated biphenyls followed years after the government expressed initial concern. Aware of this concern, the original manufacturer and other chemical companies began to search for substitutes prior to regulation. Similarly, most firms in the asbestos products industry substantially complied with the Occupational Safety and Health Administration (OSHA) asbestos regulation years before it was promulgated. This preregulation period can allow industry time to develop compliance technologies, process changes, or product substitutes while allowing leeway for it to adjust to ensure continued production or future commercial innovation.

The government's initial show of concern is often, however, an unreliable stimulus to technological change. Both technical uncertainties and application of political pressures may cause uncertainty regarding future regulatory requirements. Nevertheless, some regulatory uncertainty is frequently beneficial. Although excessive regulatory uncertainty may cause industry inaction, too much certainty will stimulate only minimum compliance technology. Similarly, too frequent change of regulatory requirements may frustrate technological development.

Regulatory stringency is the most important factor influencing technological innovation. A regulation is stringent either (1) because compliance requires a *significant* reduction in exposure to toxic substances, (2) because compliance using existing technology is *costly*, or (3) because compliance requires a *significant* technological change. Policy considerations dictate different degrees of stringency as well, since some statutes require that standards be based predominantly on environmental, health, and safety concerns, some on existing technological capability, and others on the technology within reach of a vigorous research and development effort. In the early 1970s, most environmental, health, and safety regulations set standards at a level attainable by existing technology.[18] The regulations reflected both a perceived limit to legislative authority and substantial industry influence over the drafting of standards. More recent regulations have tended toward greater stringency but still rely on existing techniques, though in minority/rare use.[19] (Examples are the technology-based standards for hazardous substances under Section 112 of the 1990 Clean Air Act, requiring the use of maximum achievable control technology [MACT] or the lowest achievable emission rate [LAER] under the new source regulations of Section 111.)

The effect of the regulatory agency's strategy on innovation is not confined to standard setting. Innovation waivers,[20] which stimulate innovation by allowing noncompliance with existing regulation while encouraging the development of a new technology, are affected by enforcement strategies as well.[21] The degree to which the requirements of a regulation are strictly enforced may influence the willingness of an industrial sector to attempt to innovate. The implementing agency ultimately may strictly enforce environmental regulations against those firms receiving waivers or, alternatively, it may adopt a "fail-soft" strategy where a firm has made an imperfect effort but a good faith attempt to comply.[22] The latter strategy is an important element of the regulatory stimulus to innovate as it decreases an innovator's risk of incurring severe agency action in the event of failure. (Additional policy instruments to encourage pollution prevention are discussed later in this chapter.)

CHARACTERISTICS OF THE RESPONDING INDUSTRIAL SECTOR

The industry responding to regulation may be the regulated industry, the pollution control industry, or another industry (see Figure 10.2). Regulation of existing chemical products or processes might elicit (1) a pollution control device, (2) input substitution, (3) a manufacturing process change, or (4) product reformulation. The regulated industry will likely develop new processes and change inputs; the pollution control industry, new devices; and either the regulated industry or new entrants, reformulated or new products. Regulation of new chemicals (i.e., premarket screening), however, will simply affect the development of new products.

Past research on the innovation process (in the absence of regulation) has focused on the innovation "dynamic" in diverse industrial segments throughout the economy.[23] The model there refers to a "productive segment" (a single product line) in industry, defined by the nature of its technology.[24] Over time, the nature and rate of innovation in the segment will change. Initially, the segment creates a market niche by selling a new product, superior in performance to the old technology it replaces. The new technology is typically unrefined, and product change occurs rapidly as technology improves.[25] Because of the rapid product change, the segment neglects process improvements in the early period. Later, however, as the product becomes better defined, more rapid process change occurs. In this middle period, the high rate of process change reflects the segment's need to compete on the basis of price rather than product performance. In the latter stages, both product and process change decline and the segment becomes static or rigid. At this point in its cycle, the segment may be vulnerable to invasion by new ideas or disruption by external forces that could cause a reversion to an earlier stage.

THE DESIGN OF STRATEGIES

The implications of this model of innovation relate directly to the design of strategies to promote innovation in three ways. First, the model suggests that innovation is predictable in a given industrial context. Second, it asserts that the characteristics of a particular technology determine the probable nature of future innovation within an industrial segment. Third, it describes a general process of industrial maturation that appears relatively uniform across different productive segments. That model does not, however, describe sources of innovation, nor does it elucidate the forces that may transform a mature segment into a more innovative one. (See Rip and van den Belt [1988] and Schot [1992] for insights into these dynamics.)

The value of this theory of innovation is that it provides a rationale upon which (1) the regulatory agency may fashion a regulation aimed at the industry most likely to achieve a regulatory goal and (2) the industry can plan its response to environmental problems. Consistently, the theory relies on the assumption that the regulatory designer may determine the extent of an industry's innovative rigidity (or flexibility) and its likely response to regulatory stimuli with reference to objective determinable criteria.

The regulatory designer must make the following three determinations:

1. What technological response is desirable? (For example, should the regulation force a product or a process change [see Rest and Ashford 1988] and, further, should the regulation promote diffusion of existing technology, simple adaptation, accelerated development of radical innovation already in progress, or radical innovation?)
2. Which industrial sector will most likely innovate?
3. What kind of regulation will most likely elicit the desired response?

The first determination requires a technological (or, more correctly, a technology options) assessment, the second a knowledge of a variety of industrial segments, and the third an application of the model considered in this chapter.[26]

A HISTORY OF REGULATION AND ITS EFFECTS ON INNOVATION

In prior work, a brief review of regulation and its effect on technological change was presented that provides empirical support for the model of regulation-induced technological change discussed earlier in this chapter.[27] The review confirms that product regulations tend to call forth product innovations, that component or pollutant regulations[28] tend to elicit process innovations, and that the stringency of regulation is an important determinant of the degree of technological innovation.[29] In addition, the respondent's technological rigidity helps explain the particular technological solutions adopted.

The review was restricted to regulation between 1970 and 1985 under the U.S. Clean Air and Water Acts,[30] the Toxic Substances Control Act,[31] the Occupational Safety and Health Act,[32] and the Consumer Product Safety Act.[33]

Table 10.1 summarizes the pertinent characteristics of the ten regulatory cases considered in the review. In no case was the industrial response to regulation uniform. Even when the predominant response was highly innovative, a few firms selected a noninnovative solution and, in some cases, chose to exit from the industry rather than comply with the regulation. Conversely, some regulatory responses characterized as noninnovative included a few innovative solutions as well, but these were the exception in those industries.

The history demonstrates that standard setting can be used to encourage all the varieties of technological innovation as well as diffusion for both product and process change. The period from 1970 to 1985 reveals significant innovation and essential compliance with very stringent regulation.[34] Product-focused regulation primarily elicits a product response (substitution by existing products or a new product). Sometimes the new product (e.g., lead-free gasoline) is accompanied by significant process innovation as well.[35] Process-focused regulation can elicit either a process response or a product change. If a process restriction is stringent enough, product substitution may be the only practical response.

Stringency of regulation can be evaluated in terms of both the extent to which it reduces risks and the extent to which it forces development of new technology. Stringent regulations that do not require new technological solutions may appear sufficient but fall far short of their potential to achieve maximum protection. For example, the failure to adopt a 0.1 fiber/cc standard, the lowest level detectable, for worker asbestos exposure inhibited development of substitute products by the asbestos industry. The industry was able to comply with the 2 fiber/cc standard simply by installing existing pollution control equipment. By failing to adopt the more stringent standard, OSHA effectively inhibited new product development and product substitution. Thus, contrary to the widely held belief that too stringent a regulation inhibits innovation, in some cases a stan-

TABLE 10.1

A Summary of Recent Regulations and the Industrial Responses

| | | Regulatory Agency | Type of Regulation | Stringency | Industry Response | |
| | | | | | Degree | Type |
Substance	Application					
PCBs	All	EPA	Product	Very Stringent*	Radical	Product
					Incremental	Process
CFCs	Aerosol	EPA CPSC	Product	Very Stringent*	Radical	Process
					Incremental	Product
Mercury	Paint	EPA	Product	Very Stringent	Diffusion	Product
Lead	Paint	CPSC	Product	Very Stringent	Diffusion	Product
Lead	Fuel Additive	EPA	Product	Very Stringent	Incremental	Product

					Incremental	Process
Mercury	Chloralkali	EPA	Process	Stringent	Diffusion	Process
Lead	All Manufacture	OSHA	Process	Very Stringent*	Radical	Both
					Diffusion	Process
Vinyl Chloride	All Manufacture	OSHA	Process	Very Stringent*	Incremental	Process
		EPA			Diffusion	Process
Cotton Dust	All Manufacture	OSHA	Process	Very Stringent	Diffusion	Process
Asbestos	All Manufacture	OSHA	Process	Mildly Stringent	Diffusion	Process

* Substantial doubt about the standard's technological feasibility at the time the standard was proposed.

dard that is not stringent enough may inhibit innovation. A more recent example, lax regulation of formaldehyde levels for occupationally exposed garment workers, similarly failed to stimulate new product development (Rest and Ashford 1988).

Stringency may be affected, in practice, by legislative directive of the agency issuing the regulation. For example, the EPA, OSHA, and the Consumer Product Safety Commission (CPSC) have different legislative mandates. The Office of Management and Budget (OMB) directed the EPA Office of Toxic Substances to construe the scope of its regulatory authority narrowly and to refer appropriate regulation to other agencies. In particular, the OMB directed the EPA not to ban three uses of asbestos, but to pass on the regulatory responsibility to OSHA. Since it has questionable authority to ban dangerous substances, OSHA could probably only regulate worker exposure in the manufacturing process or user industries.[36] Thus, the directives would provide for regulation of ambient levels, rather than a ban, encouraging the diffusion of ventilation technology rather than the substitution of new industrial products.[37]

Uncertainty in regulatory signals or agency position can also deter innovation. Faced with uncertainties that create risks that the technology developed will not ultimately be needed or will be unnecessarily costly, potentially innovative industries will simply adopt low-risk existing technology. Thus, only diffusion will occur. Both standard setting designed to encourage innovation and innovation waivers have encountered problems with regulatory uncertainty in the past.[38]

The preceding discussion focuses on the regulation of existing chemicals, though some new chemicals are developed as part of the technological response. If the EPA desires to encourage the development of new chemicals to replace toxic chemicals currently in use, it must take more definitive actions. First, it must be clear about its premanufacturing notification process by providing definite guidelines regarding the specific safety evaluations that should be undertaken on different classes of chemicals.[39] Second, it must increase the likelihood of market penetration by appropriate regulation of existing toxic chemicals. This consolidation of new and old chemical regulation is essential to effect the desired product transition.

Innovation waivers apply mostly to process change, are expressly innovation forcing, and do not promote diffusion. The regulatory designer seldom uses a waiver mechanism for promoting radical process innovation because of the long time generally necessary to develop the innovation. The waiver mechanism, however, might well encourage both incremental process innovation and acceleration of radical innovation already underway. Success requires the EPA to give early, clear, and certain signals to the developer of the technology to minimize the risk of that technology being found unacceptable. Furthermore, good faith efforts resulting in significant, though incomplete, achievement of the pollution reduction goal should be rewarded by fail-soft strategies, using appropriate and adjustable economic sanctions.

Thus, the model of the effects of regulation on innovation applied to the history of standard setting and innovation waivers can contribute to more rational and deliberate design of regulation. The design should combine an assessment of the innovative capacity of the possible responding industrial sectors with levels and forms of regulation tailored to that capacity. The entire process should reflect a realistic evaluation of the best possible achievable technological goal. In that way, regulation can be used both to stimulate technological change for health, safety, and environmental purposes and to bring about a desirable restructuring of the industrial process.

POLLUTION PREVENTION: A NEW ETHIC OR NEW RHETORIC?

The current new emphasis on pollution prevention must be understood in a historical context. The regulations discussed in brief in the previous section had their origin in the 1970s, when somewhat aggressive government intervention was in vogue. The environmental progress and technology forcing that did occur resulted from clear and stringent regulatory requirements. Understandably, industry not only did not want to be "forced" to develop new technology, it did not want to be forced to make any technological changes that were costly or that compromised production efficiency. Government regulation was criticized as being too focused on "command and control," but for different reasons. Industry objected originally because regulation was seen to require (i.e., to command) unnecessarily low levels of permissible emissions or effluents—that is, the *stringency* of the regulations was objected to. On the other hand, some economists objected because they believed that economic measures such as pollution taxes that would affect the prices of inputs and final products were superior to mandated pollution levels for achieving environmental improvement—that is, the *method* of achieving compliance was objected to. In addition, industry and the economists argued that specification standards (of which there were precious few) stifled industry's use of more innovative and efficient ways to comply. Industry should be left to choose its method of complying. Industry, in fact, was never in favor of the economists' pollution charges, although pollution credits and trading did appeal to those industries that had pollution reduction capability to spare.

The 1980s ushered in an antiregulatory federal government whose philosophy was couched in rhetoric that rejected command and control regulation in favor of voluntary action. Carrots (economic incentives), rather than sticks, would be the governmental approach. But the term *voluntary* came to mean voluntary as to whether or not a firm would choose to comply. While existing regulations (on emissions and effluents) were not reversed, they were not vigorously enforced. Instead, new government regulations focused on information and reporting requirements (such as the reporting of emissions to air, water, and land in the Toxics Release Inventory [TRI] and the requirement to inform workers of toxic exposures) and on negotiated rather than government-dictated rule making. Given this antiregulatory era, how did it come about that pollution prevention was eventually endorsed by both government and industry? And just what kind of pollution prevention did they have in mind?

Although companies such as 3M had long argued that "pollution prevention pays," that rhetoric became identified with the idea that pollution prevention made good sense because it was grounded in the economic rationality of the industrial firm. It was argued that the firm, faced with its own hidden costs of pollution, and presented with the correct information, would change its operations to reduce environmental pollution. Industry began to embrace pollution prevention (initially without any deep understanding of what it meant), partly because the costs of waste disposal were becoming prohibitive and partly because pollution prevention contributed to a positive corporate image.[40]

Government, faced with renewed citizen demands for reduction of environmental pollution but still ideologically committed to economic instruments, began to realize if economic incentives were to reduce environmental pollution, those incentives had to be fashioned as supplements to, rather than as wholesale replacements for, regulations. Regulations continued to adhere to traditional emission and effluent restrictions and actually went even further in entertaining product phase-outs (e.g., for chlorofluorocarbons) and product bans (e.g., for asbestos). Rhetoric continued against command-and-control regulation, but now the objection that was voiced concerned overspecification of the means of achieving pollution reduction rather than the stringency of levels of pollution control. Government became increasingly committed to stringent (but flexibly implemented) regulation backed up by tough enforcement. How did industry come to accept this return of government to more serious concern with the environment?

The credibility of chemical-using and chemical-producing industries suffered greatly in the 1980s, and the fact that industrial product and emissions information was now accessible to citizens and workers through so-called right-to-know legislation (see Chapter 8) convinced companies that they must do something. The increasing prohibition on landfilling, cleanup costs at contaminated sites, and citizen action ended the do-nothing period for pollution prevention. But what, in fact, did industry do during the 1980s while waving the pollution prevention banner?

Several studies, to be discussed subsequently, throw light on the question. It turns out that, while pollution control technology was in situ, most industrial firms were not using the pollution prevention options open to them. Their first response was to undertake housekeeping changes and equipment modifications that could have been instituted much earlier had they perceived the federal government to be serious about environmental regulation. The firms also discovered that they could save money. Recycling increased and was financially attractive, partly because it was accompanied by material reclamation and partly because off-site waste treatment was becoming expensive. In other words, firms had been so suboptimal in their industrial operations that almost anything they did yielded an improvement in the efficiency of pollution abatement; referring to Figure 10.1 and the earlier discussion, firms were above the efficient frontier in their pollution control efforts (see also notes 5 and 6). What the record shows, however, is that input substitution, process redesign, and product reformulation were rare events. They were rare events because environmental requirements were not stringent enough on their face and/or because there was inadequate enforcement to force technological change.

Although a number of specific self-reports of individual accomplishments of "pollution prevention" in industry are found in the open literature,[41] three comprehensive and critical overviews compiled since 1985 discovered little fundamental technological change (INFORM 1985; OTA 1986; and EPA 1992).

The EPA has initiated several activities or programs that focus on pollution prevention: (1) the creation of the Office for Pollution Prevention, emphasizing source reduction in the manufacturing or use of chemicals and materials; (2) the creation of the Technology Innovation Office in the Office of Solid Waste and Emergency Response, emphasizing remediation technology; and (3) the creation of the National Advisory Council for Environmental Policy and Technology (NACEPT), addressing diffusion and innovation of all environmentally relevant technologies from pollution control to pollution prevention. NACEPT was created by former EPA administrator Lee Thomas to complement the science-oriented EPA Science Advisory Board with a technology-focused advisory committee. The council is working with various offices and divisions in the EPA to effectuate a cultural shift from preoccupation with risk assessment to promoting technological change.

The effects of all the above pollution prevention activities on the regulatory signals given to industry by the EPA are yet to be realized. Specific projects include: (1) negotiating pollution prevention responses into enforcement agreements with polluters, (2) revising water effluent standards to encourage pollution prevention, and (3) a "voluntary" program with industry to reduce emissions to air, water, and land of seventeen solvents and heavy metals by 33 percent and 50 percent by the end of 1992 and 1995, respectively, using source reduction and in-process recycling. (The seventeen solvents are among 189 hazardous substances whose emissions to air are to be regulated under the 1990 Clean Air Act. Thus, there may be regulation spurring the voluntary effort.)

BARRIERS TO POLLUTION PREVENTION

Even if strong signals are sent to a company to undertake pollution prevention, there may be both regulatory and industry barriers to a desired response. An appreciation of these barriers is important if successful pollution prevention policies are to be designed and implemented. The regulatory barriers for environmental technology innovation were recently addressed in a report by NACEPT focusing on permitting and compliance policy (EPA 1991a). Since the emphasis of this chapter is on the response of the firm, regulatory barriers are not discussed in detail here. The NACEPT report emphasizes a need for technological considerations in regulatory permitting and enforcement, to remove disincentives to innovate. A second NACEPT report (EPA 1991b) addresses regulatory barriers for the diffusion of technology and information relevant to pollution prevention and policies for overcoming them. (However, neither report addresses incorporating technological considerations in the design of regulation to stimulate innovation. Future work of NACEPT is expected to address that issue.)

In a report addressing problems with achieving waste reduction in the electroplating industry and in degreasing processes (New Jersey Report 1988), the authors identified a long list of mostly nonregulatory barriers to technological change and categorized them as follows:

1. *Technological:*

- Availability of technology for specific applications.
- Performance capability of technology under certain economic requirements and process design standards.
- Lack of (some) alternative substances to substitute for the hazardous components.
- Higher degree of sophistication with operation of some waste reduction technologies.
- Skepticism in performance of certain technologies and therefore a reluctance to invest.
- Process inflexibilities.

2. *Financial:*

- Research and development costs of technology.
- Costs related to risk of process changes with regard to consumer acceptance and product quality.
- Noncomprehensive cost evaluations and cost-benefit analysis as well as cost calculation method.
- Lack of understanding and difficulty in predicting future liability costs (e.g., of waste disposal).
- Short-term profitability calculations resulting in low tolerance for longer payback periods of equipment investment.
- Alleged drawback in competitiveness as other companies are not investing in waste reduction technologies.
- Lack of capital investment flexibility due to low profit margin.
- Economies of scale preventing smaller companies from investing in waste reduction options (e.g., in-plant recovery technologies).
- Possibilities that investment in process modification can be inefficient for old companies.
- Company financially (and even technically) tied up due to recent investment in wastewater treatment plant.
- Actual cost of current technologies masked in operating costs.

3. *Labor force–related:*

- Lack of person(s) in charge of management, control, and implementation of waste reduction technology.
- Reluctance to employ trained engineers for the alleged time-consuming design of waste reduction technologies.

- Inability to manage an additional program within the company and, therefore, reluctance to deal with a waste reduction program.
- Increased management requirements with implementation of waste reduction technologies.

4. *Regulatory:*

- Disincentives to invest in reuse and recovery technologies due to RCRA permit application requirements for recycling facilities in addition to compliance requirements, application costs, and so forth (work-intensive).
- Depreciation tax laws.
- RCRA waivers available only for hazardous waste treatment technology or process.
- Uncertainty about future environmental regulation.
- Regulatory focus on compliance by use of conventional end-of-pipe treatment technology (may result in investment in those treatment technologies rather than waste reduction technologies).
- Compliance with discharge standards, thus having "EPA off your back" provides no incentive to invest in waste reduction.

5. *Consumer-related:*

- Tight product specifications (e.g., military purposes).
- Risk of customer loss if output properties change slightly or if product cannot be delivered for a certain period.

6. *Supplier-related:*

- Lack of supplier support in terms of product advertising, good maintenance service, expertise of process adjustments, and so forth.

7. *Managerial:*

- Lack of top management commitment.
- Lack of engineering cooperation to break hierarchical separation of areas of responsibility (e.g., production engineers do not cooperate with environmental engineers in charge of the treatment and disposal of hazardous substances).
- Reluctance on principle to initiate change in the company ("Uncle John did it this way; therefore we are doing it the same way!").

- Lack of education, training, and motivation of employees (e.g., in good housekeeping methods or operation and maintenance of recovery technologies).
- Lack of expertise of supervisors.

Most of the barriers listed above can be disaggregated to a more detailed level. One could ask, for example, why there is a lack of top management commitment. This might be caused by various factors: (1) lack of information from the financial department to top management concerning the profitability of waste reduction technologies in general; (2) lack of confidence in performance of new technologies; (3) lack of managerial capacity and capital to deal with the transition costs of reorganizing the production process, educational programs, consumer demands, or discharge waivers; (4) lack of awareness of long-term benefits of waste reduction approach, resulting in waste reduction being a low-priority issue.

In discussing barriers and incentives for "waste reduction," the Office of Technology Assessment (OTA) concluded that:

Proven technologies and the opportunities industries have for waste reduction do not themselves guarantee these technologies will be used. Factors that affect the ability and willingness of companies to implement waste reduction measures include:

(1) the nature of the company's industrial processes,
(2) the size and structure of the company,
(3) technology and information available to the company,
(4) attitudes and opinions that affect company operations,
(5) the economics of waste reduction, and
(6) government regulations.

Whether these factors serve as constraints or incentives for waste reduction will vary even among different plants within the same company.

Because the Federal Government's current waste minimization program is *voluntary* . . . , the degree to which these factors motivate or deter industry from waste reduction has determined the amount of waste reduction accomplished to date. Understanding these constraints and incentives is therefore essential for formulating Federal policy. They will affect regulatory options, for example, because the economics of waste reduction in different industries may influence the decisions government makes about mandating levels of waste reduction. However, these elements of industrial decisionmaking are particularly important in assessing nonregulatory Federal policy options. Nonregulatory programs rely on persuasion rather than on coercion to influence decisions. (OTA 1986, 94)

The reason for articulating the earlier long list of mostly nonregulatory barriers is to emphasize that significant government intervention, including carrots and sticks, may be necessary to stimulate change in industrial sectors bogged down with inertia and attitudinal problems. In the next section are addressed those policy mechanisms most likely to (1) give a clear, unambiguous regulatory signal, so that what is expected of a firm in terms of environmental performance becomes a definable goal for the firm, and (2) effect changes in managerial knowledge and attitudes toward undertaking technological changes both to improve productivity and to reduce environmental pollution. It should be emphasized that these policy mechanisms will not reduce all barriers. However, they will change the total environment in which the firm makes decisions and thus promote pollution prevention over end-of-pipe approaches to pollution reduction.

POLICY IMPLICATIONS

In twelve interviews conducted for this chapter with state and federal personnel administering pollution prevention initiatives, the overwhelming opinion was expressed that *stringent and certain* regulatory demands (such as emission, effluent, or exposure standards, or product bans and phase-outs) were necessary to effectuate pollution prevention. Economic instruments were seen as complements to, not substitutes for, regulatory requirements. The proper combination of stringent requirements with flexible means must then be designed with something specific in mind.

It was argued earlier in this chapter that regulations must be explicitly designed with technological considerations in mind—that is, they should be fashioned to elicit the type of technological response desired (see, for example, Rest and Ashford [1988]). Again, both stringency and flexibility (through innovation waivers or enforcement practices) are important. Enforcement and permitting procedures must augment, not frustrate, the regulatory signals. Regulatory design and implementation are largely in the hands of government, the exception being negotiated rule making or voluntary compliance efforts involving an industry-government effort.

Once the regulatory signals are crafted, a firm must be receptive to those signals that require change. It was argued earlier that a key to success in changing a firm is to influence both managerial knowledge and managerial attitudes affecting decision making involving both technological change and environmental concerns. Managerial knowledge, managerial attitudes, and the technological character of the firm are not actually independent factors, although policies can be devised to affect each directly.

Relevant to managerial attitudes and decision processes, Karmali recently reviewed three different theoretical approaches that are useful in understanding what influences managerial attitudes that affect the willingness (or even the ability) of the technology-based firm to undergo change:

> *Technological determinism* is based on the principle that technological developments have their own dynamics and constraints that determine the direction of change even when stimulated by external forces.[42] *Economic determinism* considers the market and economic competition to be the main driving forces behind technological innovation. Essentially, this approach treats technology as a black box. Unlike the first two approaches, *social constructivism* attempts to move away from such unidirectional models and suggests that different social groups, such as the users of the technology and those potentially affected by it or its impacts, are able to exert influence on those who develop the technology. Any technological change is thus seen as the product of a dynamic interaction, rather than one driving force from inside or outside the firm. Social constructivism can thus be viewed as a means of bridging the gap between the organizational internalists and externalists discussed above. (Karmali 1990, 71)[43]

All these factors may well influence managerial attitudes and, hence, decision making toward environmental demands, but further, policy instruments that *per se* affect technology, as well as economic incentives and social relationships, can be used to influence the firm toward a more socially optimal technological response to environmental problems.

Decisions, of course, are also affected by the knowledge base of the firm. This can be improved by requiring the firm to identify technological options for source reduction and conduct throughput analysis (i.e., a materials accounting survey) (Hearne and Aucott 1991; National Academy of Sciences 1990) and by providing for technical assistance to firms, demonstration projects, continuing education of engineers and materials scientists, and the use of appropriate engineering consulting services (New Jersey Report 1988).

Table 10.2 lists the elements of solutions, both micro- and macro-policies, for employing a technology-focused risk management approach, coupled with policies that align important forces. (See also Chapter 9 for a discussion of similar policy initiatives utilizing government agencies and firm-focused prevention teams.) The policies fall into five groups: regulatory initiatives, technical assistance, economic instruments, stakeholder participation, and international policies.

TABLE 10.2
POLICIES TO PROMOTE CLEAN TECHNOLOGY

Regulatory Initiatives

- Shift attention from risk to risk reduction
- Focus on the appropriate target
  - —Individual hazards
  - —Industry sector
  - —Industrial processes
- Source reduction
  - —Input substitution
  - —Product reformulation
  - —Process redesign
- Multimedia focus, including worker health
- Coordination of environmental, energy, and industrial policies
- Design regulation to get the technology wanted
- Strict standards with flexible provisions

Technical Assistance

- Technical assistance to firms

Economic Instruments

- Tax policy
- Taxes on inputs and production
- Liability and financial responsibility

Stakeholder Participation

- Involve citizens and workers

International Policies

- Devise international policies

REGULATORY INITIATIVES

First, it is necessary to shift attention from assessing risk to identifying technologies for risk reduction. Second, the focus must be on appropriate targets. Risk assessment and federal regulations have focused historically on individual hazards. It is essential to think about whether regulating a whole industry would not be preferable, whether substituting one industry for another would not be preferable, or whether focusing on industrial processes, such as degreasing, that are common to many industries would not be preferable. Third, source reduction must be an integral part of a successful strategy—that is, changing the inputs, changing what industry makes, and changing how industry makes it. Fourth, a multimedia focus is needed—not just on air, water, and waste, but taking the opportunity when redesigning technology to include concerns for worker health and consumer product safety, because worker exposure and indoor air pollution are generally the two greatest sources of human exposure. It would be a mistake to design technology optimally for reducing external pollution without optimizing the reduction of worker and consumer exposure. Environmental, consumer, and worker interests should be aligned with those of the firm. Fifth, coordination (i.e., co-optimization) of environmental, energy, and industrial policies is needed. In this case, interests that have gone about their goals independently in the past would be aligned. The common theme is the design of technology, not the control of hazards. The challenge is to meet energy needs, industrial growth needs, and environmental needs by means of new technology, a new deployment of resources, and the use of process engineers, chemists, and materials scientists to design safety into technology. Sixth, as already discussed at length, it is necessary to design regulation to get the technology desired, not simply to encourage adoption of the technology that exists. Strict standards are needed, but with flexible provisions to allow and encourage innovative responses by industry.

TECHNICAL ASSISTANCE

It is essential to provide technical assistance to the firms that are not in a position to innovate. This includes information transfer, demonstration projects, the education of consultants, and joint ventures.

ECONOMIC INSTRUMENTS

Although instruments might be described as economic incentives, they must have the force of law behind them in order to work. Tax policy for investment must be seriously reconsidered. In the United States extra tax incentives are given, in the form of accelerated depreciation, for pollution control equipment. Investments in new production technology are not similarly treated, so firms that have a choice whether to adopt a pollution control device or to change their technology are better off, dollar for dollar, buying from an environmental technology vendor at present. It is necessary to consider taxes on inputs and production to provide incentives to shift away from harmful materials. It is essential to emphasize liability and financial responsibility for both property/environmental and public health damage (Ashford, Moran, and Stone 1989; Ashford and Stone 1991). Nowhere have the effects of economic and financial incentives been seen as powerfully as in the liability area. The hazardous waste industry in the United States has been dramatically restructured as a result of forcing companies to come up with insurance policies or adequate collateral to pay for cleanup, and that has caused a dramatic shift in who stays in the business (Ashford, Moran, and Stone 1987). The same must be done for industries that produce and/or use chemicals.

STAKEHOLDER PARTICIPATION

Citizens and workers need to become involved. Especially where workplace hazards are concerned, "technology bargaining" must be encouraged between management and labor (Ashford and Ayers 1987). Whatever dramatic successes have been seen in the United States are in no small part due to the fact that the nation has an active consumer and labor movement and an informed citizenry through freedom of information. Even in other countries with Anglo-Saxon legal systems, such as Canada, England, and Australia, the same success has not been seen.

INTERNATIONAL POLICIES

Finally, international policies must be devised that focus on encouraging technology innovation and not on the transfer of inappropriate or environmentally outdated technology. Here interests are aligned on a global basis.

All these policies together—regulatory initiatives, technical assistance, economic instruments, stakeholder participation, and international policies—are the key to effecting technological and human behavioral changes through information transfer, regulation, and economic incentives. All are necessary elements, but in the last analysis it will take an artistic rather than a technocratic effort to bring about success.

NOTES

1. Technological innovation is the first commercially successful application of a new technical idea. By definition, it occurs in those institutions, primarily private profit-seeking firms, that compete in the marketplace. Innovation should be distinguished from invention, which is the development of a new technical idea, and from diffusion, which is the subsequent widespread adoption of an innovation by those who did not develop it. The distinction between innovation and diffusion is complicated by the fact that innovations can rarely be adopted by new users

without modification. When modifications are extensive, the result may be a new innovation. Definitions used in this chapter draw on a history of several years' work at the Center for Policy Alternatives at the Massachusetts Institute of Technology (MIT), beginning with a five-country study, *National Support for Science & Technology: An Explanation of the Foreign Experience*, CPA No. 75-121 (Cambridge, Mass.: MIT Center for Policy Alternatives, August 18, 1975). Some definitions appear in that study at pages 1–12.

2. R. Stewart, "Regulation, Innovation, and Administrative Law: A Conceptual Framework," *California Law Review* 69 (1981): 1256–1377; W. Magat, "The Effects of Environmental Regulation on Innovation," *Law & Contemporary Problems* 43 (Winter-Spring 1979): 4–25. For a review of earlier research at the MIT Center for Policy Alternatives and elsewhere, see N. Ashford and G. Heaton, "Regulation and Technological Innovation in the Chemical Industry," *Law & Contemporary Problems* 46(3) (Summer 1983): 109–57; and Ashford, Ayers, and Stone (1985). See also Irwin and Vergragt (1989); Kurz (1987); OECD (1985); and Rothwell and Walsh (1979).

3. Environmental, health, and safety regulation, as seen by economists, should correct market imperfections by internalizing the social costs of industrial production. Regulation results in a redistribution of the costs and benefits of industrial activity among manufacturers, employers, workers, consumers, and other citizens. Within the traditional economic paradigm, economically efficient solutions reflecting the proper *balance* between costs and benefits of given activities are the major concern.

4. The work of Burton Klein best describes the kind of industry and economic environment in which innovation flourishes (B. Klein, *Dynamic Economics* [Cambridge, Mass.: Harvard University Press, 1977]). Klein's work concerns the concept of dynamic efficiency, as opposed to the static economic efficiency of the traditional economic theorists. In a state of static efficiency, resources are used most effectively within a fixed set of alternatives. In contrast, dynamic efficiency takes into account a constantly shifting set of alternatives, particularly in the technological realm. Thus, a dynamic economy, industry, or firm is flexible and can respond effectively to a constantly changing external environment. Several conditions are critical to the achievement of dynamic efficiency. A dynamically efficient firm is open to technological development, has a relatively nonhierarchical structure, possesses a high level of internal and external communication, and shows a willingness to redefine organizational priorities as new opportunities emerge. Dynamically efficient industry groups are open to new entrants with superior technologies and encourage "rivalrous" behavior among industries already in the sector. In particular, dynamic efficiency flourishes in an environment that is conducive to entrepreneurial risk taking and does not reward those who adhere to the technological status quo. Thus, Klein emphasizes structuring a macroeconomy containing strong incentives for firms to change, adapt, and redefine the alternatives facing them. Regulation is one of several stimuli that can promote such a restructuring of a firm's market strategy.

5. The "existing technology" curve represents (the supply of) lowest-cost technologies from among less efficient existing technological options for achieving various levels of environmental risk. This curve is thus the present efficient frontier of existing pollution control and production technologies having different degrees of environmental risk.

6. If a particular firm was not using the most efficient existing technological option to achieve a certain level of risk, it would lie above the existing technology curve. The firm could improve its efficiency in risk management by either using better end-of-pipe control technology or engaging in pollution prevention, which could be accomplished if the firm changed its inputs, reformulated its final products, or altered its process technology by adopting technology *new to the firm*. This would be characterized as *diffusion*-driven pollution prevention, and the changes, while beneficial, would probably be suboptimal because the firm would achieve static, but not dynamic, efficiency.

7. See Ashford and Heaton, note 2. See also Ashford, Heaton, and Priest (1979, 161) and N. Ashford and G. Heaton, "The Effects of Health and Environmental Regulation on Technological Change in the Chemical Industry: Theory and Evidence," in *Federal Regulation and Chemical Innovation*, edited by C. Hill (Washington, D.C.: American Chemical Society, 1979), 45–66; Kurz (1987); and Rip and van den Belt (1988).

8. The statutes from which these regulatory systems derive their authority are as follows (in the order described in the text): Clean Air Act (CAA), 42 U.S.C. Sec. 7401–7642 (1990); Clean Water Act (CWA), 33 U.S.C. Sec. 1251–1376 (1982); Resource Conservation and Recovery Act (RCRA), 42 U.S.C. Sec. 6901–6987 (1982); Federal Insecticide, Fungicide, and Rodenticide Act (FIFRA), 7 U.S.C. 136–136y (1982); Federal Food, Drug, and Cosmetic Act (FDCA), 21 U.S.C. Sec. 301–392 (1982); Toxic Substances Control Act (TSCA), 15 U.S.C. Sec. 2601–2629 (1982); Occupational Safety and Health Act (OSHA), 29 U.S.C. Sec. 651–678 (1982); and Consumer Product Safety Act (CPSA), 15 U.S.C. Sec. 2051–2083 (1982).

9. Technology forcing here refers to the tendency of a regulation to force industry to develop new technology. Regulations may force development of new technology by different types of restrictions. For example, air and water pollution regulation focuses on end-of-pipe effluents. See, for example, CAA, Sec. 111, 112, 202, 42 U.S.C. Sec. 7411, 7412, 7521; CWA, Sec. 301, 33 U.S.C. Sec. 1311. OSHA, in contrast, regulates chemical exposures incident to the production process. See OSHA, Sec. 6, 29 U.S.C. Sec. 655. The FDCA, FIFRA, and TSCA impose a premarket approval process on new chemicals. See FDCA, Sec. 409, 505, 21 U.S.C. Sec. 348, 355; FIFRA, Sec. 3, 7 U.S.C. Sec. 136a; and TSCA, Sec. 5, 15 U.S.C. Sec. 2604. The degree of technology forcing ranges from pure "health-based" mandates, such as those in the ambient air quality standards of the CAA, to a technology diffusion standard, such as "best available technology" under the CWA. See CAA, Sec. 109(b)(1), 42 U.S.C. Sec. 7409(b)(1); CWA, 301(b), 33 U.S.C. Sec. 1311(b). For a discussion of this issue and a comparison of

statutes, see B. LaPierre, "Technology-forcing and Federal Environmental Protection Statutes," *Iowa Law Review* 62 (1977): 771.

10. See FIFRA, Sec. 3, 7 U.S.C. Sec. 136a; FDCA, Sec. 409, 505, 21 U.S.C. Sec. 348, 355; TSCA, Sec. 5, 15 U.S.C. Sec. 2604.

11. See FDCA, Sec. 505, 21 U.S.C. Sec. 355.

12. See TSCA, Sec. 6, 15 U.S.C. Sec. 2605; OSHA, Sec. 6, 29 U.S.C. Sec. 655; and CPSA, Sec. 7, 15 U.S.C. Sec. 2056.

13. See OSHA, Sec. 3(8), 6, 29 U.S.C. Sec. 652(8), 655.

14. See generally CAA, 42 U.S.C. Sec. 7401–7642; CWA, 33 U.S.C. Sec. 1251–1376; and RCRA, 42 U.S.C. Sec. 6901–6987.

15. In practice, product and process regulations may be difficult to distinguish. If a process regulation is stringent enough, it effectively becomes a product ban. Product regulation generally gives rise to product substitution, and process regulation generally gives rise to process change. See *Federal Regulation and Chemical Innovation*, 58. See also, generally, Ashford and Heaton, note 2.

16. Note, however, that component regulations normally specify elements of the production process designed to prevent undesirable by-products. See note 29.

17. N. Ashford, D. Hattis, G. Heaton, et al., *Environmental/Safety Regulation and Technological Change in the U.S. Chemical Industry* (March 1979), Report to the National Science Foundation (CPA No. 79-6) (hereinafter cited as *CPA Chemical Industry Study*). Results of this study were published in *Federal Regulation and Chemical Innovation*.

18. See LaPierre, 837.

19. This historical review concentrates on regulations under the CAA, CWA, OSHA, CPSA, RCRA, and TSCA promulgated in the period 1970 to 1985.

20. See Ashford, Ayers, and Stone (1985).

21. The EPA has also recently initiated a pollution prevention element in enforcement negotiations for firms in violation of standards.

22. See Ashford, Ayers, and Stone (1985).

23. In particular, the work of Abernathy and Utterback offers an important model of the differences in the nature of innovation across industries and over time. See W. Abernathy and J. Utterback, "Patterns of Industrial Innovation," *Technology Review*, June-July 1978, 41. For a fuller discussion of the model in the context of regulation, see generally Ashford and Heaton, note 2.

24. Automobile engine manufacture would be a productive segment, as would vinyl chloride monomer production, but neither the automobile industry nor the vinyl chloride industry would be a productive segment since they both encompass too many diverse technologies.

25. It is typical for the old technology to improve as well, although incrementally, when a new approach challenges its dominance.

26. A research report by the MIT Center for Policy Alternatives may be useful to provide a further conceptual basis for designing regulation. See N. Ashford and R. Stone, *Evaluating the Economic Impact of Chemical Regulation: Methodological Issues* (February 1985) (CPA No. 85-01) (hereinafter cited as *CPA Economic*

Methodology Report). This research reviews and develops methodologies for assessing past and future dynamic regulatory impacts involving technological change.

27. See Ashford, Ayers, and Stone, note 2.

28. Component regulations specify undesirable elements of the production process, and pollutant regulations specify unwanted by-products of the production process. See *CPA Economic Methodology Report*, 26.

29. More precisely, a relatively high degree of stringency appears to be a necessary condition for inducing more innovative compliance responses. When stringency arises from technology-forcing characteristics of the regulation, the response tends to be more innovative.

30. See CAA, 42 U.S.C. Sec. 7401–7642 (1982); and CWA, 33 U.S.C. Sec. 1251–1376 (1982).

31. See 15 U.S.C. Sec. 2601–2629 (1982).

32. See 29 U.S.C. Sec. 651–678 (1982).

33. See 15 U.S.C. Sec. 2051–2083 (1982).

34. Compliance was achieved even though, in many cases, industry argued that compliance with the regulation was doubtful or impossible.

35. In the case of lead-free gasoline, the process innovation was a new cracking process.

36. Whether banning a substance for which a suitable substitute exists is a "feasible" regulatory action under OSHA is an untested subject. See OSHA, Sec. 6(b)(5) .29 U.S.C. Sec. 655(b)(5) (1982). Unlike OSHA, the CPSC has clear authority to ban dangerous products. Its authority, however, extends only to consumer products and not to the largely industrial products that were the subject of the proposed EPA referral. See CPSA, Sec. 2.8.15 U.S.C. Sec. 2051, 2057 (1982).

37. In Sweden, where asbestos has been banned in many applications, several substitutes have been introduced, many of which (particularly gaskets and friction products) have been developed by U.S. firms. See, for example, *Wisconsin Business Journal*, September 1972, 47.

38. See, for example, *International Harvester Co. v. Ruckelshaus*, 478 F.2d 615 (D.C. Cir. 1973), where the court remanded the EPA's decision to deny a one-year suspension of the deadline for strict auto emissions standards. The court observed that if the deadline were strictly enforced, and if any one of the major automobile manufacturers were unable to meet the deadline, "it is a likelihood that standards [would] be set to permit the high level of emission control achievable by the laggard" (638). In that event, the technological leader (Ford Motor Co.) would suffer detriment, having "tooled up to meet a higher standard than [would] ultimately be required" (638). The court was "haunted by the irony" of this situation (637). This kind of uncertainty over whether deadlines will be strictly enforced creates a disincentive to innovate.

39. See TSCA, Sec. 5, 15 U.S.C. Sec. 2604 (1982).

40. Increasing interest in pollution prevention is evident in the spawning of three new journals: *Pollution Prevention Review* (New York: Executive Enterprises Inc.); the *Journal of Clean Technology and Environmental Sciences* (Princeton, N.J.:

Princeton Scientific Publishing Co.); and the *Journal of Cleaner Production* (Oxford: Butterworth Heinemann).

41. For a critique of efforts at 3M and DuPont, see Donahue (1991) and Doyle (1991), respectively.

42. Managerial attitudes and responses obviously are influenced by incentives and by the knowledge base, general practices, and procedures (i.e., culture) of the firm. Management's attitudes and responses to environmental problems may also be determined or constrained by the particular technology of the firm itself. There is a kind of "technological determinism" that influences not only what can be done, but also what *will* be done. For example, firms that have rigid production technologies (i.e., processes that are infrequently changed) are unlikely to have managers confident enough to embark on process changes. Certain technologies beget specific management styles—if not particular managers per se. There is probably also a managerial selection in and out of the technology-based firm. For example, if changing or reformulating the final product requires a process utilizing a different scale of production, the firm may not have managers experienced at operating at smaller (or larger) scales. Although much has been written on the influence of the organization of the firm (Karmali 1990; Kurz 1987; OTA 1986, 97–98 and 100; Schot 1992), it is the author's contention that the technology of the firm can determine corporate structure and attitudes as much as the other way around.

43. The reader is referred to research relied upon by Karmali in constructing his views. See Cramer et al. (1989); Cramer et al. (1990); OECD (1989); Rip and van den Belt (1988); and Schot (1992).

REFERENCES

Ashford, N., and Ayers, C. 1987. "Changes and Opportunities in the Environment for Technology Bargaining." *Notre Dame Law Review* 62(5): 810–58.

Ashford, N.; Ayers, C.; and Stone, R. F. 1985. "Using Regulation to Change the Market for Innovation." *Harvard Environmental Law Review* 9(2): 419–66.

Ashford, N.; Cozakos, A.; Stone, R. F.; and Wessel, K. 1988. *The Design of Programs to Encourage Hazardous Waste Reduction: An Incentives Analysis.* Trenton, N.J.: New Jersey Department of Environmental Protection, Division of Science and Research.

Ashford, N.; Heaton, G.; and Priest, W. C. 1979. "Environmental, Health and Safety Regulation and Technological Innovation." In *Technological Innovation for a Dynamic Economy*, edited by C. Hill and J. Utterback, 161–221. New York: Pergamon Press.

Ashford, N.; Moran, S.; and Stone, R. 1989. *The Role of Insurance and Financial Responsibility Requirements in Preventing and Compensating Damage from Environmental Risks.* Final Report to the New Jersey Department of Insurance, Center for Technology, Policy and Industrial Development, CTPID 89-1.

Ashford, N.; Moran, S.; and Stone, R. 1987. *The Role of Changes in Statutory/Tort*

Law and Liability Insurance in Preventing and Compensating Damages from Future Releases of Hazardous Waste. Report to the Special Legislative Commission on Liability for Releases of Oil and Hazardous Materials, the Commonwealth of Massachusetts, October.

Ashford, N., and Stone, R. 1991. "Liability, Innovation and Safety in the Chemical Industry." In *The Liability Maze: The Impact of Liability Law on Safety and Innovation*, edited by R. Litan and P. Huber. Washington, D.C.: Brookings Institution.

Cramer, J.; Schot, J.; van den Akker, F.; and Geesteranus, G. 1990. "Stimulating Cleaner Technologies Through Economic Instruments: Possibilities and Constraints." *UNEP Industry and Environment*, Paris, May-June, 46–53.

Cramer, J.; Schot, J.; van den Akker, F.; and Geesteranus, G. 1989. "The Need for a Broader Technology Perspective Towards Cleaner Technologies." Discussion paper for the ECE Seminar Economic Implications of Low-Waste Technology, The Hague, October 16–19.

Dieleman, H., and de Hoo, S. 1993. *PRISMA: The Development of a Preventative, Multimedia Strategy for Government and Industry*.

Donahue, J. 1991. "Mischief, Misdeeds and Mendacity: The Real 3M." *Multinational Monitor*, May, 29–31.

Doyle, J. 1991. *Hold the Applause! A Case Study of Corporate Environmentalism as Practiced at DuPont*. Washington, D.C.: Friends of the Earth.

Environmental Protection Agency (EPA). 1992. *Improving Technology Diffusion for Environmental Protection*. Report and Recommendations of the Technology Innovation and Economics Committee of the National Advisory Council for Environmental Policy and Technology (NACEPT). Washington, D.C.: Environmental Protection Agency.

Environmental Protection Agency (EPA). 1991a. *Permitting and Compliance Policy: Barriers to U.S. Environmental Technology Innovation*. Report and Recommendations of the Technology Innovation and Economics Committee of the National Advisory Council for Environmental Policy and Technology (NACEPT). Washington, D.C.: Environmental Protection Agency.

Environmental Protection Agency (EPA). 1991b. *Pollution Prevention 1990: Progress on Reducing Industrial Pollution*. October. EPA 21P-3003. Washington, D.C.: Environmental Protection Agency.

Environmental Protection Agency (EPA). 1990. *Toxics in the Community: National and Local Perspectives*. Washington, D.C.: Office of Toxic Substances, Economics and Technology Division.

Hearne, S., and Aucott, M. 1991. "Source Reduction versus Release Reduction: The Need for National Materials Accounting Reporting for Pollution Prevention." *Pollution Prevention* 2(1): 3–17.

Heaton, G.; Repetto, R.; and Sobin, R. 1991. *Transforming Technology: An Agenda for Environmentally Sustainable Growth in the 21st Century*. Washington, D.C.: World Resources Institute.

INFORM. 1985. *Cutting Chemical Wastes: What 29 Organic Chemical Plants Are Doing to Reduce Hazardous Waste*. Washington, D.C.: INFORM.

Irwin, A., and Vergragt, P. 1989. "Re-thinking the Relationship Between Environmental Regulation and Industrial Innovation: The Social Negotiation of Technical Change." *Technology Analysis and Strategic Management* 1(1): 57–70.

Karmali, A. 1990. "Stimulating Cleaner Technologies Through the Design of Pollution Prevention Policies: An Analysis of Impediments and Incentives." Manuscript submitted in partial fulfillment of Master of Science in Technology and Policy degree, Massachusetts Institute of Technology, Cambridge, Mass.

Kurz, R. 1987. "The Impact of Regulation on Innovation. Theoretical Foundations." IAW Discussion Paper. Tuebingen, Germany: Institute for Applied Economic Research.

National Academy of Sciences (NAS). 1990. *Tracking Toxic Substances at Industrial Facilities: Engineering Mass Balance versus Materials Accounting.* Report of the National Academy of Sciences Committee to Evaluate Mass Balance Information for Facilities Handling Toxic Substances. Washington, D.C.: National Academy Press.

Office of Technology Assessment (OTA). 1986. *Serious Reduction of Hazardous Waste.* Washington, D.C.: OTA.

Organization for Economic Cooperation and Development (OECD). 1989. *Economic Instruments for Environmental Protection.* Paris: OECD.

Organization for Economic Cooperation and Development (OECD). 1987. *The Promotion and Diffusion of Clean Technologies in Industry.* Paris: OECD.

Organization for Economic Cooperation and Development (OECD). 1985. *Environmental Policy and Technical Change.* Paris: OECD.

Rest, K., and Ashford, N. 1988. "Regulation and Technological Options: The Case of Occupational Exposure to Formaldehyde." *Harvard Journal of Law and Technology* 1 (Spring): 63–96.

Rip, A., and van den Belt, H. 1988. *Constructive Technology Assessment: Toward a Theory.* Zoetermeer, Netherlands: Office of Science Policy, Ministry of Education and Sciences.

Rothwell, R., and Walsh, V. 1979. "Regulation and Innovation in the Chemical Industry." Paper prepared for an OECD workshop, Paris, September 20–21.

Schot, J. 1992. "Constructive Technology Assessment and Technology Dynamics: Opportunities for the Control of Technology." *Science, Technology & Human Values* 17(1): 36–56.

PART V

❦

The Greening of
Interfirm Relationships

11

Environmental Comakership Among Firms as a Cornerstone in the Striving for Sustainable Development

Jacqueline Cramer and Johan Schot

Since the issuing of the report *Our Common Future* by the World Commission on Environment and Development (1987), the drive for sustainable development has become a central issue in national and international environmental policies. The concept of sustainable development has worked very well as a mobilizing agent. It is now referred to in many policy documents. Although the concept itself is accepted at the rhetorical level, its incorporation into practical environmental policies is highly contested. Particularly, the question of how economy and ecology should be brought into harmony with each other leads to major disputes. To give concrete form to the drive for sustainable development, the Dutch government has incorporated the concept into its National Environmental Policy Plan (Tweede Kamer 1989) in terms of three objectives:

- Closing substance cycles in the raw materials production process-product-waste chain and associated emissions.
- Saving energy along with increasing efficiency and using renewable energy sources.
- Improving quality (above quantity) of products, production processes, raw materials, waste, and the environment to extend the use of substances in the economic cycle.

From these objectives, the cornerstone for operationalizing the concept of sustainability can be derived: the effective control of the entire life cycle of products from raw material to waste forms. The need to manage the waste chain as a whole (the so-called cradle-to-grave approach) calls for government product policies and business product strategies extending over the whole life cycle of a product.

In the past, neither governments nor industries have developed an environmental product policy.[1] Governments have been accustomed to focusing on regulatory measures directed toward limiting the release of contaminants by individual firms (for example, through standard setting) or branches of industry. Such policies are rarely designed to influence the choices of individual firms as to the materials and technologies they use and the products they make. Nor have these policies had an influence on the relationships between firms, from the producers of raw materials to the producers of intermediate products and the end-user firms. At best, firms have complied with government regulations, but chiefly by using add-on technologies (Cramer et al. 1990; Heaton et al. 1991).

In the past decade, most multinational corporations and some small and medium-size firms have begun to pay more attention to environmental concerns (see the Introduction). The actions taken, however, seldom involve a willingness to experiment, improve, and substitute products, except under public and regulatory pressure. Firms do not follow an innovative product strategy.[2] Such a strategy does not involve a single effort to produce an environmentally sound product. Instead, an innovative strategy aims at improving the company's *capability* to produce environmentally sound products. To develop this capability it is important, for example, to incorporate environmental considerations into the business strategy of the whole firm, including departments responsible for innovation, such as research and development (R&D) and marketing, and to create organizational conditions for synergy between the environmental function and other functions involved in formulating the business strategy.[3]

In addition, the shaping of an innovative product strategy implies that the firm should no longer be concerned only with its own production process but also with other phases of the product life cycle. Since most firms are not themselves involved in all phases of this cycle, cooperation among firms is necessary. This need for cooperation is not limited to the development of environmentally sound products. Innovation processes of any kind most often do not occur within companies, but between companies. Innovations are the result of an interplay between, for example, users and producers. By cooperating, companies can mobilize external resources and experience that is lacking within just one company (Hakansson 1987). This chapter does not discuss product innovation as such, but one important precondition and aspect of it—namely, the way firms interact on environmental aspects of products. This interaction is called environmental comakership (for original use, see Schot [1992]). Currently, environmental comakership consists of two steps. The first step is the exchange of information between firms about the environmental aspects of their (semifinished) products. A second, more committing step is the setting of demands on suppliers by user firms. Both steps could result in more structured cooperation between suppliers and users aimed at joint development of environmentally sound products.

Do these forms of environmental comakership among firms already exist? Is there already a tendency among firms to broaden their conventional business strategy toward an orientation to the whole product life cycle? These questions form the major issues discussed in this chapter. More specifically, the chapter addresses the following questions:

1. Is there already a visible tendency toward environmental comakership among firms? Two indicators are used to examine this tendency: increasing information exchange between firms about environmental aspects, and the setting of demands on suppliers by user firms. In addition, the chapter assesses which possibilities for improving current environmental cooperation are considered useful and practical by industry.
2. What role can governments play in stimulating environmental comakership among firms?

In answering these questions, the chapter makes use of two empirical studies. The first study addressed current methods of environmental information exchange among producers in the Netherlands and the possibilities for intensifying this process (Cramer, Dral, and Roes 1991). This research consisted of case studies of four industries: wood preservatives, printing inks, cosmetics, and carpeting. For each case study an average of eleven interviews were carried out with representatives of the various stages in the production chain. The second study focused on the role of environmental aspects in the strategies of a broad variety of company actors both inside (R&D, marketing, quality control, etc.) and outside (banks, insurance companies, trade unions, etc.) companies in the chemical industry (Schot et al. 1990). One part of the study was devoted to the purchasing policies of firms. The study included eight multinational chemical corporations and five small chemical firms with less than 100 employees. The results are based on company documentation and an average of three in-depth interviews with officials in each company. The results of both studies were discussed in a workshop attended by representatives of industry, government, research institutes, and consulting firms.

This chapter proceeds as follows. The next section discusses current methods of environmental information exchange among producers and the possibilities for further structuring this exchange. Existing practices for setting demands on firms, motives for doing so, and obstacles to further development are then addressed, as are possibilities for environmental comakership. The question of how government can stimulate environmental comakership and therefore bring about needed product policies is discussed thereafter, and a combination of supply and demand policies are put forth, an important part of which is the orchestration of sustainability strategy formulation. A plea is made also for a new role for governments as lead users who can influence innovation.

INFORMATION EXCHANGE AMONG FIRMS

CURRENT METHODS

For the study of how exchange of environmental information among firms currently takes place, the selection of the four industries—wood preservatives, printing inks, cosmetics, and carpeting—was based on the following considerations. First, products and product groups were sought that are regarded as priorities in Dutch environmental policy because they are highly polluting. A consideration was the inclusion of both manufacturers that produce semimanufactured products for professional markets and those that produce consumer products. Finally, a branch of industry was sought that already has experience in the development of a product information system. The carpeting industry turned out to be a good example.

From the four case studies it can be concluded that the exchange of environmental information among firms is still fairly unstructured. The formal system of data exchange is derived mainly from specific legislation or government directives. In the four industries it is compulsory to divulge certain product data under such regulations as the Environmentally Harmful Substances Act, the Hazardous Substances Act, the Food and Drugs Act, and the Pesticides Act. This product information relates mainly to risk and safety aspects, however, and only to a limited extent to environmental aspects. In the European Community (EC), requirements for the disclosure of product information are being developed for the industries. It is likely that the release of product information will increasingly be coordinated and structured at the European level, a trend that is in fact already noticeable.

Aside from regulatory requirements, some environmental information is also formally exchanged on a voluntary basis by means of certificates as part of a certification program. Although these certificates do not contain detailed information themselves, firms know the detailed requirements to get a certificate. In most industries certificates are primarily oriented to quality and safety aspects. In the wood preservatives industry, however, the so-called SKH (Stichting Keuringsbureau Hout) quality certificate constitutes an important channel of information for environmental aspects as well. Since quality aspects (such as the leaching power of the wood preservation agent) in this industry are so closely connected with environmental aspects, this certificate functions in part as an environmental certification. In most of the other industries studied, this is not so clearly the case, since their certificates are primarily oriented to quality and safety aspects.

Other than these formal mechanisms, information is currently exchanged mainly in an informal way. Examples are written formats such as product data sheets, brochures, leaflets, and letters, and oral exchange by informal consultation. The intensity of such informal exchange varies. In the industries studied, informal exchange tends to occur more easily with suppliers than with clients. The suppliers are mainly chemical firms that provide raw or auxiliary materials (see also Chapter 12). The larger companies in these industries certainly maintain good informal contacts with supplier firms. Consequently, they tend to be generally satisfied with the current form of environmental data exchange with their suppliers. The situation is different for some of the slightly smaller companies, which sometimes lack sufficient expertise to impose requirements for environmental product information on their suppliers.

The four industries tend to exchange less information with their clients about the environmental aspects of their products. Information is exchanged only if clients specifically request it. In the wood preservatives and printing inks industries, such communication is more common than in the cosmetics and carpeting industries. One reason is that the former industries supply products that are designated as priority items by the Dutch Ministry of Housing, Physical Planning, and Environment. The environmental problems in these industries are consequently discussed more from a social point of view than in the cosmetics and carpeting industries. Furthermore, the wood preservatives and printing inks industries both supply to industrial end users in particular. These users tend to set clearer environmental requirements than those in the retail trade, which supplies directly to the consumer (as in the case of the cosmetics and carpeting industries).

It can be stated that information exchange among producers about the environmental aspects of their products is still rather ad hoc. It is as yet not common practice in industry to provide environmental information to customers or to request such information from suppliers. These conclusions are supported by similar experiences of representatives of participating countries at a workshop on this topic, organized by the Economic Commission for Europe (ECE) in April 1991 (ECE 1991).

Possibilities for Further Information Exchange

Is it considered useful and practical to structure more carefully the current methods of exchanging environmental product information between firms? If so, how could this be achieved most successfully? These questions were asked of the persons interviewed in the four industries. To help assess their views, a tool called the environmental matrix was used. This matrix provides a format for full environmental information on all the phases in a product's life cycle (see Figure 11.1). The matrix was discussed with those interviewed by asking whether the information outlined on the matrix should become part of the information exchange.

Most of those interviewed were not familiar with the environmental matrix or the life cycle approach. They consequently found it difficult to envision immediately how the information exchange system would function in practice and what the drawbacks would be. Some feared that by providing information on environmental effects throughout the entire product life cycle they would be held liable for all the environmental effects in the entire cycle. Some even pointed out that the introduction of such a system of information exchange could be effective only if it were coordinated at a European and/or international level. Otherwise, problems of competition might arise.

Despite these objections, most of those interviewed said that they were prepared to collaborate, subject to certain conditions, on the introduction of a product information exchange system encompassing the whole product life cycle. In general it was thought that such a system would be useful only if limited to specific environmentally harmful products and the chief environmental problems connected with these products. Almost everyone interviewed rejected the idea of setting up such a system for all products, which seems an impossible task in, for example, the cosmetics industry, where a multitude of different products are manufactured.

FIGURE 11.1
MATRIX OF ENVIRONMENTAL PRODUCT INFORMATION

ENVIRONMENTAL ASPECT	PRODUCT CYCLE				
	PRODUCTION I	PRODUCTION II	DISTRIBUTION AND TRANSPORT	USE OR CONSUMPTION	DISPOSAL (INCLUDING RECYCLING)
Use of natural resources (energy, water, raw materials)					
Water pollution					
Air pollution					
Soil pollution					
Waste production					
Noise and other nuisances					

In general, the industry representatives expressed reservations about making such an exchange system compulsory. They preferred to acquire experience with exchange of information first. Only afterward should compulsory information exchange be considered.

In an EC context as well, caution seems advisable concerning the introduction of statutory information exchange. There is a chance that the EC would view such a requirement as an obstacle to trade. To avoid this problem it seems preferable to make agreements on a voluntary basis.

All those interviewed expressed a marked preference for developing a system of exchange that is in line with initiatives already in progress in each industry. In the wood preservatives industry, for example, it has been proposed that environmental aspects be added to the SKH quality certificate. Despite reservations, representatives of the carpeting industry saw opportunities in the long term for incorporating environmental aspects in the PIT (Produkt Informatie Tapijt) label, which is geared to providing consumers with information on the quality aspects of products. First, however, they wanted to refine the PIT system that the industry introduced in August 1989. Representatives of the cosmetics and printing inks industries believed there were opportunities for expanding the category of "toxicological and ecological information" in their product data sheets, although they also believed there would be problems obtaining this information. Ecological effects in particular are difficult to document scientifically, and research in this area is very costly.

In view of these points, it is understandable that the four industries are not in favor of a universal system of information exchange. The industry representatives argued that, in general, a separate system would have to be set up for each industry in close consultation with those involved in the industry.

The views of suppliers and clients in the four industries agreed in part with the views of the manufacturers. A number of suppliers (particularly chemical firms) saw no reason to expand the current system of exchanging product information in view of the close contacts they have with their clients. A limited number of suppliers were more positive on this matter.

Among clients, there was a marked difference between the professional end users and those whose own end user is the consumer. The professional clients, or end users, attached greater importance to expanding product information on environmental aspects than did the retailer clients. The professional end users operate within legal frameworks that force them to take note of the environmental aspects of their products. They also frequently have more expertise than clients who supply directly to the consumer. The latter group of clients tends to respond to environmental issues only when the consumer raises them. Many of these clients therefore considered it more useful to encourage the introduction of an environmental label directed at consumers. In their view, this kind of label would have a more profound impact on the market than mandatory information exchange between manufacturers.

In sum, the four industries envisioned certain possibilities for further structuring environmental information exchange among firms. However, the development and type of exchange should depend on the particular branch of industry.

SETTING REQUIREMENTS FOR SUPPLIERS

From a study of the environmental behavior of the chemical industry in the Netherlands it appears that there is at least a tendency to integrate environmental considerations in purchasing policies by end product manufacturers. However, initiatives in this direction are still ad hoc. The following are the kinds of stipulations imposed on chemical firms by their users with regard to environmental aspects:

1. Restrictions pertaining to substances that have environmental effects that are considered problematic or that receive a great deal of negative publicity. Firms request that their suppliers provide products or materials without these particular substances. Examples of such substances are polyvinyl chloride, cadmium, and chlorofluorocarbons.

2. Requirements that increase the possibilities for the reuse or recycling of the firm's product at the waste stage. The automobile industry, for example, is investigating ways of recovering the plastics used in automobiles when they are ready for scrap. One of the conditions is that all the plastics used have the same chemical structure, which makes it easier to recycle and reuse them. The automobile industry is consequently exerting pressure on the chemical industry to supply plastics that meet these demands for reuse (see Chapter 13). To cite another example, various companies are investigating methods for increasing reuse of their own packaging materials. For instance, studies are being carried out to determine the possibilities for returnable butter tubs and detergent containers.

3. Specifications as to method of delivery. Waste disposal and storage is becoming an increasingly high-expense item, and waste storage involves risk. Therefore, a growing number of companies are implementing strict stock policies. The objective is to keep the amount of stock as low as possible. Suppliers are requested to deliver the exact amount required, preferably in returnable packaging; they are also requested to forward the

order so that it arrives on the day it is required for use. There are two areas in which waste will be eliminated through improved inventory control practices: firms will no longer have to dispose of material that (1) has been in stock so long that it exceeds its shelf time, or (2) is no longer needed. The second situation can arise when the formulation for making a product changes (Hunter 1989).

The use of checklists containing specifications for suppliers' products is not yet standard practice by end product manufacturers. Nor are any requirements specified for the way the suppliers produce their products. The persons interviewed in the study of the chemical industry, however, expected that such requirements will be made in the near future. Two arguments were given for this. First, it is impossible for an end user to sell its product as ecologically sound if the raw materials used in that product are produced in a very polluting way. Second, experiences with quality care were also mentioned. In the past, users mainly set quality requirements for products. In recent years, however, they have begun to impose requirements relative to the process and system used in the manufacture of products.

There are three main motives for end users to set environmental requirements for their suppliers: (1) reduction of cost—for example, waste storage; (2) shifting of responsibility for the consequences of regulations; and (3) anticipation of reaction to market demands.

The persons interviewed in the chemical industry study mentioned four barriers to the establishment of requirements for suppliers:

- There is a risk that those putting out work to contract will be held responsible for the conduct of their suppliers.
- Setting environmental requirements is the responsibility of suppliers.
- Some suppliers hold such a strong market position that the user is unable to ignore them, and with these suppliers there is insufficient freedom to set demands.
- Setting requirements implies that the characteristics of the product to be supplied will change, which may affect the supplier's production process.

At least the first signs can be observed of a growing interaction among firms concerning the environmental quality of the products they supply or use. In the majority of cases, users do not exert pressure on suppliers unilaterally. The interaction is more like a consultation process that sometimes even results in a joint effort to solve a particular environmental problem or leads to the joint establishment of a new company. These developments are clearly forms of environmental comakership. However, they are still exceptions. It is not yet common practice for firms to jointly seek a more environmentally sound product development strategy.

FUTURE OPPORTUNITIES FOR ENVIRONMENTAL COMAKERSHIP

Environmental comakership is a relatively new phenomenon. Although information exchange still occurs on a rather ad hoc basis, companies do envision certain possibilities for further development of information systems. In addition, firms have started to impose requirements on their suppliers and to cooperate in solving environmental problems. These trends clearly relate to another trend in industry in the field of quality control. Since the 1980s many large user firms have decided, due to increasing international competition, to contract out more work to fewer firms (Hagedoorn and Schot 1988) in an effort to build strong relationships with a small number of suppliers. The strengthening of these relationships includes a substantial upgrading of quality standards. As a result, quality has started to take on a different meaning as well.

In the 1960s and 1970s, quality was monitored by quality control personnel or departments whose task was to spot, often by random checks, products that failed to meet established quality standards. Firms are now trying to integrate responsibility for quality control throughout the organization. This movement is often labeled total quality management. Quality control methods have also undergone enormous change. No longer are random checks made at the start of the process, halfway through the process, and on the finished product. New quality control methods imply a continuous process of checking. Suppliers that fail to meet quality standards and do not establish needed quality control systems are pushed out of the market. Closer relationships between users and suppliers have also resulted in growing interaction in the design of products, a development labeled as comakership.

The general trend of closer cooperation among firms offers a good starting point for environmental considerations. Environmental comakership could become part of this trend and consequently gain more momentum. Although environmental comakership is still in its infancy, there is fertile ground for tightening the social interaction among firms around environmental issues. Firms have already begun to exchange data, set requirements, and in some cases develop new products, and this trend could profit from already established relationships in the quality control area. Despite the fertility of the soil, however, environmental comakership will not come to full bloom by itself. There are many obstacles, including a lack of information on the environmental aspects of products and a lack of clearly articulated demand from industry for this information. In this area government could play an important stimulating role.

THE ROLE OF GOVERNMENT IN ENHANCING ENVIRONMENTAL COMAKERSHIP

PROVIDING AND STIMULATING THE SUPPLY OF INFORMATION

The environmental assessment of the whole life cycle of a product is not easy. The first obstacle is the enormous lack of data. Second, even when data are available, it is often difficult to decide how to combine, rate, and aggregate it. There is also the trickier problem of how to evaluate and compare various environmental effects. Aluminum provides a good example. Considering the enormous amount of energy needed to make aluminum, it cannot by this standard be considered an environmentally sound product. However, aluminum lends itself admirably to recycling. The energy balance of this material shifts, therefore, in a positive direction. Thus, if a high percentage of aluminum were to be recycled, it could be considered an environmentally sound product.

To help address the need for more information and methodologies for managing it, governments should take an active approach in setting up environmental data bases and helping industries develop methodologies. In fact, such initiatives are already being taken in some countries, including Germany and the Netherlands, and by the EC. These initiatives are important in creating a supply of information, but they are not enough. One problem is that firms, especially small and medium-size firms, do not easily make use of formal data bases set up by the government (Allen et al. 1983). These data bases usually have high thresholds because of administrative procedures or high costs, but even more important in gathering information, firms rely on personal contacts and their own network, which includes suppliers, users, and competitors (Hakansson 1987; Von Hippel 1988). One important reason for this is that firms need specific information for their own situations. The information stored in data bases is most often general, and thus, firms still must tailor it to their own needs and questions. In addition, given the enormous number of different products and substances, government will be able to gather information on only a few; thus, government data bases will be limited to information on certain products.

One way to avoid these problems is to let firms themselves gather information on the environmental aspects of products. Therefore, it is essential that the trend described in this chapter and in Chapter 12 toward increased information exchange among firms on the environmental aspects of products gain momentum. If this trend continues, firms themselves will provide the information to their customers or suppliers. Government would focus less on developing data bases and more on stimulating the development of a system of information exchange. From the authors' research it is also clear that the idea of a uniform system of information exchange for all industries should be rejected. Information exchange should be tailored toward specific industries. At this time, the best option is to link environmental information exchange to existing systems. There are two obvious possibilities for accomplishing this. The first is to piggyback on the movement toward total quality management. If information about the environmental aspects of products is integrated into firms' quality control systems, some environmental information will be transferred automatically among firms by means of certificates. The possible disadvantage is that environmental data will be overlooked because other quality characteristics are considered more important. A second possibility is the incorporation of environmental data into material data sheets. Present material data sheets are already often required by law, but basically contain safety data. Some firms have already experimented with this idea by introducing environmental data sheets. Material data sheets typically do not contain information that covers a whole product life cycle. This problem could be solved by making it mandatory that for every phase of the product life cycle, manufacturers add information about their production processes (including emissions and energy use) and the environmental (waste) problems that are added to the product (Assies et al. 1991).

ORGANIZING DEMAND THROUGH SUSTAINABILITY STRATEGIES

The supply of information by governments or firms themselves is not enough to provoke environmental comakership that will force firms to develop and maintain an innovative product policy that results in environmentally friendly products. Most firms will react to the supply of information by storing it, without making any real change in the way they innovate. If supply-oriented policies are to work, they should be complemented with demand-oriented policies. A demand-oriented government policy aims at stimulating the articulation of demand for specific products. One way government can accomplish this is by making manufacturers responsible for their own products through the whole life cycle. Although this would be an important impetus for innovation (see Chapter 13), this discussion focuses on possibilities to organize demand articulation by more actively aiming at specific environmental targets.

Von Hippel (1988) showed that user firms in some cases have great influence on the nature of innovation processes in supplier firms. In the innovation literature, great emphasis has been placed on the fulfillment of user needs as one of the characteristics of successful innovation (Freeman 1982, 124–25). It is therefore advantageous for suppliers to have access to lead users who will inform them about demand specifications. These lead users must be competent—meaning, according to Jervan et al. (1989, 7), users who can define the problems, distinguish the trivial from the more fundamental problems, and assist actively with technical knowledge. Access to lead users is essential in the case of a new technology with vague and undefined performance.

Governments could act as lead users themselves or stimulate and help firms to formulate user needs. The best-known and most successful examples of governments acting as lead users are from the military and telecommunications areas.[4] In these fields governments have been able to elicit rapid technological development in specific directions. Suppliers are willing to take high risks because their market is secured. This advantage is lacking with regard to environmentally friendly products. Further, government regulation has not resulted in stable, long-term markets for such products. On the contrary, markets are often vague and undefined, and what counts as an environmentally friendly product is rather unclear.

A useful tool to articulate and organize demand is the development of "sustainability strategies" (for original use, see Cramer 1991). A sustainability strategy means the conscious selection and application of a particular technological trajectory and products because they are preferred over other technological trajectories and products in view of their sustainability. Such sustainability strategies should be formulated at the level of a specific product group or a specific social activity, such as transportation or recreation. The strategy should be directed primarily toward reaching explicit environmental objectives in a time span of five to fifteen years. For example, the following sustainability strategy might be stated: "The objective is that by the year 2000 the recycling capacity of the most commonly used plastics will reach at least 60 percent. This implies a standardization of types of plastics and the establishment of an infrastructure for collecting and processing plastic waste." An example of an attempt to formulate a sustainability strategy is the U.S. Environmental Protection Agency's industrial toxics project. This project targets specific chemicals in the manufacturing sector and develops focused pollution prevention strategies for them. The project offers industry the opportunity to participate on a voluntary basis.

The design of sustainability strategies reaches beyond the level of individual firms and focuses, for example, in the case of product groups, on the whole production chain. Furthermore, such strategies should focus not only on environmental and technological aspects, but on socioeconomic and infrastructural changes, which will accompany product changes as well. On the basis of a comparison of different technological trajectories and products it can be decided, in the end, which trajectories and products should be preferred in view of sustainability and therefore be put into practice.

In the design of sustainability strategies, government's role is twofold. Government should influence the process by setting the environmental objectives to be attained. Government should also keep watch over the particular industries, which all tend to defend their own survival, acting as an arbiter and distinguishing individual from collective interests. It should set the targets, and the industries should elaborate the best sustainability strategies under these boundary conditions. Government can also act by structuring action to make things work, focusing on the establishment of networks among firms and of user-producer relations in which environmental criteria have a place. The building of networks will result in increasing pressure by firms on one another to solve environmental problems, and in this way markets will force new environmental products to come about.

Formulating sustainability strategies will not be an easy task. Problems related to a lack of environmental information and methodologies for handling it will recur. Despite these problems, the authors believe it is better to clearly choose a particular sustainability strategy. The advantage is that the current, often scattered environmental efforts of government, industry, and research institutes can be concentrated on specific main issues that are commonly agreed upon and further articulated. In addition, a specific strategy offers firms more certainty about future market prospects. This means that an important obstacle to innovation will be removed (see Chapter 10).

CONCLUSION

The early sections of this chapter discussed a tendency toward environmental comakership among companies. Although current information exchange is still ad hoc and is not yet common practice, it is clear that it will expand in the future. In addition, companies have started to set requirements for one another. It is expected that this trend will gain momentum as well. One route for this could be through linkage with changes in the field of total quality management. The chapter also discussed various points of departure for governments to stimulate environmental comakership, addressing such policies as developing data bases and methodologies for life cycle analysis, stimulating data exchange among firms, making firms liable for their own products (see Chapter 13), and orchestrating the formulation of sustainability strategies. The combined implementation of these policies will result in an increasing pressure on firms to develop innovative responses. In the long run, this could lead to the incorporation of environmental aspects of products into the structure and culture of the firm.

NOTES

1. The need for a product policy can also be argued on the basis of actual pollution involved. According to an article titled "The Problem Is the Product" in *The Economist* (September 8, 1990, p. 16), in the best chemical companies effluent accounts for perhaps 4 percent of output. It is in the hands of consumers that large amounts of waste are created.

2. For classifications of environmental firm strategies, see Petulla (1987), Steger (1988), and Schot (1992). Coming from different angles, all three authors identify the importance of a strategy that is based on the expectation that, in time, excelling in environmental management can lead to competitive advantages. In that case, innovation in the environmental aspects of products is essential. Such a strategy clearly differs from, for example, an offensive strategy that does aim at improving existing practices, but not systematically. Firms that follow an offensive strategy focus on environmental problems identified outside the firm, either by government or by the public. They do not try to enhance the firm's structural capability to deal with environmental aspects.

3. In multinational corporations environmental considerations do play a role in product development, as a check afterward. These checks make it possible to block certain developments, and they have a defensive nature. In most firms, however, environmental considerations do not play a large role in the selection and formulation of, for example, R&D projects (Groenewegen and Vergragt 1990; Schot 1992). The defensive character of firms' environmental policies can be derived from the position of the environmental function within firms as well. Environmental officials are concerned primarily with regulation and implementation of external or internal requirements. The time they spend on strategy formulation is restricted (ECOTEC 1990; Schot et al. 1990).

4. An informative example of technology forcing in this respect occurred during the development phase of the transistor. The military explicitly selected and promoted transistors made from silicon (which withstood nuclear radiation

better than germanium) as well as particular designs capable of high-frequency operation. Radiation resistance and high-frequency operation were performance characteristics unique to the military (Misa 1991).

REFERENCES

Allen, T. J.; Hyman, D. B.; and Pinckney, D. L. 1983. "Transferring Technology to the Small Manufacturing Firm: A Study of Technology Transfer in Three Countries." *Research Policy* 12: 199–211.

Assies, J. A.; Groenewegen, P.; Korenromp, R. H. J.; and Vergragt, P. J. 1991. "Milieuprofielen en de praktijk" (Environmental profiles in practice). Internal report. Groningen, Netherlands: University of Groningen.

Cramer, J. 1991. *De Illusie Voorbij; Op Weg naar een Brede Aanpak van de Milieuproblemen* (The illusion is over; On the road to a broad approach to environmental problems). Utrecht: Van Arkel.

Cramer, J.; Dral, P.; and Roes, B. 1991. *Produkt Informatieuitwisseling over Milieuaspecten tussen Producenten* (Product information exchange about environmental aspects between producers). Leidschendam, Netherlands: Ministry of Housing, Physical Planning, and Environment.

Cramer, J., and Schot, J. 1990. *Innovation and Diffusion of Environmental Technology: Opportunities for Research from a Technology Dynamics Perspective*. Publication No. 44A on Nature and Environment. Rijswijk, Netherlands: Advisory Council for Research.

Cramer, J.; Schot, J. W.; van den Akker, F.; and Maas Geesteranus, G. 1990. "Stimulating Cleaner Technologies Through Economic Instruments: Possibilities and Constraints." In *UNEP Industry and Environment* 13(2): 46–53.

Economic Commission for Europe (ECE), Working Party on Low- and Nonwaste Technology and Re-utilization and Recycling of Wastes. 1991. *Minutes of the Meeting of the Task Force on Environmental Product Profiles* (EPP). April 3–5. Geneva: ECE.

ECOTEC. 1990. *The Impact of Environmental Management on Skills and Jobs*. Birmingham, England: ECOTEC.

Freeman, C. 1982. *The Economics of Industrial Innovation*. London: Pinter Publishers.

Groenewegen, P., and Vergragt, P. 1990. "Environmental Issues as Threats and Opportunities for Technological Innovations." *Technology Analysis & Strategic Management* 3(1): 43–55.

Hagedoorn, J., and Schot, J. 1988. *Co-operation Between Companies and Technological Development*. Apeldoorn, Netherlands: Studiecentrum voor Technologie en Beleid/TNO.

Hakansson, H., ed. 1987. *Industrial Technological Development. A Network Approach*. London: Croom Helm.

Heaton, G.; Repetto, R.; and Sobin, R. 1991. *Transforming Technology: An*

Agenda for Environmentally Sustainable Growth in the 21st Century. Washington, D.C.: World Resources Institute.

Hunter, J. 1989. "Waste Minimization Through Inventory Control." Paper prepared for Waste Minimization Conference, New Brunswick, N.J., May 10.

Jervan, H.; Onsager, K.; and Aasen, B. 1989. "The Role of Public Sector Users in the Development of Environmental Technology." Internal report. Policy Group No. 755. Oslo: Resource.

Misa, T. 1991. "Constructive Technology Assessment: Cases, Concepts, Conceptualizations." Paper prepared for conference on Constructive Technology Assessment: Policy Implications of New Directions in the History, Sociology, and Economics of Technical Change, University of Twente, Enschede, Netherlands, September 20–22.

Petulla, J. 1987. "Environmental Management in Industry." *Journal of Professional Issues in Engineering* 113(2): 167–83.

Schot, J. W. 1992. "Credibility and Markets as Greening Forces for the Chemical Industry." *Business Strategy and the Environment* 1: 35–44.

Schot, J.; De Laat, B.; der Meijden, R.; and Bosma, H. 1990. *Geven om de Omgeving. Milieugedrag van ondernemingen in de chemische industrie* (Care for the environment. Environmental behavior of chemical firms). Report No. 15. The Hague: Netherlands Organization for Technology Assessment (NOTA).

Steger, U. 1988. *Umweltmanagement: Erfahrungen und Instrumente einer umweltorientierten Umweltstrategie* (Environmental management: Experience and methods of an environmentally oriented strategy). Wiesbaden, Germany: Frankfurter Allgemeine/Gabler.

Tweede Kamer (Second Chamber of the States General of the Netherlands). 1989. *Nationaal Milieubeleidsplan* (National environmental policy plan). 1988–1989 Session. 21 137, nrs. 1-2, The Hague: SDU.

Von Hippel, E. 1988. *The Sources of Innovation.* Oxford: Oxford University Press.

World Commission on Environment and Development. 1987. *Our Common Future.* Oxford: Oxford University Press.

12

Forces Shaping the Development and Use of Product Stewardship in the Private Sector

Patricia S. Dillon and Michael S. Baram

During the past twenty years, U.S. corporations have made significant progress in reducing routine pollution and accident hazards at their manufacturing facilities. Increasingly, however, manufacturers recognize the need to extend their responsibility beyond the plant boundary to encompass environmental concerns throughout their products' life cycles. Many large manufacturers are in the early stages of designing improved management systems and product stewardship programs aimed at the systematic identification and reduction of environmental risks associated with their products.

Companies employ a number of strategies to achieve safer and more environmentally acceptable products, including product redesign and the transfer of expertise to their suppliers and customers. The application of risk management strategies varies, depending on the product and the forces influencing the company. Product characteristics, such as type of environmental risk and commercial life cycle, affect decisions. External forces that shape the nature of the corporate response include cradle-to-grave and other regulatory requirements, market forces, liability, customer demand, and public pressures. Since it appears that companies selectively apply risk management strategies, it is possible to provide incentives or develop public policy tools that would increase the use of private-sector initiatives.

This chapter examines the concept of product stewardship, the forces promoting the development and use of product stewardship in the private sector, and current practices of U.S. corporations with particular emphasis on technology transfer. Technology transfer is defined as the purposeful transfer of technical and environmental management information and know-how from one organization to one or more others where it is needed to achieve environmental protection objectives. Technology transfer is emphasized because of its potential to provide direct benefits to the recipient as well as to diffuse expertise throughout industry. The chapter concludes with suggestions for how policy makers can use this analysis to enhance technology transfer in the private sector to reduce environmental risk.

Two research projects, which include data from more than twenty companies, are the basis for the analysis presented here. The first project examined the voluntary initiatives of companies in response to the U.S. Emergency Planning and Community Right to Know Act (also known as SARA Title III), which requires companies to publicly disclose an unprecedented amount of information on their chemical use and emissions (Baram et al. 1992). On the basis of interviews with numerous company officials, case studies were developed for eight companies involved in various life cycle stages (for example, chemical production, processing, and use) of three chemicals and operating in diverse industries. The study was designed to determine the voluntary initiatives companies are taking to reduce accidental and routine releases of chemicals and the scope of interactions among chemical producers and their industrial customers.

The second study examined product stewardship and related developments such as "design for environment" in the private sector. This study had three principal objectives: (1) to examine the scope, design, and implementation of corporate product stewardship programs; (2) to identify approaches to the design of environmentally responsible products and services; and (3) to identify similarities and differences in the activities of companies that can be ascribed to product attributes such as environmental risk or commercial characteristics. Three product sectors—consumer electronics, pesticides for home use, and chlorinated solvents—were chosen for study based on differences in their commercial life cycles and the environmental risks they posed.

DEFINING THE CONCEPT OF PRODUCT STEWARDSHIP

While any company activity to improve product safety and environmental compatibility could be interpreted as "product stewardship," the authors consider product stewardship to be systematic company efforts to reduce product risks over all or significant segments of a product life cycle—that is, from raw material acquisition through ultimate use and disposal (see Figure 12.1). At the front end of a product's life cycle, companies can design more environmentally compatible products and packaging through strategies such as materials selection, design for disassembly and recycling, and product life optimization (for example, increasing product durability and repairability). At the back end, once the product enters commerce, companies can promote the safe use and disposal or recycling of their products through the provision of technical expertise and services to distributors and end use customers in the form of know-how and other technology transfers. Although the remainder of this chapter focuses on

FIGURE 12.1.
PRODUCT AND COMMERCIAL LIFE CYCLES

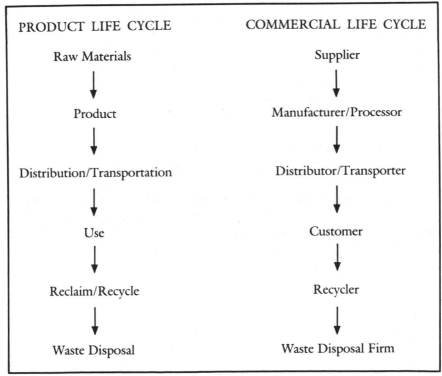

NOTE: This figure oversimplifies the product life cycle. Some products have fewer or additional stages in their life cycles (for example, the product is not recycled or there are two manufacturing steps). There are often multiple firms operating or customer types within any given phase of a product's life cycle that play different roles in the life cycles of different products.

technology transfer, in most cases a comprehensive strategy to reduce product risk will combine product design and technology transfer efforts.

Technology transfer can occur among the numerous players involved in the commercial life cycle of a product (see Figure 12.1) and can flow upstream and downstream. For example, a chemical supplier may provide training on the safe use of hazardous chemicals to its industrial customers, or a customer might request that a supplier conduct a safety audit at its plant. Increasingly, customers are also exerting pressures on manufacturers to supply more environmentally acceptable products. In addition, the horizontal transmission or sharing of risk management expertise between similar types of firms (for example, chemical manufacturers), which is often facilitated by trade and professional organizations, plays a role in the diffusion of knowledge throughout industry and influences technology transfer activities within individual product life cycles.

A variety of formats are used in the transfer of risk management information and expertise, including training, technical assistance, targeted information dissemination, and audits. The content of the information can range from very specific (for example, how to handle a specific product safely) to general (for example, how to do community relations) and can target different audiences, including environmental and safety professionals as well as public relations and sales personnel.

EXTERNAL FORCES STIMULATING THE DEVELOPMENT OF PRODUCT STEWARDSHIP

Technology transfer has reached unprecedented levels in recent years as suppliers voluntarily provide information and expertise on safe handling and use of their products to customers and as customers demand more services and more environmentally acceptable products from suppliers. The increase in technology transfer can be attributed to a number of forces, most of which converge on the ultimate corporate goal—to maximize profits and reduce losses. Companies' efforts are aimed at reducing liabilities and regulatory costs, improving their competitive positions in the marketplace, and avoiding publicity that could negatively affect product sales or create public pressure for increased regulation of industrial activity. These external forces are stimulating fundamental changes in the attitudes of corporations, bringing about a recognition of their corporate responsibility as well as efforts to reduce the environmental impacts of their products.

In general, environmental risks associated with the use and disposal of harmful products can threaten the economic well-being of companies. Injurious products stimulate product liability and other tort litigation as well as worker's compensation claims, which result in losses to manufacturers. Harmful products also can trigger media coverage; negative publicity can directly affect product sales or overall company profits. In addition, public pressure can stimulate new laws and regulations to control or reduce the impact of products on the environment, imposing additional costs on companies. These forces, therefore, result in cost-avoidance behaviors by companies.

Technology transfer is one approach that companies are taking to reduce liability arising from the use of their products. Some companies seek to improve the capacity of the end user to handle and dispose of products safely to prevent incidences that may result in lawsuits and to create more "sophisticated" users. By increasing the knowledge of the product user, in the event that a product liability suit arises, the product manufacturer can try to defend itself by claiming that the user had sufficient expertise to prevent the incident from occurring.

A number of regulatory developments also provide incentives for companies to become more involved in the commercial life cycles of their products and to initiate product stewardship and technology transfer efforts. For example, cradle-to-grave regulations such as the Resource Conservation and Recovery Act establish corporate responsibility for the disposition of hazardous wastes beyond the plant boundary; the Comprehensive Environmental Response, Compensation, and Liability Act (also known as Superfund) makes companies accountable for the cost of hazardous waste cleanup; SARA Title III mandates disclosure of chemical hazard and risk information to the public, necessitating increased communication about chemical risks between chemical suppliers and user firms. The complexities of SARA reporting requirements also provided companies with an opportunity to expand their technology transfer efforts.

There is growing recognition that the environment creates market opportunities for companies in addition to legal and economic consequences. A recent survey of top corporate executives found that they believe that their greatest opportunities in the management of environmental affairs come from producing environmentally friendly products and services to differentiate their companies from competitors (Booz, Allen and Hamilton, Inc. 1991).

From the authors' research, it appears that there are three underlying forces creating the market opportunities. First, increased legal liability and an expanded regulatory framework have created opportunities for companies to improve marketing and sales through the use of value-added environmental services that increase customer appreciation and loyalty. Some companies, for example, offer to take back used chemical products or containers; other companies provide services such as safety audits or training programs. Second, companies are responding to the growing environmental awareness and demand among consumers and industrial customers for more environmentally friendly products and labels. Although the response to market demand appears to have achieved environmental benefits in some areas,[1] it also has led to green marketing or environmental claims that sometimes seem to be of questionable accuracy and significance for technology transfer. Third, the adoption of total quality management principles by corporations, coupled with increased customer need and demand, has enhanced the technology transfer process. Closer customer-supplier relationships have increased the feasibility of technology transfer, and the elevation of customer satisfaction on the corporate agenda has increased the desirability of providing expertise and services to customers.

By and large, the technology transfer initiatives in the private sector are voluntary, although some regulations in the United States and Europe do require companies to engage in some form of technology transfer. For example, the Hazard Communication Standard of the Occupational Health and Safety Administration (OSHA) requires manufacturers to provide material safety data sheets (MSDSs) and labeling for their customers. Some countries (for example, Germany, Japan, and Canada) have established national environmental labeling programs designed to inform consumers and to promote the manufacture and sale of consumer products that are more environmentally friendly than other products. It is predicted that in the next few years most European countries will have established labeling programs (Organization for Economic Cooperation and Development 1991). Germany also passed an ordinance that requires producers and sellers of packaging to take back and to reuse or recycle used packaging material.

The effect of regulation and liability on technology transfer is not always positive, however. Sometimes, they can create obstacles. For example, a manufacturer of telecommunications equipment considered providing a take-back service for the nickel/cadmium batteries used in its consumer products (for example, cordless telephones). However, U.S. hazardous waste regulations are an impediment. While household hazardous waste is exempt from the regulations, a collection site becomes subject to these regulations if institutional customers deposit multiple batteries. Another example is found in the area of labeling. Concerned about being held liable for false or misleading claims, some companies in the United States refrain from providing environmental information (for example, the term "recyclable") on their products because there is a lack of consistency and standards for making such claims.[2]

CONCEPT TO REALITY: RECENT INITIATIVES IN THE PRIVATE SECTOR

Although some company efforts to address product risks are ad hoc (for example, in response to a specific incident or need), others are part of a systematic effort to reduce risks associated with their products. Some companies, particularly those in the chemical industry, have developed formal product stewardship programs that emphasize technology transfer.[3] For example, as part of its Product Stewardship Program (PSP), Dow Chemical makes its technical expertise on safe handling of chemicals available to its downstream industrial customers. Dow's PSP uses several means of technology transfer, including the provision of MSDSs (required by OSHA) with supplemental safety information, the provision of training materials and seminars for customer personnel, and industrial hygiene surveys conducted by Dow personnel at the facilities of selected customers to assist these firms on occupational health and safety matters. Product stewardship is not limited to large companies such as Dow. Through its CLOUT program, Hydrite Chemical, a small chemical manufacturer and distributor, promises its industrial users of chlorine and other products access to regulatory, environmental, and safety information, training, and technical services.

Although some companies have initiated product stewardship and technology transfer programs independently, the state of the art and the pervasiveness of product stewardship efforts particularly within the chemical industry have been advanced by the Responsible Care program of the Chemical Manufacturers Association (CMA) and its members' commitment "to counsel customers on the safe use, transportation and disposal of chemical products" (CMA 1990). In addition to this general commitment, the CMA adopted Codes of Management Practice for product stewardship and product distribution that are an obligation of CMA membership.

Large companies appear to be more active in initiating technology transfer activities than smaller companies. Size and resources put large firms in a better position to offer services to customers and to demand changes of their suppliers. Because of their lack of resources, smaller companies are often the recipients of information and services. In addition, it is reasonable to expect that once a large firm forces technological changes in a product of a supplier firm, the new technology will diffuse or become available downstream to other customers, including small firms.

To further illustrate and analyze the technology transfer initiatives of both supplier and user firms, it is useful to categorize the mechanisms these firms employ and provide some example of the scope of such initiatives.

PRODUCT WARNINGS, LABELS, AND OTHER PRODUCT INFORMATION

Although some product warnings and labels are required by law, some companies are routinely providing additional information, either on labels or in product inserts, on the safe handling, use, and disposal of their products to customers downstream.[4] For example, a small chemical company studied by the authors added a special environmental section to its MSDSs that provides supplemental regulatory and chemical information. Manufacturers of plastic packaging now use a voluntary coding system that identifies the type of plastic used in making the container to assist in recycling the product (Council for Solid Waste Solutions n.d.).

EDUCATION AND TRAINING PROGRAMS

Suppliers are educating customers and other downstream users on the proper use and disposal of specific products and about more general concerns, such as risk communication and regulations (for example, reporting requirements under SARA TITLE III), through various written materials developed by the company, by trade organizations, or by government agencies and training programs. Some companies use visits to the customer's facility by sales personnel or technical representatives to educate the customer; some sponsor training programs at the customer's facility or provide videotapes; and others may invite customer personnel to attend training programs at their facilities alongside their own personnel. The following are specific examples from companies the authors studied: a small manufacturer of industrial gases provides customers with technical representatives who conduct seminars on gas handling and emergency response; a large chemical company sends its customers information kits dealing with SARA Title III and community relations and sponsors one-day seminars on regulatory requirements for its customers as well as its distributors' customers; and a paper company provides users of its carbonless (chemically coated) paper with written information and videotapes about workplace health hazards such as chemical dusts.

SERVICES

With purchases of their products, companies are providing customers with a diverse array of value-added services that promote the safe use, handling, and disposal of the products. These services are often made available upon customer request. Companies interviewed by the authors provided the following examples: a paper company requested that its supplier of chlorine perform safety audits of chemical storage areas and handling practices at its facilities; in the event of an accidental chemical release, a small manufacturer of specialty gases will provide its distributors and end use customers with emergency response assistance; and a computer manufacturer takes back used equipment from its customers for recycling.

ACCESS TO COMPANY PERSONNEL AND GUIDANCE DOCUMENTS

Realizing that information previously available only in house can be a valuable resource for customers, companies interviewed are increasingly making in-house resources such as company personnel and guidance documents available to customers. For example, representatives of a paper company spent the day with personnel from its chlorine supplier's research and development department discussing dioxin and technologies for its removal from paper products and wastes. On request, a manufacturer of telecommunications equipment provides its customers with guidelines for the identification of hazardous materials in its products for use in equipment disassembly, materials recovery, and disposal; these are the same guidelines that are used internally.

PURCHASING CONTRACTS AND PRODUCT SPECIFICATIONS

Both suppliers and customers are incorporating environmental performance standards into standard business vehicles (such as purchasing contracts and engineering specifications) for ensuring delivery of desired goods and services. For example, through a purchasing contract, a chemical supplier secured access to its distributor's customer list (which is usually kept confidential) in order to send information on the safe handling and use of its chemicals directly to the end use customer. In purchase orders and contracts, a manufacturer of telecommunications equipment now stipulates that it will accept no packaging materials (for their products or for products purchased by them) that contain or have been manufactured using chlorofluorocarbons (CFCs). In addition, they have incorporated a general clause into all contracts with suppliers and vendors requesting a reduction in the use of hazardous materials in the manufacture of products. A computer manufacturer developed engineering specifications for packaging materials purchased and used by the company that prohibit the use of CFCs, restrict the use of heavy metals, and promote recycling and the use of recycled material in packaging.

NOTIFICATION, SCREENING, AND SELECTION OF SUPPLIERS, DISTRIBUTORS, OR CUSTOMERS

Several companies studied by the authors have notified suppliers or customers of their preference for doing business with firms that adhere to good operating practices or conduct their operations in a manner consistent with the environmental policies and goals of their companies. One chemical supplier notified its distributors that it would reduce the number of firms handling its product by one-third. To continue to distribute the supplier's product, a company must adhere to "good industry practice." A manufacturer of telecommunications equipment has notified all suppliers and vendors that it prefers to purchase components and packaging that do not contain or were not made using CFCs.

PARTNERSHIPS

Not only are customers turning to their suppliers for assistance, but they are also forming partnerships with their suppliers to seek solutions to environmental problems. Unlike the other forms of technology transfer cited above, these partnerships result in a two-way transaction—that is, the mutual sharing of knowledge or services. For example, in its quest to eliminate the use of an extremely toxic chemical, a semiconductor firm worked with two of its equipment manufacturers to develop alternative technologies. A supplier of dry-cleaning solvents teamed up with an equipment manufacturer to bring the latest in clean technologies to its customers. Since a single company generally does not operate in all or multiple phases of a product's life cycle, finding a solution to some environmental problems may necessitate the creation of partnerships among firms within the product's life cycle and possibly with other markets. A good example is a partnership formed by a computer firm to recycle the plastic components of equipment traded in by its customers. In this case, the supplier of virgin resin buys back the recycled material from the computer firm and remanufactures it into resin, which is purchased by another company for the manufacture of roof panels.

PRODUCT CHARACTERISTICS INFLUENCING COMPANY DECISIONS

The particular patterns of technology transfer and the type and quality of the information provided vary depending on a number of factors related to the product—in particular, the product's environmental risks and commercial characteristics. Following are some commercial characteristics that appear to influence the scope and quality of technology transfer activities:

- End use customer. A number of characteristics of end users seem to influence a company's decision, including the end use customer's knowledge and expertise; the number of end use customers; and the relative importance of a particular end use customer or product line to the firm's overall profits.
- Value of used product or components. Materials that maintain their performance characteristics and their economic value after use in the initial product (and after incorporating the cost of material recovery and scrap recycling) are good candidates for the voluntary initiation of technology transfer services from suppliers to downstream customers.
- Control of product life cycle. Technology transfer may be facilitated if the company has ownership over any given phase of a product's life cycle (for example, in the case of in-house customers or leased equipment).
- Use of distributors. Direct contact between suppliers and customers facilitates the transfer of knowledge and expertise. If information is provided to a distributor for distribution to an end user, there are often no assurances that it reaches the intended audience.
- Competitive nature within the life cycle. If competition on the basis of price is limited (for example, with commodity chemicals), value-added services such as chemical risk management information and counseling can emerge as a competitive factor.
- Proprietary information. Proprietary information (for example, process secrecy) can inhibit technology transfer; safety and regulatory advice might be shared to the extent that it does not impinge on proprietary information or competition.

POLICY IMPLICATIONS

As part of its product stewardship effort, a manufacturer can select from a number of strategies to reduce risk throughout the life cycle of its product.

Each product life cycle contains a combination of variables that appear to determine the scope, patterns, and quality of technology transfer activities. Since companies selectively apply technology transfer methods to certain product lines and customers, it is possible that technology transfer activities can be extended to additional customers and a broader range of formats included.

Illuminating the technology transfer process for particular products provides the foundation for a potential strategy to enhance existing patterns of technology transfer and to stimulate new technology transfer patterns or intercompany linkages. For example, regulators could evaluate the level and type of current initiatives in a product sector to determine whether additional efforts are needed to improve safety or environmental compatibility over part or all of a product's life cycle. The evaluation might also include an examination of the influences (such as external forces or the product's commercial characteristics) on the companies' selection or avoidance of certain technology transfer strategies.

The initial goal of this evaluation would be to encourage voluntary efforts by providing industry with the opportunity to apply its expert knowledge of its products and markets to the issues and to the formulation of response strategies. This could be achieved through dialogues among the appropriate stakeholders in a product's life cycle and, if necessary, education about the environmental concerns and potential solutions. Regulators also could work through customers to apply pressure on their suppliers to alter their products or to provide environmental services. The evaluation process and dialogues also might identify regulatory barriers to the implementation of technology transfer that might be addressed by policy makers. As a last resort, policy makers could consider developing market-based incentives or imposing regulatory requirements on firms to stimulate technology transfer. On a more general level, government agencies also could disseminate information on technology transfer options and best practices to companies that want to develop new efforts or expand their voluntary efforts.

NOTES

1. For example, the coding symbols that identify the composition of plastic (e.g., PET is labeled with a number 1 and HDPE is labeled with a number 2) facilitate the sorting and recycling of postconsumer containers and plastic components of such products as computer terminals.

2. The attorneys general from a number of states formed a task force to study green marketing claims and published recommendations for industry in *The*

Green Report: Findings and Preliminary Recommendations for Responsible Advertising. More recently, the Federal Trade Commission issued guidelines addressing environmental marketing claims that are a step closer to national standards, although they are not enforceable nor do they supersede state regulation.

3. The formal product stewardship programs being developed by manufacturers of durable goods such as telecommunications and computer equipment focus more on designing safer and more environmentally friendly products than on technology transfer.

4. The transfer of chemical hazard information from chemical producers to downstream chemical processors and end user firms was established by common-law product-liability doctrines and the OSHA Hazard Communication Standard (effective in mid-1985). Common-law product-liability doctrines establish a product seller's duty to warn and provide safe use instructions to purchasers and users. OSHA's Hazard Communication Standard requires chemical manufacturers and importers to provide MSDSs and labels on chemical substances to their downstream customers.

REFERENCES

Attorneys General of California, Florida, Massachusetts, Minnesota, Missouri, New York, Texas, Utah, Washington, and Wisconsin. 1991. *The Green Report II: Recommendations for Responsible Environmental Advertising.*

Attorneys General of California, Florida, Massachusetts, Minnesota, Missouri, New York, Texas, Utah, Washington, and Wisconsin. 1990. *The Green Report: Findings and Preliminary Recommendations for Responsible Advertising.*

Baram, Michael S.; Dillon, Patricia S.; and Ruffle, Betsy. 1992. *Managing Chemical Risks: Corporate Response to SARA Title III.* Chelsea, Mich.: Lewis Publishers.

Booz, Allen and Hamilton, Inc. 1991. *Corporate Environmental Management: An Executive Survey.* Bethesda, Md.: Booz, Allen and Hamilton, Inc.

Chemical Manufacturers Association. 1990. *Guiding Principles for Responsible Care.* Washington, D.C.: Chemical Manufacturers Association.

Council for Solid Waste Solutions. n.d. *Plastic Codes Help Recyclers.* Washington, D.C.: Council for Solid Waste Solutions.

Organization for Economic Cooperation and Development (OECD). 1991. *Environmental Labelling in OECD Countries.* Paris: OECD.

13

Solving the Automobile Shredder Waste Problem: Cooperation Among Firms in the Automotive Industry

Frank den Hond and Peter Groenewegen

Several European car manufacturers, including Volkswagen, BMW automobiles, and Peugeot, are creating publicity about the recycling of automobiles. In a recent Dutch advertising campaign, BMW used the slogan "Imagine that your car will return as a BMW!" Several automobile manufacturers have announced that they will take back vehicles at the end of their useful life.[1] To implement this policy, automobile manufacturers are initiating disassembly or dismantling projects to learn about vehicle recycling. Recovery of materials already averages 70 to 75 percent of vehicle weight. The remaining 25 to 30 percent, called shredder waste, is an acknowledged environmental problem. Shredder waste is often contaminated with mineral oils, heavy metals, and PCBs, and until now most of it could be landfilled relatively cheaply. In the near future, however, it will no longer be possible to landfill shredder waste in a similar manner to municipal solid waste, as it is being classified as hazardous waste in an increasing number of countries.

The automobile dismantling projects resemble one another in important aspects, such as their emphasis on recycling of polymers and on learning about the cost of disassembly and possible improvements in design. They differ in the choices of specific technologies used. In a number of projects new technologies are being tried; some are add-ons to existing shredding operations, and others replace traditional operations. In other projects the improvement of sorting and dismantling operations is a central goal. A second important difference among these projects is their inherent view of the industrial structure. They may focus on cooperation with existing waste-handling organizations or attempt to create new linkages with organizations currently outside the shredder industry.

This chapter contributes to the discussion on closing the materials cycle as a way to solve environmental problems (see also Chapters 11 and 12). It will show that closing the cycle is not simply a technical issue on which firms cooperate to identify new solutions. More is at stake here. Closing the cycle can require a change in the network structure of the industry. In the case of the automotive industry, recycling requires the involvement of two networks. The first, the production network, comprises the automobile manufacturing firms and their suppliers. The second, the disposal network, consists of automobile dismantling and shredding companies, which seek to cash in on the remainder value of automobiles. Automobile dismantlers especially depend on design choices, because ease in dismantling reduces labor costs and increases the reuse of certain parts. For shredding companies, the value of car hulks depends on the amount and value of materials that can be extracted from them. For example, galvanized steel is worth less than nongalvanized steel. The increasing use of plastics and integrated parts and components affects the profitability of both dismantling and shredding companies. Both types of companies are therefore dependent on materials and design choices in the manufacturing industry. Despite this dependency there are no direct links between automobile manufacturers and dismantling and shredding companies, although presently some linkages are emerging. Integrating the production and disposal networks into one network is an essential element in solving the shredder waste problem. But this is not without problems. For example:

- Some of the possible solutions of benefit to dismantling and shredding companies require changes in materials and/or construction. Automobile manufacturers perceive such requirements as restrictions on the design process.
- Recycling and reuse, which automobile manufacturers propose as the most important solutions to the shredder waste problem, are more or less the business of dismantling and shredding companies. Therefore, these companies criticize pilot recycling projects, claiming that the manufacturers are "reinventing the wheel" and "doing our job." There is serious concern about a shift of power from the vehicle dismantling sector to the vehicle production sector.
- Automobile dismantlers have made money from automobile dismantling for decades, but all too often at the expense of health and the environment. Automobile manufacturers do not want to get involved with, or be connected to, corporations that run environmentally haz-

ardous operations. In fact, the major concern of manufacturers is to show that they are environmentally responsible.

INDUSTRY STRUCTURE AND THE WASTE ISSUE

A wide variety of firms are involved throughout the life cycle of automobiles, from producers of materials, parts, and components to assemblers and retailers, repair and maintenance shops, and dismantling and shredding companies. Figure 13.1 shows the major network linkages between these actors. The dotted arrows represent the emerging network linkages between manufacturers and dismantling and shredding companies.

The production part of the network involves a number of different actors. A particular automobile manufacturer may be linked to hundreds or thousands of different suppliers of materials, parts, components, and systems. The complexity of this subnetwork reflects the complexity of the product, the automobile. The division of labor in this subnetwork is constantly changing, depending on the manufacturers' production cost calculations and changing needs for technological expertise. The current trend is to use an increasing number of ready-to-assemble parts, such as seats, brake systems, and engine electronics, from outside suppliers. Changes in the structure of the network result from a combination of factors: the manufacturers' need to control and benefit optimally from the supply system, changing consumer demand, technical changes, and an extended range of design options. The general direction of change is resulting in diminished control over the actual materials composition of automobiles by the end producers. The retailing system, linking the manufacturer to the customer, is of less importance here and will not be discussed.

The vehicle disposal system, organized by dismantling and shredding companies, is only weakly linked to the production subnetwork. Within the disposal subnetwork the arrangements are rather stable. They reflect typically national traditions of metals recovery and waste management.

DESIGN AND MANUFACTURING

The automobile production system is very complex. The trajectory from inception to production involves the conception of new models; their design and engineering; the development of a production system; the supply of materials, parts, and components during production; final assembly; and finishing. Clearly, automobile manufacturers are the dominant actors in this system. They accept new concepts, develop them into

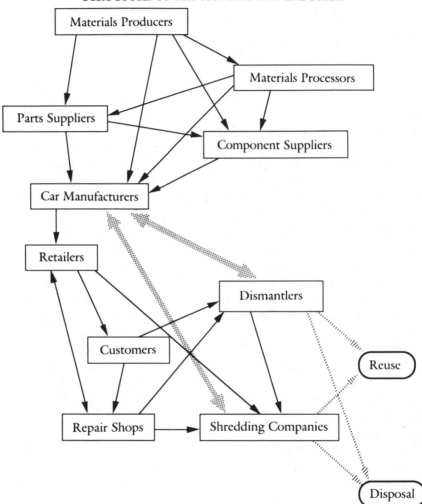

FIGURE 13.1.
STRUCTURE OF THE AUTOMOTIVE INDUSTRY

technically sound design, and orchestrate the assembly of automobiles. Although they may rely on outside expertise from engineering consultants and supplying firms for some design and conceptual work, they will always treat some elements of the manufacturing process as proprietary for competitive advantage. The production of parts and components is less a function of the manufacturers themselves, although the organization and management of the supply system is a major issue for the manufacturers.

Also of importance is the degree of hierarchical control the manufacturer has over the production system. At one extreme is an integrated manufacturing system in which the manufacturer produces most of the needed materials, parts, and components. Numerous small suppliers that compete solely on price are hired to produce specific parts. This approach tends to limit the manufacturer's flexibility, because the design of parts and components must be specified completely before bidding is opened, well in advance of actual manufacturing. Such an approach might be justified to reduce uncertainty and to reinforce the stability of relationships with external suppliers, as was the case in the early days of the American automotive industry.

At the other extreme of hierarchical control is a recent alternative in which the manufacturer engages in long-term contracts with a relatively small number of companies. This approach is used by Japanese automobile manufacturers. They try to collaborate as much as possible with their suppliers, to gain optimally from the suppliers' experience, flexibility, and knowledge, and to limit administrative procedures to an absolute minimum (Clark and Fujimoto 1991).

Given these two extremes of control, resulting from historical and regional traditions, it is not surprising that a range of models exists for the organization of automobile manufacturing.[2] The differences may be described in terms of degree of vertical integration, of the amount of value a car manufacturer adds to the end product. Examples of companies with a high level of vertical integration are FIAT and Mercedes-Benz. Other automobile manufacturers—for example, the Japanese companies—are known for their low levels of vertical integration (Chanaron 1988).

The entire manufacturing system is periodically reevaluated by the car manufacturers. Womack et al. (1990) argue that the "ideal" car manufacturer today should consider the management of relationships with suppliers very carefully, because it is a key factor for competitive success. Relationships with external suppliers must be an integral part of a manufacturing system that emphasizes speed and effectiveness on several dimensions, including design, manufacturing, and dealing with customers. This integration results in a "lean" production system with an emphasis on swift and responsive communication during all phases of the design and development of new vehicles. The suppliers, incorporated into the production and design systems of the main manufacturer (the assembler), should have much of the knowledge and experience needed to develop new parts and subsystems according to exceedingly demanding specifications. Technological innovation, resulting in new products and processes, must be incorporated rapidly into design and manufacturing to ensure the manufacturer's economic health. A lean production system not only incorporates innovations more quickly than the more traditional mass production system, but it also triggers innovations because it is more open to outside signals (Womack et al. 1990).

Changes in the organization of manufacturing take place in response to changing competitive demands from the automobile market, which is increasingly a global market with an emphasis on the specific wishes of relatively small groups of customers. These customers tend to be attracted to more "individual" cars, which necessitates smaller production series and shorter production times for certain models. Smaller series and shorter production times favor the use of new materials that require relatively low investment costs for tooling and the ability to make rapid tooling changes. These demands favor more flexible manufacturing operations and have wider effects on various other aspects of the technology employed. All of these elements add up to a justification for links between design and production and markets. Included in this spectrum are the application of manufacturing technologies such as automation and robotics; the use of computer-processed information in design, engineering, and manufacturing; improved management of logistics; and—of importance for automobile recycling—changes in choices of materials. The choice of materials by design engineers is embedded in the broader aspects of the manufacturing system, such as the size of production runs and the type of tooling used in specific plants. With the increasing emphasis on flexible production, plastics are becoming favored materials for increasing numbers of applications (Busch et al. 1987).

It is important to note how changes in production and in the market affect the materials composition of automobiles. Automobile manufacturers claim that the increasing application of plastics and lightweight materials has environmental benefits by reducing overall vehicle weight and hence fuel consumption. Trends in automobile manufacturing also contribute to the increasing use of plastics in automobiles. These include easy assembly, integrated components, smaller production series, shorter production runs, lightweight materials, and diverse, tailor-made materials for specific applications.

DISPOSAL

When automobiles break down, or rather, when the cost of repairing them exceeds their value, they are discarded. Currently, most automobiles, when they are no longer useful, go to automobile dismantlers, who disassemble and sell some of the valuable parts in the secondhand market and then sell the remaining hulks to shredding companies.

The environmental burden automobile dismantlers pose is well known. At the edges of most large cities, stacks of rusty, oil-leaking automobile wrecks are commonplace. The dismantler makes a profit by reducing the amount of labor needed to an absolute minimum, by having clients remove the parts they want to buy and by doing virtually nothing to protect either the discarded wrecks from degradation or the environment from pollution.

Under the pressure of regulations, however, automobile dismantlers are increasingly doing business in a more environmentally acceptable way. This is especially the case in the Netherlands and other countries in northwestern Europe. The firms in this sector have organized themselves in trade associations that have a role in certifying their members according to higher than average standards. New business practices include the removal of environmentally hazardous components, such as fuels and hydraulic and brake fluids, as well as some parts and components, such as batteries, air conditioners, and air bags.

The drained and partially stripped hulks are sold to shredding companies, which use heavy machinery to crush and shred metal-containing products. Shredding companies operate increasingly complex processes in which metals are separated from other waste and ferrous and nonferrous metal parts are collected separately. The nonferrous metal parts are further processed by specialized companies.

After the separation of metals, an increasing amount of nonvaluable material (the remnants of plastic parts, glass, rubber, coatings, and paints) remains and is known as shredder waste. About 25 to 30 percent of the weight of the automobile remains as shredder waste and must be disposed of, usually in landfills. (See the Appendix at the end of this chapter for a more detailed description of the shredder waste problem.)

The "technology" of automobile dismantling is relatively simple, consisting of the manual disassembly of parts, using ordinary tools and aids such as lifts to gain better access to portions of the car. The shredding operation is technically more advanced, using expensive heavy machinery and separation equipment. The separation of nonferrous metals requires advanced technologies, although, in some cases, hand-picking of copper and brass still takes place. New technologies for separating nonferrous metals include, for example, an eddy-current repulsion process, which is based on differences in electrical conductivity and specific weight. Rousseau and Melin (1989) provide an overview of the state of the art in nonferrous metals separation.

With these new technologies, substantial quantities of both ferrous and nonferrous metals can be recovered: 95 percent of ferrous metals, 53 percent of aluminum, 98 percent of zinc, and 39 percent of copper (Vos and Meiling 1991; Rousseau and Melin 1989). Yet, because of the increasing number of vehicles to dispose of, the quantity of shredder waste that remains to be disposed of still increases. Moreover, inadequate operations in steps prior to shredding—such as incomplete drainage of fluids or failure to remove electrical equipment such as small transformers containing polychlorinated biphenyls before shredding—leads to chemical contamination of shredder waste. As a result, this waste will be classified in some countries as hazardous waste, increasing its disposal costs. In fact, European shredding companies are finding their profits declining because of decreasing amounts of metals for resale and increasing disposal costs for a greater amount of shredder waste. To address this problem, shredding companies must be informed about the technical details of manufacturing and dismantling operations.

NETWORKING

As described earlier, automobile production and disposal take place in separate networks of the automotive industry. The only link between these networks is through the retailing system. The automobile dealer is an important actor who deals with both manufacturers and dismantlers (see Figure 13.1).

Two different types of network interlinkage are established through dealers:

1. When a customer comes to a dealer to buy a new automobile, he or she can sometimes get the purchase price reduced by leaving an old vehicle with the dealer. The dealer sells or delivers some of these old vehicles to a car dismantler or shredding company. In France, Renault, Peugeot, and Citroën have subsidiaries that handle the transport of discarded automobiles to shredding companies.[3]
2. BMW and Mercedes-Benz use the dealer network to collect parts such as bumpers and starter engines, which they refurbish and sell as qualified BMW or Mercedes secondhand spare parts. This secondhand parts market is profitable because the high-quality image of BMW and Mercedes brings high prices for replacement parts.

Regardless of these two connections, the link between automobile manufacturers and the actors involved after sales tends to be weak. Why has this occurred, and why is the situation changing? A number of reasons can be noted. Until recently, automobile manufacturers had no specific interest in connecting with automobile dismantlers or shredders. They probably even tried to avoid association with dismantling activities, which are dispersed, sometimes semilegal or illegal, and often directly competitive with dealers for the spare parts market.

This attitude is changing under the pressure of expected or announced government legislation.[4] Fears of product liability that would hold the end producer liable for waste management, as well as the positive publicity that can be generated with a more proactive attitude, have prompted German car manufacturers to take the initiative to set up pilot projects for automobile dismantling. An additional reason is the expectation that customers will regard "recyclability" as a selection criterion in their future decisions to buy new automobiles. Pilot dismantling projects allow the automobile manufacturers to learn about disassembly and to identify limitations from financial, logistic, and design perspectives. At the same time, as it is not yet clear which solutions will be adopted for the problem of shredder waste, manufacturers can experiment and try to influence policy makers. By demonstrating efforts in recycling, automobile manufacturers hope to convince governments that legislation is not necessary to solve the shredder waste problem (Association des Constructeurs Européens d'Automobiles [ACEA] 1991; Von Manteuffel 1990).

Automobile manufacturers are interested in solutions that are acceptable from an environmental point of view and at the same time do not interfere with their independence in design and manufacturing decisions. In the projects discussed below, the manufacturers aim to learn—in technical, strategic, and financial terms—about the operation of the waste management network.

AUTOMOBILE MANUFACTURERS' PILOT DISASSEMBLY PROJECTS

In developing strategies for reducing shredder waste, automobile manufacturers are seeking long-term solutions. Disassembly of vehicles is a major element of these strategies; therefore, a number of pilot disassembly projects have been initiated. The projects aim, among other things, to assess different methods of bolting and welding automobiles together. Current design and manufacturing operations require thinking that differs from that needed when reuse and recycling are the issues. For example, many manufacturers lack precise information about the materials composition of the complex parts that are supplied to them. And only since initiating disassembly projects have they learned in some detail about the materials composition of their automobiles. Other things to be learned include the effects of construction techniques on dismantling speed. In these projects, manufacturers tend to concentrate on current models, as they are obviously more interested in those that more closely resemble models currently in development than those produced fifteen to twenty years ago.

BMW A.G.

In June 1991, BMW began to disassemble vehicles in a pilot plant in Landshut, Bavaria. The objectives of the BMW project are as follows: developing and maintaining technologies for the reuse and recycling of hitherto unexploitable materials and components in order to achieve, for the medium term, an adequate reuse potential; providing a disposal struc-ture for the entire materials volume of scrap automobiles that will be acceptable under future conditions; and gaining knowledge of recycling-oriented design concepts and their application for new generation of vehicles. In this project, BMW will develop model-specific dismantling methods based on current disassembly technologies. The experience gained will be transferred to a nationwide network of 200 to 300 auto-mobile dismantlers in Germany that officially cooperate with BMW in the dismantling and recycling of old BMWs. The network should be expanded to other countries such as Great Britain as well.[5]

As mentioned earlier, since 1965 BMW has collected components such as starter engines, transmissions, and alternators from damaged BMWs to rebuild and sell in the secondhand market. Recently, BMW also started collecting damaged bumpers, catalytic converters, and waste fluids from its dealer network in Germany and other countries.

FIAT Auto

FIAT cooperates with Peugeot S.A. and with chemical companies such as ICI, Enichem, in the Eureka/RECAP project on the problem of end-of-life waste from automobiles. The company has developed a plan to treat scrap automobiles that is comparable with other dismantling concepts. One difference is that the concept makes use of the Italian legal possibility to create a *consortio obligatorio* (compulsory consortium), which could make it possible to exclude other segments of industry, such as automobile dis-mantlers, as is feared by the Commission des Fédérations et Syndicats Nationaux des Entreprises de Récupération de Ferailles du Marche Common (COFENAF), the European association of ferrous scrap recovery associations. FIAT has not widely publicized its system.

In the Eureka/RECAP project, production waste is also an issue. FIAT is responsible for this part of the project. The basic idea is to set up a series of waste treatment sites near the FIAT plants and those of its suppliers where production waste will be separated and made ready for reuse or—if reuse is not possible—for distribution to specialized and integrated waste treatment centers. These centers could also be used for treatment of remaining shredder waste.

FORD EUROPE

The approach of Ford Europe is to help stimulate the establishment of an infrastructure for the collection, separation, and reuse/recycling of plastics waste. This is to be achieved through the economic stimulation provided by new markets for the recycled plastics. In practice, however, Ford first concentrates on the operational requirements of the material and only secondarily addresses the improvement of removal and recycling of parts. For collection, identification, and separation of plastics, Ford opts for sophisticated techniques rather than relatively labor-intensive dismantling. As yet it is unclear with what type of companies Ford would cooperate, because the company is still developing new technologies. Ford has also started an automobile dismantling project in Germany.

MERCEDES-BENZ

Mercedes-Benz developed a "total recycling" scheme for scrap vehicles in cooperation with Voest-Alpine Stahl in Austria. The process comprises the following steps: draining of the vehicle (removal of fuels and fluids); disassembly of the engine, starter motor, transmission, and other useful parts such as the battery and catalytic converter (so that nonferrous metals can be recovered); disassembly of easily removable plastic parts; crushing of the hulk; and feeding of the crushed hulk into a so-called melt reactor. In the melt reactor the energy content of the organic components, such as the remaining plastic parts, is used to melt and separate the steel contents. Lead, zinc, and other heavy metals evaporate. Oxygen and natural gas are supplied for heat and to prevent the formation of furans and dioxins. Flue gases are purified from heavy metals, and the thermic energy is transformed into useful energy. In principle, with this new option it would be possible to bypass shredding companies in vehicle disposal operations; no references are made to dismantlers.

Peugeot S.A.

Peugeot (including Citroën and Talbot) is cooperating with CFF (Compagnie Française des Ferailles, the largest shredding company in France) and Vicat (a cement works) in a pilot project for treating discarded automobiles. The participants are investigating methods of recycling and recovery (including incineration with recovery of heat) of the various materials in automobiles that will leave minimum quantities of waste for final disposal in landfills. A pilot plant has been built in Saint-Pierre de Chandieu, near Lyon, to handle three stages: draining and disassembly of automobiles, shredding of the hulks, and treatment of shredder residue. Model-specific disassembly of about 7200 cars in two years will take place. The economic and technical feasibility of the dismantling is being studied, as well as the actual recycling of the separated materials. In the third stage of treatment the energy value of shredder residue will be recovered for cement production. This final process has been developed by CFF and Vicat. The project is part of the Eureka/RECAP project in which Peugeot cooperates with FIAT.

Volkswagen A.G.

In Volkswagen's project, implemented in Germany, the disassembly of discarded automobiles includes removal of fluids, separation of plastics and metals, treatment of the metals content in a shredding operation, selling or shredding of aggregates, recycling of batteries, and removal of recyclable plastics. The materials recovered in this way could go to the originating industries for further treatment. To further develop this system, Volkswagen has initiated a project in Leer, Eastern Frisia, in cooperation with the shredding company Evert Heeren GmbH, local authorities, and two large chemical companies. The project has a threefold assessment goal: to determine the cost of dismantling automobiles, which parts can be sold again, and which parts and materials can be recovered in such a way that they can be recycled. As of this writing, mostly bumpers have been collected; it has been reported that new bumpers can be made out of recycled bumper materials.

Nedcar B.V.

Nedcar, located in the Netherlands, has set up an environmental program that includes engineering guidelines and recommendations.[6] The following are examples of these recommendations: choose thermoplastic over thermosetting materials; avoid chlorofluorocarbons; make simple-to-disassemble components of a single material; and mark plastics according to the VDA 260 identification system. Other recommendations are that plastic waste from cars should be reused at as high a quality level as possible, preferably for the original application, and, if necessary, component specifications should be changed to make reuse possible. Since January 1992, Nedcar has participated in a dismantling project by providing about 100 Volvo 440 models for disassembly. In this project, Nedcar cooperates with a plastics producer (GEP), the plastics industry trade organization, the Dutch Ministry of Environment (VROM), the vehicle producers and importers trade association (RAI), and StiBA, the Dutch trade organization of automobile dismantlers. Disassembly is done at the site of one of the StiBA members. From their participation in this project, Nedcar wants to learn about easy-to-disassemble vehicle construction.

This discussion of pilot projects is not exhaustive, as other automobile manufacturers are also participating in vehicle recycling. For example, both General Motors (Opel) and ADAC (the German Automobile Association) in Germany have initiated collection and disassembly schemes, Renault in France wants to collect parts and materials for reuse through its dealer network, and Rover in the United Kingdom cooperates with the Bird Group, the largest shredding and nonferrous metals recovery company in the United Kingdom, in a dismantling scheme. The Japanese automobile manufacturers, notably Nissan and Toyota, also work on vehicle recycling.

The producers of luxury sports cars, such as Porsche, Ferrari, and Jaguar, are less involved in automobile recycling. This is partly because it is questionable whether many vehicles of this type ever end up at a shredding operation. Rather, they usually last a very long time as collectors' items. In addition, most of these makes are not independent, hence they can profit from the experiences of their parent companies—for example, Jaguar from Ford and Ferrari from FIAT. Only Porsche is an independent company, and it participates in the joint recycling program of the German automobile manufacturers.

The choice of the examples described is based on the availability of empirical information, diversity of strategies, and diversity of the manufacturers themselves in terms of volume producers versus specialty producers[7] and the amount of their dependence on their home markets.[8] Although it is not a complete review of recycling projects, it is representative, as the projects and strategies of other automobile manufacturers are composed of the same elements.

CLASSIFICATION OF STRATEGIES

For a classification of the various recycling strategies, two dimensions are considered. The first is the level of change in the technology basis of the complete chain of activities: is the technological change incremental or are other, more radical innovations sought? The second dimension concerns the type of network extensions the automobile manufacturers pursue: do they try to reinforce the current waste management network or do they propose important changes to it?

A change in the technology basis is considered incremental when it simply improves on existing waste-handling operations through activities such as disassembly of a certain number of parts for reuse and subsequent shredding and separation of metals. Examples are the Nedcar and Volkswagen projects, which work completely within the existing tradition of waste treatment technologies. In contrast are the Mercedes-Benz project and some of the attempts by Ford. These projects are considered radical because they seek to develop technologies that deviate from the current technology basis in the waste management network.

Some change in networking is clearly part of most projects. The authors consider networking adaptive whenever automobile manufacturers establish links with existing types of firms in waste management. The networking strategies of Nedcar and BMW are adaptive because they cooperate with automobile dismantlers, companies already involved in the disassembly of vehicles. By contrast, if automobile manufacturers seek cooperation with firms that are currently not involved in dismantling, such as shredding companies and steel works, this is called an evolutionary change in networking. An example is Mercedes-Benz cooperating with Voest-Alpine Stahl. As a consequence of the latter, waste management networks themselves will change. These dimensions are combined in the matrix shown in Figure 13.2.

FIGURE 13.2
CLASSIFICATION OF STRATEGIES

		CHANGE IN NETWORKING	
		Adaptive	*Evolutionary*
CHANGE IN TECHNOLOGY BASIS	*Incremental*	Nedcar BMW	Volkswagen, Peugeot/FIAT
	Radical	Ford	Mercedes-Benz Ford

Developments in networking and in technology are not strictly independent. Tushman and Anderson (1986) pointed out that radical innovations in a sector tend to be introduced by new firms in that sector. Therefore, it is not surprising that Mercedes-Benz, working with a radically new technology, has established evolutionary network relationships. However, because the current technological basis of vehicle dismantling is known, incremental changes in the technological basis can be pursued more or less independently of changes in networking. This suggests that of the four possible combinations in the matrix, two are more plausible than the others: radical technological change and evolutionary change in networking, in the lower right of the matrix, and incremental technological change and adaptive networking change, in the upper left of the matrix.

Some limitations to this classification of strategies should be pointed out:

1. The term *strategy* is used in one specific sense. It is difficult to be definitive in identifying a company's strategy because it may be composed of several elements. First, written strategies (or plans) can exist solely for the company's internal use, or just for publicity, or for something in between. Second, there can be rather significant differences between plans and actions. Therefore, the question arises as to whether what the company states or puts in writing should be considered its strategy, or, rather, what the company does. The authors tried to address this problem by defining a strategy as a *position*, according to the following definition: "Specifically a means of identifying where an organization . . . locates itself in what is known . . . as the environment" (Quinn et al. 1988, 13). The authors' information is based on company reports, press releases, and interviews with representatives. Outside documents were used to check and amend the primary sources.

2. Automobile recycling is very much in development. It is not possible to make definite statements because the strategies of automobile manufacturers are still evolving.

3. The description of projects suggests that there is no horizontal cooperation between automobile manufacturers. This is only partly true. At a political and strategic level, the manufacturers do cooperate. For example, in Germany, the car manufacturers' trade organization, VDA, is developing a plan for vehicle recycling that is based on collection of automobiles via dismantlers, draining of the fluids, disassembly of useful parts and materials, and recovery of the metal content by shredding or in a melt reactor. At the European level, the ACEA, the European automobile manufacturers' trade organization, promotes a very similar vehicle recycling concept. At the level of practical work, however, which is the focus of

this discussion, there is very little horizontal cooperation. Peugeot and FIAT, which are mutually profiting from each other's experiences, are an exception. This lack of horizontal cooperation can be explained by the very competitive character of vehicle design.

In the classification of strategies for the projects described (which are not necessary to the final solutions), some interesting points emerge (see Figure 13.2). In the majority of the projects, the automobile manufacturers are not seeking changes in the technology basis that would be radical departures from existing dismantling and materials separation technology. Instead, the primary aim is to integrate the manufacturing and waste disposal networks by coopting new partners and strengthening the disposal side of the network with new actors. In this sense the tightly linked manufacturing network is expanded on an experimental basis to encompass the entire life cycle of the car. A second striking point is the association of small automobile manufacturers with an adaptive networking strategy, while the larger ones are associated with an evolutionary approach.

Finally, in line with the earlier-mentioned observation of Tushman and Anderson (1986) that radical innovations are usually brought about by new firms, radical changes in the technology basis for the most part are not being sought by existing manufacturers. Ford and Mercedes-Benz seem to be the only ones now tinkering with rather futuristic possibilities.

The strategies can thus be described as focusing more on organizational change and less on technological change. Therefore the following section looks more closely at the three aspects of the automotive industry discussed earlier in the chapter—design and manufacturing, disposal, and networking—but this time with an eye toward future solutions to the waste problem.

FUTURE TRENDS

DESIGN AND MANUFACTURING

It is difficult to predict whether the emerging technology for solving the shredder waste problem will reinforce the current technological basis of the automotive industry. Most experts suggest that the pilot projects will result in the dismantling of a number of parts and that the materials will be reused in the same applications. The plastics content of shredder waste will be usable after bulk separation, but only for low-quality applications. These predictions do not suggest very radical technological changes.

Nevertheless, it can be argued that combinations of solutions may be found that could significantly change the structure of the automotive industry. One consistent line of argument might be the following: let us presume that the dismantling of automobiles with the aim of parts and materials reuse will be implemented on a large scale, and also that it will not be limited to a few easy-to-recycle materials and parts such as bumpers and fuel tanks. Rather, complete dismantling will occur, and recovered parts and materials will be reused in the industry. Then the roles of many actors in the industry will change. For materials suppliers, such as polymer producers and compounders, the sources of raw materials will change dramatically. These suppliers will have to learn to work with different and widespread sources of materials and to handle varying mixtures of virgin and recycled plastics. In this situation, it might be beneficial for an automobile manufacturer to aim for production of a "totally" recyclable car as a marketing and manufacturing strategy. The manufacturer could assume a role in the disposal side of the business as well.

Such radical changes in the technological basis are not, however, necessarily compatible with current trends in design and manufacturing discussed earlier (den Hond and Groenewegen 1991). Potentially conflicting technological trends and environmentally sound features of automobile design are identified in Table 13.1.

TABLE 13.1

POTENTIAL CONFLICTS BETWEEN TRENDS IN DESIGN AND MANUFACTURE AND ENVIRONMENTALLY SOUND WASTE MANAGEMENT

DESIGN AND MANUFACTURING TRENDS	ENVIRONMENTALLY SOUND FEATURES
Easy assembly	Easy disassembly
Integrated components	Easy repair
Smaller production series	Universality of parts
Shorter production runs	Universality of parts
Lightweight materials	Easy recyclability
Diverse, tailor-made materials for specific applications	Smaller variety of materials

DISPOSAL

In the future, the quantity of shredder waste can be reduced by the application of various technological solutions. One set of solutions addresses the problem in the stages before shredding takes place. These are aimed at improving the disassembly process, with total dismantling as an end. Disassembly currently is done by manual labor with simple tools, but there is a push toward reducing the labor required. The Volkswagen and BMW projects employ manual disassembly. In contrast, Ford is working on physical processes for removing plastic parts from the body, hence eliminating labor. In addition, some solutions focus on selective removal and reuse of parts and materials, notably plastic materials.

A second set of solutions focuses on the stages after shredding. Examples are sophisticated separation technologies. In the future, a reduction will take place in the amount of parts and materials that remain in car wrecks to be shredded, due to prior disassembly of some parts and materials. This prevents some shredder waste, but disassembly cannot be the ultimate solution. Efficient reduction of shredder waste will require economic integration of the two steps of disassembly and materials recovery after shredding that might allow one player to reap all the benefits.

Incineration or thermal technologies are considered an improvement on landfilling. Thus, solutions to the shredder waste problem must include economically and technically feasible incineration. Perhaps some bulk separation can take place to enable the use of some of the fractions in shredder waste. Both of these solutions require "clean" materials, which means avoiding the use of certain additives in plastics or the use of substances that would require expensive incineration technology. Current opinion is that because of the mix of materials, incineration will never be economical.

Radical solutions to the shredder waste problem could turn the current technological basis of vehicle disposal upside-down. The approach Mercedes-Benz and Voest-Alpine Stahl have chosen is an example. With their approach it could become possible to feed automobile wrecks into a melt reactor to directly produce ferrous metals. This would make the shredding business obsolete.

NETWORKING

The technical solutions suggested above, for both the design and manufacturing stage and the waste disposal stage, require communication between the two networks involved. It is clear that properties of the network will change in response to changes in technology. Automobile manufacturers are extending their network to include actors involved in vehicle disposal. Currently, Nedcar and BMW are the only automobile manufacturers cooperating with vehicle dismantlers. The others, including Volkswagen, Peugeot, and FIAT, have established contacts with shredding companies.

The solution to the waste problem will require some way of dealing with the operations in the final life stage of the automobile. Dismantlers (in most cases small enterprises and, in a few German and Dutch cases, larger companies) will probably be involved in the final network. In their publications, VDA and ACEA see a role for automobile dismantlers. The increased level of project activities and possibly permanent solutions implemented by automobile manufacturers, dismantlers, and shredders will certainly lead to a more integrated network.

A different route, however, might be the development of an entirely new network. Mercedes-Benz and perhaps Ford may be aiming for such a development in working together with companies that traditionally have not been involved in vehicle disposal.

Two further situations suggest future trends. First, the network extension sought by most automobile manufacturers to deal with vehicle disposal seems to be directed at larger, well-operated companies. Therefore, the authors expect the waste issue to lead to a shake-out of small vehicle dismantlers and suboptimal shredding operators. Integrated companies might even develop that cover all aspects of shredder waste handling. Second, as manufacturers must learn about the specific requirements for dismantling their own vehicles, the integration of solutions to waste problems into the design of automobiles will certainly be on the agenda for years to come. Via the establishment of extended ties between the production and disposal networks of the industry this trend will be reinforced. The solutions sought by some actors will certainly result in viable industry-wide solutions in the long run. However, the authors cannot predict which will be the winning strategies.

CONCLUSIONS

At least one important aspect of the pilot vehicle dismantling projects is that automobile manufacturers are seeking firsthand experience with the problems of vehicle dismantling and waste handling. Thus, they are gathering knowledge about both the financial and logistical aspects. Taking the issue one step further, the authors have suggested that what really will be at stake is control over the vehicle disposal network. The technological directions explored in the various pilot projects, as well as the relationships involved, have been presented here to indicate how solutions might affect the industry in the long term.

Another significant aspect of these projects for automobile manufacturers apparently is that they may contribute to thwarting the efforts by government and green consumers to directly influence the design of automobiles. Also, by stressing their recycling efforts, manufacturers may distract attention, whether deliberately or not, from the issue of the increasing volume of automobiles. The existence of these two factors makes clear that the strategies manufacturers seem to have chosen cannot be characterized easily.

The efforts of automobile manufacturers are certainly defensive in part, as reactions to the threat of regulation. Although some of the vehicle-dismantling projects may be defensively motivated, their realization would certainly be an offensive strategy, since the companies themselves would have to take the lead and develop a solution. Whether any player in the current industry will regard the waste issue as an important opportunity for an innovative strategy, reasoning that excellence in the environmental field will lead to competitive advantages, is unclear.[9]

The question of *why* there are different strategies for managing scrap car waste has no definitive answer yet.[10] However, it appears that the following factors are relevant to automobile manufacturers:

1. The market position of the manufacturer in the regions it operates in. A larger market share might make the logistics of collecting parts and materials easier. The size of the manufacturer may also be relevant.
2. The value of the product, such as spare parts. Even before recycling became an issue, BMW and Mercedes-Benz, for economic reasons, were collecting some damaged parts from their dealers, either to rebuild and sell in the secondhand market or for reuse as raw materials for parts production.
3. The attitude of the national government. German automobile manufacturers, who have to deal with stringent regulations, have responded more quickly than others to proposed waste management policies.[11]

The greening of the automotive industry cannot be understood, however, just by looking at individual strategies toward vehicle recycling. It is clear from this industry's example that solutions to environmental problems, such as waste issues, involve cooperation among a number of differently located industrial actors. To understand greening, technical and organizational solutions must be assessed in an integrated way.

Appendix: Shredder Waste

Shredder waste is both an environmental and an economic problem. It is an environmental problem because of its growing volume and its composition. Increasing numbers of vehicles on the road inevitably result in increasing numbers of discarded automobiles, and the length of time that consumers keep their automobiles before discarding them is likely to decrease in Western Europe. After dismantling, which includes the sale of some parts and the recovery of ferrous and nonferrous metals, and after shredding, some shredder waste remains. Disposal of shredder waste is increasingly difficult because of rising landfill costs and lack of adequate incineration plants. The composition of shredder waste is largely unknown, but the amounts of heavy metals, mineral oils, and polychlorinated biphenyls can be high enough to classify it as hazardous waste. Indeed, increasingly, shredder waste is being landfilled separately from municipal solid waste as "special" waste, as it is, for example, in Germany. Moreover, national and European Community policies aim to minimize the quantity of waste landfilled. Industry views incineration as an alternative to landfilling, but in most European countries, waste incineration has met with severe difficulties because of its environmental effects and public opposition. Economically speaking, increasing quantities of shredder waste impose a cost, particularly for shredding companies. They are pressured by the increasing volume of waste on one side and increasing restrictions on landfilling and incineration on the other. In addition, because the proportion of nonmetals (especially polymers) in automobiles is increasing, the financial returns to the shredder per ton of input are diminishing. These problems result in lower profits (Henstock 1988; Whittaker 1991). Therefore, various national governments in Europe emphasize prevention of shredder waste as the main strategy for solving both the environmental problem and the socioeconomic problem.

About 25 to 30 percent of the weight of the automobile when shredded becomes waste, called shredder waste. The quantity of shredder waste is increasing for several reasons. The amount of nonreusable material, much of which is plastic, has increased from about 2 percent in the 1960s to about 12 percent currently, and this percentage is expected to increase.

Three trends are contributing to the increase. First, plastics are being substituted for metals and natural materials. Examples of seemingly irreversible substitutions are the use of high-density polyethylene for fuel tanks and the use of polymers (notably polypropylene) for bumpers and virtually the complete interior trimming and dashboard. Second, with the introduction of high-strength steels, steel parts can be made, often of better quality, with less steel. Thus, the decline in percentage of steel results in a relatively higher share of other materials. Third, parts that enhance safety and increase comfort—such as sound-insulating and heat-insulating plates, electronic equipment, and underbody coverings—have been introduced in automobiles, and very often these are made of plastics. In addition, market trends, such as consumer preferences for "individual" car models, result in smaller production series and shorter production times that favor the use of plastics. Relatively low investment is needed for the production of plastic parts in small series when compared to steel parts.

The estimated quantity of shredder waste in the European Community is about 3.25 million tons. This number is based on the disposal of 10 percent of the 13 million automobiles currently on the road, each weighing about 1000 kilograms (2200 pounds), 25 percent of which remains as waste after shredding.

ACKNOWLEDGMENTS

The observations in this study are based on work commissioned by the Netherlands Organization for Technology Assessment (NOTA) and for the Commission of the European Community, DG XII/SAST unit. The authors thank Alan Irwin of Brunel University in London and Brandan Barker and Paul Hooper of the Department of Policy Research on Engineering, Science, and Technology at Manchester University for the collection and organization of the material on Ford Europe.

NOTES

1. Volkswagen promised to take back Golf models sold since the beginning of 1992 at no cost to the customer. They are not expected to come back until after ten years ("Volkswagen bereid tot terugname wrakken" [Volkswagen agrees to take back wrecked cars], *NRC Handelsblad*, August 17, 1991). BMW was the first manufacturer to announce take-back of automobiles for dismantling outside Germany, their origin of production ("BMW May Recycle Car Parts," *Financial Times*, June 29, 1991). At the 1991 Frankfurter Motorshow, BMW announced that it will take back any disposed BMW offered to the company.

2. A description of Italian, French, English, and German automobile production systems is provided in E. De Banville and J.-J. Chanaron, *Vers un Système Automobile Européen* (Toward a European system of automobile production) (Paris: Economica, 1991).

3. Assainauto for Peugeot, Place Nette for Citroën, and Sococase for Renault.

4. For a description of German, Dutch, and European Community regulations on the disposal and subsequent treatment of discarded vehicles and shredder waste, see: for Germany, Bundesminister für Umwelt, Naturschutz, und Reaktorsicherheit—BMU, *Zielfestlegung der Bundesregierung zur Vermeidung, Verringerung oder Verwertung von Abfällen aus der Kraftfahrzeugentsorgung* (concept) (Bonn: BMU, 1990); for the Netherlands, VROM, *Notitie Inzake Preventie en Hergebruik van Afvalstoffen* (White paper on prevention and reuse of waste). Tweede Kamer 1988–1989, 20877 no. 1-2 (The Hague: Staatsdrukkerij, 1988); for the European Community, H. Erasmus, *Doorlichting van Prioritaire Afvalstromen—Voorstel voor een Nieuwe Benadering van Preventie en Hergebruik van Bepaalde Afvalstromen* (Proposal for a new policy on prevention and reuse of waste streams). Brussels: Commission of the European Communities DG XI.

5. "BMW May Recycle Car Parts," *Financial Times*, June 29, 1991.

6. Before January 1992, Nedcar was called Volvo Car. The change in name marked a change in the partitioning of stocks among the shareholders—Mitsubishi, Volvo AB, and the Dutch State—each of whom obtained one-third of the shares. Nedcar produces the Volvo 400 series and also plans to produce Mitsubishi models from 1994 onward.

7. Annual production of passenger cars for the manufacturers chosen: Volks-

wagen, 2,882,870 (for 1990, from 1990 annual report); Ford Europe, 2,157,908 (for 1989, from Organisation Internationale des Constructeurs d'Automobiles [OICA]); FIAT, 1,958,990 (for 1989, from OICA); Peugeot, 1,977,885, including Citroën and Talbot (for 1990, from Comité des Constructeurs Français d'Automobiles [CCFA]); Mercedes-Benz, 542,160 (for 1989, from OICA); BMW, 511,087 (for 1989, from OICA); Nedcar, 121,343 (for 1990, from 1990 annual report). Volkswagen, FIAT, Ford, and Peugeot are considered volume producers, having models in all market segments; BMW, Mercedes-Benz, and Nedcar are considered specialty producers, selling only in the upper middle class and luxury market segments.

8. Share of FIAT sales in Italy in 1990: 52.9 percent ("New Car Sales in Western Europe Slip," *Financial Times*, January 21, 1991); share of Peugeot/Citroën sales in France in 1990: 41.8 percent (1990 annual report); share of Volkswagen sales (including sales of Audi and SEAT) in Germany in 1990: 33.3 percent (1990 annual report); share of Nedcar sales in the Netherlands in 1990: 16.2 percent (1990 annual report).

9. For example, Volkswagen wants to reuse fuel tank materials to make new fuel tanks and bumper materials to make new bumpers.

10. For this classification of strategies, see Steger (1988) and Chapter 5 of this volume.

11. For a discussion of the influence of environmental regulation on solutions chosen by industry, see Chapter 10 of this volume.

REFERENCES

ACEA. March 20, 1991. *Position of the European Automobile Industry on Automobile Waste Management*. Brussels: ACEA.

Anderson, P., and Tushman, M. L. 1990. "Technological Discontinuities and Dominant Design: A Cyclical Model of Technological Change." *Administrative Science Quarterly* 35: 604–33.

Busch, J. V.; Field, F. R.; and Clark, J. P. 1987. "Economics of Automobile Body Panels." Paper prepared for Innovation in Materials for the Transportation Industry conference, Turin, Italy, November 4–6.

Chanaron, J.-J. 1988. "Productivity, Vertical Integration and Competitiveness—Some Methodological Reflections and Empirical Evidence." In *Die Zukunft der Arbeit in der Automobilindustrie* (The future of labor in the automobile industry), edited by B. Dankbaar, U. Jürgens, and T. Malsch. Berlin: Edition Sigma.

Clark, K. B., and Fujimoto, T. 1991. "Product Development Performance: Strategy, Organization, and Management in the World Auto Industry." Boston: Harvard Business School Press.

Commission des Fédérations et Syndicats Nationaux des Entreprises de Récupération de Ferailles du Marche Common (COFENAF). 1991. *Preliminary Remarks on the ACEA Position Paper on Automobile Waste Management.* Brussels: COF-ENAF.

Henstock, M. E. 1988. "The Impact of Materials Substitution on the Recyclability of Automobiles." *Resources, Conservation and Recycling* 2: 69–85.

den Hond, F., and Groenewegen, P. 1991. "Implications of Future Scrap Car Handling for Design of Cars." Paper prepared for Third International Conference on Materials Innovation and Their Applications in the Transportation Industry ATA-MAT, Turin, Italy, June 5–7.

Quinn, J. B.; Mintzberg, H.; and James, R. M. 1988. *The Strategy Process, Concepts, Contexts and Cares.* Englewood Cliffs, N.J.: Prentice-Hall.

Rousseau, M., and Melin, A. 1989. "The Processing of Non-magnetic Fractions from Shredded Automobile Scrap: A Review." *Resources, Conservation and Recycling* 2: 139–59.

Scholten, A. H., and Kanis, H. 1987. *Is levensduurbeleid levensvatbaar?* (Is a policy to expand the life of products sustainable?) The Hague: SWOKA.

Steger, U. 1988. *Umweltmanagement: Erfahrungen und Instrumente einer Umweltorientierten Unternehmens-strategie* (Environmental management: Experiences of and tools for an environmentally oriented corporate strategy). Wiesbaden, Germany: Frankfurter Allgemeine and Gabler.

Tushman, M. L., and Anderson, P. 1986. "Technological Discontinuities and Organizational Environments." *Administrative Science Quarterly* 31: 439–65.

Von Manteuffel, P. 1990. *Konzept zur zukünftigen Altautoverwertung* (Concept for a future scrap car treatment). Frankfurt: VDA.

Vos, J. J., and Meiling, K. 1991. *Informatiedocument Afvalstoffen—Autowrakken en shredderafval* (Information document on waste streams—Car wrecks and shredder waste). Bilthoven, Netherlands: RIVM.

Whittaker, J. R. 1991. "Energy Transfer from Shredder Residues." Paper prepared for Recycling Plastics from Automobiles, Packaging and White Goods: Plastics Recycling—Meeting the Challenge conference, London, March 13-14.

Womack, J. P.; Jones, D. T.; and Roos, D. 1990. *The Machine That Changed the World.* New York: Rawson Associates.

Conclusion

Research Needs and Policy Implications

Johan Schot and Kurt Fischer

The economic goals of companies are concerned mainly with profit and continuity. Profit serves as the means to secure income and safeguard investments, thus making it possible for a company to remain active in the constant competitive struggle and to adapt to changes in its surroundings. Environmental factors are becoming more dominant in those surroundings. Several chapters in this book have shown that environmental concerns are becoming progressively more important in the market, that regulations are being tightened, and that there is growing pressure on companies for environmental credibility. All these trends appear to be irreversible.

Companies can act on these changes through strategy formulation. The cases and surveys presented in this book make clear that many firms currently follow a defensive environmental strategy. They do their best to comply with regulations and react to public pressures. This may involve substantial investments in end-of-pipe technologies to achieve required emissions and waste reductions, although most firms do not have dramatically high net costs for pollution control when these costs are expressed as a percentage of revenues (see Chapter 4). Firms that take a defensive strategy regard environmental concerns as external problems and restrictions on company operations. Environmental concerns are not integrated in the overall (product) strategy, or in R&D and marketing policies (see Chapter 5). These firms do not try to identify possibilities to excel in environmental protection to gain a competitive position. Many lack information about the nature and volume of their emissions, and comprehensive and continuous monitoring procedures for waste and emissions are frequently absent. Of course, there are differences between industry sectors and, more important, between large firms and small and medium-size firms. With a few exceptions, small and medium-size firms are relatively less affected by regulatory and public pressures and have not seriously considered the environmental impacts of their production systems, although some small firms have developed new, environmentally friendly products for specific market niches (Potter 1992).

Due to increasing pressures, however, some firms have moved from a defensive strategy to a more innovative strategy. The starting point for such a strategy is a firm's pursuit of its own policy to achieve substantial reductions of waste and emissions, often to levels far below those stipulated in government regulations. Solutions are sought in the organizational sphere as well as in the realm of technology. Top management plays an active role in stimulating the search for solutions and making sure that appropriate measures are implemented by conducting audits. As argued in the introductory chapter, a firm's implementation of an innovative strategy is based on the expectation that environmental excellence is necessary to secure continuity and could lead to competitive advantages. This approach implies that efforts will be made to improve the company's structural ability to innovate and to develop new, environmentally friendly products and processes. In this way, more radical changes in existing production and consumption patterns are anticipated. To be sure, in many cases firms begin to develop an innovative strategy as a means to reduce uncertainty in the face of unpredictable or destabilizing actions by the government or environmental pressure groups. However, the implementation of elements of a more innovative strategy will put into motion processes in the company that could eventually lead to the development of a complete innovative strategy and the subsequent greening of industry as a whole.

In the preceding chapters, significant obstacles to implementing an innovative strategy are identified. As the book's editors, we wish to highlight the following obstacles:

- Due to growing competitive pressures that are bringing about all kinds of changes, firms are already confronted with a lot of uncertainty. The inclusion of environmental criteria in strategic considerations adds more uncertainty and complexity, and thus, firms are reluctant to do so. Moreover, some global business trends, such as shorter production life cycles and smaller production series, are not easily compatible with environmental requirements (see Chapter 13).
- Companies must develop a new shared interpretation in which environmental problems are no longer perceived as external and costly. In

a way, firms and corporate managers must develop a new identity (see Chapter 2). For example, automobile manufacturers should no longer think of themselves as car makers but as producers of transport.

- Implementing an innovative strategy is hard and challenging work, partly because it always involves changing power structures within the company and among companies (see Chapter 6).
- The existing external incentive structure encourages a defensive strategy. Most government regulation is geared to the implementation of end-of-pipe technologies (see Chapter 10).

In this book, several driving forces for overcoming these and other obstacles are identified. Until recently, government regulation and public pressure were the most important driving forces (see Chapter 4), to such an extent that companies have directed their efforts completely to meeting requirements set by public pressure and government regulation. Regulations are becoming tighter, and new regulations are forcing firms to be more open and transparent (see Chapter 8), which will make them more vulnerable to further public pressure. Simultaneously, opportunities in both the consumer and industrial supplier markets are increasing (see Chapters 11 and 12), and it is becoming clearer that implementing cleaner technologies could lead to cost reductions (see Chapter 9). In addition, there is a growing tendency among actors such as investors, insurers, workers, unions, user firms, and consumers to integrate environmental concerns into their activities. All this implies that, in the future, firms will be confronted with a wider range of pressures from many more sources. Despite the obstacles, an innovative strategy could become a necessity for dealing with these pressures.

POLICY IMPLICATIONS: REGULATIONS AS A CATALYST

For governments, speeding up the process of change in firms from a defensive to an innovative strategy will be a difficult and challenging task. The central task of government action could be described as the deepening and broadening of existing pressures.

Deepening of pressures implies that regulatory pressure should be tightened in two ways. First, the use of different instruments and actions should be seen as complementary. Stringent and certain regulation is needed and should not be replaced by voluntary action. Voluntary action is necessary but will work only when it has the force of law behind it. Voluntary action should take the form of agreements between industry and government (see

Chapter 10) and the appointment of regional prevention teams to stimulate, supervise, and advise companies (see Chapter 9). Second, the existing
regulatory trend to force firms to become more open should be intensified.
Firms should be forced to publish waste and emissions figures, environmental plans and targets for the future, and results of environmental
audits. Thus, the formulation and implementation of prevention plans
should be made compulsory.

Broadening of pressures implies that government action should be
explicitly focused to elicit pressures from other and new sources, such as
investors, insurers, user firms, workers, unions, and the public. For example, insurance companies are increasingly looking for ways to abandon
policies that restrict them from insuring against environmental risks. If
insurers develop this market in greater depth, they are certain to impose
various requirements, coupled with checks and inspection, on how companies behave. Government could speed up the process by introducing
strict liability or could make it mandatory for firms to cover specific risks
through insurance. Firms are also exerting pressure on one another
through supplier-user contracts (see Chapters 11 and 12). Governments
should encourage this trend (Schot 1992).

RESEARCH NEEDS: OPENING UP THE BLACK BOX OF THE FIRM

Until now, most regulation has not been based on a solid understanding of
how industrial firms operate. There is a tendency to look at companies as
completely homogeneous entities with clear outer boundaries. The chapters in this book show that various groups inside and outside the firm
conjointly shape its behavior and strategy. These intradynamic and inter-
dynamic processes should be seen as processes of organizational learning.
The proposed movement toward deepening and broadening of regulation
requires a basic understanding of these learning processes (Alm 1992). In
this book, research proposals and ideas are set forth that would bring
about the needed understanding. To conclude the volume, we wish to
highlight the following research needs.

1. More in-depth case studies are needed to determine how learning
processes that lead firms from a defensive mode of action to a more
innovative one occur within and among organizations. This work should
employ and be inspired by theories developed within the framework of
strategic management, organizational, and innovation studies. Eventually,
this research could lead to a classification of groups of companies that go
through similar learning processes under specific conditions.

2. Companies develop different approaches and care systems for safety, environment, and quality. There is a strong need to work toward the potential integration of these approaches.

3. To tackle environmental problems during the entire life cycle of products, companies need to work together more closely. It was concluded (see Chapters 11 and 12) that cooperation among companies on the environmental aspects of products is a growing trend, but it is still in its infancy. Investigations are needed on the forms of environmental cooperation that develop, on the kinds of barriers that are encountered, and on the kinds of driving forces that work. The particular patterns of cooperation will depend on a number of factors, such as product and commercial characteristics. Research should identify those factors.

4. Research should be focused on how government policies can induce the transition from a defensive to an innovative environmental strategy in firms. In this respect, comparative research on national environmental policies can greatly improve understanding of the appropriate types of government intervention.

5. The discussions in this book deal with the behavior of firms in the Western world. More research is needed into interfirm and intrafirm dynamics in non-Western countries. This research should take into account the effects and implementation of policies set by companies that are based in the Western world.

6. Public pressures have been among the most important driving forces for changes in firm behavior. This will continue to be so because the public is becoming more and more sensitive to environmental concerns, and regulation is forcing companies to become more open and transparent. To deal with these pressures, firms and trade associations have developed codes of conduct and programs that have led to a new kind of social interaction and learning process between firms and the public and to changes within companies. Research is needed to map these evolving new relations and their effects on company behavior.

REFERENCES

Alm, Alvin L. 1992. "Science, Social Science, and the New Paradigm." *Environmental Science and Technology* 26(6): 1123.

Potter, Stephen. 1992. "The Design and Commercial Success of Green Products in Small Firms." Paper presented at the Greening of Design Seminar, Institute of Advanced Studies, Manchester Polytechnic, England, February 29.

Schot, Johan W. 1992. "Constructive Technology Assessment and Technology Dynamics: The Case of Clean Technologies." *Science, Technology and Human Values* 17(1): 36–56.

Index

About the Contributors

Nicholas A. Ashford is Professor of Technology and Policy at the Massachusetts Institute of Technology, where he teaches courses in regulatory law and policy, and technology and law. He holds both a doctorate in chemistry and a law degree from the University of Chicago, where he received graduate training in economics. For several years, Dr. Ashford was a public member and chairman of the National Advisory Committee on Occupational Safety and Health and also served on the EPA Science Advisory Board. He is a fellow of the American Association for the Advancement of Science and is currently chairman of the Committee on Technology, Innovation, and Economics of the EPA National Advisory Council for Environmental Policy and Technology.

Michael S. Baram is a professor and director of the Center for Law and Technology at Boston University School of Law. He is also a partner in the law firm of Bracken and Baram, a Boston law firm specializing in environmental law. His work is focused on corporate environmental management, environmental regulation, risk communication, product stewardship, process safety, and related subjects. His publications include numerous articles and several books, including *Managing Chemical Risks* (with Patricia Dillon), *Corporate Disclosure of Environmental Risks: U.S. and E.C. Law* (with Daniel Partan), and *Alternatives to Regulation*.

Peter Cebon is a Ph.D. candidate in the Organization Studies Group at MIT's Sloan School of Management. He holds a bachelor's degree in civil engineering from the University of Melbourne and a master's degree in technology and policy from MIT. He has also worked in government and for a water resources consultant. His research focuses on organizations' management of innovation concerning energy, environment, and safety and the impact of that management on the organization and its relationship to the institutional environment.

Jacqueline Cramer studied biology at the University of Amsterdam from 1970 until 1976, specializing in environmental research. She remained at the university until March 1989 as a staff member in the Science Dynamics Department, where she primarily taught biology, concentrating on environmental policy. She now works for the Centre for Technology and Policy Studies of the Netherlands Organization for Applied Scientific Research (TNO), where she conducts research on the question of how government, industry, and social organizations can stimulate the development and use of

385

clean technology. Since November 1990 she has also been a professor, occupying an endowed chair in the Environmental Science Department at the University of Amsterdam.

Hans Dieleman is Assistant Professor in Environmental Sciences and Environmental Sociology at the Centre for Environmental Studies, Erasmus University, Rotterdam, the Netherlands. He has published several works in the field of environmental policy, pollution prevention and waste minimization, and technology transfer toward medium-size and small companies.

Patricia S. Dillon is a research associate at the Tufts University Center for Environmental Management, where she specializes in corporate environmental management and community right-to-know issues. Her current research examines product stewardship and related developments in the private sector, such as design for environment and industrial ecology. Recently, Ms. Dillon coauthored (with Michael S. Baram) a book, *Managing Chemical Risks: Corporate Response to SARA Title III* (1992), and the chapter "From Design to Disposal: Making the Environmentally Responsible Product" in *Managing for Environmental Excellence: The Next Business Frontier* (forthcoming).

Kirstine Drew is a research manager at ECOTEC Research and Consulting Limited. She is an economist and, prior to joining ECOTEC, worked for the Society for Appropriate Technologies, assessing the viability of intermediate technologies in India. Ms. Drew has a keen interest in environmental policy and has been involved in a number of studies for local authorities and the central government in the United Kingdom. She is currently involved in running the Technical Assistance Unit for ENVI-REG, which ECOTEC is managing on behalf of the Directorate General for Regional Policies of the Commission of the European Communities.

Melissa Everett, a researcher at the Center for Psychology and Social Change at Harvard Medical School, is the author of several journalistic studies about work and values, including *Breaking Ranks*, a study of conscientious objectors in the 1980s.

Kurt Fischer is associate director for Program Development at the Tufts University Center for Environmental Management (CEM). In this capacity, he leads the development of strategies for the integration of university-wide environmental programs, coordinating research, policy, education, and outreach activities. He is CEM's liaison to the U.S. Environmental Protection Agency for Tufts' cooperative agreement with the Office of Research and Development and manages the development of the center's annual program announcement and request for proposals. Mr. Fischer joined CEM in 1985 as a senior research analyst, conducting research and writing reports in areas of environmental policy, regulation, and government-industry relations.

Thomas N. Gladwin is Professor of Management and International Business, and director of the Global Environment Program at the Stern School of

Business of New York University. He has authored five books on corporate environmental management, including *Building the Sustainable Corporation: Creating Environmental Sustainability and Corporate Advantage* (1992), commissioned by the Corporate Conservation Council of the National Wildlife Federation.

Peter Groenewegen is a chemist and holds a doctorate in science studies from the University of Amsterdam. He has done research on company strategy and technology development, as well as on research and development cooperation between corporations and universities. Currently he is coordinator of a research program on science, technology, and the environment at the Free University of Amsterdam in the Netherlands.

Frank den Hond is a chemist and is currently working on a doctoral dissertation concerning the role of technology development within environmental strategies of companies, focusing on the automotive industry. He works at the Unit of History, Philosophy, and Social Aspects of Science, Faculty of Physics and Astronomy, at the Free University of Amsterdam, the Netherlands.

Sybren de Hoo is the deputy secretary and program coordinator at the Netherlands Organization for Technology Assessment (NOTA). He is a sociologist and civil engineer whose main field of study has been decision-making processes. Some of his former positions include construction designer, scientific staff member of the Institute of Sociology and Environment of the University of Leiden, senior staff member of the steering committee for the Dutch Debate on Energy and Policy, senior staff member of the Scientific Council for Government Policy, and senior staff member of the Ministry of Education and Sciences.

René Kemp studied econometrics at the University of Brabant in Tilburg, the Netherlands, until 1987. Following this, he worked for two years as a research fellow at the University of Limburg, studying the diffusion of technologies and their impact on employment and occupational structure. In 1989 he became a research fellow at the Maastricht Economic Research Institute on Innovation and Technology, where he has been involved in research in the area of economics and environment, especially on the topic of technological change for environmental protection.

John E. Mack is Professor of Psychiatry at Harvard Medical School and a widely published author whose works include *A Prince of Our Disorder*, the Pulitzer Prize–winning biography of Lawrence of Arabia.

James Medhurst is a director of ECOTEC Research and Consulting Limited. He was trained as an economist and chartered town planner prior to joining ECOTEC. He has a strong professional interest in evaluating and advising on the development of rational environmental strategy and improving the efficiency and effectiveness of policies. To this end he is responsible for directing research into the effects of environmental policies on the economy and industry. He has been a consultant to the European

Commission (DG XI, DG XII) and U.K. government departments and local authorities and is currently retained as an expert by EROSTAT to advise on the development of environmental accounting frameworks.

Robert Oresick is an assistant dean at Boston University's College of General Studies and holds a doctorate in psychology. He is the author of numerous articles on moral development and self-consistency.

Johan Schot joined the research and teaching faculty of the University of Twente in Enschede, the Netherlands, in 1991. Previously, he was senior research analyst at the TNO Centre for Technology and Policy Studies (STB/TNO) at Apeldoorn, the Netherlands. He studied social history at Erasmus University in Rotterdam and graduated with distinction. His specializations were the history of technology and technology policy. He assumed his research position at STB/TNO in 1985 and initiated the strategic clean technology program there in 1987. He has held the position of secretary for the Environmental and Safety Studies Group of the Dutch Council on Research for the Environment and Nature. Dr. Schot's research projects include theories of technological change and options for policy making; technology assessment; technological risk; evaluation of innovation effects of environmental policies; environmental management within firms; and strategic cooperation among firms.

Peter Simmons is a research fellow at the Centre for the Study of Environmental Change, Lancaster University, England. He has been researching business responses to environmental problems and is currently engaged in a study of consumption and environmental concern.

Ulrich Steger is presently a member of the board of directors of Volkswagen at Volkswagen AG/Wolfsburg, Germany, where his responsibilities include environment and traffic. He is also chairman of the supervisory board of the Mitteldeutsche Kali AG as well as a member of the executive committee of "Partnerschaft in der Wirtschaft" and several other similar supervisory boards. In 1976 Dr. Steger was elected to the German Bundestag and from 1984 to 1987 served as the Hessian Minister of Economics and Technology. In 1987 Dr. Steger became a full professor at the European Business School, where he holds the Chair of Environmental Protection and Business Management. Since 1991 he has been manager of the Institute for Environmental Management and Business Administration.

Hugh Williams is a chartered engineer and an economist. He is joint managing director of ECOTEC Research and Consulting Limited, which advises companies on the commercial implications of environmental regulations and market pressures and also provides business services and management consultancy to the Environmental Protection and Waste Management Industry. He is also retained by the Commission of the European Communities as an expert advisor on energy and waste issues and is currently conducting for them a major strategic review of the water industry in Europe with emphasis on product development and competitiveness.

Brian Wynne is a reader in science studies at Lancaster University, England, where he is director of the Centre for Science Studies and Science Policy and research director of the Centre for the Study of Environmental Change. A scientist turned sociologist of science, Dr. Wynne has published extensively on the subjects of the authority of science and public perceptions of risk. He has acted as a consultant to a number of national and international organizations.

Island Press Board of Directors

SUSAN E. SECHLER, CHAIR, Director, Rural Economic Policy Program, Aspen Institute for Humanistic Studies

HENRY REATH, VICE-CHAIR, President, Collector's Reprints, Inc.

DRUMMOND PIKE, SECRETARY, President, The Tides Foundation

GEORGE T. FRAMPTON, JR., TREASURER, President, The Wilderness Society

ROBERT E. BAENSCH, Senior Vice-President/Marketing, Rizzoli International Publications, Inc.

PETER R. BORRELLI, Executive Vice-President, Open Space Institute

CATHERINE M. CONOVER

PAUL HAWKEN, Chief Executive Officer, Smith & Hawken

CHARLES C. SAVITT, President, Center for Resource Economics/ Island Press

PETER R. STEIN, Managing Partner, Lyme Timber Company

RICHARD TRUDELL, Executive Director, American Indian Resources Institute